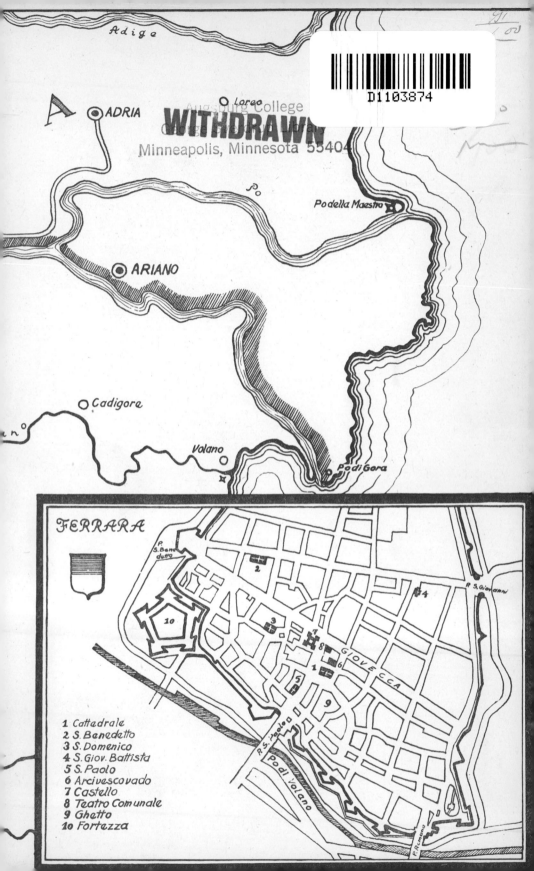

Adige

ADRIA

Loreo

Po

Po della Maestra

ARIANO

Cadigore

Volano

Po di Gora

Po di Gora

FERRARA

P. S. Bene-
detto

2

4

R. S. Giovanni

10

3

7

8

6

GIOVECCA

1

5

9

R. S. Paolo

Po di Volano

1 Cattedrale
2 S. Benedetto
3 S. Domenico
4 S. Giov. Battista
5 S. Paolo
6 Arcivescovado
7 Castello
8 Teatro Comunale
9 Ghetto
10 Fortezza

P. Reno

A SHORT OUTLINE OF EVENTS AND DATES
IN ITALIAN HISTORY FROM 1814-1870

AT THE beginning of the 19th century the Italian Peninsula was anything but a unified nation. Divided in states belonging to the Austrian Hapsburgs, the French and Spanish Bourbons, the Kings of Sardinia and the Popes, it resembled a quilt of motley patches, most of which were under foreign rule. At the turn of the century, repugnance for foreign and clerical rule created growing unrest among the nobility and the educated middle classes. The French revolutionary armies, invading Italy in 1796, found ready allies among many Italians. Napoleon ousted the Austrians and the Spaniards, annexed the Papal States, including Rome, created a Kingdom of Italy of which he was the king, and his stepson, Eugene Beauharnais, the viceroy. He was the first to visualize a united Italy, if only as an annex to the French Empire.

After the collapse of the Napoleonic Empire, in 1814, Austria took the upper-hand and attempted to re-establish roughly the Italy of pre-Napoleonic days. Not only did she govern Lombardy and Venetia directly, but Austrian princes also ruled the Duchies of Modena, Parma, and Tuscany. Austrian garrisons were installed in fortresses guarding cities which belonged to the Papal States, ostensibly to protect the weak Papal government against revolutionary uprisings, in reality to defend the territories under Austrian rule against the rising tide of new ideas such as Italian unity and constitutional government. However, revolutionary sentiment grew and took on the form of secret societies. The most famous, 'the Carbonari (Charcoal-Burners), aimed at the elimination of foreign rule and the establishment of a unified Italy. The Carbonari engineered risings in Naples (1820), in Piedmont (1821), in Modena and Parma, and in the Papal States (1831). In 1832, however, the Austrians had restored order everywhere. It was at this time that Giuseppe Mazzini, a former Carbonaro, realized that the Carbonari methods were ineffectual, and started a movement of his own, "Young Italy."

In 1846, Pius IX (Cardinal Mastai Ferretti), was elected Pope. In contrast to his predecessor, Gregory XVI, Pius had Liberal leanings and was sympathetic to Italian attempts at national independence. He proclaimed an amnesty for political prisoners and exiles, instituted various reforms, and was furiously opposed by the reactionaries in the clerical camp. In 1847, Ferrara was occupied by Austrian troops. In 1848, under the pressure of Liberal agitation, Liberal constitutions were promulgated in Piedmont, Sicily, Tuscany, and the Papal States. 1848–1849 sees the first Italian War of Independence. After an uprising in Milan (Lombardy) against the Austrians, Piedmont declared war on

Austria. The Piedmontese were smashingly defeated in the Battle of Custozza and, again, in 1849, in the Battle of Novara.

In 1848, Pius IX, alarmed by a popular insurrection in Rome, fled to Gaeta, and Rome was proclaimed a Republic. Now France intervened to restore the Pope to power and sent a military expedition to Rome. Rome was defended by Giuseppe Garibaldi and his militia, but the situation proved hopeless and ended in his retreat. By August, 1849, the revolutionary movement had again been suppressed everywhere. Only Piedmont, ruled by the House of Savoy, had retained its Liberal constitution, and therefore became the focus and hope of Liberal Italy. The leading spirit in the Piedmontese government was Cavour, founder of the newspaper *Il Risorgimento,* which agitated for Italian independence, a league of Italian princes, and Liberal reforms.

Cavour became Prime Minister in 1852, engaged Piedmont in the Crimean War on the side of France and England, and, as a result, had the opportunity to voice the grievances of Italy at the Congress of Vienna (1855). Cavour succeeded in allying France to Piedmont, with the aim of ousting the Austrians from Italy and organizing Italy as a federation of States. Provoked, the Austrians invaded Piedmont. As a result, Tuscany, Modena, Parma, and the Papal Legations (territories belonging to the Papal States and governed by Apostolic Delegates), Ravenna, Ferrara, Bologna, saw violent insurrections. The war ended with the Treaty of Zurich, which ceded Lombardy to Piedmont. Venetia was to remain Austrian. Cavour resigned, but returned to power in 1860. In this same year, Garibaldi and his Thousand Redshirts sailed to Sicily, took Palermo and Naples, and were joined by Piedmontese troops. Naples, Sicily, the Marches, and Umbria voted for union with Northern Italy. In 1861, the Kingdom of Italy was proclaimed by the first Italian parliament, with Victor Emmanuel of Savoy, King of Piedmont, as first king, and a government based on the Piedmontese Constitution of 1848. A vast national agitation now clamored for the annexation of Rome, where French troops were still in garrison.

In 1866, the new Kingdom of Italy declared war on Austria. The Italians were again defeated at Custozza and their fleet destroyed near Lissa. However, under pressure from the French, Austria ceded Venetia to Italy. In December of the same year, the French withdrew their troops from Rome. Garibaldi again assembled a volunteer army and began the invasion of the Papal territory around Rome, with the aim of taking Rome. The French came to the assistance of the Pope and defeated the Garibaldians at the Battle of Mentana (1867), mowing them down with their new rifles, the breech-loading *chassepots.* In 1870, however, as a result of the Franco-German War, the French withdrew their troops again, Italian troops entered Rome, a plebiscite declared Rome part of Italy, of which it became the capital.

RICCARDO BACCHELLI

THE MILL
ON THE PO

Translated by
FRANCES FRENAYE

PANTHEON

Endpaper maps reproduced by courtesy of
The New York Public Library, Map Division

TITLE OF THE ITALIAN ORIGINAL

IL MULINO DEL PO

The English edition combines the
first two volumes of a trilogy

Printed in the United States of America
by Belgrave Press, Inc.

Published simultaneously in Canada
by McClelland and Stewart, Ltd., Toronto

CONTENTS

Prologue   7

RUSSIA—1812

The Bridge Over the Vop   13
Saint Martin's Day   36

I. GOD SAVE YOU

The Treasure of the Virgin of Spain   45
Dosolina   102
The Day of Tribulation   157
The Reckoning   190
The "Libertines'" Revolution   229
The Finest Trade in the World   272

II. TROUBLE TRAVELS BY WATER

The Siege of Bologna   331
The Smuggler of the Po   361
Of Trickery and Greed, Intrigue and Blackmail   404
Cecilia Scacerni   444
The Break-Through   551

With the author's assistance and approval, certain historical passages of too local an interest have been cut in the English version of The Mill on the Po, *as it was felt that the foreign reader could not follow events familiar and fresh only in Italian memories.*

PROLOGUE

THE MILLS on the Po! There are hardly a dozen of them left, and less with every year that goes by. The traveller, unless he makes his way up the river by boat, must seek them out one by one. Because they are so few in number amid the mighty flow of the winding river they are hidden here by an elbow or steep bank, there by a tuft of trees growing out of the sand or a curve in the river road. They are old and dark and their dilapidated air illustrates what is meant by the ruling issued by the National Bureau of Waterways to the effect that their use is permitted until they have fallen to pieces. This ruling, now dating back many years, which sealed the fate of these last survivors of a pre-mechanical age, was intended to protect the riverbed and banks from the mud suction produced by the mill wheels. Mechanical milling is an old story by now but the river mills resist their fate and will not die, increasing thereby the reputation of the honest workmanship of their builders. But for whose benefit do they proclaim their builders' integrity? For that of the few remaining millers who know only that their fathers or grandfathers had them built many long years ago and who still respect the builders for having finished them so well and enduringly in every part, both above and below the water, from hulks to millstones. Or for the distracted eyes of ignorant travellers, of whom, however, I am not one, since my eyes have been ever watchful and attentive, and every time I have come back to the mills I have been deeply moved by the thought of all that has happened during the interval of time that they have grown to an honorable old age on the river, thinning out and disappearing one by one, until only these last few remain.

The great wheel, or ulà as it is called, turns with the motion of the stately river and its slow cadence is immeasurably quickened in the flying rotation of the millstones above (whose outer circumference the millers call a "wing"). And this cadence of the wheel imparts to the coupled hulks a vigorous liveliness, an energy, a vital rhythm, a tremor which is in harmony with the lively and almost vibrating motion of the twin prows, which dip into the stream in which they are anchored. The river mill is as alive under the miller's feet as a ship under those of a sailor. The miller claims that there is no better flour for making bread than that evenly and gently ground by the turn of a wheel in the water, and in a region such as Ferrara, known for the best bread in the world, his words carry weight.

7

The floating mills that still survive are the very last of their line and so dear to me is the highly poetical theme of their decay that for many years I was reluctant to lay hands on it, for I too respect a job well done and aspire to the same reputation as that of their builders. Of these, surely not a single one is now alive to tell how he laid the keel of a new mill. And soon enough even the memory of the customs and language inherent to the miller's trade will in its turn disappear.

In order to convey the poetry latent in such a heartfelt and hopeless struggle against the inevitable march of time I would call, if I dared, on behalf of his own river upon Virgil, the most delicate of poets. For he is master of that tender respect for the past which is best defined in the Latin word pietas, *as we find it in his* Georgics.

A miserable modern novelist has not the courage to appeal so high. But I can state with assurance that not even a novel can have a life of its own without some poetical idea behind it. This cries out for saying because never before as today has this necessity been obscured by such a flow of sterile intellectual talent designed to conceal in a thousand scientific simplifications the lack of any idea at all. I am aware in so saying of the condemnation that will fall upon my book if I myself fail to respond to this necessity, that is, if my ability is not commensurate with my passionate intent.

It is with passion and affection that I now return to say another word about the water mills and a certain historical and geographical theory that I have derived from their study. I must expound this theory before I give rein to my imagination, and as a matter of fact it forms a prelude to my story.

From the two stones rubbed together and the primitive mortars devised by savages and barbarians to the cylinders of a modern industrial machine, from the millstones turned by the arms of slave laborers in ancient civilizations to the windmill and the millrace (which is said to have been introduced by the Saracens), we know that the technique of milling is one of the distinctive marks of every people and its development. In the Middle Ages, for instance, the mill run by a local lord for the people's use was a characteristic accessory of the feudal power exercised from monastery or castle. But in the great plain of the Po, where man-made banks contain the majestic waters from the Alps and those more turbulent from the Apennines, there are few small tributaries propitious to feudal monopoly. For the vassalage of a feudal lord's dependents grew out of the concentration around a castle or monastery not only of mills but of all the other appurtenances necessary to their daily life, which fell necessarily under his protection.

The water mills, mobile in both construction and function, were scattered along rivers, the greatest of which was a natural boundary line between rival states and a contested strategic position. Thus they were destined by nature and necessity to bring about a freer relationship between millers and their clients, and emancipation from dependence upon the mills owned by the feudal lords. They came under no domination other than that of the ruler of a whole state, or monarch,

8

as we call him when we contrast with feudal lordship that wider governmental power installed by royal houses as they proceeded to weld large territories into nations.

The millers, because of their life on the river, formed not a mere hereditary guild or corporation, but a whole class with customs and interests of its own grafted upon those of the larger national community. Their clients, on account of the universal need for daily bread, whose satisfaction required free and safe communication and commerce between themselves and the millers, had the same interests as they did. And these interests (since every social liberty is only the recognition of a useful form of servitude) made up the fabric of a social institution.

In the Po Valley, then, the servitude imposed by the feudal lords, who did not seem to be aware of its exaggeration, soon came to be considered abusive and rapacious. I go so far as to believe that the existence of the water mills, bound up as they were with the daily needs of the people, contributed to the rapid transformation of the feudal system into an economy based on reclamation projects carried out by the abbeys of the region and into a form of centralized government and an ideal of universal application. Thus in the region between the Po River, the Apennine mountains, and the sea, we see the early development of a movement which was destined later to spread through Europe but which meanwhile had in Ferrara its first and most shining example. The necessity of bettering communications with the mills hastened the resurrection from overgrown swamps of Roman roads, which had once served both local and Imperial traffic, in that province of Emilia, whose name is taken from one of the most famous of their number. And the fact that bread is a humble necessity does not make it an any less cogent one. In reading the chronicles of this epoch we often find that the lord or ruler of a certain locality, upon setting out to subdue some rebellious fief or castle, first cut off its access to the water mills, thus reducing the local population to a diet of boiled wheat, which the chronicler, as a lover of good bread, found particularly pitiful. This same stratagem was used, of course, in partisan communal strife and by violent and greedy tyrants.

But, limiting ourselves to the history of Ferrara, the major seat of civilization in the Po Valley, we shall see that with the advent of the Este family a feudal lord took on the stature of a monarch, protecting the mills of the region and causing an Ariosto and a Muratori to profess themselves respectively poet and historian of his dynasty. And so we arrive at the encouraging truth that quarrels and wars and all the most violent human passions, when there is good will on the part of God and man, actually contribute to the achievement of unity among men and the profit of civilization.

Here is a fitting conclusion which will, I trust, win me the reader's indulgence for my discourse on the water mills of the Po. And going back to the beginning of this preface, it is to this feeling of poetry and history that I dedicate my life and work, all that I have and am. I add *only that this story entitled* The Mill on the Po *covers a period of just over a century, from the year when the Italians who followed Napoleon to Russia suffered a defeat in the passage of the Vop River, which preceded on a smaller scale the imminent disaster of the Beresina, to the victorious crossing of the Piave and the victory of Vittorio Veneto at the end of the First World War.*

Quod bonum, felix faustumque sit. *Let this be my augury.*

Russia = 1812

THE BRIDGE OVER THE VOP

C AN YOU BELIEVE it's the same?" the officer asked his men, pointing to the river. They looked at it without answering, sappers and pontoniers together, forming a sparse vanguard of the Fourth (Italian) Army Corps, led by Viceroy Eugene and escorted by Marines of the Royal Guard. The river was the Vop and the date November 8, 1812. Lean and exhausted, Captain Maurelio Mazzacorati was one of the few officers still in possession of a horse after the disastrous crossing of the Dnieper, the battle for the eleven times lost and then recaptured Maloyaroslavets, and twenty days of retreat before the pursuing Hetman Platov. On top of all these vicissitudes had come, forty-eight hours before, a wind and snow storm, which had wrecked the encampment of the Fourth Corps and caused the loss of all its vehicles.

One look at the bony horse, which stood shivering with its head hung low between its knees, was enough to make it clear that soon enough Mazzacorati, too, would be obliged to proceed on foot. Meanwhile he repeated, half to himself:

"Can you believe it's the same river we saw last summer?"

The river was broad and its waters gray and sinister, with a sort of angry vapor hanging over them. Slabs and blocks of ice, piling up and shattering against one another in the whirlpools, made a heavy, dull noise of breakage and suction. But the river, however hostile, was not half so fraught with danger as the insidious snow, which lulled the weary men into a sleep certain to end in their being frozen alive. The snow spread out as far as the eye could see, all the way to the low horizon, under a gloomy sky which as early as noon presaged the arrival of night and another snowfall, while a freezing blast, as sharp as a razor blade, whipped the men's exposed faces. Silence and gloom closed in with greatest intensity from the north, while the outlook in other directions was one of deathlike monotony.

"With due respect for military discipline," one of the group, stepping forward, replied to the captain, "our bellies were full last summer when the river was empty and dry."

The appearance and accoutrement of the speaker were in harmony with the slightly gruesome nature of his joke. He was skinny as a ramrod, but this was due to his youthful age rather than to the hardships he had recently endured, for the cold had only brought out a healthy glow on his beardless cheeks, giving him a highly cheerful expression. He was wearing a leather cap and a great fur coat, spattered with mud, which looked as if it had seen better days. Instead of a gun he carried a stick, and hanging from a loop on his belt was a large frying-pan.

Some of his hearers laughed, but not the gaunt captain, with fever-ish eyes and traces of bile in his yellowed complexion. At the place where they had come to a halt the road turned and ran up along the Vop to a cluster of wretched log cabins not far away. The Russian guide addressed a long rigmarole to the captain, who caught from it one word that he had heard before: "Sloboda." The guide made signs to indicate that in this direction the river narrowed and probably there was a ford.

"Sloboda!" the captain interrupted him. "To these rascals every vil-lage in the world is called Sloboda!"

Because none of them knew that this was the generic term for vil-lage in the guide's tongue they were in a state of constant fear that he might betray them. And pondering now upon the swollen and savage river coursing between its frozen banks, the desolate wastes of snow, broken only by the dark cabins and clumps of birches or firs, they had a strong suspicion that he had led them astray in order to make them an easy prey to the Cossacks, who had a way of swooping down on their fiery horses from the white desert with wild cries and muskets and lances upon the flanks of the retreating army.

The company of Marines from the Royal Guard, which was a picked body of men, proud of its valor and of the distinction bestowed upon it by the Emperor in becoming honorary colonel of the regiment and dispensing its members from obedience to any officers but their own, stood to one side in good order and looked disdainfully at the medley of sappers and pontoniers. These bore all the marks of having suffered a crushing defeat, and when the captain ordered them to start cutting down trees and demolishing huts in order to obtain material for a bridge they obeyed listlessly and showed reluctance to break up their close formation. As a result, some of the Marines were detached to protect their squads.

As soon as Mazzacorati tried to budge his horse the animal's knees crumpled and it fell down and rolled over on its back. The young sol-dier who had spoken up a minute before ran to free the rider, calling out that this evening there would be a feast of chops and steaks. To Mazzacorati the loss of his horse meant death and he watched it draw its last breath without pity. The soldier, on the other hand, unob-servant or heedless of the officer's plight, rapped his knuckles against the frying-pan and pranced about trying to warm his feet, until finally his restlessness annoyed an older companion, who wore an angry and frowning look on his face in spite of the promised steaks.

"Go on! Tread the snow all you like, but you won't get any wine out of it!"

"You don't like my Russian dance? Your feet are going to freeze, do you know that? And your nose and your . . ."

"Curses on you! Where did you learn to be so fresh with an old soldier?"

14

"Old or new, I don't care a hang for you or your nose or any other part of you."

"I'll cut off something of yours if you bring it back whole from the wars! But I don't know who you are or if you're a soldier at all, much less whether I can pay you the compliment of challenging you to a duel."

"Lazzaro Scacerni," said the other, laughing and continuing to prance about. "Of the second company of engineers of the Royal Guard."

"I'll remember," said the other seriously, for he belonged to the select guard of honor, which was jealous of its reputation and known for the number of duels its members engaged in.

It was hard to know whether to deride or to admire a challenge issued under circumstances like these. Meanwhile the captain raised his voice in order to hasten the execution of his orders and Scacerni walked away, saying:

"If I live to see the end of this campaign I'm going to have some fun!"

Mazzacorati heard him singing as he swung off in the direction of the village:

> *In summer when only the trees are green*
> *I'll fall in love with the first man to be seen.*

These were the words to a refrain sung by the peasant girls of his own country, in the Po Valley, when the fields were dried up by the heat of the sun and they had to pull down leaves from the trees to feed the cattle.

> *Summer has come and summer has gone,*
> *My handsome lover fled with the morn,*

the song went on. The plaintive, dragging tune, which gave a curious flavor to the words, worked so effectively upon Mazzacorati's imagination that he could see the great plain of Ferrara under the sun of the long summer days, so far away from this Russian land where death lay waiting relentlessly in ambush. A wave of annoyance and bitterness and despair swept over him and something like hate for his sturdy and unscathed fellow-countryman. He didn't envy him, but he wanted to die in peace. Now all he could hope for was not to see him again.

Soon General Poitevin of the Fourth Army Corps arrived on the scene with the bulk of the engineers. He gave orders to build the bridge in continuation of the road approaching the river and to start levelling the banks in order to make the approaches. Tools and material alike were insufficient for the task. The blades of the sappers' light axes slipped out of alignment and there were not enough flares to enable them to see in the already encroaching twilight. Mazzacorati's pontoniers worked with the few nails and hooks they had at their disposal to make pontoons out of hastily assembled logs and pieces of wood, while other troops continued to straggle in from behind them, lighting fires by the side of the road and preparing to strike camp until the bridge should be ready. The general was impatient, for he was anxious to have it finished before sunrise and the expected arrival of Viceroy Eugene.

The first pontoons held up, but they were in shallow and relatively quiet water, for the main force of the river was thrown against the opposite bank. Mazzacorati found Scacerni perched at the farthest extremity of the bridge, briskly pounding piles into the mud and laying planks across them.

"Have a piece of roasted horse meat!" said the soldier. "It's yours by right."

Hammering away at the planks as he jumped from one to the other he put to good use every moment of the misty and rapidly declining day. It seemed almost as if he alone, shouting and laughing and swearing, were keeping up both the pace of the work and the morale of his comrades. The job was progressively more difficult as the river deepened and stronger currents offshore whirled their way downstream. Scacerni fell silent and proceeded more cautiously, feeling out the riverbed with a long pole before lowering the pontoons carried to him by his fellows.

"Things are taking a bad turn," he observed to Mazzacorati, who only shrugged his shoulders in reply.

A few minutes later the swift current carried away first one pontoon and then another, and Mazzacorati notified the general. The general came onto the bridge and ordered the placing of a third pontoon, which immediately broke loose and followed its predecessors.

"Generals are doubting Thomases," mumbled Scacerni half to himself. "With them seeing's believing."

"You must drive in a semicircle of stakes upstream," said the general, "in order to deflect the current."

"Easier said than done!" Scacerni exclaimed. "What are we to hammer them with? And we'd have to swim out to set them in place."

But in spite of these mocking words, which showed what a strain it was for him to submit to military discipline, he was the first one to set out some extra stakes and pound them with a long-handled hammer. Finally three more pontoons were laid down and these held firm. In his effort to make the supports of the fourth touch bottom Scacerni leaned so far over that he almost somersaulted into the water.

"We have to get the bridge across, come what may," the general was saying to the group of officers gathered around him on the riverbank. "It's a question of saving the Fourth Army Corps and the Viceroy himself to boot."

But at the farther end of the bridge work had come to a halt. A raw, cutting fog had come down over the river, hiding both men and nature, so that the former were more intractable and the latter more hostile than before. A few weak flares were still burning, but the voice of the river grew louder and louder in the darkness and struck fear into men's hearts. The rumor had reached even those who were farthest away that

16

the bridge could not possibly be finished that night and the general was perfectly aware that the hammering of piles and planks had stopped even though he kept up a pretense of firmness and went right on saying:

"Gentlemen, the bridge must be finished before dawn."

"We'll do what's possible," said an officer who had heard him repeat the same statement a dozen times before.

"And what's impossible, too!" the general exclaimed. "Isn't this the army of Napoleon?"

Silence greeted these fine words. The cold was almost unbearable.

"No use combatting the darkness," ventured another officer. "Tomorrow morning . . ."

"But the Fourth Corps is arriving tonight, and you know what condition they're in, short of ammunition and supplies, with their only hope of replenishing them at Ducóvchina on the other side of the river."

"If the Russians haven't destroyed the town behind them, just as they have every other place between here and Moscow," put in an old colonel, a friend of Poitevin, who had been in the army all his life and was a brave man but an unlucky one.

"Come, come!" said Poitevin. "How can you be downhearted, when I know you've never been afraid of any man?"

"Man is not our chief enemy, General!"

"Well, nature, if you will. Nature is the engineers' concern. We owe it to ourselves to get the best of her!"

"We need more tools," said a lieutenant of the sappers. "The axes are unserviceable."

Suddenly anguished cries arose out of the dark river, echoing gradually farther and farther away until they died out in the distance. Although they were used by now to almost every sort of horror these piercing shrieks out of the night froze the blood in their veins. A moment later Captain Mazzacorati came to report that the last pontoon the men had attempted to place had broken loose, carrying several of their number away with it. At this point he had ordered them to stop work rather than lose more lives and material.

"But what about the Viceroy?" exclaimed the general in consternation. "I promised him a bridge over the Vop for tonight."

None of the officers replied. They seemed to indicate by their silence that the Viceroy's ill humor was strictly his own affair. Standing close together with their heads hanging low, stiff with cold in spite of their heavy coats and boots, they waited for the time to go by. Meanwhile fires sprang up on the bank of the river and along the road, one of which, in the direction of the village, seemed to blaze with particular brightness.

"What's that?" asked the general.

"They must have set fire to some of the cabins in order to keep themselves warm," answered one of the officers apathetically, barely raising his head to look where his superior was pointing.

17

"We must stop them! That wood is our salvation!"

"General," said a young officer who stood to one side, out of the light cast by the flare, voicing the opinion of his companions, "if we could get the sleeping soldiers to take up arms they'd only turn them against us, or else chase their comrades away from the burning cabins and enjoy their warmth themselves. We'd have a fight on our hands all night long among those who are already installed and the newcomers, and all over a few logs. Is it really worthwhile?"

He spoke these unpleasant truths in an annoyingly deliberate manner.

"The Emperor is waiting for us at Smolensk," mumbled Poitevin. "Are we to fail him?"

"There'll be good reason if we do," retorted the same young man.

And with this sarcastic parting shot the officers separated in silence, begging for places around the scattered fires. With the onfall of night both discipline and common humanity vanished. The general took Mazzacorati with him to inspect the work that had been done and the condition of the river. Holding a flare up over the water they perceived that it was now at a lower level than before.

"As it freezes harder," Scacerni explained, "the volume diminishes."

"Let's hope so," sighed Poitevin, who was now resigned to waiting for dawn. "Captain, you and your men must see to it that none of the logs that have been chopped and made ready are put on the fires. I give you formal orders to protect them."

Mazzacorati shrugged his shoulders, considering that he would be lucky if his men didn't give in to the temptation of building a bonfire themselves. Meanwhile they all lay down close together in order to keep warm. Scacerni had once more disappeared and Mazzacorati didn't know whether to be glad or sorry. He had a dry cough deep in his chest and a stabbing pain in one side which kept him from sleeping. The bodies of the men around him seemed to bear down upon him as if in a nightmare and squeeze the breath out of his body. His teeth chattered and he shivered all over with fever, musing in a state of semidelirium how he had never loved anyone or anything, not even himself, and least of all just now when he had come all this distance only to die. "Why?" he asked himself. "For whom?"

But the bitterness and hate he felt toward Napoleon were vaguer and less direct than the disgust he aroused against himself. "Napoleon's furthering his own ambitious and tyrannical interests. What's stupid is to have faith in him, or worse yet, to follow him without faith. I've got exactly what I deserve."

He went back in his feverish memory to his childhood in Ferrara, where he was born, to the straitened circumstances and humiliations of a noble family that had fallen upon evil days, to the cruelly exaggerated discipline imposed by his father, and his mother's stupid way of rebelling against it by boastfully comparing to the thieving and worthless stock of the Mazzacoratis her own very ancient lineage, famous for its great soldiers, its connection with royal and imperial families, and the fact that it included one saint, two beatified holy women, one Pope and a contemporary candidate for the Papacy. The elder Mazzacorati did not care a hang for this genealogical tree and when his patience was exhausted he did not hesitate to prove his indifference by administering a sound whack to the illustrious female scion that he saw before him. The boy, who loved neither of his parents, did not sorrow over this sight, indeed if he hadn't been afraid of getting himself into trouble he would have laughed at it quite openly. Because it was less expensive he was sent to a seminary rather than a private school and there he claimed to have acquired a vocation for the priesthood, simply because he was sure in this way to annoy his father, who, had he not been an only son, would probably have forced him into it. His main object, in short, was to escape from the limitations of his family, but he became conscious of this too late, after he was already a priest, a wicked and sacrilegious priest with just enough mysticism left in him to poison his soul with a fear of hell and a gloomy aversion to God, Whom he held responsible for his own mistake. He took refuge in a fierce pride, mingled with rancor and boredom, which he passed off among the ignorant as ascetic severity. He was not without intelligence and his success as a scholar and preacher made him fatuous and pedantic. The only joy he got out of life was in contempt for everyone and everything around him, which raised him to heights of exaltation, only to dash him down into greater prostration and unhappiness than before. Thus his priesthood was offensive to both his own soul and its Creator.

The few Masses that he was called upon to say (and God knows in what spirit he said them) brought him in very little money, so that he had to live at home, and his father reproached him for the expense of his upkeep. The old man was trying to turn all his possessions into cash, and having sold every last painting and piece of furniture he had even taken down the carved panels of the ceilings, leaving yawning holes over the vast, cold, dirty rooms, or rather caves, below. In the course of this dismantling an Englishman who had settled down in Ferrara, a hemp merchant and lover of old things, came to frequent the Mazzacorati establishment, and with him his youthful accountant, Antonio Roncaglia, who was as gay and dissipated as Maurelio Mazzacorati was embittered and gloomy. These two were Freemasons and Roncaglia was amazed to see that the young priest responded eagerly to some of his most daring so-called philosophical sallies. As a result he introduced him to the leader of the Masonic lodge of Ferrara, Giovan Battista Boldrini, who fanatically professed the most modern ideas and was active in the fight against religion. Thus it was that there came into Maurelio's hands a group of philosophical works—books smuggled into Ferrara from Venice, hidden in bales of merchandise stored at the depots of Italian, Dutch and English traders in the river port of Lagoscuro.

It was with fierce joy that Maurelio fell upon these books, abandoning the company of Roncaglia, who cared only for their obscenities, in favor of that of the anticlerical Boldrini, who flattered him in the most pompous terms, both as a priest and a nobleman, for having thrown off the yoke of superstition and tyranny. Boldrini's flattery tickled his scholarly pride, and the persuasion that he was an individual victim of the religion that had for centuries victimized all of human kind added to his feelings of hatred and revenge a vainglorious satisfaction in his own enlightenment.

These personal considerations meant even more to him than the hopes aroused by the latest news of France and the French Revolution. Hard upon Maurelio's emancipation, filling all Europe with mingled hope and terror, came the victories of the Republican armies of France over those of the allied kings. Boldrini and Mazzacorati, when they heard that the French were pouring into Italy, could see in their imagination a guillotine erected in the Piazza Grande of Ferrara and the naked goddess of Reason enthroned on the altar of the Cathedral, while Roncaglia burned with impatience to leave his goose-quill pen, account books and scales for weighing hemp, and to enlist in the service of General Bonaparte. On June 21, 1796, when the French troops did arrive, the tree of liberty was planted beside the Castle and on the church squares, and the gloomy Mazzacorati, wearing a Phrygian cap, went around from morning till night with the carefree Roncaglia for a companion, knocking feudal coats-of-arms off the façades of the palaces, although sparing, at the general's orders, all those of the Papacy whose government was still nominally in power.

Behind the two zealots came a crowd of solemn and foul-mouthed idlers carrying axes, hammers and ladders. They had already distinguished themselves for the amount of their destruction when they thought of the fine statues of the two Marchesi d'Este, former rulers of Ferrara, to one side of the Cathedral. These popular figures had been celebrated by the poet Ariosto, a fact which to a rabid Jacobin like Maurelio Mazzacorati was totally indifferent.

"Too bad our Englishman closed his shop and went back home," said Roncaglia, while their followers were throwing a noose around the figure of Niccolo d'Este on horseback and the seated Marchese Borso. "He would have paid good money for these two pieces of bric-à-brac."

"Remember this, Roncaglia, we must not let ourselves be softened by the fact that these symbols of slavery may be beautiful to look at, or corrupted by the possibility of exploiting their value. I'd rather see every statue in Italy perish!"

With these memorable words, which he alone was to remember, Mazzacorati gave the signal to pull the statues down from their pedestals and hammer them to shapelessness on the pavement below. While a group of French soldiers looked on, the mob sang and danced around the ruins of these two noble bronzes, which later were melted into cannons for the use of the French liberators. The mob's rejoicing was to endure no longer than the length of time it took for these Republican arms to pass into the service of the despot Napoleon. But not even

20

that night when Mazzacorati lay at death's door on the Vop River did he repent of the statues' destruction.

Meanwhile, when the statues were magnanimously disposed of, the French army began to requisition silver and jewels to pay for the necessities of war and Boldrini preached civic duties to the women who had flocked shrieking to witness the plundering of the great municipal pawnshop or Monte di Pietà. Even the sacred vessels of the Cathedral, after having been de-consecrated *pro bono pacis* by Cardinal Mattei, were confiscated along with the rest, but no one of the clergy would admit to having saved from the pile the ancient heavy silver busts of the beloved patrons of Ferrara, San Giorgio and San Maurelio, and Mazzacorati, as a reader of *Priests Unmasked,* rose up in the sacristy to accuse them of fraud. The priests defended themselves in mild tones, by comparing Mazzacorati to Menelaus, the sacrilegious minister of God, of whom it is told in the apocryphal Second Book of the Maccabees that he led Antiochus to defile the Temple of Jerusalem: "He (Antiochus) presumed to go into the most holy temple of all the world; Menelaus, that traitor to the laws and to his own country, being his guide, and taking the holy vessels with polluted hands, and with profane hands pulling down the things that were dedicated by other kings to the augmentation and glory and honour of the place, he gave them away."

Mazzacorati went around boasting that he had broken the spell of superstition, or, when he was in humbler company, that he had cooked the clergy's goose. But the common people, who did not go in for subtleties, had already begun to say that freedom to steal was the only benefit brought by their liberators and that they wanted the loot for themselves. Boldrini, as Commissary, did everything humanly possible to enlighten the benighted and regenerate them, and because Mazzacorati had given proof of being a true Jacobin and of having firsthand experience of both the tyranny and wile of the adversary, he made him his right-hand man. The Commissary had sent out an open letter to the nuns of every order, exhorting them to throw off the veil, quit their convents, and enjoy their rights as citizens and women. The disappointing response to this invitation made him suspect that the mothers superior or confessors had kept his letter out of the hands of its intended recipients and he sent Mazzacorati, decked out in a Republican scarf and cockade, to read it out loud in their parlors, where he was listened to in fear and trembling, as if he were the Antichrist in person. His own five sisters Mazzacorati chased out of the convents quite unceremoniously and led them home amid the plaudits of the crowd. These five timorous creatures had all very slender appetites, but their return brought with it a strain upon their father's resources. The old man, however, was now completely at the not very tender mercy of his son.

Maurelio now became a lieutenant of the Civil Guards, with the mission of protecting the famous trees of liberty, under which, in the name of "liberty, equality and fraternity," baptisms and marriages

21

were celebrated and official banquets were held, to the scandal of the ill-fed population, which was harassed by taxes and requisitioning. These trees, especially in the country, were subjected to all sorts of injury on the part of priests, aristocrats, and the superstitious majority of the plain people. So exaggerated were the penalties imposed by the city government upon those caught in the act of defiling a tree that they inspired to satire all those malcontents who did not dare speak up against the Frenchmen but exercised their wit upon the Frenchmen's awkward and fanatical local collaborators. The penalties had been decreed in the hope that their very enormity would discourage offense and that there would never be any necessity of carrying them out. But there was growing resistance to requisitioning and indeed widespread rebellion against the invaders. The French authorities, in revenge, insisted upon strict enforcement of the law, including that of the city of Ferrara aimed at the defilers of the trees of liberty.

Don Pietro Zannarini, the parish priest of San Pietro Bolognese, one of the Church's most stalwart defenders against the Jacobins, had boasted from the pulpit of having been twice guilty of this crime. Finally, for having publicly incited the faithful to uproot for the third time the tree in front of the church, he was arrested and brought to court. When he refused to deny either his words or his deeds the judges were compelled, by virtue of the local law, to sentence him to be shot by the Civil Guard outside the Porta San Paolo, near the small church of the Paroni. A horrified crowd, considering him a holy martyr, saw him pass along the street, with head held high and a crucifix between his untrembling fingers, escorted by soldiers of the Civil Guard who looked as if they rather than their prisoner were being led to the slaughter. He knelt down to say his prayers to Our Lady of Consolation at the Porta San Paolo, then stood up to face the firing squad, of which Maurelio Mazzacorati happened to be in charge, like a Christian militant. There were only a few onlookers left, for the crowd had melted away as if in the face of a threatening storm. Even the soldiers did not have the heart to make any response to their lieutenant when he waved his plumed cap over the dead body in priest's robes and shouted in harsh and inappropriately pulpit-like tones:

"Fraternity or death!"

His voice rang out in the silence like that of a man who has made a loud noise in order to dispel his fear, and the echoes lingered in his ear. Robespierre, the Incorruptible, was his idol, and soon after the priest's execution Maurelio came to consider himself as a victim of the same sort of betrayal. Believers branded him as Judas, making him a scapegoat for the popular ire, idlers pointed him out on the street as "the fellow with the plumed cap who shot down a man in return for a tree," and even his Jacobin companions avoided him. The city chose to honor him at a banquet held at the tree in the Piazza Grande in order to celebrate the Republic of the Human Race, and he later realized that the real purpose must have been to make him conspicuous in the eyes of his enemies, to heap infamy on a reputation hitherto merely ridiculous, and to cause the dead priest's blood to be on his head alone. He arrived at a full understanding of his position in the public eye when he saw how his own family looked at him in stony silence. At the banquet of the Republic of the Human Race, which was attended by the lowest and most oafish class of merrymakers, male and female, everyone had heaped compliments on him as a defrocked priest, a new Brutus and a champion of the tree of liberty. Since the result of the banquet, then, was to crystallize public opinion against him, even his most fanatical companions were glad to see him leave Ferrara with a commission in the engineering corps of the expeditionary force that started out with the names of Cispadana and Cisalpina and ended up as the army of the Kingdom of Italy.

To Ferrara he returned only once and briefly, when his father died. It was a summer day and one of popular celebration, for a man from Bologna was demonstrating the first man-carrying balloon, which took off from the open space in front of the Fortress to the applause of the crowd. The day ended with artillery salvos, banqueting, wine, and a lottery of seven hundred crowns, which was won by the wife of a tavern keeper and gambled away by her again that same evening amid the carousal. Mazzacorati's sisters had gone back to the convent, taking their mother with them, and refused so much as to see him. And the artillery salvos proclaimed the Imperial victories in Austria, the Emperor's birthday, and a saint newly discovered or rediscovered while Pope Pius VII was in prison: Saint Napoleon. It is easy to imagine in what state of mind these events left the Republican Mazzacorati, but how did it happen that their memory had lingered on so long and now came back to haunt him as he lay, half dreaming, but as angry as if he were fully awake, on the bank of the Vop River? Was it perhaps because the intense cold recalled to him by contrast the heat of that festive summer day? Or because he himself was astonished how little it mattered to him either that his father was dead or that he had only a very slim chance of returning to his native land? Or because, when he had left Moscow, in the shadow of impending disaster, he had relished the prospect of going back to Ferrara to false friends like Boldrini and Roncaglia, who were now slaves to the tyrant? More likely the approach of death, as it so often happens, had sent his thoughts back to the remote past.

Yes, he had been right, in spite of all of them, but it had taken the disastrous Russian campaign to prove it, and now as he lay cold and exhausted he knew that he would not live to enjoy his justification. He no longer believed in God, and Fate was too vague and uninteresting an object for his resentment. He despised himself for the ill luck that had befallen him. "To die like this, in my prime!" he thought to himself.

Did he really hear something or had his fever carried him from delirium to hallucination? The deep, cold night, the silence of the snow and of the men huddled about the half-extinguished fires seemed to convey a sound like that of breathing, a slow creaking of wheels and a voice of sorrow and anxiety and human travail. There were faint calls and scattered groans of despair, the rumble of wagons and the dragging sound of weary feet, the collective sigh of a multitude of the exhausted and dying.

Mazzacorati knew the sound. He recognized the lament of the mob of fugitives that had trailed out of Moscow after the army, their numbers swollen by soldiers who had lost their units, harassed by the Cossacks at their heels and the tortures of hunger and fatigue and cold. But this mob had been far in the rear, Mazzacorati reflected, it was out of the question that they should reach the Vop so soon. He did not know that the Viceroy's staff had decided to push them on ahead so that they should not create disorder or impede the progress of the troops and the crossing of the river. They had proceeded at an unusual and indeed incredible speed, spurred on by the news that a river lay just ahead and by fear lest they should not get across it before the bridges were burned. They too were prey to the cruel hope that beyond the river lay abundance and safety. In their flight they had trodden down those of their number who had fainted away on the ground and those who had stumbled and fallen over them. Now they were a bloody horde and few were those among them who could remember their own fathers or brothers or wives or sons. Some of them were mothers who had lost their children on the way and did not have the heart to linger behind to search for them. Perhaps they had trodden them down themselves amid the snow and mud in a moment of starvation and madness.

With Fate at their heels like a lash they had finally arrived, and now they poured onto the approach dug out of the river bank to the bridge, while the warning voices of those who saw where they were going served to push them on rather than to hold them back. They stumbled raving over the ice of the ramp and piled over one another onto the narrow bridge, which had no railings, without knowing that it came to an abrupt end in the darkness. They shrieked with fear and indignation, and those of them who slipped on the icy boards were shoved or crowded into the water. Now it was too late to stop them and besides they did not understand the shouted warnings of those who had perceived the danger. Anyone who tried to halt, to plant his feet on the ground, arch his back and retreat, was pushed off the bridge by the man coming after him, who only a moment later was a victim of the same fate and in his turn shouted and struggled in vain. The impulse of the reaction before the fatal jump off the end of the bridge travelled back through the mob, creating the impression that someone was trying to block their passage and making for a new wave of anger and fear among them. Some resorted to murder in order to open up a way before them, working their way forward with kicks and punches, and pitilessly trampling down their fellows until they came themselves to the brink of disaster and called for the pity they had not shown to others, vainly clinging with their fingers and teeth to those who had pushed their way behind them. Everyone, in his fall, pulled another with him.

Shouts mingled with prayers and curses with death rattles. Fortunately the ice was merciful and closed over them more relentlessly than if it had been water. Many never touched the bridge with their feet but were swept along by the compressing motion of the mob even after they were dead and thus were propelled, still upright, on their feet, into the ranks of those who were alive and struggling in the black river. This agony endured until a company of soldiers formed a barrier with their rifle butts at the approach to the unfinished bridge. But they would have been kinder in the long run if they had pushed the whole mob into the icy water.

The faint glimmer of the late dawn cast a somber light over the wastes of snow, the river, the half completed bridge and a disorderly mob, which was quite possibly too far gone to remember the events of the night, spread out along the road to the village with its burned cabins. A decision was taken to ford the river, even if it was running at full tide and the water came up to the horses' withers. General Lechi and General Pino (the latter sitting as straight in his saddle as if he had not been seriously wounded in the last battle) arrived on the scene; the standard-bearers raised the Imperial eagles and the flags of the Kingdom of Italy; the drums rolled and the troops went through the river, directed on either side by two officers famous for their tall stature and vigor, Colonel Millo and Captain Ferrari, who stood knee-deep in the water to direct operations. The passage of the most orderly troops went on for several hours, with a considerable number of men collapsing from fatigue or being carried away by blocks of ice. The low temperature caused the road leading up to the ford to become glassy and slippery and the river had begun to rise. At this point the Viceroy rode up and the soldiers acclaimed him with hurrahs for Napoleon and the cry: "On to Smolensk!"

"They'd do better to save their breath and take off their clothes before they plunge into the water," said a voice next to Mazzacorati, who was sitting or rather lying on the snow and looking on from the sidelines at the work of breaking up the slippery ice on the road.

"Oh, it's you again, is it?" mumbled the sickly captain, recognizing the crystal-clear tones of Scacerni.

"Yes, here I am," replied the young soldier. "If any river's to be the death of me it's the Po! At least that's what a gypsy fortune-teller once told me. Did you see those poor fellows last night? A fine way we received them with that bridge of ours!"

He seemed rested and well-fed, eager and gay, with the healthy color on his cheeks and the youthful appearance that had aroused Mazzacorati's wrath the preceding evening. He felt like ordering him to set to work breaking ice along with the rest, but instead he said:

"Wasn't it perhaps the best thing for them, after all?"

"Well, you know how the proverb has it: 'There's a cure for everything except a broken neck.'"

25

Now the artillery pieces and other horse-drawn vehicles were fording the river. The horses, egged on with whips and spurs, pawed the
ice and as often as not slipped into the river with their wagons behind
them, amid much shouting and splashing. Under so much weight the
riverbed was gradually deepening. After the lighter pieces came a
five-inch howitzer, which got stuck halfway across. The horses were
tangled in the harness and had to be cut loose, and the vehicles coming immediately after were caught in the swirling current around this
obstacle and carried off, bearing men and animals with them. The ford
was blocked and water began to ooze slowly under the wheels of the
wagons and gun-carriages now piled up in the middle of the river.
Whenever the drivers were able to pull a vehicle out of the mud they
invariably ended by enmeshing it with its predecessors and throwing
it back onto the pile. Orders were given to nail the guns down securely
to their carriages and leave them on dry land, to unharness the horses
and get them by hook or crook across to the other side.

Meanwhile the hapless civilian fugitives, with everything conspiring
against them, seemed to have a premonition that they would never
cross the Vop alive and they stood on the bank, shouting, weeping, and
imploring the soldiers to help them. Every horseman had a cluster of
them around him and a few did manage to hang on to someone's coat-
tails and get over. But many were lost in the water and the greater part
of them stood in a state of weariness and stupefaction, aware of the
hopelessness of their position, amid the gun-carriages and wagons
abandoned on the road leading up to the river.

Already dusk was falling. A squad of Cossacks, shouting and shooting their guns off into the air, galloped onto the scene to attack the
burned village. They were thrown back by the gunfire of the rear
guard, but when they repeated their attack a little later they found the
ruins abandoned and they set up on sleds some of their light artillery
pieces. Then they opened fire on the crowded road and their shots
awakened Mazzacorati, who was lying half unconscious on the snow.
They raked the road from one end to another, making a bloody furrow
in the crowd of fugitives, who did not dare come out from behind the
illusory protection of the wagons. By now, suffering had stripped them
even of their sense of fear. Between one volley of shots and another the
savage horsemen galloped up to dip the points of their swords and
lances in their victims' blood.

Mazzacorati no longer cared to be alive. He only regretted that they
had awakened him as he lay near the ford at death's door. For some
reason, perhaps because they were not wasting ammunition in these
last minutes of daylight or else simply because the place where he was
lying was not within their range, their shots did not reach him, but
stopped at the edge of the road.

Scacerni had apparently got hold of some booty, for he reappeared
with a sack on his shoulder.

"Those devils shoot straight, but I've been able to do some foraging,"

26

he said. "Oh, nothing of value, just practical stuff. You'd be pulling death by the whiskers trying to lug gold over this snow. Now it's high time for us to cross the river. Get up and strip off your clothes; there's no time to be lost."

"Why?" Mazzacorati asked.

"In this north wind we'll need to keep our clothes dry for the other side."

"I mean why should I think of crossing? Why are you bothering about me?"

The young soldier seemed to be surprised.

"Why, indeed, I wonder? I can't say . . ." Then he thought of something and laughed. "The horse! That's it! The good steaks that came off that horse of yours, don't you remember? You can't imagine how hungry I was last night, and your horse saved my life. It's only fair; one good deed deserves another. Take off your clothes and I'll roll them up with mine. After that horse meat it's only right that I should save your life in return."

Mazzacorati's teeth were chattering with fever and cold while Scacerni rolled up each successive piece of clothing.

"Look at that, will you!" he exclaimed all of a sudden.

A tall woman had jumped down from the riverbank onto the shore and stood there leaning over the water and shouting:

"I'm afraid! I can't do it! Oh! Oh!"

Then she fell flat on her stomach and sobbed loudly.

Naked as he was and of slender build, Scacerni was muscular and redblooded enough to resist the cold. He went over to the woman and spoke to her, half in Italian and half in the crude French that had been picked up by most of the soldiers of Napoleon's armies.

"What are you doing?" he asked. "What sort of a childish trick is this?"

"I wanted to drown myself in the river, but I didn't have the courage to do it," she answered in French, lifting up her face.

The Cossacks had ceased fire but their shouts could still be heard from the ruins of the village. The woman closed her eyes.

"Please kill me," she said. "Don't let them catch me alive!"

"Come along with us then," said Scacerni. "Take off your clothes."

When the woman seemed not to understand he pulled her up off the ground and started to tug at her wet furs.

"I only want to help you to get across," he said.

People were roaming up and down the shore without daring to wade into the water while the soldiers continued to pour through the ford. Whenever the Cossacks were silent and wheeled momentarily away, as was their custom, the air was filled with weeping and shouts and lamentations. The woman stood there in her undershirt, for Scacerni had packed the rest of her things in his roll.

"Hold onto one of my shoulders and float after me," he said. "You may as well keep your shirt on."

Convinced that he really meant to save her she took his hand and to his great surprise kissed it. But he did not have time to open his mouth.

"Isn't that enough?" Mazzacorati interrupted angrily. "What do you expect to do with this woman?"

"Exactly what I please, my fine sir!" answered Scacerni with aroused insolence. "That's a pretty question! What am I going to do with you, in the state you're in? But I'm helping you all the same. Only don't ask too much of me at the last minute. If you try me any further . . . well, I'd like to see how you'd make out alone! But at this point it's only a waste of time to quarrel. Your clothes are in my sack and I'll show you I'm not a thief. Hold on, both of you," he added imperiously, walking in surefooted fashion into the water and lifting the sack high above it in his hands. "One hand on either shoulder. But don't grab my neck or arms, especially if I have to swim. If you do, I'll knock you off into the water, and there's an end to it. Let's have that down in black and white and stay friends. When we get to the other side I'll give you your clothes, Captain, and each of us will go his own way. You've given me trouble enough already. What a filthy world and what damnably cold water!"

Laughing and talking to himself Scacerni had arrived up to his chest in the water, which was already around Mazzacorati's neck.

"*Sacraméstul!*" Scacerni exclaimed in dialect. "This is what you call cold! Hold on, you two, and keep up your courage! Brr!"

Now Mazzacorati could hardly touch bottom.

"Easy! We'll make it!" said Scacerni, feeling the depth with one foot before stepping forward.

The swift black water formed a whirlpool around his stalwart body. The opposite bank was not far now, but this was where the river was deepest and the current especially strong. It swirled around Scacerni's throat as he dragged his two charges along, with their nails digging into his shoulders, and every now and then one head or the other drooping under water. Now the bank was within reach. Scacerni threw the sack up onto the shore and pushed the woman ahead of him.

"Here we are!" he exclaimed with relief.

But at this very moment Mazzacorati lost his grip. A big sliver of ice struck him in the ribs and his body slipped under water and started to drift downstream. Scacerni swam out, caught hold of him and pulled him back to shore unconscious. The current had taken them both some yards down the river and when he walked back along the shore in his bare feet with Mazzacorati's body across his shoulders he found the woman with her furs on her back.

"Did you think you weren't going to see me again?" he asked laughing.

"What would I have done without you?" she answered.

"Good. Now we must get dressed and cover this fellow up. It's lucky the sack came through dry."

"Wait a minute before you dress."

She picked up two handfuls of snow and began vigorously to rub down Scacerni's back, chest, stomach, hips and legs. The blood began to flood through his chilled veins and steam rose off his warm skin. He laughed aloud and since she too was naked under her furs he massaged her at the same time from head to foot. They rubbed each other's necks and ears and noses, standing face to face, chest to chest and stomach to stomach, in a harsh and chaste intoxication that rose out of the vital heat now restored to their bodies. Then they put on their clothes and leaned over Mazzacorati.

It took some time for the captain to come to, and when Scacerni decided to follow the soldiers until they should strike camp he stumbled along some distance behind, too proud to ask for assistance. Every few steps they waited for him to catch up, and he could hear them talk and laugh together. When they had covered less than a mile they found themselves farther ahead of him than usual and there was no sign that he was still following. Scacerni retraced his steps and found him flat on the ground biting his fingers in order not to call for help.

"Cheer up, Captain," he said heartily, pulling him to his feet. "We're almost there. But why didn't you call out?"

"That's my own affair. If you'd shot me where I lie you'd have done me a favor."

"Come, come," said Scacerni with gruff kindness. "I didn't know the cold could drive a man daffy."

To leave those who had fallen by the wayside to their fate was so common a practice that many of them no longer wasted their strength calling for help. But Mazzacorati had been so cantankerous that Scacerni was bent on saving him in spite of himself, as if by so doing he could go him one better.

"Who is he?" the woman asked in a low voice.

"One of our officers, who comes from the same part of the country as I do. I told him to lean on me but he's stubborn and insisted on fending for himself."

With the sharpened perception resulting from his fever Mazzacorati overheard their whispered words.

"Are you particularly fond of him?" she asked.

"I don't even know his name. It's from the way he talks that I understood where he comes from."

"He would have left me on the other side."

"Oh, did you notice that?"

"You are a good man, but he isn't."

"Don't pay attention to what he says. All of us are bad under circumstances like these."

"But you're not bad."

"I'm stronger, that's all."

"No, that's not all. You've done more for me tonight than I could have expected of a brother. What made you do it, I wonder?"

"It wasn't so hard. Don't take it too seriously."

Mazzacorati was asking himself the same question. "I haven't much time now," he thought to himself. "The end is near. Now it's up to me to show how a man of my kind can die. But why did this fellow do it? Just because he is strong? That's no reason." He questioned himself angrily, fearful, for some reason, of learning the answer.

It had begun to snow hard. Now the air was less cold, but walking was more difficult. They had been going in the direction of a faint red glow in the distance, which they took to be the Fourth Corps encampment. But they could no longer see it and the heaviness of the snowfall rapidly covered up the footsteps ahead of them. Scacerni stumbled over something and bent over to see what it was.

"A dead body," he murmured. "We're on the right track."

Guided by a succession of such abandoned bodies they finally reached the first scattered and flickering fires. Sleeping men were packed closely around them under the falling snow.

"You can't expect anyone to make a place for us here," said Mazzacorati, still more cynical than he was weary. "It would have been better for us to throw ourselves down without making the effort to come so far."

"Captain, watch out, you'll goad me too far!" said the soldier, now openly disregarding their difference in rank. "You'll see who finds a place for us!"

The first man he took hold of started spasmodically, cursed and tried to get up on his feet, but fell back, mumbling:

"Heaven help me! I'm a mass of wounds and my legs are frozen."

"That's because he wet his clothes in the river and now they're frozen to his skin," Scacerni observed impassively. "Brother," he added to the crouching man, "we need to share this fire too."

The other did not hear him, but went on groaning with his head falling gradually between his knees as if he were congealed all over and had fainted away. As for the next three men that Scacerni shook by the shoulders, they gave no sign of being alive, and he took hold of their legs and pulled them away.

"They can afford to give us their place," he said. "It can't do them any good at this point."

He poked the fire and they sat down beside it with the snow covering their heads and shoulders.

"What is she to look at? A beauty?" Mazzacorati asked all of a sudden, jerking his chin in the direction of the woman, who was holding out her hands and feet to the rekindled flame.

"Don't judge either a woman or a piece of cloth by candlelight," said Scacerni sententiously.

"You're always speaking in proverbs, aren't you?"

"She has soft, white hands, so she must be a lady or have lived like one. Those hands have never known hard work. Yes, she is a beauty, I'd say."

"Then I see why you rescued her," said Mazzacorati sardonically. "There was a very good reason." And he added in a didactic manner: "I approve."

30

The woman understood that she was the subject of their conversation and smiled at Scacerni. Her smile was a becoming one. Scacerni brought some roast horse meat out of his sack and poured some crude brandy from a flask into a tin. The woman ate and drank but Mazzacorati could not swallow.

"It won't go down," he said.

"That's a bad sign."

"Tomorrow, if I live that long, I have something to tell you."

They sank down to rest. Scacerni and the woman put their arms around each other under the snow, which soon covered them up and kept them warm. When they woke up the next morning the hollow eyes, shrunken nose, blue face and gasping breath of Mazzacorati were all too eloquent symptoms of his condition.

"Oh!" said Scacerni, looking at him unhappily.

"Don't say a word. I know. I have something to tell you," the captain said.

"Anything I can do . . ." Scacerni began sympathetically.

"You can't do anything. Be quiet and listen."

Around the fires all the men that had sufficient strength were struggling to their feet and going over to respond to the call of faint drums. Others either faltered and fell or else could not get up at all.

"Listen to me," said Mazzacorati, with a sort of malicious sweetness in his voice that contrasted with the feverish and angry light in his intent eyes. "You're going to get home alive."

"I only hope your words are a good omen!"

"It's not that I wish you particularly well. Just be quiet and answer my questions. I don't know that I can trust you, but come, see if you can tell me the truth. I'm too far gone for it to cost you anything and it may even be to your advantage."

"Ask me what you will," said Scacerni, recovering respect for his officer now that he saw him at death's door. "I am listening, Captain."

"When we first met on the other side of the river you thought that I had money on me, gold stolen in Moscow, or that I had a wealthy family at home, didn't you? I'm not reproaching you for imagining such things. Quite the contrary. Just tell me the truth. If you don't I shan't believe you. You thought you had struck it rich, isn't it so?"

"You're raving," said Scacerni with annoyance. "If you have a wealthy family, that's your good fortune. As for your having gold on you, well, I had your clothes in my sack but I didn't keep them and let you drift down the river!"

"Stubborn hypocrite that you are! Well, I have nothing on me, you know that, and I've nothing at home, either. I've no home at all, and no family. Now what do you say? Your pains were all wasted. I'm poor as a church mouse."

"Then we're both in the same boat."

"Are you sorry, then, for what you did? Look me in the eye!"

"There's not much profit, that's true," said Scacerni, laughing. "But

I wasn't counting on that. I'd have done the same thing for anyone that was in your pickle. Cheer up, now."

The woman had heard them talk, without understanding what they were saying, and now she touched Scacerni's arm:

"Don't do anything violent. Tell him that he'd better make peace with his God."

Mazzacorati laughed.

"One of your pious women, eh? That's just what I need to die a holy death! No doubt she'll read me a sermon! Perhaps I was right when I said you'd have better left her behind!"

With his face contorted by a perversely reinvigorating anger Mazzacorati was so ugly that she turned away, making repeated signs of the cross in the Russian manner, to which he replied with blasphemous laughter, until he was taken by a fit of coughing which brought bloody saliva to his lips.

"Are you too a good Christian?" he said jeeringly to Scacerni as soon as he had pulled himself together. "Good for you! I'm glad! Do you believe in God?"

"Captain, I don't have to tell you what I believe. All I can say is this: If you had the treasure of the Kremlin in your pockets, a thousand sunny acres in Italy, and more gold than there is in the ghetto of Ferrara I'd change it all for a good pork chop! Because what we ate last night, welcome as it was, was only horse meat!"

"My family and I always lived in extreme poverty," murmured Mazzacorati, paying no attention to what had gone before.

"Very bad indeed."

"What? Are you showing your true colors at last? Do you confess?"

"You're the one that's ready to make a confession if there were a priest to hear it. The time is short, I tell you. And from the look on your face I'd say you must have some bad sins on your conscience."

"That's not your affair! Now that you know there's not a penny to get out of me you'll show yourself up for what you are. I'll have the last laugh yet!"

He lifted himself up on his elbow and leaned forward. The look in his eyes and the spittle that streamed out of his dying lips lent his face a horrifying expression.

"Go away!" he repeated. "I'm perfectly happy! Leave me here and let me die! But of course you're a *good* man, just as she was saying; you're full of Christian charity. You wouldn't dream of doing unto others . . ."

He fell back with a convulsive cough, closed his eyes and gritted his teeth. Then he waved his hand to signify that he was still alive and unrepentant.

"Let me laugh, you cursed hypocrite!" he said. "Do you want me to believe there is a God? Have you too set your mind on my dying a holy death?"

And he drew himself into an upright position, impelled by a mixture of rage and fright which momentarily took the upper hand over his pain.

"Well, now that you make me think of it," said Scacerni, "perhaps it was for the love of God that I saved you."

The dying man twisted and writhed with repulsion, then he returned to a stony calm.

"So you'll insult me to the very end with your Christian charity, will you, you hypocrite? But I'm stronger than you are and I have means to take you down a peg."

He searched for something under his clothes, murmuring in a philosophical and fanatically pedantic vein that seemed under the circumstances singularly inappropriate and pitiful, something to the effect that egoism was the only motive of human behavior.

"Have a sip of this," said Scacerni, holding out the flask of brandy, "and see if it gives you the strength to go on. It's time we were moving."

"I won't drink with you!"

"Then I'll drink alone."

Mazzacorati had found what he was looking for, a tiny ivory case with a screw lid that he wore on a chain around his neck.

"There's no miraculous medal or scapular in it," he said with a final jeer, holding it out to Scacerni. "I don't deal in fakes of that kind. I'll die the way I've lived, just as you see me, without fear of God or man."

The rumble of drums had died out in the distance, amid the silent snow. Only those who had fallen to rise no more now remained around the dying fires. Scacerni poked the ashes thoughtfully, straining his ears to catch some sound. The dying man guessed at his preoccupation.

"Am I taking too long to die?"

"I don't say that, but the fact is that the Cossacks may be here any minute. Are you quite unable to walk? I've heard there's a village nearby where we might stop to rest and recuperate."

"Yes, Ducóvchina they call it."

"If we're the last to arrive there we shan't find much left for us. Can't you possibly? . . ."

"I neither can nor will. If I don't die of fever then the Cossacks will finish me. That's all I ask for. But take this case. There's a fortune waiting for you in Ferrara if you have the nerve to lay your hand on it. Do you know how to read?"

"No."

"Then get someone in whom you have absolute confidence to read you the paper you'll find inside. It's a receipt signed by a Jew in Ferrara, who promises to give to the bearer of this paper and the half coin that goes with it and fits the other half in his possession a whole treasure of gold and pearls and diamonds, which I, Captain Maurelio Mazzacorati, left in his care. I'm leaving it all to you, do you understand?"

He spoke rapidly, taking advantage of the momentary respite from suffering that so often precedes the arrival of death.

"What's the Jew's name?" Scacerni asked thoughtfully.

"It's written on the paper. Everything's in good order. Now I've repaid your kindness. But listen to me. If you're a good Christian you must know that it's all sacrilegious plunder, all stolen from convents, from the Virgin's altar. These jewels were thank offerings of the faithful. And in order that you shan't give the excuse of being ignorant, when you reach Ferrara you must look up some member of the Phrygian Cap infantry regiment, preferably Captain Antonio Roncaglia, if he's still alive, for he was with me when I plundered that altar. You'll hear plenty about the Caps and what fine gallows birds they were! We didn't have any use for priests' cassocks and cowls and tonsures, I can tell you, and no threat of excommunication ever bothered us. You must hear the whole story, and not let the Jesuits teach you how to get around your scruples, if you have any. It happened during the war in Spain, when we were laying siege to a convent called Santa Maria del Cerrito, which was defended by Spanish monks and soldiers. I set off a mine and broke in through the hole it made in the wall. You know how we did things in Spain, don't you? The men were shot or hanged and as for the women, nuns or not nuns . . . well, you can imagine the rest. Their Virgin was handsome enough and covered with jewels, of which I obtained my rightful share. The others drank and gamed theirs away or wasted them on women. I had more sense; in fact, I meant to go into business with the proceeds when this Russian campaign was over. But, as you see . . ."

"There's many a slip . . ." said Scacerni, in his usual proverbial way of speaking.

"Bravo! It almost makes up to me for everything to see that my treasure has at least the effect of making you drop your pose of virtue. That's why I'm leaving it to you." He spoke in tones alternately spiteful and fatuous, whose incongruity might under different conditions have been laughable, and inevitably returned to his chief fixation: "If I tell you that these things are under a ban of excommunication you must believe me! We did violence to the Church in its buildings, possessions, and in the persons of its representatives; we were guilty of profanation and sacrilege. So you too will be subject to excommunication *latae sententiae,* as they say in Latin. You can take my word for it. If you approach the sacraments after you have accepted my inheritance you are profaning them and damning yourself to eternity. So either you care for money or else you're afraid of hell! And don't be surprised that I should know all these fine points of ecclesiastical law. I haven't been talking nonsense, you know. I studied for the priesthood, that's how I came by my Latin. Yes, I *was* a priest. Doesn't that put the fear of God into you? Shall we burn this paper and save your soul? Or shall we hang on to it?" He made as if to throw the ivory case into the fire, but Scacerni brusquely held him back.

"I say let's wait and see, Captain."

"Ah, if that's what you say I see I wasn't so far from wrong in my estimate of your character. Keep it then and enjoy your state of excommunication the way I did. I had to submit you to this trial. For a moment, do you know, I nearly doubted you! And I'm the man that shot the priest of San Pietro Bolognese for his offense to one of our trees of liberty! You can imagine what doubt means to me!"

He was talking not so much to Scacerni as to something deep down inside of himself, in the mystery of the nature around him and the fast-approaching shadow of death. Mingled fear and rage came into his eyes as he shouted:

"I die as I have lived. If God exists then I shall be judged as a renegade priest and hell won't be wide enough to hold me! No! I'll keep faith with myself!"

A great clot of dark blood spurted out of his mouth and he fell back lifeless.

"An ugly death!" Scacerni muttered gloomily, putting the ivory case in his pocket. "And the time he made us waste with his chatter! Not that I mean to speak ill of him now that he's dead."

The woman leaned over Mazzacorati, murmured a prayer, closed his eyes and pulled his coat up over his face.

"He lived longer than these others," said Scacerni, pointing to the dead bodies around the half-extinguished fires. "And perhaps he deserved it less."

"It's not up to us to judge his deserts."

These words stirred something in Scacerni's conscience and softened the growing irritation he felt against the dead man.

"Quite right," he said, baring his head. "I'll take care of him now. But first let me bind up your feet. We've a long walk ahead."

He bent down on one knee and asked her while he worked:

"What is your name?"

"Lisaveta Fyodorovna."

His head was still bare and she ran her hand affectionately through his thick hair. There was no more time to be lost. They set out, taking as long strides as they were able in the clinging snow, having turned their backs after one lingering last look upon the dead man's body, which seemed longer than before but frail and slight. The snow was falling on his face and had begun to shroud him all over.

SAINT MARTIN'S DAY

As THEY caught up with the columns of soldiers, who were advancing slowly over the snow, an officer shouted to them in Italian:

"Is there no end to these damned creatures? If only they'd stayed home instead of cluttering up our way!"

Scacerni was startled to realize that the officer must think neither of them had understood him. Then he remembered the leather Tartar cap and fur coat that he was wearing and knew that the officer had taken him for a native of the country. He smiled to himself, for it would be easier for him to obtain his freedom if he was not recognizable as a soldier.

He feigned stupidity and fear at the impatient words of the officer, who beckoned to them to move faster. The fugitives and stragglers had, in fact, been lined up farther on, just behind the advance units, with skirmishers, or velites, as Napoleon had baptized them, of the Royal Guard to contain them. As they went along Scacerni did not see any of his old comrades. The fording of the Vop had cost as many men as a battle and practically eliminated all that were left of the engineers. From the rear there came every now and then a short and weak crackle of gunfire, which served to quicken, if only for a moment, the dragging steps of the fugitives. As he trailed along behind them Scacerni wondered how there could still be such a long black line of these wretched creatures when so many of them had been lost in the river or had never even tried to cross it. He was ill at ease to be once more part of the herd and began to figure out how he would get away.

They had just come out of a stretch of woods, piled high with snow, when they saw the sprawling village of Ducóvchina before them. This was the first civilized place, untouched by the war, that they had seen since Moscow, the first houses that had not been plundered and destroyed by peasants, Cossacks, or soldiers of one army or the other. A loud shout of joy and longing rose from the multitude. In the cold air they could see chimneys smoking, and these meant shelter against the cold and food to satisfy their hunger. And the fugitives were arriving first and would be the first to enjoy them, thus staving off for a day the prospect of a painful death. They pointed gaily to the village, laughing as if they were drunk, and in defiance of the velites broke out of line, raving with excitement. They had managed to run ahead of the cautious cavalrymen of the advance units, when out of the village charged a group of Cossacks, who fell upon them with musket fire and thrusts from their swords and lances.

36

These were, as they learned later, the Cossacks of General Ilovaiscoi, who had been ordered to lie in ambush in the village in order to harass the remnants of the Fourth Army Corps. Instead they met up with the wretched fugitives, who stopped in their tracks, as if their bewilderment at the perversity of fate were greater than the fear of being massacred. But soon the velites with their rifle butts and the light cavalry with the broad side of their swords pushed them back into line, screaming and cursing. A moment later arrived the first columns of foot soldiers, with their arms in readiness, and when the Cossacks came up against this organized resistance they scattered in their usual way underneath a hail of bullets, while the infantrymen prepared to enter the village in a more prudent manner.

Luck would have it that Scacerni, who had been at the rear of the line of fugitives, did not join the first rush toward the village and now found himself in the forefront of those who had been driven back into formation. The cavalry had deployed in pursuit of the Cossacks, and the infantrymen were closing their ranks and reloading their guns. Scacerni saw that only an open space separated him from the village, a snowy field littered with fallen bodies. He did not stop to reason but moved instinctively. Taking the woman by the arm he started to plunge through the deep snow to the nearest houses. Someone called out to him in French and Italian, but he pretended not to notice and did not turn around. He heard one of the velites shout to another: "Shall I shoot him down?" and a companion tell him to save his ammunition and let the fellow come to his rightful end on the gallows. This made him smile. In a few minutes he was out of their range and among the outlying wood or mud huts of the village, which stretched out along an empty main street, where the snow was trodden down and covered with slime. Here, with Lisaveta at his heels, he broke into a run until, near the end of the street, he ducked into a miserable side alley. The first door he tried was unlatched. The woman stopped to lean panting against the doorpost of the rude, dirty hut. Outside, in a roofed-over pen, a pig squealed.

"I don't want that pig to attract other guests to this inn," said Scacerni, drawing a knife from under his coat. "Go in and see if we can start a fire. I'll see to the chops for dinner."

The pig squealed but once more. Scacerni came in holding it up by the hind legs, dripping blood on the floor.

"We've no time for making blood sausages, so we'll have to let the blood go. But chops will do very well instead. What are you doing? Twiddling your thumbs?"

Lisaveta shook herself, but no more than to change the melancholy look on her face into a wan smile as she watched young Scacerni, puffing and laughing, busy himself with putting wood in the open fireplace and the stove, striking a flint and lighting up. He started to cook some thick slices of pork, keeping one ear cocked for any noise from outside. The walls of the hut were dilapidated and covered with smoke, which even now had begun to fill the room. Whether continuing good luck or instinctively keen judgment had led Scacerni to pick this forlorn place, the fact was that they had so far been undisturbed, while all around them soldiers were laying sack to the village. Soon the smoke made them cough and cry. Scacerni looked for bread, but all the cupboards were bare.

"We'll have to do without," he said regretfully, going back to watch the pork, which sizzled appetizingly on the embers.

Lisaveta had stretched out on the wide, flat heating stove, attached to the wall. Suddenly the door was flung open and a corporal and two soldiers appeared at the threshold.

"Ah!" Scacerni explained. "The smell of broiling meat has brought them."

The bitter fumes of smoke made the intruders pause.

"I can't breathe!" said the corporal. "Who's in here, anyhow?"

Scacerni towered up out of the smoke, unmistakably a rough fellow, spattered with blood and mud, still pretending that he was a Russian. His eyes were bleary and the expression on his face so evil and threatening as he stood there brandishing his knife that the corporal raised his gun.

"What's this? Have we uncovered a partisan in his lair?" .

This was the name given to Russian irregulars and hostile peasants and Scacerni knew that the word alone, without even so much as a suspicion behind it, was enough to warrant a summary execution.

"I'm an Italian like yourself," he said, making a quick choice between two evils. "And I've meat to eat. How many of you are there?"

"A dozen in all, but we have two kids and some chickens to add to your roast. Is it pork?"

"Yes. Glad to have your contributions! But we'll be packed in here like sardines."

"There I agree. But the best places are all taken. We'll post a sentinel at the door to keep this one to ourselves. Meanwhile, lay down that knife; your meat is burning."

The corporal and his companions were all men of a certain age and a mellow disposition, whose chief desire was to satisfy their hunger. After he had put away his knife Scacerni pointed to Lisaveta, saying that he had acquired her as a camp follower, and they were content to congratulate him on this new recruit. What really interested them was the odor of the meat, which gave them cramps in their empty and constricted stomachs. They ate greedily, and only when they had taken the edge off their appetite did the corporal open his mouth to say:

"It needs salt. But it's good, all the same."

The corporal wore the heavy beard which among Napoleon's armies was the distinguishing mark of the sapper or specialist of some kind. He and his fellows sucked even the clean bones, so great was their hunger. Then the heaviness of the meal, the heat of the room, and fatigue all conspired to overcome them with sleep. They lay down on the floor, and some of them dropped off with their mouths still full.

It was the eve of Saint Martin's Day and the Viceroy had ordered forty-eight hours of rest in Ducóvchina for all that was left of the Fourth Corps.

Scacerni, certain that the others would not awaken for many hours from their stupor, climbed up on the stove beside Lisaveta. All of a sudden he remembered that he had touched her when she was stark naked in the snow and slept with her soft, womanly body in his arms. Now she was trembling.

"These are friends, I told you. You needn't be afraid. Or are you afraid of me? That would be very ungrateful of you."

"Neither one nor the other. It's my own people that terrify me."

"What a woman won't think up! And I thought you were so brave! Are you afraid of the Cossacks? I wonder where they've gone."

"You don't know . . ."

"What should I know? What a handsome creature you are? I can see that in spite of the smoke."

But she stared at one corner of the hut and said:

"Do you see the empty niche over there? That's where the peasants kept their icon. Perhaps they didn't have time to save anything, even the one pig in the sty. Somewhere they may be starving this minute. But they took their icon away in order that it should not be touched or even seen by the soldiers of the Antichrist. That's what you are, you and your comrades. And do you know who I am and what I stand for in the eyes of my own people?"

She spoke with mingled fear and sorrow. Scacerni was intrigued, but he did not know what to do except to hold out his flask of brandy.

"Perhaps this will cheer you up. Have a drink and forget about the Antichrist. What wild ideas you have in your head!"

She drank deeply and her face passed from pallor to a ruddy glow. Now that the smoke had gone down the light from the dying fire fell on her beautiful and anxious face with the eyes enlarged by terror.

"Did that brace you up?" he asked in a kindly voice, taking back the flask.

The reflections of the fire in the half-dark room, the heavy odor arising from the sleepers, the silence of the surrounding village, where the snow was once more noiselessly falling and every house was crowded with tired and replete men all contributed to making him feel warm and lazy and oblivious of all but the present. He took hold of her hands and she proceeded to pour out her confession.

"If you only knew!" she said. "If you had seen what I have! But I understood too late. Why do you think I fled from Moscow? Since I was living in sin, I had every comfort anyone could want. I had admirers who provided me with everything: servants, horses, jewels, furs . . ."

"I knew that!" said Scacerni awkwardly. "I said to myself when I first touched you that you had quality."

"I was known all over the city. Nobles and officers came to my house. Many a wife was jealous on my account, I can tell you . . . Did you see Moscow burn?"

"How could I have missed it?"

"The fire didn't reach where I lived, and I stayed. I didn't want to lose my wealth and all the precious things I had in my house. And so I stayed on. I received your French officers. I didn't see what was coming. They too made me handsome gifts and told me I was beautiful. They said their Napoleon was invincible and soon the Czar would sue for peace. They had their orderlies wait on me. I thought I was safe. And they had charm, I must say I liked them. We were very gay, we ate and drank and made love. Then when I realized that the French were leaving Moscow! . . . Before they had come I had seen foreigners and traitors of every description marched under my windows. I had seen them beaten and spat upon by the population. With my own eyes I had seen them, and yet I had learned nothing. Now I remembered, and knew that my turn had come. The Russians would soon be back and hear of my hospitality to the enemy. They would whip me to death. That is why I ran away. But I shan't escape them."

"Don't say that."

"All of us will die."

"Where I'm concerned, that remains to be seen. Don't speak too soon."

"And will you help me to safety?"

Scacerni felt a twinge of conscience. To take her for his own, by sheer force, seemed to him no more than right after what he had done. But it was not like him to make a promise that he had no intention of keeping. And the undertaking seemed to him too serious an affair with so long a way to travel. He kept silence and she mistook it for consent.

"I don't want to die! I'm afraid! Save me! I still have my looks!"

This was true enough. Her long, soft, black hair fell over the rounded shoulders emerging from her loosened blouse. Her neck was smooth and fair, and her lips were red from drinking the brandy. Scacerni put his arms around her yielding waist, between the wide hips and full bosom.

"Moscow's gone up in smoke," he said. "They won't remember you there after all they've been through."

"You don't know," she said in a mood of sorrowful resignation. "But I want to go on living! If you save me I'll be rich again some day and reward you with a fortune."

"You too!" said Scacerni laughing. "Just like the captain. Strange, isn't it, how everyone here in Russia wants to be my benefactor!"

There was a feeling at work in him much stronger than lust, which insistently bid him get away from this place and save his own skin. Just outside of Ducóvchina, at the moment when he had heard the velite say behind him: "Shall I shoot him down?" he had resolved not to let himself be caught up again in the mob of fugitives but to trust to his own strong legs to carry him alone through the forests and across the rivers, defying frost and starvation. Even now he had a tickling feeling between his shoulder blades. How could he carry out this resolution with the responsibility for a woman to impede him? His reticence did to some degree alarm her. Perhaps, after all the attention she was used to receiving, it hurt her womanly pride. And perhaps she thought it an easy matter to enmesh such a rough sort of fellow in her toils when she suddenly slipped off her clothes and offered herself to him.

"Silly! Can't you see how much I like you? I'm not asking you anything, for tomorrow we'll all be dead."

The glow of the fire cast bright lights and deep shadows on her body. In this atmosphere of warmth and inebriation Scacerni really did attract her. In a low, hoarse voice she murmured inviting, lascivious words of her own language. He took her over and over again until they were both exhausted and fell asleep, side by side.

Scacerni did not know what time it was when he woke up, but his first thought was to get away. A moment later he was greedily sorry to leave the woman beside him, for the sight of her aroused renewed and more brutal desire. But if he delayed she would surely awaken. And all through his sleep he had kept before his eyes not her image but his firm resolve to escape. He slid down onto his feet, fastened his clothes, packed up a good part of the meat to take with him and glided in swift silence out into the open air.

It was dawn of the feast of Saint Martin, patron of soldiers. On this November day, in his own country, they drew off the new wine, amid spirited and often rowdy festivities. Perhaps the corporal and the other old soldiers asleep in the hut behind him were dreaming of the parades and extra rations and fireworks with which this holiday was habitually celebrated in their home garrisons. Or perhaps their memories wandered still farther back to scenes of peasant revels, late on the eve of the holiday, with lusty wine spilling out of the newly-filled vats and drunk with a dish of roasted chestnuts to the accompaniment of bawdy serenades to inconstant widowers and deceived husbands. But as they lay immersed in sleep, and the happily exhausted woman of Moscow beside them, Scacerni had already put them out of his thoughts. He was all eyes and ears as to how to creep out of Ducóvchina without running into any sentries who might hold him for questioning or shoot him down as a partisan or spy.

Thirty thousand Italians went to Russia with the Viceroy Eugene's Fourth Army Corps, and of these only two thousand came back alive. It is proof of their valor that in spite of everything they did not surrender to the enemy a single one of the military ensigns and banners they had so proudly borne with them. A week after the fording of the Vop the Marines of the Royal Guard, attached to the rear guard of Marshal Ney, were wiped out to the last man during the three terrible days of Krasnoy which preceded the complete rout of the Grand Army as it crossed over the Beresina.

1
God Save You

THE TREASURE
OF THE VIRGIN OF SPAIN

1

A<small>T THE TIME</small> when Lazzaro Scacerni forded the Vop River and ceased to take part in the Russian campaign, the people of Ferrara no longer counted the years in terms of the floods in the Po Valley but according to the repeated levies of the Napoleonic armies. The most calamitous of these, in 1813, had netted eighteen-year-old boys for combat service and orphans and foundlings of an even more tender age to serve as midshipmen and drummers. The people were physically and spiritually exhausted, underfed and disheartened. For lack of seeds and farm hands the crops of the years 1813 and 1814 were dismal failures. When the levies ceased, after the Emperor's abdication, everything was dated from the years of famine, and poverty peopled with thieves and adventurers the plains and lagoons and seacoast of the land between the Po and its tributary, the Reno.

Now Napoleon reigned on Elba and few of the inhabitants of the village of Ariano on the Po remembered a ferryman by the name of Scacerni, who disappeared during the disorders of 1809, much less his son Lazzaro, who had just come back from Russia. Hardship and danger and violence had hollowed his cheeks and hardened his eyes and acquaintance with foreign tongues seemed to have stripped him of the use of his own, leaving him taciturn and melancholy in contrast to his former lighthearted self. A still youthful, unkempt, silky beard fell down over his chest and gave him the appearance of a bandit. In the course of his interminable and hungry travels he had had recourse to every sort of trade and expedient until finally in Dalmatia he had found passage on a sailing ship from Ragusa that was carrying wood to Venice. The master of the ship, when he heard that Scacerni was on his way to Ferrara, spoke to him of a certain Michele Bergando of Ragusa, formerly a well-known pirate and smuggler. The continental blockade aimed against Napoleon had led him to go in for smuggling along the lagoons of the Comacchio region and the mouth of the Po. At this occupation he had made so much money that, so the master had heard, he had retired from his evildoing and settled down to live like a gentleman in Ferrara. Nevertheless, the master said, without revealing how he came to know the man's affairs so well, he still received and disposed of smuggled or stolen goods, not because he needed the money, but simply in order to keep a finger in the pie and because, frankly, his tastes ran in this direction. He was known by the nickname of Raguseo and dressed in Turkish style in memory of some youthful years he had spent in the Levant, where he had gone native and taken unto himself three wives. He was a man of medium stature but unusual strength, with a placid, non-committal face, hooded eyes, and a straggling mustache.

This information Scacerni tucked away in his memory, all the more retentive because he was illiterate. More and more frequently, especially now that he was closer to home, he wished that he had wrung from the unfortunate Captain Maurelio Mazzacorati the name of the Jew to whom he had consigned the treasure. Of course the name was written inside the ivory case, but it was of little use to him because he did not know how to read. He had in mind to procure himself instruction in this art, because he did not feel he could trust knowledge of the name to anyone. As for the sacrilegious origin of the treasure and its spiritual consequences he had not forgotten them but had resolved with the considerable willpower at his command to think about them as little as possible. The north wind carried him faster than he had expected to his native land, for after unsuccessful attempts to cast anchor the ship was laid up to wait for better weather in the inlet known as the Sacca dell'Abate. Thence through the woodlands of Mesola and the valleys of Belbosco and Goro it was but a short distance to his native Ariano. Every inch of this countryside he knew well, for here he had been brought up by his father, who came of a long line of dwellers in the Po Valley and was a ferryman by trade and a fisherman and poacher by avocation.

From the still waters of the inlet, where the ship now lay at anchor, Lazzaro gazed at the narrow beach sloping down from the very edge of a clump of trees, whose waving branches were reflected in the water. The branches rustled wildly from time to time in a blast of the bitter north wind and this familiar noise caused him to leap back in his memory to the days when he and his father (of his mother there had for some reason never been any mention) used to go out with bows and arrows and nooses to catch birds and other small woodland game or to lower fishing nets into the streams of the valley. He had learned to know not only the beaten paths but every secret trail and thicket as well, every marsh and hidden passageway in the neighborhood of Ariano, which was almost an island among a network of waterways between the main body of the Po and the branch called the Po di Goro. He knew too the becalmed salt-water inlets along the coast, with their shoals of shifting sand amid the myriad muddy rivulets of the delta. Here he had acquired sharp eyes and ears and familiarity with the use of the harpoon and the navigation of a punt propelled by a long pole touching the river bottom. Along with his acquaintance with the ways of birds and fish went the ability, in case of need, to disappear noiselessly among the tall reeds and grasses, once he had placed his own clandestine net or appropriated the contents of the teeming wicker basket of another unlicensed fisherman.

Now he looked out at the woods bordering the inlet and thought back to the free and easy life he had led as a boy. It was to something like this that he wished to return, all the more so because, as far as he could make out from what people were saying, the combination of old rulers and new, Papists and Austrians, went in for strict policing on both sides of the Po. Everyone had to account for his movements and show his papers, wherever he travelled or chose to stay. Such restrictions, which had never been to his liking, now went very much against his grain. Moreover the priests and organized religion must have re-acquired considerable power and Mazzacorati's explanation of the consequences of his sacrilegious act came vividly and threateningly back to mind. Night was falling and everyone on the ship had sunk into a happily exhausted slumber. Lazzaro was just as glad, for the bond between the ship master and the retired thief who was a receiver of stolen goods seemed to him to bode some evil. His aim was to have as little to do as possible with either enemies or guardians of the law, an intent which he expressed in the motto: "Stay honest and fancy-free." So strong was his yearning for independence that he took off his clothes, tied them up in a bundle around his head, dropped silently over the side of the ship and swam ashore. Once on the deserted beach he gave a quick look back to make sure that everyone on board was still sleeping and then plunged into the woods.

The woods and valleys of this region were at the beginning of the last century far more extensive than they are today, when so much land has been reclaimed for farming. Now nothing is left of the Mesola forest but a narrow strip, between the Valle Giralda, where woodland animals go after dark for a drink of fresh water, and the brackish Sacca dell'Abate. The sun had long since set when Lazzaro started to walk among the silent trees. He had a knife and a dagger and these were quite sufficient for his needs. It would be easy enough to harden pieces of wood in the fire for a primitive harpoon and twist horsehairs into nooses for catching wild birds.

He had no reason to go hungry, even in the dead of winter, and the prospect of malaria during the summer months did not frighten him. He built a rustic cabin, hidden among the tall reeds of the valley, and lived there at his ease for the time being, with less concern for the difficulties of everyday existence than for the possibility of finding a way to move further on and put to use the precious paper left him by Mazzacorati. He turned this question over and over in his mind, while he lay in wait for fish or game or when he had nothing at all to do. The few other human beings he ran into were as silent and unsociable as himself and they understood each other at first glance. The last thing in the world anyone of them dreamed of asking another was where he came from or where he was going. Meanwhile Lazzaro's fixation on the subject of the mysterious piece of paper was based half on curiosity and half on defiance. To think how quickly the secret would be revealed to anyone who knew how to read a few letters! He wondered very often whether there was not somebody to whom he could entrust his burning question, but could think of no one except perhaps a priest in the confessional, and there were obvious reasons why he could not have recourse to the Church. His father, as far as he remembered, had no close friends, and he himself had left his native village of Ariano as a small boy, under circumstances which we shall relate below.

2

One day in the year 1807, after the battle of Austerlitz and the peace of Tilsit, at the height of Napoleon's glory, Scacerni, the ferryman of Ariano, had business in Ferrara and took his young son Lazzaro with him to the city. The boy was overwhelmed by the experience, all the more so because on the same day Marshal Masséna was passing through, at the head of twenty thousand crack troops and amid a dazzling martial display, which was announced by cannon salvos from the Fortress and greeted by eager crowds in the streets. There paraded before the wide-eyed country boy the magnificent horses of the Piedmontese cavalry, the brilliant red uniforms of the strapping Swiss infantry, the proud and ferocious-looking recruits from Corsica, and last of all, to the general astonishment, a battalion of American mulattoes. The paving stones rang with the soldiers' cadenced steps and the drumbeats echoed through empty houses, whose inhabitants had all gone up to the roof to see the unaccustomed sight. Tall drum majors in conspicuous dress twirled their batons, threw them up higher even than the roof tops and caught them again without falling an inch out of the line of march, and all the while the regimental bands outdid themselves in blaring martial airs.

Among so many marvels it did not escape young Lazzaro that the drummer boys were hardly a day older than himself and he began at once to envy them.

The boy felt as if he were in a fairy tale come true. These troops had come from every corner of the globe and now, victors of a hundred battles, they were marching, so people said, to the Kingdom of Naples. With fifes and drums and crackling guns they had routed whole armies, taken cities even larger than Ferrara by storm, crossed rivers wider than the Po and mountains higher than the familiar Apennines, which he had so often looked at in the glow of the sunset and longed to explore every time he had a chance to hear them talked about by shepherds who brought their flocks to graze during the winter in the valleys.

Now streets and houses shook to the rumbling passage of the artillery. All over the surface of the earth they went, these soldiers of Napoleon, and when they met the enemy, Napoleon himself, mounted on a white horse, led them into battle. Drummer boys no older than himself sounded the signal to attack and Napoleon was certain to win the day. With gleaming eyes Lazzaro confided to his father that he wanted to be a soldier.

48

"That's a trade for desperadoes, and your Napoleon is a sinister rascal. When you're called up you'd best take to the woods. But there's plenty of time before they call you. And many a slip 'twixt the cup and the lip. No use crossing that bridge before you come to it."

They knew plenty in Ariano, perhaps more than anywhere else in the Ferrara region, about Napoleon and his government. Seven years earlier there had been popular disturbances, directed against the innovations brought by the French Jacobins, and these had been punished with military reprisals, which were occasions for violence and theft, insults to the men and insolence to the women. The wealthy people of the village (for Ariano, small as it was, had considerable business) were forced to pay heavy taxes, which led indirectly to the impoverishment of all. Rich and poor alike had a distinct memory of the abuses of this time and felt particular bitterness against those who had outraged their religion, although there had been no mention of "trees of liberty" since 1803, and baptisms and weddings were celebrated according to Christian rites and in the churches.

Liberty and its trees, republics, kingdoms, empires, these were all mere words for a man of Scacerni's condition. What spoke louder were the facts, that is requisitioning, confiscation, taxes and military conscription, all of which grew more burdensome every year. As far as words were concerned, the elder Scacerni had heard the hatred expressed by malcontents, fugitives, political prisoners and draft evaders, who came to him for transportation and shelter. These paid him well, but he served as their ferryman and guide for other motives than that of mere profit.

Just as the valley people counted the years in terms of floods, so did they judge governments by the works they left behind them. And the most recent flood, in 1801, which had submerged both the hilly region of Bondeno and the so-called "Island of Ariano" in the valley, had given them reason to complain that the Papal government was lax in its preventive measures and miserly in its remedies. It was natural enough in this part of the world that they should not know (any more than the professional historians) what was the outcome of the battle of Marengo. But there was one thing that interested every man jack of them, and that was the upkeep and patrolling of the riverbanks both before and during the high tide of the flood. And as for the remedies that should have followed after, these gave them still more cause for disappointment. When a committee of citizens of Ferrara went to seek aid in Milan the ministers told them that they had no intention of abrogating the heavy new taxes which had taken the place of the old. All that the government could suggest was that they reinstate the former local imposts in order to raise funds for their own relief.

News of this answer reached the frozen and half-starved victims of the flood in the melancholy month of *brumaire*, as the Republicans had renamed November. Perhaps on this occasion the ferryman of Ariano, which by virtue of its position was invariably one of the most vulnerable points of the flooded valley, did hear mention of the capital city of Milan, and in what terms it is not hard to imagine. Poverty and taxes; taxes and poverty.

Then came the continental blockade, which interrupted commercial traffic of every kind and cut off the market for the hemp and cereals that had formerly been the mainstays of trade along the Po. With the general increase in prices poverty turned into hunger and famine. At the end of 1807 came a repetition of the difficulties of 1801 and when Ariano once more asked to have its taxes lightened it received another humiliatingly negative answer. Increasingly sweeping levies of new troops deprived the land of farm workers, and the government compelled parish priests to draw up the hateful lists of those eligible for the draft.

These troop levies came to be celebrated in song and story. A hundred years later our grandmothers could still remember the words to a melancholy song sung by girls whose sweethearts had been taken away:

> *Napoleon, in truth,*
> *Has carried off the flower of our youth.*

There was an end, too, to the shaky religious truce between Emperor and Pope. The report came to Ferrara that on June 12 a wagoner called Mengacci had been brave enough to nail on St. Peter's door Pius VII's excommunication of Napoleon. But Pius was to undergo the same captivity as his predecessor.

News that Prini, the Minister of Finance in Milan, had decreed a new tax on milled grains was the last straw. From every village and parish and crossroad a swelling crowd of peasants marched to a chorus of church bells upon Ferrara. On the morning of Sunday, July 9, six thousand men stood in front of the hastily barred gates of San Benedetto, San Paolo and San Giovanni, to the west, south, and east of the frightened city. The instigators of the march were counting on the fact that the city's regular garrison was in large part absent, either in the wars against the "fifth coalition" or in unconquerable Spain. But they had little command over the motley crowd that stood now before the gates. There were farmers with forks and scythes, fishermen with their harpoons, a few hunters with shotguns and some "rebels of 1799" who had brought out their old carbines. Their vaguely unifying motive was to avenge the Pope and retaliate against famine and high taxes. Most of them had tagged along with only the vague idea that there were great riches stored up by the Jews in the ghetto. To lay their hands on these would be not only blameless but meritorious, a fitting punishment for heathen usurers, who had on their heads the blood of the Saviour.

Faced with barred gates and threatened by a sortie of the national guard, which had sprung to arms at the signal of alarm given by rolling drums, the mob withdrew and turned to sacking some of the outlying villages. But the next morning most of them were short of food. A con-

50

siderable crowd gathered in the Borgo San Giorgio, just outside the gate of the same name, attracted by a large firing piece which some enterprising fellows had hoisted up among the bells in the church tower. Every now and then they took a random shot at the Porta San Giorgio, in spite of the fact that their weapon was better suited to mowing down ducks in a pond than to making a breach in the walls of a city that had been in its time one of the mightiest strongholds of the continent.

Among those perched in the church tower was the ferryman of Ariano. His son, who had grown excessively tall and thin in the two years since Marshal Masséna's passage but possessed the solid bony structure of the powerful man he was later to become, stood among the crowd in the church square, half overcome by hunger and sleep.

Midsummer heat swept across the plain, and the Borgo San Giorgio, together with the remains of the monastery attached to the church, was overflowing with people. Some of the earliest recruits, after having plundered a few farms in the surroundings, had gone back to their homes. Those who remained plus some latecomers, drawn by the dull thud of projectiles against the gate, were men inured to the hardships of a rough and independent sort of life, who might have taken for a motto the local saying to the effect that no man is so poor that he hasn't a knifeblade with which to provide for himself. They had large, rugged bodies, primitive, harsh faces and thick mustaches and many of them showed the ravages of malaria in their rough, somewhat bilious complexions. Their arms were not merely the tools of their trade, but guns, pistols, knives, picks and axes. They stretched out to rest in the open square in front of the church or in the old monks' graveyard, in silent expectation or whispered colloquy. In their eyes were courage and cupidity, acute fanaticism and an even more acute hunger. If there had been a chief ready to lead them in an attack they might well have captured the city, which was in a state of consternation on account of both the siege and a dire accident within the walls.

Seven or eight soldiers had accidentally set fire to an explosive mixture which they were grinding in mortars in the powder magazine of the former Charterhouse, now an arsenal. Enveloped in flames, with their clothes and skin burned off their bodies, they rushed madly outside and rolled in the grass, "amid such complaints and lamentations as were never heard before," as a local historian has it. Their agony soon ended in death at the Sant'Anna Hospital.

Meanwhile the peasant mob continued, with greater stubbornness than might have been expected, to lay siege to the Porta San Giorgio. As their numbers lessened, so their discipline grew, and they organized themselves into squads, built up on a basis of family relations or friendship, with the best among them as leaders. Some of them had got hold of a bag of flour and were busy mixing and cooking it under the arcades of the half-destroyed monastery. In this way the siege went on for a week. On the fourth night they went so far as to try to batter down and set fire to the gate, but it stood fast against their battering rams and torches, and the guns of the defenders caused them several casualties. Meanwhile the firing piece they had mounted in the tower fell short of ammunition. On July 15, the ferryman came down from his post and stood with his son, listening to what people had to say in the square. The crowd had thinned out considerably and those who were left had begun to disagree, when suddenly a shout went up and they fell apart in every direction, most of them huddling around the tower or door of the church, while hoofbeats and rifle shots rang out among them. A few sporadic efforts to re-group the dispersed peasants and induce them to draw arms only served to increase their disorder, while the attackers, French dragoons under the command of General Grabinski, who had been summoned posthaste from Bologna, rode them down without mercy.

The dragoons had cut their teeth in the savage guerrilla warfare of Calabria and the mere mention of bandits or brigands was enough to make them see red and strike with sabers and broadswords about them. Hundreds of refugees piled into the church, while others wisely took to their heels in the open country where Grabinski's men were not numerous enough to pursue them, especially as everyone wished to be in at the kill of the bulk of the victims. Galloping back and forth across the square and shouting at the top of their lungs, they trod down living and wounded and dead alike under their rearing and foaming horses, whose chests and hooves were splashed with human blood.

The bell tower had one door opening onto the graveyard and another, which still exists today, into the church. Here the press of the crowd was the greatest. Lazzaro was separated from his father, whom he last saw running up the stairs of the tower. He himself had found refuge on the roof of the church where he squatted down so that the dragoons should not see his head sticking up and use it for a target. The square in front of the church was piled high with the dead and wounded, when the peasant who had reached the top of the tower opened fire on the dragoons, now engaged in herding their prisoners into the church below. The dragoons ran furiously to the door of the tower, whose narrow stairs were jammed from top to bottom with men who could hardly breathe or keep their eyes from popping with the pressure of their fellows around them. Those on top of the tower lost their heads completely and began to throw down bricks on their enemies, and the dragoons, in turn, decided to force the stairs by hacking their way up, step by step, through the solid mass of living flesh that now occupied them, throwing the pierced and inanimate bodies down the well behind as they advanced from landing to landing. The blood, sweat, stench, shouts and general madness brutalized them completely, as laughing and swearing they hastened to accomplish their horrible slaughter. Meanwhile the line of horses which they had left in front of the church gradually lengthened until it stretched almost around the square. From the top of the tower came a deafening roar, an atrocious sob that echoed in vain against the pitiless blue sky.

Lazzaro had been paralyzed with fear, but now that the massacre was nearly over he remembered that he had last seen his father disappearing into the tower. The dragoons had reached the summit and the few peasant survivors were swinging from the bells and hanging out from the narrow barred windows, as if they were seeking escape from an all-devouring fire. Among the outcries of terror and the death rattles of these unfortunates the boy heard, or imagined he could hear, the savage laughter of the dragoons as they forced their victims with the points of their swords to drop off their perches to certain death below. Some fell upon the roof of the church, which lay directly under one of the tower's four windows, while the rest piled up in a bloody heap on the ground.

When night came the street was peopled only with corpses. Lazzaro crept down into the empty church. The door was wide open but there was not a living soul inside. He wanted to search for his father's body but the difficulty of the task was too much for him, and he was afraid of being caught and killed without explanation. The night was clear and the sky was clustered with stars. He knew that if he let himself go in tears and despair it would be all up with him. And so, pulling himself together, he set out by foot for Ariano. But he had not gone far before a civilian patrol laid hands on him and took him back to Ferrara. The city prisons were spilling over and the deconsecrated churches of San Romano, San Niccolo, and Spirito Santo were put to use to house the influx of captives. There they lay, many of them wounded, on piles of rotting straw, under the eyes of armed guards posted in the pulpits, with only a few loaves of bread, which chance rather than charity had put in their way, to sustain them. A military court sat for the next eight months in judgment, sentencing them by twos and fours every week to be shot in front of the Fortress. Lazzaro Scacerni was sent, along with a group of orphans and foundlings of his own age, to serve as cabin boy in the navy. Then, on account of his experience in river navigation, he went over to the army pontoniers and took part in the Russian campaign with the second company of engineers of the Royal Guard.

3

Now Lazzaro Scacerni had come home. The inheritance of Mazzacorati might be, for all he knew, a very great treasure, but so far, for reasons that we have already seen, it was inaccessible. Moreover, for him to turn up in any village after months of living in the wilds, might throw him in a suspicious light and even lead to his arrest as one of the numerous outlaws who now infested the region. But one day, after having hidden the precious case in a tree trunk, he went as far as Codigoro, where he saw some almanacs in a stationer's window and decided to inquire inside as to how he should go about learning to read.

He went in timidly and kept one eye cocked on the door, for he had lost the notion of how to behave between four walls and he could read in the eyes of the stationer and his customers what they thought of his uncouth appearance. There was, indeed, something of the savage about him, as if he would feel more at home in stormy weather than under a clear sky.

"I wanted to find out the price of your almanacs, if you would be so kind . . . in case I wanted to buy one."

"Four pennies . . . in case you have the money," said the stationer, a tubby fellow who loved to tease and was emboldened by the newcomer's obvious uncertainty to throw off the mask of subservience and treat him with outright rudeness, winking at the other persons present in the shop as he did so.

Scacerni pretended not to notice.

"The question is how to read them," he said.

"What? You don't know how to read?" said the stationer, raising his eyebrows with feigned surprise.

"I'm thinking of my little niece."

"Of course you know how to read," said the stationer, taking him for a complete fool. "As soon as I saw you I knew that you'd had your share of schooling."

"I'm thinking of my niece, I said, and she doesn't know." Scacerni perspired with the effort of holding himself in.

"Well then," said the stationer scornfully, "buy your niece a book of ABC's. Here's one, for twelve pennies."

"Oh, it's not the price that worries me . . ."

"Of course not. What are twelve pennies to a gentleman like yourself? You, with your knowledge of reading, can be your niece's teacher. Have you more than one niece, by the way? A whole happy family?"

"I see. Because the book alone, without a teacher, won't do the trick, is that it?"

"Exactly. Look for yourself."

The stationer laid it before him upside down and Scacerni looked greedily down at the printed page, unaware of the joke that was being played upon him.

"It's good, clear print," he observed, trying to think of something to say, and gave a deep sigh.

"You're a man of letters, I can see that, since you can read them every which way!"

The provocation was strong, but Scacerni was not tempted to anger. When a man has resolved, not out of weakness but out of strength, to be patient, then he can outlast the insolence of a gadfly such as the tubby stationer. Lazzaro was wrapped up in a feeling of superstitious awe of the mystery and virtues of the mass of little signs on the page before him. He had looked at them with such intense desire that his head was reeling and he put his hand up to his forehead. Never before had he known such embarrassment. The gloating expression of the little stationer and the amused complicity of his customers left him very humble. After all, they could read. A cold sweat broke out on his brow, as if he were a schoolboy caught unprepared for his lesson.

"Is it quite impossible to learn alone?" he said modestly, casting aside the pretense of a niece.

"It pays to be sincere!" said the literate and sarcastic stationer in a highly condescending manner. "Try for yourself, and you'll see. Look here, this letter is called A and pronounced Ah. Now read it."

"Ah."

"And it's called a vowel. It's the first vowel. The second letter of the alphabet is B, and it's called a consonant. Read it, please."

"B," said Scacerni, and he repeated dreamily: "A, the first vowel; B, the second letter of the alphabet, a consonant."

"Good. You are very promising. Here are C and D, the third and fourth letters respectively."

"The third and fourth letters, C, D," repeated Scacerni docilely.

"Now comes the hard part. And then we'll stop for today, so as not to tire you out completely. Combine the three consonants you've just learned with the first vowel, just the way it's printed here. Go ahead."

"B, A," Lazzaro said stumblingly, amid general laughter.

"Now you see why you need a teacher! B followed by A makes Ba. When you've said that, then you've started to read!"

"You have every right to laugh," Scacerni said with a forced smile. "You know how to read and I don't. But if this is all a joke, then I say it ill becomes those who know to trick those who don't."

He had a sudden suspicion that these strange sounds they had made him say were just part of a ridiculous rigmarole. B, A, Ba . . . The blood rushed to his head and his eyes gleamed. Still he kept himself under control.

"What's that about a joke?" said the stationer with condescending superiority. "When you've learned how to put consonants together in every possible order then you'll know how to read. But don't go imagining it's so easy. The alphabet contains all of twenty-four letters, two dozen, do you understand?"

This bit of information puzzled and overwhelmed the ignorant Scacerni and re-enforced his deference toward the stationer.

"Two dozen, you say . . ."

"Yes, in every possible order and combination."

"Very well, then," Scacerni admitted, "I need someone to teach me."

These resolute words were in such contradiction to his vagabond appearance that they awakened the stationer's inveterate curiosity.

"To teach you how to read?" he said with a malicious glitter in his eyes. "What use is that to you? So it's not for a little niece, after all. Or for a pretty sister-in-law, either."

It was clear enough what he meant. What can a poacher or a highwayman want with book learning? But the very irony of this implication put Scacerni on his dignity. He extracted twelve pennies from his pocket and picked up the book of ABC's.

"Look here, man, why should you take an interest in my affairs?

Have you heard the story of the fellow about to be hanged who asked: 'Does the rope slip easily?' Well, what if I am doomed to end up on the gallows? Can't I have taken a notion to read the death sentence with my own eyes? I might even find it written in the book that you're a perfect jackass. Do you follow me? I'm fussy, just like the fellow who inquired about the rope. And here's hoping you swing from one yourself some fine day."

For years and years the stationer said that the strangest thing that had ever happened in his shop was when a bandit with a price on his head came to buy a book of ABC's in order to be able to read his own death sentence. As for Scacerni, he derived no great satisfaction from having put the fear of God in the little stationer. On the contrary, he was left with a feeling of shame for his ignorance, of which he could not rid himself until he happened to find a companion who was leading the same wild life as himself and by some strange chance knew how to read. So, after a time, the ABC book came into its own, although he had not dreamed that the job could be so difficult. Eventually he was able to read the name and address of the possessor of Mazza-corati's jewels: one Ezekiel Annobon of the Via Vignatagliata in the ghetto of Ferrara. And because his newly acquired learning did not degenerate into pedantry, he did not pursue it further.

Scacerni had no definite idea of the year of his birth. He supposed that he was about twenty years old, although on account of the vicis-situdes through which he had passed he felt considerably older. At times he was overcome by a feeling of laziness and indifference, as if he had lived long enough already. This feeling came over him most often when he rediscovered in the valley of Mesola some half-hidden woodland glade or refuge among the tall swamp grass which reminded him of the quiet and uneventful years of his boyhood, which had gone by as swiftly and smoothly as a punt over the stagnant river waters, leaving no wake behind. At times like this he felt ageless and fell into a mystified daze, as if everything in the present had already existed before and were beginning again, not just for the second time but out of eternity. Now that he knew the Jew's name he had lost all desire to go look for him, and it wearied him to even think of the treasure. He could not properly think of it at all without remembering the curse that hung over it, which stood out more vividly in his imagination now that he had put behind his wild military career and buried himself in this lonely existence, filled with memories of the fear of God that had been instilled in him by his father. He had returned to saying his prayers, and thinking back to the dying words of the depraved Mazza-corati he could not pretend to have misunderstood the threat of excommunication. The offense to the Virgin Mary seemed to him both hateful and presumptuous. Is she not the merciful Mother of us all, and who is there to intercede for us on the day of judgment with her Son if we have turned our hand against her? Now he remembered how his father, after many vain attempts to change the subject, had finally answered his insistent questioning about the identity of his mother:

"You have no mother but the Blessed Virgin Mary; see to it that you are worthy of her protection."

More than ever before he felt the undertone of sorrow and terror in the words of his father, who lay buried now in a ditch alongside the other victims of the slaughter at the Porta San Giorgio.

Even when he had one eye on harpooning a fish or picking a game bird off the branch of a tree, he mulled over all these things and wearied of them in his mind. And yet it irritated him to think that such riches should lie idle in the hands of Ezekiel Annobon. If there were only a way, neither profane nor sinful, to do something about them, and surely, with God's aid, there was something he could do; indeed he was quite set upon doing something and the fact that he did not know exactly what only made the prospect more alluring. There were moments when the wild and lonely life he was leading seemed so tedious that he was strongly tempted to join one of the straggling bands of outlaws who were molesting the countryside with their acts of robbery and violence. Many of their number chance had already thrown in his path, and when they had put his discretion to the test they did not hesitate to ask him to join in the nefarious enterprises of which they boasted so freely. Lazzaro stuck strictly to his own business, but he knew that the longer he lived in the wilds the harder it would be for him to steer clear of their highly objectionable company, especially since by his very silence he had made himself to some degree their accomplice. Such was to some extent the attitude of all the country people. They were prudent by nature and traditionally averse to playing the spy or turning in anyone to the government, whose powers were still divided between the overbearing Austrian army and the incompetent and chickenhearted Papists.

Then came the foggy season. Already for some time the morning sun and the fresh breeze that went with it had been hardly sufficient to lift the wisps of white mist exhaled from the floating swamp grasses and other vegetation that clouded over the clear water surfaces among the clusters of reeds in the river. In the evening there were indescribably gorgeous autumn sunsets, when the bright red and vermilion and emerald green of the sky were reflected in the burnished blue of the lagoons until all these brilliant colors faded away together in the heavens over the faraway and enchanted Apennines. Then once more a murky fog reigned over the waters, and the breeze, whether from land or sea, instead of carrying it away only added to its volume. Now the sun, even at noon, only whitened and lit up the fog, but was powerless to drive it away. There was a rustling of the wings of migrant birds and the chatter of wild ducks, which gathered in greater numbers every day to usher in the winter. Then the white shadows of the fog grew wet and heavy and frigid, especially when they were propelled by a gust of north wind. Their kingdom was as wide as the world, and apparently never-ending. Scacerni shivered with uncertainty rather than cold, in his wattle cabin, on his mattress of dry leaves with the damning paper between his hands. He was torn between a desire to burn it and the temptation to set off without further delay to seek out Annobon, the Jew.

It was the autumn of 1814, and the war and famine had given way to a third tribulation. The doctors called it typhus and plain people the plague, but under either name it had a way of carrying away its victims in the space of twenty-four hours. Gaunt, hairy, ragged and pale from living in the swamps, Lazzaro Scacerni looked suspiciously as if he bore its poison in his veins when he came at last to the Porta San Giovanni. It was already dark, on account of the heavy fog, although evening had not fallen, and as he strode along a deserted road through the invisible countryside he felt as if he were approaching a city of the dead. Then all of a sudden the massive, dark, round towers of the ancient fortified gate stood out of the mist in front of him. A treacherous wind pushed the dense, cold mass of fog with an almost crackling sound against the walls and the iron-barred gate. Only a small door at one side was open and Scacerni stood in front of it uncertainly for a moment before he decided to stick in his head.

"Hello there, my man, where are you going?" called out a cloaked Papal guard, who stood just inside, sheltered from the blast of the wind.

"To the hospital," Scacerni replied deliberately. And seeing that the guard was extremely loath to being brought face to face with him he added: "I feel something or other in my bones. . . . Never mind, I hope I'm wrong, but of the four of us there were in the family a week ago, three have gone already and I'm left alone and afraid to be so far away from any neighbor. You know what they say: perhaps it's a good idea for you not to come too near me, if it's true that it's so catching. . . ." And he came closer to the guard, swaying from one side to the other and putting one foot inside the door.

"A very good idea indeed!" said the guard, drawing back in haste, for people said that the plague was communicated not only by contact with infected persons and their belongings, but even by the breath that came out of their lips. "Have you your papers on you? What's your name? Where do you come from? Three from the same family, all in one week, did you say?" There was a tone of rising anxiety in his voice.

"I come from Focomorto," said Scacerni at random, assuming an expression of vacancy. "Focomorto . . . There were four of us in the family. . . ."

"I understand, God help us! Is the plague so bad at Focomorto too? So very close by?"

"Very bad indeed. If you let me through I'll go straight to the hospital, because I'm almost sure I have it. Otherwise I'll just lie down on the ground here outside the gate. After all, what does it matter?"

"Speak for yourself on that score, my friend!"

The bitter wind swept under the arches of the gate and was sucked in through the door, chilling and irritating the guard's throat and chest. He was moved by a mixture of pity and fear, predominantly the latter.

"Go on through," he said, "and hurry up about it."

Scacerni did not wait for a more pressing invitation. But as he was darting through the door the sergeant in charge stuck his head out of the guard room.

"Who's there? Are his papers in order? Where are you going, man?"

But the first guard cut short his zeal.

"He comes from Focomorto and he's got the plague."

"Heaven preserve us! The plague, you say?"

"I'm on my way to the hospital," said Scacerni, stepping closer and beginning to tell his whole story over again.

"Good luck, then!"

"The same to you!"

The sergeant began to make vague gestures of incantation against the plague and on the strength of these Scacerni pushed ahead.

"Have you a couple of pennies in your pocket?" the first guard called after him.

"Let me look and see," Scacerni replied, thinking that the fellow wanted him to pay toll. But now that the danger was gone the guard could afford to show real pity.

"For one penny you can get a bowl of hot soup from the Brothers of Charity."

"What do you know about that?" Scacerni said to himself. "A decent man in uniform!" For he had no very high opinion of the police.

Thanking the guard for his good advice he hurried on, as if he were afraid to leave the other enough time to repent of his good deed. At this point he was suffering so from hunger that he almost wished he were a weaker man in order to feel its pangs less acutely. He had so little money in his pocket that even one penny was a considerable expense, and he did not meet anyone of whom he could inquire about the good Brothers. He was walking along a broad and deserted street near the wall, where on account of the mist he could see no more than a few steps ahead of him and not even a ray of light came out of the closed windows above. Only through the gardens, which abounded in this section, could he hear an occasional church or convent bell, ringing in a broken and suffocated manner. Stricken by a succession of dire events, the once noble city seemed to have lost almost all its population.

Groping his way through the straight streets of this modern section Scacerni soon came to an open space where he could hear a murmur of voices and see the shadowy figures of a group of men and women. They were poor people waiting for charity at a monastery gate and he fell into line behind them. He took the last place, partly out of natural modesty and partly because this was the first time he had been in the position of a beggar and he was mindful of the respect in which, for Christ's sake, we should hold the poor. But his exemplary behavior did him little good, for he could hear them muttering resentfully that it was hard enough to get what they did out of the miserly monks without having to share it with intruders. The women voiced a shrill protest and some unkempt, bearded men who had been disputing among themselves for the first place momentarily suspended their quarrel in order to close ranks under the church porch against the newcomer. Scacerni could not help indulging in a bitter laugh as he stood his ground in the place where he belonged. And he had his reward. The monk who finally came to the door with a bucket of steaming bean soup was thoroughly annoyed by the shameless insistence displayed by those at the head of the line.

"How many times have I told you to let the women in ahead of you?" he said angrily.

Grumbling to themselves, the men gave way, but a moment later they were quarrelling again over who should have precedence.

"Miserable wretches! Can't you understand? Then the last shall be first!"

Repeating, in an annoyed manner, these words of the Saviour, he started to give soup to Scacerni, who, however, had no recipient in which to hold it.

"What? Did you come without a bowl? Do you expect us to give you one? That's fine appreciation for you!"

"I'm a stranger to the city, Father," Scacerni said modestly, somewhat amused by the monk's irascibility, "and very hungry."

The others were quick to catch him up on this.

"A stranger, did you hear? Send him away! Why should he come take the bread out of our mouths? There's no charity here for strangers."

"Oafs!" shouted the monk, overhearing them. "Shameless oafs and pigs! Where did you get such an idea? You're animals, not human beings!" And he added, to the two lay brothers who were holding the bucket: "Get the biggest bowl we have in the kitchen and fill it with soup for this poor fellow. If kindness teaches them nothing, let them learn from hunger. It's no more than they deserve."

The beggars quieted down and Scacerni had a bowl of steaming soup, which was one of the best he had ever tasted. When he had finished he gave back the bowl and spoon with a few words of appreciation.

"Thank the Lord, not His servants," the monk answered.

Scacerni had only dim memories of Ferrara, and the fog further prevented him from finding his way, but he was able to see well enough to know that he was going in the general direction of the four towers of the Castle and the center of the city. As he went along he was attracted by a cheerful light coming out of an open shop. But soon he guessed the reason. The shop was that of a baker, who wished to make sure that no one would lay hands on his bread or his cash box, and just outside Papal Carabinieri regulated the entrance of prospective buyers and saw to it that they did not sack the place as they had recently sacked many of its kind. A small crowd of people stood in front of the bakery and did not hesitate to proffer bloody curses at bakers and millers together. Inside the lighted shop the proprietor's two plump daughters were quick to wait on the customers and even quicker to take their money.

"They're battening on our hunger," cried voices from the crowd. "They sell us the bran and keep the white flour for themselves. Just look how they shine! They're well fed, sure enough! Four pennies and a half for a twelve-ounce loaf of bread, the thieves, and they fill it with rotted flour and sawdust, sharpers that they are! But things can't go on like this forever; we'll put them straight. You won't always have the police to guard you, you murderers. One day we'll settle accounts. One day you'll see!" And the threatening voices grew louder: "One day you'll see!"

Within the shop there was silence, although on both sides of the counter faces were eloquent. The baker and his daughters concentrated fiercely on their business, but their assumed air of remoteness from the loud voices and disturbance outside only accentuated the real nature of their feelings, which were divided between uneasiness and irritation. Almost everyone of their customers had something to say, as he weighed the bread in his hand before paying for it.

"Yesterday it was four pennies."

"Well, today it's four and a half," answered the baker dryly.

"Because there's more bran in it?"

"And it may be five tomorrow," the baker said, with something like a grin.

"Thanks for the good news!"

"We don't set the price of flour, you know; that's the miller's affair."

"Then God give him his just deserts, too! He must be another noble soul like yourself!"

After having had their say, right under the nose of the impassive Carabinieri, the customers went away satisfied, at least for the present. Scacerni had stopped to look and listen, but he did not sympathize with the murmurs of the crowd. The baker's plump daughters were to his liking, and besides he had no use for people who talked without putting their words into action. Had things actually taken a violent turn he would have been willing enough to take part in sacking the shop, but for the present he admired the *sang-froid* of the baker and envied, after what he had just overheard, the power and prestige of the miller, who set the price of flour.

Soon he found himself behind the Cathedral and on the Strada dei Sabbioni. All of a sudden he laughed at the thought of Ezekiel Annobon and the astonishment that would come over his face when he received this unexpected visit.

Recently some of the old laws against the Jews had been restored. They were not obliged to wear a yellow badge sewn over their hearts, but there was talk of putting back the gates at the three entrances to the ghetto and meanwhile they were obliged to be in their houses when the curfew sounded. Those who did not comply with this rule were liable to run into trouble and extortion on the part of the police, and insults, catcalls or even stonings from the common people, who found a distraction from their own misery in making others miserable.

The ghetto was thickly populated and the Strada dei Sabbioni, which led into it, was redolent of kosher cooking and buzzed with the exchange of greetings among Jews hurrying home. The great bells of the Cathedral and of San Paolo were ringing out the fall of night, when Scacerni stopped a man on the street and inquired for the house of Ezekiel Annobon.

"How early it grew dark today!" the Jew replied with the throaty voice and nasal tone peculiar to his nation.

Scacerni repeated his question more loudly, believing the man to be slightly deaf.

"A most worthy and benevolent man and one well acquainted with the Law, one of the leaders of our Spanish School."

"What does that matter to me?" said Scacerni impatiently. He was supremely indifferent to the fact that Annobon was apparently descended from the Sephardic Jews, expelled from Spain, who were the élite of Ferrara's Jewish community. "Where does he live, that's what I'm asking."

"Don't you know?"

"I wouldn't be asking you if I did."

While they talked in this vein they came to the corner of the Via Vignatagliata.

"Anyone who's going at this hour to the house of an honest man ought to know the way," said the Jew.

"There's a Jew's reasoning for you!" Scacerni exclaimed, echoing a popular phrase descriptive of any form of punctiliousness or evasion.

The little Jew had disappeared into the darkness, rejoicing that he had saved an honored fellow countryman from a *goy* of very doubtful intentions. But Scacerni found a less bigoted and suspicious informant and soon knocked at the ancient nail-studded door of Ezekiel Annobon.

"Who's there?"

"A friend."

"Your name?"

"My name wouldn't mean anything. I come from Captain Mazzacorati."

There was a long silence, as if his interlocutor were searching his memory.

"Mazzacorati, did you say?"

"Captain Maurelio Mazzacorati."

"The captain is dead."

"Yes, he died in Russia, I know. But I'm very much alive and my patience is almost exhausted."

"Are you alone?"

"Yes, for the present. But I'll come back tomorrow with means of forcing my way in."

"Wait a minute. After all, I don't know you."

"Then you must take me for Jesus Christ!"

"What need is there to raise your voice?"

"I have just told you that this evening I am alone. But I'll be back tomorrow with the police."

As a matter of fact, no one could have been less desirous than himself of getting entangled with the law. But meanwhile Annobon had decided to choose the lesser of two evils and opened the door just wide enough for his visitor to slip in sideways before he closed it behind him. Scacerni looked around and saw that he was in a long, low-ceilinged groundfloor room, feebly lit up by the lantern carried by his host, a very short, bent old man wearing a robe that came down to his feet and on his head a skull cap, from which emerged a few locks of yellowish-white hair matching his straggly beard. All his vitality seemed to be concentrated in his bright, sharp eyes, which had such a mild and melancholy expression that Scacerni was sorry he had spoken so insolently. This pathetic old man with the thin, curved nose bore himself with such dignity that he inspired respect. Scacerni took off his cap and the cape that he wore, according to local custom, with the right side tossed over his left shoulder.

"I beg your pardon for the late hour and my bad manners. One of your people out on the street made me lose my temper. If it is not inconvenient, I have something to say to you."

"You must pardon me, likewise. These are perilous times for our people. Follow me."

He led Scacerni into a small adjacent room, illuminated by a brass lamp, and seated him beside a table.

"What can I do for you?"

"Well then," Scacerni began, "it's true that Captain Mazzacorati is dead, but how, may I ask, did you know it?"

"Anyone that hasn't yet come back from Russia is not likely to be coming. And how do *you* know?"

"I closed his eyes,"—(he remembered the gesture of Lisaveta Fyodorovna)—"that is, I almost closed them. In short, I saw him die."

"Peace be with his soul."

"Amen, although he died in sin. Do you admit to having something that belongs to him?"

"I don't deny it."

"Good. Then we shall get along splendidly. I have with me the list and your receipt. Here they are. Your signature's at the bottom."

"I recognize it," said the old man, after he had looked attentively at the paper in the light of the lamp.

"And here's the half coin as a further guarantee."

Annobon drew the other half out of a drawer and fitted the two pieces carefully together.

"Is that right?" asked Scacerni. "Do they match?"

"They do, perfectly."

"And what does the agreement say?"

"Everything is yours."

There was a dryness to the Jew's voice that intrigued Scacerni and at the same time intimidated him. He felt vaguely uncomfortable and wished to explain things further.

"Of course you'll want to know how I came into possession of these tokens."

"I don't want to know anything at all," said Annobon emphatically, stroking his beard with one thin hand and raising the other as if to defend himself.

"You don't see anything strange about it?"

"I go by these documents, and they release me of all responsibility."

"There weren't any pen and ink handy out there for making a will, I can tell you. He died of cold and exposure after we crossed a river called the Vop. In fact, I may say without boasting that I saved his life in that river and that's why he made me his heir. . . ." Then, because he did not like to tell a lie, he added: "That's not exactly why either. But now, is the stuff mine or isn't it? When I pulled him out of the river, he was a dead dog, I can tell you."

"All I need are the paper and the half coin you have brought me."

"Capital! You're an honest man! If you knew what we went through in Russia! Yes, he was a dead dog, all right. It wasn't much use my dragging him out of the water because the cold air was too much for him. It sounds queer in the telling, but that's exactly how it went. Do you know the story of these things and where they come from?"

He disapproved of his own loquacity, but it was beyond his power to stem it.

"I don't know and I don't want to know," the old man repeated.

"You're too cautious! After all, you're a Jew; what can it matter to you?"

And he added, laughing and half closing his eyes, with an air of mingled guile and stupidity:

"But you're right, what can it matter, after all? . . . It was just a manner of speaking. . . . I'm the only one that need know."

"Exactly. It's not my concern. Now I'll bring the things out and you can check them with the list. And after that you'll do me the favor of going away."

"Good. I know how to read, you know. I learned for this very purpose."

When Scacerni was left alone a tumult of unexpected and contradictory emotions swept over him. He wanted to confide still more fully in the old man and thus absolve himself of he knew not what guilty feeling, and at the same time he was annoyed that he should have spoken so freely when the other did not even care to listen. And it surprised him to realize that, with the treasure almost in his hands, he was moved not to joy but to dissatisfaction. To come back into society after so many months of isolation, he reflected, was like a glass of heady wine.

Then Annobon came back, carrying a little leather bag.

"It's up to you to count. I wash my hands of them."

Greed lit up Scacerni's eyes and made his fingers tremble as he counted the jewels and the gold. When he had gone over the whole list he wiped the perspiration off his forehead.

"What can be the matter with me I don't know. I never imagined these things would have such an effect. Perhaps it's because I'm weak from lack of food. I feel as if I were drunk. But everything's there. You're an honest man, an honest Jew."

"I know that without your telling me."

"Proud, aren't you? But never mind. I trust you. Can you give me an idea how much this stuff is worth?"

A notion had come into his head that he should sell it all to the Jew, thus ridding himself of a great deal of trouble and transferring to another the weight of the excommunication that he superstitiously imagined was attached only to material ownership of the sacrilegiously stolen goods. What harm could excommunication bring upon a Jew?

"I can't tell you," Annobon said. "And now it's getting late. I should be happy to see you go about your own business."

"You can't tell me? Come, now; not even if I say that because I trust you I'm ready to sell it here and now at a fair price? You've given me proof of greater honesty than that of many Christians. . . . I can just hear them saying: 'How did it happen? Where was it and why? . . .' Yes, they'd probably accuse me of having killed Captain Mazzacorati in order to lay hands on his treasure! But I feel I can count on you as if you were one of my own family. Just give me a fair price and it's all yours, without further discussion."

"Not for anything in the world," exclaimed Annobon with such horror in his voice that Lazzaro looked at him apprehensively.

"What's the matter with you? Even if there were some sort of curse hanging over it, what do you care, since you're fated, in any case, to go to hell? What is it? What are you imagining? Do you really believe that I . . ."

"I speak before Him who sees and knows all. If blood has been shed, then I refuse to take blood money. If there has been a crime, let punishment fall upon whoever committed it. Let Him judge who alone has power to sit in judgment."

Scacerni began to understand.

"Then you really do take me for a murderer," he said slowly and as if with difficulty. "You too!"

As a matter of fact no one had taken him for a murderer before. But he felt tired and depressed and had a presentiment that he would never be able to throw off the burden of this suspicion.

"Then, Ezekiel Annobon, farewell. I'm sorry, because I have come to hold you in high esteem."

"Farewell."

"And what do I owe you for your trouble?"

"Nothing. Nothing at all. Only go away!"

Once more he was aware of the old man's horror and repulsion.

"Very well then, nothing. And yet I could tell you the whole story . . . I could prove . . . But I don't know exactly how. Mazzacorati is dead."

He realized even more strongly than before that he could prove nothing. Pulling his cap down angrily over his eyes and drawing his cape about him he went away without saying a word. Once outside he could feel danger closing in upon him. The Papal police and the Austrian soldiers who held the Fortress must surely send out patrols to make the rounds of the city streets. There he was with no papers to establish his identity and the treasure in his pocket. He knew now what accusation might be brought against him. The only witness to the recent transaction suspected his guilt and might be preparing at this very moment to report it. All of a sudden the dark walls of the city took away his breath, as if they were those of a prison. He was uncertain of which way to go and surprised to find light still streaming from between the shutters of tavern windows, midway between San Romano and San Paolo. The hour he had spent with the honest Jew had seemed so long that he could not believe the night to be still so young. Yes, Annobon was an honest man, and for this very reason he should have taken greater care not to offend him. The confusion and discomfort he had felt a few minutes before were now turned into anger and anxiety. Meanwhile a tempting, greasy odor came out from the taverns and reawakened his appetite, which had been stimulated rather than assuaged by the monks' soup. He was in the oldest section of the city, among narrow, winding alleys and low houses, inhabited for the most part by people of ill repute. The few of them with whom he came face to face showed no inclination to waste their time. Standing in a half-open door with the light behind her a prostitute invited him in. Scacerni could not help laughing.

"If they knew what I had in my pocket,"—(and he fingered the bag as if he were afraid it was lost)—"they'd have a knife in my back quickly enough! But it would be even more of a joke, now that I'm such a rich gentleman, if I were to die of starvation!"

After crossing the wide streets of San Romano and San Paolo, with which he was already acquainted, he made a vague effort to keep away from the Cathedral, the Castle and the crowded Giovecca, the three places in the middle of the city where he might expect to run into the greatest number of people. Suddenly there loomed up out of the fog in front of him one of the four towers of the Castle, with its thick walls and the drawbridge over the moat around it. A military patrol marched close by him, but since it was too late for him to step aside he walked straight ahead and they did not disturb him. On the other side of the Castle he started along the Strada dei Pioppponi, lined with princely palaces, which seemed to him so endlessly long that it was all he could do to overcome the urge to run. He felt as if the whole city were at his heels, intent on taking the treasure, proclaiming him an assassin and carrying him off to prison.

A full moon had climbed up in the sky, penetrating the fog and lighting up the façades of the magnificent palaces, relics of another age. Scacerni walked with the stealthy tread of a thief or a hunter, his ears cocked for the sound of another patrol. But fortune was with him to the end. He climbed up on the city wall, on whose summit stood a row of trees, and there he found himself on a level with the fog, which lay over the city and spread outside, like a vast blanket, over vast stretches of underbrush, woodlands and marshes all the way to Lagoscuro on the Po. There was an early-winter paleness in the damp, moonlit air and a stillness so complete that the leaves of the poplars along the street Scacerni had just left behind him were silent. The plane trees planted on the wall had begun to lose their foliage, which was strewn on the ground below.

In this region outside the city walls the scions of the House of Este had once had villas and pleasure gardens, long since overgrown and finally submerged in the water, destroyed along with all their artistic treasures. Only the name *Il Barco* lingered on, kept in usage by people who no longer understood its meaning. And because the poor, in an effort to sanctify their own misery, are wont to associate power, opulence and worldly beauty with sin and damnation, they imagined this region as the site of a witches' sabbath and all sorts of other diabolical legends. And they especially believed in the existence of one particular and very noisy devil, Urlon del Barco, or Blow-hard, whom Scacerni could vividly remember as a terrifying nightmare visitant of his youth.

Now he smiled as he remembered this devil, who was famous all over the countryside for his practical jokes and other escapades. He would appear at a peasant woman's door dressed as a friar or beggar and when she went to fetch him a crust of dry bread he would break all the eggs in her kitchen or transform them into cabbage stalks or pieces of coal. When the women went to market he would squeeze into their baskets in the guise of a bearded baby and then, to their fright, disappear into thin air, hurling a shrill laugh and a string of obscenities behind him. Even those among the peasants who had never laid eyes on him and doubted his existence blamed him for the hail that destroyed their crops, and millers and boatmen held him responsible for sudden squalls on the river. For this good reason, before going to bed, they raised a rough cross or lit a fire of olive branches in front of their dwellings in order to bar his way. To scorn or forget this rite would have been both foolhardy and stupid.

Scacerni, then, had never doubted Blow-hard's existence. Now, as he prepared to lower himself over the wall, near the old and decrepit Porta degli Angeli, into Il Barco, the devil's domain, he went through a moment of chill and hesitation.

"A dry mist, that's a sign of good weather," he said to himself reassuringly. "If Blow-hard knew how hungry I was he wouldn't come anywhere near me."

Then he crossed himself and slid down the rough and worn surface of the wall, which offered any number of jagged places to which he could catch on. Below, the fog, in spite of being lit up by the moon, was thick and blinding. He crossed the muddy ditch and struck out on a path that promised to lead away from the city in the direction of Lagoscuro. He could hardly see a step before him and the path pursued a winding course among the bushes and tall grass, even seeming at times to disappear among the reeds or mingle its track with another. But Scacerni had taken his bearings by the stars before going down the wall, and he had as a plainsman an instinctive bump of direction, even in foggy weather, among the overgrown marshes. He was quite sure of being on the right way to Lagoscuro and somewhere between the main highway, which he wished to avoid, and the road to Francolino. It did not surprise him to find a path so freshly beaten in this sparsely inhabited region, for he knew that both Il Barco and the woody Diamantina on the other side of the highway were passageways for smugglers operating between Ferrara and the Po and refuges for the daring bandits who fell upon travellers, often those who were going on official business between Rome and Venice and Vienna. Scacerni had heard some of these bandits whom he had met while he was hiding out in the valley brag of the profitable "jobs" that could be pulled off by a bold hand in the vicinity of Lagoscuro. He had no particular reason for going there himself, other than to escape from the city, and now, as he thought about the lay of the land, he was smitten by the fear of being held up and robbed of his treasure. He had brought his knife and with it cut a stout, gnarled stick from the first tree along the way. Thus he was sure of being able to defend himself against two or three assailants. But what if they were to ambush him in larger numbers?

"Fancy that!" he said to himself somewhat excitedly, trying to pierce with his eyes through the thick, milky fog. "I've been a rich man for only an hour and already I'm afraid my wealth will be stolen. That's natural enough, though; I could hardly have known such fear when my pockets were empty. What's unnatural is that I should be afraid of both thieves and the police. Well, there you are; a man must take things as they come, and this is the way they've come to me. Even that old Jew, an honest man if ever there was one, was convinced that I had murdered Mazzacorati. No matter how solemnly I swear to the truth of my story I'll always meet with the same incredulous and shocked reception. So how shall I transform this treasure into money? And even if I do, to what good use can I put it? Money's not like wheat that grows if you put it in the ground. How am I to go about spending it? Queer that I should have so many worries, just because I'm a rich man!"

The mere thought of the fact that he was now a rich man tickled him somewhere between the ribs, gave him a warm feeling deep down inside and made him want to kick up his heels with happiness. Then, a moment later, some rustling leaves, the shadows of a clump of trees, or the sudden appearance of a solitary trunk in his line of vision caused his hand to go automatically to the hilt of his knife, while with his

68

other arm he brandished the stick fiercely about him. At such a moment he started talking to himself again:

"Here I am, rich, and what use is it to me? Look how hungry I am! God knows I've been hungry in my time, but never the way I am now with this gold in my pocket. Hunger . . . Hunger . . ." (The word alone was enough to bring up a yawn from his empty stomach.) "Just see what a mess things are in this world of ours! There's no place for me among honest men, and I'd be even worse off among thieves. Aside from the fact that I have no intention of playing the fool or the floater. So what am I to do? Who's to speak up for me? That Russian woman, Lisaveta! Who knows where she is or what end she's come to, poor creature? A good bit of water has gone down the Vop since then! And even if, by some miracle, I could produce her as a witness, who would believe her? The only thing that can save me is for that devil Blowhard to be so obliging as to pull Maurelio Mazzacorati's soul out of the hellfire where it's now burning!"

These unspoken joking words, which had become cruder and more blasphemous as they went along, were frozen by a sudden fright, which sent shivers running up his spine and made his scalp tingle. With his eyes staring and his hair standing on end he gripped the stick in his hand spasmodically, but there was not enough strength left in his arm to raise it an inch from his side.

"Holy souls in purgatory, have pity on me," he murmured between chattering teeth.

The complete and oppressive silence around him served only to increase his terror. Not a breath of wind was stirring, and yet a faint, deathlike current of air had brushed his face. It did not occur to him that it might be caused by the silent and invisible passage of a bat or other nocturnal bird, because he had it on his conscience that he had called upon the devil to help him and having done injury to a dead man's soul.

"In the name of the Father and of the Son . . ."

But he was unable to lift his arm, even to make the sign of the cross. Something that might have been the bark of a lost dog sounded in his hallucination like an outburst of unnatural and inhuman laughter, a threatening and yet sorrowful cry of hate, anger and despair from the throats of damned souls and fallen angels together. Gradually it was transformed in his mind into the typical wild and fearsome cry of Blow-hard, the devil of Il Barco, and now it ran all around the horizon, echoing from everywhere at once and nowhere in particular, spreading itself out but growing no fainter. Because his nerves were on edge and his imagination was aroused by the darkness, the least rustle, perhaps caused in reality by an animal's cautious progress over the dry leaves, was enough to persuade him that he was hearing mysterious footsteps, first fast, then with an interval between them that made his blood run cold. And before he could count them the direction from which they seemed to come shifted brusquely from north to south. Fear made a nauseous taste in his mouth.

69

"This is just the hour for Blow-hard to be abroad," he thought to himself.

But the flesh-and-blood man who came to meet him was walking quietly along with a pack on his back.

"What brings you to this place at this time, my good fellow?" asked the stranger calmly.

"I come from Focomorto," said Scacerni with indescribable relief, recovering his aplomb as quickly as he had lost it. "The plague has killed off my whole family."

"Then, if you don't mind, keep your distance."

"I've left home," Scacerni continued, "without any idea as to where I am going. I have no work and must find some way to earn my daily bread."

"And it's out here that you're looking for work? You're more likely to run into something that will cure you of wanting or needing such a thing as bread forever."

"I'm looking for anything I can find. At this moment I've lost my way."

"Just tell me this: have you had the plague yourself? They do say it leaves people a bit touched in the head."

"I hope I may be wrong, but I think I have it this very minute."

"Then stay away from me! Now I begin to see why you're here, although, to tell the truth, at first I suspected you of something quite different. If you take the first turn to your left you'll be on the highway and there, mind my words, you'll travel faster and more securely."

"And does the highway lead to Lagoscuro?" asked Scacerni, bent on confirming the other's conviction that here was a man either delirious or outright crazy.

"Yes, and as I told you, it's the only safe way. With which, I say goodbye."

"And what might you be carrying over your shoulder?"

"Ha, ha!" said the stranger, without answering his question. "Now I know for sure that you're not a spy. You wouldn't be so brazen as to ask me such a question. Have you ever heard of the 'salt road'?"

"No, never."

"Just as well that you haven't. Be sure to stick to the highway, now. What's your name, incidentally?"

"They called me Blinker, because there are days when I can't stop my head from shaking," said Scacerni, who was enjoying the farce thoroughly.

"Well, I'm known as Big Brother," his interlocutor said proudly, fully convinced by now that he was dealing with an idiot. "I can't tell you just why, but that's an honored name in Ferrara. Look here; have you a strong back and can you keep your mouth shut?"

"I can carry a two-hundred-pound pack all day long, if you must know. And as for keeping my mouth shut, well, if you hadn't spoken to me, I'd have gone by without saying a word."

"Good for you," Big Brother said in a mellifluous manner. "As one

man to another, I want to do you a favor. If you don't find work at
Lagoscuro, go look in Ferrara for a man called Raguseo. If you have
the qualities I have specified he'll give you honest work to do."

"What do you mean, honest work?"

"Not the work of a spy, that's certain. And now goodbye."

"Goodbye."

Scacerni reflected, as he went his way, that this was the second time
this man Raguseo had been called to his attention. As for the salt
road, he knew that this was the name given to a network of smugglers'
communications among Ferrara, Venice, Tuscany and the Papal States,
complete with letterdrops and posting houses for the change from one
relay of horses, mules, oxen or human bearers to another. The contraband might be almost any sort of goods on which the dealers desired
to evade taxes and duties, but the old and flourishing trade in salt between the Adriatic ports and the interior had given its name to the
whole agglomeration of secret roads.

Scacerni arrived quickly enough at Lagoscuro and at the beginning
of his stay there fortune somewhat treacherously smiled upon him. He
came at a time when the port was handling a heavy traffic in grain
bought up and shipped out by the Austrian soldiery. Longshoremen
were in demand and in this capacity Scacerni soon earned enough to
exchange his ragged clothes for a new mohair suit, into whose seams
he sewed his precious treasure. Then this temporary hum of activity
in the port came to a sudden stop, for the supply of grain was not
sufficient for the needs of the country, much less for exportation
abroad. Scacerni became acquainted with a new kind of poverty, one
that dulls a man's body and demoralizes his spirit in involuntary idle-
ness and indifference. His stomach was heavy with protracted hunger
and he passed his time yawning and sleeping, happy enough when it
was a bright day to curl up at the foot of a sunny wall with his companions. He managed to live by going from house to house and about
the docks and doing odd jobs for which he received slices of corn
bread, given to him in charity rather than in payment for his often un-
solicited services. His sluggish condition was the effect not only of his
forced inertia and the skirmishes he had with malaria and pellagra, but
also of the precariousness of his newly acquired riches and of the concern he felt about them after so many years of careless day-to-day
living. Every now and then he let himself be carried away by wild
dreams, in which he became so involved that it made his head ache to
try to puzzle a way out of them. He was beginning to acquire the
mentality of one of those eccentric beggars who pile up some miserable
treasure in a filthy, flea-ridden mattress and die still sleeping upon it,
to the amazement of those who find out what was their true condition.
He could see no way out of his troubles except by recourse to Raguseo,
and this went against the grain because it was tantamount to declaring himself a thief, while he strenuously protested to himself that he
was innocent. And his reluctance stemmed also from the fact that he
was ignorant of the real worth of the treasure (here he invariably

cursed softly at the Jew who, with all his honesty, had refused to put any value on them) and therefore afraid that Raguseo would blackmail or cheat him.

At night, in the chilly dockside warehouses, where he and his fellows among the unemployed were allowed to make their lodging, he hunted mice, which some of the men considered a very delicate food, claiming that a grain diet had purged them of any uncleanliness or impurity and made their flesh particularly tender. Scacerni could not bring himself to eat them but he whiled the long, sleepless nights away by devising all sorts of ingenious ways to catch them and offering them to those who relished them as the mainstay of their diet. But eventually the mice became slyer and more agile at escaping his grasp. They too grew thinner and increasingly nervous with hunger, and connoisseurs declared them less and less tender tidbits.

"Do you know any trade?" Scacerni was often asked when he was looking for work.

"I'm Jack-of-all-trades and master of none," he would reply.

"Then go to Occhiobello. That's where there are shipyards and drydocks, where they build boats and water mills for use on the Po. Hundreds and hundreds of them there are, and almost all of them built at Occhiobello. In the old days when merchant ships from as far away as Holland and England came here for cargoes we used to send to Occhiobello for caulkers. That's the place to go if you really want to find work!"

They talked so much about Occhiobello that the very idea of it bored Scacerni almost as much as Lagoscuro, where apparently they considered him only an extra mouth to feed and were anxious to get rid of him. Occhiobello was only five miles or so away, but on the other side of the river, and the Austrian guards stationed at the pontoon bridge had a way of asking every traveller where he came from, where he was going and why, who were his parents, where he was born and how he made a living. The Austrians had strong garrisons at Ferrara and Comacchio and kept a watchful and jealous eye over the Papal government. Around Ferrara, where they had taken to requisitioning food for their troops, people said that the Austrian eagle had two heads, the better to eat with, whereas Napoleon's eagle had only one. Joking is a form of consolation, and the evils of the present always seem to surpass those of the past. Of course these garrisons were given to the Pope for love and protection, but the fact was that he had no choice but to accept them, for they ensured Austrian passage over the Po in case revolution were to brew once more in Italy. Napoleon was at Saint Helena, having left bewilderment rather than peace behind him, for the magnitude and singularity of the events of recent years made it seem unlikely that things stay long settled or that any peace endure.

In March the Austrians started to engage men to work on a bridgehead which they had suddenly decided to throw up in Vallonga, just across from Occhiobello. The project entailed filling in and levelling the ground, cutting down trees, and making the prescribed sort of embankments, and since the Austrians offered generous and punctual pay it attracted Scacerni and such of his fellows as were really anxious to find work. For several days Scacerni wielded a shovel, but when he heard that at Occhiobello itself the Austrians were building pontoons for a bridge he offered his services as carpenter and diver, having indeed had considerable experience along this line before.

Captain Hauptmann, who was in charge of the bridge building, soon singled him out for his skill and found out that he had been a pontonier in the Imperial army. Veterans of the Napoleonic wars, and particularly of the campaign in Russia, were already looked upon with curiosity and astonishment, and such a reaction was very natural in Captain Hauptmann, who happened to have lived through them at a desk behind the rear lines.

Of his own personal affairs Scacerni told the captain no more than was necessary in order to substantiate his story that he had not ever really known where he was born. As a faithful soldier of Metternich and the Holy Alliance and an enthusiastic supporter of the new Restoration, the good captain was quite ready to see in Scacerni the son of an obscure martyr, a ferryman who had died in the tower of San Giorgio for the sake of legitimacy and religion. And as a result of these sentimental considerations Scacerni received a testimonial to the good work he had done on the bridge, which was obviously a useful identification paper on either side of the Po. Meanwhile Captain Hauptmann had warmly recommended him to the parish priest of Occhiobello and forced him, for the first time in many years, to go to confession.

Scacerni was a believer and took the sacraments seriously, for which reason he would much rather have put off the accomplishment of this duty. He finally managed to excuse himself for passing over in silence the story of the treasure stolen from the Virgin of Spain on the grounds that it had not yet yielded him any profit (he had hidden the jewels under a stone in the attic where he had taken a lodging) and that it was not yet too late to restore it. This was a very weak argument and the omission of the fault from his confession was a grave one. But we are not called upon to judge him here, and besides it may be said to his credit that although he felt justified in this line of reasoning, he was not, strictly speaking, happy about it.

In the long idle shipyards of Occhiobello men worked again day and night over anchors and cables and boards for the keels of pontoons. Hammers rang, planes scraped, saws screeched and axes, wielded by expert hands, shaped pieces of wood of every size and shape. Great vats of boiling tar filled the shore, which was shaded by poplars and willows, with odorous smoke. There was a gaiety in the air such as had not been seen over a number of years, when not only poor boatmen and fishermen but even prosperous millers had carried out no more repairs on their craft than were strictly necessary.

In April King Joachim Murat descended upon Ferrara, riding intrepidly along with a plumed helmet on his head in pursuit of the mirage of an Italian crown. His men scaled the walls and besieged the Austrians in the Fortress, while two former colonels of Napoleon, Borghi and Negri by name, took advantage of the general confusion to open the city gates to him and to raise a volunteer corps for his support. With these volunteers and the few regulars he had brought with him Murat attacked the bridgehead at Vallonga. It was a clear day and the countryside was green with new leaves and grass. Visibility was good and the whole population of Occhiobello came down to the riverbank in order to watch the battle waging on the other side. Murat's men advanced over the swampy fields and along the riverbank, from Casaglia and Lagoscuro, in such thin lines that they could almost be counted one by one. Every now and then they came to a halt and fired at the Austrian embankments, from which came no reply. The smoke of one isolated rifle shot after another went up from these advancing lines; afterwards a volley of gunfire crackled all the way across the river and its smoke hid them momentarily from view. Then the cannons had their say, and Scacerni felt a familiar excitement in his legs and running through his blood. Horsemen rode between one line and another, but soon all were enveloped in smoke and the battle was invisible. Scacerni saw a cannon that had been put in place by some of the men who had been working under him hammer at the approach to the bridge. By evening it was known that King Joachim's soldiers had advanced as far as the system of breastworks, barricades and fortified farmhouses of Vallonga, but at the cost of unnecessarily high losses. The next day they courageously renewed their assault, but to no avail, and soon afterwards the Austrians made a sally in force and a decisive counterattack. Occhiobello, on the opposite bank of the river, could see nothing of the actual encounter, but witnessed the flight of the most undisciplined and demoralized of the attackers, who jumped over bushes and ditches and along whatever narrow roads or paths they could find in their hurry to leave the battlefield behind them.

King Joachim was later to finish his adventurous attempt as bravely as he had begun it. As for Colonel Negri, he escaped to America and ended his days at Saint Thomas in the Virgin Islands. This was Scacerni's last experience of the involuntary prickly and tingling sensations produced in an old soldier by the sounds of battle.

"It's all up with the brother-in-law," was Captain Hauptmann's only comment on Murat's campaign on the Po. Even Scacerni knew that Murat had married a sister of Napoleon, and understood these words as an epitaph.

A provisory Austrian government was set up in Ferrara and from a conversation between Captain Hauptmann and one of his subordinates who were pointing to a map together, Scacerni gathered that, in order better to guarantee the restoration of law and order, the Austrians had set their boundary lines on the main branch of the Po, taking for themselves part of the territory south of the river that had formerly belonged to the Papal States and Ferrara. Word went around that because the Papal delegates were better at prayer than at topography

74

the Austrian commission had persuaded them that the main branch of the river, where it divides into a host of small streams, was the one called the Goro. According to the new boundary Scacerni's native village of Ariano and the "island" around it passed into Austrian hands and he, as an Austrian subject, should, properly speaking, have been listed by the Austrian authorities as a veteran of the army of the defunct Kingdom of Italy.

Scacerni was not displeased, especially now that he personally was protected by a testimonial of good conduct, to see the Austrian police clean the criminal elements out of the region of the Po delta, a task which the Papal forces had never seriously undertaken. But he preferred to remain a subject of the Pope and to live between the two states, along the river, where he could enjoy the complete liberty to which he still felt so strong an attachment, although he no longer wished to seek it in a hermit's existence deep in the woods and valleys.

The festive *Te Deum* sung at Ferrara when the Papal legate took back the government from the Austrian protectors was singularly lacking in enthusiasm. The bridge and the bridgehead of Vallonga had long since been dismantled and Captain Hauptmann had been transferred from Occhiobello to Galicia, promising Scacerni to show him the upper reaches of the Vistula if ever he were to pass that way. Scacerni went to work for an old shipwright, by the name of Subbia, who soon came to appreciate his ability with the hammer and square and cord and chalk and to regard him not as an apprentice but as a full-fledged carpenter.

"I shall be sorry to lose the services of a man like you," he would say, sighing.

"I didn't say I wanted to leave, Master Subbia."

"And I shouldn't send you away either, my dear fellow, but after we've caulked this hull, which in better days would already have gone into kindling wood, there's no work to do and I don't know when more will be coming. Repair jobs are all that's to be found nowadays. No one dreams of building a new boat. Ah, when I was young! . . ." And out of spite he kicked the hull on which Scacerni was working.

"But until times are better I'll be content with my bed and board."

"Ah, you can lie abed as long as you like, my dear fellow. But your board's another matter. If things go on like this my old woman and I won't have enough for ourselves, and the cat will be left to dance among the cold ashes. Do you know the price of a bushel of corn? Forty crowns! And fifty for wheat! It's positively unheard of!"

"Better days will surely come."

"But when will that be? When we've all starved to death. The peasants are so badly off that they've had to take to the mills the wheat that they had put aside for sowing. And that's a sure sign of famine to come."

"Yes, that I've heard tell."

"Of course. Would I be making up such a story? As a man sows so shall he reap. The famine of last year was nothing compared to this, and next year this will seem a trifle. . . . You'll see."

His sinister prophecy was frightening and all too likely to come true. The winter of 1816 was a hard one in the Ferrara region, and typhus, or the plague, as they called it, raged again, even more devastatingly than before. Master Subbia and his wife were stricken together and no one dared enter their house, not even a nephew who lived at Porpolana, although he was the only relative they had and expected to be their heir. Without the help of Scacerni they would have died like dogs.

"Where did you get your courage?" the old man asked him when the danger was past. "Have you had a touch of typhus yourself already?"

"Not I. But the plague and I are good friends; it's even done me a good turn or two in the past," said Scacerni jokingly, remembering how he had made his way into Ferrara the year before. "And then I was with Napoleon in Russia. Death is more afraid of me than I am of death!"

"From now on there's place for three at our table, or else for none. Wife, isn't that true?"

"God's own truth," his wife nodded. "You shall be like our own son, if it had pleased God to give him to us."

"I shall leave you the shipyard in my will, Master Lazzaro!"

"Don't let's make trouble," said Scacerni. "The shipyard goes to your nephew. But not for many a year, God willing."

"To that coward at Porpolana?"

"Plenty of people were afraid of the plague, Master Subbia. If every one of them were to be disinherited, the world would be a topsy-turvy place indeed."

"There's something to what you say," admitted Subbia, perplexed. "And I see that you're just as honest as I imagined. But we owe you a debt of gratitude which I wish to discharge in one way or another."

"That's nothing. Don't bother your head about it. . . . If it's your turn today, it may be mine tomorrow. We're put here in the world in order to help one another."

"Now you're speaking like the Scriptures."

Scacerni was not really so concerned about family loyalties and the way the world went around. His heart was set on other things and he had no desire to be a carpenter or caulker for the rest of his days. Old Subbia himself had put an idea into his head when he complained about the high cost of food.

"Fifty crowns for a bushel of wheat, and the price is likely to go even higher! But no matter how bad things are your peasant can always get along. He raises his own food: wheat and corn and pigs and chickens. If he hasn't enough money to buy shoes he can go without or improvise a pair of sandals. He doesn't have to spend a single penny in the shops. But in this trade of ours, and I'm not denying that once upon a time it was very profitable, how are we to obtain supplies for either workshop or home without money? Everything has to be paid for in cold cash; there's no other way of procuring wood or iron or the tools to work them. Where there's a business, money must be in circulation. It's like the moisture that's absorbed into the air from the ocean and then comes back to earth again in the form of rain. Do you see what I mean?"

"I do."

"And that means that we craftsmen and artisans are worse off than anyone when bad times come."

"And what trade is the best, then, in your opinion?"

"The miller's, year in and year out, there's no question about it."

"Is he really so well off?"

"Just listen to me and judge for yourself. The peasant grows the wheat, to be sure, but it's no good to him until it's been ground. As long as bread is the staff of life there's need of the miller. When the shopkeeper sends his prices up then the miller increases the fee for his services, and all the while the river turns his mill wheel for nothing! Then there's another consideration that's not generally known. Every self-respecting miller enjoys the lordly prerogative of exacting a toll of the corn or wheat the peasant brings him, for his own use. The peasant takes this for granted and closes an eye to the proceeding, that is as long as the miller doesn't overdo it, for even if the peasant doesn't know how to read and write no one is quicker at calculating what measure of flour should come out of a given quantity of corn or wheat. Let the miller be moderate in his demands, if he doesn't want his profits to stick in his throat."

"In short, the miller makes his own laws and enforces them, is that it?"

"Exactly. He's his own lord and master. But, I repeat, he must clip the sheep gently, not skin them alive. Didn't Napoleon himself bite off more than he could chew?"

Subbia's words seemed to depict the miller's trade as requiring a mixture of mastery, disdain and skill at turning it to profit, and endowed it with an aura of rustic grandeur that appealed greatly to Scacerni's love of unrestrained and honest liberty.

"They say that the mill is the miller's farm, but I call it his bank for multiplying money, as well, an interest-bearing source of revenue that it's hard to beat!"

And Subbia went on to praise the miller's way of spending money almost as much as that of earning it. He described a comfortable family life, with no need for economy, and the charms of the miller's wife who is in all probability given to honest gallantry and flirtation. And Scacerni found this aspect of the miller's existence equally agreeable. But Subbia was speaking, of course, of the millers of times gone by, not of their miserable, gaunt, pinchpenny successors. In his day Subbia had counted more than six hundred water mills, all of them flourishing, along the river.

"As long as there's water in the Po," he exclaimed in a wave of retrospective enthusiasm, "I say the miller's life is a jolly one!"

"As jolly as you like! But why, then, doesn't everyone go in for the life of a miller?"

"That's a fine question! Just because teeth are good to eat with, is that any reason why a man should be made of nothing but teeth? If he were, what would he eat, I ask you? No, not every man is cut out to be a miller. It takes a very stout fellow."

"What do you mean?"

"There are bound to be some drawbacks. Not everyone can put up with a lonely life on the river. There are dangers aplenty."

"And what are they?"

"A flood may break the mill loose from its moorings, or an ice pack crush it and send it to the bottom. There are times when the miller has to struggle day and night against the elements and risk losing his life in the struggle. And then there are thieves. In his isolated position the miller can't count on the police to protect him. When bandits come in the night the miller must satisfy them with one hand and chase them away with the other; he must know when to temporize and when to tell them off; he must keep on good terms with them and yet not be afraid if they use force against him. As often as not there's gunplay involved. Are you up to that, Master Lazzaro?"

"Indeed I am!" Scacerni responded eagerly.

"There's enthusiasm for you! You're enough of a man, I can guarantee that!"

"But I haven't got the most important thing of all, the money to set me going!" Scacerni said, more prudently.

But when he grew surer of Subbia's gratitude and affection he spoke to him in strict confidence of a small sum of gold that he had found during the burning of Moscow and deposited with a Jew in Ferrara, for fear of idle gossip and the inquisitiveness of the police. Subbia gravely nodded approval of this course of action. Finally Scacerni proposed that the shipwright, for the sake of appearances, pretend to take a half-interest with him in the construction of a floating mill, and to extend credit to him for the other half of the cost, which in reality he would pay for out of his own pocket. If Subbia were to do him this favor he might consider himself acquitted of the debt of gratitude which he was so anxious to settle and leave the shipyard to his rightful heir.

"Is that all I can do for you, my friend?" said the old man. "Then I'll make you the finest mill that was ever seen on the Po. Go ahead and fetch your money from Ferrara."

Scacerni was so anxious to embrace his new trade that he did not stop to think again of the source of his money or of the probability of Raguseo's cheating him. Nothing venture, nothing have. And as for his original doubts, he dismissed them with what seemed to him at the moment faultless reasoning:

"Should I have left the treasure for Annobon to enjoy because he has no fear of excommunication? In that case I'd better have been born a Jew. And the Pope can't very well wish that on me!"

78

Meanwhile Subbia aroused in him increasing enthusiasm for the beauties of the new mill, which was to be the crowning achievement of his shipwright's career. Scacerni thought occasionally of Mazzacorati, and in no very devout manner.

"Why did that damned rascal have to tell me where it came from? If only he'd kept quiet, I could enjoy it without so many scruples. A fine way that was to thank me for pulling him out of the Vop!"

In so saying he did not realize that he himself was displaying anything but gratitude. On days like this he was so wrapped up in his passion for the mill that reasoning was quite beyond him. When money is scarce advice is always cheap and old Subbia constantly rekindled his enthusiasm by discovering new attractions in the trade of a miller.

"This is an opportunity of a kind that may never come again. The famine is sure to end"—this was in direct contradiction of himself—"just as worse ones have ended before it. How are we to prophesy? Present evils always seem to be the most dire, but who knows what our fathers endured? And one thing is certain: this too will pass away. Fifty crowns for a bushel of wheat! What do you make of that, my boy? It's something the like of which has never been seen before! But what are fifty crowns?"

This abrupt question hurled into his own argument threw him off his balance and he felt that he must answer it.

"Fifty crowns are fifty crowns, there's no denying that. But old age entitles a man to memories and I can remember the time, long, long ago, when fifty crowns would buy a brace of milk cows or an ox. Those days are gone forever. Fifty crowns haven't the same value today; they're worth thirty, or say thirty-five. And I remember when wheat cost thirty-five crowns a bushel; my father used to tell me that. It's not high prices, then, that make for famine, it's scarcity. This famine, I repeat, will go the way of the rest. And meanwhile, what do we see?"

"I am waiting for you, with your judgment and experience, to tell me."

"Oh, as far as judgment goes, that's not lacking, Master Lazzaro. And experience, well, that's what stays with us when all the rest is gone. Heed my words." Scacerni was all ears. "The present generation of poor or miserly millers (they amount to the same thing and there's not much to choose between them) have let the mills go to ruin. Of the six hundred that I once knew only half are left and they're not enough even for this year's wretched crops of grain. What will happen a year or two from now when, if God wills, it will return to abundance? The mills are wearing out and losing their usefulness. I know how they keep them going nowadays, with a patch here and a patch there to stop up the cracks and a few repairs to the machinery, all expedients that only aggravate their bad condition. I calculate that within two years at the most half of the mills that are on the river today will have gone to the bottom or started to drift or have in some way ceased functioning and have to be towed in for a long job of repairs. Even if the worst comes to the worst people can't eat less than they are eating today. And just imagine the luck of a miller who has planned for the future and appears on the scene with a brand-new mill that can work day and night, in every sort of weather, just as long as there's water in the Po to turn it! There's a prospect for you! Such a mill will be more than a farm to its owner; it will be nothing less than a gold mine!"

With which he drew back, looked at Lazzaro with childlike, gleaming eyes and began to spout proverbs at him.

"Fat sheep make a fat shepherd, I tell you. God never slams a door without opening a window. A man must know when to risk his money because if he hangs onto it too long it will simply make a hole in his pocket. The early bird catches the worm."

And he added with characteristic forthrightness and generosity:

"You've told me how I can help you, and I'm at your service. But I want to do something more than that. If you advance me enough for the immediate expenses of the job: wood, iron, machinery and labor, then you can pay my personal charges at your leisure."

"Those are the words of an honest man!"

"That's what I've always claimed to be."

"And a man of feeling!"

"It's no more than what I owe you."

The two men went scrupulously over their estimates of the costs. Five or six hundred crowns' worth of material for the twin hulks, four hundred crowns for labor, and a thousand for the mounted machinery, altogether two thousand five hundred crowns. Would the treasure of the Spanish Virgin provide this much money? At this point Scacerni was so unwilling to give up the mill that not even on his deathbed would he have confessed its dubious origin. And in his haste to get the building under way he resolved to go to Ferrara, no matter what the risk, and find out Raguseo. He who had always been able to sleep, in no matter what predicament, had not closed an eye for three nights running. He set out early in the morning and before he knew it he saw rising out of the plain the four towers of the Castle, the mass of the Fortress, and the city walls. He had again sewed the jewels into the seams of his suit, which was now that of a neatly dressed master craftsman. Captain Hauptmann's testimonial enabled him to put on a bold face at the Porta San Benedetto and he was let through without any trouble. He made his way to the Castle and the Giovecca, where people of good society passed along the narrow street between the theater and Saint Anne's Hospital on their way to keep an appointment at Tasso's Café. It was not yet the fashionable hour for such strolling, but good weather had brought people out on the sidewalks.

Scacerni's pleasure at visiting the city under circumstances so much more cheerful than before was diminished only by the embarrassment he felt over stepping out in his clumsy hobnailed boots among so many fine ladies and gentlemen. He became even more embarrassed when he suddenly realized the unforeseen difficulty of finding Raguseo. There was no one whom he quite dared accost: one man seemed too respectable to be stopped for questioning by a stranger, another passed by in too much of a hurry, many had faces that seemed to him stupid or insincere or altogether too curious. Scrutinizing and eliminating them as he went along he went beyond the crowded neighborhood of the Giovecca to a street where there were practically no passers-by. He retraced his steps, resolved to inquire in one of the shops, but those too failed to suit him, because they were either too full of customers or the shopkeeper had a forbidding expression on his face. Soon he found himself back in the center and turned to pass under the arcade in front of the theater, still without having made any progress in his search. Losing his patience he went into the first door, which was that of a tobacconist, walked up to the dark counter and bought some chewing tobacco.

"Shopkeeper," he said frankly, starting to bite into the plug, "can you tell me where to find a certain Michele Bergando, more commonly known as Raguseo?"

"Michele," repeated the tobacconist, raising his eyes from the cigars he was engaged in separating; "Bergando," and he let an astonished eye wander over his interlocutor's face; "Raguseo," and he stared into a dark corner of the shop, with a half-blank, half-interrogative expression. "There's nothing missing," he concluded with annoyance.

"And what about the man's address I've just asked you for?"

"Oh, you're asking me, are you? Is that a proper sort of a question? How should I know, is what I mean."

"I had no intention of giving offense."

The tobacconist merely shrugged his shoulders in reply. But from behind Scacerni there came a polite but disagreeably mellifluous voice:

"Perhaps I can help this gentleman."

"Go ahead," said the tobacconist, as Scacerni turned around.

Before him stood a strange, gaunt, round-shouldered individual with a pointed nose and chin in a round face with yellowish eyes, which blinked as if they were unaccustomed to daylight and made him look decidedly like an owl.

"I've heard tell of this Michele—what did you call him?—Bergando . . ." he began.

The tobacconist blew his nose.

"Does something bother you?" asked Scacerni, irritated by the shopkeeper's manner.

"I was blowing the dust out of my nose, that's all."

"Ah . . . I thought perhaps . . . I'm a stranger, you see, and I don't know the customs of Ferrara."

"I'll tell you what you ought to think, inasmuch as you're a stranger," said the tobacconist, but a look from the owlish individual made him end his sentence in a different key. "Think whatever you like," he said abruptly.

"You see, my good man, our friend the tobacconist was counting his cigars and you've mixed up his calculations," said the other. "He's an irascible fellow who takes umbrage at the least thing, especially when he's counting!"

"Then I excuse him. But I still don't know where to find . . ."

"Raguseo, is that it? Well, that I can't tell you, but since I see that you're an honest man I can give you some good advice. I don't really know . . ."

"Then why are you wasting my time?"

"If you come with me I think I can find out for you."

"Come with you? Where?"

"Just a few steps away."

Scacerni looked hard at the tobacconist, who now affected to be far removed from the scene, then once more at the other man's owlish yellow eyes. Something was very suspicious.

"Thanks for your kind offer," he said, "but I don't need your advice. I must have the address, that's all."

And he stepped nimbly out of the shop, looking behind him to make sure that he was not being followed. But the owl-faced man lingered behind, either to scold the indiscreet tobacconist or else because, having decided that Scacerni was not worth any more attention, he had turned to concerns of greater importance.

"The city would be a splendid place if it weren't for spies," Scacerni thought to himself. "Now, what next? The mention of Raguseo's name seems to produce quite a sensation. Just a few steps away, he said, and there, sure enough, is the prison!"

In front of the theater and the café were grouped a number of people, including Austrian officers in their close-fitting white uniforms and, standing a little apart, some officers from the Papal army. These were engaged in conversation with a few civilians, among them one who by virtue of his manner, dress, the cut of his mustache and the way he grasped his walking stick as if it were a foil for fencing, had a martial air, which seemed, however, forced and exaggerated, especially in view of the reserved attitude of the officers to whom he was talking. He gesticulated, spoke in a loud tone of voice and constantly hailed various passers-by, most of whom returned his greeting coldly. To every lady that went by, whether on foot or in carriage, he took off his hat and made a deep bow. Apparently everybody knew him but no one was particularly proud of his acquaintance. There he stood, occupying half the sidewalk and blissfully unconscious of his unpopularity, laughing and talking and bowing away. A young fellow of criminal antecedents, one of those known at the times as "bullies" and recognizable by their swaggering gait and the devil-may-care look on their faces, knocked against him as he walked along. The talker looked him up and down and pointed at him with his cane:

"Do you see that fellow?" he said to the group to which he was talking. "He's one of those Phrygian Caps who robbed the Virgin's altars in Spain for gold to pay for their orgies with. . . ."

"And what about yourself?" the bully interrupted, drawing himself up to attention and making an ostentatious military salute in the French manner. "Weren't you the captain of my company, Signor Antonio Roncaglia?"

The officers, in spite of their dignity, and the civilians with them, could not help bursting into laughter. Everyone looked around, but their attention did not in the least upset Roncaglia's brazen demeanor. Evidently the former Jacobin had sought out the company of the officers in order to draw a veil over the deeds and misdeeds of his past. Scacerni took note of his name, which he remembered hearing on the lips of the dying Mazzacorati, but his eyes followed the quick-tongued bully, who, preening himself on his triumph, was walking away at the awkwardly loose, swinging gait affected by his fellows, most of whom lived on the earnings of some prostitute foolish enough to be taken in by their charms.

The bully walked under the arcade, across the Piazzetta dei Camerini, by the Archbishop's Palace and through the district of San Paolo. He turned on the Vicolo Vaspergolo and arrived in front of San Romano where, pompously as ever, he started to pass under the overhanging balconies that form arches over the narrow Strada delle Volte. Before he could enter any of the dark, lowering doorways so frequent in this ill-reputed part of the city Scacerni laid a hand on his arm.

"That was a clever answer you made to Captain Roncaglia. You gave him back some of his own medicine! Good for you!"

"As a Rogue of Ferrara, I could do no less," said the bully, who was not impervious to flattery. Then, looking Scacerni over, he added: "But aren't you a bit presumptuous, my friend from the country, to stop someone on the street who's never laid eyes on you before? If it weren't that you look ignorant rather than evil, I might have been tempted to take you for a spy."

His manner of speaking was so obviously boastful, as if it were attuned to the standards of his profession, that Scacerni was amused and carried out the game by affecting humility:

"If a Country Rogue may ask a favor of a colleague from the City . . ."

"A Country Rogue?" exclaimed the bully, who as a Rogue of Ferrara belonged to an association of pimps and hired assassins. "I didn't think such things grew in the country!"

"They do, I assure you. Just ask Raguseo."

"Do you know Raguseo?" asked the Rogue, with a new tone of respect in his voice.

"If it weren't for us poor Country Rogues, what would happen to the salt trade?"

"Oh, I've heard of that. A job for broad-shouldered porters like yourself."

"Say for donkeys, and be done with it!" said Scacerni, continuing in a vein of pretended humility. "Someone must do the heavy work in this world, and if a fellow's not clever enough to be a bully he must find some more modest way of making a living. I have interesting news for Raguseo, but I haven't been able to find him at the usual address."

"On the Strada degli Armari?"

"Yes, I was just there, but they told me he was away."

"Raguseo has more than one address, let me tell you, my country bumpkin."

"I thought that on the Strada degli Armari . . ."

"You did, did you? The Palazzaccio in the Strada degli Armari is the best known of his dens. But he has other secret places."

"The one I know is quite enough for me," Scacerni said, with an abrupt change of manner, stretching himself to his full height and displaying the breadth of his shoulders. "Thank you very, very, very much. Just let me give you one piece of advice."

"Give advice to me?"

"Yes. When you're walking along with your chest thrown out in front remember to pull in that bottom of yours in the rear. Otherwise some fine day someone may prick and flatten it for you like a balloon."

"What do you mean by pricking and flattening? Is that a way for a Country Rogue to treat a colleague in the City?"

From one moment to the next his bragging collapsed and gave way to natural cowardice. Looking at the strong muscles and angry eye of Scacerni he grew pale and seemed actually to shrink in stature until he was as shapeless and yielding as a dishrag.

"And hold your tongue!" Scacerni added. "If you open your mouth again you won't be popular with me or with my friend Michele Bergando either."

The Palazzaccio, in the Strada degli Armari, was a building that had seen better days, as was witnessed by the carved marble of the doorposts and the pillars in the courtyard. Now doors and windows were walled up and the dilapidated gate hung open from hinges that had long since given away. The courtyard was overgrown with grass, which however was not tall enough to hide scattered heaps of broken plaster and garbage, peopled with filthy and hostile stray dogs. A large number of hairy half-wild cats of every color and description sat basking in the sun, heedless of the presence of a small army of fat mice which ran to hide among the weeds when Scacerni came upon the scene. The paving of the gallery running around the courtyard was half torn up and irregular and the smoke-stained arches were covered with mold as if they were the roof of a cave. Even the street outside, with grass growing between its cobblestones, as was the case practically all over Ferrara at this most impoverished period of its history, seemed blind and silent.

Scacerni went up the worn steps of the main stairway and knocked at an old and decayed door on the landing. There was no reply but he could feel eyes trained on him from a spy hole. He knocked louder and echoes rang through the building. Then the door opened, and he could see its thickness and iron rivets on the inside. A man stood there, wearing a Turkish-style robe and a round Slavic cap.

"A hard knock's a sign of a strong arm," he said pacifically.

"I've come emptyhanded," said Scacerni, holding out his hands.

Raguseo kept his right hand behind his back.

"Spoken like an honest man!" he said in a courteous tone.

"And a friend."

"That we shall see. I bid you welcome, but if you are carrying any arms you would do well to leave them here in the hall."

Scacerni laid his knife down on a carved chest and threw open his arms.

"If you like, feel my pockets."

"Since you invite me to, it's not necessary."

The former pirate spoke easily and correctly in the Venetian dialect peculiar to the Adriatic coast and the coastal islands, all the way from Istria to Corfu. He fitted in with the description of him given to Lazzaro by the ship master, and at first glance there were no marks of the strength that had made him an almost legendary character. But there was a penetratingly sharp liveliness in his keen and scrutinizing eyes, set close to his thin, hooked nose and incapable of brightening or softening his perpetually threatening frown, which was like that of a bird of prey. Birdlike too, against his dark, olive skin, was their hard, glittering light, as blind as if it were reflected by a mirror. His eyes were not so much evil as they were soulless. For this he was no more to blame than is an animal for the instincts with which nature has endowed it, but his innate naked cruelty was shocking in a human face, all the more so because it was crafty and conscious. As he was aware of the unpleasant effect he produced on other people, the astute Raguseo habitually kept his eyes half closed, with the result that the minute, gleaming pupils, which were as round and black as peppercorns, peered out from under the lids like the mouths of loaded pistols. On his thin lips he wore a hypocritical smile and when he laughed, as he often did, it was in an awkward manner. His voice, which was usually very subdued, had a false ring. The whole man was epitomized and laid bare by his grim and infinitely wrinkled forehead, where every vice and evil deed had left its trace and conflicting sinful passions had carved out deep furrows.

Scacerni's rough boots, which contrasted with Raguseo's embroidered slippers, raised echoes in the large rooms, as if the building were empty, except for its overwhelming number of unmatched rich and exotic furnishings, which made one imagine immediately that they came from a mass of loot or booty and would be at home in the hold of a pirate ship or the cave of a highway robber. Light filtered in from openings at the top of the walled-up windows, and in cloudy weather, Scacerni thought to himself, one would need lamps all day long. At every door they went through Raguseo stood ceremoniously aside, in order that his guest might not pass behind him. After they had crossed several large rooms they came to one that was smaller and better lighted, with luxurious rugs on the walls and floor and a low table surrounded by divans. Raguseo clapped his hands lightly and a boy, clad in Levantine dress and with an effete and effeminate manner, brought in a small inlaid table and Turkish coffee.

"You must excuse me," Scacerni said. "I've not had dinner."

"Coffee is to be drunk at all hours of the day. I mean that you risk offending me."

"That I have no wish to do, since I've come to propose a bargain."

Raguseo sipped his coffee and then put his cup down, while Scacerni waited for him to ask what the bargain was.

"I live in strictly Turkish style," he said, crossing his legs in front of him, "except for my wine. I like only the best and just now I have a cask straight from Cyprus. Will you have some?"

"No, thanks; as I told you, I've had no dinner. And then, if I may say so, I never drink before doing business."

Raguseo showed no signs of picking up this hint any more than the last, but Scacerni proceeded to pin him down.

"I came to ask if you would buy some gold and jewels that I'm anxious to get rid of."

Instinctively Raguseo responded.

"Have you brought them with you?" he said, his eyes gleaming.

"Do you take me for a child? I keep them in a safe place."

"Very wise of you," sighed the former pirate. "One meets such strange people. But you've made a mistake: I don't deal in jewels."

"Then I must beg your pardon and take my leave."

"What's your hurry? I like the way you talk. And your face confirms my liking. Just to oblige you. . . . It's stuff of uncertain origin, more or less stolen, I suppose."

"Suppose what you like. Actually it was left to me by Captain Maurelio Mazzacorati, an officer from Ferrara, who died in the Russian campaign."

"His name is familiar. So you were a soldier, were you?"

"I saved his life in a river, but to no purpose."

"A most praiseworthy deed! A pity that, as you say, it was to no purpose."

"So you too imagine that I finished him off, do you? Well, that's not surprising."

"I? When did I say such a thing? Do you smoke? Did I say anything about your having finished him off?"

And he held out one of the stems of a curved hookah pipe from which he had begun to inhale.

"That's not surprising," Scacerni repeated. "In fact, there you have the reason why I came to a man like yourself who I thought wouldn't ask me who I was, where the jewels came from, how they fell into my possession, and so on. But if I've made a mistake then I shall go my way."

"You have plenty of determination, I can see that, and I'm no mean judge of men. I wish I had met you years ago when I was at sea. We'd have hit it off together, I'm quite sure. We'd have done things, I tell you, we'd have pulled off certain bits of business. . . . But those times are gone. A man begins to feel his age, my boy. . . ."

He was perfectly sincere in his regret for his lost youth and his pirate days at sea, and also in the sudden liking he had taken to Scacerni.

"That sort of business isn't to my taste," said the latter coldly.

"Ah well, every man has a right to his own opinion," the pirate admitted courteously. "But those were the days, let me tell you! Oh, to be young again, and off to sea! That's a life for you!"

"And are you willing to strike a bargain with me?"

"It all depends. If you earned the stuff legitimately, then it has one value; if you found it, the value starts going down; if it's stolen goods, then it goes down some more; and if there's a dead man mixed up with it, then it goes down, down, down . . . do you grasp my meaning?" And he counted the "downs" on his fingers.

"Very well. I shan't hedge on the price. You can take it or leave it."

"What a hurry! Then you're not saying where it came from?"

"Do I ask you where you get your money?"

"I shouldn't tell you, if you did."

"But I don't ask, do I?"

"You've reminded me of something. How am I to know what is your purpose in coming to my house? I'm not curious, everyone knows that, but who are you, anyhow? Who sent you here?"

"Do I look strange to you who are no mean judge of men? Do I look as if someone had sent me? Can't you see that I have my own legs to carry me?"

"As a matter of fact, I believe you," said Raguseo, looking him over thoroughly. "What would you say to our matching the muscles of our arms?"

This trial of strength was Raguseo's way of testing friends and enemies alike, of making them feel the physical force of his arm and imposing his will upon them; moreover it catered to his self-esteem, since he had found few men that could stand up to him and none that was stronger. Scacerni was taken aback, but only for a moment.

"At your service," he said, slipping off his jacket.

Raguseo removed his robe, folded it carefully and began to roll up the sleeves of his shirt, which was of fine silk, but soiled, in contrast to the cleanliness of Scacerni's rough hemp garments. Scacerni towered over a head above his opponent, but height is not necessarily an advantage in a contest of this kind, and the retired pirate displayed a powerfully muscled arm. He laid aside his slippers and with a studiously careless gesture, as if he were getting rid of something that was in his way, took a stiletto out of his trouser pocket and put it on the table. The sheath dropped onto the floor and would have remained there had not Scacerni picked it up.

"Better cover your weapon," he said, "if you don't want it to rust."

Raguseo assented, but made sure that the stiletto slipped easily in and out of the sheath.

"Do you take the game hard?" Scacerni asked.

"No, I stay as meek and mild as a lamb," replied Raguseo, among whose many sins was a very bad temper. "Shall we stand or sit?"

"As you like."

"Then let's be free to change from one position to another," said Raguseo. His plan was to tire his opponent, then to leap up and suddenly bear down on his wrist, for he expected to outwit him even if he was the stronger.

He ordered the boy to bring two wooden benches for them to sit on, and they put their elbows on the table, one on either side of a corner. Then they put their palms together and clasped hands. On both sides the clasp was a powerful one, and they stared hard into one another's eyes.

"Ready?"

"Ready!"

Setting their feet firmly on the floor and holding the table with their left hands they felt out one another's solidity. Both were of iron. Raguseo purposely gave way for a second and managed to push his elbow forward and turn his wrist. He was more than ever convinced that he must win by sheer skill, for if it were a question of endurance the other would outlast him. Even if they were equally matched as to muscle, Scacerni had youth on his side. All of a sudden Raguseo jerked his arm back, with such a rapid and powerful movement that Scacerni's wrist was almost completely turned, and in order to save it he had to let his arm go so far that it looked as if he were done for. But when Raguseo was up against the necessity of bringing both hands down onto the table he was unable to profit by his advantage. Slowly but steadily Scacerni raised his arm to a vertical position again. Just as Raguseo had come to realize that he was the weaker of the two, so did Scacerni perceive that he must be more careful. Raguseo had hard, bony hands and a very powerful grip, with which he gradually increased the painful pressure on the hand of his opponent. At the same time, with a brief but continuous twisting motion, he sought to tire and eventually break down the other's wrist, and this bit of tactics was equally annoying. Scacerni broke out into perspiration and Raguseo breathed hard. When Scacerni brought his full strength to bear on his adversary's arm, the latter was left breathless by the effort of resisting and had no energy left with which to continue the tricks he had tried before. Both men's elbows seemed to be nailed to the table, but the muscles of Raguseo's arm quivered, and the veins stood out on his wrists and the back of his hands. He rose abruptly to his feet, knocking his bench over, and pressed with the full weight of his body upon Scacerni's arm. Scacerni clenched his teeth. He could feel the blood pulsing in his temples and his sight was momentarily clouded, so difficult was it for him to resist. He gave way imperceptibly, lowering his head, staring hard at the table and bending every muscle to the task.

Somewhere inside he still had a small reserve of resistance, whereas Raguseo had expended the last ounce of his strength. With a pained and astonished expression he relaxed, and both arms flew back to an upright position. From then on the younger man's resilience prevailed, and the outcome was only a question of time. Raguseo had the unaccustomed and incredible feeling that he was going to lose and he suffered humiliation on top of his pain when Scacerni repaid him in his own coin for the tactics he had used at the beginning, alternately loosening and tightening his grip, with ever-increasing pressure on the wrist and finally the threat of prying the elbow off its base. Still it came to him as a surprise when his strength suddenly ebbed and Scacerni pinned the back of his hand down on the table.

He bared his teeth and reached out with his left hand toward the stiletto. But Scacerni knocked the weapon into a far corner of the room, while at the same time he relaxed his grip and stood up on his feet.

"You're a very strong man, Michele Bergando," he said, pretending not to have noticed the other's treacherous gesture, but looking him straight in the eye. "It's no more than just to say that at this sport you truly excel."

Raguseo appeared to have got his temper under control. Perhaps he remembered with regret that he was no longer aboard a pirate ship where it's all very easy to get rid of a dead man's body.

"You have a right to judge," he said, still panting, but in a courteous tone of voice, "since you're the first man who's ever beat me at it. It's an honor to be defeated by a champion of your caliber."

But his passion was still inflamed and he had to give vent to it, which he did in a sudden volley of oaths and curses in *lingua franca,* accompanied by obscene gestures, all directed at himself, biting the while at his aching right hand.

"Now I feel better," he said at last. "There's satisfaction in knowing a real man. And to prove it, I am ready to offer a price for the jewels whenever you're ready."

"I have them on me," said Scacerni, struck by the sincerity in his voice.

"Ah!"

This interjection, proffered in a tone of mingled surprise and regret, made Scacerni suddenly aware of how foolhardy it was of him to have brought the jewels with him to a place like this. But he felt sure that Raguseo had no intention of robbing him, in view of the esteem he had won along with his recent victory.

"Very well," Raguseo added. "Go get your knife and we shall bargain fairly and on equal terms."

Both men laid their knives on the table, as a proof that everything was above board, but Scacerni found the bargaining long drawn-out and disagreeable. Raguseo insisted that the gold was twelve carat, or even less, and declared every one of the diamonds and pearls to be cloudy or small or ill cut or in some way imperfect. When finally he offered two thousand crowns for the lot Scacerni felt so relieved that he did not stop to think that either the pirate had cheated him out of a fair price or else, if the price was fair, there must be some ulterior motive behind it. The money was counted out to him in cash and he went back to Occhiobello with wings on his feet, in spite of the fact that his pockets were weighed down with gold.

4

"Subbia is in his second childhood," people said when they heard that he was laying down the hulks of a new mill. "He's giving credit—and for an enormous sum—to a vagabond of very uncertain origin and no particular merits!"

And others quoted a proverb that had wide circulation in Ferrara about those who come suddenly into great wealth:

"A lucky find, or a generous will, or a robber's haul."

At first the local shipwrights, especially the older ones, who had known Subbia longest, all joined together, partly out of inertia and partly because of a paradoxical mixture of friendliness and envy, in criticizing the skeleton and shell of the two big, flat-bottomed hulks at which Lazzaro and the master were hammering away so cheerfully. They could find nothing to say to the fine, seasoned woods—Slavonian oak, and selected larch and so-called Muscovite pine—that were going into the construction, so they fastened their attention on the cost of the job and calculated that it was very high.

"All paid in cold cash," they murmured. "We've got that from a very good source, although of course we're not the sort to count the money in other people's pockets."

And indeed every one of them had gone on his own, under some pretext or other, to ask the dealer who had sold Subbia the wood.

"Cash right over the counter, in times like these! And wood that no one's so much as looked at for years, because it comes so dear. Yes, 'a lucky find, or a generous will, or . . .'"

Now, not even children of the fairy-tale age believe there's much chance of finding buried treasure. And a fellow who said he didn't know where he was born or who was his father was not likely to have benefited from a rich relative's generous will.

"They say he brought back the money from Russia, that he laid hands on it in Moscow, when Moscow was burning."

"And do you believe it?"

"I'm not one to think ill of his neighbor."

"Neither am I. But no one can tell me tall tales, either . . ." and the speaker made a gesture to illustrate what he meant by tall.

"Master Subbia gave him credit because he lent a hand to him and his wife when they had the plague."

"Why didn't Master Subbia tell us that he was ill? We are old friends and know him for an honest man. Which one of us wouldn't have come to his assistance or have sent his wife and children to bring him whatever he needed? I shouldn't have hesitated for a single second. Would you?"

"I? Of course not!"

"The same for me!"

"To tell the truth, I was away at the time."

"The fact is that he treated us in a downright unfriendly manner."

"A friend in need is a friend indeed," dryly observed the man who had been away. His remark brought the others up short and touched a weak spot in their consciences, so that they changed the subject and spoke again of Subbia's financial arrangements. He couldn't possibly have enough capital himself to pay for the expenses he had already incurred in the construction of the new mill. These good people who had been so discreet and lacking in curiosity as not even to know that their next-door neighbor lay at death's door were now informed by gossip from Lagoscuro of every detail of the life led there by Scacerni. They knew that he who was now so neatly dressed had spent a winter less than two years ago in rags, dependent upon public charity and hunting mice for nourishment.

"Hunting mice? That's odd, now, isn't it?"

The oddness of this story inspired them to mockery, and the small boys of the village, as they walked by the shipyard, imitated the miaowing of a cat and the call: "Pussy! Pussy!" of its owner.

Scacerni pretended to pay no attention. First, because he felt that it would be beneath him and second, because he felt that he had certain obligations as the guest and friend of Subbia. But the latter became aware of what was going on when the small boys were bold enough to swing some live mice by their tails over the shipyard fence. He asked for an explanation, but Scacerni told him not to bother his head about such childish tricks.

"They're only brats, of course," Subbia admitted, "but someone's put them up to it."

"They'll soon have enough of such sport."

"I'll make them have enough of it myself."

The lean, spry old man lay in wait with a long whip and when the boys felt it on their bare legs they were soon cured of swinging mice over the fence. Toward evening, when his old cronies came to smoke their clay pipes with him in the shipyard and pass the usual remarks about the progress of his work, he startled them by saying:

"I've decided to give a party and invite the whole village."

They broke out in exclamations of surprise, all the more so because Subbia had the reputation of being anything but a spendthrift.

"Have you won the lottery at Ferrara?" they asked.

"No, but I'm preparing a mouse-fry that will feed everyone for miles around."

"Are we included?"

"Of course; it's in your honor."

"Are you trying to hurt the feelings of your old friends?"

"I only want to save you the effort of coming here to smoke your pipes. If you've nothing to do, there's a much more pleasant breeze on the riverbank than in this yard."

Of course they went away. The old man had dared more than the younger and braver Scacerni; that is, he had defied the evil tongues of the community. But these in due time were silenced. The hardships of the winter of 1816-17, the famine of the following spring, and the high prices that prevailed before the harvest were sufficient to take the breath away from even the most inveterate gossips.

The country people lost all hope other than that in God. But they took courage in May and June, the two months most decisive for the wheat, when rain and sun poured down in just the right measure to make up for the unsatisfactory sowing of the previous autumn, when both seed and fertilizers were lacking. During the anxious days before the harvest was sure, when the peasants wondered whether their crops would yield them enough to pay their debts, and their creditors shared their worry, Master Subbia had something to say about the price of wheat and corn, which had soared far above what he had predicted.

"When things can't be any worse, then they're bound to get better," he insisted. "You'll see!"

Then when the harvest surpassed even the most hopeful expectations, prices began to fall, and people at last took heart again, he added:

"Do you see? Didn't I tell you so? It is the will of Almighty God, Who rules all things, and mends them even when we despair!"

Now that the time of extreme hardship was over and the shipyards began to receive orders for repairing boats and even building new ones, the men of the village grew more expansive and put out feelers for a reconciliation with Subbia and Scacerni. They even went so far as to say, when a miller ordered a new mill, that it was Master Lazzaro's first order which had brought back luck to Occhiobello. None of them seemed to remember the past, except Scacerni, who added it to his experience of how frail a thing is the good will of man. But he kept this gloomy thought to himself, especially because he had no wish to mar the restored good humor of the kindly Subbia, who was so happy to have returned to good relations with his neighbors that he went around saying:

"This village has its faults, but no more than any other. After all, Occhiobello is where I was born and where I hope to die."

Scacerni had no objections, but he could hardly be expected to feel the same way. He was acutely aware of having been homeless for too long, and eager to set himself up in his mill on the Po. This was the life that appealed to him, where he could be alone and not surrounded by idle chatter, where, like the captain of a ship, he could call himself his own master. Every day his longing grew. Meanwhile, he followed the proverbial advice to ask for nothing and to refuse nothing that others asked. For the moment they asked only that he show a smiling face, and this he did not refuse them. Only when he saw a mill wheel turning in the water did he give in to his impatience. The corn crop

92

was as good as the wheat and it looked as if the famine were really over.

The twin hulks had been launched and were floating proudly on the river. With their straight sides, high bows and square sterns, they had a massive and robust appearance. Inside they had a strong framework and their bows were ornamented with arrogantly pointed iron beaks which Master Lazzaro himself had hammered out on the anvil.

"What are they for?" someone asked.

"For decoration," he answered.

Actually he knew that boats and mills whose owners had failed to take the necessary precautions were often swept by the current down the river and bumped into those which were properly anchored and moored to the shore. In such an event he had an idea that his hooked beaks might come in handy. But he was not anxious to incur animosity or to have the reputation of being overly proud or pessimistic, so he refrained from mentioning such a possibility.

The two hulks were actually of unequal size, with the larger one supporting the two pairs of millstones, one for wheat and one for corn. Three main beams connected the two hulks: one at the bow and one on either side of the mill wheel, which continually showered them with the jet of its water. On the narrow deck, at the forward part of the bridge between the two hulks, were capstans and windlasses for mooring ropes and the anchor hawsers. Another means of mooring the mill was provided by a long, jointed wooden pole, made fast to the floor of the bridge.

In coupling the two unequal hulks Master Subbia gave the smaller one a pronounced outward slant. For this reason there were those who called it a lame or a crooked mill. Master Subbia only laughed. Experience, he said, was the best teacher.

"There's more than one current in the Po," he told Scacerni. "In fact there are two, one running parallel to either bank, where we find the mills stationed, at exactly the right distance offshore. The larger hulk is on the inside, where the water moves slowly; the smaller hulk is on the outside, where the water moves quickly; the smaller catches the full flow of the current, a little farther out. When the river is high then the mill runs smoothly, but when it is low and the current is weak then the mill wheel slows up. So you can see for yourself the advantage of the outward slant of the bow of the smaller hulk. When other millers' stones have reduced speed yours will be running as fast as spinsters run after a husband."

Scacerni was amused by the comparison.

"Still the whole mill does swing out," he observed.

"It's all a question of mooring and anchoring it in such a way as to hold it firm. If it offers resistance to the current it will bring more water to the millrace. Never mind what others say. There's none so blind as he that will not see."

Meanwhile the axle was set in its locks and the spokes of the wheel fitted onto it. Aboard the smaller hulk were placed the bins for storage of wheat and corn, a small blacksmith's forge and a carpenter's bench, fitted out to make any necessary repairs. For the miller must have more than one trade at his fingertips. There was also a covered storeroom in whose upper portion were kept fishing nets, bird lure, decoys, a gun and gunpowder. And needless to say there was a cooking stove. The berth in the miller's cabin was a wide one, which afforded Subbia cause for rejoicing.

"It's clear you don't intend to sleep always alone," he said jokingly when his wife, who had taken charge of outfitting the cabin, asked what measurement of sheets she should buy.

Aboard the larger hulk, joined to the axle, were placed two vertical wheels whose strong cornel-wood teeth were geared to horizontal cylindrical racks, which accelerated the motion of the mill wheel as they transmitted it to the iron spindles and the millstones. The spindle ran through the center of the stationary lower stone and its square end fitted into a bridge attached to the top of the upper one whose heavy weight it caused to rotate briskly and thus effect the final operation of grinding. So, through a number of intermediary mechanical devices, the mighty and ceaseless flow of power from the river was harnessed. A framework of boards in the keel encased the housing of the two millstones, and the central rod rested on a base which could be raised or lowered by means of a wedge or lever. By this device the miller could regulate the grinding process. In order to produce coarse flour he raised the base and caused the upper millstone to bring less pressure to bear on the lower. This was called "grinding high," and the opposite procedure, by which a finer flour was obtained, "grinding low."

Now they began to roof over the deckhouses on both hulks and the bridge between them, whose forward deck was left open so as to afford full visibility for any necessary maneuvers.

"Look here," said Master Subbia, as he put the final touches on the roofing, "what's this mill to be called?"

"The Mice Nest."

"Come, come," said the shipwright, taking offence. "Haven't you forgotten that silly trick? It was a mean one, I grant you, but it's long since over and done with."

"I was thinking of the mice I used to catch in the warehouses at Lagoscuro. But that's no name, I agree. How about 'Hunger Mill'?"

"Well, it's your affair if you want to joke about it."

A few days later Master Subbia came back to the subject.

"What an ugly name for a mill. Unlucky, I call it. Who'd want to take his corn and wheat to a dismal place like 'Hunger Mill'? There's no use antagonizing your customers, just on account of a name."

Even the wisest and most sensible of men may stumble over a trifle, and for some reason Scacerni took Subbia's suggestion amiss.

"Isn't the choice up to me as the mill's owner?"

"Yes, up to you, entirely."

And Scacerni stubbornly told all comers that "Hunger Mill" was the name, whether they liked it or not. They remarked, not without reason, that the name expressed all the eccentricity and contrariness of the new miller. Finally old Subbia tried a different approach to the subject.

"The twenty-ninth of next month is Saint Michael's Day and by then the mill should be finished. Do you know the saying that he who eats well on Saint Michael's Day will not want for money all year long?"

"That sounds like a lucky day for finishing the job."

"Don't let such good luck escape you, Master Lazzaro. A mill is always placed under the protection of the Virgin Mary or one of the saints, so why don't you take Saint Michael for a patron? You can't find any better. Listen to the words of an old man who'll probably never make another mill in his life and who pays no more attention to gossip than you do. People being what they are, they may very well tell the parish priest what an heretical name you've given your mill and he may refuse to bless it. The name is important to you, I know, but is it worth risking your future for? Just think it over, because of course it's up to you to decide. But you know what the proverb says: When in Rome, do as the Romans do."

"Let it be Saint Michael's Mill, then," said Scacerni, giving in to common sense, although later on, whenever he was in trouble or out of sorts, he would always refer cursingly to "Hunger Mill." He wanted two mottoes, one on the small hulk, facing the river: "There's none so blind as he that will not see," and the other on the large hulk, facing the shore: "First come, first served." It was the custom to inscribe mottoes of this sort, but these two, although they contained perfectly sound advice, had a scornful and provocatory tone. They were printed in capital letters by a painter who came all the way from Comacchio to put the finishing touches on the mill. He painted the two hulks pitch-black and the various superstructures red, green, yellow, and all the other colors in the rainbow. On the front outside wall of the cabin he made a picture of the mill's patron saint, with his heel on the neck of a writhing dragon, which he portrayed with a flaming crest and the eyes of a basilisk. And in order to scare off some curious boys, he told them not to look too closely into the dragon's eyes.

"Didn't you know that the basilisk's eyes have such an evil power that if it looks into the mirror it must die?"

He was an able artist and his work aroused considerable comment, particularly the impressive figure of the archangel and the vehemence of the dragon's flames.

"And, Master Lazzaro, you can say that there was no skimping on either ultramarine blue or vermilion, the two most expensive colors on the market."

There were, to be sure, some pretentious strangers, emissaries, perhaps, of secretly jealous millers, who insisted that the painter had but scanty notions of foreshortening and perspective, and that the lance which the archangel was brandishing in his upraised right hand was aimed at his own left knee rather than at the head of the dragon. This criticism was reported to the artist, but he received it without flinching.

"He's aiming his lance at his own knee, is that what they say? They've taken the Archangel Michael for an idiot like themselves, then! Never mind, he can hold his own where a lance is concerned."

His critics were, in any case, amply taken care of by this reply, and he proceeded to paint on the larger hulk, in a slightly less exuberant manner, the bearded Saint Anthony Abbot, patron saint of all the mills on the Po, protector from the ravages of flood and fire.

At last, on the twenty-ninth of September, came the great day. The new mill sparkled in the bright, warm sunlight on the river, giving out a smell of seasoned wood and fresh varnish. Temporarily anchored near the shipyard, it stood slightly askew in the current, but Master Subbia's secret theory on this subject had been revealed and now aroused general admiration. The river was high and turned the idle wheel and millstones with a cheerful, whirring sound. The axle, vertical wheels, spindles, iron rods, and every bolt, nut and screw that held them fast, untried as they were, all settled into working in harness together.

"Here's wishing a hundred years of life and luck to the new mill!" said the good Subbia with tears in his eyes.

"And long life and health to Master Lazzaro Scacerni!" shouted in chorus all those who had been invited to a banquet in celebration of its completion.

With the pride Scacerni felt because they had hailed him in public as a master miller, came full realization that he had now accomplished his desire. His satisfaction was brimming over, and in it there was not missing even that streak of melancholy without which no satisfaction can be complete. At this moment he was stepping ashore from the skiff in which he had taken the white-robed parish priest and his acolyte around the mill and finally aboard it, in order that every part—hulks, deckhouses, millstones and propitiatory paintings—should be blessed.

"Long live Master Lazzaro! Hurrah! Hurrah!" shouted the crowd, anxious to sit down to their feasting.

Long tables had been set up close to the shore in the shade of a grove of young poplar trees, not far from Subbia's house, and five women had worked two whole days to prepare the banquet. Subbia's wife seemed to have recovered all her youthful vigor as she rolled out dough for making spaghetti, plucked chickens, which were to be served to the guests of high degree, and prepared croquettes flavored with parsley and garlic, together with *gnocchi* or potato balls, which in these days when potatoes were almost unknown, were (and still are) a Saint Michael's Day delicacy, for the host of banqueters of humbler station.

The parish priest sat at the head of the table of honor, with Subbia and Scacerni on either side, and after them the painter from Comacchio and the village dignitaries. Up in the trees small boys looked down on the scene below. There were three ample barrels of wine: two reds, one mellow and hearty *Sangiovese* and the other of the tarter *Bosco* variety, topped off by a sweet white dessert wine to wash down a caramel pudding. Rice cakes piled up on the stove and the *gnocchi* floated in great earthenware pots full of melted butter and cheese. They sat down to dinner at eleven o'clock in the morning and at three in the afternoon there were those who were still eating. Some had taken time off for a nap, but those who aroused the greatest curiosity and envy had munched for four hours without interruption. The barrels gradually emptied until they were bone-dry and made a hollow sound under the drinkers' drumming knuckles.

Halfway through the banquet, when the wine barrels were already low, a joke went around the table until it reached the painter (whose face was as flaming red as the crest of his dragon), for whom it was intended. The dragon, which he had painted so fat and well-fed, looked for all the world like an eel and the archangel's lance must therefore be a common harpoon for fishing. The painter rose from his seat, but before he uttered a word, he let out his belt several notches. The wine, as is its custom, seemed to have loosened men's tongues, and the fact that the artist's native Comacchio was famous for eel fishing strengthened their new interpretation. The painter hiccoughed and then said:

"Drink hearty, my friends! So there are still some of you who speak ill of my painting! Of course, we've seen eels enough in our time, but which one of us has ever been down to hell and seen a dragon? If anyone wants a better likeness, let him take a trip to the nether regions and if he comes back alive he'll be able to tell us every detail of the monster's appearance. Meanwhile the one that I've painted, be it eel or dragon, is acceptable to the priest, the miller and myself—oh, and I forgot to say that my wife likes it, too—so there can't be very much the matter. And Saint Michael, whether he wields a lance or a harpoon, is a very great saint, on that we all agree. Drink hearty, my friends!"

"Drink hearty!" they called back. "We all like it, eel or dragon! Hurrah for Saint Michael and Master Lazzaro! Long life to Master Subbia and the Master of Eels!"

"That's more like it," said the painter, sitting down with a sigh, because he had eaten in such abundance. Only a few of his critics, whom drink had put in a bad humor, bridled because he had politely told them to go to hell.

Toward evening a travelling orchestra came by: two violins, a harp and a horn. At the first notes of music the women and girls streamed out of the houses, and setting tables to one side the young people began to dance. But the horn blower, whose chief aptitude was creating saliva, could neither play in tune nor keep in time with the others. Fortunately a bass drum came upon the scene and covered his false notes with its ruffles, beating out the time in a masterly manner whenever the horn threatened to spoil the concert entirely.

The parish priest had gone away and the men began to joke more roughly. In the kitchen the women, tired but happy, collapsed on their chairs. A large red moon came up from the horizon, veiled by the September mist, and seeming almost regretful to have arrived only toward the end of the celebration. Master Subbia was none too steady on his legs, but he managed to say goodnight to Lazzaro.

"I'm happy that before I'm put away in my grave I've had a chance to build such a very fine mill and to have found one more old-fashioned miller."

With which it was high time for him to go to bed, for all of Occhiobello was sleeping.

5

Scacerni had already explored the banks of the river with a view to finding a suitable spot to set up his mill. The physical conformation of the shoreline had to be considered, beside the general lay of the land and the possibility of attracting customers. On his first exploratory trips he had asked the advice of the millers whom he met along the way and they had pointed out excellent sites, where the flow of water was steady and secure and where he was sure to make money hand over fist just as others had done before him. But when he asked why these predecessors had apparently left such gold mines behind them, they only shrugged their shoulders in reply.

Then Scacerni remembered how a skilled hunter inquires of his fellows where they have seen the greatest number of hares or woodcocks only in order to go look for them himself in the opposite direction. It is true, of course, that the game may be exactly where he has been told, because his informant is either an honest man or else twice as clever as the average, but then even cleverness has its drawbacks. He made up his mind, eventually, to choose his own site and his choice soon fell upon a place just before the curve between the two Guardas (one in the territory of Venice and the other in that of Ferrara), on the Ferrara side of the river. Here there was a wide beach, overgrown with reeds and rushes, where there rose out of the mud one solitary poplar, which he noticed was a refuge on cold nights for any number of chattering sparrows.

He took leave of Subbia by lantern light, before sunrise on the day after the celebration. But after his effusions of the preceding evening the old shipwright had grown suddenly mute, as if he had nothing more to say. Both men were, indeed, somewhat embarrassed.

"Master Subbia, I'll come on Saint Martin's Day every year to settle the rest of what I owe you."

"I know that without your telling me."

"Then, Master Subbia, it's goodbye."

"Goodbye, Master Lazzaro, goodbye."

But Subbia's wife, whose shyness and reserve were often mistaken for unwarranted pride, spoke up in more cordial terms:

"Master Lazzaro, now that you're striking out on your own, don't forget that you've been to us something very close to a son. I may say so, after all, because I'm old enough to be your grandmother. If we two old people are still alive when you marry, then bring your wife to receive our blessing."

"You'll live a hundred years, grandame," Scacerni said in a voice that he meant to be affectionate but that came out hoarse and unpleasant on account of his emotion. And then he turned to follow the voice of adventure and set out in search of his fate.

Up came the anchors of Saint Michael's Mill. It was towed by two boats, each one with four oarsmen, and their two separate ropes kept it going in the right direction, in a straight line and far from the treacherous shoals. Master Lazzaro, brandishing a long pole, jumped from bow to bow, sounded the depth of the water, called out orders like a boatswain and stood by, ready for any emergency. The tide had risen during the night and although there was less chance of going aground, there remained the danger of collision in the swift-running current. The low-lying shore of Vallonga disappeared first from view, then the roof tops and woods and church tower of Occhiobello. Along this stretch of the river, between Occhiobello and Paviole, the millers (and there were many of them) were still sleeping. Dawn was just beginning to redden the horizon to the east, before them, while the mountains to the west were still shrouded in fog and darkness. Then came the bridge at Lagoscuro. Here they had to aim in time for the narrow passage, before it was too late for skillful steering to avail. Scacerni had the rowers brace their oars while he sized up the way to approach it. His voice rang out strong and echoed on the shore, where a few passers-by heard it and others looked down at him from the bridge. Even some millers were now awake and stuck their heads out of the windows of their blackened mills.

"Row hard, boys! To the right! Whoa there!"

Now their aim was correct. They pulled their oars and coasted, then pulled and coasted again.

"That's it, boys. Easy does it. Straight ahead! Here we go! Now pull hard, straight ahead! With God's help we've made it!"

This last phrase he murmured to himself. The mill was in the center of the current and making good headway. Through the narrow opening it glided and Scacerni measured its speed and realized how serious it would have been to bump into either side of the bridge. Now the riskiest part of the trip was over. Saint Michael's Mill went comfortably along between the widening banks toward the Isola Bianca, or white island, whose greenness and fertility were caused by the overflow of rich mud gently deposited upon it by successive floods, which in this orderly section of the river had overrun it without causing any damage. The safety of these waters had attracted a great number of mills, which lined both the Venetian and the Ferrarese banks in double and triple file. Scacerni held to the left, on the Venetian side, where the channel was deeper. Now the sun was rising in the sky. The millers looked out scowlingly at the new arrival, but seemed relieved when he went on beyond them. They did not show any surprise because they had all of them heard of the Saint Michael's construction. Most of them lived alone or with one helper on their mills and kept their families on the shore, but where there were children aboard they were all on the deck, gaily shouting and waving, and Scacerni's oarsmen gave them back a gay reply.

As the island went by Scacerni recognized Francolino and Paviole, Pescara and Garofalo. Then came the great bend, where the Po turns to the north, as if it were no longer responsive to the call of the sea, until Polesella, where it resumes its eastward course, like the royal river that it is. There was Zocca on the first elbow and Polesella high above the second, with its houses overhanging the banks of a tributary to the Po. Lazzaro began to see the roof tops of Guarda on the Venetian side, but its opposite number in the territory of Ferrara, which he had already begun to call home, lay low in the meadows and he could perceive only the top of its ancient, dark church tower above the high bank of the river. He greeted it in his heart with mingled friendliness and respect. Now it would call him to church of a Sunday and soon, all too soon, the weary voice of its rustic bells would ring out the funeral rites of one more miller whose beard had grown white in the course of long years spent on the Po.

Just before Guarda there were the "dikes" of Nogarole and San Guglielmo; the river was divided by a wide shoal, almost an island, and the current ran swifter on either side. Here, in the deep water on the right, he had decided to anchor Saint Michael's Mill, in a position exposed to the rage of the floods, which would have seemed foolhardy to a timid man and daring to a wise one. But Scacerni had confidence in his own watchfulness and agility. In case of emergency he would move his mill to shelter behind the Guarda promontory, although it would be no short way to go, and still more difficult would be the return upstream, effected by hedging, that is carrying first one anchor and then another a hundred feet forward, before rewinding the hawser around the windlass and pulling up to a new position. But nothing venture, nothing have, as everyone knows, and he that will not work will want. Now the current swung back toward the center of the river and he could see the bank where he intended to make his anchorage. As soon as they had passed Polesella, in order not to be marooned on the reef, he had started to cut in toward the shore. Now the tall poplar tree waved its branches as if in welcome. Over went the anchors; they came to rest on a solid bottom and gripped it well.

Since the men had had no opportunity to eat along the way, they sat down in mid-afternoon to a copious combination of lunch and supper prepared by Subbia's wife, and left not a trace of either food or wine. How far away Occhiobello seemed already!

100

"To your good health and the luck of Saint Michael's Mill!" said the oarsmen, raising their glasses.

"And luck to you, my boys!"

"And here's to your first customer!"

"Here's to him!"

They meant to be back at Occhiobello by nightfall and so, pocketing their pay and the extra percentage that Scacerni gave them, they started down the river, hugging the shore, where the current would give them the least trouble. Soon a lazy and curious moon rose over the stern of the mill, mirroring itself with a golden streak in the lonely river and looking down at the new arrival, who was starting out on a voyage that would be counted not by miles, but by days and seasons and years and the flow of water under the flat keels and over the mill wheel.

Master Lazzaro made up the berth in his cabin and thought that he was quite tired enough to go to bed. But for a long time he could not sleep. He listened to the rustling and muttering of the water over the edge of the bow, along the sides, toward the stern and among the stilled blades of the mill wheel. For he was waiting for the arrival of his first customer before he released the wheel to the motion of the river and the passage of the years. Meanwhile in the light swish of the water there was something like a rapid and subdued whisper, a chattering laugh that died away in a gurgle, as if the river had come to win the acquaintance and affection of the new mill.

DOSOLINA

1

THE WATER of the Po doesn't cost a penny, and as the proverb has it, the more you take, the more profit you'll make. In calculating his probable income and expenses, Scacerni had not gone much beyond this bit of elementary wisdom. Nor had he stopped to consider that he had not so very many crowns left after making his down payment on the mill. Customers were few. Even people who should have found it convenient to come to him because they lived near by stuck to their old habits and seemed to regard a well-beaten path as the shortest. And did he know his trade? That was the first question they asked of those who had tried out the new miller.

"He has plenty of good will. He does his best." That was all they got for an answer.

One man, for instance, asked him for a coarse grind, which was what he liked best for a dish of corn meal. Scacerni milled it too "high," then becoming aware of his mistake when the job was half done, he went to the opposite extreme and came out with a grind that was too fine. Worst of all, he mixed the two consistencies in the same sack, and although the peasant didn't notice it there on the spot, his wife was quick to see the difference when she began to knead it and she voiced her dissatisfaction in no uncertain terms when she brought the steaming corn meal to the table. Scacerni repeated the same mistake more than once, and flour is a delicate thing, with which there is no trifling. The peasants told Scacerni quite frankly that they were not coming back. They were sorry, of course, because they could see that he was trying to do his best. But good will didn't make him a miller, and there was no reason why he should learn his trade at their expense. Why didn't he take on a boy who had already served his apprenticeship?

At this point Scacerni would have been glad to do so, but where was he to get the money for his pay? One peasant, a little less uncouth than the rest, decided to watch Scacerni at work. The miller was tempted to tell him to attend to his own business, but he held his tongue and submitted to inspection. The peasant kept running his fingers through the flour just as it dropped from the millstones, and all of a sudden he shouted that they were starting to heat up. He was right, and this was a serious accident, one which spoiled the flour and ruined the taste of the bread. The peasant was a bandy-legged, irascible little man, who could not help rejoicing in the mortification of a stout fellow like Sca-

102

cerni, with his martial and somewhat disdainful bearing. The little man was vociferous in his vituperation; he moaned over the waste of time and effort, the spoiled flour, the dissipation of the fruits of God's good earth. In fact, he came near to branding the miller as a herald of famine, a heretic and an abomination. Only a little over a single sack of wheat was lost, but Scacerni was momentarily helpless when it came to cleaning the choked millstones. Finally the angry peasant loaded his donkey and rode away, puffed up with righteous indignation and enjoying in advance his opportunity of giving the miller a bad name. Lazzaro looked down the road after him with a strange feeling of a kind he had never had before. It resembled the cramps that go before an attack of swamp fever and the weakness that comes after, and yet it was all in his mind: a mute and impotent anxiety, a restless urge to lay his hands on something concrete to do, without knowing where or how to begin. Poverty had held no terrors for him when he had not a penny in his pocket, but now that he was a man of property he was suddenly afraid.

The amount he owed the tavern and shopkeepers of Guarda was steadily increasing. He had lowered his fees until they were less than those of the least esteemed of his fellows, and this discredited him in the eyes of the most prosperous customers, while it attracted to his mill a host of desperate or hopeless peasants, who either would not or could not pay. There were even those who gave him moldy or mildewed wheat and then said that it had spoiled during the few days it had lain in his bins. This was outright robbery, but he submitted to it in order to keep them quiet. And even so they were among those who talked against him. Hunger Mill! Hadn't he called it that himself? His few honest customers, of course, treated him no better. What was it the bandy-legged man had said about the pictures on either side of the mill?

"Fresh paint and carnival colors won't do the trick! If you want my advice, you'd better pull teeth for a living!"

Yes, it was indeed Hunger Mill! But was it not his own defiant use of this name that had brought down a curse upon his head?

It was Saint Lucy's Day, whose night is the longest in all the year. The dark, cold, melancholy winter had settled down around him, but at least his poverty spared him the visitations of thieves, who took advantage of the damp, foggy weather to row up and down the river in piratical style, robbing grain and flour and money, if there was any, from the mills. Scacerni had made ready to receive them with two guns and three pistols, which he for a time kept carefully oiled and loaded. But now he could afford to let his gunpowder grow soggy, for the river pirates knew perfectly well that both his bins and his pockets were empty and did not waste their time attacking him. Every now and then, doling out his ammunition because he could not afford to replenish it, he took a few shots at the sparrows in the poplar tree, not merely in order to make their miserable, stringy meat into a sauce

103

for his cornmeal, but rather because their chattering, which he had once thought was an omen of good luck, now seemed to him unbearably taunting.

The road from Guarda to Ro followed the line of a former bank of the river which, after a piece of land called The Sisters' Farm, diverged considerably from the present stream. Along the river at this point were the "dikes" of Nogarole and San Guglielmo, and the land lying between was said to be one of the most exposed spots back of the river embankment. Here was a broad expanse of meadows, almost entirely empty and uncultivated, made up of a mixture of sand and clay. Once, in the course of the centuries, it had been the bottom of the river and it was still covered with silt and sediment and marshy vegetation. There were pools of stagnant water, which had accumulated from the back country or welled up from below and could find no outlet into the river. Here there was a chance for brave souls to make a killing of migrating game birds far more succulent than a sparrow. The meadows were crossed by a network of slightly raised foot-paths, running among the reeds and tall grasses, which provided an excellent way of going down to the river unseen.

The solitude of the mill had become oppressive. Scacerni had chosen this existence, to be sure, but without imagining that it could be so miserable. Now that his surroundings had become hateful he was glad to see a human face, even when it belonged to some rather dubious individuals who insisted on calling themselves his "friends." Under different circumstances he would not have wished for their company, but for the time being he had nothing better and did not contradict them. These men were connected with the "salt road," whose acquaintance the reader has made before, and, in their own words, they were "building up business" of a kind that we already know.

In some ways they were perfectly right. There were now a large number of very small separate Italian states, whose complicated taxes and custom duties were a hindrance to the development of free trade, and all the more vexatious in this part of the country, which had known the advantages of belonging to Napoleon's United Kingdom of Italy and found the succeeding restoration both anachronistic and unnatural. Under these conditions smuggling was a natural corrective, and indeed took on the proportions of a flourishing and beneficent, even if illegal business. The life-giving activity that went with this fraudulent trade brought many more advantages to the population than the deathly stagnation engendered by taxes and duties so high that they bade fair to defeat themselves and choke off commerce altogether. For in the Papal territory an internal system of tolls and licenses and other legal formalities was so hampering that in order to do business of any kind, or in fact even step out of his house in the morning, the ordinary citizen was obliged to be a law breaker.

Of course the smugglers did not look at things from any such theoretical point of view, but the fact is that neither public opinion nor their own conscience branded them as criminals, and none of the peasants, farmers, shopkeepers or boatmen who lived along the river could afford to combat them, least of all the millers, to whom they often gave protection against the robbers and highwaymen of the region. Let us only note, in closing this necessary digression, that it is easier for a man to know when he is stepping outside the law than to predict how far he will go or whether he will be able to retrace his steps. In any case it was ill looked upon to report smugglers to the police, first, because the police were notoriously inept, and second, because there was a strong feeling among the people against spying upon and denouncing any of their fellow citizens. Brave men administered a rough justice of their own and others simply submitted to whatever was asked of them.

Saint Michael's Mill offered great convenience to this group of "friends" and they made increasing use of it as a point of landing or departure, a temporary place of storage for smuggled goods, and quarters for eating, sleeping, and occasionally taking refuge from the law. Scacerni did not refuse to take the smugglers in, but he never accepted any of their money. Soon they came to esteem the taciturn miller and to pity him for his misfortunes, and they proved the sincerity of their sentiments by making him all sorts of advantageous propositions. But Scacerni only shrugged his shoulders and thought to himself: "Look at the sort of kind friends I've fallen among now!" Among them he recognized Raguseo's right-hand man, the "Big Brother" whom he had met one foggy night on his way to Lagoscuro. But he gave no signs of having ever seen him before.

Meanwhile the days were growing longer. By Saint Vincent's Day the back of the winter was broken, and then came Candlemas:

> Let Candlemas come and go,
> In the rain or in the snow,
> For the winter's over now;
> Be it snow or be it rain,
> Only forty days remain.

Scacerni's fortune changed just when he had given up all hope and come to the gloomy conclusion that in learning his trade he had lost all his customers. A certain number of peasants happened to come to him when the mill to which they usually went was either overloaded or broken down, and because they were satisfied with his milling they gave him a good reputation. Saint Michael's was, after all, the mill most accessible to the good people of Vallona, and about some six villages near by. Scacerni asked no more than an honest price for his services and took only a moderate toll of the grain for his own use, as a time-honored custom allowed him. Man is a legalistic animal and this was clearly an abuse, but the fact that its imposition and acceptance were of such long standing served to keep it within reasonable bounds, better than any amount of forced legislation. Now that the new miller had mastered his art he was spoken of in the highest terms all over the countryside, especially by those who had been the first to defame him. He had to take on first one and then two boys to help him, and the mill ran day and night, with every ounce of water the river would give it, to the delight of Scacerni's smuggler friends.

No longer did his customers come with one or two sacks loaded onto a skiff or the back of a donkey. Now they arrived from the river with barges and from the back country with wagons and wheelbarrows, whose creaking wheels indicated a good harvest and good business for the mill. They never had to call out to the miller, for, flushed with success, he was up at all hours and ready to serve them. Even peasants from the villages of Guarda and Crespino on the Venetian side and from as far as Polesine di San Giovanni in the territory of Ferrara, set a day in advance for their coming, and finally Scacerni made arrangements with Venetian boatmen to carry the wheat flour and corn meal back to the opposite shore. Popular favor being the fickle and volatile thing it is, Scacerni came to be considered the only miller worth patronizing. "A new broom sweeps clean," murmured his satisfied customers, while his hapless competitors, looking at the alluringly bright colors of the mill reflected in the water, muttered: "Good luck is better than talent, any day!" Master Lazzaro let them say what they liked and turned a deaf ear to their gossip. Of course, he could usually recognize another miller among those who went by, by the keen scrutiny he made of the mill from top to bottom. And he had a fair idea of what they were saying: that a mixture of ignorance and greed had led him to pick too open and exposed a location, but that sooner or later he would choke on his ill-gotten gains. He was a fool, they said, to think that the flood of 1811 was the last of its kind, or to imagine that the high-water marks reached in the years since were any indication of what the river could do. One day or another he would feel the impact of the unbridled waters, the sudden swell that came without bothering to announce its arrival, the whirling, battering, overwhelming strength of the Po! And to think that his smaller hulk slanted out in order to draw more water into the mill! This clever discovery of Master Subbia's particularly annoyed them, because they had not thought of it for themselves and they could see that it was really working successfully. And they vented their spite by predicting that Saint Michael's Mill would be swept away like a straw on the crest of the flood, that just because of Master Subbia's devilishly ingenious contrivance the two hulks would split apart and open up like the legs of a . . . . This daring comparison aroused so much laughter and was repeated so often that soon it came to the ears of Scacerni.

"Let them console themselves for their envy as they like," he said, "as long as they don't say such things to my face."

But needless to say none of them was so bold. News had gone around that of three men who had attacked Scacerni on the riverbank, near the meadows, one had been lucky enough to know how to swim when he took an involuntary ducking in the icy water, the second had been carried to the hospital, and the third owed his escape only to the speed of his running. The wary millers kept their distance and contented themselves with mulling over the disasters they remembered from their youth and those of which they had been told by their fathers.

"Do you remember the high water of May 29, 1810?" asked one miller with an especially precise memory. "Seventy-four inches! But it didn't overflow the banks and so we millers were the only ones to really experience it. Late spring is the most treacherous time of the year, and how the river came down upon us that day, roaring like a thousand bulls and driving our drifting mills before it until they were piled up against one another all the way across! Many a man lost his life or all his worldly goods in the water. Didn't my own cousin, whom some of you must remember, drown miserably, leaving a penniless wife and five children behind him?"

And the others chimed in with memories of the damage they had suffered at various times in the past.

"We'll see what happens to this fellow when the floods come!" they invariably concluded. "Just imagine if the south wind, scourge of the mills, starts blowing over his open anchorage and raises up a wave as wide as the river! No one wishes trouble upon him, but where did he get the idea of setting himself up in a place exposed to the full blast of the south wind? If the water is high and the south wind blows it up still higher then in no time his hulks will fill up with water and go to the bottom. Then it's goodbye flour, goodbye millstones, and goodbye Master Lazzaro! Lazzaro, isn't that it? And what's his last name? Scacerni? Who ever heard of the name Scacerni here on the Po?"

The times were, in fact, so normal, the weather so smiling, and the river so subdued in its behavior, that as one good year followed another Master Lazzaro could only tax fortune with being too kind and hope that she would not suddenly bring down on his inexperienced head one of the calamities of which the millers had spoken. Having joined the army so young and gone off with Napoleon to Russia, he had had no occasion to become acquainted with these floods, nor had he remotely considered them from the point of view of a miller and the owner of a mill, such as he had now become. Actually, it was a healthy distrust of the vagaries of the river that had led him, in making his choice of a site, to take into consideration the shelter of the Guarda promontory below him, which would serve not only in time of flood but also in case the floating ice of the spring thaw threatened to pierce his keels. But the prospect of cutting loose from his moorings, pushing out toward midstream, steering among high waves and whirlpools and shallows and kedging slowly along with windlass and anchors on such an unshipworthy bark as this one, with the fierce south wind beating on his side or stern, was anything but a gay one. It would be easy enough, under such conditions, to drift sideways down the river, or go aground, or break up and sink, as the prophets of despair (may God prove them wrong!) had insisted was most likely.

Meanwhile money continued to flow in and he settled his debt to Subbia before it was due. Subbia had aged so that he could no longer work. He was a pathetic old man, but still as kindhearted as ever, and he rejoiced almost more than Scacerni himself over the latter's good fortune.

"How goes it, Master Subbia?"

"As well as can be expected for an old man." And when Scacerni paid him the very last instalment of what he owed, Subbia added: "Come back soon, Master Lazzaro, if you wish to find us alive. From Guarda to Occhiobello is not far to go. Promise me, Master Lazzaro, that you'll come back soon. Don't wait for the next Saint Martin's Day."

And Scacerni promised. It was not far to go, true enough, but when he found himself once more absorbed by the prosperous affairs of the mill it soon seemed so. He put off the trip from one month to another, until more than a year went by, while the old shipwright and his wife had begun to count the time that was left for them to live not in years but in seasons.

It was something new in Scacerni's life that, as we have seen above, fortune should be too kind. And because this seemed almost blasphemous he turned his occasional ill humor on the millers who had spoken against him.

"It isn't as if I were taking the water away from them! After all, that's free as the air! . . . Men are worse than beasts, for when a beast has satisfied hunger and lust you don't catch it being jealous of its fellows. But with us it seems as if every man's hand were against his neighbor."

And so saying he made friends with no one, even when the bitter feelings against him had subsided. His work was quite enough to occupy his thoughts and he was glad that the two boys he had taken on as helpers were not given to talking. As for his distractions, hunting and women, both were near at hand. Hunting was by definition a silent pastime, and as for women, the more they chattered the better he liked them, for thus he had no need to answer, or indeed even to listen to what they were saying.

Thus time went by in a changeless manner, while events piled up in his memory. Its flow was even as that of the sun, which ran in the opposite direction to that of the Po, rising every morning at the mouth of the river and setting at its source, only to reappear again the next morning. During the passage of these fat years Scacerni became acquainted for the first time with a life of peace and quiet, with money that was easy to spend because it was easily come by. He paid his helpers well, treated his acquaintances to drinks at the tavern, and made handsome gifts to more than one woman, but all the while he admitted no one into his confidence and friendship.

The Ferrara region is known, and deservedly so, for its feminine beauty. Master Lazzaro sought out women with pale, warm complexions and bold, teasing eyes, which made their brusque surrender all the more to be prized and caused them to pass suddenly from defiance to pleasure. He delighted in their majestic figures, the broad shoulders and full breasts, the curved and rebellious flanks, long legs and slender waists contrasting with broad hips. Virtuous women he

108

left strictly alone, but when he met those who only pretended to be unapproachable it amused him to tempt them with his robust masculinity and his reputation for being a handsome man. With gifts he was unfailingly generous. To girls daring and unconventional enough to spend the night in his mill he gave garnet necklaces or earrings; to prudent housewives who let him in when their husbands were out of the way he brought a bushel of flour. Others asked him, in return, to grind a certain amount of wheat or corn for them without charge. Some demanded too much and he could not resist making some salacious reference to how they had earned it. But when they went so far as to watch over the process of grinding and see to it that he took no toll from their earnings then he lost patience and sent them packing.

All women, whether gay and passionate, or greedy and ambitious, were attracted by his roguish and devil-may-care attitude, his hawk-like face and jaunty dress, which consisted of wide corduroy trousers held up by a broad sash around the waist, an open shirt and a red kerchief on his head. In winter he wore a hunter's jacket, an ample cape and a wide-brimmed hat, which gave him something of a bandit's appearance. He had, moreover, a goodly share of masculine vanity, and considered his enjoyment of the peasant women as one of his privileges as a miller. Gossip had it that among his conquests were more than one miller's wife, and it was true enough that none of them had ever taken part in their husbands' resentment against him. Indeed, those of them that had marriageable daughters never failed, when they met him on the country roads or village squares or in front of the church after Mass on Sunday morning, to hint that it was time for him to give up his half-savage life on the mill and settle down to a more serious existence. He could very well let other men's wives alone, they insinuated, if he were to pick one for himself among their handsome girls. Scacerni only laughed and said nothing. The most sagacious and insistent of these good women were, of course, very often those who, if they had met him ten years before, would have talked in quite a different vein, and without their girls' entering into the picture at all. But, be that as it may, it was inconceivable, if he did make up his mind to settle down, that he should marry anyone but a miller's daughter.

The mill wheel was beginning to take on a dark color as the paddles circled endlessly around. It's the same old world but always new, a new world but always the same, as the almanacs have it. Itinerant merchants came by regularly every December with almanacs for sale, just as others came in the various seasons, making a singsong announcement of their wares or services: chair menders, sellers of ladles and pots and pans, coppersmiths, chimney sweeps and knife grinders from the mountain valleys:

> Ding-dong for the grinder man,
> He will sharpen if he can;
> Ding-dong bell,
> 'Tis a trade that serves us well.

Fast upon the almanacs came the holidays, an occasion for hailing the new year or at least for cheerfully turning one's back on the old, one more gone to join its predecessors. Scacerni bought the almanacs but he couldn't bring himself to put much stock in them. Of course there was wisdom in such sayings as: *April showers bring May flowers; Red sky in the morning, sailors (and farmers) take warning; February, short and chary.* These were safe enough guesses, and so were such simple predictions as that of a midsummer storm, a white Christmas, and a good harvest, if drought or rain or late frosts or false spring did not prevent. Thus far did Master Lazzaro believe in almanacs, and no farther.

"And why do you buy them, then?" asked the host of the Guarda tavern.

"In order to put to use my hard-won ability to read. Isn't there a proverb that goes: *Read much, write little, talk less?* There's the reason for my reading."

Although Scacerni was unwilling to confess it, even to himself, the days often seemed long and his labor vain. It was with a sudden and inexplicable melancholy that he heard the knife grinder's son sing of his succession to his father's trade:

> *My father is a grinder*
> *And I'm the grinder's son;*
> *But I shall be the grinder*
> *When my father's days are done.*
> *Ding-dong bell,*
> *'Tis a trade that serves us well.*

"Listen there, will you," said the grinder, pressing his foot on the pedal that regulated the flow of water from the tap over the grindstone. "Do you hear what that dunce is singing? That's what it is to bring children into the world! There's a son for you! And I must listen to him, just as my father listened to me."

How did it happen that, instead of sorrowing over his son's song, this man actually rejoiced in it? Lazzaro had a good trade, too, as substantial compared to the knife grinder's as his solid mill to the latter's wagon, and there were no presumptive heirs to claim his mill as their own. But when the knife grinder said: "There's a son for you!" he spoke as if this were the very last word of wisdom, and a consolation for the inevitability of death.

"As far as I'm concerned," Lazzaro tried to tell himself, "there's no one near enough to me to be counting my days for the sake of an inheritance."

But this did not serve to dissipate his melancholy. Instead, he remembered having heard that no one knows love who has not had children. And another thought, which heretofore had only aroused his mocking laughter, now assailed and humiliated him, the thought of the sons born of his amorous rovings, who were now growing up under the roofs of other men.

110

"How can you say you don't believe in almanacs?" insisted one of the peasants in the tavern. "Mine has often predicted the weather correctly, and war and peace, famine, plagues and comets besides."

"You remember the times when the predictions came true, and I the times when they have deceived me."

And so the days went by.

With Epiphany the feasting's over.

And since the year's harvest was good:

Dry cold in January:
Build a stout granary.

Already by the feast of Saint Agatha, early in February, the ground had begun to breathe again:

Saint John, the reaper,
Saint Peter, the husker,
Take wheat and corn to the mill
To make flour and meal.

As one barge or wagon went away, loaded with flour, another took its place. At this time grain was measured by the palm and three palms of wheat gave, by honest count, four palms of flour. Give me an exact measure and charge me dear, as the peasants said. A sack of grain was slit open and its contents released into the hopper, from which it passed through a valve into a trough or "shoe" that led directly to the "eye" or opening in the upper millstone. The trough precipitated the flow of grain by the jerking motion imparted to it by a shaker-arm, which was in contact with the "damsel," a four-sided iron piece mounted on the rotating spindle. A bronze bell was suspended by a cord above the "damsel" and when the grain ceased to flow then the cord, which ran through the trough, slackened and a clanging noise proclaimed that the miller was wasting his time when he should be feeding more grain into the hopper. All through the mill the air was permeated with flour dust, and there was a smell of river and fields, mingled with that of burnt oil from the machinery.

Master Lazzaro payed his helpers promptly and gave them generous bonuses, but in return he demanded their best efforts and swore at them roundly when he heard the ring that signified an irregular flow of grain into the mill. Didn't he pay them even during the months when there was least work to do, just in order that they shouldn't feel hungry noises in their stomachs like the echo of the bell?

In the hunting season he took down his shotgun and went out in a boat before dawn to stalk ducks, waiting for them among the tall grass until they were drawn by decoys to come down in those parts of the river or the adjoining swamps where it was easiest for him to mimic their call. After he had found them out by their loud quacking and they had taken flight into the air, he would lie flat on his stomach in the boat, waiting for them to come down, with his eye glued to the

111

sights of his gun and his ear cocked for the whir of their wings. The gun went off with a terrifying bang and often brought down ducks in great numbers.

When there was little to do at the mill one of the boys slept, while the other fished with a hook and line, a sport which Scacerni abhorred. He himself fished only with the harpoon, of which he was a master. It was a delight to see him crouch at the pointed prow of his boat, motionless as a statue, so that the fish were deceived by his reflection in the water, with the harpoon poised in one hand. The flash of its rapid course straight to the target was like the swift flight of the sea gulls that came up the river from the sea, driven by the heat lightning of midsummer evenings. Often the river water was muddy or there was nothing to be caught but small fish or eels, but Scacerni was intent on keeping his sharp eye and strong arm in training. Among his best catches were river pike, which he cooked with vinegar and parsley. And in spring fat spawning sturgeon swam up from the sea and right into the nets which the fishermen had spread out between two boats.

The two taciturn boys whom Scacerni had taken on as helpers were called Malvasone and Beffa. Malvasone was slow and strong, like an ox, with an ox's round eyes, narrow forehead, wide, flat nostrils and patient obedience. He was as good and honest a fellow as could be imagined, who had only three interests in life: carrying sacks, eating whatever was set before him, and sleeping when he had nothing better to do. Beffa, whom no one knew by any other than this odd name, was of quite the opposite type. No one knew where he had come from and he had such an ugly and surly face that everyone on either side of the river whom he had asked for help had got rid of him as quickly as possible by wishing him on the least cherished of his neighbors. Children instinctively ran away and peasant women kept an eye on their chickens, frightened by the leering and hungry look in his eyes.

"He's the kind that would set fire to the haystacks just for the sport of it, or in order to get a light for his pipe," people said, overcome by the same mixture of hate and fear that they felt for the wandering and predatory gypsies that occasionally passed by. He possessed none of the gypsy arts of hammering and soldering copper and telling fortunes, but everyone accused him of being a thief.

"Have you missed any of your own belongings?" Scacerni said, after he had caught a glimpse of this black sheep and heard what they were saying about him. "Since he's been about the village have you noticed anything missing?"

"Not yet," they reluctantly admitted.

"If you claim to know so much, but really know so little, why do you insist on branding him as a thief?"

"We don't want to brand him as anything. We don't want him in our homes or hanging about them."

"There you're within your rights. But don't give him a bad name for a crime he hasn't committed."

112

"He may not have committed anything so far, but some day he's bound to."

"That's fine reasoning for you!"

"It's God that's branded him!"

"Ah, do you know God's brand so well, my fine Christian gentlemen? You'd string him up just because you don't like the face God has given him? And then pat yourselves on the back and say: 'I told you so'? You'll push him into crime, I tell you. I know what hunger can do."

"As you like, Master Lazzaro, but we don't want to see his face in the village or in the fields around it."

"The village isn't your private property. And not all the fields are yours, either. I'll take him on at the mill. I've been looking for a boy to help me."

They didn't believe him, but Scacerni proceeded to confound their doubts by obstinately doing exactly what he had said. In this case he was right, at least in theory, and the act he did was a kind one. But such was his character that, right or wrong, he would have shown himself equally pigheaded.

It was true enough that Beffa was monstrously ugly. He had sparse, scrubby hair and his face was marred by smallpox, which had eaten away his nose and eyelids and lashes and swollen his pock-marked cheeks, leaving untouched only his thin lips, which by some trick of nature or else because such was the innermost nature of their owner, seemed able to smile only at his neighbor's misfortunes. This thin line of his lips added malice to the bestial passions that inflamed his bloodshot eyes, below a beetling forehead.

In the presence of Master Lazzaro Beffa was invariably hardworking and respectful, in fact obsequious, although he could never quite rid himself, no matter how hard he tried, of something of the air of a mad dog, one that refrains from barking in order to bite all the more effectively. Beffa was a good cook and the miller lodged him, along with Malvasone and the kitchen stove, in a rough cabin on the shore. Beffa's inborn malice expressed itself in the innumerable tricks he played upon his companion, leading him to stumble through cold mud up to his ankles on winter nights, laying traps that caused him to fall in the river, whence he emerged bruised and spattered with mud, putting donkey hair in his bed, red-hot pepper in his food and salt in his holiday coffee, which Malvasone gulped down with an expressionless face, attributing all his troubles to an imaginary hobgoblin of the swamps. Beffa had persuaded him of the existence of such a creature by tormenting him at night with ghostly voices and apparitions. But Malvasone seemed reassured rather than terrified by these visitations and only greeted them with a stream of obscene noises and exhortations, after which he turned over on his other side and fell asleep.

Besides being an adept of the hook and line Beffa was skilled at trapping birds with nets and bird lure. He took pleasure in watching fish writhe in the net and in crushing the heads of trapped fowl. Malvasone took the eggs of pike, carp and sturgeon, packed them in salt and dried them in the sun, thus making a rough sort of caviar, which went well with drinks of every kind. He was himself almost as heavy a drinker as he was a sleeper, and, as we have said above, a fellow as honest as the day is long.

All in all, life on Saint Michael's Mill went by agreeably enough, and robbers, knowing it was well watched, gave it a wide berth, even in the years when they might have made a profitable haul. As a matter of fact, in these years of plenty brigandage went into a relative decline.

Master Lazzaro took on a third helper, who, unlike Beffa, met with general approval. This was an orphan boy, Schiavetto by name, alert, well-mannered and of good character, whom the miller wisely quartered separately from the perverse Beffa and the simpleminded Malvasone, on a cot under an improvised board shelter on the deck of the mill. At the times when there was the heaviest work to do and part of it had to be done at night Master Lazzaro, whose ear was now perfectly attuned to the machinery of the mill, slept in a hammock on the larger of the two hulks, near the millstones. Thus if too much grain was poured down the hopper, slowing the pace of the milling operation, or too little, which caused the upper millstone to make a whirring noise, called in millers' jargon a "snore," Master Lazzaro had only to open one eye, stretch out his hand and tighten or loosen the cord that regulated the flow of grain through the valve.

Now Malvasone's sleep was so heavy that Scacerni used to say that not even the French bombardment of the Russian fortifications at Borodin (which he remembered distinctly because on that seventh of September 1812 he had worked on the construction of a bridge across the Kolocza) could have awakened him. And Beffa's hearing was not acute enough to allow him to judge the flow of the grain through the hopper. Schiavetto proved to be the best sentinel and Scacerni often put him in charge of the mill at night, thereby arousing Beffa's rage and resentment. It was not that Beffa had such a high opinion of his own skill, but he could not bear for anyone else to obtain recognition of merit.

Under Schiavetto's vigilance the warning bell never rang anymore, and this only added to Beffa's jealousy. He hated Schiavetto for his ability and good looks and for his enjoyment of the miller's especial favor, which of course he attributed to the basest possible motives. As for Master Lazzaro, he had hated him from the start because of the money he had made and his success with women. This hate was so strong and came to him so naturally that it had reached enormous proportions before he was even aware of it.

Such violent passions are to be found the world over, not only on the mills of the Po.

2

The territory lying between the Volano and the Po, together with the road to Panaro and Lagoscuro, had been known ever since the days of the House of Este under the name of Diamantina. There had never been any cultivation of this land and in the old days it had been a preserve for the wild boars of the princely house. Now it was wilder than ever, overgrown with scrubby bushes and dotted with stagnant pools of water left by the Po after it had altered its course and run closer to the city of Ferrara.

Here where there was an abundance of game, Scacerni showed himself a true son of the ferryman of Ariano, hunting to his heart's content with utter disregard of the law. Indeed, since poaching was in his blood, he hunted with greatest gusto in the spots where it was strictly forbidden. He had raised two dogs, a greyhound and a bloodhound, the latter having a particular gift for following up a wounded animal by both land and water, and trained them to be suspicious of all strangers and to sniff a representative of the law a mile away. And he had bought a horse, which he kept stabled in Guarda, for riding far out into Diamantina, when the summer's work was over and autumn tempted him to hunt. No woman had ever made his blood tingle as it did when he heard the call and saw the fluttering wings of a woodcock and stalked it along the dewy edges of the fields where it had come to seek food after the first frost had driven it away from the marshes. For Scacerni malaria held no terrors, since he had hardened himself to it as a boy. In July and August, when it usually came over him, he wrapped himself in a wool blanket and lay shivering and with chattering teeth in the sun, "sweating out the fever," as he described it.

About this time Scacerni found game in Diamantina of a kind quite different from what he had expected. For once he was curious to know what people were saying about him and interrogated the tavern keeper at Guarda, who reported that the millers and their wives merely said that in this choice he was as eccentric as usual.

"Eccentric? Why?" Scacerni asked with astonishment.

"To have chosen a girl who is a stranger . . ." replied the host, who was a compendium of universal information.

"A stranger! They've travelled the world over, these good gossips, I take it!"

"No, but they are millers and to them anyone is a stranger who was not born and raised on a mill."

"And what then?"

"They say that no one can fit into a miller's life without being born to it."

"But I wasn't born to it myself."

"Then they'd most likely say that you're a miller's son without knowing it."

"What's that? Where's your respect for my mother?"

"I beg your pardon. But don't you say yourself that you don't remember your father's trade or the place where you were born?"

"That's true."

"Then there's no reason to take offense. The supposition is a legitimate one."

115

"Mine host, you ought to be a lawyer! And what else do they say?"

"I don't want to create bad feeling."

"Go ahead and tell me. I'm in a mood for laughter."

"They say that she'll make a fool of you, if you must know."

"Of *me? Sacramèstul!*"

"You said you were in a mood for laughter, didn't you?"

"Well, am I not laughing? What reason do these paragons of wisdom give for that?"

"Oh, for no good reason at all, an idea, a superstition, a matter of horoscopes . . ."

"Let's hear this no good reason."

"Well, if their count is right, you are some fifteen or twenty—let's say eighteen—years older than she is. And you can imagine what they say about a man of forty and a girl of twenty."

"But I'm not forty!"

"And is she twenty then?"

"She's younger than that," Scacerni admitted, no longer laughing.

"And looking ahead to the time when you'll be fifty and she'll be thirty they say that crabbed age and youth cannot live together."

"It's my fate to loosen people's tongues—and to make them talk in proverbs! Do I pry into their affairs, I ask you?"

"That's all the more reason why they should pry into yours," said the host, who was something of a philosopher.

"They're envious, that's all. They didn't believe I could have such luck."

"She was brought the May, on Ascension Day," observed the host, who was still in a mood for versifying.

Scacerni frowned, but he quickly realized that the other had spoken in a proverbial rather than a personal vein. Now it is high time to let the reader in on Scacerni's secret. On the eve of the Ascension he had planted the traditional shoot of "May," or hawthorn, before the door of a young girl called Dosolina Malvegoli, who lived in the Palazzo Diamantina, once a princely dwelling, but now the squalid and dilapidated home of a number of very poor families. Dosolina was innately shy and because of her extreme youth and poverty she was too modest to take seriously the compliments she had often enough received for her beauty. For this reason she was utterly surprised to receive such a declaration of love and could not imagine who was its author.

"Child's play!" said her father, when she told him that someone had brought her the May.

A man poorer than Princivalle Malvegoli it would have been hard to find, and his poverty was so ill-starred and painful that it did not even inspire compassion. He claimed, perhaps with some right, to descend from an aristocratic family, but his only title to nobility lay in his name. People said mockingly that this was not much of an inheritance, in view of the fact that he had to support a wife and five children, but he retorted that for all their laughter they would find him a man to reckon with one day. The little money he had ever earned he spent on a legal battle to recover the title and wealth to which he laid claim, but his lawyer, after squeezing his last penny out of him, told him that this wealth had been dissipated a hundred years before. To which Malvegoli replied that if he had had more money with which to hire an honest lawyer things would have turned out in quite a different way. So people continued to mock him for his pretentions, which seemed one more preposterous than the other.

Malvegoli had been in his time an agent for grain and hemp, the latter abundantly grown in the nearby valley of the Bondeno. Because he was fairly well-educated and had a nimble tongue he had made a tolerable start along this line when he had taken a notion to go into business for himself in the city, where credit was easy. But there he came to complete ruin, which he blamed on his creditors, on high prices, poor harvests, bad luck and, in short, everything and everyone but himself. He was reduced at this point to opening shop in a part of the Palazzo Diamantina so broken down that no one else would have taken it. Exactly what he dealt in no one could say, since all that met the eye was the one large, empty, dust-filled room where he kept his unfortunate family, five ragged, hungry children of whom Dosolina was the eldest. His courageous and long-suffering wife, Donata, who never had enough food to satisfy their hunger, was somewhat embittered by her husband's shiftlessness and vanity.

"Don't rack your brain so hard to find out who's to blame for your troubles," she would say.

"Am I at fault, is that what you mean?"

"No, I'm at fault myself to have married an individual so completely useless."

"Let a man give up everything for the sake of his family and see what he reaps in the way of gratitude!" shouted Malvegoli.

"For his family, did you say, you simpleton?"

The marital disputes on this subject were long and acrimonious, and they caused considerable pain to Dosolina, a sensible, clearheaded, hard-working girl who shouldered the care of the younger children when her mother went out to scrape together, often to practically beg, food for their dinner. As for her poor father, he was always full of grandiose and confused plans, and indeed enthusiastic about their prospects of success.

"Ideas will be the death of you," said Donata. "You'd do better to dig ditches."

"What? A Malvegoli should work with a pick and shovel?"

And they resumed their eternal quarrel.

The valley of the Bondeno, as we have said, was rich in hemp and occasionally Malvegoli acted as a go-between for the sale of a sizeable lot of it. But his earnings went either to his creditors of long standing or else were spent in a tavern. The very nature of his business required that he show himself to be a good fellow, and the wine afforded a release for his natural talkativeness and fancy.

"You have plenty of friends," said Donata, "and only one enemy."

"Who's that?"

"Yourself."

"Do you mean that it would be a good thing if I . . ."

Once, after she had received considerable provocation, she came out with the end of the sentence for him:

"Yes, if you tied a stone around your neck and threw yourself into the river."

After saying this she had to admit that she had gone too far and put herself in the wrong. But the admission irritated rather than calmed her. As for Dosolina, she burst into tears.

"Do you see what you've done?" said Princivalle. "You've made an innocent girl cry."

"Oh, I'm the one to make her cry, am I?" And Donata extended her anger to her daughter: "Just be quiet, you silly girl born of a stupid father!"

More than once Dosolina had feared that her parents would come to blows, and she never saw her father come back to the house without a feeling of trepidation.

Dosolina was of a gentle and delicate beauty, a tiny little creature, that, as some of the young men were beginning to say about her, couldn't have been more perfect if she had been shaped by a turner's lathe. Her heavy, fine hair, if it had been loosened from its tight braids, would have come down to the ground; it was a glorious mass of flowing gold, lighted up by pearly reflections. Her face was that of a child, sorrowful and wise beyond her years, all but her smiling eyes, blue as cornflowers shining out among the waves of golden autumn grain. The seed of the cornflower, after the flower is gone, has a way of mingling with the wheat and embittering the flavor of the bread, but the shining honesty of Dosolina's blue eyes bespoke a true and unalterable heart. Her neck, which she playfully held bent a little over her left shoulder, was slender as the stem of a flower, and her skin was white and untouched by the sun, both because the care of her younger brothers and sisters kept her close to the house and because the preservation of its whiteness was her one feminine ambition. Her tender young hands, slightly reddened and worn from her household labors, were touching to see.

Dosolina knew nothing of boats and life on the river, or of mills and mill wheels. She was at home in the dismal Diamantina and among the fields near the Bondeno, where the hemp grew green and tall under the summer sun until, in September, its stalks were cut and put to soak, and the smell of their rotting filled the air as a signal that it was time to break the flax and card it. Perhaps, when the setting sun lingered over the poplars bordering the now abandoned roads that had once converged upon the Palazzo Diamantina, and a peasant woman's voice raised in song added to the atmosphere of desolation, Dosolina dreamed of some hoped-for yet fearful fulfillment of her presentiments and imaginings, the arrival of some knight errant from the outside world who would carry her off like Cinderella. When darkness had already fallen under the trees, their tops still caught the last rays of light and quivered in the evening breeze as if they were murmuring an invocation. Deep in her heart she must have felt akin to the quivering tops of the century-old young poplars, although she was too simple to formulate her desires or to invoke, even in secret, the arrival of a day that might change her life for the better.

The nature of her longings and the solitude of her environment had an intimidating effect upon her. She had no friends of either sex, for her blood was not the same as that which ran through the veins of the peasants' children, and her severe mother had terrified her by holding up to horror the example of girls who had fallen away from their virtue. This many of them did in the wild woodlands of Diamantina or among the fertile, sun-drenched fields of hemp around the Bondeno, where every autumn the harvesters found open spaces in which the young hemp had obviously been trodden down to provide a lovers' hideaway and material for a salacious joke or story. Dosolina's mother relentlessly held up before her the dishonor of this girl and the shame of that, the fate of one who had gone to prison and of another who had wound up in a house of prostitution. Girls such as these, she never tired of repeating, were the ruin of themselves and their families, the cause of feuds and crimes, and often murderesses in their own right who came to an untimely end on the gallows and whose souls, of course, went straight to hell. The woman involved in these horrors, whether seduced or seducer, she always held totally to blame, strange as it seemed that she should lay so much sin at the door of her own sex. Was not she herself, after all, an irritating example of feminine vulnerability, since in spite of the scorn with which she regarded her husband she was still in love with him? And the consequences of her own weakness of the flesh were the ragged progeny with which she found herself surrounded.

"But I've never even thought of any of these things you tell me about," said the innocent Dosolina, trying to escape her mother's virtuous indignation.

"That's just because you're a silly girl!"

"Then if I'm not to be a silly girl I ought to think about them, is that it?" asked her daughter with gentle irony.

"What you ought to do is tremble!" thundered Donata. "Don't you believe in the Last Judgment and Hell?"

"I've studied my catechism, Mother, and I know very well what to believe. But, with God's help, I don't really think I shall go to Hell."

Donata was silenced but on the rare occasions when a priest came to say Mass in the palace chapel or when she and her daughter went to communion at the village of Pieve di Vigarano she was rash enough to try to find out what sins Dosolina had mentioned to her confessor, with the result that he felt more than once that he must warn and reproach her.

The peasants had great esteem for Donata because of her ability to make certain plasters and herb concoctions for the care of the sick.

119

She affected to accept their esteem with a superior air, but when it came down to it she never refused to help them and thus it was that she earned enough to feed her hungry brood. This occupation kept her moving about the countryside, where she was constantly worried about the dangers that might befall her stay-at-home daughter. And her love for her children was so painful and tortured that, as we have seen, she subjected Dosolina to unjust suspicion even within the four walls of her own house.

There is no telling of what she might have suspected her on that Ascension morning when a hawthorn shoot was found planted outside the door, had not Princivalle said:

"Child's play!" And he added, betraying a vain man's secret misgivings: "Do you suppose someone is playing a joke on us?"

"Hardly!" exclaimed Donata. "They might play a joke on *you*, of course. But not on the rest of us, not on me! *I'm* here, after all, and surely no one would dare offend me. No, it was a suitor, that is certain, but if I find out who it was, he'll have to reckon with me. And, meanwhile, don't let it go to your head, Dosolina!"

But of this there was no danger, for Dosolina was inclined to share her father's suspicions and to wonder sorrowfully why anyone should trick her in this fashion. Like all thoroughly good people, she was repeatedly dismayed to perceive the existence of evil, and no matter how hardened to it she might become by experience she would never really understand it. In this instance her first thought had been: "It's a joke on me because I'm so poor," and indeed she had resigned herself to this explanation when her mother's words forced upon her the notion that someone might actually be in love with her. With all her young heart and her easily inflamed imagination she grasped at the fulfillment of her long-standing dream of a stranger, come like a fairy-tale knight to deliver her. She repudiated her first humble and timid reaction and refused now to admit that fate could play her such a sorry trick as to dash all her hopes and dreams to the ground. No, the May had been brought her by a lover!

Different meanings were attached in various parts of the country to the planting of the May, and it might signify, according to the circumstances, love, jealousy, scorn or repudiation. Because the people of the region were given to jokes, practical and otherwise, at times they brought a mock May to girls who were notoriously self-satisfied or vain and at others to those to whom, as Princivalle had feared, they simply wished to display contempt.

But, after all, no one had a grudge against Dosolina. Donata stubbornly combed the few miserable settlements in Diamantina in order to find out who had been so bold as to tempt her daughter and her excessive zeal made Dosolina the butt of a satirical snatch of song:

> Dosolina, don't you put on airs,
> As if your father sat among the peers;
> Your mother's not a peeress, after all,
> And pride goes, Dosolina, just before a fall.

A stranger, who was also a hunter, had indeed ridden very often by the Palazzo Diamantina and dismounted in order to give his horse a drink or to buy something at the shop, as if the sign swinging outside really meant that there was something to sell. He was not one of those who had worn thin the joke of asking what sort of a shop this was to have no merchandise inside. On the contrary, he kept coming back to inquire for what he wanted, but discreetly and without a smile, pretending to believe the embarrassed excuses proffered by Dosolina.

"We're expecting it to arrive within the next few days," she would say blushingly.

The stranger was unfailingly polite and as he rode away on his fiery horse with a gun slung over one shoulder and a cape over the other he cut an adventurous figure that could not but strike her imagination. He always seemed to come when her mother was away, and for this reason Dosolina cut short their conversations, which fortunately he did not attempt to prolong. All she knew of him was that he was a miller on the Po. After he had seen Dosolina's blue eyes and golden hair Lazzaro had gone to the best tailor in Crespino, a sizeable town on the other side of the river, and ordered a well-cut corduroy suit, which gave a gallant air to his trim, military figure and insured his being as pleasing to a woman's eye as he had been when he marched in one of Napoleon's parades. Then he went in his new clothes to the barber.

"Put this savage beard into civilized condition."

The barber proposed several different styles before he actually cut into the wild mass of hair.

"A sapper's beard," said Scacerni, harking back to his soldiering days, when a full beard was the distinctive mark of the engineers and only worn by privileged men in the other branches of the army. But the barber knew that now a beard of this kind was the sign of a hothead or a Liberal, and he hesitated, balancing the scissors on his thumb and forefinger. A sapper? The word meant nothing to him, and Scacerni thought with sudden melancholy of the years gone by, when any self-respecting barber would have caught on without further explanation. What did this fellow imagine? That he was a ditchdigger? Yes, a good number of years had passed, and although they did not weigh upon his shoulders they did somewhat alarm and annoy him, especially when he thought of the tender age of a certain young girl. Finally he told the barber exactly how to trim his beard.

"Lazzaro, my boy," he said to himself as he looked into the mirror when the operation was done, "have you got it in for the years just because they're so fleeting?"

In these words there was a mixture of fear and vexation, for without admitting it even to himself he knew that he was seriously in love for the first time and he was angry because he did not know how it had come about. If he could trace the exact time and place when this love had come over him, so he imagined, then he would be able to free himself of its spell. For this reason—or so he told himself—he returned over and over again to see Dosolina Malvegoli and the days when he

121

did not see her seemed very long. Tailor and barber had considerably improved his appearance, but it never occurred to either Donata or Dosolina that he was the one who had planted the May before their door. Lazzaro, on his part, was bothered by the fact that he could not find anything to say to the girl. How did it happen that a love which had entered into his heart so deeply should be so hard to declare? All the gallantries he had murmured so successfully to other women seemed to him unsuitable and positively offensive in connection with Dosolina and he was ashamed at the mere thought of trying them out on her.

"I hear that someone brought you the May," he said to her tentatively one day.

She turned crimson, and not knowing how to change the subject said exactly the opposite of what she really believed.

"Someone that has it in for me, no doubt."

"And who could that be?"

"Someone that meant it for a joke."

"And mightn't it be a suitor? An honest man who wants you for his bride?"

"Are you joking, too? Who could want to marry a girl as poor as I am?"

Scacerni was half distressed and half relieved over this answer to his question. Now he knew that she had no other lover and that her poverty was working in his favor. The miserable Princivalle Malvegoli could not afford to say no to a prosperous miller like himself. He was no longer young, if you like, but this did not faze him. Then he thought: "It's not my age, it's the difference between her condition and mine. That doesn't matter to me, but what about her?" To escape from his perplexity he finally tackled Princivalle, more brusquely than a highwayman, in the middle of the road, leaning over to speak to him from his horse:

"Look here, if it suits your daughter, I care not a fig for a dowry. If you want to know how well off I am and how well I can take care of her, just ask on both sides of the Po about Saint Michael's Mill and the reputation of Lazzaro Scacerni." So saying, he spurred his horse and rode away.

Thus it was that Dosolina learned who had brought the May to her door, and to tell the truth she was more astonished and intimidated than she was actually happy. Princivalle, on the other hand, was supremely pleased, for with so rich a son-in-law he saw prospects of carrying out some of his old plans.

"Don't you dare put on such a dire face!" he said to his daughter.

"I?"

"You look as if you were under a spell!"

"Let her think it over," said Donata doubtfully. "After all, it's up to her."

"What's that? Now that at last fortune's knocking at my door, you women threaten to chase it away! And after all I've done for my family, too!"

"After you reduced it to starvation, you mean!" his wife retorted peremptorily. "Better not harp on that! And let Dosolina alone."

"But I'm perfectly happy at home," murmured Dosolina shyly.

"Don't worry, I'll not let your father force your hand," said Donata, ruffling her feathers like a hen in defense of its chickens.

Princivalle sat in front of the dish of thin corn meal on the family supper table with a half offended, half contemptuous expression, but this soon melted away as he gave free rein to the fancies that flashed through his mind like so many Roman candles.

On a beautiful day halfway through September, when the river was majestically high, Dosolina and her parents went to visit Saint Michael's Mill, setting out early in the morning from Santa Maria Maddalena, beyond Lagoscuro, where Master Lazzaro sent a boat with two rowers to fetch them.

So many new things, the idea of marriage, the man who had asked her, and the clamor of her parents, who, protesting all the while that she must be left free to make up her own mind, had not given her a moment of peace, all conspired to disturb poor Dosolina. She did not know how things had come to a head so quickly and had a vague feeling that she had been imposed upon, so that she was reluctant to accept this marriage, even if it was obviously a fulfillment of her dreams. Even the fact that she had a suitor, and one who had brought her the May, was a cause of turmoil in the ill-fated Palazzo Diamantina. Had not her parents found cause to renew their quarrels?

"You need a beating, you do!" Princivalle said to his wife one day. But he got back even more than he had given.

"A beating? Is that how you talk to the mother of your children, you donkey? You've brought nothing but misfortune upon everyone that's had to do with you! And if I don't put it more strongly it's only because of Dosolina."

All of these painful things had been better left unsaid, particularly one last thrust when they were discussing the visit to Saint Michael's Mill. Princivalle said something about how it was time that the two young people should come to know each other better, to which his wife answered venomously:

"Young people, you say? Why, he's old enough to be her father!"

It was just as well that as they stepped into the frail boat Donata should feel a sudden fear of the water.

"Make yourselves comfortable," said the boatman, perceiving their awkwardness and embarrassment.

They moved silently in the current on the Venetian side of the river, Dosolina dazed, Princivalle ill-humored, and Donata hunched up on her seat, hanging on to both sides of the boat and giving an occasional hostile glance at the muddy water. But the silence was broken by the oarsman at the stern, who was owner and pilot of the boat and had

123

not to exert himself unduly, except to steer, as they glided with swift strokes effortlessly along.

"It won't do to be afraid of the Po," he said, "if you're going to spend your life on it! We've been hearing for some time that Master Lazzaro Scacerni was expecting a visit. And we're glad of that, because we all wish him well. Here we have a truly beautiful young girl. As for Master Lazzaro, he's a man you can swear by. An honest man, a master miller, one whose actions speak louder than his words. He doesn't stick his nose into other people's affairs, but if they were to investigate his they'd find something solid to sink their teeth into, I can promise you that. He's not afraid of hard work and he has a pair of good fists and courage to back them up with whenever it is needed. He makes good money and spends it generously and with all that he's handsome to look at. If you ask me, his wife will be a lucky woman!"

Princivalle looked triumphant and Dosolina blushed deeply. Under any other circumstances Donata would long since have cut short the boatman's eulogy, which lasted all the way to Polesella, but he was providentially silenced by the necessity of pulling hard on his oars in order to put the boat across the river.

"Sit still!" he warned his passengers as he veered toward midstream.

He hardly needed to warn Donata, who was already stiff as a board. Now that they were bucking the waves they were made really aware of the strength and speed of the river, whose yellow water swirled around the boat and made disappearing eddies on every side. Along the sides and under the bow and stern it made a gurgling noise which seemed like a greedy threat to pull them under. Staring hard at the waves made Donata's head whirl, but she could not take her eyes away from them. Dosolina clapped her hands:

"How big and wide it is! And how beautiful! Look, it's just like gold!"

It was a pale and misty gold, created by the rays of the September sun. Donata suddenly perceived that they were equally far from both banks and let out a stifled cry of fear.

"What would you say if the river were really running high?" asked the boatman.

"Wouldn't you call it high now?" asked Malvegoli hesitantly.

"Just about halfway."

"But we don't know how to swim."

"In case of an upset, just hang on to the sides of the boat. Even if it capsizes it will stay afloat."

At this joke Princivalle's face grew dark and anxious and his wife called out between tight lips, as if she were afraid the sound of her voice might rock the boat, to the carefree Dosolina, who was looking in every direction and finding one sight more marvellous than the last:

"Sit still and don't move! Are you deaf? Didn't you hear him say the boat may turn over?"

The boatman's warning only served to make Donata angry without

124

diminishing her fear. From either bank echoed the church bells of the two Guardas, ringing the angelus and signifying the arrival of noon. They seemed to portend a day as lucky as it was fair. Dosolina made the sign of the cross and began to say: *Angelus Domini nuntiavit Mariae*, but Donata did not have the courage to take her hands off the sides of the boat to cross herself.

Now they were near the shore and the boatman steered straight for the mill, whose sturdy, dark hulks seemed to rise up suddenly ahead of them and grow larger every minute so that the approaching boat was smaller and smaller by comparison. Standing on the deck, taller than ever, and with a frown on his forehead caused by anxious expectancy, stood the master of the mill. He pointed out to Donata and Princivalle the ladders which they were to climb and gave them a helping hand when they reached the top. But when it was Dosolina's turn he leaned over, bent down, caught her with his arms around the waist, hoisted her gently up and set her gallantly down on the deck.

"Dosolina, you weigh no more than a flower!" he said to her in greeting. And when she blushingly drew close to her mother, who had hardly stopped panting from exertion, he added: "Here, if you will, you may feel yourself at home."

Dosolina was too embarrassed for the moment to look around her and it was through her feet that she first came to know the mill. For the mooring ropes by which the mill was attached to the shore permitted a certain free play of the hulks, and they dipped forward first to one side and then to the other in a slow, even motion, almost a hint of imminent departure, which gave a tremor to the deck on which the visitors were now standing. This oscillating movement, in its turn, alternately tightened and slackened the mooring ropes, so that the joints of the pole that went down from amidships to the river bottom and the anchor cables over the sides all gently splashed as they rose and fell in the foaming yellow water.

The mill was in spotless holiday trim. All the windows were wide open to the light of day and so were the portholes at the forward end of the deck where a table was neatly set with four stools around it. Inside and out the mild air and temperate sun played over the scene. The slow, dripping sound of the mill wheel added a cheerful note as it blended with the swift, throbbing noise of the millstones. There was an atmosphere of animated silence, of serene repose and humble peace in a little world all its own, hung between sky and water, between the open river on one side and the mainland, hidden behind the nearby bank, on the other. Over it all hung a surprising sweetness, a sense of physical ease and comfort that added a bemused wonder to Dosolina's timidity. The pleasing smell of newly milled flour mingled with that of the fresh water and mud cast up by the river and the mustiness of the vegetation that clung to the keels. The air breathed youthful health and appetite.

"Let's sit down at the table," said Master Lazzaro. "It's late and you must be hungry. There'll be plenty of time later to show you the mill."

And he added, turning to Dosolina: "I hope that some day you will come back as its mistress."

She started and for a second her eyes met his. Before she lowered them again she had a distinct feeling, induced perhaps by the serenity of the surroundings, that she could trust him. And at the same time she acquired a sudden proud awareness of her own beauty, which had been reflected in the look he gave her. There was love in his look, and she had an abrupt presentiment of all that love could mean. She longed now for the day of her marriage at the same time that she feared it, with a fear inherent to her tender years and chaste upbringing.

Schiavetto waited on the table and the visitors did honor to a dish of pike smothered in garlic sauce, Malvasone's home-made caviar, a "miller's pie" made of unleavened pastry crust and oil cooked over the embers, and some fine peach preserve. Then Master Lazzaro showed them how he regulated the flow of water to the mill wheel, by lowering from a windlass a sluice gate which served to dam partially the mill-race or, when the current was slack, a triangular block that made it dash with greater impetus against the paddles. He pointed out the mill-stones, valves, cords, and all the rest of the mechanism in a calm manner and without looking again at Dosolina or making the least reference to the possibility of their marriage. For some reason this made her feel all the more timid and she stayed close to her dignified and approving mother.

Scacerni went on to explain that when the millstones were worn smooth they ground too feebly and their surfaces had to be scraped and chipped to make them rougher. This was called "dressing the furrows." When one of the stones bore down too heavily in the middle it was called spread-mouthed, and on the edge, spread-winged. He exhibited the hammers with which he chipped the stones, and his workshop, complete with grindstone, carpenter's bench and all the other tools needed by a good miller. Princivalle Malvegoli, who had drunk copiously at table, could no longer restrain himself.

"A fine mill, a grand mill, a wonderful mill! And you, Master Lazzaro, what a man you are! I knew who you were, of course, and the honest boatman told me more. But, upon my word, I didn't expect so much. And with a mill like this one! Here the miller's wife will be a queen. What a life, I tell you!"

Dosolina wished that her mother would say something to stop this excessively complimentary chatter, but Donata only smiled indulgently. They visited the cabin on the smaller hulk and there, amid his hunting and fishing weapons, they saw the miller's bunk.

"This is where I've slept so far," he explained to them, "and this," pointing to the stove, "is where I cooked my meals when I first came and had no one to help me. Those were hard times at the beginning."

"And from now on, where do you intend to sleep?—God bless you," asked Princivalle.

Dosolina made a gesture of embarrassment.

"From now on," said Lazzaro, "if things go as I hope . . ."

"And you have reason to hope, I tell you . . ."

"Then, as I say, I have in mind a house not far from the shore. Nothing very large, but it's enough, as they say, to have a roof over one's head . . ."

"And to own all the land in sight!"

"Come, come! There's not so much as that. You're going too fast. There's enough for a vegetable garden, a modest bit of land, but sufficient to live on comfortably. My wife will have to look after that, because a miller's farm is his mill. That is, if the wife I want will have me."

"And how could she turn down a man like yourself?"

"Who can say? And in any case the decision is up to her, by your leave."

Malvegoli nudged Dosolina with his elbow, but she was silent and edged away. Standing there in front of the miller's bunk her father was even more indiscreet.

"For two people, this would be a narrow bed, wouldn't it? But it's true," he added, winking at Lazzaro and Donata, "that the newly married like it narrow."

"Come, now!" said his wife, not too unkindly, "what a beast you are!"

"Have you already bought the house you just spoke of, Master Lazzaro?" Malvegoli went on.

"I've spoken for it and made a deposit, but it's not too late to withdraw."

"And why should you withdraw?"

"Because I've set my heart on one girl and if she won't say yes I'll have no other."

"Lucky creature! Did you hear that, Dosolina?" burst out Malvegoli. "He won't have any other!"

"How can she hear," interposed his wife calmly, "if you never stop talking?"

"You've made a deposit, eh?" repeated Malvegoli, somewhat dizzy with wine.

"But I can perfectly well give it up and live the rest of my life here on the mill."

These words on the lips of a man like the miller filled Dosolina with mingled shyness and pride. But soon her father put his foot in it again.

"Go along with you! How can she say no? Not unless she's quite daft! There can't be a girl as mad as that."

"Remember, please, that it's not up to you to say."

Master Lazzaro's voice was curt and dry, for which Dosolina was grateful, hoping that it might persuade her father to be quiet. But he was not a man to be so easily discouraged and would have gone on talking had not his wife interrupted.

"Don't tease her, now," she said.

"Of course not," put in Lazzaro, mastering his impatience. "That wouldn't be right. I've had my say, and now it's her turn to think it over and give me an answer. Of course, as far as I'm concerned, the sooner the better."

Now Dosolina really wished to say something, but she could not get out a single word. She blamed her father for having embarrassed her and herself for being incapable of a minimum of politeness. Little did she know how charming she was as she stood there, speechless and angry, while Master Lazzaro took his meddlesome future father-in-law by the arm and led him up on the deck under the pretext of showing him some piece or other of machinery. The gratitude in Dosolina's heart was very close to love, and looking down at Lazzaro's rumpled bunk she thought to herself: "His bed would be better made if he had a wife to make it."

Meanwhile her mother said with more than her usual seriousness and affection:

"He would make a good match, I'm sure of that. Now it's up to you."

"I'll do whatever you say."

"Whatever we say?" said her mother smilingly. "And what if we say you're to marry him."

"I'm always happy to obey you."

"And this one time you wouldn't be unhappy?"

"I never have been before."

"Well, then . . ."

"Well, then, I'm perfectly happy."

Malvegoli had not been able to stay away for even this short moment and now he leaned through the cabin window just in time to hear these last words. Because he was at bottom a good man, concerned for his daughter's happiness and sure that this was the best way for her to achieve it, he had a moment of real emotion, which made up to him for many of his misfortunes and left him temporarily speechless.

"Then you can tell him yourself," Donata said to her daughter.

"I shouldn't presume . . ."

"I'll tell him, then," Malvegoli burst in, returning quickly to his usual intrusiveness. "I'll tell him! Master Lazzaro, come here!"

"Idiot, can't you understand that he'd like to hear it from her own lips?" Donata interrupted him.

Princivalle saw the truth of her words and scratched his head with mortification. Scacerni came into the cabin, and the smiling mother and father drew to one side and leaned out a porthole to look at the river.

"Am I to believe, then, that you've chosen to make me happy?" Lazzaro asked Dosolina.

"If you can be happy with a simple girl like myself."

"Then God be praised for giving me this comfort!" he exclaimed, taking her hand.

"May He be praised and magnified for ever," she chimed in, pulling her hand gently away in order to make the sign of the cross.

"And may He bless our marriage," Scacerni concluded.

Now Princivalle's satisfaction was no longer out of place and he said joyfully to his wife:

"Come now, my dear, admit that for once I was right! I saw right away that this would be a wonderful son-in-law!"

"I'm glad to admit it, and happy for Dosolina. May God bless them both."

"He's a lucky man, too, this son-in-law of ours! He's found a pearl of great price, and I don't say so just because she's my daughter. It's God's truth that Dosolina's worth her weight in gold."

"She's worth more than that," said Scacerni, remembering how light he had found her to be when he hoisted her up on the mill. In his strong, horny hand he held the delicate, hardworking hand of Dosolina.

Meanwhile Malvasone and Beffa had climbed aboard and Scacerni called all three of his boys together to celebrate the good news.

Schiavetto smiled in his usual winning way; Malvasone shifted awkwardly from one wooden clog to another, repeating over and over again how happy he was, while Beffa skulked behind him and kicked him in the ankles.

"I'm very happy, I say . . ." Malvasone muttered for the third time, then he turned on Beffa: "Stop it, will you, you idiot!"

The news of someone else's happiness brought out on Beffa's face only a leer, which caused Dosolina to draw back with fright.

"Beffa's an ugly fellow," said Lazzaro, "but he can't help it, after all."

"You're too kind, sir," Beffa answered, even uglier than before in his effort to make himself agreeable.

"Our marriage won't bring him bad luck, you can tell him that," said the miller.

"Bad luck? It won't bring that to anyone, God willing!" said Malvegoli.

"That's what I say, too," said Dosolina, compassionately holding out one hand to the ugly monster, who pressed it and said hoarsely:

"With God's help I hope to serve the mistress as well as I've served this kind master."

Again his lips drew back over his protruding white teeth in a ghastly grin.

It was sunset when the Malvegoli family started to go home, having set the wedding just for three months away. In order to spare Donata the trepidation of recrossing the river Scacerni had hired a horse and cart to take them back, and he waved to them from the riverbank until they had disappeared from view. As evening fell he became aware of how far advanced was the season and how much of the year was already gone. He had a vague and uncomfortable presentiment of the bad weather and short days to come, when the sun would only flicker briefly in the autumn and winter sky. Lazzaro lingered on the deck, thinking that soon Dosolina would come to bring cheer to every season.

"It's time to light up already," he reflected, "and yet less than a month ago we should have had a full hour more of day!"

And he looked ahead in his imagination to the time when he would be married, to the winter evenings beside the fire and the nights with Dosolina beside him. Then he wished the winter nights might be even longer, and his vague feeling of discomfort turned into a shiver of joy and anticipation.

3

Princivalle Malvegoli knew no one whom he could ask to be the bride's witness at the wedding and so it was that Master Lazzaro suggested his old friend Subbia, the shipwright of Occhiobello. As he rode to see him he reflected how pleased the old man would be by the news of his marriage. He had not thought of Subbia for a long time and had no idea of how he was faring. Subbia must be offended by this neglect but perhaps a visit upon this particular occasion would induce him to forgiveness.

All along the way he smiled to himself at the prospect of giving pleasure to this good friend of his time of trouble. Already he could hear the old man's sententious comment: "Who can find a virtuous woman? For her price is far above rubies." Yes, Dosolina would surely please him. But at this point he remembered another one of the shipwright's favorite sayings: "The anvil outlasts the hammer." This was a gloomy proverb, and all the more so when the anvil was by so many years the younger. And yet, to tell the truth, he had never felt himself to be in such good health, so strong a hammer, if you like, as since he had fallen in love. He laughed to himself at the memory of how when Subbia had a glass too many he would tease his wife by quoting this same proverb. It occurred to him that the old woman might have gone to heaven, but he quickly dismissed this thought from his mind. He crossed the bridge at Lagoscuro, rode on to Santa Maria Maddalena, and soon saw the roof tops of Occhiobello below the riverbank, with the church tower above them. From the shipyards hidden by the grove of poplars and willows on the shore came the sound of axes and hammers and he could see, and very nearly smell, the steam from the huge vats of tar. It must have been only yesterday, not years ago, that he had left these parts. He tied his horse and began to ask the passers-by whether Subbia had much work on order in his yard. The first people to whom he addressed this question merely shrugged their shoulders, but finally an old shipwright recognized his face and said, without making any direct answer:

"I know you. Aren't you the man who built a mill during the last year of the famine?"

"Exactly."

"Saint Michael's Mill, wasn't that the name?"

"Right."

"I remember now. I was there at the banquet. So now you travel by horseback, do you? That shows fortune has treated you well."

"I can't complain, but . . ."

"Then I congratulate you."

"But where can I find Subbia?"

"Subbia, eh? Then you don't know?"

"Ah!" said Scacerni with a sudden chill in his heart. "Has he had an accident of some kind?"

"Well, my friend, he was eighty years old, or more. You can't call it an accident at that age. But, excuse me, are you related to him that you should be so concerned?"

"No, I'm not a relative, only a friend."

As he spoke the words seemed only to add to his embarrassment, so great were his sorrow and regret that he had been neglectful for all these years. Now other shipwrights gathered around and recognized him and his interlocutor said:

"If you want news of Subbia, his heir is working on a boat just over there."

Scacerni thanked them with a nod and walked over to the stoutly built young man who was tarring a keel. More than ever he was aware of the passage of time as he said to him:

"Forgive me for disturbing you. You don't know me, but I feel as if I knew you. I was a friend of poor Subbia. . . . Yes, I heard the news just now. You must be the nephew from Porpolana of whom he spoke so often."

"Himself," said the other disagreeably, grinning unpleasantly without taking his eyes off his work, although he was performing it rather listlessly. "Do I owe you anything?"

"Owe me anything?" exclaimed Scacerni, surprised by these words and even more by the manner in which they were spoken. "What do you mean?"

"I mean cash. What else do you think? That weak-minded uncle of mine left so many debts behind him that I had to pay a lot for the house and tools he supposedly left me. If you're another creditor, then you're too late. I'm through with paying up for him. Let the devil take and roast him, for all I care!"

Scacerni listened to these outrageous words with a bowed head and a deep feeling of shame and remorse, as if part of the fault, he did not yet know how much, was his. So great was his discomfiture that he murmured weakly:

"For my part I was very fond of him. I beg you to speak of him in more Christian terms, especially in view of the fact that he's dead."

"I don't give a hang for him or for you either!" sneered the other, who was delighted to see such timidity in so big a man.

"He was a real friend!" exclaimed Scacerni sadly.

"And how do you think he treated me, his own nephew? All during his dotage he had me support him. When I first came no one thought

131

he could live more than three months, but as soon as he began to eat bread from my table he got it into his head to go on living just to spite me. I wish that you who are so sympathetic could have seen my wife! She never was very softhearted and with him she was hard as a stone. Every mouthful of corn meal that my uncle ate was that much iron in her soul."

His manner of speaking gave an eloquent description of Subbia's last days.

"And what about your aunt?" Scacerni asked.

"She had better sense and lost less time in going to push up the sod. Is there anything else you want to know?"

"Yes. Where are they buried?"

"In the cemetery, of course."

"I mean is there any stone to mark their graves?"

"Now, my man, you're making me laugh. Since you were such a great friend of his, I suggest that you speak to my wife about buying a tombstone! Just look at who's come to see me today, a friend of my uncle, a very great friend! Leave me alone, that's what I say! If you knew how little I cared to work myself to death when I was born to be a gentleman. Ha, ha!" he added, looking Scacerni up and down. "Is that your horse? And you're well dressed, aren't you? You're a wealthy man, I can see that. Congratulations! And his friend, eh? You're the kind of a friend that turns up when the need for him is over! Isn't that true? See to it yourself that he has a tombstone!"

Scacerni was so angry that he would gladly have stuck the fellow's face in his vat of tar. He left him abruptly, jumped on his horse and went toward the center of the town. As he rode along the wide-paved streets the first person he met was the parish priest. He got down from his horse and took off his hat.

"Do you remember me, Reverend Father?"

"Yes, indeed, and I'm happy to see you again. It's plain that God has made you prosper."

"I only wish that I deserved my good fortune," Scacerni said bitterly.

"Come, Master Lazzaro, if God were to reward us only according to our deserts it's a fine fix we'd be in!"

"Yes, Father, I know. So you even remember my name, do you?"

"Of course."

"Then I needn't tell you how I felt when I found out that Subbia and his wife are dead and that their house has passed into the hands of such a nephew. Just think, Father, I came to Occhiobello to ask my old friend to be a witness at my wedding. And what do I find!"

The priest was a soft-spoken but observant old fellow, and now he looked hard at the indignant Scacerni, who stood before him holding his horse by the bridle.

"Poor Subbia fell into evil hands, to tell the truth, during his last years. His business was going badly and he grew weak-minded and got himself into debt."

"And did his nephew pay off the creditors?"

"Who says that?"

"He hints at it himself."

"Not a bit of it. He exposed the old man to every sort of humiliation in order to discourage his creditors or arouse their compassion. But he didn't pay a penny."

"Just as I thought."

"But his wife was egging him on all the while. She's a woman with a chip on her shoulder. There's no end to what people will do for money; it's little wonder that avarice is among the mortal sins. She and her husband made Subbia beg for charity from door to door and you who knew him can imagine how he enjoyed that. If he didn't bring something back with him he found the door locked and had to sleep outside—and at his age, mind you!—or else they didn't even give him the crust of bread they told him he stole out of their mouths. But that's not all."

"Did they beat him?"

"Poor old codger!"

"And did no one stand up for him?"

"I tried to bring them around to more Christian sentiments, but without much luck. Old age is bad enough, I tell you, but when poverty comes along besides! . . ."

"Those two brutes deserve a hiding, that's what. It can't help the old man now but at least it will be a fitting revenge."

"Do you forget with whom you are speaking?" asked the priest severely.

"And then I have it in for the people who used to call themselves Subbia's friends," Scacerni went on indignantly. "Everyone in the village claimed to be among them and no one ever received anything but good at his hands."

"Do you think people have so few troubles of their own that they're apt to take on those of others?"

"Very well, but I say they're a lot of cowards, and I'll be happy to tell them so to their face before I leave Occhiobello."

"Oh, yes? Stubborn fellow, aren't you? Then let me tell you this. When old Subbia used to come to confide his troubles in me he often said: 'I have one friend who would surely help me if he could, that is if he knew to what a pass I had come.' Mind you, he never taxed this friend with forgetting him. All he ever said was: 'He has his own business to attend to. . . .' Do you know of whom he was speaking?"

Scacerni's anger subsided and he fell into a mood of even greater bitterness and self-reproach than before, while the priest went on:

"Subbia never for a moment doubted this friend or spoke ill of him. Now, Master Lazzaro, you who are so prompt to throw other people's sins in their teeth, what have you to say for this man? Look into your conscience and give me an answer."

"You're quite right, Father; it's all too true," Lazzaro answered with mortification. "This friend, as you choose to call him, is worth even less than the people he rants about."

133

"Now you're going too far. But when it comes to judging our neighbor it's better to think twice about it, especially as Our Lord has warned us against it. I am just on my way to the cemetery and I can show you where the two old people are buried. Come with me and say a prayer over their grave. I know you'll put your heart into it."

"That I will, Father, my whole heart. I can promise it as faithfully as if I were saying it at confession."

"Then your prayer will surely be heard in heaven. Come along, now."

Later on, as he rode with slack reins back to Guarda, Scacerni turned over in his mind thoughts that were both old and new. The newer they seemed at first to be the more quickly he had discovered that he had been thinking them as far back as he could remember. He did not notice that night had fallen and that his horse was finding its way alone in the dark.

For the first time in his life he thought of his old age. He would be old before Dosolina; did he have it in him to leave her provided against hunger and beggary? Might he not die too soon, before he had accomplished his task? Or mightn't the world treat him as cruelly and indifferently as it had treated Subbia? Would he and Dosolina have children? This idea consoled him, but only for a moment, as he saw in his imagination a poor widow, burdened with children who were perhaps ungrateful, or even worthless altogether.

Lost in these mournful thoughts he began to feel he had lost courage. His simple and direct soul was not tolerant of prolonged melancholy and he did not know how to account for it. Suddenly he had a presentiment that he was due to be punished for the sacrilege of having made money out of treasure stolen, amid bloodshed and blasphemy, from the Virgin's altars. It seemed to him now as if he had always known that punishment would eventually overtake him. Had he any right to involve Dosolina in his sin and in the reprisal that was certain to follow? Or should he give her up entirely? He quivered all over at the thought, realizing more than ever how much he loved and desired her. He broke out into a cold sweat and suffered so acutely that his discomfort had to come to a head and find a solution. With all his strength he rebelled against the idea of renunciation, impetuously daring to defy God's justice. With passionate joy he proclaimed that no harm could come upon an innocent head and that he took whatever punishment might impend all upon himself.

"Punish me, Lord, if You are just! And if You are not just, I have no reason to respect or fear You!"

He arrived at the mill dead tired, as if from a far longer journey, and fell asleep like a stone. The next morning he woke up thinking that before he met Dosolina the old shipwright was the only person he had ever cared for. And as for Dosolina, he resolved to make her the happiest woman on the Po and, indeed, in the whole world.

At the end of the year they were married, and their house was in a locality known as Poplar Bridge.

134

Princivalle Malvegoli's exhilaration and the high hopes he had entertained of his son-in-law had subsided ever since the day when he had asked him in vain for a loan of ten crowns with which to celebrate the wedding in proper style.

"I'd rather make you a gift of two crowns than a loan of ten," the miller said.

"But it's ten I'm asking for, and I'm ready to sign a promissory note for them if you don't trust me!"

"I said I'd give you two. Loans have a way of breaking up friendships."

"Two crowns to a man like me?"

"There's not the shame in honest poverty that there is in doubtfully acquired wealth."

"But I wanted to ask my friends to the wedding."

"You told me you had no friends."

"No true friends I meant."

"Well, false friends aren't worth bothering about."

"And what about music?"

"Your real friends don't need to be entertained with music; in fact, it would only attract a crowd of loafers, carrion crows, I call them."

"But do you realize, my dear fellow, that you're marrying into the Malvegoli family?"

"My wife will be called Scacerni. Suppose we ask her opinion on the matter."

Dosolina would express no opinion at all, but she made it known that she preferred the ceremony to be as simple as possible. And as for Donata, she said to her husband's face:

"What money has a down-at-the-heel individual like you to spend on wedding festivities?"

"Everyone's against me, as usual! After all that I've done for my family!"

This kind of talk never failed to get on Donata's nerves.

"There is one thing I should like to say to my son-in-law," she said, turning to Scacerni, who had remained silent during this painful exchange. "If my old man ever dares ask you again to lend him money, please don't give him a penny."

"What makes you think I may ask him for money?" Princivalle protested, winking doubtfully and distressfully in the direction of the silent Scacerni.

"It wouldn't be the first time!" said Donata scornfully. "But never fear, I'll see to it that the wedding is all it should be."

And provide she did, an abundance of cakes and wine and the traditional almonds. She even hired a couple of musicians, who escorted the little procession to the church and back, and as for friends, plenty of them came without waiting upon an invitation.

The years since 1817 had gone quietly and prosperously by in the region of Ferrara, while an Austrian garrison still manned the Fortress and the ambitious aims of the Hapsburg Empire were masked under a devout allegiance to the Pope. In the city itself the pious Papal legate, Cardinal Arezzo, and the good Archbishop Fava steered both temporal and spiritual affairs with great tact and discretion and the province was reputed to be one of the most tranquil in the Papal domain. The Papal government, lulled by this feeling of security, had decided to put to use the unwelcome Austrian police by exiling or jailing in Ferrara various hot-heads, malcontents, conspirators and political prisoners who in this remote spot could do no harm. The Austrians, for their part, watched with interest the increasing unrest among the population and the low esteem in which it held the government of Rome, which more than any other in the Italian peninsula was in a position of apparent sovereignty and yet absolute dependence on a foreign power. For despotic as the Papal government appeared to be, in reality it relied quite obviously on Austrian support, which fact not only undermined its dignity but endangered its safety as well.

Under these temporizing conditions, then, there were in Ferrara large numbers of old Jacobins, Napoleonic veterans and officials, freemasons, constitutional Liberals, Republicans, members of various religious sects and disbelievers, some of them natives of the place and others in exile or imprisonment, who were busily murmuring and conspiring against the priestly rule.

Lazzaro Scacerni, whose mill was not too far from the city, and indeed right on the strategical boundary of the Po, could hardly miss hearing of this state of affairs. For some time he had noticed that the smugglers were dealing not only in salt, tobacco, silk and other such goods, but also in parcels of printed matter. At one time or another they had also taken advantage of the shelter offered by Saint Michael's Mill to bring across the river persons of respectable enough appearance, but whom he recognized in spite of their disguise first as political agents and emissaries and then, after the disturbances of 1821, as refugees from justice. Because he wanted nothing to do with either of the two governments and had only tolerated the smugglers in order to keep out of trouble, this traffic in printed matter and persons trailed by the police gave him considerable annoyance, and he said as much to Big Brother, who was an increasingly important personage among all those who dealt in illegal affairs.

"Surely you can understand that I want to steer clear of complications."

"Yes, I understand."

"Especially now that I'm married and have even more reason than before for leading a quiet life and attending strictly to my own affairs."

"I see perfectly well what you mean," said Big Brother, scratching his head, "but our chief must be making a mint of money out of this new business, at least to judge from the way he pays us. To tell the truth, I haven't much taste for it myself. Speak to me of salt and things like that, and I'm your man. But our chief is never satisfied."

"I don't know who your chief may be," said Scacerni, who was perfectly aware that it was Raguseo, "and I don't want to know. But I've never made trouble for you, have I?"

"No, you haven't, that's true."

"Then you too must use discretion."

"Quite right."

"Moderation in everything, especially, as I was just saying, since now I'm a family man."

"I understand your reasoning and admit that it deserves consideration."

"Good. But I ask more than your understanding. You must pass the message along. A word to the wise is sufficient."

Big Brother went on scratching his head, without making an answer. Whether he actually passed on the message or whether the political traffic naturally waned, the fact is that soon afterwards the smugglers returned to their usual business, in which, as we know, Lazzaro saw no harm. Indeed, to his way of thinking, it would have been a sign of undue tenderness toward the government to combat them. And it would have been all too easy for them to bore a hole in one of the keels of the mill and let the weight of the millstones carry it to the bottom, or throw a pitch torch aboard which would set fire to the sacks of milled grain or the dry wood of the mill above the water line. There are two incentives to saintliness, as the proverb has it, one love and the other necessity. And at this moment, just after his marriage, Lazzaro was under the sway of an all-engrossing passion.

Everything contributed to keeping alight its flame: the fragile delicacy of Dosolina's youthful charm, the tender light of her bright eyes and shimmering hair, her fresh complexion, gentle ways, and the memory of their wedding night, when her profound timidity had made him pause at the entrance to their nuptial chamber, fearful of doing her harm, at a loss for words with which to cheer her and almost ashamed of his own strong hands, in which, as he used later to tell her, he had felt her heart beating like that of a bird. And just as he had been inordinately pleased by her modesty on that occasion, which had caused him to discover something new and good in himself and life and to alter his former rather casual idea of women, so now he was equally taken by the affectionate and sensual intimacy that under the influence of his caresses had replaced her original shyness, while she gradually grew up to love and learned all its ways. Another thing that somehow united them was the disparity in their sizes, the contrast between his immensity and her delicate proportions, which nature often seems to make into a motive of attraction.

The property at Poplar Bridge, between Guarda and Ro, half an hour from the mill, was composed of a modest but comfortable house, a vegetable garden, chicken coops, a pigsty, and a yard suitable for threshing in which there was a woodpile and an oven for baking

137

bread. Malvasone was supposed to look after the vegetables, but his place was soon taken by Beffa, who turned out to have had some practice as a gardener. In order to get on with the sowing and pruning and picking Dosolina was frequently obliged to call upon his services, although she never got over her repulsion for his ugly, leering face, and indeed felt an increasing fear, mingled with she knew not what dark presentiment. She upbraided herself and tried unsuccessfully to overcome her misgivings, but she was still too shy to confide them to Lazzaro. As a matter of fact, Lazzaro was equally timorous, without being aware of it, of his wife and of her air of refinement, doubtless inherited from the Malvegoli family, which was all the more impressive because of its very unconsciousness. He felt this way whenever he saw her hesitatingly put her foot down in the winter mud or lay hands on some homely and dirty domestic object with the intention of cleaning it. So strong were his feelings of tenderness and admiration that he was annoyed with himself and could find only a gruff and teasing way of expressing them. On such occasions he taxed her with being a "young lady" who had thrown herself away upon a boorish miller. She thought he was reproaching her and felt hurt and confused, while on his side the fact that he had not managed to convey his complimentary meaning often irritated him in an unreasonable manner. When he scolded her because she had not called Malvasone to do some of her heavy cleaning or Beffa to look after the pig in the sty she thought that underneath he was resentful of the fact that she was too delicate to do her own work and must call his helpers away from the mill. After all, she had not brought him a penny of dowry.

"Just give orders for what you want done," Scacerni said. "You were born to be waited on and your delicate hands aren't fitted for such tasks. Don't you understand? Is it so difficult to have other people serve you? It would be more understandable if you had just the opposite inclination."

Scacerni's intentions were of the kindliest and best, but his impatient tone of voice seemed to belie them, and Dosolina got the impression that he was almost sorry to have acquired so useless a helpmeet.

"I know perfectly well what I owe you," she said, biting her lip with mortification. "You took me without a penny."

"Go along with you! I took you for yourself, not for a dowry. Whoever said such a thing?"

"That's why I'm under all the more obligation to you."

"When you're as beautiful as you are, must you have a dowry besides? You're too proud, that's all. I'm very nearly angry with you!"

He was actually annoyed and his annoyance stuck in her mind and made her more fearful of him than ever.

Now that Master Lazzaro lived ashore Beffa and Malvasone slept on the mill. Scacerni was so used to having one ear cocked for the turning of the millstones, the splash of the water on the paddles of the wheel, and the direction in which the wind was blowing that at first he found it hard to go to sleep with four walls around him.

138

"Some people are kept awake by noise," he observed, "but what disturbs me is the silence of the country."

Finally he put up a weather vane on the roof—a wheel the metal blades of which creaked as it turned in the wind and gave him an idea of what was blowing up outside. This noise did not disturb his sleep, but it did bother and sadden Dosolina, who found it prophetic of evil, like the hooting of an owl.

Schiavetto slept in a small room in the house, except for the nights when there was work to be done at the mill. Now he was no longer a boy but promised to be a very handsome young man. Because of the frank, lively nature that shone through his eyes he was just as attractive to Dosolina as Beffa was distasteful. She might have been his elder sister and it was as such that she affectionately laughed and joked with him. Lazzaro was not displeased to hear them laugh together, although they stopped in an abrupt and almost guilty manner, as if they were afraid of giving offense, whenever he appeared on the scene.

"May I ask what you're laughing over?"

"Oh, nothing at all."

"How's that? One can't laugh over nothing."

"I don't remember. Something silly. Do you remember, Schiavetto?"

When the trivial cause of their mirth was told in plain words it seemed so utterly insignificant that they could hardly believe it and Lazzaro might well have believed that underneath it there was some joke of a much more daring kind. The fact is that he never joined in their laughter and when once he ventured to say: "I'd like to laugh with you," they stared at him with amazement and then burst into gales of merriment.

"What's that?" he said. "Did I say something so out of the way? Am I not allowed to laugh too?"

They only laughed all the harder and with a vague feeling of uneasiness he gave up questioning them.

"The mistress has found herself a second father," Beffa said to his master, "and the kindliest one can imagine."

Sullen as he appeared Beffa indulged in exaggerated compliments, most of them as unwelcome as the preceding. But talking to Schiavetto he spoke in a more malicious vein.

"Clever boy! You know how to get on in the world. The mistress makes certain eyes at you . . ."

And when Schiavetto blushingly protested he went on:

"Cleverer still! That's the thing to say, of course. But I know something about women. The mistress will be a widow one of these days and you may as well prepare the way to your succession. If you turn the trick you'll have a prosperous mill and a handsome woman to boot. In fact, you may not have to wait for the master to pass away, because pretty soon he'll need help. With time the millstones grind more and more slowly, and one of these days you may be called on to keep the miller's wife happy. Why do you take it so hard, my innocent lad?"

"Your talk's as ugly as your face."

139

"Then why don't you report it to Master Lazzaro?"

"I'm no tattle-tale."

"Good. That's an ugly thing to be, and then the master might open his eyes and be of my opinion rather than yours. Then the mistress would get a beating and you, not I, would be sent away."

Schiavetto knew that he was not strong enough to give Beffa the thrashing he deserved and so he went to the other end of the mill and shed tears of anger. When Beffa found him alone, inside or outside the house, with Dosolina he pretended to withdraw in embarrassment in order not to disturb them. And later on he said to Schiavetto:

"I'm not one to throw the light on a pair of love birds."

Second to his ruling passion, which was malice, Beffa was subject to overwhelming gluttony. The smell of a spicy dish was the only thing that could touch his heart, and it was amazing the way a melting look came into his eyes and he stretched his neck out to see where it came from. Master Lazzaro was amused and since Dosolina did all the cooking she tried to make up for her unconquerable repulsion by preparing for his benefit something particularly tasty, such as blood sausages, which he fell upon with greed.

"She's very wise to feed me well," he said later to Schiavetto, licking his cracked red lips. "That's the way to teach a watchdog not to bark at thieves."

Master Lazzaro had instructed Beffa and Malvasone that whenever Big Brother and his fellows came to make use of the mill they were simply to shut an eye, without taking part in anything. But while Malvasone invariably slept through their visits, Beffa soon made himself their active accomplice and turned Saint Michael's Mill into a sure hiding place not only for smugglers but for all the evildoers who wandered up and down the river. Although criminality was in general on the decline there was still much bad blood in the countryside and an abundance of evil passions which often overflowed into violent crimes and reprisals, all these favored not only by social and political conditions, but also by the fact that safety and impunity were assured anyone who could cross the boundary line of the Po. By virtue of good luck or of the healthy respect in which they held him Scacerni had managed so far to have no dealings with bandits and thieves. But while he was lulled to carelessness by his matrimonial joys, Beffa had entered into the favors of Raguseo and was a rival in Raguseo's service to Big Brother, an honest enough smuggler but at the same time a lost soul, a desperado and assassin.

One misty, moonlit night, although there was no work to be done, Schiavetto went back to the mill for something he had forgotten. He was just about to give his usual whistle when he saw that the two larger rowboats were both tied up on the shore, the millstones were turning and there was light in the cabin. Strangers must be aboard, but then why were the boats beached? He jumped on the skiff and pulled himself along by one of the mooring ropes that was attached to the stern of the mill, with the intention of seeing what was going on.

The first thing he saw was that two strange boats were tied to the smaller hulk. It seemed unlikely that anyone should have brought grain to be milled at this hour and so he proceeded cautiously, under cover of the noise of the mill wheel. Standing balanced on the slender prow, which dipped into the foam thrown out by the turning wheel, and holding on with both hands to the rough surface of the hulk, he pressed his eye to a hole in a board which allowed him to look down into the hold below the cabin. Two kerosene lamps swung from a beam to the vibration of the mill, so gently that their flames were never diminished but merely quivered and occasionally burned brighter. And what he saw in their light made the boy think he must be dreaming. He could see four faces, one of which was Beffa's while the other three were those of strangers. There was another figure, a stocky barefoot young man who lay with his arms and legs tied with strong ropes on the floor. Two men were sitting on his knees, with totally indifferent expressions that were even more frightening than the expectant looks of Beffa and one more of their number, bending over a roaring coal fire in the stove. They were all so still that their shadows moved on the walls of the hold in the same rhythm as that of the swinging lamps. What they were up to Schiavetto could not guess, nor why the bound man did not cry out, unless he were still suffering from the effects of a violent and prolonged struggle which caused him to breathe painfully, with his head turned so that nothing could be seen of it but his chin. A moment later he twisted in his bonds and raised his neck from the floor. Then Schiavetto saw that he was gagged, in such a way that only a stifled, faraway murmur came out of his throat.

"Quiet there, stay quiet," said the two men who were sitting on top of him, in the same tone of voice as that of a blacksmith addressing a restless horse.

But Beffa and his companion turned around from the fire.

"Patience, Big Brother, we'll soon take proper care of you," said Beffa. "Just wait a minute, and you'll have no reason to complain, Big Brother."

Schiavetto's heart was in his throat and he could not take his eyes off the scene.

"Big Brother," said Beffa's companion, who had a pair of pincers in his hand, "you'll soon come down from your high horse. You'll learn better than to disobey Raguseo and try to put something over on your friends. You ought to know already what it means to be in Raguseo's bad books. But we'll cure you of all that!"

These words imprinted themselves on the boy's mind as brightly as the coals of the fire, which flamed and crackled as Beffa stooped to blow into them. He too held a pair of pincers, with which he now drew out a glowing horseshoe nail.

"Here's one ready," he said. "And the animal is in the stocks. Just lift up his foot."

Stocks is the name given by blacksmiths to the apparatus in which they confine a horse that is unwilling to be shod. One of the two men who had been sitting on the victim's knees got up in as leisurely a fashion as if really only an animal were concerned, and sat now astride his stomach, grasping his leg in both hands and holding up the foot. His fellow, with the same awkward sluggishness, drew aside, hunched over like a sculptured figure holding up a shelf. Beffa was heating his nail over the flames.

"Is yours ready?" he asked his companion.

"Pretty nearly. Stick yours in first."

"All right, Big Brother, here you are."

Schiavetto wished he could run away and yet he was not able even to close his eyes. Big Brother stretched out his neck to look at the glowing nail between the pincers, while Beffa walked with bent shoulders toward the rear of the low-ceilinged hold, knelt down before the bare foot, measured it with his eye and drew very close. The foot contracted convulsively at the approach of the nail, but upon actual contact it sizzled and a cloud of thick, acrid smoke filled the hold and cut off the sight of the horror. Even the gag could not entirely stifle the victim's moaning.

"Howl away, Big Brother," Schiavetto heard Beffa say. "If you lose your toe nail you'll grow a callus in its place."

But a fit of coughing interrupted his cruel joking.

"Hurry up," said his accomplice. "There's no breathing in this hole."

"We must get some of the smoke out," said Beffa, raising the trap-door above his head.

Schiavetto did not see the rest, for the skiff had begun to drift away. He almost fainted and before he knew it he had lost his grip on the mill. There were no oars on the skiff and the river carried him away in the dark night. He shook all over and his teeth chattered with a confused feeling of horror for what he had seen and for those who were responsible, for himself as a spectator and mankind in general. His eyes stared unseeingly through the darkness, dazzled by the sparks of the fire, while the stench of the smoke in his nostrils made his stomach turn over. The current carried him ashore beyond Guarda. Fear lest Beffa and his friends notice the skiff's absence and come after him, mingled with an indignant pity that threatened to cause him to break out sobbing, drove him instinctively along the shore in the direction of Poplar Bridge. A moving light on the river, not far from the mill, caused him to quicken his pace.

Master Lazzaro had gone to bed and it was quite a job to awaken him by tapping at the window. Schiavetto was afraid that Beffa was just behind him and the noise of the knocker on the front door seemed to him likely to put him and his fellow assassins on the trail.

"Why are you coming home so late?" asked Scacerni as he opened the window. "You should have been in bed long ago." But hearing the boy's panting he added: "I'll come let you in."

It took some time and a drink of brandy to help Schiavetto catch his breath, but once he had started to tell his story he was overcome by almost hysterical excitement and words poured out of his mouth, with

142

numerous interruptions and repetitions, as if he were drunk. He was waiting for Master Lazzaro to take his gun down from the wall and go to administer revenge and justice. For himself, he now felt quite capable of returning with his master to the scene of the crime and putting the torturers to death like the wild beasts they were.

Scacerni listened to him coldly, with an increasingly grim look on his face, interrupting only to confirm the names of Big Brother and Raguseo. He seemed almost glad that the boy's account should be a rambling one because it gave him more time for reflection. Twice he clenched his fists, and at the end of the story he raised his eyes with a desperate expression that struck further fear into the boy's heart.

"I should have come to tell you even sooner," Schiavetto was saying, "but at first I didn't catch on to what they were up to, and afterwards I was carried down the river."

"So much the better, Schiavetto. It's over with now, and we'd best not interfere. If you had come earlier I don't know how I could have held myself back."

"But Master, that poor fellow? . . ."

"Oh, that one? Probably he's done the same thing to others in his time. They're all of a kind."

"And what will you do?"

"I'll keep quiet, and so must you, with the mistress, and Beffa, and everyone else. You must pretend nothing has happened. Do you think you can do it, Schiavetto?"

Schiavetto looked upon Scacerni like a father, and he had never imagined that anyone or anything could impress or humiliate him. For a minute he thought that his idol was afraid, but then he realized that he was only depressed and that his apparent indifference was born of impotent despair. He felt like a son who becomes aware for the first time that his father is smarting under the injustice of fate and his fellow men. Almost painfully ashamed he lowered his head, so as not to have to look him in the eyes. Scacerni interpreted this gesture as assent to what he had just said, and added:

"Are you sure you can manage to pretend nothing has happened? Will you be able to look at Beffa without blinking an eyelash, after you have seen him with those pincers in his hand? That won't be so easy, you know. I don't mean that you'll be afraid; on the contrary, I know that you're a brave boy, but you may be carried away by disgust and anger. And if you can't put a good face on the matter and meet him without flinching, then the best thing for both you and me is that you leave here before tomorrow morning and avoid meeting him at all. Think it over, and if you don't feel you can do it, I'll gladly give you money enough to tide you over until you find another job, but one that's far away, I tell you, far from the river. I have the money right here in the house. So think hard before you decide. There's no time to lose, because if you go it must be before dawn."

"I'm not going to desert you, Master," said Schiavetto, with indignation added to his horror. "But why do you make me such an offer?"

"Because I want you to think over the situation well. The night is nearly over and tomorrow it will be too late. I'm just as fond of you as you are of me, and so I want to make sure. . . . Yes, I saw you look up at my gun a minute ago! Don't you think I'd like to take it down and punish that wretched Beffa, who's raising hob in my house and causing me to risk the gallows? I was the only one to give him a crust of bread when everyone else chased him away; I took pity on him when they treated him like a dog. In fact, they were angry with me for taking him in; they said I'd be sorry, and they were right. But what can I do now? You have good judgment even if you're only a boy; just tell me what's a man in my position to do? Should I move the mill to some other anchorage? I couldn't go very far, and wherever I went I should lose my customers and not succeed, even at that, in shaking off these murderers. You've seen with your own eyes what they're capable of doing to anyone who stands in their way. And what's more serious is that I have a wife. Now I'm talking to you as man to man, Schiavetto. My wife is pregnant and I'm fearful of trouble for her and the child. It's not poverty alone that I fear! Those villains are capable of blackmailing me and taking out their spite on a woman. Now that you've seen them at work I need hardly say more. They have me just as tightly in their clutches as they had Big Brother tonight. And I only hope that he pays them tit for tat another day!"

Schiavetto's accumulated horror found vent in a flood of tears, which actually relieved the tensity of the situation and softened Scacerni's bitterness. He had become more and more heated in his peroration and the final words had come out of his mouth boiling with bitterness and resentment. Now he patted the shoulder of the weeping Schiavetto.

"Look here, Schiavetto, would I keep you here if you were my son?"

"And if you were my father would I leave you?" the boy answered with a new strength in his voice.

"Very well, Schiavetto. As man to man, I value your friendship. Dry your tears and let's shake hands."

They shook each other's right hands, while Schiavetto wiped his eyes with his left sleeve.

"Don't worry about me, Master Lazzaro. I've cried, to be sure, but I know my own powers. I promise you that I shall behave tomorrow as if I had seen nothing."

"Come, come," said Lazzaro with a smile. "I have no worries on your account. And perhaps things won't always go like this. Life spins around like a wheel and if today you find yourself at the bottom, tomorrow you may perfectly well be at the top. It's all a question of patience. Those fellows won't always be in a position to threaten us with a knife up their sleeve. We'll get rid of them somehow."

But deep down in Lazzaro's heart there was a dark fear, which he did not put into words and perhaps did not even clearly perceive, a fear that he was in disgrace with God and with God's Mother. His impulse of revenge turned into a shiver of terror. He was weary but he

144

knew that he would not find rest either this night or for many nights to come.

"Go to sleep now, Schiavetto," he said sadly. "And what will you do tomorrow morning?"

"I'll go straightaway to the mill."

"Good," said Scacerni approvingly, with an attempt at a smile. "Where your arm offends you, cut it off! But what you saw was enough to take anyone's appetite away."

There was a pale and wintry sun the next morning, which lit up a frost that had covered every leaf and branch of the trees and every blade of grass on the ground. When from the riverbank Schiavetto first caught sight of Saint Michael's Mill he thought that all he had witnessed the night before must have been no more than a bad dream or diabolical vision, particularly as he saw the skiff tied up in its usual place. Scacerni noticed the skiff, too, but said nothing. He gave his usual whistle, and Schiavetto was so astounded to rediscover everything that he had last seen under such extraordinary circumstances that he forgot the trembling of his heart.

"Good morning, Master!" said Beffa, as he came to fetch them with the boat. "Frost came last night and it's a cold morning! And, do you know, the skiff slipped away and drifted more than a mile down the river. I found it beached and half full of water. Malvasone must have tied it insecurely when he came back from drinking wine at the Guarda tavern."

He seemed to be trying out the effect of his words, which to Schiavetto signified only that he had not been dreaming after all.

"You must learn to tie it up better in the future," Master Lazzaro said coolly.

"That's something you needn't tell *me*. Meanwhile I worked over bailing it out until I was in a sweat. But you, Schiavetto, you look quite blue and trembling with the cold."

"I am cold, that's a fact," said Schiavetto.

"This is no matter of hot and cold," Scacerni interposed sternly. "If you let another one of my boats drift away I'll have to discharge you. I can't afford to lose them just because you've had too much to drink."

"Quite right, Master, but we weren't drunk last night. It has even occurred to me that someone loosened the skiff for a joke as he went by."

"Rubbish! I've said what I have to say. Just remember."

Aboard the mill Scacerni found everything awry; dirt, disorder, carelessness and neglect. He lost his temper and included all three of his helpers in his rage.

"I've been too easy with the lot of you," he shouted, "and you've taken advantage of me. A man has to keep his eye on you all the time, and to treat you well is sheer folly."

All this swearing and angry talk were calculated to draw off Beffa's suspicions, if he had any, from Schiavetto to himself. Usually he paid no attention to any murmuring around him, but this morning he seemed to prick up his ears just in order to jump on one of his helpers.

"Master Lazzaro got up on the wrong foot this morning," Beffa whispered to Schiavetto. "Is his wife making life miserable for him so soon?"

"Insolent bastard and clown!" Scacerni thundered. "I picked you up when you were starving and worse off than a mad dog, and now you talk about me behind my back, do you? Just say these things to my face so that I can have the pleasure of leaving my mark on you beside God's other curses!"

He took the dour Beffa by the chest and shook him violently. And before Schiavetto could recover from his astonishment the miller turned on him also.

"And you were listening to him, were you? Hypocritical timeservers you are, the lot of you! Some day I'll beat the hides off you all and send you packing."

Of course, after what he had learned of the events of the previous night, he could hardly hope to be rid of Beffa so easily, but his feigned violence had helped the fearful Schiavetto to get over the shock of the first meeting and at the same time intimidated Beffa and distracted him from any intentions he might have had of trying to find out what Schiavetto knew. Indeed Schiavetto had been so impressed by the master's haste to clean up the mill that he had already gone twice down in the hold in search of soap and brushes which were not within reach as they should have been, and so hurriedly that he had not had time to think again of what had taken place there the preceding night. Scacerni's scolding made for a general shake-up of everything on board. Dust flew from every corner and mice scurried about, while the three cats retired to the top of the deck and sat there in a posture of ruffled dignity. All this commotion dissipated something unhealthy in the air; it took Schiavetto's mind off things too horrible to think about and revived his spirits.

They all joined in chasing the mice, which were fat as all mill mice should be and particularly appealed to Malvasone. For once Beffa did not tease him for putting them to one side. The housecleaning went on until the churchbell rang out noon and Lazzaro called a halt.

"From now on Saint Michael's Mill must be always spick and span; it must shine like polished glass. I shan't merely keep an eye on things during the daytime hours; I shall drop in at night to see how they are going. That's the way I want to be worked for, and if anyone can't fall in with it let him feel free to go. I'll not keep him under constraint and there's plenty of room left in the world. Is that clear?"

Schiavetto noticed too that Lazzaro had begun to carry a pistol in his jacket pocket. When the miller went home that night he took with him a gun that hung on the cabin wall, leaving behind him only a flint-lock used for duck shooting, from which he removed the flint. Before a week was up he kept his promise of making nocturnal visits to the mill. The result of his new severity was an increase of efficiency and hence of profit in the mill operations, and he even thought of either buying another pair of millstones or setting up a second mill at the same spot. But at the bottom of his heart there still lurked a dark consciousness of sin and a secret fear of future ill luck and chastisement. His prosperity, instead of making him happy, seemed to him treacherous and accursed, as if it had originated with the devil in person. Still he was unwilling to search his conscience too deeply for fear of being forced to make a restitution that would have cost him dear. He was increasingly a slave to his passion for Dosolina and to the comfort and ease of his married life. And at the same time, the more profit he made the more he was anxious to make. Now that he felt some obscure threat from Raguseo hanging over his head he was anxious to put aside enough money to move somewhere far away if necessary. Meanwhile, although the smugglers continued to avail themselves of his tolerance of their use of the mill, they did not go beyond the bounds of what he called discretion and decency. Beffa afforded him no reason for complaint, but of course he was acting as a spy for the nefarious crew whose heavy hand Scacerni seemed to feel on his shoulder even when he was asleep; he was an agent of Michele Bergando, whose nickname of Raguseo derived not only from the city of his origin but also from a local expression applied to anyone who was given to the pitiless greed for gain that had made this man a backer and leader of every sort of evil trade. Scacerni could not deceive himself; from one day to the next, for business reasons or willful caprice or the sheer terrorism that went with the exercise of his power, Raguseo might order administered to him the treatment recently visited upon Big Brother.

Schiavetto wondered why the miller never spoke of this subject again and seemed indeed to have forgotten it. Yet he felt that behind his master's increasingly reserved manner there was a mixture of rough affection and fatherly solicitude. All this while Scacerni felt uneasy in his conscience and angry with himself for having been a party to crime and having temporized with Michele Bergando. "I've acted as if I didn't know the price of striking a bargain with the Devil," he said to himself; "as if my soul were money that could be converted into change and spent in small parcels. I ought to know, after all, that salvation and damnation are all of one piece. I knew perfectly well that there was a curse on the treasure."

As Dosolina's pregnancy advanced he became troubled lest his child should be born under an evil star and doomed to misfortune. The unbelievable tender emotion he had felt when Dosolina had informed him of her condition was with him at every moment, to his greater despair. He was tempted almost to be sorry that he had married and begotten a child, for if it were not for her, his beloved, and the creature about to be born of their union, he would by now have moved the mill away or sold or sunk it, and left for some remote corner of the globe. Instead, here he was, bound to the site of his affliction.

"I'm not the man I was," he said to himself; "I'm no man at all. And Dosolina, poor girl, is to blame. Or is she?"

147

Every new face that appeared at the mill, not to mention that of Beffa, made him suspect that here was an emissary of Raguseo.

"Yet, who knows?" he told himself. "Raguseo may have forgotten my existence. If he knew how he was preying on my mind he'd have a good laugh and say it was a fitting revenge for my victory in the match of our muscles. He has the jump on me now; he's playing with me like a cat with a mouse! . . . Nonsense! Can it be that I am afraid?"

At such times he was plagued by the idea the Bergando was lying low only in order to keep him in suspense, or that he was toying with him quite absent-mindedly and teasing him with the least possible effort. This came into his mind one day when he was watching the grim gallantry and fierce feints of one of the cats stalking a mouse on the deck of the mill. Beffa, too, was at the scene and Scacerni could not help bursting out in spite of himself, as he looked into Beffa's shifting eyes:

"I used to know a man in Ferrara who practiced the tactics of that cat. A queer fellow, half Turkish, who knew very well how to play with the rats and mice around him."

"Who was that?"

"Michele Bergando, a former pirate, but he was known under another name. In fact this cat reminds me of him so strongly that I think I'll give him the same handle."

Beffa's eyelids were too eaten away by smallpox for him to blink them, but the pupils were bathed in a viscous fluid as if they were affected by the glare of a bright light. There was a strange tone to his voice when he managed to swallow his saliva and say:

"And what was the nickname then?"

"Raguseo."

"Then let the cat be Raguseo, too," said Beffa with a forced laugh.

Yes, from time to time the whole thing seemed to Scacerni like a game, like his favorite pastime of hunting, which never failed to sharpen his eye and quicken the beat of his pulse. Only in this case the roles were reversed and he was the prey; his was the wild and frightened look of the fox in the trap. But was he really trapped? The last word had not been spoken.

His passion for Dosolina was gloomier and more desperate than ever, as if the nights that lay ahead of him were counted. By day he hardly spoke to her at all, but was lost in his own thoughts, among which one was compellingly recurrent:

"If Raguseo touches my woman, I'll wring his neck for sure."

Dosolina was almost intimidated by his taciturn gaze. First she thought that false rumors must have made him jealous and suspicious, but she did not dare question him about them; then, once the first disturbances of her pregnancy were over and she had begun to fill out, she imagined that he found her ugly, no longer cared for her, and regretted their marriage. Because of her natural shyness she could not understand why, under these circumstances, he still sought after her so passionately at night, unless, perhaps, under cover of darkness he saw her as she was before her figure had spoiled.

In reality she was more beautiful than ever now that violet circles rimmed her blue eyes and her rosy complexion had turned into a pearly white. Now he knew how under his kisses her cheeks glowed and the light of her eyes grew darker and more intense, bearing more eloquent witness than her hesitant words to the love she bore him. The new heaviness of her waist and hips, which was not yet cumbersome and tiring, only made her seem to him sweeter and more surrendering than before. As his fierce lust caused her to be aware of this inexplicable appeal that she made to his senses Dosolina felt ashamed and half sinful, afraid of her own weakness rather than of his strength, because she was unable to resist a wave of blind desire whenever he approached her.

These nights of love were like a dream, like a guilty secret of the flesh that they shared between them. When the blonde Dosolina fell asleep with her head on his chest and in his still unsated exhaustion he was filled with the fragrance of her hair and felt for her a tenderness that he could never manage to put into words, then often Lazzaro lay awake in a state of unspeakable anxiety, fearing to hear Raguseo or one of his emissaries knock at the door. He even wished that this might be true, in order to settle the matter once and for all without delay. The nights were still long, even when winter gave way to spring, and the creaking weather vane turned slowly in the breeze as if to punctuate his alternate nightmares and insomnia. The only thing that hastened their passage was the occasional outburst of a storm, foreboding a changeable and angry season. Often when he got up to answer what he thought was a rap at a door or window, he found that the wind was rattling them. On one such night he ran into Schiavetto.

"I thought I heard someone knocking," said the boy.

"And who could it be at an hour like this? Are you mad? I came to see if everything was properly locked up." And then he added, more gently: "Go along back to sleep. A young fellow like you needs more rest than an old man."

Even when it occurred to Lazzaro that his fears were excessive or ill-founded, that things might go on as they were for years, the old pirate would come suddenly and disagreeably into his mind again. He could hardly forget him for long because, as we are told by the chronicles of the period, there was constant rumor in city and country alike of armed hold-ups, thefts and extortions. Poverty and prolonged vicissitudes of every kind had barbarized the people of this region, where once the warlords of the House of Este had raised levy after levy of soldiers—the people that had kept their successors, the Popes, in healthy fear. No one is so poor, they had always said, that he has not a knife blade with which to defend himself. Perhaps if poverty had been the only trouble they would now have known better how to mete out their own justice. The trouble was that they were not poor, but harnessed to the cart of prosperity.

149

Meanwhile Lazzaro's thoughts turned around and around like the weather vane on the roof. The weather grew increasingly erratic; on account of a late freeze the level of the Po was first so low that there was not enough water to drive the mill wheel, and then swollen by the melting snow that poured into its mountain tributaries.

"The fat years are over," murmured the old peasants. "Now come the lean ones. That is the way of the world."

They looked at the flooded fields, the heavy clouds in the sky, and the sun that gleamed fitfully, when it came out, over the steaming, damp earth.

"A gleam in the air means rain is there," they said, according to the proverb.

A variable and snowless winter was succeeded by a treacherous spring, filled with dire forebodings.

Another affliction in Lazzaro's house was Dosolina's father. He was even more extravagant in his speech than before and seemed to resent the consideration Lazzaro showed for his wife by taking a maidservant to help her. An unnecessary expense, said Malvegoli, pretending to be a stern, old-fashioned father, who had not accustomed his daughter to such luxuries. What really bothered him was that there should be money enough in Lazzaro's house for a servant, but not for his father-in-law. Every time there was a market day or fair near by he had some wild proposition to make to Lazzaro: a consignment of hemp or worm-eaten wheat, or corn that turned out to be covered with mold, a piece of land that would have been a bargain were it not for the fact that it was heavily mortgaged, and so on. He tried to persuade him to finance a lottery in Ferrara and the project of building a flying ship, with sails and a rudder, held up by two balloons on either side.

"I'm just a miller," Scacerni replied. "How do you expect me to have so much money?"

"All I need is enough to make a deposit."

"And what about the rest?"

"Oh, the rest . . ." Malvegoli would add distractedly, "the rest will do in promissory notes."

"And who's to pay for them when they fall due?"

"Before that time comes we shall have made enough to repay capital and interest and have a big profit besides. It's a sure winner."

But the miller was not so easily persuaded.

"You have no faith in me, that's it!"

"No, I haven't."

"And you say so to my face, do you?"

"Yes, I do."

"And to think that I came to you on account of my daughter, because you're one of the family, and I didn't want to give the profit to an outsider."

"Never mind about that."

"What do you mean?"

"Just go ahead and ask an outsider for the money."

Princivalle almost burst with rage. He took his complaint straight to his daughter, with no regard for the discomforts of her pregnancy, and succeeded in causing her to feel very depressed.

"If your husband really loved you he wouldn't treat me like this. I'm sorry I ever advised you to marry him. It was a great mistake."

Dosolina was already overinclined to feelings of this sort. And jealousy contributed to her woe. She had not escaped being told of all the women whom the miller had courted before his marriage, and indeed some of them had been pointed out to her. If, however, she seemed to fall in with her father's resentment he would turn against her, and remind her that he had favored the match and that she was an ungrateful daughter to say that it was not all it should be. He almost went so far as to reproach her for every piece of bread she had eaten before she was married, and meanwhile he ate and drank away, wailing all the while that the close-fisted Donata was slowly starving him to death. Dosolina, knowing perfectly well how things were at home, sent gifts to her mother and plied her father with good food and drink, in order to soothe him and put an end to his humiliating recriminations. But when Malvegoli was stoked up with good food his talk grew all the more heated. When Lazzaro came back from the mill he found Dosolina red-eyed from weeping and insisted on her telling him the reason. Of course Malvegoli was more foolish than he was evil-hearted, but Lazzaro told him off in a few hard words. As for Dosolina, he told her to go on helping her poor mother, but he added a warning that if ever he found her red-eyed again he would see to it that her father did not set foot in the house again.

"Your mother is always credited with being right!" wailed Princivalle. "And you have allied yourself with her against me. But the bread I receive from your husband's hands sticks in my throat."

Meanwhile, however, he went right on eating. And Dosolina, like the good daughter she was, thought that both her husband and mother showed too little consideration for Princivalle Malvegoli.

One morning she woke up under the influence of a dream, which was not clear in her memory but had left a strong impression upon her that she would die in childbirth. At first this idea, which is not uncommon among women bearing their first child, was not altogether displeasing. She felt a mild, erratic tenderness toward herself for dying so young and toward her husband who would love her too late and one distant day tell their child of its poor dead mother. She imagined the mourning of her dear ones and her funeral procession, pervaded by the odor of burning candles. But her imagination broke down when it came to picturing as a boy or girl the creature that she now with love and wonder felt stirring within her. Another time her dream ended with her feeling herself nailed irrevocably into her coffin and lowered into the grave. From this nightmare she woke up in a cold perspiration, with her teeth chattering, powerless to call her husband. This marked the end of the playful resignation with which she had spoken of the impending danger to Lazzaro, who shrugged his shoulders in order to conceal his inner perturbation, and to the housewives of the neighborhood who came occasionally to visit her. Now she was overcome by a desperate, unreasonable fear, which she did not dare confide to anyone, and which bid fair to spoil all her anticipation of motherhood and the preparations she was making for the care and clothing of her baby. This fear would grip her all of a sudden so realistically as to make her believe that already her last hour had come.

As soon as she had caught her breath she would beat her breast and mumble a *mea culpa* and a *miserere,* inwardly rebelling, with a slavish and corrupt bitterness, against the husband who continued even under these dangerous circumstances to induce her to sin. Because Scacerni had left Schiavetto at the house to serve her and, in case of need, to call him back from the mill, Dosolina had the horse hitched to the cart and went to Guarda to make a confession and set her soul in good order.

The parish priest, Don Bastiano Donzelli, was a good, simple fellow, and all of a piece. He approved Dosolina's zeal, but not her excessive scruples. Moreover, at certain hours of the day he went to work, with hoe and plow and pruning hook, on a small piece of his own property.

"Daughter, the fear of God and of damnation is always a healthy thing. But this fear of yours is carnal and not of the spirit. Watch out, daughter, for the pureness of heart is the first requisite of true contrition."

"But I'm sure I'm going to die."

"How very startling! That's one thing we're all sure of!"

"I shall die in childbirth."

"Look here, my good woman, what does all this mean? If you need me, here I am. Unworthy as I may be, that's what I'm here for. Bring me your sins, your mortal sins, if you like, and I'll not spare you first penance and then absolution, if you deserve it. But don't be over-scrupulous, that's a sin of pride, if you must know it. And don't come tell me fairy stories that have no place in the confessional, such as that you're sure of dying in childbirth. You're in God's hands, just like the rest of us. You're going to die, are you? Very startling news that is! If that's all you have to tell me, let me go back to my work. The weather's bad this year, as you know, and the sowing difficult. I'm needed on my land, because if I hire others to do my work then the harvest will be theirs, not mine. And don't go thinking ill of me. This work is just as acceptable to God as any other. He doesn't want any of us to idle, not even His priests."

He was himself an active man, perhaps almost too active for his ministry, and known besides for his honesty and competence in agricultural matters, so that he was often called upon to settle disputes in the market place. Dosolina admitted her fault and accepted his upbraiding humbly, but her fears did not for this reason cease to torment her.

The women of the neighborhood, when they looked her over, found

152

signs, to which they gave a superstitious interpretation, that her travail would be a hard one. Even if they did not put this prophecy into words they looked at Dosolina so pointedly that she came to take the hooting of the night owl or the sight of a black cat as messages of misfortune. Dosolina particularly missed her mother, who lately had sided with her husband in handing out the most despotic sort of advice to her son-in-law. Scacerni was increasingly irritable and perhaps now he really did regret having taken such a timorous wife, one who would surely cost him a fortune in drugs and doctors. In his impatience he managed to offend mortally both his wife's parents.

"We'll not set foot in this house again!" they shouted.

"Exactly what I was hoping for!" he answered.

Of course he had no sooner spoken these words than he realized that he had put himself in the wrong, without, however, wishing to admit it. And Dosolina steeped herself more deeply than before in her feeling of resentful humiliation. "It's because I'm poor, and ugly now beyond recognition, and half an invalid that he treats me so," she said to herself. "And now that I'm married there's nothing to do but stick it out. Luckily I haven't much longer to live."

As for the neighbors, one of them, called Venusta Chiccoli, who coupled common sense with a kind heart, put the other women properly in their place:

"If you come here just to pull long faces, my friends, and have nothing better to offer, you'd best stay away."

Venusta was a jovial, energetic, outspoken sort, practiced in midwifery as in every other domestic art, especially in view of the fact that she herself had borne so many children that she said she could not keep track of them.

"And now with this girl here," she said, after she had come to have a great affection for Dosolina, "I feel as if I had added one more child to my collection, as if I didn't have more than enough to do already."

So saying she smiled with a mixture of lightheartedness and pity for herself and humanity in general, seeking to conceal her generosity and to pretend that she was sorry for any kind act she might have done. This characteristic attitude she accompanied by beating her hand on her forehead, as if to say: "What a queer one I am!" Then, when it came to talking about her brood of children and the faraway days of her own youth, she would clap both hands to her belly, which was shapeless from hard work and childbearing and also from a certain natural carelessness, which seemed in her case to speak for the fact that she was kept so incessantly busy that she had not time to take thought for appearance. She was goodnatured and always ready to help as far as she was able those who needed her, but at the same time she never stopped scolding them for having got into trouble and herself for having come to their assistance:

"Of course, you're out of your mind," she would say, "but I'm even madder to have let myself in for sharing your trouble for no good reason!"

Beside taking care of her own house and any other house in Guarda where care was needed, she functioned as midwife, nurse and seamstress. She was always hurrying breathlessly along, as if she were late to her destination, but actually she never failed to arrive where she was wanted in plenty of time. The ageing of her sturdy peasant body made it hard to picture the well-rounded but agile figure she had had in her youth, but her plump face still kept its original contour and there was a keen, resolute, intelligent look in her deep, well-cut, black eyes. Her nose had thickened, partly from the use of snuff, but the nostrils still quivered with sensuality, in contrast to her tightly drawn lips, which turned down with unconscious bitterness whenever her face was in repose. At a time like this if anyone asked her what she was thinking about she looked up in astonishment, as if she were coming back to herself, and asked mordantly how she could possibly have time to think.

Chiccoli, her husband, was cobbler for both the villages of Guarda, since the inhabitants of the Venetian side traditionally crossed the river to have their shoes mended. He was a man remarkable for his success with women, a success which none of them could account for, least of all Venusta, who as a girl was pretty, charming, proud, hard to please, and sought after by a number of far more attractive suitors. Chiccoli was the last man that it ever occurred to her to beware of, much less to fall in love with, for there was nothing in his favor. He was short, fat, ugly and mellifluous, but in his dull eyes there was reflected an overwhelming propensity for women, not for this one or that but for the whole sex; he desired them all indiscriminately and was content with any of them. There was in his eyes a sort of sublime abnegation, so that even if a woman could not admire him, she was sure that she could twist him around her little finger, that she could obtain from him whatever she wanted either in the way of petty whims or desperate follies. He was a man who asked for only one thing in exchange and thought that it could not be paid for too dear. His power over women, then, came from the fact that he had a vocation for love and exercised it in a humble yet irresistible manner.

Be this as it may, he had caught Venusta behind a hedge at a favorable moment—for men of his kind have a sixth sense for feeling out propitious occasions and turning them to advantage. Before she knew it she was pregnant. Even now, as she looked back, she could remember only his first words immediately after her fall, which still made her blush, half in satisfaction, half in disdain.

"Now you won't think me worthy of marrying you," he had said.

"Now I'll have to marry you, stupid," she had answered, laughing amid her anger and shame.

Every time she reproached him with some violation of his marriage vows he would seek her pardon by saying:

"As the father of your children . . ." and she could never resist laughing.

Master Lazzaro had taken his shoes to Chiccoli and his mending to

154

Chiccoli's wife ever since he had first set up the mill and, to tell the truth, when Venusta first heard of his intention to marry she could not help saying to herself: "There's the sort of man that I should have married myself!" Which did not in the least prevent her from having friendly and almost maternal feelings toward Dosolina. She had not hesitated to tell even her husband of the weakness she had for Scacerni and he had answered in his usual joking fashion:

"Quite right, but it's too late."

"Because I'm no more than an old shoe by now, is that it?"

"Because you're too virtuous a woman!"

It so happened that, for very different reasons, Chiccoli and his wife were the only real friends Lazzaro had made since leaving Occhiobello.

"She's a good woman and one with a head on her shoulders," Lazzaro used to say. "As for him, he keeps his counsel and steers a straight course between the reefs. He's a 'navigator,' as they used to say in Lombardy when I was a soldier."

This was one of the rare occasions when he mentioned the days of Napoleon. How remote Lombardy seemed to him now from this side of the Po! For a moment he was lost in memories, seeing in his mind's eye the marching soldiers of Marshal Masséna on that faraway day in Ferrara when he had first had an urge to travel about the world wearing Napoleon's uniform.

"When the pear's ripe it's bound to fall," he warned Chiccoli playfully.

But they never had any serious differences and in the days when Scacerni had run after the women Chiccoli often went with him as a rearguard, to hold the bag for him or to fill it with eggs of his own, like a cuckoo that places its brood in another bird's nest. Although Scacerni didn't know it the cobbler had more than once stolen a march on him or supplanted him. One of Chiccoli's best cards was the fact that he never boasted of his successes with women, but gratefully accepted whatever they were willing to give him. Now these escapades lay behind them and Lazzaro was given to moralizing in the presence of his friend, bidding him lay aside his former impulses and stop stepping out the door of his shop with an unsoled shoe in his hand to make eyes at a passing woman.

"Stick to your last, cobbler, and let Venusta have peace of mind. You don't deserve such a wife in the first place."

"Very well, I don't deserve her."

"You should worship the ground she walks on."

"Very well, I worship it."

During exchanges of this kind they took care not to look at one another, for if Lazzaro at such a moment caught the cobbler's mock-serious eye his usual frowning expression would melt into open laughter, to the detriment of the morality he had just been preaching. And Chiccoli would join in. His laughter always outlasted Lazzaro's, as if to underline discreetly his final triumph. For under a delicate appearance the cobbler had vast reserves of health, while that of the outwardly stalwart Scacerni had begun to fail, as if it were somehow sapped from within. His malarial pallor was accentuated and streaked with a sort of bilious yellow and the whites of his eyes were often clouded over. His hair was still black, but soon after his marriage whole tufts of white appeared in his beard.

"Because I have been too much alone," he said jokingly.

Venusta quite unceremoniously advised the young wife to exercise a certain prudence. Maturity may have as much vigor as youth, she said, but it cannot have the same resiliency. Dosolina blushed and was at a loss for what to reply.

"What's that you say? Whatever do you mean? . . ." she protested.

"You know very well what I mean."

"Not in my present condition! To tell the truth I don't even think he loves me any more!" And Dosolina burst out crying.

Venusta exclaimed and insisted, but could not convince her of the contrary. In the last month of Dosolina's pregnancy husband and wife were occupying separate rooms and Dosolina was disconsolate as she lay alone in the wide double bed. As for Scacerni, he knew perfectly well, without confiding it to a soul, what was making him so liverish. He would not even attribute a reasonable share of his ill health to a recurrence of malaria, which in the course of this damp, hot summer attacked him more violently than before, so that his customary cure of what he called "sweating it out of his system" was no longer effective. This, too, he insisted on attributing to Raguseo, and even took a certain baleful joy in considering his enemy the source of all his evils.

"But it can't end like this," he said to himself. "The day will come when I'll pay him back in full measure. Then the usurer will see how faithfully I discharge my debts! I may go to prison, but he'll go straight to hell!"

THE DAY OF TRIBULATION

1

ONE NIGHT in mid-October Scacerni was sleeping heavily after several days of wearisome work. The river had risen with astonishing rapidity, only to subside again equally fast upon the heels of a sudden cold wave, in a totally unexpected manner. Lazzaro had spent several nights on the mill, but now, after a look at the clear, starlit sky, he thought it was safe to go to bed at home. Because of the cold he had covered himself with an extra blanket, but in the middle of the night he woke up bathed in perspiration. The temperature had risen abruptly, a heavy, hot south wind was whipping around the house and the weather vane was turning like mad. He thought at first that the change in the weather had awakened him, but during a lull in the wind he heard Venusta, who had come to stay with Dosolina during these last few days before the expected birth, walking about the kitchen and pouring water from a pot into a basin. She went into Dosolina's room and through the open door a low moan, like the complaint of a child, reached the sleepy Scacerni's ear and made him curse the erratic weather as he leaped out of bed. The plaintive tone of the moaning was so pronounced that for a moment he tried to persuade himself that Venusta had with her one of her younger children. Pulling on his trousers he slowly left his own room. In the dark kitchen he saw glowing coals on the brazier and a glimmering light before Our Lady of Sorrows. Soon the ray of light from the crack of the half-open door into Dosolina's room informed him whence the complaint was coming. He felt a tender, sorrowful, impatient compassion, as if he were saying: "Don't cry, the pain will go away," to a child.

In Dosolina's room Venusta snuffed her tobacco noisily and sneezed. The moaning had ceased, but a sudden gust of wind shook the house to its foundations. Lazzaro heard Dosolina say:

"Venusta, you mustn't stay up all night. Go to sleep now; I feel better."

Her voice was so sad and sweet that Lazzaro stopped in the middle of the kitchen to listen.

"A pinch or two of good snuff, and I can stay awake as many nights as I please, my beauty," Venusta answered.

"Venusta, I'm going to die. I can feel it."

She was crying again and Lazzaro expected Venusta to make a rough but affectionate denial, but instead she laughed and said, stroking Dosolina's forehead:

"You know that the first time I was sure I would die myself, and

157

then just look how many times I went through it! In fact, my first-born arrived only three months after we'd gone to the altar, Chiccoli and I. Does that surprise you? It's an odd story and one day I'll tell it for your amusement."

"I'll not be there to hear it, Venusta. I'm not going to live much longer."

"Come, come! What silly talk!"

Venusta tapped Dosolina affectionately across the back of her hand, but Lazzaro was overcome by a sudden and enormous fear that Dosolina was really going to die. Just as he was about to enter the room he heard her say:

"Don't go thinking that I'm afraid. At first I was, I must admit. But now that I'm so close to death—and it's no use your saying I'm not!— I've put my fear behind me. I've confessed my sins and put my soul in order. Why should I stay in this world any longer? God will forgive me."

"Why should you stay, indeed? What about your husband?"

"His love for me didn't last long. Not even a year."

"Now you really deserve a spanking! If you weren't such a baby I'd be angry at you."

"You don't know. You can't know . . ."

"I know very well, my dear, that men have worries of their own, and when they don't tell us about them, as often as not it's to save us from worry. I'm so positive that you're the apple of Master Lazzaro's eye that I'd stake my own two eyes upon it."

"Very well, then, it's his worries. . . . I don't want to contradict you. And what does it matter now, anyway?"

"What do you mean by 'now'?" muttered Venusta.

Lazzaro was completely taken aback by this revelation. His wife thought that he no longer loved her and if she were to die he would be left knowing that she had carried this misconception to her grave. He clenched his fists. Here was one more thing to be added to the hate he owed to Raguseo. He could not see Venusta's face, even when she came back to the kitchen with a basin in her hands, because the light of the bedroom was behind her. But he knew that it had clouded over.

"Has her labor begun?" he asked in a low voice.

"Are you here? Pain may sharpen her ears."

She put down the basin and shut the door.

"What have you to say?" asked Scacerni. "What can you tell me?"

"There's nothing to be afraid of, but . . ."

"But what?"

"I'm not sure. Her labor . . ."

"Has it begun?"

"Let me finish what I was saying. By this time I wish it were further advanced, that's all."

"Why so?"

"Because the stronger and more persistent the labor pains the better. But it's too soon to worry."

158

"You're worried, all the same."

"My dear man, you're just like the rest of them. You'd like to settle it in double-quick time, with no more effort than you put into it yourselves! We know how little effort it costs you, while we women are let in for the worst of it. It's something to think about, I can tell you, Master Lazzaro, especially the first time. That's why you see me concerned."

"Venusta!" called out Dosolina, "who's there?"

"Didn't I tell you that pain might sharpen her ears?" And she called back: "Your husband, Dosolina."

"How's that? Didn't he go to bed?"

"Yes, but he's awake now." And she added, to Scacerni: "Go say something to quiet her."

"The wind woke me, Dosolina," Scacerni said as he came into the room. "Did you hear it? Now it's blowing up again. There's no peace to be had in this uncertain weather."

"Yes, I heard," Dosolina answered painfully. "After all the work you've had these last nights, you may have to go back to the mill again, my poor Lazzaro."

"Whatever happens, tonight I'll not budge from here."

"Don't worry about me. I'll be all right."

"God grant it, Dosolina."

She was telling a lie, and he knew it. She was lying like a child, and the drawn, sorrowful look on her face caught at his heart.

"God grant it, Dosolina, because otherwise . . . I can't bear to think of it. I've never found words to tell you how much I love you, Dosolina, and the idea of losing you drives me to despair."

Dosolina's eyes opened so wide that they lit up her whole face.

"Lazzaro, you can't imagine what good you're doing me. Now I shan't want to die any longer."

"What's that? You wanted to die?"

"Yes, Lazzaro; forgive me. Some day I'll explain. But now my pains are returning."

Venusta came back into the room.

"Let her be quiet, Master Lazzaro. How's your fear now, Dosolina?"

"I'm still afraid," Dosolina answered, "but he's given me courage."

"Good. How fear and courage can go together we shall have to see. Meanwhile, Master Lazzaro, light a candle to the Most Blessed Virgin and one to Saint Anne who bore her and is the protector of all women in childbirth."

Scacerni obeyed, but just as he was about to light the two candles his own words "I may go to prison but he'll go straight to hell," surged up in his mind, written in flaming letters against a background of eternal darkness. Infuriated and at the same time dismayed he held the candles out to Dosolina.

"You light them," he said, adding to himself: "I'm not in a state of grace."

Now the wind whistled and roared without ceasing and rain poured

159

down on the dark, wet fields. From the river came the sound, now near, now far, of gunfire. Men from the villages along the river were mounting guard on the banks in order to discourage those from inland from taking advantage of the darkness to cut through the embankments and let the impact of the river run off into the valleys. They fired their guns to warn anyone with such mistaken intentions and to dispel the shadows of hate, suspicion and fear. Well did Scacerni know the meaning of their shots.

"The river's swollen again."

When the river was high vagabonds and thieves often swarmed out in boats, hoping to loot someone in trouble. It was good policy to warn them that there were powder and lead with which to beat them off. Then came a mysterious deep, heavy yet winged sound that could be heard above everything else, a short note alternating with a long one, that gave a feeling of power and rang out not a prayer but a command.

"They're blowing the horns," Scacerni said. "They're calling the emergency squads to the riverbanks. The river must be many inches above the danger line."

Even Venusta knew that during the last days men had been staving up the embankments in order to keep the river from spilling over and to contain the jets of water that had already begun to flood the low meadows.

"Help us, O Lord!" she murmured.

"It's still a wind from the south," Scacerni thought to himself. "That's bad enough, but if it veers around and waves come in from the sea it will be worse still." And he added out loud: "Ugly weather."

The horns echoed urgently now from several directions, under the continuous rain. They seemed like an ancient voice expressing the anxiety of a land bound for life and death to the river. Every man heard the voice in his heart's blood as his father and his father's father had heard it before him, and with it came a deep feeling of trouble that broke out into curses and prayers. But over all the voice of the horns still sounded, higher and farther away, summoning up a desperate but pugnacious fatality that was beyond human woe, beyond the battle to which it called, beyond either hope or resignation. This voice was entuned to the forces of nature and sang bravely out on the dark wet wing of the south wind that what must be must be.

Lazzaro sat with his elbows propped up on the kitchen table, looking into the fire and listening intently. His inclination was to follow the call of the horns, but every now and then a low groan from Dosolina made him quiver.

"Things are going as they should," observed Venusta.

"How long will it be?" Scacerni asked.

"Ten or fifteen hours, perhaps twenty, since it's the first time."

He had a sinking feeling at the pit of his stomach and a fear that he did not put into words: "She'll never live through it."

160

"The mill will be lost before then," he said out loud. "But what does that matter?"

"Lost?" exclaimed Venusta.

Someone knocked at the front door. "They're coming to bring me the bad news," Scacerni thought to himself, without moving. The knock was repeated, louder than before.

"Are you asleep, Master Lazzaro?" said Venusta.

"I'll open the door," said Lazzaro, shaking himself.

Beffa stood at the threshold, wrapped in a cape and dripping all over.

"It's a fierce night, Master. The river has swollen faster than anyone has ever seen it swell before. And you can still see it rising."

"You can see it in darkness like this?"

Beffa stopped swaying back and forth like a bear and squinted at the miller with one eye.

"Do you feel like joking, Master?"

"What am I to do if the Po is rising? No matter how fast . . ."

"As you like. But I thought it was my duty to tell you. You really should come have a look."

"I can't move from here."

"Because it's raining so hard, is that it? Pardon me, Master, I presume you must be joking."

"I said that I can't move."

"Of course you've the last word; you're the master."

"You and Malvasone must see to it that the moorings hold. There's plenty of extra rope aboard. Better double the hawsers. Later on I'll send Schiavetto for news. Day can't be very far off now."

So saying, he looked out the door. The sky was so black that it seemed as if dawn would never come.

"Schiavetto?" Beffa was mumbling. "You'll send Schiavetto to bring you news? I've brought news already. What else can he find to tell you? If you want to know the naked truth, St. Michael's Mill is in a bad way. As I see it, the prospects are bad. Apparently you don't want to understand."

He was astonished that Scacerni should let him talk on so long and even more astonished to hear him burst into laughter.

"I understand quite well that you're scared to death!" the miller answered. "Now get along with you and do what I say."

Beffa went away, muttering something about people who risk other people's skins in order to keep their own out of the rain.

"Master Lazzaro!" called Venusta. "Dosolina wants a word with you."

Schiavetto had slid silently into the kitchen.

"Master, I'll go to the mill," he said, "and I'll report to you if anything happens."

"Wait for daylight. And, Dosolina, don't worry; I shan't leave you."

By now he found something like a malicious joy in the fact that the mill threatened to go to rack and ruin. Let the worst happen, as long as it was over quickly! And at the same time the thought of Dosolina was a harrowing one. The look on her face stopped him at the bedroom door. Somehow the distortion of her features caused by labor pains had given her an unrecognizable and yet sanctified expression. In her suffering he seemed to see his own mother, whom he had never known, even by name. Now, while the tension of her body beneath the sheets revealed the extent of her pain, she opened her eyes wide and her face was lit up with loving kindness. She was very close to him and unspeakably dear.

"Go, Lazzaro, go where you are needed, to the mill," she gasped. "I know that the river is high. All the good that you can do me you've done already. I have courage now, Lazzaro; you've given me that. They need you now at the mill. Go there for my sake, and for the sake of our child. Schiavetto will carry messages between us. Go, I beg you."

Venusta looked up thoughtfully and said:

"Dosolina is right. At the point she is now a man is only in the way."

"Then I'll go for sure," said Lazzaro. "They do need me at the mill, that's true. Beffa has lost his nerve and Malvasone hasn't much of a head on his shoulders. If you need me just send Schiavetto and I'll be back in a hurry. Cheer up, Dosolina, I'll go. And thank you."

He started to give her a kiss on the forehead, feeling almost physical resentment and sorrow for her suffering. But a sudden access of pain seemed to tear her away from him. She stared at him with wild, animal-like eyes, as if with aversion.

"Go away! Don't touch me! Go away, man, I tell you! Have you come to look on at my pains? Just stay away. It's all your fault, but you'll not do it again, now that I know. O my God, let me die, and put an end to my suffering! Never again, man! Never again!"

She fell back panting on the pillows. Was she delirious? She had closed her eyes; did that mean she would die? Lazzaro gave a terror-stricken and questioning look at Venusta.

"Don't bother your head about what she may say," Venusta said, laughing. "We all say the same thing, don't you know that? Of course, if there were any justice in this world you ought to have a share in our pains. We all say something of the sort, especially the first time. And then, never fear, we forget it! You men have a way with you!"

"Do you think it is right for me to go, then?" Scacerni asked as soon as they were out of the room.

"Of course you can go."

"But there's something serious underneath your joking. What is it that's going wrong? Didn't you say it was best that her pains should increase?"

"True enough. But I'm afraid these are what we call cold pains."

"What does that mean?"

"Pains that wear a woman out without accelerating the birth. But you can go, just the same. Schiavetto's here and it's not very far away."

"Very well. I have complete confidence in you, Venusta. And, needless to say, you mustn't worry about expenses. If you want to call a doctor from Ferrara, for instance, just send Schiavetto on horseback."

"No doctor can know as much as a woman, that is, unless he's borne half a dozen children himself."

Rightly or wrongly, Lazzaro agreed.

"Do whatever you think best. I only want to have a clear conscience. But is she suffering very much? Tell me."

He could see Dosolina's face and her closed eyes, and he was terrified lest they should have been touched by death.

"Oh yes, she's suffering," said Venusta.

"I mean, is there any danger of her dying?"

"Come, come, what big words! Why don't you make a vow to Saint Anne? She can help more than any of the rest of us. Promise her half a dozen candles and three weeks of fasting on both Wednesdays and Fridays."

"That I promise, gladly," he said, looking at the image of Our Lady.

"Go now, Master Lazzaro," murmured Venusta.

Outside the wind had blown up into a stronger and stronger storm. The faint light of dawn lit up the dripping green fields, where the excessive summer rains had produced an over-abundance of leaves and grass. When he heard a clap of thunder Lazzaro was incongruously reminded of the proverb: "Saint Luke's Day chases thunder away." Saint Luke's Day must be close at hand, and he tried to remember what day of the month it was, but to no avail. After crossing the road to Ro, he wanted to take a short-cut across the meadows, but they were already submerged. The wind blew first from one direction and then from another, and in the house he had left behind him Venusta whispered a prayer: *Sancta Maria, ora pro nobis.*

Lazzaro was grateful to Dosolina for having let him go out to face the dangers of storm and flood. If he had stayed on to witness her suffering he would have surely lost his mind. He had a strange sensation in his eyes and throat. Now he remembered that he had not felt any urge to cry since the day when his father had died, at the foot of the church tower in the Borgo San Giorgio, and then he had held back his tears in order to keep up his courage. What relief there was, at this moment, in the tears that streamed down his face. He was only a weak specimen of humanity, but these were tears of love.

2

The only thing left to do was to skirt The Sisters' Farm and go up the road as far as the crossway at the beginning of the "dikes," and Scacerni hurried along in this direction. The horns were no longer sounding, but heaven and earth were still in travail. Scacerni wished suddenly that he were with Dosolina and had almost started to turn back when he saw Malvasone coming toward him, wrapped in a soaking, muddy blanket.

"Come quickly, Master . . . The mill . . . the mill!"

Between one clap of thunder and another and among the gusts of wind and rain there were occasional blank silences, when the intermittent gunfire aroused dire suspicions of the possibilities of armed violence, which would surely lead to armed reprisal and to feuds among the villages along the river. The church bells of Guarda and Ro slowly rang out a storm warning in order that everyone should be on the alert. If their tempo were to quicken it would mean that people should seek refuge in high places, on the upper floors or roofs of their houses. Scacerni's house at Poplar Bridge had only one floor, and hardly had he started to pull his cap down over his forehead and run the rest of the way to the mill when the thought of Dosolina's being in danger stopped him short in his tracks. If the water were to rise and engulf her . . .

"The mill, Master!" shouted Malvasone.

"To the devil with the mill!"

Malvasone was taken aback.

"The road to Guarda is crowded with people. They're gathering from all over the countryside because they are afraid."

"What are they afraid of?"

"The dikes. The old men are saying that the dikes can't hold."

"What about this road then?"

"They say that it's built along an old embankment of solid construction."

Could a woman in childbirth possibly be carried out of the house in weather like this? If the river came through both the dikes and the embankment she was done for. They were in God's hands, both of them.

"God, if the river breaks through, grant that I die with Dosolina!"

Rather than a prayer this was a solemn compact, and because he was sure that God had heard him Lazzaro grew suddenly calmer.

"And now to the mill, Malvasone."

"Good," said the faithful helper. "I'll see it through with you."

"What if the river breaks over?" Scacerni asked as they started on their way.

"It's apt to break just where it's least expected. And God will provide. I'll not leave you in trouble after serving you when times were good. I'm no Beffa, after all." He muttered these last words so low that Lazzaro did not understand them.

"Thank you, Malvasone. I knew you were an honest man."

As Malvasone ran along his big feet splashed mud for several feet around him. But soon he had to slacken his pace, because even before The Sisters' Farm the road was crowded with refugees in miserable clothes, who had loaded their household goods on carts and wheelbarrows and brought their animals with them. The two men went on as fast as they were able, until they were stopped by two gendarmes and representatives of the Waterway Commission, who forbade passage on the unsafe dikes, where bands of volunteer workers had been enlisted to stave up the banks, stack bags of earth on top of them, and

164

seal off any holes, leaks, or infiltrations. For some days past the watchers appointed by the Commission had taken up their station in hastily repaired shelters on the widest portions of the bank, where, like sentinels guarding against an enemy, they surveyed the height of the river and the flow of the currents. Above all, since the enemy was both before and behind them, they kept an eye on the landward side of the embankment and especially on the pools of water that had accumulated, when the normal escapes were choked, just below them. Their practiced eyes could see danger in a sudden jet or fizzle from underground, a new trickle or the appearance of a lighter or darker shade of water in one of the stagnant pools. For by now the meadows between the dikes and the road running along the old embankment were filled with water, submerging the reeds and high grasses and even reaching the low-hanging branches of fruit trees. The earth, which had been prepared for sowing on Saint Luke's Day, was no longer visible; only the occasional head of a stalk of marsh grass stuck out above the water.

When Scacerni said to the gendarmes: "I'm the owner of the mill there in the river," they stared at him as if he had announced himself as the closest relative of a dying man and drew aside to let him and Malvasone go by. Silently the two men hurried along a path that ran at a level halfway up the embankment, keeping out of the way of the carriers and shovellers who were working at the top, piling up earth and supporting it by a net filled with stones and cutting branches into piles to be driven into the ground if necessary.

The sight of this orderly and vigorous work would ordinarily have given Scacerni comfort, but he had not the heart to go up on the ridge and see how high was the river. He was distressed enough by the note of condolence in their greetings, for most of the volunteers were from the neighborhood of Guarda and knew him well. He walked with lowered eyes along the slippery path and at first he did not recognize the mill as it loomed up, bigger and blacker than ever, over the rim of the embankment. The mill was close to the shore and just as they arrived the current drove it even closer. It was shaken from bow to stern and appeared to be out of control entirely and about to catapult into the water.

"Who's on board?" he shouted to Malvasone, pausing to gasp for breath.

"Nobody."

"Bastards!"

"Didn't Beffa come to your house?"

"Yes."

"Well, he came back saying that you had ordered him to take charge." Malvasone beat his hand against his forehead. "I should have known that he was telling a lie."

"Never mind, Malvasone. I should have thought of it myself."

A group of volunteers, with long poles, pushed the mill away from the bank, where the suction of water caused by its bulky mass might

165

have carried away earth and caused a break-through. A young man from the Waterway commanded them, and he was listening to Beffa at the moment when Scacerni unexpectedly appeared. But the miller did not come forward for a minute, choosing to hang back and listen to what was being said. There was a brief lull in the fury of the storm; the rain was falling less heavily and the wind was almost silent.

"The dikes are too weak already, sir, you know that," Beffa was saying. "My advice is to cut the last moorings and let it drift away."

"But where will it go?" asked the other, who was not really an expert on the river, although Beffa treated him as such for the sake of flattery.

"That's easy. It will go with the river and be carried over to the sandbanks on the Venetian side. Over there, do you see, sir, where the water is racing?"

"And then?"

"There, if it goes to the bottom, no harm will be done. The beach is wide and the bank behind it solid. All the danger, as you have just told me, is here at the dikes, which may easily give way."

"He's cleverer than I thought, the rascal," said Scacerni to himself, suddenly appearing at Beffa's side.

"Oh, it's the master!" Beffa exclaimed. "I'm glad you're here, even if it's so late."

"Just in time to catch you red-handed." And he added to the young man from the Commission: "I'll see myself to keeping the mill away from the bank where it can do no damage. And you, Beffa, bail out the boat."

The rowboat and the skiff were half full of water, the mill was loose and its bow dipping deep into the water. Now that it had been pushed away from the shore the current had started to impel it toward the center of the stream.

"Master, do you want to go aboard?" Beffa asked.

"Who loosened the mooring ropes?" countered Scacerni, without answering his question.

"They were already loose by the time I got here," said the young man from the Commission.

"I loosened them," Beffa said boldly, "so that the mill would stand farther out from the shore."

"That was not just ignorance but malice aforethought," said Scacerni, paying no attention to Beffa but addressing himself directly to the other. "You can see for yourself that the thing to do was to double the ropes, to throw out an anchor in the direction of the river, then to pull in the other two anchors, which evidently had been dragging, and throw them even farther out toward the mainstream. I'll see to all that myself. Meanwhile someone has been trying to ruin me." And he added abruptly, turning to Beffa: "Didn't I tell you to bail out the boat?"

"But . . ."

"No buts about it! You're under contract to work for me until next

Saint Martin's Day; to work, I said, not to play the coward and the knave. Go to it now, and keep whatever you had to say to yourself. The next word that comes out of you will mean the last crust of bread from my table, you can be sure of that."

Soon Beffa and Malvasone had emptied the boat, and Master Lazzaro had it towed along the shore until it was well above the mill, which continued to bob up and down and to edge out toward the center of the river. It seemed almost certain that somewhere in it there was a leak.

The muddy, foaming river ran turbidly under the heavy, gray sky, like a bull, pricked at the flanks, rushing with lowered horns to destruction.

"Good luck, Master Lazzaro!" called the men from the banks as he passed below them in the boat, steering it with one oar from the stern. And when the two boys jumped in and started to row, a graver voice said: "God be with you!" For a good way along the embankment they looked down at the boat as Scacerni set the bow against the current, and under the impulsion of the oars it took a diagonal course outward, so as not to be pulled by the current into collision with the mill. They had hardly left the shore when Schiavetto appeared, waving from the crest of the bank. Making a trumpet of his hands he called out:

"Venusta sends word for you to be of good cheer, Master!"

Heavy as they were, the oars bent with the strength of Scacerni's arms as from the rear end of the boat he rowed and steered at the same time, nodding his head to show that he had heard Schiavetto's message. The heavy boat sank its bow stubbornly into the raging water and plowed its way through it until, just as the steersman had calculated, it reached a point upstream where the rowers could rest their oars and let it drift down parallel to the mill. Everyone on the bank followed their course with trepidation.

Now they drew alongside the mill. Malvasone leaped aboard with one end of a rope, which he wound around the first capstan that met his eye at the bow of the large hulk. And after him came Beffa and Scacerni. Once aboard they had reason for fear. The mill was rolling so violently that they had to take off their shoes in order not to fall down on the wet and slippery deck. The wheel, with many of its paddles broken or loosened, had come to a stop, and a tangle of split branches from trees was enmeshed in it, creating a turmoil so great that water was pouring through the joints of the smaller of the two hulks, which at the same time received more water from the other side, where it got the impact of the waves from the river. There was serious danger that it would soon be filled to capacity and start sinking. The roof over the deck, the walls of the cabin, the three connecting beams, and indeed the whole structure creaked alarmingly, while the water gathered in the hold made the dismal swishing sound that strikes fear into a seaman's heart.

"Find two buckets and take off your clothes," Scacerni ordered.

While they searched among the objects piled up in the corners of

167

the cabin, he took an axe and made openings first in the wall and then in the floor of the cabin. Up through the floor surged the water collected in the hulk. The two boys lowered themselves into the hold and standing up to their chests in water they began to bail it out with the buckets, whose contents they threw through the opening the miller had made in the cabin wall. Meanwhile Scacerni took a harpoon and poked furiously at the clogged paddles of the mill wheel, until he had freed it of encumbrances and the water could flow unimpeded between the two hulks. With this the mill stood higher above the water and seemed to be in far less dire straits than before.

The storm still darkened the sky, but the wind had turned and now blew toward the sea, thus helping the mighty river to rush to its natural outlet. Had the wind veered and come *from* the sea instead of toward it, the river might well by now have overflown its banks and flooded the land for miles around. And if the huge sea waves had beaten on the stern of the mill it would have long since gone to the bottom. Instead, as we have seen, it was gradually regaining its balance.

"And to think that I hoped to see the mill go for firewood after the storm!" snarled Beffa under his breath, while fear of drowning on the one hand and of a beating from his master on the other kept him hard at work bailing out the hold.

Just at that moment the rotted and swollen carcass of an ox was swept by the current between the two bows and when Lazzaro, unable to turn it aside, stuck his harpoon in its flank in order to sink it, it burst open, exhaling a foul smell into the surrounding air and water. In the hold the water was down to the boys' knees as they continued to bail it out with buckets. Scacerni pointed out to them the various cracks in the sides of the hold and they stopped them up with some old rags that he had found here and there in the mill. Finally the two helpers could put on their clothes.

Meanwhile Scacerni was readying the extra anchor and pulling in the one that had previously been thrown out but was now tangled up in its own hawser and lying flat on the bottom without any grip in the sand. Now he could maneuver the mill and move it out where the water was a little calmer. When he had put it just where he wanted, farther out than usual, so that there was no more danger to the dikes, he threw a rope to the workers on the bank and they attached it to a stake driven into the ground. This replaced the ropes that had been lost when the poles to which they were tied had been carried away. Holding onto this rope anyone could easily go to or from the shore in the skiff. Now communications with land were re-established, the mill was once more fast, and hope was reborn. Malvasone was sent to wind another heavy rope around the poplar tree, which stood out sturdily and in full foliage above the swollen water. In one of its brusque changes of phase, particularly noticeable when a flood has pushed it up against the banks, the water, having overrun the sand bars in the middle of the river, now flowed fast but evenly along without there

168

being any wind to raise waves in either one direction or the other. No swirling current now threatened the dikes, and under the tepid rain the river looked for all the world like the sea, with the darkness still so heavy that except in an occasional flash of lightning the opposite shore could not be seen. Although it was now nearly noon it was still as dark as night. Just then a watchman on horseback rode along the embankment and shouted out a bit of encouraging news which could be heard even by those aboard the mill.

"Up at Lagoscuro the river has stopped rising!"

A wagon loaded with sacks of bread began to pass among the volunteers, prompting Beffa to ask Malvasone if this was to be a day of fasting on the mill. The two boys were busy putting things in order, while Master Lazzaro went on patching the cracks in the hulk and boarding over the hole he had made in the cabin. Beffa spoke out in a new and irritatingly cocky manner:

"It was all very well in years when the river didn't rise very high. But this time it was a close shave. . . . The other millers have always said that this was a dangerous anchorage."

"There are scoundrels that haven't even the decency to keep their mouths shut!" Scacerni could be heard murmuring from the hold, while the good-natured Malvasone observed:

"It's a good thing there wasn't any flour or meal stored in the bins or it would have had a good soaking."

Just then Schiavetto appeared on the bank, calling:

"Master Lazzaro, here's lunch for all hands."

Beffa lost no time in going to get it and Schiavetto came back on board with him.

"How is the mistress?" Scacerni asked.

"Still the same, so Venusta says. But you're not to worry."

Scacerni felt his appetite fail him. But when Beffa, without waiting for permission, stuck his hands into the basket and stuffed his mouth full, the miller burst out at him:

"Who told you to help yourself?"

Beffa stared at him insolently without making answer and Scacerni angrily snatched the basket away.

"There'll be no eating today," he said, hurling it into the river.

Poor Malvasone looked after it longingly.

"That wasn't exactly good manners on your part," he said mildly to Beffa.

"What message shall I take back to the house?" Schiavetto asked timidly, after an awkward pause.

"That I'll be there soon. You can go now."

Hardly had Schiavetto reached the shore when the top branches of the poplar began first to rustle and then to shake all over. From the north side of the river came a wild, whistling whirlwind that bent the trees over and pulled the mill toward shore, while angry waves rose up and started to beat mercilessly against the side of the outer hulk. Leaning over the rail of the deck Scacerni tested the hawser of the anchor

169

he had just thrown out in order to make sure that it was not dragging but would keep the mill from being thrown against the dikes. But just as he ascertained that it was holding fast the whirlwind shifted abruptly halfway around the compass and began to blow from the southeast, bucking the current of the river and raising up a great wave that crashed along the sorely buffeted dikes and broke against the upright poops of the mill, which were not built to resist it. Water swept up over the sterns of both hulks and threatened to break them to pieces, while the bows dipped crazily into the river. The whirlwind was full of twists and eddies that sucked up the water and sprayed it over everyone and everything on the mill. Work was halted on the embankment as the wind drove the wave against it and topped it with a shower of foam. Aboard the mill the only thing to do was to lie flat and hold on to the first fixed object that came to hand; if anyone so much as raised his head he could feel himself being swept away. Water had again poured into the hold and rocked the mill back and forth, threatening to sink it. The first gust of the whirlwind had carried away the skiff, which perhaps Schiavetto had failed to tie up tightly, and the larger boat was loose and knocking against the stern of the smaller hulk in such a way that one or the other bid fair to stave in at any moment. Scacerni jumped onto the connecting beam at the stern, called out to Malvasone to untie the rope altogether, and holding on with his arms to the broken and motionless wheel he managed to kick the boat with his feet until it drifted away. But the wheel, released by Lazzaro's weight and that of the water rushing against it, suddenly began to move and pulled him under. Entangled in the broken paddles, loose timbers, and the waste thrown up by the river, Lazzaro seemed certain to drown. On his neck and shoulders he could feel the murderous strength of the river, crushing and stifling him under the wheel, which made a half turn before it came to a stop. His last thought was of Dosolina, as he had seen her in the pangs of childbirth.

"Be with her, Holy Mother of God; no one else can save her!"

A sharp pain in his leg, which was enmeshed in the wheel, made him think he was going to faint before he even had time to drown. He tried to cry out and instead filled his mouth with water. Meanwhile Malvasone had with superhuman effort turned the wheel the rest of the way around and brought him to the surface. Throwing himself astride the beam the boy took hold of his master, pulled him up and dragged him into the cabin of the large hulk, where he lay on the floor and spewed out the mud and water he had swallowed. The agony of his leg prevented him from being aware of the bruises and bleeding scratches that covered most of his body. His leg hung heavy and inert and he would not even have known it belonged to him were it not for the stabbing pain that was all too vivid a reminder. He saw as if in a dream the faces of Beffa and Malvasone hanging over him in the semi-darkness and his wet clothes made a chill come over him which he mistook for that of death.

"Save and take care of her, Our Lady of Sorrows, when she is com-

170

fortless and alone!" he murmured, closing his eyes and seeing in his delirium a face so sorrowful that it might have belonged either to Dosolina or to the Virgin.

The whirlwind had died down as suddenly as it had arisen and now the river flowed with comparative calm, gurgling among the wreckage of what had once been the proud Saint Michael's Mill.

"Brace up, Master Lazzaro," said the kindly Malvasone. "You've come out of it alive."

"Did you pull me out?" asked the half-unconscious miller.

"Somehow I managed to move the wheel, which was pinning you down. But it was no easy job to get it turning."

"Thank you, Malvasone, although it might have been better . . ."

"Nonsense! There's nothing that can't be mended, except a broken neck. And all that needs mending of you is your leg."

Malvasone's unaccustomed loquacity almost made Scacerni smile. His fundamental vigor reasserted itself, like a fire that flickers in the wind but is not extinguished.

"In the storeroom there must be an old suit that I used to put on to go hunting. See if you can find it," he said, opening his eyes.

They did, and with the help of Malvasone he changed his clothes, clenching his teeth with every motion of his swollen leg, which was not bleeding but covered instead with ominous black splotches. He then asked for two boards and tied the leg up between them, so that the broken bones would not splinter any further. The rain had stopped but cold air poured through the cracks in the walls and the storm continued to play at various points of the horizon.

"Hail must have fallen in the storeroom," said Malvasone, "but I found some other things that may come in handy."

These were a half bottle of brandy, which went far to revive their spirits, and a sack of coal that had luckily escaped soaking. While Scacerni pulled himself up to a sitting position against the frame of the millstones Malvasone made a small fire.

"Thank you for everything, my boy," Scacerni murmured.

"Not at all. One good turn deserves another. What would be really welcome would be some corn-meal cakes and herrings to fry over this fire!"

So saying he sighed heavily at the thought of the lunch that had been thrown to the fish, and even Beffa could not help smiling wryly.

"Yes, I'm sorry now that I threw it away," said Scacerni. "But surely you understand, Beffa, that with my mind divided between my wife and the mill I couldn't help losing my temper when I saw you were so greedy."

The mill was still a cause for concern, for there was more water in the hold and hence danger that it might sink lower and lower into the river. Scacerni decided to send both boys to bail out and stop up any new cracks they could find. Just then Malvasone emptied the sack of coal on the fire.

"Hold on!" he exclaimed suddenly. "What's this?"

And he pulled an iron object out of the sack and examined it closely.

"Here's a strange thing to find on a river mill! If we did our business on land then I'd say a horse or a mule had lost it. But we've no blacksmith aboard, have we?"

Scacerni shot a glance at Beffa, who had donned an expression of curiosity and astonishment. For the moment he believed that this affectation was a cover for real anxiety and remorse and in his newly saved condition an almost violent Christian charity inclined him to feel pity for the sins of his luckless helper. And Malvasone's joking words a second later increased his pity because, quite innocently, they called up the author of all evil.

"Then the devil himself, with cloven hoofs and all, must have been aboard," Malvasone said, laughing.

"Come, come, surely you can't make so much fuss over a horseshoe," Scacerni put in, anxious to change the subject.

"It comes from a mule or a donkey, that's what I say, Master."

"Since it came in the coal it must have been brought aboard by the charcoal burners. Don't they come down on their mules from the mountains at this season?" These words brought to his memory the bells around the mules' necks, which announced the coal men's arrival. "Just throw it in the river, Malvasone, if you don't like it," he added. "Now, boys, I'm sorry to ask you to do more work, when I can't lift a finger to help you, but you've got to go to it with the buckets and bail out the hold again. And plug up any holes you may see, like good fellows."

Malvasone started to obey. But Scacerni had been mistaken in interpreting Beffa's affected surprise over the horseshoe as a sign of shame. The hardhearted rascal had only imagined that his master was winking at his misdeeds and indeed treating him like an accomplice.

"Let this confounded carcass go to the bottom!" he shouted with insolent familiarity and perverse joy. "Do you want to break your back working like an honest man, when you know very well how many better ways there are to make money? That is, if you're not afraid of hell-fire or the gallows!"

"An easy conscience doesn't need to speak so loud," said Malvasone as he went along.

But Scacerni was frightened by the depths of infamy he perceived in Beffa's lost soul and he said in a voice that was more despairing than it was imperious:

"To work, Beffa! I don't want to hear another word out of you!"

"To the devil with the work, and let me have my say! For whom do you take me? You'll not order me about, and I'll not sweat for you any longer. Did you think you could keep the upper hand forever? From now on I have you in my power and I'll lead you like an ox with a ring through its nose. If you still want to go on working, then you can do my work too. You don't like that? Then speak to my master in Ferrara. He rewards those who serve him well and punishes those who betray him. To the devil with wheat and corn, with the mill wheel and stones and all the rest of them!"

Even before the beginning of this outburst, for which the brandy gulped down on an empty stomach may have been partly responsible, Malvasone had disappeared into the hold and started bailing. Scacerni and Beffa glared at each other face to face and quite alone, while lightning still flashed on the horizon.

"I took pity on you . . ." Lazzaro began.

"Pity?"

"You may well sneer! My pity was wasted, both when I first took you on and now."

"But now . . ."

"Enough for now, I say!"

"What? Do you think you can still? . . . You make me laugh!"

"You won't laugh for long! By my word as an honest man, although that's something beyond your understanding, I swear that you won't laugh!"

"You mean to say that even in the state you're in today you dare to defy me?"

"I'm a match for you even in the state I'm in today, and for your villainous master in Ferrara besides—yes, for Raguseo. I'm not afraid to call him by name."

The storm still thundering on the horizon seemed to draw nearer and once more it grew dark. Malvasone called from the hold:

"Beffa! Come give me a hand!"

"I'll see you hanged before I do! Scacerni and you together!" shouted Beffa.

The fact that, wounded as he was, this man had strength enough to dominate the situation, turned his rage into something like homicidal fury. Leaning on the framework of the millstones, Scacerni pulled himself to his feet, grasped the hands that Beffa was holding out to choke him, and twisted them in his own iron fingers.

"On your knees, you coward!"

Beffa whined and tried to resist; he made vain efforts to kick and choke his captor, but finally the pain of the grip made him bend his knee.

"Now to work!" Scacerni said, throwing him back against the opposite wall.

Beffa wanted to attack him again, but Scacerni had picked up an iron bar and held it threateningly over him.

"To work, I say, or here's what you'll get." Then he shouted to Malvasone: "Beffa will do the hold of this large hulk. See if you can finish the other by yourself."

Scacerni sat on the millstone, with the bar in his hand, watching Beffa bail out below.

"You may think that's all there is to it, but it's not so," Beffa mumbled. "We'll see who comes out on top! We'll settle accounts!"

"I'm ready to settle with you and with anyone else, wherever you

173

say! But now just work and keep your trap shut, if you don't want to feel the taste of this iron!"

Evening was still far away, but the horizon was encircled by sporadic bursts of lightning. There was no rain, but the thunder clapped ominously like a rumble of distant guns.

"Master Lazzaro! Are you there?" Schiavetto called from the embankment. At the same time Malvasone stuck up his head:

"I've finished bailing, Master, and plugged all the holes I could find."

"Then we're safe and sound."

"Master Lazzaro!" Schiavetto called again from the shore.

"Take his message for me, will you, Malvasone?" Scacerni said quietly. And a minute later, when Malvasone came back: "Well, what is it, my boy?"

"He says . . . but I don't know whether it's true. . . . These are women's affairs and they always see the black side of things. . . . He says . . ."

"Well, what does he say?"

"That things are not going too well. Her pains have stopped and she can't seem to come to the point. . . . So says Schiavetto, or rather Venusta. In short, she's far gone, she's in danger of dying. Venusta says you must pray to God, because she's in His hands."

"Beffa, never mind. It wasn't for myself that I wanted to save the mill," groaned Scacerni, his face turned to an earthen color. Then he recovered his self-control. "No," he said, "as long as there's life God bids us not to despair. Give Beffa a hand, Malvasone. But first tell Schiavetto to find a boat and come take me ashore."

Malvasone delivered this message and Schiavetto set off running along the bank. The volunteer workers were gradually drifting away as the river began to subside.

"What did Schiavetto say?" Scacerni asked.

"He's gone to look for a boat, but there's none in sight. Of course it's too dark to see very far."

"How stupid that I can't swim! But I could always pull myself into shore by holding onto the rope around the poplar."

Just then Beffa called up from the bottom of the hold, where he was safely sheltered behind the mill machinery.

"There's our great Goliath for you! Our conquering hero! Upset over a woman! And a woman who's played him false and made a fool out of him, so that no one knows whose child it is that's brought her to death's door. But everyone does know, of course. . . . It's Schiavetto's! There! I've been wanting to tell you, and now I feel the better for it!"

"I shan't feel better till I've killed you!" cried Scacerni, trying to drag himself into a position where he could get at him with the bar.

But he was held back by another hurricane blast of the southeast wind and by the strange appearance on top of the poplar of a ball of flame which rapidly set fire to the whole tree. There was a tremendous crash and the flaming poplar started to fall on the mill, which would surely have been destroyed along with all those aboard if the slacken-

174

ing of the rope that held it to the tree had not allowed the wind to push it forward. The poplar fell just off the stern, causing the mill to leap forward like a piece of cork, then sizzling it disappeared under the water. The characteristic odor of lightning hung heavy in the air.

The mill sprang away from the bank as far as the anchor on the riverward side would permit, and when this anchor did check it there was such a jolt that Scacerni was thrown off his already precarious balance and slid along the deck until he was miraculously able to grasp a stanchion. With his body hanging half overboard he could see how the mill, pressed hard by the fierce blast of wind and barely held fast by the anchor, was turned sideways. While the wind blew the mill up the river the anchor hawser grew taut and threatened to pull the smaller of the two hulks over, while the current gurgled under and against the larger hulk, acting as a lever. The danger was not so much that the mill would actually capsize as that the connecting beams and the axle would be broken and both hulks damaged beyond repair. As he lay almost diagonally across the extreme end of the highest part of the tottering structure Scacerni caught a glimpse of Malvasone's ruffled head:

"Loosen that hawser if you possibly can!" Scacerni called out.

Malvasone crawled out on the bow of the smaller hulk, whence he caught a terrifying glimpse of the abyss of water opened up below, and managed to release the anchor. The mill straightened up, and with the wind blowing at it hard from behind started to shoot upstream, almost as quickly as a sailboat, drifting at the same time farther and farther away from the shore. It was held now only by two small anchors at the bow whose long hawsers allowed it to travel several hundred feet before they swung it around completely and left it with the bow now pointing downstream and the stern bucking the current. There it stayed, rolling and dipping into the water, caught between the opposite forces of wind and river and following with its every movement whichever one momentarily prevailed, very much as if it were a ball tossed to and fro between them in the semidarkness.

Just as the pale and panting Lazzaro had exhaustedly dragged himself into a position where he could lean against the cabin, the contorted face of Beffa appeared before him.

"There you are!" Beffa exclaimed, beside himself with thwarted rage. "That pride of yours has come a cropper now! Look what a graybeard fool you are, and made a fool by a boy who has barely a hair on his chin. Hurrah! And you wanted to stay on this cursed mousetrap and keep me here with you! I've eaten my heart away long enough, I tell you! Now even the mice are deserting Saint Michael's Mill, and you and your leaky boat will go to the bottom! Your leg's gone and you'll drown, you . . ." and he made the obscene gesture of sticking his thumb between two fingers. "You'll see! I . . ."

This outburst struck Scacerni with such astonishment that he failed to react immediately and Beffa thought for a moment that he could go on with his vituperation without fear of reprisal. But all of a sudden the miller reached out for him with both arms and held him in a crushing grasp around the middle. Beffa's feet dangled over the edge of the deck, his eyes popped out of their sockets, and he could not even muster up a whispered plea for mercy. Malvasone looked on gaping, having come upon the scene just in time to hear Scacerni say:

"My leg may be done for, but I've still a pair of arms, you dog! Let's see you swim now, if you can!" And with these words he lifted up Beffa's helplessly kicking body and threw him, still spluttering curses and obscenities, into the river.

"Serves him right!" said Malvasone. "Maybe that will teach him a lesson! I don't go so far as to say I hope he drowns, but rather than see that snickering face of his again . . ."

"No, don't say that," Scacerni panted.

His anger fell, almost as quickly as the wind, which had suddenly gone down, leaving the mill free to float back to its anchorage. Scacerni was prey to a turmoil of memories, all of them tormenting, but like a man awakening from sleep he could not pin down the one he wanted most to recapture. He felt himself shrouded in darkness like that which was now falling, after a day of trial and tribulation, over the land and water about him. His leg, no longer so acutely painful, dragged inertly as Malvasone, with hands that were, for all their clumsiness, incredibly gentle, dragged him onto an improvised couch of sacks on the deck. Relieved of his pain he watched Malvasone coiling ropes and preparing to tie the mill up to some other object on the bank. But what was the use of it all, if Dosolina? . . . The thought of Dosolina was too much for him to bear. Her image was overhung by a twilight even denser than that of the thunderstorm, which was now definitely retreating into the distance. The sky had been swept clean by the wind and rain and now it was clear and almost wintry, so that he could glimpse stars among the scudding clouds. Involuntarily his eyes wandered to the hole in the earth left by the poplar that had been for so many years his companion. He remembered the sparrows which had built their nests there and flown home to it every evening, never abandoning him, even when the going was hardest. But what were his former troubles compared to those that assailed him now? Here he lay bereft of everything and forsaken by God and man, while Dosolina perhaps was dying. He tried to keep thinking of the poplar, but the empty place where it had stood was like that left by an amputated limb, a spent passion, the death of a dear one, the dearest of all, whose image he was trying desperately to keep out of his mind. He did not believe the outrageous slander with which Beffa had mocked him, but the poison of it had left cruelly lingering a bitter taste in his mouth. And all of a sudden this bitterness mingled with a consciousness of crime. Had he not thrown Beffa to death in the river? And back of all his misfortune was there not the sacrilegious theft of the Virgin's jewels with which he had allowed the Archfiend to tempt him? Fearful words broke out on his lips and overcame his despair, but words that spoke of repentance and hope in the mercy of God, and he prayed as if he were at this instant before the Seat of Judgment.

"Behold me, my God, on top of all my other sins, a murderer! An ignoramus, a thief, and a murderer! But I know that it's not a sinner's death You're after. You will listen to what I have dared tell no one. . . ." The turmoil of all his previous reasoning seemed to have led to nothing until he hit upon this simple fact that he was a prodigal son seeking forgiveness. "Yes, Lord, I am Your son, even if I am a sinner and a murderer. . . . Do not cast me out, but have mercy on me! The wrong that I have done, the Virgin's stolen treasure. . . ." He knew quite well what he must do, and raising himself painfully onto one knee he said slowly and deliberately: "Lord God and Most Holy Mother, I, Lazzaro Scacerni, a most unworthy sinner, hereby bind myself to abide by whatever the priest may enjoin me after I have made a complete confession. But meanwhile, if it's not too late, Lord, do not let Dosolina pay for my misdeeds. You know the innocence of her heart; do not allow her to suffer. Yet in all things let Your will be done. I put myself, Lazzaro Scacerni, in Your hands."

So saying he made the sign of the cross, as if to seal his vow. Although his anxiety for Dosolina was greater than his fear for the mill at the height of the storm, now his mind was clear and a new strength flowed through his wearied frame. He lay on the deck for an indefinite length of time while Malvasone, thinking it best that his master should take what rest he could, went about by the light of a lantern, putting the mill in order, yawning all the while with hunger. The embankment was deserted, for the volunteer workers had been sent home and the watchers were resting in their sentry boxes or shelters, confident now that the danger was over. The river flowed peacefully and majestically along, and even the mill, at least to judge from external appearances, stood ready to go to work again. When Malvasone finally made up his mind to rouse him, it seemed to Scacerni as if he had been lying on the deck for no more than a few minutes. Before he was thoroughly awake he heard a boy's clear voice calling from the embankment:

"Ahoy there, on Saint Michael's Mill! Master Lazzaro! You have a son!"

"Did you hear, Master?" said Malvasone, coming out with the lantern in his hand.

"Yes, wait and hear what else he has to say."

Scacerni's heart was in his throat and he clutched Malvasone's arm as if he were drowning, fearful to inquire any further.

"Can you hear me, Master Lazzaro?" Schiavetto called.

"Yes, he can hear you," answered Malvasone.

"Venusta says for you to thank God Almighty . . ."

"I bless Him and thank Him always," murmured Lazzaro, putting himself once more in God's hands.

"Dosolina is safe and sound!"

Malvasone could contain himself no longer.

177

"A little more of this, Master Lazzaro, and I'll be dead of hunger!"

But perhaps this was just his way of expressing his satisfaction. Meanwhile, from the bank, Schiavetto showed astonishment over the disappearance of the poplar. And this was the end of the day of tribulation.

3

Scacerni's steadfast resolution to accomplish cheerfully his vow was strengthened when he heard one particular detail of the often repeated accounts given by Venusta and Dosolina of what they had gone through during those hours when the mill was in peril. He took more pleasure in hearing their story than he did in telling his own.

"Do you know, we went through some black moments that day!" Venusta said for perhaps the twentieth time, during one of the frequent visits she paid to the slowly recovering Dosolina and her wounded husband. "We thought the game was up, for sure. Saint Anne did eventually save her, but for a while her pains had stopped and that's the worst possible sign. . . ."

"Yes, you sent word to me of that," Scacerni said, turning almost apologetically toward Dosolina. "I was adrift in the river, with both boats gone, and in a very bad way."

"I know that," Dosolina said with a gentle smile. "I know that you couldn't come."

"She gave us cause for worry, this girl, I can tell you!" said Venusta. "Her pains came back only after I had given up all hope."

"When did they come back, exactly?" Scacerni asked.

"Wait a minute. Let me think. Yes, I have it! Didn't we hear a tremendous crash, louder than any other during the storm?"

"Yes, that was the stroke of lightning that hit the poplar."

"Is the poplar gone?" Dosolina asked.

"Yes, and you'll see for yourself what a gap it has left."

"I'm sorry for that."

"Are you really?"

"Yes, somehow I am. I have an idea that it used to keep you company. And I remember it from the first time I came to the mill."

Scacerni smiled indulgently at these touching words, while Venusta went on:

"It was just at the moment of that crash that her pains began again, and that's what saved her."

"And at what time was Giuseppe born?"

"Toward evening, when the weather had begun to clear."

Then divine grace had preceded, not followed, his vow. At a moment when he was still far from any thoughts of salvation, God in His mercy had preserved his beloved wife, whom he felt more than ever to be flesh of his flesh. He could still see the scene of that night when Malvasone and Schiavetto had carried him in to where Dosolina lay, her face bloodless and pale, but with a radiant smile upon it. The smile

178

was not for him, he knew, it was for the newborn babe for whom she had endured such travail, and yet, strangely enough, instead of being jealous he only felt all the surer that she was his alone. He thought of the angry words with which she had accused him of being responsible for her suffering and wondered whether she too remembered them. It was clear enough, in any case, that she harbored no resentment against the baby. If this was injustice, he was content to bear it. And perhaps it was by way of compensation for her harshness that she said so gently to Venusta:

"Aren't you going to show him to his father?"

Yes, a new Dosolina was superimposed upon the old, making her more dear to him than ever before. For a moment his hands seemed to him too rough and heavy to caress her when she was so weary and frail and holy. She had not the energy to lift her head up off the pillow, and indeed it was all she could do to keep her eyes open. All the strength there was in her was concentrated in that maternal smile. Yet when he stooped to kiss her forehead she murmured:

"Was it a hard day, Lazzaro?"

"Yes, how you suffered, my poor girl!"

"I'm not speaking of myself. I mean was it hard for you on the mill in that terrible weather? . . . Oh, have you hurt yourself?"

"That's nothing. The important thing was to save it for you and the baby. And it is safe now."

He hid from her the fact that his leg was broken and his chief worry when the surgeon came the next morning was that she might find out. With the leg propped up on a bench in the kitchen, he could see how black it had turned overnight.

"Many's the wound I've seen, Doctor, as a soldier," he said. "And I recognize this kind of discoloration. Are you ready to amputate, if necessary?"

"Let's hope it's not so bad as all that. Just now I'm going to set the broken bone."

"Very well. But I don't want my wife to hear any noise."

"That's up to you! Can you keep from crying out with pain?"

"You do your part and I'll try to do mine."

He ground his teeth and broke into a cold perspiration when the surgeon stretched the leg, fitted the ends of bone together and put on the splints. But not a sound came out of him. Afterwards he told them to put him in the big bed, beside Dosolina. Before she had seen the splints on his leg the look on his face told her what he had been through.

"Lazzaro, you did hurt yourself yesterday! . . ." she exclaimed.

"It's nothing to speak of, compared to your pain . . ."

"I thought of you, Lazzaro, do you know that? And I know even without your telling me what danger you were in."

The familiar and affectionate way in which she addressed him, forgetful of her usual respectful formality, touched him even more than the words themselves.

Malvasone had told everybody that Beffa had swum away from the mill at the height of the danger, and they seemed all to rejoice over his disappearance. Now Master Lazzaro would learn, they said, how useless it was to set himself up as a reformer. If he had heeded their advice and taken on a proper sort of boy—and there were plenty of these to be found—he would not have found himself deserted in his hour of need. But knowing his stubborn character they said to his face no more than:

"A good riddance!"

During these days the whole of Guarda, which consisted of some two dozen families, came to visit Scacerni. One of their motives, of course, was curiosity as to how he would manage to meet the heavy expense of repairs to the mill. But they went home with their curiosity unsatisfied, and the best they could do was to take the road along the dikes as often as possible and to linger near the anchorage of Saint Michael's Mill, where the hole left by the poplar was still gaping.

"Who could have imagined such a thing? A tree of that size! There's the power of lightning for you! A frail thing, this life of ours; it hangs by a thread!" Thus they philosophized as they looked at the improvised workshop set up by a shipwright from Crespino, with the help of Malvasone and Schiavetto, in order to work on the mill. There he boiled tar and worked with hammer and saw to caulk and patch up the two hulks and their cabins and to repair the damage to the millstones and wheel. Where, the onlookers wondered, did Scacerni get the money? The shipwright did not give them any information as to the cost of the job. He was a taciturn man who crossed the river every day to come to work and went back at night without having spoken to a soul; indeed he even brought his lunch with him tied up in a big handkerchief. It seemed as if Scacerni had purposely chosen a man from the opposite bank, ignoring the worthy craftsmen he could have found nearer home. But by now his neighbors knew what to expect of him; he was a good man but a hardheaded one.

Malvasone did the heavy labor and Schiavetto was nimble-fingered and quick to learn. The shipwright knew his business, even the men of Guarda had to admit that, and twice a day he sent Schiavetto to tell his master of the progress of the work.

When Dosolina went to church to give thanks after childbirth, Lazzaro, who was still in splints and walking on crutches, went in the cart along with her. It was planned that they should call out to Chiccoli, the cobbler, and Venusta, and that all of them should enter the sacristy together for Dosolina to receive the priest's blessing. After she had said a prayer of thanksgiving, lit a candle and left some money in the poorbox Scacerni said:

"Leave the cart to this helpless cripple and go on ahead, all three of you. And no trifling with my wife, mind you, Chiccoli!"

This was quite enough to make the gallant Chiccoli preen himself happily and the other two joined in the laughter.

180

"If Don Bastiano has time, I'd like to exchange a word with him," said Scacerni. "I'll join you shortly."

"Good," said Chiccoli. "Venusta has made some raisin cakes and put out a bottle of white wine. Hurry up if you don't want to find nothing but empty plates and glasses. And if Don Bastiano will honor us with his presence, so much the better."

"Delighted," the priest said cordially.

Don Bastiano was accustomed to seeing Scacerni at Mass every Sunday and feast day of obligation, but he had never known him to come to the confessional except at Easter, and had intended to tax him with this remissness. Great was his astonishment when Scacerni asked if he might then and there make a general confession. Whereupon, without any omissions, distortion or apology the miller told him the story of the sacrilegious legacy of Mazzacorati, the blasphemies that had accompanied it, and the excuses with which he himself had tried to still the voice of his conscience, as if he were not fully aware of the implications of his acceptance. He told of his sale of the treasure to Raguseo, of Schiavetto's discovery of the torture of Big Brother and of his accumulated resentment against the old pirate and his hireling, Beffa. Whether Beffa was dead or alive he did not know, but he must admit that he had thrown him into the river with the express purpose of putting an end to him. And he ended by telling of the vow of which this confession was the fulfillment and of the undeserved grace that God had showered upon him.

"Here I am," he concluded, "to do whatever penance you may lay upon me."

"You have committed grave sins, mortal sins," said Don Bastiano with an unusually gruff voice, "sins that put you in danger of excommunication, *latae sententiae*. But you were aware of that from the start, even if you don't know Latin. Your tempter, *instigator et instrumentum iniquitatis*, took pains to inform you. Your eyes were open to the implications of your act, you have just said so yourself."

"Yes, I knew. I was fully informed."

"Then all I can say is that I'm sorry for you."

Scacerni thought it best to make no reply.

"I'm sorry for you," the priest repeated, "because I believe your repentance is sincere. And in order that you may size up the sincerity of your conscience, let me tell you this: the other day in the woods"— Don Bastiano was a great hunter—"I saw Beffa in person. So he is alive."

"That's lucky for him."

"And for you?"

"God be praised, then! But, to tell the truth, I wanted to kill him."

"Then you are quite right to say so frankly, my son, and I praise you for it. The fact is that he had a more wicked look on his face than ever. You'd better watch out. Sinner that you are, you are an honest man. Whereas he . . . but *imperscrutabilis mens Dei;* the ways of Almighty Providence are hidden from us."

181

"I know no Latin, Reverend Father," Scacerni said modestly.

"True. Let us return to your sins."

So saying he counted them and distinguished between those of greater and lesser importance, the venial and the mortal sins, the examples of negligence and omission, of fraud and offense to conscience. Scacerni listened with a sincerely repentant air, assenting with genuine humility to every accusation. Don Bastiano appeared to be discouraged.

"Quite a number of sins we've put together!" he exclaimed with mingled regret and disdain. "And one of them, my son, I must tell you quite plainly, I don't feel I can absolve. But don't be disheartened. God, in His mercy, can forgive anything. And just as He can pick out a flaw in what the world esteems as virtue, so can He see a grain of good in the worst vices. But to have knowingly pocketed the proceeds of a sacrilegious theft, in which persons belonging to holy orders were subjected to violence—of that I cannot so easily absolve you. I must consult someone more versed than myself in theology, and indeed I shall do so tomorrow, when I go to the Archbishop's Palace in Ferrara. Meanwhile you had best meditate on the enormity of your sins. Repent, and pray, and hope for God's mercy."

"That I can promise you, Reverend Father."

"Before God Almighty, remember. For He hears all."

"Before God."

Still the priest did not make any move to let him go.

"Listen, Scacerni," he said after a pause. "Those excuses you made for yourself, those cavils with which you sought to justify your action . . . have you named them all?"

"I don't understand you, Reverend Father."

"Isn't there one that you have forgotten?"

"Not that I know of . . ."

"Didn't it ever occur to you that there might be others . . . one in particular? . . ."

"No, I can't say it did."

"Think hard."

"No, in all conscience, I know of no other."

"Very good. That betrays an ignorance which does you honor. It testifies to a commendable lack of guile."

"Ignorance of what, if I may ask?"

"What? Have I offended you?"

"Not a bit of it."

"Well, you were a soldier of Napoleon! Does that name convey nothing to you?"

"Nothing. What should it convey?"

"So much the better, my son. But surely you know all that he stole from the Holy Church, right here in Ferrara, for instance."

"I've heard tell of it, yes."

"For that reason and because he persecuted the Holy Father in person, he was excommunicated. But later on he received absolution and pardon. He was not the only one, of course, and not the worst of his kind, either; at least he didn't cloak his robbery and violence under a pretense of protection or religious zeal. Perhaps he was a wolf, but he didn't wear sheep's clothing."

"Excuse me, Reverend Father, but I don't see the connection between my misdeeds and those of Napoleon."

"Didn't you ever think that your having been subjected to his bad example might excuse you?"

"No, I never did, I swear it. How could an ignorant man like myself think of something of the sort?"

"Oh, blessed ignorance! I praise you for it, my son! Do not be mortified by your ignorance, but rejoice in it! You did not maliciously calculate that if so many could be forgiven for so much then your little sin would pass by unnoticed."

"Ignorant I may be, but I know very well that other people's sins are no excuse for mine."

"Good! Spoken like a man! Now I'm sure of your repentance. I can't absolve you until I've consulted a higher authority, but because you are an honest man, let me shake your hand." With which he came out of the confessional and Scacerni rose up on his crutches to meet him. "You've taken up so much of my time," the priest added, "that I can't go with you to Chiccoli's. Please ask him to excuse me. And come back to see me in three days."

Scacerni came back at the appointed time to receive his penance. Don Bastiano ordered him to recite certain acts of contrition and to contribute to a fund for the erection of a new church. On his part Scacerni volunteered to make a pilgrimage with Dosolina to the miraculous altar of the Madonna dell'Atrio in the Cathedral of Ferrara and to leave there some *ex voto* offering as a token of gratitude and expiation.

"Don't forget to pray for the soul of that blasphemous miscreant who came to such a bad end there in Russia," the priest said in parting. "Even if he is beyond saving, the prayer may stand you in good stead some day."

Newly blessed and restored to good standing Lazzaro went away. But he had a half disappointed feeling that he had got off too easy. Had he perhaps wallowed, almost vaingloriously, in his sin? Perhaps it had catered to the very human desire of being different from anyone else and there was less flavor in his new-found conventionality than in the restless torment to which over so many years he had been accustomed. He had come to think of himself as an extraordinary sinner, and now penitence and pardon seemed dull beside his former perplexity. Even the mill meant less to him now that there was nothing guilty about his possessing it. But such hair-splitting is proper to the narrator rather than to his hero, whose main preoccupation at the moment was how to cope with his debts. He had already paid for the repairs to the mill, which were a large item in a year like this. The last harvest had been a poor one and the next already boded ill. Saint

Luke's Day, when the proverb says: Wet or dry, sow wheat and rye, had gone by with the fields still submerged in water, and even by Saint Martin's the seeds had not yet been put in the ground. This was a very bad start.

The first time that Scacerni put his foot on the ground after the surgeon had removed the splints, the leg hung stiff and heavy, quite unresponsive to his will.

"Slowly now," said the surgeon. "You'll have to re-train it gradually to its old ways."

"What do you mean, re-train?" grumbled Scacerni, sinking despairingly back on his bed. He had noticed without wishing to admit it that his bad leg was shorter than his good one.

"The knee isn't moving yet," said the surgeon. "It may look shorter, but it really isn't."

"Yes, it is. Just look." Scacerni had taken it in his hands and laid it on the bed beside its fellow. "You've crippled me for life, you idiot! Murder, I call it!"

"And I tell you you're a lucky man," the surgeon answered, holding out the crutches that Scacerni had thrown into a corner, hoping never to use them again. Now, if he hadn't stepped aside, Scacerni would have hit him over the head with them. "Is this your gratitude?" he called back from the door.

"What? Do you actually expect me to pay you?"

"Of course I do."

"Then here's your pay!" And he threw the crutches after him.

Later the miller calmed down and soon, day by day, he recovered his strength. He even got used to having one leg shorter than the other and saved himself from discouragement by never making any comparison between them. Many a time, however, he thought to himself: "I wish I'd gone under with the wheel!" Sitting somberly in a corner he did not see the affectionate yet piercing look with which Dosolina read his mind. Finally one day she came close to him with the baby in her arms.

"Lazzaro, don't you think I understand?" she said, summoning up her courage to say what was in her heart. "Don't you think I know what it costs a man like you to be hampered in this way? The first thing I shall tell this boy when he has reached the age of reason is that you sacrificed your leg in order to ensure us a living."

"Dear, dear heart . . . Dosolina . . ." said Scacerni hoarsely, pulling the two dear heads within the compass of his strong arms and looking at them tenderly.

Eventually he even sent money to the surgeon, who had not dared set foot near Poplar Bridge again. The surgeon was a donkey, but what could he do about it? Good or bad, one must take a doctor as he comes. Like bad weather and the caprices of the government he was not worth a man's worry.

With the aid of a cane he could walk well enough, and little by little he acquired enough confidence to roam over the mill. The road was too long for him to walk so he went every day on horseback with a gun slung over his shoulder. Mindful of Don Bastiano's advice he kept his eye alert and his finger on the trigger whenever he rode by any clump of bushes or thicket such as might provide an ambush for the ill-starred Beffa. Astride the saddle of his horse Scacerni had something of his former youthful and nimble air. Dosolina's eyes were still bright with love for him and he recovered his spirits so far as to have the barber trim his beard and thin out some of the gray hairs in it. After all, he philosophized, there's nothing but a broken neck that can't be mended. God tempers the wind to the shorn lamb and when He appears to slam a door He may open a window.

The restored mill showed signs, too, of the day of tribulation but its scars were less visible than those of its master. Patches of new wood spotted the gray walls of the deck and cabins and the keels were black with fresh tar. Because he was trying to cut down on expenses Scacerni had decided against any more decorative paintings, and of the gaudy originals only a few worn traces were left, along with some scattered letters from the defiant mottoes that had adorned the sides. The peeled and faded Saint Michael, still proudly pressing his heel on the dragon's neck, could now add to his legendary triumph the true story of a long fight against hardship and poverty, bad luck and human malice, heavy work and discouragement, temptation and sin. Scacerni thought back over these things, not with undue pride, but with awareness of all the lessons he had learned, of which the last one had been the most illuminating, leaving him as it did with confidence in the Almighty's protection. This was the idea he tried to express to the artist in Ferrara whom he commissioned to paint an *ex voto* picture for him to offer up at the Virgin's altar. The subject was to be the mill tossing on the wild waves of the rising river and the poplar tree riveted by lightning. In one corner was a detail showing himself dragged under by the mill wheel, while in the other Dosolina lay in childbed, holding the newborn baby in swaddling clothes in her arms. At the top center the Virgin and on either side of her Saint Anne, watching over Dosolina, and Saint Anthony over the mill.

"Which Saint Anthony do you mean?" asked the artist.

"The patron of millers, Saint Anthony Abbot, the one with the little pig, walking over fire and water."

This Saint Anthony was, indeed, an object of particular veneration on the part of all the millers along the Po, who never failed to celebrate his feast day on the seventeenth of January. Scacerni had hardly left the artist's studio when he came back to add:

"Put a man in the river, too, will you? But make it clear that he's swimming and will safely reach the shore."

"Well, well!" the painter said jokingly. Because he specialized in *ex voto* pictures he claimed a close acquaintance with graces and miracles of every kind. "You did have your share of blessings that day!"

"I wasn't the one who came so close to drowning," Scacerni answered quite seriously. "But the miracle of his escape was all for my benefit and I wish to give thanks for it."

"I've never had to cram a picture with so many different things!"

"Well, I'm not quibbling over the price, am I? I've made a down payment already."

"That's true."

"Then, if you're any sort of an artist, you must get us all in."

Scacerni smiled to himself, remembering the painter from Comacchio, the "Master of Eels," and came to the conclusion that all artists were slightly touched in the head. But the *ex voto* satisfied him completely when he came to call for it. Meanwhile a strong suspicion had been aroused in his mind which made him almost wish to have the drowning man taken out of the picture. For some time there had been no word of Beffa in the Guarda region and Scacerni thought that he must have gone to the dogs somewhere far away. But one day near the beginning of the year, when the river was fairly high, a boatload of ruffians went by, shouting and shooting off guns in every direction, perhaps because they were under the influence of wine. They looked like troublemakers or bandits in search of a quarrel which might serve as a pretext for some act of robbery or extortion. Such figures were familiar ones, especially when the high water enabled them to row away at more than ordinary speed. Scacerni might never have paid them any attention had they not swerved from their course and made catcalls and obscene gestures toward Saint Michael's Mill. Crouching in the bottom of their boat one fellow in particular, whose face could not be seen, appeared to be egging them on, and Schiavetto, who had very keen sight, pointed him out to his master.

"I'm not quite sure," he said, "but that looks to me suspiciously like Beffa."

"Quiet, there!" shouted Scacerni, making a trumpet of his hands, in the direction of the river. "Or I'll get after you with my gun!"

The instigator of the abuse apparently told them that he really had such a gun hanging in the cabin or else they were frightened to have anyone examine them so closely. At any rate they pulled hard on their oars and glided quickly away over the waves, singing an insulting song.

"I have no reason to believe that Beffa is in these parts," said Master Lazzaro to Schiavetto, "but do you know how to use a gun?"

Almost immediately he started to give Schiavetto and Malvasone instructions in shooting. He set up a target on the riverbank and taught them how to handle rifle and pistol alike. In his enthusiasm he felt as if he were carried back to his soldiering days.

"As long as there's no more than an exchange of ugly words, just restrain yourselves and keep your powder dry," was his final advice. "But if someone comes at you with an upraised gun don't stop to ask what are his intentions. Take aim and shoot. When a knife's the weapon, there may be some point to gaining time, but with firearms it's a question of who puts in the first shot."

186

"What if he does come with a knife then?" Schiavetto asked.

"First let me finish telling you about guns. Don't let anyone come nearer than three yards to you if you have a rifle and four feet if you have a pistol. Because if he can put out an arm and snatch it from you then you're done for. Of course knife to knife makes for a manlier fight."

"What if the gun won't go off?" Malvasone asked. His question was laughable in view of the martial stance he had assumed, holding himself proudly at attention but with the mouth of the gun barrel leaning on the ground.

"You want to study every possibility, don't you?" Scacerni answered in a kindly manner. "Good for you. If the gun sticks, turn it around and perhaps you can strike out with the butt. If you have a patron saint, that's the time to say a prayer to him. Then hit your enemy if you can. Since you're fighting in self-defense Heaven may help you!"

"Oh, I've a patron saint, never fear," said Malvasone gravely.

And so a well-appointed miniature armory was set up in the cabin of the smaller hulk. Schiavetto brought aboard a watchdog and Malvasone, who had trained his ear to the sound of the millstones, kept a gun at his bedside, near the cord with which he regulated the flow of grain through the hopper at night. God helps those who help themselves, as the saying has it. The police would haul a malefactor to justice readily enough, but there was no guarantee that they would arrive in time to catch him. When they arrived on the scene they might find corpses strewn about or the mill burned to the ground, for Scacerni had reason to believe that Beffa was quite capable of taking such sudden and violent revenge.

Strangely enough Lazzaro was no longer afraid of violence or blackmail on the part of Raguseo. He was not a man to indulge in shadowy fears and the shooting lessons and target practice he had given his helpers had proved to him that he still had a keen eye and a wrist steady enough to hold a gun. A song, the only one he knew, had come back to him from his youth and although his voice was better suited to shouting orders concerning the mill than to keeping a tune, he sang it as a lullaby to his son:

> *Ferrara, Ferrara,*
> *That excellent town,*
> *Where eating and drinking*
> *And joy do abound!*

Many a city, in Napoleon's time, had been toasted in these words by arriving or departing soldiers. And now little Giuseppe, who mortified his mother by crying all the louder when she sang to soothe him, would fall asleep only to the strains of this song.

"Do you suppose he wants to be a soldier?" his father said smiling. "I want to see him a miller, so that he can take care of you when I am gone. Of course my father, too—God rest his soul!—was dead set against my soldiering. And then, as I've told you, Dosolina, he died at the hands of General Grabinski's dragoons in the bell tower of the Borgo San Giorgio and I ended up in Napoleon's army: Fourth Corps, Second Company of Pontoniers of the Royal Guard of Viceroy Eugene. How strange are the ways of the world!" His smile was lost in his beard, and as for his eyes, they never smiled at all, so that Dosolina took his words more seriously than she was meant to.

"What are you saying, Lazzaro?"

"Isn't it likely, my dear, that I shall die before you?"

"Come, come, now; must you be thinking of such things as that?"

"I must think about leaving you well taken care of, so that you'll not repent, even when you're a widow, of having married a man such as me."

"Repent? Not even if I were reduced to beggary! You should know me better than to say that, Lazzaro! I love you better every day."

"And what about me? Haven't I loved you more than I can say ever since I first laid eyes upon you?"

But Dosolina, as a tender mother with her firstborn at her breast, was prey to the fear traditionally aroused by any mention of the Napoleonic levies.

"You won't run off to be a soldier, will you?" she whispered. "Napoleon has gone far away beyond the seas and, God willing, we'll never see him again. You'll always stay with your mother, won't you, my little boy?" And she tried out one of her lullabies: "Ding dong, the bells are ringing. . . ."

But little Giuseppe, as if he were bound to be a soldier to spite her, shrieked even louder than before, until his father intoned:

> *Where eating and drinking*
> *And joy do abound!*

When the time had come to baptize him Scacerni had fruitlessly ransacked his memory for the first name of his own father, which he would have liked to hand down to his son. It was Don Bastiano who finally suggested that they name him for the earthly spouse of the Mother of all good Christians.

"Call him Joseph and you can't go wrong."

5

Saint Anthony Abbot was, as we have seen, patron of all the millers along the Po. No one on the whole river was too poor to observe his January feast day, to bring out smoked *salame* or fresh sausage to turn the usual dish of corn meal into a festive dinner. The wealthy ate their *salame* with a rich sauce and followed it with roast meat and chicken, raisin cake and puddings. Anyone who failed to set out what he could on the table was branded as a miser, the kind that gives away nothing but the bones left from his corn meal. Every member of the millers' families bought new clothes for the occasion or put on the best he had to display when he went out walking in the clear, cold air. Farmers' boys in their turned-up caps led droves of domestic animals, their workaday harness laid aside and their horns and tails decked out with bows and streamers, to receive a blessing. For the piglet traditionally portrayed at the feet of the Egyptian Saint Anthony as a symbol of his victorious struggle over the temptations of the flesh had transformed him in the peasants' minds into a placid patron of the farmyard. In every mill and stable his bearded terracotta image, draped in the long tunic of an abbot, seemed startlingly mild to anyone who recalled the fearful torments with which he had paid for his asceticism.

Toward evening the millers came home to banquet, making note that already the days were growing longer. On the night following, a bearded old man, legendary as far back as the Dukes of Ferrara, brought gifts to the children.

Master Lazzaro could not afford to feast as lavishly this year as he would have liked. But with Dosolina, Malvasone, Schiavetto, Chiccoli and his wife at the table he nevertheless enjoyed himself thoroughly, pitting Saint Anthony against Saint Crispin, patron of cobblers, who he declared must be benevolent indeed to take such a wild fellow as this particular shoemaker under his protection. When the dinner was over they all said riddles and jokes and poems of the kind traditional to the region.

The mill had been left unguarded during this simple banquet and someone maliciously cut the ropes that moored it to the bank. Thanks to Saint Anthony, it was found the next morning on a sand bar not very far away. Close upon this warning Scacerni received an anonymous letter telling him to give proof of his good will by taking Beffa back into his service. Otherwise he would find himself in the clutches of someone whose arms were long enough to reach him wherever he might try to go. And at the end there was a postscript saying that target practice was useless and foolhardy and firearms were dangerous toys.

THE RECKONING

1

PARADOXICALLY ENOUGH, Scacerni's first reaction to this threatening letter was one of relief. He preferred to come to grips with his adversary as man to man than to go on with blackmail hanging over his head. The short interval in which he had not worried about these things was no cause of regret now that he could look back and see it in its true light, as a lull before the storm. Now, knowing perfectly well the source of the danger, he had no intention of bowing his head supinely before it. If he were to take Beffa back he would be at Raguseo's beck and call. The best course was to lay his cards on the table and declare open war. He had not sought to provoke it and so his conscience was clear. After the other had struck the first blow, there could be no question of trying to reach an agreement. And so his first move was to ask Don Bastiano Donzelli to draw him up a will in which he left everything he had to Dosolina.

"When a man's just escaped from the jaws of death, Father," he said in reply to the priest's astonishment, "he can't help being aware of the thread his life hangs by. It's wise to put one's affairs in order, isn't it?"

"Of course, my son."

"And if my wife and child were ever to find themselves left alone in the world—as God forbid—would you, for the sake of Christian charity, see to it that they are taken care of and sell the mill?"

"Do you mean that you wish me to be your executor?"

"Is that what it's called?"

"Exactly."

"And must I put it into my will?"

"Yes, you must."

"Well then, as the good Christian priest I know you to be, put it down that you're to sell the mill and pay off my debts before anything else. After that there should be enough left for Dosolina to live on until Giuseppe is grown, whether she chooses to stay at Poplar Bridge or go back to her family or take lodgings with Venusta Chiccoli, who would treat her as if she were her own daughter."

"Look here, my man, what's put all these ideas into your head this fine morning?"

"I told you that at the start, Reverend Father."

His precise motives, after all, were strictly his own concern. Meanwhile he decided to postpone until a more propitious time the pilgrimage to the Madonna dell'Atrio. Of course, if he had thought there was any chance of intimidating Raguseo once and for all and bringing

190

him to definite terms, then he would have behaved less defiantly. But Raguseo, not content with holding him by the collar, was attempting to throw a noose around his neck. It was ridiculous to imagine that such a foxy individual would live up to any promises. Even if he were to force momentary good conduct upon him, the man would be all the more inclined to extort revenge for his submission, to do everything he could to reduce Scacerni to the same degree of vassalage as that of Beffa, Big Brother, and the rest of their kind. There was nothing to do but take up the challenge. Fate had forced him against the wall. The motto with which he had twice before dared the old pirate to do his worst came back to him:

"I may go to prison, but he'll go straight to hell!"

And yet at bottom he did not imagine that he would come out of this trial of strength alive; what mattered to him was that his enemy should not come out alive either. He gave up the idea of facing him with a gun and inspected the knives, some of them strictly utilitarian, others decorative trophies, of which he had quite a collection. Among them were a stiletto from Brescia, a spring dagger from Campobasso, and a couple of plain, honest blades whose handles afforded a good grasp to a man with an agile wrist and a firm resolve to fight bravely and at close quarters. He chose one of these last and sharpened it on a stone.

He put his conscience at rest by telling himself that he had not wanted this crime, that the enemy had declared war against him and that he was only acting in self-defense. If he did not free himself once and for all, then he would be forced to commit other and graver crimes in Raguseo's service. That was his choice: to strike out for liberty or to resign himself to becoming a bondsman. In all this reasoning he did not think of freeing the countryside from Raguseo's oppression. Now that he had taken measures to provide for Dosolina and the child his thoughts were concentrated strictly on his personal rebellion. He was sure that he was fighting in the right cause and that the Lord would punish him with nothing more than a term in purgatory.

He could see no flaw in his reasoning. After all, the phrase: "I may go to prison, but he'll go straight to hell," was no more than a manner of speech. The law was very severe for crimes of violence and he risked having his head chopped off and set up for an example in the square near the Porto San Paolo, known as the Piazza del Travaglio. In view of this circumstance he thought to amend his motto to:

"I may go to purgatory, but he'll go to hell."

Indeed, if it came to a choice between jail and the gallows, he preferred the latter as a quicker and more definitive solution. He let another drop of oil trickle over the stone and sharpened the point of his knife before slipping it back into its leather sheath.

It was a cold, clammy evening, with the north wind penetrating every chink it could find in the walls and almost blowing down anyone who might be on the road outside as it whistled through the low, blinding fog.

"Fog without rain, and the temperature below freezing," said Scacerni as he came into the house. "That means it will be cold and clear tomorrow. By the way, did I tell you I must go to Ferrara in the morning?"

"What? With the earthquake?" asked Dosolina uneasily.

She did not often question her husband about his comings and goings, but the earthquake was something unusual. It was the recurrence of an earthquake peculiar to the region, not so destructive as it was persistent, coming back at regular intervals and trying the patience, as history informs us, of the citizens of Bologna and Ferrara. This time, for over a month past, its tremor had come every third day between two and three o'clock in the afternoon, and people had begun to take it almost as a matter of course. Nevertheless Dosolina felt some apprehension.

"Tomorrow is the regular day," she said.

"So it is, to be sure," Lazzaro said laughing. "As a matter of fact, if the earthquake would go at it with a little more vigor there'd be less work for the hangman."

"What do you mean by that, Lazzaro?"

"That it would be better if some people were dead than alive. But the earthquake is as feeble and slow as the arm of the law."

"You have a strange way of talking this evening, and of looking, too. . . ."

"It's just love, my treasure, that's all!"

True enough, for the first time after the long abstinence imposed by Dosolina's painful labor Scacerni's thoughts were thoughts of love and as soon as these words had escaped him he could think of nothing else.

"Didn't you promise me," he added, "that this evening . . ."

"Yes, I did," she answered, "but you seem so strange . . ."

"Haven't I reason to seem strange after all the time I've waited? You don't know how impatient I've been!"

"It seems almost as if you had a fever."

"I've reason for that too, haven't I? I'm burning, my precious Dosolina!"

This was the truth, but not the whole truth, for he was feverish chiefly over the idea that this was perhaps the last time he would make love to her. She seemed more desirable than ever and his passion was so intense that there was no room left for regret. His pleasure knew no yesterday and no tomorrow, but just this one night before he must die.

Everyone in the house was sleeping and outside reigned the silence of a midwinter night. No leaves rustled, every stream was frozen over and every furred or feathered creature had taken refuge in its lair or nest. In the fireplace a great oak log, cast up by the Po, had burned ever since the feast of Saint Anthony and now it was gradually sizzling out on top of a bed of ashes. Lazzaro's eyes sparkled like the fire as he looked lustfully at his young wife, while Dosolina's, despite her emotion, glowed with a milder and purer flame. Either because she was cold or because she wished to withdraw from the vehemence of Laz-

192

zaro's desire she got up from her chair, took the copper bed-warming pan with its enclosure, known jokingly as the friar and the nun, and filled it with burning coals, chosen among those that were almost totally consumed and would turn to ashes after they had given out their heat rather than emit flames and smoke. She leaned over the fire with the tongs in one hand, holding up the other—which was so slender as to seem transparent in the light cast upon it—to protect her face. One tiny foot stuck out from under her wool skirt and rested on the edge of the fireplace. As she leaned over her waist seemed slenderer and more alluring than usual under her rough bodice. Lazzaro looked at her greedily for a moment without touching her, then he stretched out his hand.

"Let me warm up the sheets, first," she said.

"What do you mean, 'first'?" he asked mockingly, pulling at his beard. And he carried the joke further: "You're teasing me with pretending to feel the cold. But let me tell you this: I'm not coming to bed before I smoke three pipes of tobacco."

He took a clay pipe down from the mantelpiece and pretended to fill it from a tobacco pouch.

"Good!" she retorted, jumping up to put the warmer in the bed and see if the baby was sleeping. "I'll be more comfortable alone, you nuisance!"

"Oh, I'm a nuisance, am I?"

He caught her in his arms and sat her on his good knee, then when she made a feint to escape him he held her all the tighter. She wound her arms around his neck and her thick hair glittered like gold in the light thrown up by the fire as he voluptuously kissed her laughing face.

"You're a beauty, you are; you're a flirt!" said Lazzaro, breathing hard and plunging his big hand into her mass of soft hair. "I've had my fill of life if I can say that you've loved me."

"Don't say such things, Lazzaro. What should I do without you?"

With candid carnality they stimulated their already overripe desire, pretending to spurn it, in words too concrete and intimate to be printed. Suddenly Dosolina started.

"Did you hear that, Lazzaro?"

"It's the wind."

Instead, someone was knocking at the dark, massive kitchen door, which was lit up only by the reflection of the fire and the hair of Dosolina.

"At this time of night!" Lazzaro grumbled.

"What if it's robbers?"

"Never, never be afraid!" he said, taking a pistol off the mantelpiece and calmly making sure that it was loaded. "Who's there?" he called out in the direction of the door.

"A friend!" came the answer.

"I have no friends at this hour unless they say their names."

"It's Rizzoli, whom you know as Big Brother."

"And what do you want?"

"I'll tell you when you let me in. It's devilishly cold and I can't say it through a closed door."

Dosolina hurriedly knotted her hair.

"Light the lantern, Dosolina, the one with the cover. And then stay in the corner or else go into your room."

"Hurry, Master Lazzaro," called out Big Brother. "You'll not be sorry that you let me in."

Scacerni was more worried than he wished to admit. Opening the door a crack he flashed the lantern in Big Brother's eyes and pointed the pistol straight at him. Big Brother blinked as he came in the room.

"You're wise to be so cautious!" he observed.

"Can't be too careful with a fellow like yourself," said Lazzaro, refusing to be taken unaware by either violence or joking.

"I mean what I say," said Big Brother, holding out his empty hands. "I told you I came as a friend."

"Then warm yourself at the fire," Lazzaro said, more hospitably, but still not letting down his guard.

Big Brother moved nearer the fire, putting his feet down stiffly like those of a duck and swaying as he limped along.

"I owe my crippled feet to someone who did a thorough job on me aboard your mill," he said. "Do you know that, Master Lazzaro?"

"I know something about it. Dosolina, you'd best leave us to talk alone."

Looking around him, Big Brother saw Dosolina in the shadows, near the wall.

"Oh, the mistress of the house! Forgive me for disturbing you."

His stocky body swayed from one crooked leg to another and his hairy hands swung down from his powerful, short arms. Under his piercing gaze Dosolina was conscious of the fact that she was still warm and dishevelled from her husband's embraces and she ran her hands over her clothes to put them in order.

"A miserable night!" said Big Brother. "One's better off in a warm house. Mistress, I shan't disturb you for long."

"Bring us some brandy, Dosolina," said Lazzaro. "I've lived through worse nights than this one."

"You've been a hard worker, everyone knows, and that's all to your credit. Now you have won a right to stay with your beautiful wife by the fire."

"Might you be envious?"

"No one can help envying you, Master Lazzaro. But perhaps with me it's a matter of sour grapes."

"Then let's have a drink upon it."

Dosolina was pouring brandy into their glasses.

"To your good health, Mistress!"

"Thank you."

"Well then . . ." said Scacerni brusquely.

"I have a few words to say to you in private . . . a mere trifle . . ."

As Dosolina went out of the room he added:

194

"If she's as virtuous as she's beautiful, then I must compliment you . . ."

"Thank you. She is. Sit down."

"Let's get down to business," said Big Brother, warming his hands at the fire. "I must admit that I had it in for you after the job they did on me that night on your mill. But, thinking it over, I realized that you couldn't say no to the long-armed Raguseo."

"I didn't know what was going on until too late."

"Yes, I came to realize that too. They ruined my feet, but they seem to have sharpened my brain. I can't move around very fast, but I can still lie low behind a hedge and get my man. Just ask Beffa! He's been swimming, if you can call it that, for the last two hours in the Po, with six inches of knife between his ribs. It took some time, but I've settled my accounts with him at last. Now it's Raguseo's turn. Are you interested?"

"I don't say no. But how do I come into it?"

"Because as soon as I've sent him where he belongs, I'll have to get across the Po in a hurry. I'm speaking to you as a friend and laying all my cards on the table. I have a horse ready in Il Barco, but when it comes to crossing the river I can trust no one. Surely you can see what I mean. I'll have the police at my heels and although I'm sure of dropping them in the open country they'd most likely stop me at the Lagoscuro bridge. What's more, Raguseo's men will be after me too. They can make it hot for me all along the line."

"I see your point. But is there no one to ferry you across but me?"

"Who could there be, Master? They're all in league with Raguseo and it's only right that they should do his bidding. He knows how to command their obedience even after he's dead. So when I heard that you'd received a letter and were on guard against him . . . Wasn't I right to come to you?"

"No one says the contrary."

"Well then, I said to myself: Master Lazzaro is a real man, one who won't let himself be put upon, and I'm rendering him a service. I needn't tell you what Raguseo's capable of doing. On that subject my feet are eloquent enough. And as long as you were dealing with me you found me to be an honest man, didn't you?"

"That I did."

"Good. I could expect you to say no less. So I said to myself, I'll free the whole countryside from oppression, including Master Lazzaro. Surely that's to his benefit. And in return, as soon as I've disposed of Michele Bergando, you'll ferry me to the other side. Isn't that a square deal? You have everything to gain by the bargain. Isn't it true? How could you rid yourself of him more cheaply?"

"Look here, Big Brother. What you say may or may not be true. How am I to know that Raguseo has not sent you to trap me? How did you find out, for instance, that he sent me a letter?"

"You are wise to be cautious, Master Lazzaro. Your hesitation does your intelligence credit. But events will prove the truth of what I have told you. Just come to the corner of the Strada degli Armari, just below the Palazzaccio, tomorrow. Of course the old fox is far too wary in his own house to be taken by surprise. The thing to do is to catch him outside his lair, but then he's all the warier. Well, what do you think? Do you know that he's afraid of the earthquake? You see, the earthquake has its uses, after all. As soon as Raguseo hears the earthquake rumble he's beside himself. Without waiting for the walls of his own house to tremble he rushes out into the open air as if a ghost were after him. Just imagine! Even the most timid souls, people who wouldn't hurt a fly, have accustomed themselves to the quake by now, and that old villain can't sleep or eat on account of it! It would be a capital joke if tomorrow, with the very first quiver, I weren't waiting for him there at the corner. He'll put his own neck in the noose, I promise you. Now I've laid my cards on the table. Is it a bargain? Will you trust me as I trust you? Will you ferry me over? As for the letter, I can tell you that I spy on him day and night. And I have my accomplices."

"What if there were no earthquake tomorrow?"

"It's the day for it," Big Brother rejoined calmly.

"But what if it were over? It can't go on forever, can it?"

But so strong was Big Brother's passion for revenge that he would hear nothing of this objection.

"What do you mean, it can't go on forever?"

"I mean it's bound to come to an end one day or another," said Scacerni, who was tempted to laugh at his visitor's vehemence.

"But not tomorrow, by all that's holy!" shouted Big Brother in his fury. "Tomorrow it will shake again, it will shake as much as I need it to, and I shan't let such a good chance escape me. Because you're quite right, now that I stop to think about it. It can't wait forever if I sit with folded hands."

"What do you mean?"

"The earthquake, by God," said Big Brother with serene confidence. "But tomorrow . . . you'll see . . . The earthquake won't let me down."

"Well, Big Brother, let's leave it like this. I shan't come to Ferrara tomorrow, because I don't want to be involved in something that's not my affair. But just because it's no concern of mine I promise that, earthquake or no earthquake, I'll take you across the river. I've never refused anyone that knew how to hold his tongue."

"Here's my hand on it, then, and the devil take whoever breaks his word!"

They struck their right hands solemnly and resoundingly together, like traders who after a long and loud argument have finally come to terms.

"And the devil take whom, then?" asked Lazzaro smiling.

"What's that?"

"Shall the devil take me or the earthquake?"

"Oh, you like to joke, do you? So do I, when the spirit moves me! The devil take you, or me, whichever one of us fails to live up to the

196

bargain. But I have complete faith in the earthquake, even more than in you, Master Lazzaro, and that's saying a lot!"

To anyone unacquainted with the subject of their conversation it would have seemed that they were bargaining over a calf to be sent to the butcher, a sack of grain to the mill, or a load of contraband across the river. Scacerni believed in good faith that this handshake bound him only to ferry Big Brother over the Po and that, once he had expressly instructed him to "hold his tongue" about what had gone before, he was free of responsibility for the murder. "I'll free the whole countryside from oppression," Big Brother had said, like Caiaphas, the high priest, saying: *unus pro populo,* that one man be sacrificed for the good of the people. Scacerni had not had recourse to this excuse at the height of his own homicidal rage against Raguseo, when his reason had led him not altogether illogically astray. But now he unconsciously repeated the gesture of the ill-famed Pontius Pilate when he released Barabbas.

"Let me make it clear once again. I know nothing of what you're up to. I wash my hands of it."

Like Pilate he believed himself to be sincere, but from out of the darkness he could hear hollow laughter and the half scornful, half condescending voice of the departing Big Brother:

"It's perfectly clear. Go ahead and wash your hands of it."

The shiver of joy that he had to restrain while he locked the door, as if it were an access of dizziness or intoxication, should have warned him that Satan's restless and deceiving spirit had brought Big Brother on this fatal errand. But Lazzaro's thoughts were all of the beautiful Dosolina, whom he could enjoy from now on without fear that she be taken from him. He laughed softly to himself, thinking of how gently he would awaken her. But when he quietly opened the bedroom door he found that Dosolina was not sleeping.

"Why have you kept me waiting so long, Lazzaro?" she asked.

"I may have kept you waiting," he said, as he hurriedly undressed, "but after tomorrow I'll never leave you alone again! By the way, I'm not going to Ferrara in the morning." He spoke lightly, as if a great weight had been lifted off his shoulders. Everything was for the best. And it was no more than just that Raguseo should die. His own evil deeds had condemned him.

2

The next day, well before the hour when the earthquake was usually felt, Scacerni stood, wrapped in a long cloak, at the corner of the Strada degli Armari. In order to justify the change of mind which had brought him thither he said to himself:

"I want to see whether the earthquake will keep its appointment with Big Brother."

As a matter of fact, the idea had come into his mind at the crack of dawn (which was already half an hour later than it had been on Saint

197

Anthony's Day), while Dosolina still lay asleep with her head on his shoulder, weary from a night of exasperated passion. Outside the fog had lifted, leaving every blade of grass bathed in sunlit dew. Once he had begun to think of what was supposed to happen during the day he could find no rest until he had got himself up, with a mumbled excuse to Dosolina, and mounted his horse without admitting even to himself where he was going. He trotted along from one village to the next, from Ro to Zocca to Francolino, where the road left the river, until he found himself at the Porta San Giovanni. That settled it: he might just as well spend another couple of hours waiting to see if the earthquake was as good as its word. Moving somewhat as if in a dream he put his horse in a stable. At the corner of the Strada degli Armari he passed in front of an individual with his hat pulled down over his eyes and his collar turned up almost to his nose, but the day was cold, so this did not surprise him. The man had no resemblance to Big Brother and did not even look up from where he was leaning against the wall. In order to conceal his own purpose, Scacerni peered about him as if in search of an address, and finally decided to take up his stand at the door of the Church of San Domenico, on the other side of the street. Just as he started to go across a low voice called him from above. Scacerni remembered the grated openings over the walled-up windows of the Palazzaccio and in spite of the heavy silence that had returned to reign around him he knew instantly where it had come from. The man with the turned-up collar began to move slowly along the wall and from his gait Scacerni recognized him as Big Brother, realizing at the same time that it looked very much as if he himself were on his way to betray their secret to Raguseo. Just as he started to enter the palace in response to the call from above he met Big Brother's veiled stare and murmured to him under his breath:

"The devil take whoever breaks his word!"

Big Brother slid on along the wall, talking as if into the air.

"One more, or one less, it's all the same to me," he muttered.

If Scacerni failed to respond to Raguseo's call he would only arouse his suspicion, yet by responding he had a part in lulling him into a false sense of security and was to an even further measure than before a party to the crime of which he had tried to wash his hands. As he went up the stairs Scacerni prayed that the earthquake would stay away and cursed the curiosity that had brought him to this spot.

Raguseo met him, clad in his Turkish robe, at the door, more ceremoniously than upon their previous meeting.

"This is a stroke of unexpected good luck, most excellent Master Lazzaro," he said in welcome. "Does it take an earthquake to bring you to call on your old friends in Ferrara?"

Scacerni thought to himself: "You'll see what tricks the earthquake has in store for you," but all he said was: "I came on business, Michele Bergando. I'd have gone by without stopping if you hadn't called out. I have an appointment at the Three Crowns Inn in the Strada della Rotta."

"You'd have gone by, would you. That was not the thing to do! Just think, if I hadn't happened to look out one of the peepholes of this miserable hovel, just to pass the time of day, you'd have gone on without stopping! And you have the courage to tell me so to my face! Yes, I was looking out from my cooped-up existence (I have to watch out for my enemies, good Master Lazzaro!) and there I saw you on your way to the church. Were you going to say your prayers? A praiseworthy idea, but no excuse for neglecting your old friends!"

Raguseo clapped his hands and one of his exotically dressed, effete-looking serving boys answered.

"Cyprian wine!" Raguseo ordered, and he added, turning to Scacerni: "This time don't tell me that you can't drink on an empty stomach!"

"Empty or not, I must say you have a remarkable memory."

"Better than yours, at any rate, since you've forgotten your friends. And how is your beautiful wife, Mistress Dosolina Malvegoli?"

"Very well, I thank you," said Scacerni, who was not surprised to find the old pirate so well acquainted with his private affairs.

"We know, you see, that you are a husband and father . . . we never forget . . ."

"You never forget your friends . . ."

"Exactly."

And Raguseo brought out a string of compliments for Scacerni's hearty and youthful appearance and the fortunate healing of his leg after the disaster of the storm.

"We know all about it," he said. "Now try this wine straight from Cyprus and tell me how you like it. You'd never find anything so good at the Three Crowns Inn, even if it is an establishment of the first order. Here's to your good health!"

"And to yours!" answered Scacerni, thinking to himself: "You'd do better to commend your soul to the Almighty."

The wine was heavy and flavorful, with a tang of resin; it shone and flowed like light oil. The wide-hipped boy had poured it from a decanter of Bohemian glass with rich silver ornamentation into two flagons of different but equally elaborate design, which seemed but samples of the old pirate's stolen treasure.

"To your wife's health and that of her poor father!" he said, raising his flagon again.

"What? Do you know Princivalle Malvegoli?"

"Yes, and I know that there's no love lost between you. But a man seldom finds it easy to get on with his father-in-law, we all know that. I've been glad to oblige him with a loan or two, and for your sake I've asked very little interest. . . . Does that make you laugh?"

"Yes, it does. I thought I knew the old man's wiles, but I never thought he'd go so far!"

"Well, not everyone has the ability of the master of Saint Michael's Mill. . . . By the way, here's to the health of Beffa, now that he's returned to your service!"

Scacerni put down his glass. He had been on the point of throwing his wine on the floor as a sign that he could not join in any such toast, when he remembered that Beffa was floating down the river with a knife between his ribs. He looked hard at Raguseo and saw that he knew nothing. Which meant that if the earthquake did not fail he was as good as dead.

"Here's to Beffa and to his protector!" he said, picking up his glass and laughing to himself to see the old fox so blissfully unaware of the trap that was laid for him.

Indeed, Raguseo grew increasingly self-confident and expansive.

"That's the way to talk!" he exclaimed. "That's what I like to hear. I've always had a good opinion of you and I was sure you would see reason. Only, just lately, it seemed to me that you were a little dilatory, a little stubborn. Forgive me for suspecting you unjustly. I'm glad for your sake to see you here, yes, and for the sake of your father-in-law, too. Just between ourselves, he's not too keen-witted, and he came not long ago to complain that he couldn't meet this one and that of his obligations. And because I had a bone to pick with you I was just about to close in on him, to do him in for good. Do you see what your stubbornness might have led to? A man has to take care in this world or else he may quite unintentionally get himself into trouble. Just a passing whim, you may say to excuse yourself; I always meant to come around. All very well, Master Lazzaro, but I didn't see it in the same way; I was exceedingly angry and thought you were going to try my patience beyond what I could endure. Because I have a weakness for you, Master Lazzaro! Didn't I tell you before that I wish I could have met you when I was young so that we could have sailed the seas together? And from an old sea dog these words are not to be taken lightly. Oh, to be young, Master Lazzaro, and with a deck under one's feet!"

The old pirate sighed in a strangely sincere manner and went on:

"The past is dead, and so is the resentment I felt toward you. I forgive your father-in-law, too. . . . Indeed, I'm very happy to see you. . . . Only I'd be happier if it weren't for the earthquake. It's got into the habit of . . ."

In Raguseo's face Scacerni could read the fear of which Big Brother had told him. Yes, without his suspecting it, Raguseo's hour was at hand.

"I've had my drink," he said, "and now I must go."

"Oh, no," said Raguseo, and it was amazing how gray and wrinkled was his face, with the fear of the earthquake upon it. "I don't want to be alone. I don't like being closed in by four walls at a time like this. I've never been afraid of anything or any man on land or sea, and yet the earthquake makes me tremble. When I was a boy in Ragusa my father's house crumbled around me. Now I feel an urge to commend myself to Almighty God's protection. But I can't help remembering that I made myself into a circumcized Turk—there's a story for you if you had time to listen—and I don't know exactly what God to call upon. I'm not the man I once was, Master Lazzaro!"

"Commend your soul to God, anyhow," Lazzaro enjoined him.

"But to which God, I ask you?"

"To the Lord of Mercy."

"Mercy? Yes, there's something to what you say. I stand badly in need of mercy."

"So do the rest of us. But now that I've given you this good advice, Michele Bergando, I must leave you. I told you before that I must go."

Scacerni was in as much of a hurry by this time as if he too were afraid of the quake.

"I can't go out of the house because of the enemies who lie in wait for me. I know that some of them have sworn to lay me low. But here, inside, I can't bear it. When the floor trembles under my feet and the walls start to buckle . . . They'll fall in on me, for sure."

The wretched fellow's lament was awkward and pitiful together. Now his tone became more plaintive still:

"Stay here; don't leave me alone. You're stronger than I am and for you the earthquake has no terrors. There's no one I can trust, either inside the house or out. Now you know under what conditions I am living and why I have to keep an eye on the street. Out there they're waiting to rob and kill me!"

Scacerni felt almost as if the impatience of the assassin waiting in the cold and lonely street below were coming up the stairs. "Little do you know what's in store for you," he thought to himself. And meanwhile Raguseo caught at every pretext for detaining him further.

"Don't think that I deal only with such crude specimens as your friend Beffa," he said.

"My friend? After all, he's more your friend than mine."

"Alas, you're right. Mine is a terrible trade, full of compromise and blackmail. I order people around and make use of them, to be sure, but they make use of me in their turn. And then they envy me for my riches! Well, as I was just saying, I have other dealings besides. Do you know the Carbonari, or 'good cousins'?"

"No, I neither know nor care to know."

In spite of his accumulated irritation he could not seem to get away; it was as if he were fated to deliver Raguseo into the assassin's hands. And Raguseo rambled on, with all the volubility of a man who is deceiving himself rather than others and trying in vain to allay his own fears.

"They're people of breeding and education, noblemen and merchants, doctors and lawyers, all conspiring together to unseat the priests' rule, get rid of the Austrians and set up a Republic. Yes, conspiracy is the only word for it."

"Whatever the word may be, it's not in my province to know."

"Strictly speaking, it's not in mine either. But sometimes one of these gentlemen conspirators has to change climate without a passport or a ticket on any public conveyance. Then he has to have recourse to someone who can procure him passage over salt and sweet water, who has relays of horses in the plains and mules in the mountains, with guides to help him cross the Po into the provinces of Venice and Lombardy, the Panaro into the duchy of Modena, to take the sea route to Dalmatia or scale the Apennines and come down on the other side in Tuscany. I'll warrant you've not so much as heard of places like these!"

"Come, come! You forget that I went with Napoleon as far as Moscow."

"True enough. The thought of the earthquake has driven everything out of my head. I'd even forgotten the hold I have over you."

"What hold?"

"The gratitude you owe me. Because I treated you fairly and squarely, you can't deny that. If it hadn't been for me, who would have bought your treasure? It came from Muscovy, you said, but how were you to prove it? It had an odor of stolen goods about it. . . . Do you laugh?"

"Yes, I can't help laughing, even if you are making me waste my time."

"The hour is coming soon. . . . God help us. . . . No, it's quite useless for me to call upon God; I have too many sins on my conscience. Yes, conscience, did you hear? It took the earthquake to remind me I had one."

Fear rather than repentance made conscience stand out like a specter on his face. Then a wave of raging pride came over him.

"See to it that you obey me, man, like a slave pulling his oar in the galley. Little do you know the power of Michele Bergando, commonly called Raguseo! One word from me and your mill is smashed, your house set afire, your son taken from you and your wife given to the biggest brute among all my henchmen. After that you'll come and beg me to let you die. You've a family now, so think it over well!"

"I'm thinking it over," Scacerni said coldly, resolved now to deliver Raguseo into Big Brother's hands himself were the earthquake to fail.

"Good for you!" jeered the old pirate. "Go to an old man for advice and to a young one for action! Had you not met me you'd not be a miller; that much you must grant."

"Perhaps I'd be better off if I hadn't met you!" exclaimed Scacerni with exasperation, disgusted less with Raguseo's attempt at intimidation than with the prospect of having to listen to more of his mellifluence. "And mind you, *I may go to prison, but you'll go straight to hell!*"

And he might then and there have anticipated the gesture of Big Brother, had he not been interrupted by the rumble, far away and yet very near, lost in the air and at the same time deep underfoot in the ground, of the earthquake. Just as Big Brother had said, Raguseo clapped his hands to his head, like a man pursued by a ghost, and rushed with his Turkish robe around him down the stairs. The Palazzaccio creaked and groaned, and Raguseo emitted a stream of shrill but unintelligible words, running so fast that Scacerni could not keep up with him. The stray dogs in the courtyard bristled, stretched out their necks and howled as if in the presence of death, and as Scacerni reached the bottom step of the stairs he heard Raguseo shout hoarsely from the gate.

The blow struck Raguseo with such lightning speed that he thought for a moment it was the earthquake which had made him lose his balance and fall back against the wall with a sickening taste in his mouth and a sinking feeling in his stomach. Big Brother's hand was still held out as it had been to strike his foe, but now he raised it to lift the brim of his hat and stare into the other's eyes. Meanwhile Raguseo remained nailed to the wall, almost as if he were frozen.

"Look at me!" commanded Big Brother. "See who it is that's finished you and croak of anger!"

Raguseo fumbled at his chest and left shoulder.

"The knife is clean through you," jeered Big Brother. "Have no doubt of that. It's too clean a death for you, after the way you made me suffer."

Stiffly and almost without breathing, the depraved old man made a supreme effort to walk away. Moving like a piece of wood he managed to take a dozen steps as far as the corner, where he leaned his back against the wall again, closed his eyes and ground his teeth together. Big Brother and Scacerni stalked him every foot of the way and when he stopped the former hissed into his face:

"I want you to look at me until you draw your last breath! Open your eyes, Michele Bergando!"

Raguseo opened them, but he fixed his gaze not on Big Brother but on Scacerni, standing behind but head and shoulders above him.

"With you accounts are even, Big Brother," he gasped, "but not with the miller!"

His eyes glowered with hate and a harsh laugh broke out on his blood-stained lips. He sobbed convulsively and blood foamed up from his throat. Then he gave one of the imperceptible deep sighs that Scacerni had heard before from men dying on the field of battle. He dug his nails into the interstices between the bricks of the wall, finally pointing one forefinger at Lazzaro before he let his head sink, choked for lack of air and collapsed in a heap at the foot of the wall. He who had been so powerful and feared lay there like a bundle of rags, like a homeless beggar sleeping in the shelter of a gateway.

On the street there was no sign of life. People had become hardened to the visitations of the earthquake and did not run in panic out of their houses. The howling of the dogs had covered the first cry of the stabbed Raguseo and now the earthquake was over, without a single window's having been opened to witness the scene below. The winter day was already drawing to an end and fog had started once more to roll through the empty streets.

Big Brother kicked the dead body tentatively with one foot.

"I must admit that it gave me a start to see you hanging about here," he said, "after you'd said that you wouldn't come to town and washed your hands of the whole business. But you did a truly professional job as a decoy. Now let's each go his own way and I'll see you next when I need to be ferried across the river. Only let me thank you again for your help before I say goodbye."

As if a long-standing, mysterious bond somehow tied him to the murderer, Scacerni joined right hands with him over the dead man's body. Then Big Brother disappeared into the fog and Scacerni went through the alley of Malborghetto in the direction of the Castle. He walked slowly along, with his mind quite empty except for an oppressive feeling of shame that he had not been strong enough to rebel against the accusation which both the murderer and his victim had made against him. Indeed he almost wished that he were really guilty, for then the death of the foulmouthed and tyrannical old extortioner would have afforded him a real satisfaction instead of just the misplaced scorn in that last look. He might just as well be damned for a sheep as for a lamb. This regret must be at the bottom of his anxiety, or rather the unfulfilled pledge to abet Big Brother in his escape, the prospect of the murderer once more holding out his blood-stained hand and the certainty that he would lower himself to shaking it. Still this was not all. This dissatisfaction was the beginning of his damnation, the stench of hell in his nostrils. His pulse beat as if he had a high fever and underneath his cloak his hand was so hot that he did not dare pull it out and look at it for fear that it might be tinged with blood. Wearily he limped along, dragging his short leg behind him, to the stable at the Porta San Giovanni.

3

But Giovanni Rizzoli, known as Big Brother, did not come to be ferried across the river. Betrayed by a false friend or by his own carelessness, he was caught by the police in the bed of a prostitute of the Strada delle Volte that same evening. The circumstances of the crime and the capture of its author aroused considerable comment in every place where the old pirate had connections, including Guarda, where both Big Brother and his dead master were well known. There was gossip about the guilt of those in high places, about the obvious advantages to be reaped by "certain people" from Raguseo's disappearance. There was even talk of the most reprehensible passions and the fierce jealousies which they had aroused. The boy who had poured Scacerni's Cyprian wine was mentioned most often in this connection, and he told of a visitor in whose company his master had fled from the terrors of the earthquake. So garbled was his description of the visitor and his errand that it aroused the most far-fetched conjectures of a political or conspiratorial crime. Some persons went so far as to say that the mysterious bearded character described by the confused boy was a disguised emissary of the Sultan of Turkey in whose service Raguseo had enlisted as a young man. The aspiring writers who congregated in the literary cafés of the Strada del Gesù and Giovecca wove this theory into a story of Mohammedan revenge, Harem rivalries, and deliberations of the Divan or Turkish council of state. Paradoxically enough, it was Master Lazzaro's beard, the one exact detail in the whole fantasy, that led to the greatest aberration. But such is the power of rumor. Even in Guarda, where Scacerni's beard was an everyday phenomenon and some people might have guessed at more than they cared to say, the suspicions most noisily bruited about were of the wildest kind, and everyone insisted that Raguseo's mysterious visitor, Turkish or not, must have been some very important personage. Knowing individuals in Ferrara whispered about the vast number of Raguseo's accomplices and the notoriously big pieces of business in which he had a finger. The Liberals swore that he had been killed by the Sanfedisti,* followers of Cardinal Rivarola, and the reactionaries accused the Carbonari.** Others whispered that Raguseo had had dealings with the whole lot of them: Sanfedisti, Carbonari, smugglers, customs guards, officers of both the Austrian and Papal police, and evildoers of every kind. He had played one against the other and eventually betrayed them all, so that the wonder was not that he had come to a bad end but that he had not come to it long before. Except for the Sultan of Turkey, all those spoken of in connection with the crime, including both police forces, to which Raguseo had impartially purveyed information, were quite content to hush it up and accept Big Brother's confession. In this way the truth actually served those who were trying to hide it.

As for Big Brother, he did not for a moment deny his guilt, first because the knife had been identified as his and next because it was known that he had a grudge against Raguseo. Moreover the magistrate had dug up a record of so many of his past crimes that he would have needed a dozen heads to be chopped off or the nine lives of a cat to serve all the jail sentences that were rightfully due him. He had committed housebreaking, highway robbery, blackmail, kidnapping, assault and battery, rape and a considerable number of murders, including those of a watchman, a priest, and a Papal guard, most often quite unnecessarily and simply because he could not control his brutality. All in all there were eighty-seven solid accusations against him. Big Brother had an accomplice, a certain Battista Toselli, known as Tough Hide, whom the police laid hands on soon after and found to be just as excellent a fellow. After this, talk of the crime died down.

Master Lazzaro Scacerni was tormented night and day, not so much by fear of actual arrest as by surprise that Big Brother had not attempted to implicate him in the crime. Such an attempt would have been only natural since everyone said that Big Brother had a way of

* Sanfedisti, or *bande della Santa Fede* ("bands of the Holy Faith"), a secret society, made up for the most part of the dregs of the populace, combating Liberals, often in very brutal form.

** Carbonari ("charcoal burners"), a secret society of Liberal tendency, demanding a constitutional government, and fighting for the overthrow of foreign rule in Italy.

making unnecessary trouble for himself and others. Had he not killed the priest of Cogomaro simply because the good old man had given him something to eat? He himself had boasted to various people in Guarda that this was his only motive for committing the murder. Similarly he had quarrelled with and injured several of his companions for no other reason than their fidelity to his person. Of course his strange silence might be attributed to a perverted sense of honor, because he had always taken pride in violence for its own sake. At the same time Scacerni dimly felt that there was something else behind it: both scorn of having had an accomplice and at the same time satisfaction in sealing by his discretion the silent pact they had struck over the dead man's body.

For the first time he appreciated the truth of the saying that a large part of sin lies in intention, that whoever desires to kill his neighbor has, in his heart, killed him, just as whoever looks covetously at another's wife has committed adultery. His sleep was restless and interrupted by nightmares, from which he woke up in a cold sweat with the fear written on his face that he might have spoken aloud of what was on his conscience. And yet what had he to fear if in the eyes of the law he was innocent? But real innocence was something very different indeed! True enough, he had an innate mistrust of the law. But if Big Brother did choose to denounce him he could easily prove how insignificant had been his complicity; it had amounted to nothing more than a promise to keep silence and to ferry him across the river, and he himself was no more an instrument of the murder than was the earthquake! But conscience told him that he had desired Raguseo's death even more ardently than the actual murderer and without the excuse of having suffered the same atrocities at his hands.

In a melancholy and sterile manner he frequently called to mind the motives of his own bitterness against the dead man and wearily sought thus to revive the hate he had felt for him. But the harder he tried to remember them the more they eluded him, and he was left with the unflattering suspicion that more than anything else he had been afraid of Raguseo and fear had magnified his resentment. The only thing that stood out clear in his memory was the passion for bloodshed that he had felt along with his strongest accesses of sensuality. This was what he had insincerely called an instinct to defend his own liberty and the possession of Dosolina.

It came to the point where he wished that at Big Brother's instigation the court would call for his testimony. Only a legal judgment could still the pitiless voice of his own conscience that persisted in calling him a murderer. Yes, only by publicly confessing his share in the crime and serving the number of years, months and days to which the court might sentence him could he throw off the far graver and more insistent accusation that an inner judge was bringing against him. There was something unhealthy and poisonous about his self-torment. The priest taxed him not so much with his confessed homicidal desires but with the weary and desperate probing into his own feelings, in which anger and pride played a large part. By wallowing in his despair he offended God's mercy at the very moment when he declared himself unworthy to receive it.

"No one is unworthy," said Don Bastiano, "unless he despairs. Don't be so difficult!"

This sin of the spirit was so much more complex than the sins of the flesh with which the good man was accustomed to deal that he had to get down his copy of Saint Alphonso Liguori's *Moral Theology* and manual for the use of confessors.

"Do you know who it is that teaches us to be so difficult?" he asked finally, in exasperation.

"The devil."

"You've taken the words out of my mouth."

But in spite of being aware that the devil was back of his tormenting thoughts Scacerni could not manage to shake them off, and indeed he only seemed to suffer from them the more deeply. During the day he was distracted by hard work, and weariness sent him off to sleep at night. But every morning he woke up with confused noises in his head and a vague memory of bad dreams that was more terrifying than a clear one. Visions of interrogation, imprisonment, the gallows and damnation danced before his half-open eyes. He could hear infernal laughter, no doubt that of the devil in person, and the jaws of hell seemed to open before him.

First thing when he woke up he turned anxiously to Dosolina.

"Did I say anything?" he asked, and then, regaining control of himself: "Did I talk in my sleep?"

Dosolina herself had told him that he tossed about and sometimes muttered to himself, but now she was almost sorry.

"Exactly what do I do? What words do I say?" he had insisted.

"I don't know. I can't make them out. All I know is that they don't make sense."

"But what do they sound like?"

"As if you were afraid. As if you thought you were falling into a bottomless pit, or as if someone were trying to strangle you. That's when you're worst, when you seem to be choking and you say . . ."

"Then sometimes you do understand what I am saying?"

"Oh, you swear like a trooper and laugh . . . Perhaps it's silly of me, but it's an ugly kind of laughter."

That he could believe, for the echo of it was still in his ears.

"And do I mention any names?"

"Yes, but very indistinctly, as if in a dream."

"Never mind. One never knows what one's saying in a dream. And what then?"

"How do you mean, what then?"

"Have you told me everything?"

"Yes, everything . . . except . . ."

"Except what?"

"Sometimes you shout quite distinctly: 'I didn't do it!' or 'Off with his head!' "

"I'm sorry that I disturb your sleep this way, especially when you're nursing the baby and need all the rest you can get. If you like, I'll go sleep in another room."

"Now what's got into your head? You don't want to make me sad, do you?"

Then, to take his mind off this painful subject and free herself from further questioning, she added evasively:

"You did ramble on a bit, of course, but that was some time ago. Lately you've been quieter and I haven't heard you talk in your sleep. Last night you slept as soundly as little Giuseppino."

This was not true and Lazzaro knew it, but he did not choose to sadden and alarm Dosolina any more. What if his dreams had revealed to her? . . . What could they reveal, except the fact that he was a murderer? His spirits sank and his arms fell to his sides. Perhaps the revelation had already been made and Dosolina knew the worst. He began to mistake her discretion, which was actually founded on pity, for horror and disgust, and yet he did not dare ask her outright: "What do you know?"

"What did I say? What did you hear?" he asked her with angry obstinacy. "You must tell me, do you hear? You must tell me everything."

"That's exactly what I have told you."

"Everything, do you understand? I command you to be frank with me."

"I've always obeyed you, Lazzaro, you must admit that," she answered, dismayed by his overbearing and capricious manner.

"Yes, I know."

"Then why do you torment me? If you attach such importance to mere dreams it must mean either that you're not well or that you have . . . well, I'd rather not say."

"That I have something on my conscience, is that it?"

"I didn't say so."

By this time he was afraid even of what he said in his waking hours and reluctant to question her any longer. When he could contain himself no more, he would start out by joking about it and end in a quarrelsome and insulting fashion.

"A wife should not have any secrets from her husband!" he would wind up by saying.

"I've come to the conclusion that you are keeping a secret from me, and a very ugly one!" she retorted.

Scacerni paled. He was beginning to know what the real secret was. It was not merely that he was curious for news of the crime, although with apparent carelessness he ceaselessly interrogated everyone who came by from Ferrara or returned from the weekly market, as well as all those along the river who had anything to do with the business of smuggling. No, it was an unwarranted but deep wish to know something about Big Brother, how he was getting along in prison and what he thought of the only actual witness to the murder.

The criminal investigation was long-drawn-out; not that there was anything new to discover, but rather because the police were anxious to have the case forgotten before it ever came to court. This is one of the more common reasons why the machinery of justice turns so slowly. The very factor that would naturally tend to make such an affair simple and easy to solve is the most easily turned to making it seem mysterious. Even in Guarda they knew that. As the seasons rolled around, winter, spring, and summer, Scacerni was haunted by the question: How was Big Brother getting along in the cold weather? How did he like it when it was hot? Did he find long nights or long days more tedious? What were the waking and sleeping feelings of a man who was waiting to lose his head? Were they the same as those of any normal human being? None of the scraps of news Scacerni managed to put together could give him an answer. From month to month he grew surer that he himself was not going to be arrested, but this surety only added to his terror, because it meant that for him there was no earthly expiation but only eternal punishment, his abandonment by God into the hands of the Archenemy. His feelings vacillated, then, between his despair and his idle and unsated curiosity as to the condition of Big Brother. In his efforts to guess at what the prisoner was thinking Scacerni identified his thoughts with what he guessed might be the other's; he shivered with the anticipation of cold steel at the back of his neck as if he were the one going to execution, in a courageously resigned state of mind or, more likely, in one of stunned oblivion. Meanwhile he strained every nerve not to cause his wife unnecessary pain and at the same time he perpetually saddened and offended her. In short, he was no longer his own master, but merely a tool in Satan's hands.

Without reaching any such recondite conclusion Dosolina had asked Don Bastiano Donzelli, when he came to bless the house at Easter, to recite an exorcism of the devil. As for Lazzaro he found little relief in his Easter confession.

"I am damned!" he said brutally to the priest.

"What? After all you've told me, that's nothing!" replied Don Bastiano, trying to turn the whole thing into a joke.

"Without hope of pardon," said Scacerni, with such genuine sorrow that the priest was roused to answer sternly:

"That's plain ignorance, my man, even greater than I can allow on account of your lack of education!"

"Father, I don't make any claim to wisdom."

"Well, I should hope not! Otherwise you'd be in danger of dying impenitent and being damned in dead earnest!"

"I don't know what else to say."

"Look here," said Don Bastiano, moved to compassion for such misery. "Do you realize, my son, that you're the first man in this parish —and you have only to look at the church tower to see how old the parish is—to have such wild ideas. If I weren't administering a sacrament to you I'd come straight out and say you must be joking."

"But I'm not joking . . ."

"I should hope not! But what am I to do?"

The untutored Scacerni's confession aroused in Don Bastiano the memory of long forgotten questions that he had debated as a seminarian, arguments over the various degrees of heresy, predestination, free will, salvation and damnation. For a moment he felt as timid as a young student of theology up for examination, then travelling back to the present he was once more moved by pity for the man kneeling before him. How had this poor fellow got himself into such a tangle?

"Come, come, my son," he said, returning to concrete considerations, "don't you believe that Our Lord has the power to save your soul if you sincerely repent of your sins?"

"He has the power, but He doesn't want to use it."

"What's that?" But he was stirred by mercy rather than anger. "There is the great mystery! Our Lord chose to be crucified in order to save you, and yet He has left you free to lose your soul, to reject His grace. He, the All-powerful, will not impose salvation on you against your will. Of course, if you persist in your despair you will lose your soul in spite of Him."

"I have lost it already."

"If you insist on judging your own case, then don't come to the divine tribunal," said the priest severely. "You are sinning against the Holy Ghost. I can only tell you to pray, if you are capable of doing so."

So incurable was Scacerni's disease that no words of prayer would come to him. As soon as he opened his lips to pray he was assailed by morbid curiosity about the state of Big Brother's soul. Had he repented? Was he in a state of grace? Like Cain, Scacerni raved against God for preferring another.

Aside from this, everything was going well. The mill was working day and night and soon he would have enough money to pay his debts. Dosolina kept house most efficiently and she had made arrangements with a peasant who had a mulberry tree to raise silk worms the following year. Lazzaro enjoyed excellent physical health and he had so accustomed himself to having one leg shorter than the other that whenever anyone mentioned his disability he said:

"I can't even remember the time when both legs were the same."

There was something defiant about this reply, as if it were intended either to cover up a lasting discomfiture or to express an exaggerated austerity. In either case it indicated an attitude of scornful indifference toward the comforts and consolations offered by his neighbors, which could not fail to offend them. His customers preferred the aggressive and bold manner with which he had spoken to them in the old days, when he used to say that there were two distinct varieties of grain, that which he was milling for them and that which he was taking out for his own consumption, the "miller's toll," as he called it.

Now, instead, Scacerni had become scrupulously honest and would not take so much as a cupful of flour, the smallest measure that was used on the mills. People crowded to make use of his services, but they found him cold and disagreeable.

"He's an honest man," they said, "too honest. Why is it that cheats are always gay and honest men wear long faces? He's honest, but far too proud."

When some fellows who were in their cups hinted as much to him one evening at the tavern he answered them rudely:

"Have I asked you whether you're honest men or cheats? And yet I notice you're always very gay."

Yes, too honest a man, this reputation spread over the whole province and Scacerni began to think of setting up a second mill at the same anchorage in order to take care of his new business. He looked forward to this possibility with the same disconsolate resignation that clouded his vision of the world in general. Before experiencing such a feeling he would never have suspected its existence and even now there were times when it seemed to him quite incredible.

"It's the Evil One," he muttered to himself. "Big Brother breathed him into me and put him in possession of my body and soul when we shook hands."

For he had seen pictures and heard stories of how the devil enters into a sinner at the very moment of his sin. Lacking any other means of information he could not have failed to see the obscene, jeering devils pictured in the Last Judgment in the Cathedral of Ferrara, carrying away their prey tied up like big game. When he went with Dosolina to take a thank offering to the Madonna dell'Atrio, he stared at these devils as if he were seeing them for the first time; indeed, he had eyes for nothing else except the figure of Christ sitting in judgment, who seemed to be motioning him toward the left, along with those who were sentenced to the flames of hell. All this time he was acutely aware of the vicinity of Big Brother, languishing in prison near by. As for the devil, he never actually saw him, nor did he need to, since he could hear his evil laughter in the water around the mill, in the woods at night, and in the gutters around the roof of his house whenever it was raining. Once he heard the devil emit the same frightening cry as that with which old Blow-hard had terrified him in Il Barco; he seemed to be gliding along the riverbank, perching an instant on the mill and disappearing over the water. Schiavetto heard him too, and his hair stood up on end, while Malvasone laughed not very convincingly at the whole story. Another time, when he was alone on the deck, Lazzaro thought he could see Beffa's body with a knife between the ribs floating face up on the water in the direction of the two bows of the mill. Of course he knew perfectly well that Beffa's corpse had long since disintegrated and gone to rest in the mud either midstream or farther down, at the mouth of the river. But a chill ran through him as he looked at this vision and then at the mill wheel, for he remembered hearing tales of damned souls who came to dance on the wheels of accursed mills. When he looked back there was nothing left to see but the usual current of water, ever old yet ever new.

"Lord Jesus, I can't go on like this; I am too unhappy."

Not long after, news came that Giovanni Rizzoli, alias Big Brother, and Battista Toselli, alias Tough Hide, the partner of most of his crimes, had been sentenced to death on the guillotine in the Piazza del Travaglio near the Porta San Paolo.

"On the other side of the Po," observed one local figure, "they'd be hanged and the hangman would give the worse character of the two, Big Brother, the benefit of a knotted rope."

This rope was an accessory much used at the time by the Austrian police.

"Not such a bad idea," said a timorous soul, "with all the criminals who infest the country."

"Don't go imagining that in Austrian territory, gallows and hangman and the rest, people are any more undisturbed than they are here. If anything, they're worse off. There are desperate characters who think that where there's more risk there's greater profit." With which the timorous soul was effectively silenced.

On the cold December eve of the execution Scacerni told his wife that he was getting up early the next morning and would be away all day on business.

4

Dosolina had suffered considerably in the course of the past few months from seeing her husband upset without being able to ask what had upset him. She saw him grow gaunter and gloomier every day, while a lost look in his eyes, almost like that of a madman, often accompanied the mournful sigh with which he woke up in the morning. She could not give in to her natural impulse to cry or ask him what was the matter, for he was quick to take offense if she so much as appeared to notice that anything was wrong. How far from his former restraint was the uncontrolled anger he now vented against her.

"What's this? Why do you look at me as if I were some strange animal? Must I feel myself spied upon in my sleeping hours as well as my waking ones?"

Venusta agreed that there was something seriously wrong with the man, but whether it was physical or mental illness or simply some stroke of bad luck she was unable to say. "Bad luck" was a diagnosis which both women refrained from mentioning. In local parlance, when a man who was not a professional criminal found himself accidentally the author of an act of violence and had for the sake of his health to go into hiding, "bad luck" was the term used to describe his condition. Had Scacerni run into luck of this kind or was it hanging over his head for the future? This unspoken thought occupied the anxious minds of

212

both women, causing Venusta to sigh to herself and Dosolina to weep in despair.

"And to think that I'm perfectly helpless, that I can't even look at him! If you could see how susceptible he is!"

Scacerni's last bout of malaria had affected his blood and he had acquired the yellowish skin and dull eyes of a man suffering from disturbances of the liver and spleen. He had shooting pains and cramps, of which he pathetically tried to make light. Indeed these were the only things that ever caused him to smile.

"No doctor or druggist's going to get my good money. What can doctors do? Take this leg of mine, for instance; I could have patched it up just as well myself. As for druggists, they're useful only to expectant heirs who want what's coming to them in a hurry. There are only two kinds of illness: one that goes away on its own and the other that kills you, and in either case a doctor is superfluous."

For the pains in his back, which he called lumbago, Scacerni would never have anything but mustard plasters and a hot toddy mixed with cinnamon and cloves. These pains he attributed to the dampness of the air in the vicinity of the river and said they were of the kind that was bound eventually to go away. But the stabs he felt in his side he classified as incurable; sooner or later, he said, they would lay him low. His malarial fever he refused to admit was in the tertian or pernicious stage, insisting that it was of the blandest and most harmless variety. He sat in the sun, either against the south wall of his house or on the forward part of the deck of the larger of the two hulks of the mill, with the cord to regulate the flow of grain through the hopper in one hand and his ears alert for the rhythm of the grinding. Tertian fever (which he knew perfectly well was what he had) was reputed to kill off an old man and rejuvenate a young one. The question was, then, whether he was old or young. When the druggist sang the praises of the wonderful "bark from Peru," or quinine, as a sovereign cure for fever Scacerni stuck by his guns and repeated that all medicines were superfluous. And so it was that he spent the summer and autumn.

In the preceding spring Dosolina had laid her hopes in the popular rhyme:

> The shining sun of May
> Restores her beauty's sway.

Indeed her slender figure and the blooming color in her cheeks were even more beautiful than before, but anxiety ruined what pleasure they might have afforded her. Instead of being a source of womanly pride her beauty was actually an offense. Scacerni never spoke an affectionate word or caressed her; in fact he rarely looked at her at all except from one corner of his eye, with a gloomy and yet lustful expression. He had a way of falling upon her as if he were a tracked animal or a savage, snatching at a drunken satisfaction of his desire before the fear of death overwhelmed him, and in the middle of the night he

213

burst into sardonic laughter. Dosolina felt that this was anything but love, and she was afraid without actually knowing why. She had a feeling of exactly this kind the night in December when Scacerni told her that he would be off early the next morning.

Venusta and Dosolina had put their heads together to concoct an innocent plot for Lazzaro's benefit. Dosolina happened to know a nun who had the reputation of being somewhat of a saint. Indeed, Princivalle Malvegoli claimed her as a distant cousin and once a year he took his family to pay a solemn visit to her convent. For various reasons these annual visits had left Dosolina with unhappy memories and a sense of shame. For one thing, Mother Eurosia was a wizened, very dark little woman with round shoulders and skin that was wrinkled all the way to the tips of her fingers and she reminded Dosolina of nothing so much as a turtle, an animal which as a child she had cordially disliked. The nun's head, bound in the bands prescribed by her religious order, was flat; she had a pointed face and a long neck, and the motions of her aged, bent body accentuated the resemblance. Her singularly penetrating bright eyes could at a moment's notice dart disapproval or become as hard and boring as gimlets, while her humble and meditative air was transformed into an impenetrable and bristling armor of disdain. This armor she put on—whether on purpose or no—every time she received a visit from what Princivalle Malvegoli pompously announced as "the saint's family." The first time he did this Mother Eurosia reproached him jokingly, the second time she asked him to stop it, and the third she begged him in the humblest way imaginable to realize that the careless appellation of saint was a device of the devil to tempt her to undue vanity.

As she spoke her eyes glittered with ascetic pride and seemed to Dosolina more than ever like those of a reptile. Princivalle accused Mother Eurosia of condescension toward her poor relatives, but nevertheless he took the whole family to see her again the following year. With Donata Malvegoli the nun had a tacit understanding and she never failed to draw her apart, doubtless in order to whisper into her ear that she should bear with patience the tribulations of her life with such a fatuous husband. Dosolina had never doubted Mother Eurosia's saintliness in spite of the bitter memories she had of these family visits, the affronts to her filial pride, the repulsive image of the turtle, and the fact that the nun also reminded her of a so-called witch woman who lived deep in the Diamantina woods and told fortunes from burning coals, pools of water, mirrors, and other cabalistic symbols. Mother Eurosia had always been put off by the timidity with which Dosolina concealed her wounded pride and had treated the younger children much more agreeably. Meanwhile the nuns glorified Mother Eurosia's heroic virtues and sacrifices and rumored her saintliness abroad. They told tales of the illuminating advice she could give on the thorniest problems, the unexpected conversions of hardened sinners, the cures of sick persons long since given up for lost, the driving out of evil spirits, and her own enjoyment of ecstatic visions during which she

214

uttered words of inspired prophecy. The convent parlor was crowded during many hours of the day with people who varied from a poor woman asking her to influence Saint Anthony of Padua to restore some lost household object to a high ecclesiastical or political dignitary seeking her counsel. To one and all she gave the same patient and kindly attention and in her Christian charity proved herself truly of saintly virtue.

Venusta Chiccoli knew also of the good nun's existence and advised Dosolina to find some pretext for sending Lazzaro to pay her a visit. So it was that on this December night as Dosolina was tossing sleeplessly in her bed after hearing that her husband would be gone all the next day she suddenly got up her courage to say:

"Listen, Lazzaro, have you ever heard of Mother Eurosia?"

"No."

"She's a saint."

"Ah well, people are never as saintly or as rich as rumor would have them . . ."

"Everyone swears she's a saint. But that's not the question. I've known her since I was a child. And there's a favor I'd like you to do for me tomorrow."

"If I can."

"Oh, you can do it easily enough. Will you go by the Ursuline Convent, ask for Mother Eurosia, and recommend our Giuseppino to her care? It's on account of a promise I made, almost a vow," Dosolina said haltingly, hoping that her good intentions would make up for her telling a lie. As a matter of fact she still had the same feelings toward Mother Eurosia that she had had as a child.

"Very well then, I'll look up this Mother Eurosia," said Lazzaro, rolling over on one side to go to sleep. "But how am I to find her?"

"I tell you, they speak of her as a saint. Anyone you meet can show you her convent."

"Still you haven't told me where it is," said Lazzaro in a singing voice that denoted a certain boredom.

"In Ferrara, of course."

"And what makes you think I'm going to Ferrara?" Lazzaro asked. His voice coming through the darkness had taken on a note at the same time harsh and compassionate, as if his anger were suffocated in despair and he were at the end of his tether.

"It seemed to me . . . I supposed . . ."

"What seemed to you? And what's all this supposing and imagining and spying on me: where I am, where I'm going, what I dream about? I know what I'm saying; you spy on me even when I'm asleep. Yes, I know!" (The very violence of this assertion served to deny it.) "And I say it's gone far enough. I'll go where I choose. And not to Ferrara!"

"Then, Lazzaro, I was mistaken. But that's no reason to take it so hard. I thought I heard you say so."

Now Lazzaro was moved less by compassion than by fear. He could not remember having declared any such intention and wondered suspiciously how she could have guessed it. But fear caused him to conceal his suspicion.

"You're right and I'm wrong," he said. "I don't know what's the matter with me this evening. I don't feel quite well."

"Then stay at home tomorrow," she said gently, mistaking his fear for repentance for the hard words he had spoken.

"I must go. There's nothing serious about the way I feel. A good sleep will cure me. And I'm not going far, only to Crespino."

But the apparently trivial thoughts he had on his mind prevented him from closing an eye. Why hadn't he said he was going to a village on this side of the Po? Because now, in order to carry out the lie, he must have himself ferried across to the other side. But who was there to follow him, and what did it matter? "If I'd killed Raguseo with my own hands," he thought to himself, "I'd not be so cautious, or to put it frankly, so fearful as I am today."

Just then the baby cried, and when Dosolina went to soothe him Lazzaro pretended to be asleep. A few hours later, when Lazzaro got stealthily up as if he were a prisoner trying to elude his guards, Dosolina in her turn thought it wise to pretend she did not hear him. But when he bent over to ascertain from her breathing whether she was really sleeping he felt quite certain that it was all a pretense intended to deceive him. Mingled with his anger was a sense of disgust with himself and the world in general and a weariness that was almost suicidal in its intensity. He rode to the mill and got Malvasone to ferry him and his mount across the river. It was still dark when they touched the other side.

"Shall I come back for you later in the day?" Malvasone asked before he started to row back.

"No," said Scacerni, who was already in the saddle. "I'll take the boat from Polesella. In fact, I may return by the bridge at Lagoscuro, since I have business to attend to there."

He stuck his spurs angrily into the horse's flanks. How stupid it was to have to invent stories for the benefit of Malvasone. Now morning was not far away and in the eastern sky the stars had begun to pale. The horse trotted briskly along and the cold, dry air to some degree revived Scacerni's spirits. His feet were congealed in the stirrups, one shorter than the other, and his hands on the reins. But the cold air cleared his head and sharpened his sight. His lungs breathed it in deeply and the warm air that he breathed out again moistened his beard and whiskers. Every now and then he looked up at the sky above him to see what it foretold of the weather and at the constellations now disappearing over the western horizon which told him the time of day. He spurred his horse again, lest he arrive too late in Ferrara.

Scacerni's ingenuous wonder at the vast galaxy of stars above him and the precise movements of their machinery was akin to reverence, but of an intimate, almost daring kind. The cold air and the steady gait of his big, bony horse combined to drive away the nausea of the sleepless night he had now left behind him. He was less morbidly conscious of his sins and more sincerely repentant for having committed them. His remorse was clear-sighted and increasingly courageous. It was healthy to emerge from the futile meanderings of thought that had entangled his spirits through the night and to breathe in the cold air and watch the procession of the stars.

His attitude toward Dosolina also underwent a change for the better. He felt a rough tenderness for her and unconsciously he forgave her for the ugliness of the thoughts he had had about her and begged her forgiveness for having let them steal into his mind. He was grateful to her for having pretended to be asleep instead of bombarding him with unwelcome questions, and little by little his tenderness and gratitude turned into passion. In his memory he leaned again over her dear, kind face and in her gentle breath his hate of himself and of mankind in general was changed by imperceptible degrees into love.

Now that the constellations of the night had gone and the morning star was rising he knew that Dosolina must be up and about. By now she would have pulled a heavy gray wool skirt over her nightgown, made her bed, poked the fire, put on the coffee and tidied the kitchen. How industrious a wife she was, and how wise beyond her years! His tenderness was mingled with something like anger, and he swore silently that never again would he bring tears to those beautiful blue eyes. In spite of the errand that was taking him by this roundabout route to Ferrara he was actually happy.

These thoughts were still in his mind when the sun rose and he saw before him the bridge of Lagoscuro. Many of the pontoons were resting on the sandy bottom of the river, for the winter frost had brought the water down to an unusually low level. The last stars faded out and the pale winter sun lit up the scene. The countryside was bare, the river shrunken and muddy; both the mud of the uncovered riverbed and the water flowing in the narrow central channel were dark in color and almost icy. Most of the mills anchored in the vicinity were high and dry and looked like shipwrecks.

The sleepy Austrian guards barely glanced at Scacerni's worn safe-conduct and a few moments later he was halfway across the bridge, where a blast of cold wind struck his face. On the other side the Papal guards were warming their hands over a smelly, smoking peat fire in the guardhouse.

The Piazza del Travaglio, or Travail Square, a small open space behind the massive walls to one side of the Porta San Paolo, rang with the noise of hammering. The executioner's assistants were putting a few last nails into the wooden platform, no higher than a man's chest, and lifting into position the square, heavy guillotine, whose usage, introduced by the French, had remained in both Bologna and Ferrara. The city was still asleep, but as Scacerni rode along a narrow street toward the square the hammering gave him notice of what was going on and every blow seemed to strike at his heart. The carpenters, just like any other workmen, had breakfasted on bread dipped in a mixture of cheap rum and brandy and now were laying strenuously about them

217

in order to warm up their still stiff and sleepy bodies. They spoke in the dialect of Bologna, whence the guillotine had been brought especially for the occasion. One of them was a great prankster and when he saw Scacerni looking on he said:

"Hello there, my good man! We're putting up the stage for a puppet show!"

He put his head in the place where soon the knife would fall and made faces like String Bean, a favorite character in the puppet-show repertory of Bologna.

"Go along with you, you fool!" said one of his companions, giving him a stout spanking.

"Come back in a couple of hours, my good man. It's too early for the show."

From the Church of San Paolo the bell tolled. Scacerni was relieved to see several other people arrive on the scene, among them a talkative lay brother in the black hood of the Brotherhood of Comforters, who gave himself considerable airs as he inspected the progress of the work. The prisoners had made their confessions and received the archbishop's blessing, he told the bystanders; now they were at Mass in the chapel belonging to the Confraternity. His hearers stamped on the pavement and blew into their hands to keep warm.

"How many of them are there?" asked Scacerni, who had forgotten about Big Brother's accomplice.

"Don't you know?"

"I shouldn't ask if I did," said Scacerni remissively.

"People have been talking about them for months, and since yesterday the whole city has been buzzing!"

"I'm from far away, from the country. I just happened to be passing by," said Scacerni, pointing to the platform.

"Then there's some excuse for you. Well, there are two of them: Giovanni Rizzoli, known as Big Brother, and Battista Toselli, called Tough Hide. And do you know what's charged against them?"

"Some important crime, I imagine."

"The proud sum of eighty-seven charges against Big Brother and almost as many against his companion, all duly checked, proved, and confessed."

"He'll need more than a tough hide to save him today," said another onlooker, laughing.

"This is no time for jokes," the brother observed severely.

"Did they work closely together?" asked Scacerni.

"Most of the time, but Big Brother was the only one involved in the murder of Raguseo. Of course, they say he did have some sort of accomplice or instigator . . ."

"A fellow with a long beard like yours, my good man," the joking carpenter called out from the platform. "A Turk, some people said, didn't they? I heard him mentioned last night at the tavern."

"They said all sorts of things," replied the brother.

"Well, if you were a Turk I'd say you'd better keep that long beard of yours at a safe distance from this machine!"

Even the brother smiled condescendingly at this sally.

"They said all sorts of things," he repeated, "but the fact is that Raguseo was killed by the Old Man of the Mountain, because he betrayed both Christ and Mohammed."

"And who might this Old Man be?"

"That's too long to explain. Secrets of state."

"So only one of them was involved in the murder of Raguseo," Scacerni continued. "And as to other crimes . . ."

"Most often the two of them were partners."

"Like you brothers of the Confraternity of the Guillotine," joked the carpenter.

This stung the lay brother to the quick. "We brothers go in twos to perform our errands of mercy, while this pair went to perform the most hideous misdeeds. I know what I am talking about, because it is my humble task to be present when their sentence is read to the criminals, with the list of their crimes. It was enough to make your hair stand on end, I can tell you, and make you think that the end of the world must be very near indeed, in fact just around the corner."

"We know their crimes," said someone who perhaps knew how long-winded the brother could be and hoped to prevent him from reciting the whole list.

"I heard it said that several men were anxious to see the end of Raguseo. And men from these parts, too, rather than any Old Man of the Mountain," said another.

But he was half sorry to have spoken and looked around him suspiciously. The rest of the group looked equally ill at ease, and this gave the brother a chance to take the floor again, with a resolute air which seemed to signify that he would not relinquish it quickly.

"Those who rejoice in others' misfortunes won't find much pity for their own," he said sententiously. "But that's not the way in our Brotherhood. This much I can tell you, that after all their misdeeds Rizzoli and Toselli are ready to die as good Christians. And whose is the merit?"

"Of Our Lord, Who had shed His grace upon them," said a little man standing inconspicuously in the background, whose remark drew favorable attention.

"Of course!" retorted the brother impatiently. His frequent attendance at sermons had influenced his manner of talking and given him oratorical ambitions, so that the question he had just asked was a figure of speech. "Of course!" he repeated. "And after that?" At this point he expected his listeners to make an appropriate reply but since none of them would give him this satisfaction he made it himself. "It is *our* merit, the merit of our Brotherhood." His listeners remained noncommittal and he continued indignantly: "You should have seen the evil faces of those two fellows when we went to visit them in prison. I've seen faces of every kind, old and young, handsome and ugly, good and bad, but when these two appeared in the room where we work over the souls of those who are sentenced to execution I said to myself: "Here are two that are determined to die unrepentant! But I was mistaken; I am glad to say it out loud: I was mistaken!"

"Now how could that happen?" asked someone in a subdued voice, but the speaker apparently did not hear him.

"I was mistaken, because I didn't reckon with . . ."

"With the grace of God," said the same little man, who seemed to have a taste for controversy. (Lucky for him that he was not alive when Calvin came to Ferrara and made converts there!) But the brother's oratory was not to be dammed so easily.

"I didn't reckon with our canon, Don Buzzoni. All of you have heard him from the pulpit, but you should have been there when he congratulated them upon their repentance and us on the good work we had done to accomplish it. We deserve it, I may say, because if it weren't for us, who knows how many more souls would go to hell? The canon said that no one is too wicked to share the hope of the Good Thief that hung at Christ's side. And let me remind you that only a short time before these two fellows were anything but sorry for their misdeeds. What more can I say? Of course all of us who were present wept!"

"It sounds as if the brother might have committed half a dozen murders himself, if you ask me," said one of the audience, amid a general snicker.

"The two repentant sinners were the only ones with dry eyes. Then, after this incomparable speech, we escorted them to the chapel to pray, after which we all came back to the main room for a rest. As the humblest of our Brotherhood I was charged with the modest task of ministering to their material needs . . ."

"And what might those be?"

"The preparation of their last dinner, for instance."

This announcement seemed to re-awaken the flagging interest of the audience.

"Don't go thinking it's such an easy job, now. Last night, when we came back from the chapel, Toselli, who's a little shrimp of a man, sat hunched up on his chair while Rizzoli sat up straight and looked self-confidently around him. The canon asked if they wanted to make their confessions and Toselli said, looking up at his companion: 'I've always done what you said, and so I shall do to the end.' Here Rizzoli gave a smug smile. 'Are you going to confess?' Toselli went on. 'Yes, I am.' 'Then I am too.'"

The onlookers were struck by this graphic description of the scene and hung eagerly on the lips of the narrator.

"Then it was my turn to ask what they would like to eat in the newly-found state of innocence in which they would be after they had confessed and received Communion. Let them ask for anything they liked, I said, and it would be given them. 'Whatever Rizzoli says,' was

220

Toselli's answer. And Rizzoli began to order with a smile: 'Noodle soup, boiled fish, calf's liver, sausage, chops, truffles, roast squab, bread, white wine, fruit, and a sweet of some kind.' Now I ask you, what do you think of that? A couple of the other brothers and I smiled, at which he got up on a high horse and said: 'If you don't really want to give it to us, why did you tell us to order what we wanted? I'll take nothing at all, then, if you please!' 'It's not that we don't want to give it to you,' I said, 'but the shops are closed at this late hour and, yes, I admit that I wasn't expecting such a large order.' 'Very well,' said Rizzoli, 'in view of this explanation we'll eat whatever you give us.' His companion still sat hunched up in his chair, looking straight ahead of him. So I left them with their confessor and went out to shop for their dinner, which I brought back to them around midnight: Noodle soup, roast squab, sausages, truffles (which happen to be in season), cheese, fruit, white wine and a sweet to finish off with. There wasn't everything they had asked for, but quite enough to take the edge off their appetite, wouldn't you say? They thanked me quite contentedly and sat down at the table. Toselli ate with real gusto and polished off his friend's portion as well as his own. For the fierce Rizzoli had no more got down a few spoonfuls of soup and a breast of squab than he stopped short, and even a glass of wine was powerless to help him swallow another bite. 'I'm not hungry,' he said, pushing away his plate. Then Toselli piped up: 'I wouldn't mind a slice of ham; it's something I've always had a weakness for.' Some people have no sense of proportion, now, have they? It was two o'clock in the morning and he had eaten a double portion of dinner and there he was asking for ham! Well, that's all. After dinner they went back to their cell and slept soundly. We said the *miserere* and the *de profundis* all night through until it was time to light the candles on the altar and wake them. I left them a few minutes ago hearing Mass in the chapel with true Christian piety. And they'll be along any moment."

Just then the executioner appeared on the platform and tested the smoothness with which the blade of the guillotine moved in its grooves. To the slow tolling of the bell there was a rumble of wheels on the paving stones and the tumbril turned the corner at the far end of the street. The crowd of people who were now tightly packed into the small square fell silent and craned their necks all together to see its arrival. The tumbril passed close to the gate, on which hung a small image of Our Lady of Good Comfort, to which the two prisoners addressed a final prayer.

An imperceptible rustle went through the crowd. Many people went down on their knees and stayed there until the cart had left the gate behind it. Scacerni had listened to the brother's story of the prisoners' last hours with such flattering attentiveness that the narrator had been moved to look at him as if he were telling it to him personally. Now he found himself enclosed and pushed about by the last-minute crowd. In the eye witness's description Scacerni had recognized Big Brother exactly as he had known him. Nor was there anything incongruous

221

about his sudden inability to eat his dinner and his dramatic repentance of his sins. But the most lifelike trait of all was the fellow's smug smile over the subservience of his accomplice, Toselli.

Meanwhile the tumbril was near the end of its journey and the black-hooded brother frayed a passage through the crowd.

"Let me by!" he called out. "I must go to do my duty!"

He managed to arrive at the platform at the same time as the tumbril, which was preceded by a group of guards and soldiers who cleared the way.

Toselli looked into the faces banked around him with a stupefied smile and he was heard to ask the brother standing on the platform steps and holding a crucifix up before him:

"How does it happen that my heart isn't beating any faster?"

"Because God is giving you strength, my son."

But the attention of the crowd was riveted on Big Brother, who sat looking down at his knees, with his hands tied behind his back and a vague but not absent look in his eyes, as if at this moment he were for the first time revealed to himself. He was smiling, and Lazzaro while he greedily drank in the sight of him, felt a shock of recognition and at the same time had the impression that he was seeing him for the first time. Big Brother got up from his seat before anyone had to tap him on the arm, and looking out over the crowd as if there were something there to attract him he met Scacerni's eyes. Whether or not he really saw him does not matter. In Big Brother's eyes there was something like a smile, which seemed to bear a message of courage and peace in answer to Scacerni's questioning and pitiful stare. Meanwhile the blade had already come down on the neck of Toselli.

Walking straight but not stiffly and with a firm but not overbearing expression on his face Big Brother climbed with his mutilated but apparently no longer painful feet up to the platform. The executioner went through the rite of begging his pardon.

"I've done my part," said Big Brother, "now you do yours."

There was a deep silence that seemed to reach up into the sky. Scacerni heard Big Brother's voice as if it too were new and for the first time sincere. The executioner received the pardon and embraced his victim, who with his hands still tied behind his back kissed the executioner on the cheek. He asked him not to blindfold him, looked humbly at the surrounding walls, the clear winter sky above him, and the crowd of people below.

"I beg forgiveness," he said simply, "from both the living and the dead."

"Pray for us all," answered a voice which so perfectly expressed the sentiments of all those present that perhaps not even its owner was aware of what he was saying.

The Capuchin held up the crucifix.

"Help me to make an act of contrition," said Big Brother to the executioner's assistants. He knelt down, with someone holding his arms, lowered his face to the floor of the platform and traced the sign of the cross with his tongue. Then when he got up again he kissed the crucifix and called out in a loud voice:

"Lord Jesus, have mercy on my soul."

If Lazzaro could have distinguished among the medley of conflicting thoughts that assailed him as he stood with his eyes glued to the guillotine, he would have felt chiefly a boundless envy of his accomplice, who stepped forward as resolutely as if his feet were swifter than they had ever been before. Scacerni and the others made the sign of the cross and bowed their heads. A second later they heard the slight noise of the release of the blade, its whirring through the air and then an abrupt stop and the thud of the victim's head on the floor. The executioner bid his assistants put the heads and bodies of the dead men in two long sacks. Then, to the continued tolling of the San Paolo bell, the crowd gradually melted away.

5

"I should like to speak to Reverend Mother Eurosia," said Lazzaro Scacerni to the woman who opened the spy hole at the Ursuline Convent. And feeling perplexity in her hesitation he added: "If this is not a good time I'll wait upon her convenience outside."

"No, that's not it. On days when there's a public execution Mother Eurosia stays in her cell to pray. But I'll tell her that you're here."

Scacerni leaned against the doorpost of the simple and unadorned house. He had come to it from the Piazza del Travaglio without remembering whether he had actually stopped to ask the way, almost as if his visit had been long premeditated.

"Come in, my good man."

He found himself in a small, shabby parlor, lit up by a large south window.

"Oh, it's you, is it?"

The nun had glided into the room by a small door and greeted him with a local expression that was used only between intimate acquaintances. But to this Lazzaro paid no particular attention. He saw her black habit and wide white headdress, but took less notice of her old age and deformity than he did of her piercing yet gentle eyes, which smiled at him in the festive yet serious manner of an innocent child. Without causing her the least astonishment Scacerni bent one knee to kiss the hem of her habit. All she did was to murmur *laus Deo*, praise be to God, as if to recognize that his homage was due not to her but to her Creator. There was something majestic in her mien as Scacerni started to explain the motive of his visit.

"I'm Dosolina Malvegoli's husband; Lazzaro Scacerni is my name, and I have a mill near Guarda on this side of the river. We have a son hardly a year old, called Giuseppe, and my wife has asked me to recommend him to your prayers."

He thought that this was the extent of his errand and that he had nothing more to say. And yet from the moment the saint had entered the room (and he was quite sure now of her saintliness) he had known that he would be surprised and disappointed if their conversation amounted to no more than this. Meanwhile she looked at him with an air of playful and almost exaggerated courtesy.

"So my good Dosolina remembered this poor old woman!" she exclaimed. "That gives me a great deal of pleasure. Of course I'll remember Giuseppe in my prayers. First because he's a Christian soul and then because he's a cousin."

Seeing a look of astonishment in Lazzaro's eyes she added: "You look surprised."

"Forgive me, Reverend Mother, did you say a cousin?"

"Oh, it's a distant relationship, but Dosolina's father claims that we are cousins of a kind. Didn't your wife tell you?"

"All she told me was that you are a saint."

"Don't say that, I beg of you!" she said. Her smile froze on her face and her eyes seemed outwardly blind yet inwardly more piercing than ever. "Don't say that," she repeated with sorrowful humility. "But how do you account for the fact that Dosolina didn't tell you of our relationship?"

"I can guess why, even if I can't wholly understand."

"Let us try to understand together. Dosolina thinks of me as a saint and to be related to a saint (if I were any such thing) would be considered by most persons a worldly gratification, a source of vanity, as we say in the convent. Something she might puff herself up about."

"Puff herself up? Dosolina?" said Scacerni, smiling and shaking his head. "You can't know her very well if you say that."

"Ah, you see, we are making progress in understanding her together. And now it is up to you to tell me more about her."

"Up to me?"

"Yes, you. After that I'll tell you the little of her that I know."

"All I can say is that she's the best of wives, just as she was the best of daughters."

"For this news I must thank you!"

"Thank me, Reverend Mother?"

"Yes, I must thank Him who sent you to give me a lesson in humility. And then I thank you and Dosolina."

"Dosolina . . ."

"Now you must listen to me. When Dosolina used to come see me with her good father and mother. . ." She paused for a moment to look at Scacerni, with unexpected humor in her eyes. "I see!" she exclaimed. "This much I can understand for myself. You're not on the best terms with Princivalle Malvegoli!"

"Nothing serious," Scacerni replied, "but I must admit, that father-in-law of mine . . ."

"Oh, I know him well enough. And I tell you, my son, that you must forgive him."

"Things haven't gone that far. There's just a certain lack of harmony, but it amounts to no more than the exchange of a few hard words. In

224

my trade we say that either the millstones fail to make contact and whirl too fast, or else they come too close together and one bears down too heavily on the other. That's the way it is between us."

"And what do you say when the stones are properly adjusted?"

"That the mill is clicking as it should."

"Then you must make things click between you!"

"I'll try, Reverend Mother, I'll do the best I can."

"You can learn from my example. I've always been aware of Princivalle Malvegoli's faults and yet until today I was quite unaware of Dosolina's virtues. That's how much easier it is for any of us to see his neighbor's bad points rather than the good. No, don't deny it; that's the way it goes. When she used to come pay me a visit as a child, with that lovely golden hair and those innocent eyes—I can see her before me this very minute—she would sit curled up in a corner without opening her mouth the whole time. I thought she was stubborn and contrary, what's called a spoiled child. I didn't realize that a sport of nature like this unwomanly ugliness of mine was enough to terrify anyone so young. Or perhaps"—she seemed to be talking more for her own benefit than for that of Scacerni—"deep down inside I did realize and—alas for my poor soul!—I resented it. And when she was a little older it was only natural that she should be annoyed, as I was, I must confess, by her father's vanity. That blessed man!—Do you know that I had to give him a good scolding for announcing his visit as that of 'the saint's family.' That makes you laugh, does it?"

Indeed, so comical was the old nun's mimicry of Princivalle that Scacerni had not been able to resist bursting into laughter.

"Well then, let me tell you as a final confession of human frailty that I never dreamed Dosolina loved me enough to look me up again, since after all I didn't love her on my side, either. And instead . . . Let it be a lesson to us to mind our own business and repent of our own sins. That way we may learn the meaning of Our Lord's parable of the Pharisee and the publican. You know it, I suppose."

"Forgive me, Reverend Mother, I am a very ignorant man."

"Never mind. Just ask your parish priest about it. The point is that we must forgive our neighbor not seven times, but seventy times seven, and even then, as it is in this case of mine, we may still be in the wrong. . . . And what news can you give me of that poor fellow whose head they chopped off this morning?"

Scacerni started, but he could not escape the compelling question in her eyes.

"He died like a good Christian," he answered with a sigh. "I wish I could be sure of the same sort of death for myself."

"May he rest in peace, in the name of the Father and of the Son and of the Holy Ghost! I knew it all along. This morning while I was at my prayers I could feel a soul taking wing toward heaven. I knew then that you would come to give me this news."

"I, Reverend Mother?"

"Yes, I was waiting for you."

225

Scacerni was taken aback and ill at ease. The old woman abandoned her visionary and prophetical attitude and gave a strange, harsh laugh, pulling her head in and out as if in a shell. Then she pointed a crooked finger at him and said:

"I know what you're thinking this very moment. This old hag is in a plot with my wife and they've staged a farce here in order to convert me. Well, I have no way of proving to you that you are mistaken and even if I had I shouldn't make use of it. The Holy Ghost didn't say to the apostles and martyrs: Go out and give demonstrations of the truth of what you say and of your own good characters. No, he merely told them to bear witness to their faith. But what am I saying? Here we have no apostles and martyrs and this is not meant for a sermon. Here we have a little old nun and a big, rough miller and neither one of them is a genius. If you don't believe me, so much the worse for you, my man! I don't want to cheat you at the game of buying and selling. When I speak the truth and know that I am speaking it then I am entirely satisfied. As for the rest, *transeat*, let it pass!"

She shrugged her shoulders and pursed her lips to illustrate her meaning. Scacerni was baffled and mortified.

"I wasn't aware of thinking any of these things, Reverend Mother, but if I did it was very foolish of me and I am ashamed."

Such a humble confession on the part of this taciturn, grizzly, powerfully built man, standing a little awkwardly on his unequal legs, to whom his rough country clothes and manner of speech lent a decidedly savage air, struck the nun as so incongruous that she laughed benevolently and said:

"You might just as well say that I put 'these things,' as you call them, into your head myself! Do you realize that you seem to have done nothing but mortify me ever since you came? That is very good for me," she concluded seriously, "it's the greatest gift you can make me, and I fear I have nothing to give you in return."

"A little peace of mind," said Scacerni with a long-restrained bitter sigh. "You can give me a little peace of mind. Listen to me, Reverend Mother, when Raguseo was killed . . ."

"My son, I am not your confessor."

"What does that matter? I have no confidence in what he told me. Whereas in you . . . The fact is that I have suffered greatly and I am still very unhappy."

"What is it that irks you?"

"The. . . I don't know."

"Speak up and you'll hear for yourself what a mistake you're making."

"It's the devil himself. . . ." said Scacerni in a low voice, looking at her as if he were not sure whether she would scorn or smile at what he was going to say. But she crossed herself and answered him with a seriousness that matched his:

"Come, come, you big, strong, stubborn man. Don't you know that

the devil is within these holy walls this very minute, that he is between the two of us, as we stand here, miserable sinners that we are?"

"Did I bring him in with me, is that what you mean?"

"Do you think he waited to come in with you? Don't you know
what great powers have been given him? Just let's reason again together, my friend. As long as we live and the trial of our souls endures
God permits the devil to tempt us. That's nothing very new, is it?
Didn't you know it before? God lets the devil go wherever he chooses,
into your soul and mine."

"Why so?"

"Why so? Are you really asking me? You really don't know?"

"No."

"Now I understand why I was waiting for you and what I can do to
help you. Your ignorance is such that even a child . . . But never
mind, it will be easy enough to teach you."

"I ask no more than to learn."

"Come, come, is that a dare? I really believe you're suffering from
forgetfulness rather than ignorance. Tell me, now, upon whom does
Our Lord visit the greatest tribulations? The answer's so easy that
you're ashamed to say. But just tell me, anyhow!"

"Upon those whom He loves most."

"And has he visited many tribulations upon you?"

"Upon me?" said Scacerni, bemused, as if he were going back over
a long chain of circumstances and suddenly understanding all of them.
"Oh, not enough for that!" he exclaimed.

"Leave the measurement of them to Him, my son! He knows better
than either of us, doesn't He? Haven't we both a great deal to thank
Him for? When you came here you thought that your troubles were
too much for you and now you find them too little. But His love for you
and me and all of us, there's something so great that we can never hope
to understand it. We can only praise Him and give Him thanks for
having embraced the Cross for our sake. Do you feel, here and now,
that we can thank Him?"

"How must we go about it?"

"Nothing is easier and at the same time more difficult. Think it over
and don't answer me lightly."

Scacerni meditated for a moment and then raised his eyes to those
of the holy nun, who was waiting patiently, with her arms crossed over
her breast.

"Yes, we can thank Him," he said.

"Well then, it's as if He were thanked already. Come, come, was it
so very difficult?" she added jokingly.

"You know whose is the merit, Reverend Mother."

"Let us say rather that the smaller our merit, the greater is divine
grace. But I have no right to keep you here any longer. Tell Dosolina
that I shall most assuredly remember your little son in my prayers and
that she must find a way to come see me before I die. And now, Master

227

Lazzaro, farewell. When trials and tribulations beset you, never say, It's too much, or, It's too little. Put yourself in God's hands and give Him thanks."

"Farewell, Reverend Mother."

This was the end of Lazzaro's visit to the saint. He might well have said, after he got back home, that she had said nothing he had not been told as a child. Yet somehow it had all seemed fresh and new. He faithfully reported her message to Dosolina, and Dosolina thanked him without observing that, in spite of what he had said, he had gone to Ferrara.

The painting on the cabins of the mill was all cracked and faded, including the Saint Michael and the dragon. Master Lazzaro did not wish to invest in a new job so he merely replaced the old mottoes with a new one, which was very common along the Po, but seemed to him to summarize a long story of vicissitudes. The words were simply: "God save you, Saint Michael's Mill!"

THE "LIBERTINES'" REVOLUTION

1

WHEN WE EMERGE from a period of storm and stress, the rumble of thunder is still in our ears and the flashes of lightning on the distant horizon dazzle and dim our memory to the point where, for a time, we may think it is irretrievably lost.

Thus it was that Lazzaro Scacerni, after groping in persistent and awestruck fashion to retrace the course of his varied fortunes, was on the point of giving up the effort to remember. The words of the saintly old nun, while helping him to recover his peace of mind, had at the same time impelled him to give up trying to understand, and to forget all that was past. But where Lazzaro's reasoning was weak his feelings and sensibilities were strong and this solution did not content him. In this predicament, with reason powerless to help him and memory apparently on the point of abandoning him forever, his luck seemed to him more mysterious than ever. When he had been beyond the succor of himself or others Providence had intervened in his favor. But why? In asking himself this question he was aware that divine grace cannot be bought, but his own good works were few and he thought with perverse pride that he was not the man to accept an unearned gift. During the long hours he spent over the white flour of the wheat and the yellow meal of the corn the thought of how God had saved him rose up in his mind again and again, and always he asked himself: "Why?"

Somehow, of course, he vaguely understood that an act of grace was the only answer. After the deaths of Raguseo and Big Brother fate seemed to have sent him a period of calm, like that which usually follows after a storm, when man seems to have obtained a breathing space from nature and his fellow men. In these days, then, Lazzaro Scacerni stepped out freely, with his unassuming confidence in himself regained. One thing was clear in his mind, that God had saved him from crime and despair and the fulfillment of a pact sealed in blood, when all the time he himself had done everything he could to lose his soul.

The disappearance of the unfortunate Beffa, the violent death of Raguseo, and the edifying end of Big Brother had lightened the atmosphere of Guarda and many other places along the Po, where their tyranny had been oppressive. Secret alliances and understandings among knaves of every description and the shameless demands they had made upon the populace suddenly slackened and timorous souls dared to breathe again. Raguseo had been an important backer of criminal enterprises and Big Brother a ruthless executor of his wishes, and their disappearance did much to bring about this relief. But there was another and more generic cause for it as well, namely, the softened character of the whole business of smuggling. The Papal government continued quite futilely to multiply customs duties, monopolies, concessions and barriers to free trade, which gave annoyance to honest men without endangering the commerce of thieves. As a result smuggling turned into the most frequent form of commerce, the only one, in fact, and the most perfectly regulated. As one historian has it, this trade "was sanctioned even by theologians" and had its own "banks, officers, insurance agencies, accountants, shippers, and an organised militia, with officers, guides and escorts for a shipment going in any direction." Because they enjoyed this semilegal status the smugglers had become milder in their ways and in order to make honest gains they let up their practice of blackmail and extortion. At the same time bandits and highwaymen underwent a like transformation and came to exercise a protective patrol of the roads and fields. Boatmen were no longer forced at pistol point to transport men and goods across the Po but were hired and paid in conventional fashion, and there was no more need to store contraband merchandise in Master Lazzaro's mill. If his "friends" of times gone by met him riding along the path between his house and the river or saw him on the deck from a passing boat they would hail him respectfully or else give him a wide berth and go quickly by. Even Beffa's disreputable companions, whom Schiavetto recognized one day as he had before, now affected an entirely different demeanor. Scacerni was puzzled by this new turn of things and in his search for an explanation he called out one day to a veteran smuggler who he knew had been an intimate of Big Brother.

"How does it happen that I haven't seen you for so long, Bones?" he asked him.

"Ah, well!" answered the smuggler with an embarrassed but mellifluous smile, drawing his boat up alongside the mill.

"What do you mean by 'ah, well'?" Scacerni insisted.

"Well, well . . ."

"Is that any answer?"

"It's as good as any other!"

"Then you'll have to enlighten me, because I fail to understand."

"Are you joking, Master Lazzaro? Surely I needn't enlighten a man who's just recently showed talent of such a very particular kind!"

"How's that? What sort of talent do you mean? Are your brains addled this morning, Bones?"

Scacerni was sitting on the bow of the smaller hulk of the mill and Bones was standing up in his boat, grasping the nearest cleat in one hand. This brought them face to face and eye to eye, which was closer than either of them actually wanted to be, but there they were and so they continued talking.

"Are my brains addled, did you ask, Master Lazzaro? Now you're joking, for sure! But go ahead and joke, if you like, and if you have any serious orders to give me, bear in mind that I'm the man to serve you. That's something I've wanted to tell you for some time."

"Thank you," said Scacerni, looking at him intently to see if he could discover the hidden meaning of these words. "But I'm sure I don't know what I could order you to do."

"That's no concern of mine," said the smuggler. "I just wanted to tell you, that's all. And you can count on the rest of us as your 'friends' too."

"Haven't you, rather, something to ask of me?"

"We? Our needs are such trifles that we shouldn't dare bother a man of your caliber with them."

Scacerni looked at him askance, but the fellow was not joking.

"Forgive the liberty, Master Lazzaro, but that was a masterly stroke of yours to net a big fish like Raguseo and a tadpole like Beffa, not to mention that brute of a Big Brother, all together! We've talked of nothing else, you know! What really astounds us is that Big Brother should have kept his mouth shut, or if he did talk, that nothing should have come out about it. You must have very long arms indeed, Master Lazzaro, to stop the law in its tracks! But that's not the half of it! To silence a man with the knife hanging over his head and nothing to lose by talking, that goes to show that the devil himself must have been at your elbow!"

He spoke with such patent admiration that Scacerni did not even try to contradict him. What others might think or say did not worry him, especially when his own conscience spoke to him so loudly. The saving of Dosolina's life and of Saint Michael's Mill had been almost routine examples of divine grace. But mercy had been showered on his own person after he had first sought to elude it and then abused and profaned it with cavilling that was more sinful than even an act of outright violence. Looking back at how perdition had first crept into his soul on that long ago night after the fording of the Vop River and how it had blandly and insidiously taken possession of him and led him to the brink of murderous rage and suicidal despair, he was more and more humbly convinced that mercy and mercy alone had been his salvation. In this new frame of mind he fell to his knees and sincerely repented his former rebelliousness. He had learned from the catechism that no good work is worthy of even the slightest visitation of divine mercy and now he saw that God had indeed acted toward him like a vigilant father holding out a hand to a wayward son. Thus was his memory, which had for a time been dulled with pain, restored to him. The calm which he was now enjoying seemed to him the crowning gift of all, the one which had finally opened his eyes to the truth, and his gratitude expressed itself in the invocation: "God save Saint Michael's Mill!" Now he could go back to his millstones, for after all he was a miller, and that which he had found at the bottom of his soul needed no further expression. By redeeming Big Brother on the eve of his execution God had released them both from the pact of blood they had sealed together.

And so the years went by, one after the other, on the mill, prosperous years, which increased Dosolina's savings and the number of Lazzaro's ailments. In his case as in many others, a robust and vigorous body was no bulwark against the onslaught of time, and besides he had the poison of malaria in his blood. When he felt an attack of tertian fever coming over him he no longer said that although it might kill off an old man it would rejuvenate a young one. And he had given up the idea of building another mill.

"If I were to leave you, good Mistress," he said to Dosolina, whom he addressed in an increasingly respectful manner, "if I were to leave you before little Giuseppe is of age, you'd make a better living off the land than the water. No woman can be expected to handle a mill."

He said this so often that finally Dosolina's feelings were hurt and she struck back at him.

"What if I took a notion to marry again?" she said provokingly. "I might marry another miller and he would give me a hand!"

"Very well," said Scacerni, between clenched teeth. "If that's your good pleasure there's nothing I can say."

"Don't take it so hard, Lazzaro! After all, you put me up to saying it yourself!"

"I've had to take a good bit from you, it seems to me! Isn't it rather strange that you should say something like that to my face?"

"But why do you always talk about leaving me, when you know it makes me sad?"

"Don't you think it makes me sad to be growing old as I am?"

"But you talk as if it were all my fault."

"I never said that, did I?"

"Oh, there are ways of expressing things without words, you know."

The slender and delicate Dosolina had filled out and acquired a rosy complexion and an outspoken and decisive manner. She was a fine figure of woman, aware of the fact that she had reached the best, and, alas, all-too-fleeting years of her life. Now it was at an accelerated pace that every passing season accentuated the difference of age between husband and wife. But if, on the one hand, this inclined Lazzaro to jealousy, on the other it made him aware of his obligation to provide so well for Dosolina that she would have no cause for complaint against him. Dosolina, for her part, was annoyed to hear any mention of this discrepancy between them and then ashamed of her own feeling of annoyance, although deep down inside she was as aware of it as anyone else. There were times when she woke up with an aching head and hot flashes and a languorous feeling, all of which were quite clearly connected with dreams of love-making. All day long she kept herself so hard at work that she had no time for letting her imagination run riot, but night found her prey to a restlessness which no amount of tossing in her bed could cure. She was unfailingly kind and attentive, but it required considerable patience to minister to her husband's rheumatism and fever and to take care of him as if he were a semi-invalid when she was so palpitatingly aware of being in her prime. What was it that the late lamented host of the tavern at Guarda had once said about crabbed age and youth? No, no, not yet! Lazzaro thought to himself. And may God forgive the tavern keeper his untimely jokes now that he's under the sod! And this thought led to another, which was even more troublesome, especially now that other old friends from Guarda were embarking in increasing numbers on their last voyage, the thought of the water that was gradually seeping into the cemetery, just behind the river embankment. After all the humidity in which he had lived on the mill he had an unreasonable wish to be high and dry when he was dead. How remote was this morbid preoccupation from the pungent desires which paradoxically enflamed his wife when she saw him in the midst of his afflictions!

Dosolina found some outlet for her feelings in a jealousy of her own, in which she indulged with a lack of restraint that was surprising for one habitually so close-mouthed and prudent. Because Venusta scorned her curiosity she sought out Chiccoli in his shop and questioned him. And the old cobbler was only too delighted to pull up his stool beside so shapely a woman, to ogle at her and inflame her imagination with his scabrous stories. With gluttonous pleasure he listed Scacerni's former conquests and his own, and described their charms, excusing the mention of so many details on the ground that everything he was telling had long since been over. He added that all these beauties had now faded, while hers still dazzled the eyes of Scacerni, the lucky fellow! At this point he stopped short and looked up at her from his stool with a gleam in his eyes that brought her back to a realization of what she owed to her own dignity. But it irritated her, thereafter, to hear Venusta and all her other friends and acquaintances lift their voices in a chorus of praise for the reformed and irreproachable miller, whose mended ways made him a model husband.

She pretended to make light of it all and laughingly to deny that there was such a great difference between the lady-killer of yore and her staid and respectable spouse. And the good neighbors would add fuel to the fire by exaggerating his youthful exploits and punctuating their stories with understanding nods and smiles that gave them an even more salacious turn than was strictly in accord with the truth. Dosolina was touched to the quick and felt a strong physical spite or resentment, as if these unknown and superannuated rivals had cheated her of the flower of her husband's vigor. Scacerni was at first surprised by this reaction, but he soon found it flattering to his self-esteem that Dosolina should have reason to be jealous of his past, since the present afforded her no motive at all for admiring his amorous prowess. He might have been less smug about it had he realized that her apparent jealousy was only envy in disguise.

They had both hoped to have more children, but this hope was deceived as the years went by. Dosolina brought up Giuseppe with tireless devotion and, as we already know, she managed her household

233

affairs with praiseworthy efficiency. Lazzaro put all his savings into gradually increasing the area of his land. He enlarged his pigsty and chicken coops and began looking ahead to a still more considerable enterprise, the purchase of some cattle. This meant building a barn with an ample hayloft, providing fields for grazing and the place for a dunghill, and finally engaging a cowherd and finding quarters for him to live in. All this Scacerni proceeded cautiously to do. He hired by the day a fellow nicknamed Hayseed, half peasant, half gardener, who rented a small house, or rather cabin, on Scacerni's farm. Not that Scacerni ever referred to it as anything more pretentious than his "bit of land," for he had a healthy superstition that it was tempting fate to brag about one's dearest possessions. Hayseed was married to an ugly but industrious woman known, because of a pun on her husband's name, as Haysack. Dosolina, always kind and unhurried, ruled wisely over her little barnyard world and Lazzaro looked on indulgently at the work in the fields, for which he had no taste whatsoever.

"The mill is my farm," he would say. And then, harking back to the pride he had always taken in his freedom, "I'm a river man, after all!" he added.

There was an open space in front of the house where boys and girls from neighboring farms came to husk the corn, to exchange the amorous quips and rhymes that were traditional on such an occasion and, when the work was over, to dance until dawn of the following day. Scacerni and some of his cronies looked on from a bench on the sidelines while in the house Dosolina poured the wine. Before corn-husking time Hayseed had threshed the wheat, only a few bags of it, but all their own. And then one day both wheat and corn were taken to Saint Michael's Mill.

"Today the miller is working for his wife," Scacerni said proudly.

"Ah no!" Dosolina retorted jokingly. "You millers are all rascals! I want a written statement of the weight, so that you won't take too much of a toll from me!"

"Today the toll is your approval of this old man, Dosolina!"

Under his heavy beard Scacerni blushed like a boy when he came out with this gallantry, while Schiavetto, now a blooming young man, and Malvasone, who was getting on in years, applauded. The evening celebrations that followed the days of threshing and husking usually included a good dinner served up to the miller's friends, with Chiccoli and his wife the first among them, and all those who worked either on the farm or the mill. Later on, to provide music for the dancing, Schiavetto played the accordion, with a harp and a violin to accompany him.

Soon after this, the heat of the dog-days was over.

> *With the first August rain*
> *I love my poor husband again.*

Then came September, and it was time to call the cooper to examine and repair the barrels for holding the season's wine. And October meant, as the rhyme had it, that

Now the heat no more is found,
Pick the apples off the ground.

Toward the end of November came the pork butcher from Fossa-samba, who had no peer in the art of castrating, slaughtering and bleeding hogs, and turning them into sausage and salt meat. He announced his arrival by singing:

Catch your hog by the foot for Saint Andrew's Day,
Here is the butcher come your way!

The feast of Saint Andrew was the last day of November, but if the mistress of the house for some reason wanted to fatten her hogs further he had another verse ready:

If you will not catch him now,
Until Christmas let him grow.

His song had something of a spell or incantation about it and never failed to pull at Dosolina's heartstrings. To her as to many another housewife, no other domestic animal endeared itself as much as the homely hog and she could not check the flow of her tears when the vein in his neck was severed and he bled piteously to death. Wallowing and grunting in the mud of his sty, the pig seemed so happy to be alive that it struck her as a crime to kill him. But regardless of her pity, sooner or later sausages were strung up over the hood of the fireplace to absorb the heat and smoke, while bacon and hams hung from the beams of the ceiling and jars of pure white lard were stored in the cellar. Soon enough, when Christmas was over, came the feast of Saint Anthony, patron of millers and protector from fire and flood.

Hayseed had some notions of wine-making and every autumn Dosolina had him tread a small mountain of local grapes which she put up in kegs and barrels and brought to various stages of fermentation. But Scacerni, while he appreciated her laudable motives, held that the place to enjoy a bottle of good wine was the tavern. His wife's vintages he accused of being tasteless or musty or having a flavor of sulphur or of the barrel about them. Every year he resisted her attempts to overcome this prejudice.

"You know how to do so many things, good Mistress," he told her, "that you mustn't complain if there's one you can't do. Look at me: I have to content myself with being only a miller!"

Deep down in his heart he was resentful of anything that curtailed the full enjoyment of his freedom, the proud and independent existence that was his on the mill. He became more and more attached to it as time went on and justified his distaste for inland life with the old superstition: "Build a house and soon death will come to call." He wasn't really afraid, but every now and then the four walls of the house gave him a feeling of being shut in and tied down. At times like these this superstition came back to haunt him, along with an unexpected nostalgia for the faraway places whose names he had long since forgotten, which he had known in his youth. He wondered what had become of the Russian girl, Lisaveta, whom he had abandoned at the ends of the earth, in Ducóvchina, and longed to go to lands such as America that he had never seen. Or he thought of the valleys and swamps near the mouth of the Po, the forest of Mesola and the Adriatic Sea. And yet none of these things, even the nearest, did he actually wish to see with sufficient intensity to go see them. Only whenever he had a feeling of being stifled and shut in it occurred to him that death would be freer and airier and weigh upon him less oppressively amid the lonely wilds where he had lived before.

He laughed, remembering how the old rogue Raguseo had confessed to yearning for the seas he had sailed as a pirate when he was young. Now he could understand him, the old madman! Who was really the madder—Raguseo, God preserve his soul!—or himself? To this question there was no answer.

Dosolina had taken to spouting bits of wisdom. She had a proverb to fit every event or occasion, every change in the weather, every month and season of the year. Frankly, this was rather a bore, especially as she was always right, and if one proverb was out of place she had another ready to make up for her mistake, or at least to prove that every rule had its exceptions. She had become a counsellor and peacemaker and arbiter of quarrels and conflicting interests in Guarda and its surroundings. Because her good offices were not always requested such intervention often antagonized one or both parties to a dispute. Then she would quote in her own defense:

"Advice is ill spoken only when it is misunderstood."

"Far better say nothing," Scacerni grumbled, "and avoid all risk of misunderstanding."

"Why so?"

"Because if a man can understand a piece of advice then it means that he can see the point of it for himself without being told."

"Forgive me, Lazzaro, but what you are saying is very stupid."

"Then you were right in the first place: I've wasted my time giving you a piece of advice and you've misunderstood it."

"Are you calling me a goose?"

"You see, I was right, after all, when I said that it was better to say nothing!"

Venusta usually took Dosolina's side, just to aggravate Scacerni, and Chiccoli, on general principle, did the same. Dosolina knew a long stream of riddles, rhymes and conundrums with which she had entertained Giuseppe as a baby and put him to sleep. They were amusing to hear once or twice, but when it came to the tenth time or the hundredth! . . . Giuseppe, now a grown boy, was vastly bored.

"What travels taking its own house with it?"

Was it possible that once upon time he had not known enough to answer: *"A snail."* And there was one about the snow:

"I am high as a house; fair until I am dirtied; I fall to the ground without bruising myself and everyone treads me down."

236

"*She sells sea-shells by the seashore,*" the boy would say, twisting his tongue over the sentence or pretending to do so in order to please his mother.

Dosolina's stories were amusing enough, but they were marred by constant repetition. And her rhymes were endless:

> *As my rhyme begins it ends:*
> *Relatives cannot be friends:*
> *Friends cannot be relatives:*
> *The soil is fertile where wheat lives:*
> *Fertile soil makes wheat increase:*
> *War is not the same as peace . . .*

And so on, almost indefinitely. Nothing of any importance, but Master Lazzaro was annoyed with himself for feeling bored and tried to find some less trivial reason for his impatience. Little Giuseppe, who hung constantly at his mother's apron strings, seemed to him to have the makings of a hypocritical and disagreeable man. There was no affinity between himself and his son, who was short and bandy-legged, lazy, timid, bad-tempered, and ill disposed toward the river, the mill and everything else that interested his father. The boy's only sport was to lay traps baited with corn meal in the winter snow with which to catch hungry sparrows.

In order to train him to something better Scacerni took him out duck-shooting in his boat, but the gunfire paralyzed the boy with fright and the cold early morning air gave him a cold in his chest. One day he tied two hollow pumpkins to Giuseppe's shoulders and tried to teach him to swim. When the boy kicked and protested he was so aghast at having a coward for a son that he struck him across the face and threw him, along with the pumpkins, into the river. If Schiavetto hadn't had the presence of mind to plunge after him Giuseppe would surely have drowned, for he had started to drift downstream with his legs in the air and his head under water. When he was taken aboard the mill he showed no desire to learn the trade, but hung back sullenly in one corner until his father swore at him and sent him home with a kick whose force was in no way impaired by the fact that it was given by his lame leg.

"He's sullen only with you," said Dosolina, who could not help feeling distressed, even if she recognized the necessity of bringing up the boy to give a good account of himself.

"Do you mean that with you he never acts that way?"

"No, not with me."

And there was a defiant expression in her eyes like that of a setting hen. The silent and sullen Giuseppe was always underfoot, asking her for fruit or sweets and suffering from either indigestion or diarrhea because she had not the heart to refuse him. Ever since he had an attack of convulsions she had lived in mortal terror that he might be an epileptic, although she knew that in reality he had nothing worse than worms. Her nervousness increased as he grew up and was more often out of her sight. She was afraid of illness and accidents, of fire, water, and animals of every kind. What frightened her most of all were the periodical visits of gypsies. As soon as she heard that one of their wagons was coming through the village, while the men mended copper pots and pans and the women told fortunes, she would run wildly after Giuseppe and shut him up in his room until the danger of kidnapping was over.

"What would they do with such a useless fellow?" Lazzaro asked her.

This was no way to talk to a mother. But in Lazzaro's opinion a man was either a miller or a good-for-nothing.

The boy had only one passion, and that was for knowing how much things cost and for buying and selling. Nothing interested him unless it could be turned to profit. From this point of view he showed curiosity enough about the products of both his mother's fields and his father's mill and an astonishing memory for figures and accounts.

"I'd like to know where he gets that," said Scacerni, laughing at this precocious stinginess.

It was a strange thing to see Giuseppe with his grandfather, who found in him the only audience for his extravagant plans for making money. The boy's eyes opened wide and he listened with rapt attention.

"Have you the cash, Grandfather?" he would ask.

"Oh, that's easy enough to find."

"Easy to find?"

"It's always easy to find cash if you have an idea."

"Just an idea? Is it really so easy?"

On the boy's narrow, colorless face were written childish disappointment and prematurely adult scorn for the old man's glib promises. And yet he never failed to listen eagerly every time that Princivalle, who had made peace with his son-in-law, came with his head full of new fancies to make a call at Poplar Bridge.

One day, not long after Big Brother's execution, Princivalle dropped a remark to the effect that he had suffered a personal loss in the death of Raguseo.

"What? You?" gasped Lazzaro.

"Yes. He may have been a bandit of the first water, for all I know, but he had brains and refinement. He was open-minded and farsighted, that much I can tell you! In this country of mossbacks he was the first and only man to understand me. The rest of them are spineless and spiritless creatures, reactionary Sanfedisti, every last one of them."

Princivalle knew how to read, and having moved in upon his oldest son, who had a house in the city, he had taken to newspapers of every kind, and even books. He tried to scrape acquaintance with educated men and notables and the slightest nod from a distant acquaintance was enough to persuade him to sit down at a table in the Tasso or Pacini Cafés. Then if the waiter importuned him for an order he would save his face by saying: "I'm with this gentleman."

Using the same tactics he pushed his way into various gatherings and acquired a number of half-digested ideas which he passed on with an air of great importance to the countrymen who came every Monday to the city market. Thanks to his kind son and daughter-in-law he had bought himself new clothes and wore a top hat of the kind considered at the time most respectable. Donata, with her other sons and Argia, her one remaining daughter, had stayed in the Palazzo Diamantina, where the shop, together with the work the boys did in the fields, gave her enough food to live on. Princivalle's trouble, according to his own story, was that his family did him injustice; even now they chose to plow fields, tend stables and dig ditches rather than follow his rising star in the city. Donata had told him off properly when he went away, indeed she had put him out of the house so unceremoniously that on the rare occasions when husband and wife met in their son's house in Ferrara they exchanged no more than a cold how-do-you-do and goodbye.

The name of Malvegoli still aroused a certain respect and facilitated Princivalle's frequentation of society, although he did not go so far as to claim any title of nobility or even a cousinship with Mother Eurosia, who had died, in an odor of sanctity, not long before. If Princivalle concealed these connections it was because he was now convinced that he could make his way on his own merits. He had struck up a democratic pose, inspired by his reading of forbidden, that is, Liberal and progressive literature of the kind cultivated by the Carbonari.

In all the Papal territory, and particularly in Ferrara and other cities of the Romagna region, those who held varying shades of radical opinion, and even many moderate constitutionalists and good Catholics, were led by their opposition to the clerical government into a strong distaste for the clergy in general. All this was because the Church had interfered with politics and priests were instruments of censorship and repression, a state of affairs which was repugnant to the general conscience and a profanation of the Church's holy mission. Not only the princes of the Church but even the humblest parish priests turned into tyrants of the confessional and branded any hint of opposition to the government a sin. Under a theocratic rule this was to some degree inevitable, but the clash was made more painful by the fact that philosophic thought had taken great strides ahead and reforms and revolutions had changed the face of Europe, leaving the spirit of the Papal government more backward and hence more narrow and suspicious than ever. The government was in an inescapable predicament: by severity it aroused hate and by indulgence scorn. "Better be ruled by Turks than by priests," as a notorious popular saying had it. One thing, however, this weak and despised government had to its credit and that was the soft-spoken tenacity with which in 1815, 1821, 1831 and 1848 it held the line of the Po. If the Austrians failed to conquer or hold Italy entirely in these years it was undoubtedly because of the unconquerable passive resistance of the Papal State.

During the brief month of life enjoyed by the provisory Liberal government of 1831, who should put in an appearance but Giovan Battista Boldrini, whom we last met as the terror of convents at the period of the trees of liberty, along with other Jacobins and admirers of Napoleon who were still to be found in military and other official capacities. Together with the Carbonari they included the members of diverse strange, small, religious or anti-religious sects so variegated and unpredictable that they were given, without offense, the name of "Libertines" rather than Liberals.

Among these were many youths of noble or upper middle-class families who held conspiratorial meetings in houses known to have Liberal sympathies, where in some cases, however, a disapproving elderly father reported them to the police. Other favorite meeting places were the *Casino dei Nobili* and the shop of a fashionable dressmaker called La Bendani. The conspirators were for the most part inspired by hotheadedness, a craving for adventure, and an unsatisfied love of a roving or military career. They were restless and devil-may-care, with a touch of cynical gloom and satanism, in the tradition already known from its great prototype as Byronic. One of these youths, indeed, was nicknamed by his friends and admirers for one of Byron's poems, the "Giaour."

Because many of the high-class conspirators were great horsemen they patronized Princivalle's son, the saddle maker, who had won a solid reputation in his trade. But Princivalle went out of his way to avoid being known as a saddle maker's father. He preferred to wait upon the waves and nods of such noblemen as remembered his antecedents, and when the leaders of the revolutionary movement snubbed him he had recourse to the feckless lawyers and wastrels who, together with a large number of spies, filled the Tasso and Pacini Cafés with their chatter. It was from the abundance of such as they that the uprising of 1831 was called not only the Libertines' but also the Lawyers' Revolution. In another and less pretentious conspiratorial gathering place, the Pellegrino Tavern, Princivalle held forth with half a dozen commonplace slogans and a world of mysterious, unfinished sentences as an authority on matters political. However, at the least impulse to get up a game of cards or billiards, his open-mouthed audience would desert him.

This explains how it came about that Princivalle Malvegoli brought news to a village like Guarda of the state of terrestrial progress and of untrammelled human thought, both of which were closely connected in his conversation with the development of his own pet projects. He proposed to erect a kiln in a locality where the earth could not possibly be made into bricks or tiles; a granary at Lagoscuro, where every other building was already a warehouse; and a hydraulic mill for weaving hemp on a dried-up or frequently flooded stream. Still more extravagantly he raved of a fleet of steamboats navigating on the Po, of steam-operated pumps for firemen, and of an irrigation project based on artesian wells and windmills in a valley where there was no wind and plenty of water. He was always wanting to sell unheard-of and unnecessary objects of every kind, and in order to facilitate their sale he suggested levying taxes on rival products of proved usefulness. Whenever he picked up a description or picture in some stray newspaper or magazine from England, France, Germany or America of a new artistic or scientific invention he had an urge to introduce its benefits to the region of his native Ferrara. From publications of this kind he had also picked up the notion of stock companies, which required no capital to start with because a few sheets of printed paper brought capital running. The undigested and incoherent ideas which he derived from this miscellaneous reading led him to reduce all political and social systems to the same fundamental and imperative postulate: how to spend money without having it.

To have an idea, that was the main thing, as he so often told his grandson. And, after all, it is quite likely that some of his ideas really deserved success instead of the recurrent bad luck by which they were hounded.

Meanwhile, he had revealed to his son-in-law the fact that he had known Raguseo.

"If he hadn't been killed, I had in mind a stupendous plan which I meant to submit to his approval."

"What was that?"

"A mill run by steam."

"By steam?"

"Exactly. They have them in England and France and in some parts of Italy already."

"Look here, I haven't the vaguest notion of what you're talking about, but it sounds as if you wanted to run our water mills out of existence!"

"That's what you backward people are always saying!"

"I don't know what you mean by 'backward' people either! But tell me this: did Raguseo lend you any money?"

Princivalle hesitated a moment between truth and falsehood before he opted for the latter.

"He was ready to give me some, that's all."

"You're better off if he didn't."

"Tell me, since you speak of Raguseo in such a positive manner: did you know him or know who he was?"

Now it was Scacerni's turn reluctantly to tell a lie.

"I didn't know him personally, but like everyone else I knew who he was."

"Then you only knew a lot of common gossip!" Malvegoli exclaimed with a self-satisfied air that annoyed his son-in-law vastly.

"So Raguseo's heirs haven't any signature of yours on a promissory note?" he asked roughly.

"I didn't know he had any heirs," said Malvegoli evasively.

"Excuse me, but I asked whether you signed any papers for his benefit."

"I'm not obliged to answer you, am I? You're not a judge, are you? Or the executor of his will, either!"

Scacerni was on the point of asking his father-in-law whether or not, since he was after all an honest man, his conscience would allow him to keep silent about the money which he obviously owed Raguseo. But it would have been unwise for him to show too much interest in the old pirate's affairs. Irritated because he could not have the last word he felt his own conscience prick him and wound up by saying:

"Right you are. All I can say is that here on the river Raguseo had a bad name. That's why I said that the less you had to do with him the better."

Princivalle was overtaken by a sudden vague fear of having got himself into trouble and would have liked to ask more questions. But discretion bid him to maintain his reserve. He remembered how Dosolina always said to his rash plans:

"Start out slow if you've far to go."

This proverb was typical of a region traversed by numberless rivers and canals, where people were wont to travel by water rather than by land, with a mule and a tow rope to pull their boats along.

3

Donata Malvegoli's earthly days came to a sudden end one morning when she had gone to a canal near the Palazzo Diamantina to do a heavy week's wash. Before going out she had murmured something about feeling the accumulated weariness of years upon her. She had told her daughter Argia to attend to the shop and not to waste time in idle talk with any customers who chanced to come by.

"I shan't always be here with you, my girl, and you must learn to take care of yourself. You can't imagine the number of snares and delusions there are around us. One word leads to another, soon the word is a wink, and then before you know it you're done for. It's the old story of the moth and the flame. And that means dishonor in this world and damnation in the next."

But it was a sign of Donata's approaching end that she was too tired to put much spirit into this often-repeated warning. She had a premonition that this youngest daughter, who received her words with downcast eyes and apparent submissiveness, was laughing to herself and turning the dire picture which had been laid before her into food for her precocious sensual curiosity. Every time the old woman had one of her increasingly frequent dizzy spells, she was torn between reluctance to leave her defenseless daughter alone in the wicked world and a wish to die before suffering too much disappointment from her future behavior. For it was written for all to see that Argia was her own worst enemy. In her bewilderment Donata did not know to whom to turn, for if she voiced her worry to Dosolina the latter would have had every right to say that, at least in her case, her mother's fears had turned out to be groundless and indeed ridiculous. She had reproached the young Dosolina for talking back to her and so it was hardly logical that Argia's humility should be a cause for alarm.

"Yes, mother," Argia always answered, looking demurely at the ground, "you're quite right." Perhaps Donata credited Argia with more irony than she really possessed, but the girl's invariable: "Yes, mother, I'll be careful," got on her nerves. She was glad that her boys were growing up accustomed to honest work, even if they seemed likely to turn into rough country fellows whose manners and tastes were utterly lacking in refinement. But once she, Donata, was dead, there was little chance of Argia's staying with her brothers. She was not a bad girl and no one could say that she wished for her mother's death, but it was plain that she was anxious to leave the Palazzo Diamantina. As soon as her mother would be buried she would be off to that abode of iniquity, Ferrara. Argia had a physical resemblance to her father and ever since childhood she had hung upon his idle chatter. When she was a child the effect his stories had upon her imagination was visible in the heightened color of her cheeks. Now her face no longer betrayed her emotion, for she was adept at dissimulation. But when she said, "We Malvegolis," or made some other reference to the family, her voice and manner were identical to those of Princivalle.

"That ill-fated family of theirs, as usual!" Donata exclaimed to herself as she dragged her way along with the wash.

But whereas Princivalle's capital consisted only of windy words Argia had something substantial to offer. It was sufficient to see how she looked at the men and they looked back at her, while she received their looks with an innocent air that only attracted them the more strongly. Once she would have lost her mother, put her affected modesty behind her and gone to join her father in the city, there was no telling what would happen. O misbegotten race of Malvegolis, created to make Donata miserable!

Muttering under her breath Donata perspired and panted along beneath the burden of her years and the sack of wash over her shoulder. The sun blinded her eyes and beat down upon her neck, and the air was heavy with heat and humidity. The path ran parallel to the canal, between two stretches of marsh, without a single shade tree to relieve it. All around there were only reeds, apparently dry, but rotted away underneath by stagnant water, and twisted, writhing stalks of vegetation whose contorted shapes seemed to express an enmity to man. In the distance were the tall poplars along the road leading to the Palazzo Diamantina and even farther away areas of woodland whose cool shadows were like a mirage created before her tired eyes by a mind that was addled by the relentless glare of the sun.

Donata went down the bank toward the narrow, sluggish canal, wiped the perspiration off her face, and knelt on the slippery board from which she habitually did her washing. The water in the canal was muddy and tepid on her hands and arms when she immersed them. Not very far away a group of ducks were swimming slowly along dipping their beaks into the mud in search of something to eat.

As she leaned over under the blazing sun the blood ran up into her head. She had a distinct feeling that if a dizzy spell came over her now she would never get up again and she commended her soul to Almighty God, suddenly gladdened by the assurance that His arms would open wide to receive the soul of a weary old mother.

Before her eyes the ribbon of water stretched out, endlessly dazzling, and seemed for a moment like the road to heaven. Then the world seemed to turn over. Before she had time to feel fear or pain old Donata slipped on the slimy board head first into the muddy water. She fell so discreetly that not even the timid ducks were disturbed, and about her death there was nothing ugly or offensive. When they found her body it was swathed in her heavy peasant skirt, and had it not been that her head was under water they would have thought that she was sleeping.

Princivalle Malvegoli made a great to-do about his misfortune, which he attributed to everyone's fault but his own. Dosolina's affliction was deep and lasting, but stoical. As for Argia she had an outburst of almost hysterical sorrow, but lost little time in moving into the house of her brother, the saddle maker, in Ferrara, where her father was also living. The general public, as ever inclined to pass hasty judgments upon matters of which it was totally uninformed, showed equal surprise at Dosolina's reticence and Argia's extravagant sorrow. A fortnight had hardly gone by when Argia began to quarrel over trifles with her sister-in-law and six months later she set up housekeeping on her own account with her father for a lodger.

Argia was possessed of what can only be described as a stupendous animal beauty. Like Dosolina she was blonde, but her hair had copper reflections and her eyes were large and black, soulless, but gleaming with passion and vivacity. It was evident from looking into them exactly what their promise, and equally evident that the promise would be maintained abundantly. Having, then, set up her own establishment she found it easy enough to persuade Princivalle that as his daughter she must dress in the latest metropolitan style (the black of her mourning clothes was for the moment extremely becoming) and wear hats that would distinguish her from her working-class sister-in-law. As she swished along at her father's side with lowered eyes and alert ears, in a graceful and somewhat provocatory manner, along the Giovecca, under the arcade of the theater, across the Piazza Grande and by the Archbishop's Palace, during the hour when fashionable people came out to promenade, she was the object of considerable attention and comment.

"Where on earth did such a beauty come from?" the young blades asked one another, unable to believe the rumors about her rustic origin.

Argia had a high waist, long legs, and exquisitely small feet, and walked with an agile step, slightly swaying her firm, rounded hips and shoulders, which harmonized with a slender neck and a not yet fully developed but already alluring bosom. Another striking element of

244

her charm was the contrast between her blonde hair and brunette complexion, with the warm tint of its olive pallor. Everywhere Argia went she left a ripple of interest behind her and the very timidity of her earliest appearances and the simplicity of her black dress aroused first the curiosity and then the desires of a whole circle of wealthy rakes, each one of whom was intent upon winning the first taste of what it was generally agreed would be a royal mouthful.

The saddle maker's customers, who heretofore had never deigned to notice Princivalle Malvegoli, now went out of their way to greet him. And Princivalle fatuously imagined that he had at last won the esteem he deserved. Of this he became fully convinced when "Giaour," a wealthy, middle-aged rake, notorious for his Liberal ideas as well as for his numerous female conquests and his prowess at horseback riding and duels, insisted upon making his acquaintance and listened to him enlarge upon some of his more extravagant notions. Giaour indeed went so far as to offer to finance Princivalle's latest brainstorm, which was concerned with the excavation of peat from some valleys which happened to be included among the illuminated and progressive rake's vast possessions. It was with this financial aid that Princivalle was able to leave the house of his son, the saddle maker, and live in more elegant style. The conditions of Giaour's generosity can easily be guessed at and are not of the main fabric of our story.

One of the uses to which Princivalle proposed to put the peat was to furnish gas for the street lamps of Ferrara, in this way bringing the city into line with no lesser places than Paris and London. While Giaour fell more and more under the spell of the fair Argia her father started to experiment with lamps of the sort invented by the Frenchman Lebon, which he ordered from Paris and set up in front of the rake's summer place in the country.

When the time came to actually carry out the experiment Giaour appeared on the scene, together with a group of carousing friends and Argia, who was now publicly known as his mistress. Princivalle had set up in an abandoned stable a big box for the distillation of the gas while four burners on the façade of the main house and two in the surrounding gardens were waiting for him to light them. Fortunately he left no one in the stable when he came out holding a bit of flaming tow at the end of a long rod with which he expected to produce the first gas flame ever to be seen in the Po valley.

"You're going to see something very beautiful!" he told the onlookers. "Something that will sweep you away with sheer wonder!"

They did see it, there was no doubt of that, and the sound of it was heard over a mile away! The explosion shook the stable walls and made the same effect upon the bystanders as lightning and thunder. The peasants who had been watching from behind the surrounding hedges ran as if they were escaping from an earthquake. But when the din was over and they saw flames coming out of the stable windows and threatening to spread to the house they came back with tubs and buckets of water to put out the fire.

245

"Malvegoli," Giaour said, half in anger and half in amusement, when the danger was over, "you and your gas lighting have cost me a pretty penny. But you shall be forgiven. The point is that you're mightier in theory than in practice and from now on I beg you to stick to the former."

Malvegoli smiled with all the pride of a sorely tried but indomitable pioneer.

"I was thinking," he said, "what a wonderful chance this would have been to try out the steam-operated fire-fighting apparatus they use in England and America."

"Well, when you get your steam-operated pumps we'll set fire to the house and try them out on that," Giaour retorted. "But please spare me from the necessity of buying the pumps for you!"

Dawn was on the horizon and the excitement had kindled hunger in both Giaour's boon companions and the exuberant Argia. The pantry and cellar of the country house had been replenished in view of just such an occasion and now Argia, playing the mistress of the establishment, called the guests to enjoy a feast of cold meat, salad and exotic fruits. Thus the episode had a happy ending and the rising sun found all present with forks and glasses in their hands. Argia's natural grace had been increased by the lessons in dancing and deportment offered her by her protector and she had quickly taken on all the airs of a lady. People said that sooner or later she would persuade him to marry her, but for the time being she seemed content to enjoy the luxuries that were hers for the asking.

4

When the saddle maker came to inform Dosolina of the scandalous behavior of their sister, Argia, he found that his news had preceded him. Soon afterwards Dosolina decided to speak to her father.

"Who's keeping an eye on Argia?" she asked him.

"Why must someone keep an eye on her?" was his reply.

"Because she's too beautiful. And she is exposed to danger."

"What danger can there be if I'm at hand?"

"That's it! A man can't understand certain things until it's too late to understand them."

"There you go, just like your good mother! I suppose you women understand everything!"

"Argia has begun to dress like a lady, have you noticed?"

"Well, I'm paying for it. There's no secret about that. At last I've found someone who appreciates my intelligence."

"And who might that be?"

"What do you mean? The intelligence is mine, isn't it? Do you want to know what makes you talk this way?"

"Yes. Tell me."

"Envy, that's all! You and your brother and sister-in-law are eaten up by envy."

"Come, now!"

"You're envious, living the way you do, to see Argia and myself live like true Malvegolis. And here you go, making insinuations, after all I've done for you! What else is that but envy? As a matter of fact, Argia's the most sensible of all my daughters."

"Who says that, I wonder?"

"I do. Isn't that enough?"

It was actually too much. As for Lazzaro, he refused to take Dosolina's concern very seriously. He laughed at the story of Argia's adventures and said that if such was her instinct she had best follow it. When he was in Ferrara one day he went to call on her and enjoyed himself immensely, while her protector sized him up as an unusual and interesting type of countryman. Dosolina read into her husband's attitude a long-standing contempt for her whole family. As a result she pulled a long face but kept her troubles to herself. Neither Princivalle nor Argia had been mentioned for some time between them, when one morning the former made a sudden appearance at Poplar Bridge, weary, mud-spattered and beside himself. It was the spring of 1831 and Ferrara had been the scene of a small revolution. A provisory government was in the saddle until such time as the Austrians should clamp down on it. Lazzaro and Dosolina took Princivalle in with mingled worry and compassion and tried to persuade him to warm himself by the fire and have something to eat.

"Hide me! I'm a marked man!" was all that he could say, trembling all over. "France is betraying us!"

"Why should you be marked? What are you raving about? What has France got to do with it?"

"The soldiers, the gendarmes, the police! If they catch me they'll hang me or cut my head off!"

"Your head!" said Scacerni. "That's going to fast. First they'll have to bring you to trial."

"*Lèse majesté*, conspiracy . . . that means the hangman's noose or the guillotine! France has broken faith and now Austria will step in!"

Scacerni nodded at Dosolina as if to say: "The poor old codger's quite daffy."

Not long before, inspired by the hope of a constitution like that of Louis Philippe in France and relying on the much touted principle of Non-intervention, the city of Bologna had staged an uprising and on February seventh Ferrara had done likewise. Demonstrators had marched through the city and gathered in front of the heavily barred Fortress, a few Papal soldiers and gendarmes were disarmed and some notorious spies given a beating. And during all these proceedings the war cry shouted at the Austrians barricaded in the Fortress and the terrified Papists down in the city was: "Non-intervention!" Because the Austrians had wisely loaded their big guns and made the powder trains ready, a reactionary wag said that he was waiting to see the outcome of the battle between the cannons of the Fortress and the canon of Non-intervention· Which pun caused his temporary banishment from his native city, where they took Non-intervention very seriously.

This principle of international law had a number of passionate defenders at the Tasso and Pacini Cafés, but at the Pellegrino Tavern its chief exponent was Princivalle Malvegoli who marshalled all sorts of evidence to prove that Austria was powerless to move.

"If Austria does anything, then France will have to follow suit, because of the sacred principle of Non-intervention," he proclaimed.

"And what about us?" someone asked.

"We're making a revolution and since Austria is the bulwark of tyranny our ultimate aim is freedom. And this time Austria can't intervene to tip the scales against us. Is that clear? Isn't it mathematically certain?"

And so people streamed into the open space in front of the Fortress to sing the Carmagnole and:

> *If the Austrians don't go away*
> *We'll celebrate their funeral day!*

In spite of the fact that the Austrians kept their powder trains ready and showed no signs of withdrawing, faith in Non-intervention persisted, particularly in Princivalle Malvegoli. The Liberal government lasted a month before Austria took drastic steps. Some of the revolutionaries fled and others were arrested; the Austrian garrisons were re-enforced and there were rumors of repressive measures and sentences to prison and execution.

While Princivalle was still meditating upon the possibilities of Intervention and Non-intervention, Giaour knocked at his door and asked if he could stay in hiding long enough to disguise himself and escape from the police. With the aid of the startled but eager Argia, Princivalle helped him rig himself up in borrowed clothes. In this way Princivalle got it into his head that the authorities were after the leaders of the Libertines or Liberal Party and wondered only why they had not yet sought him out among them. Argia held up a flickering candle in front of a mirror and Giaour nervously glued a false mustache onto his upper lip and tried on a wig. While he was in this delicate posture and in a state of anxiety for his immediate future Malvegoli came up with the fruit of his own meditations.

"As for my mustache," he said, "I suppose I'd better shave it off."

"That's a good one!" said Giaour, with half a false mustache clinging to his fingers. "Why should you?"

"In order to escape the tyrant's grasp!"

"You? What should any tyrant have against you?"

"My good sir," said Malvegoli with pique, "if they're looking for the leaders, the hotheads, the . . ."

"Don't 'good sir' me, if you please! I'd like to know what right you have to address me in this manner! And what right you have to call yourself a leader is really beyond me!" Giaour was aware of being insulting, but could not contain himself further. "As a matter of fact,"

248

he added, "I've been meaning to ask you for some time what part you were playing in this comedy."

"Comedy? What comedy? What part should I be playing, in your estimation?"

"I'll tell you that right away. Either you're a fool, but I didn't think there could be *such* a fool as you, or else you're pretending to be one, and I hardly think you're clever enough for that. And now I must say goodbye. If you think you're a very important character let me tell you this much: if the police catch us we'll swing our heels from the gallows, and if we run up against the Sanfedisti they'll stick a knife into our bellies. . . ." Then he added, turning to Argia: "Take care of yourself, my beauty, and we'll meet again when the atmosphere's a bit more healthy. And keep up your good spirits, because when I come back I want to find you more beautiful than ever. We'll celebrate, never fear. Now give me a kiss and light my way down the stairs."

Argia lost no time in responding to this invitation. Probably Giaour's delight in teasing the old man, frightening him to death, and then kissing his daughter under his very nose was the result of some hitherto unconscious and concealed antipathy, which had suddenly found a malicious outlet. Malvegoli stood rooted to the floor with consternation. When Argia came back upstairs he recovered his tongue.

"What did he mean by that, now? What was all that nonsense about? Was he drunk? But then you must be drunk too! The insolence of him to kiss you at a moment like that! And you let him do it, I saw you! You can't deny it!"

Argia was so agitated that she did not even listen and at this moment Princivalle's imagination hovered again over Giaour's reference to the gallows. He could feel the rope around his neck and his heels swinging to and fro in the breeze. He gasped for breath and threw his hands up in the air. There was a knock at the downstairs doors, which made him all the more fearful. Could it be the fanatical hordes of the Sanfedisti, armed with sticks and guns and knives? But the intruders were police, who without so much as a "Stay where you are!" ransacked the whole house.

"He's not here," said one who seemed to be the captain of their band.

"And for whom, may I ask, are you gentlemen looking?" asked Malvegoli, drawing himself up into a position as dignified as possible.

With the captain were five or six stupid boors and one gaunt, loose-jointed fellow with an owl-like face which the reader may remember having met before. He looked now as if he were perched on a tree, blinking at the lights in the room.

"Can't you guess?" he asked with a sneer.

"No, I honestly can't."

"Aren't you Princivalle Malvegoli?"

"Yes, I am." Here we are, he thought to himself, they've come to arrest me, soon I'll be swinging . . .

"Then how can you ask for whom we are looking in your house?"

"I am asking you, though, that's just it."

"Why not ask your daughter?" said the owl-like individual. But this was too subtle for his fellows, one of whom laughed offensively and said in crude terms:

"We're looking for the chap that makes the wheels go round!"

"Wheels? What wheels?"

"Listen here," interrupted the captain. "Are you trying to pull the wool over our eyes or are you really only half there? Just in case the man has been here recently let me tell you this: We're after him for political crimes, *lèse majesté* and conspiracy. His head's at stake, I'll have you know, and the same holds true for his accomplices."

In order to dispel Princivalle's last doubts one of the other fellows made the gesture of a blade coming down on the back of his neck.

"They'll chop it off as clean as you please," said the owl-faced individual. "You might as well tell us everything you know, because he won't pay your bills any longer. You've drawn the last allowance you'll ever have from him. Good times are over! Do you catch on?"

"What good times?" exclaimed Malvegoli, whose pride would not allow him to understand. "What allowance? Who has an allowance around here?"

"You tell us!" they all said together, opening their eyes wide.

"And what about my genius?"

There was a general outburst of hilarity. The captain held his sides with laughter, tears streamed down the owl-like face, and the other rude fellows roared until they were choking from the strain.

"Who could have imagined we should have such a lark!" said the owl-faced spy. "It was actually worthwhile to stay up so late!"

"Enough now," said the captain, striving to recapture his dignity. "You know how the proverb has it, Malvegoli: A word to the wise is sufficient. And I beg the young lady's pardon. We know when to be discreet. But if the chap we're looking for has been here, we shall surely meet again! And now let's be on our way."

The image of death danced in front of Malvegoli's eyes again. Deciding to bluff it out he took on an injured air which, mingled with his quite obvious fear, produced a very strange effect indeed. He placed his trembling legs far apart and raised his voice to stutter theatrically:

"And was it necessary for you to come at this late hour?"

"What do you mean?" asked the captain, turning back from the door.

"Looking at this late hour for a man in my house. You've forgotten that I have a daughter. I say that you owe me an explanation."

"What?" exclaimed the spy as if astonishment made him talk out loud to himself. "Is it really possible that you're the only one who doesn't know?"

"Didn't you yourselves . . ." Malvegoli began, but then he stifled the rest of what he was going to say. In his confusion he wondered when he had lived through or dreamed all these events before and hesitated to believe the evidence of his own senses. His crimes, even if they existed only in his imagination, caused him just as much fear and torment as if they were real. With that rash "You yourselves. . ." he had come within an inch of giving himself away, and he still had a presentiment that something very disagreeable was about to happen. He was a foolish man, but have foolish men no right to suffer? He was jolted now by the bass voice of the crudest of his interrogators, who took up the owl-faced spy's last question and shot it at him in even plainer language:

"Do you mean to say you don't know who is the lover of this truly lovely daughter of yours?"

There was a chorus of laughter from one corner of the room and Argia's eyes blazed with indignation.

"I'll tell you a thing or two!" she shouted. "You have no right to insult me!"

The men realized that a beautiful woman could silence them quickly enough and that they had gone a step too far. Only the officious spy could not resist trying to have the last word.

"I beg your pardon," he said, "but it's our painful duty to take into consideration the fact that Argia Malvegoli is notoriously the concubine of the man we are after. You *are* Argia Malvegoli, aren't you?"

The captain, who did not relish this legalistic irony, cut him short.

"That has nothing to do with the case in point," he observed.

"I beg your pardon," said the spy stubbornly. "As pertaining to the fugitive's activities it is entirely within the scope of our investigation."

"Meanwhile we're wasting our time here while he's giving us the slip. We're supposed to bring him back, dead or alive, have you forgotten that? Let me remind you that you guaranteed our catching him red-handed in this house. And is this all your guarantee amounts to?" Professional jealousy made the captain give a sarcastic smile. "I shall tell Cavaliere Flaminio, since you inveigled him into taking you under his protection. A fine figure you'll cut then! But now it's high time for us to go. Forgive us for disturbing you, young lady, and as for you, Princivalle Malvegoli, remember that we are keeping an eye on you, that we have papers ready to serve on you at a minute's notice!" He raised his voice as he spoke these threatening words. "If a certain person did pass this way tonight you'll find yourself in trouble. And if it comes out that you know where he had gone then you'll pay for it with your head. That's all I have to say. Now let us go. Your head, Princivalle Malvegoli, remember!"

His little band obeyed, hiding their chagrin over the loss of their prey behind scornful looks cast in the direction of Malvegoli. One by one, like figures in a nightmare, he saw them file out, with the spy the last one to go. Failure and outraged pride were transformed on his face into an incongruous expression of moral censure for a lost woman and her worthless father. Coming from him this smug assumption of superiority was such as to arouse grim laughter.

Poor Princivalle was incapable of any sentiment but shame. Meanwhile Argia had speedily recovered the natural aplomb and self-assurance of her kind and come to the conclusion that the only antidote to the upheaval of the night lay in a sound sleep and a fresh outlook on life the next morning. Her father fell into a chair and beat his forehead with the palms of his hands like a man who is aware of having understood too little and too late. Then he stumbled out of the room without casting either a word or a look behind him. Argia followed, and perceiving that he was about to venture out just as he was into the night air, she fetched a cape and ran down the stairs to throw it over his shoulders. In her own way she was not a bad-hearted girl, but what could she say to him at a moment like this? With a sigh of resignation over the fact that the inevitable had come to pass and her father's eyes had been brutally opened she retired to her own quarters. There her sigh soon became a lazy yawn, for after all the possession of a well-furnished and comfortable room and a soft, warm bed, inviting to both love making and leisure, had been among the prime incentives for her embracing a courtesan's career.

The luckless Princivalle wandered aimlessly about the deserted city, hoping only to get away from it before his shame was exposed to the cold light of day. He did not know exactly how he was going to elude the vigilance of the Austrian soldiers and the Papal carabineers, but it turned out that his very vagueness was the best safe-conduct. He slipped out the half-open small door in the Porta San Giovanni while the sleepy sentinel thought that either he had already shown his papers or else he was *persona grata* to the officer of the guard. He walked, still dreamily, across the fields in whatever direction his legs chose to take him, which was to Poplar Bridge, where he would not have had the courage to go of his own volition. Finally he arrived, or rather collapsed, at the door.

"Lazzaro," he groaned as soon as they had let him in, "close the door, for the love of heaven!"

Lazzaro closed it and gave him a drink of brandy, while Dosolina prepared a cup of hot milk. Sitting beside the fire Princivalle came slowly around, repeating between one swallow and another:

"Hide me, Lazzaro! Save me, Dosolina!"

"We'll hide you," Lazzaro answered, "and if necessary we'll save you as well."

"I should say it is necessary! They're after my head in Ferrara."

"Why so?" asked Lazzaro, exchanging with his wife a further look of mingled doubt and pity.

"Because I took part in the revolution, I made a demonstration in the streets, and now France has let us down."

"Ah well," said Lazzaro, shrugging his shoulders, "even in this out-of-the-way spot we've heard that you didn't get anywhere with your revolution. So you were one of the demonstrators, were you? You don't suppose the government will bother to cut off your head for so little, do you? I don't say that anyone who gets mixed up in a mess like that just for the pleasure of shouting his head off in the streets shouldn't be given a chance to think better of it in jail. But the guillotine would be an exaggeration. And what has France got to do with it? Why should they be concerned with you in France?"

"But I played a conspicuous part, I was a friend and leader of the conspirators. . . ." Then he added ruefully: "No, that's not it. The fact is that I can't go back to Ferrara. I'd rather die than go back. And I thought he was a friend! . . . Shame upon me! And with my gray hair! To think that I was the only one who didn't know that my daughter had dishonored me! That is why I came to you, to hide my shame. Your mother was right, Dosolina. I made my family endure every kind of hardship and never realized that I was causing their ruin. It's all my fault, including what's happened to poor Argia . . . My fault, all mine . . ."

These were the words of a defeated man, and the tears that oozed out of his reddened eyes over his rough cheeks were almost more than Dosolina could endure.

"Say no more, father dear!" she exclaimed, "you've said too much already. Don't you suppose that mother has long since forgiven you? I can't bear to see you crying, and I'm sure that if she could call down from heaven mother too would tell you to dry your tears. Don't cry any more, I beg of you!"

"Dosolina is right," said Lazzaro with rough tenderness. "Say no more, for we've understood enough already. If you can be content with the company of farmers and millers then you may as well consider this house your own. It's not so grand here as in the city, but we welcome you with all our hearts. And now, if you'll excuse me, I'll be getting on to the mill. But look here, if the police are really after you, we must think of a hiding place."

"Never mind," said Malvegoli humbly. "I don't really think they're on my trail. The danger was mostly in my imagination; I made it up in this poor old head. Even if they did come for me I'd most likely get off with only a few days in jail, and that's no more than I deserve."

"I always said that those lights we saw in the sky at the beginning of the year boded something evil!" Dosolina exclaimed. "Here we are, with misfortune after misfortune, and who knows whether we've seen the last of them. What a weary world!"

The lights to which she referred were those of the *aurora borealis* of January 7, 1831, which among the country folk had been the object of considerable speculation.

"Didn't I tell you so?" she added. "There's no telling what new affliction may be in store!"

"Let's hope that we don't get mixed up with the police," said Scacerni. "Cheer up, Dosolina, we've weathered worse things than this!"

The police did not pursue Princivalle and as for Argia, no one at Poplar Bridge mentioned her name again. The fact is that shortly afterwards she entered into the good graces of an influential gentleman connected with the new provisional government and used the gifts nature had bestowed upon her to clear her father's name, whom no one

253

had ever taken very seriously anyhow. This, then, was the end of Princivalle Malvegoli's political career.

During the first months after his father-in-law's arrival Lazzaro frequently questioned him about the political events of this fateful year, but the accounts he got gave him little satisfaction. Many of the miller's friends and neighbors fell into the way of dropping in of an evening, attracted as if by the presence of a great storyteller and pleased to have an occasion to discuss within the privacy of four walls matters which it would have been unwise to air at the tavern. Little was known at Guarda of the severe treatment accorded to the Liberals and Libertines by Pope Gregory's government, and the country people observed a traditional caution where political discussion was concerned. With all this and their general illiteracy to boot, they managed none the less to pass a certain amount of news from mouth to mouth when they were sure that no one could overhear. And so it was that they enjoyed listening to the wild words of Princivalle Malvegoli.

"How else could you have expected things to turn out?" Lazzaro asked. "I can see that you might reasonably have hoped to bump off the Pope's wooden soldiers, but you forgot about the Fortress and the fact that it was garrisoned by Austrians. They're a different matter! As a veteran of the army of Napoleon I think I know more about them than your lawyers in Ferrara, who know no other weapon than the pen. What else could you hope for?"

"For Non-intervention!" answered Malvegoli, but with a much milder voice than that with which he had held forth in the Pellegrino Tavern.

"What's that? Black Magic?"

Faced with the wrinkled and bewildered expressions of his interlocutors Malvegoli attempted to explain.

"France with its glorious three days of July . . ."

"How now? Are you talking Turkish? Tell us in plain language . . ."

And they continued to interrupt him in this rude fashion, for the sake of teasing, even when they had understood him perfectly well.

"France is over the mountains, first of all," said Scacerni, "while Austria is right here on the Po. Surely you didn't think the French would risk their necks out of sheer brotherly love, did you?" And he went on, amid general laughter: "And what would have been gained if the French had come to help you? After all, they were here before and not so long ago that you can't remember. Under their rule the common people were far worse off than they are now. But it may suit you city dwellers to forget those years, since for you they were fat ones."

"Fat years? Not for me," whined Malvegoli.

"I don't say for you personally, since if you'll forgive me for being so frank you've always been a fool. But the brutal way the French had of putting down those who disagreed with them. . . . Let me remind you that I saw my father thrown down from the bell tower of San Giorgio!"

254

"The French are enemies of God!" interposed Dosolina.

"We don't want either the French or the Austrians to rule over us in Italy," Malvegoli suggested timidly.

"Then why shouldn't we be satisfied with the Pope, since he's neither Austrian nor French?"

"Because if Italy is ever to be strong it must unite and be one country. Have I made myself clear?"

"All too clear."

"Why so?"

"There you go again with your magic spells and incantations! What do you mean by 'Italy,' anyhow? Who's ever seen or heard of such a thing? How can it be united?"

"I can explain well enough, if you'll give me a chance," Malvegoli began, but the other interrupted him.

"Let *me* explain. Our fine gentlemen are bored with their prosperity. They are too comfortable and eat too much rich food. No wonder they are so hot-blooded that not even a beautiful girl can cool them off. I needn't tell *you* that!" (Here Princivalle bowed his head in mortification.) "And so they are looking out for some new form of excitement."

"But there are intellectual people . . ."

"I was just coming to them, to the lawyers and such like, who want to take the government into their own hands. If they did take it over would they pay the taxes? Would they volunteer to fight? Or wouldn't they just line their own pockets the way they did when the French were here? Here in the country, where we are ignorant, we have to rely on our memories. When the intellectuals were at the helm they imposed taxes and levies of soldiers such as we've never seen since. Mark my words: a big fish is bound to eat a little one. Put men of letters to rule over us and they'll be no better than the rest. At least those who are in power now have already eaten their fill; new rulers would have more of an appetite. And since in either case we have to foot the bill, whom are we to prefer, I ask you?"

"Bad weather and whims of the government aren't worth worrying about," said Dosolina, quoting the old proverb.

Scacerni could not help turning over in his mind those strange new words "Italy," "freedom," "unity" and "independence," which his father-in-law had timidly introduced to Poplar Bridge in the face of such stubborn opposition.

"Do you know what I think of this 'Italy' of yours?" he asked him. "I think it must be something like that steam-operated mill you wanted to put up for the ruination of us poor millers."

"That would have been for the good of all," Malvegoli protested. "It would have meant progress and prosperity."

"I'm busy enough watching over my own affairs. And I have no desire to be ruined for other people's benefit. You told me something of how it worked and I am sure it would burn the flour in the process of grinding."

The faces around the fireplace and out on the porch turned dark and unfriendly and Malvegoli dared defend the steam mill and the cause of progress no further.

Dosolina and Lazzaro were good people, of course, as is proved by the fact that they did not envy Argia, who was reputed to have capitalized on her vice to the extent of setting up a magnificent house of her own, complete with horse and carriage and liveried servants. But, for all their goodness, they could not refrain from heaping coals of fire upon the head of poor Princivalle. As a crowning affliction his health had begun to fail and he suffered from all the most trivial and humiliating ailments of old age, not daring to complain lest he give trouble in a house where he was eating the bread of charity. For some time now he had been disappointed in his little grandson, Giuseppe, who gave clear signs of feeling nothing but scorn for anyone who did not have money. But all these sorrows he kept to himself and Dosolina was so busy watching over his soul and seeing that he did not suffer a relapse into sin that she did not even notice.

Don Giuseppe Romagnoli, the new young priest, was by nature more zealous than intelligent and he was inspired by the "political precepts" of Cardinal Rivarola to abuse religious practices and turn them into the tools of a veritable inquisition of those who were supposed to be in error. He bore down so hard upon the enfeebled Princivalle that the old man returned from his frequent visits to the confessional in a state of hopelessness and terror, which led his daughter to think that his repentance was not yet complete.

There was nothing left for old Malvegoli but to die, and this nature attended to in the quietest and kindliest way. One morning he failed to appear at the breakfast table and when they went to look for him they found him asleep in his bed, never to rise again.

Political unrest, added to its former troubles, had made things harder and harder for Pope Gregory XVI's temporal government. Increased taxes, scarcities, and high prices were felt even among the peasants, who were usually spared them because they were to some extent self-sufficient and had little traffic in money. Under these circumstances the clergy spread the news that the Liberal revolutionists were to blame. There followed bad weather, widespread earthquakes, and insufficient harvests. The government had to step up the tax on salt, and along the Po, where it was still fresh in the poor peasants' minds how much better off they had been under the Emperor Francis, known to them as Francis Fatloaf, there was open envy of the Austrians on the other side of the river.

"Hurrah for Fatloaf!" some of them said. "And death to the Liberals!"

The impiety of the Libertines, they said, had brought down divine punishment upon the whole population.

In Ferrara and its surroundings reaction to the abortive Liberal uprisings never took on the ferocious character it assumed in the notoriously conservative city of Faenza and its bloody suburb, Urbecco. But everywhere political differences became on both sides excuses for passion and violence. The various groups and sects of both the oppressors and the oppressed indulged in countless crimes of vengeance. The Carbonari had their "squads" and "maquis," who were matched by the "volunteers" and "centurions" organized by the Sanfedisti. The former ill served the liberty they claimed to be fighting for, and the latter discredited the religion they were supposedly defending.

All in all, the years of repression after the revolution of 1831 were bitter ones for the Papal rule, both in Bologna and Ferrara where Cardinal Spinola, the Papal legate, and his lieutenant, Monsignor Asquini, made themselves hated for imposing their power with such brutality and in the province of Romagna where the Church virtually committed suicide by accepting the support of the mobs of fanatical Sanfedisti. Even the leaders of the excesses came to realize dimly that these were paving the way for anarchy and that they themselves could not hope for much protection from the Papal government after they had unwittingly undermined its authority and caused the people to rise up in hate against it. Although they could not refrain from trying to carry out the wild program of total extermination of the Liberals, they were nevertheless aware that in case of failure they could not hope to escape popular ire except through the intervention of the Austrians.

Influenced by a last flicker of reason they came finally to the point of giving up the cause they had served in such a mistaken manner. The fiercest and most uncompromising Papists were eventually the first to become traitors. Among the most notorious of these were Virginio Alpi, leader of the centurions and Sanfedisti of Faenza and Forlì, and the personage whom we have already met under the name of Cavaliere Flaminio, the police chief who made the pun about cannons versus canon. We shall not reveal his real name, first because it is not essential to our story, and next because thus we shall spare from further dishonor the memory of a man who of whatever crimes he may have been guilty, came to an undeservedly sordid end. Alpi, on the other hand, did not pay for his political excesses but was sentenced as a common criminal. Both men will appear again in these pages.

The first years of Pope Gregory XVI's reign, marked by the restoration of absolute temporal power of the Papal government after the uprisings of 1831, antagonized all those who had hoped for reforms, embittered those who had tried to promote a revolution, and made traitors out of many Papal officials. These and the Sanfedisti furnished Austria with any number of spies, confidential agents, and professional trouble-makers. Men who had set themselves up as loyalists betrayed their loyalty, legitimists defied the principle of legitimacy, Sanfedisti did not keep faith and Papists, by outpoping the Pope, only lowered his reputation. And all this because they committed the unforgivable crime of seeking foreign aid.

As for the modest characters of the present story, let us here reveal that the man who had become Argia's protector after the flight of Giaour was none other than the police chief Cavaliere Flaminio.

Princivalle Malvegoli was buried in the cemetery at Guarda and Dosolina had Masses said for his soul. A good man, everyone said, in spite of his eccentricities, one who had lived a simple life but preserved his honor. When Lazzaro thought of the mild expression he had seen on the dead man's face he could almost hear him saying: Now I'm no longer a bother to anyone.

At such moments he felt a need of repeating to himself that there was nothing on his conscience in regard to the way he had treated his father-in-law. Surely Princivalle had said and done enough foolish things in his time! The memory of them left Scacerni slightly discontented, not only on account of the political events which had had repercussions even on life along the river, but also because the old man's ravings echoed even more strongly in his ears now than they had when he was alive. Now there was no way of contradicting them, and the gentle, penitent look on Princivalle's dead face would not efface itself from his memory. Those notions of a free, united and independent Italy, which under any other circumstances would have gone in one ear and out the other, had stuck irritatingly in his mind. As resentfully as if Princivalle were still before him he threw them back in his face and asked himself how an educated man could have lived in such a disorderly fashion and have died without ever having finished anything that he had begun. Still, he soliloquized, of the dead one must think no evil and his father-in-law had died like an honest man, with penitence and forgiveness written on his face.

In the last analysis, Lazzaro was himself of a thoroughly independent turn of mind, quite apart from any considerations of Italy or the Papacy. This side of his nature derived in part from his feeling of being a river man, and the enthusiasm with which long ago, at Occhiobello, he had embraced the life of a miller. He was never one to second the cry of "Long live Francis Fatloaf!" nor did he raise a cheer to Ferdinand, who in 1835 succeeded Emperor Francis on the Austrian throne. As far as he was concerned the Austrians had better stay on their own side of the Po, and, besides, there was something cowardly about the adulation of their Emperor that did not go down with him at all. The notion of "Italy" had made less of an impression upon him than that of the steam-operated mill, but had impressed itself upon his mind, and the very fact that it was irritating proved that it had a certain pungency and efficacity. His poor country, old and new, past and future, beset during these years by injury and scandal!

Meanwhile one year passed by after another and Lazzaro Scacerni was among one of the oldest millers on the Po, none of whom, as contemporary records attest, had ever seen the river so dangerously high as it was between October and December of 1839. The Panaro was equally swollen, and finally both rivers broke together over the Bondeno region. There, many villages were left with nothing but their church towers sticking out of the water, while all around Ferrara there were two months of fear and false alarms. Lazzaro moved Saint Michael's Mill behind the protection of the Guarda peninsula, where neither the rushing water nor all the wreckage that it carried in its path could sweep it away. He had reason to worry about his house at Poplar Bridge, but the break-through of the Panaro, while causing destruction in the hills, lightened the danger to the main Po Valley.

Aboard the mill things were not running altogether smoothly. Malvasone had become deaf as he advanced in years and hence he was incapacitated for work that required good hearing. Of course the bell could not rouse him, and even a salvo of guns would have had little more effect. The worst of it was that the poor fellow insisted that he felt very well and was quick to take offense if anyone reproached him.

Most of the reproaches came to him from young Master Giuseppe Scacerni, who had grown up to be a cold-blooded youth, as frigid as a mysterious blast of wind that leaves one with a crick in the neck without one's ever knowing where it came from. He was short and pot-bellied, with spindly legs, fair hair, and a yellowish complexion. He had the unpleasant, watery, red-rimmed, pale blue eyes of an albino and the general effect of his face would have been dull and colorless had it not been that its shape was like that of a rabbit and its expression like that of an angry cat. In it could be read a sort of spiteful resentment, a mixture of craftiness and stupidity, and a resolve to return every annoyance that was given him in double measure.

He felt no vocation for being a miller, but he had quickly mastered all the secrets of the trade and without putting any art or skill into it he had got himself into a position where he could cheat and antagonize the customers and make life miserable for his subordinates. Among the latter his first victim was Malvasone, who faced the prospect of beggary in his old age if he were to be sent away from the mill, and the next Schiavetto, who controlled his feelings only in order not to give pain to his old master. Giuseppe had already begun to tyrannize over his father, leaving him torn between surprise and indignation. The son's way of doing things was always the same: he used his malevolent craftiness for saving a trifle here and there, fraudulently exacting an extra penny for his services and looking with suspicion on everyone and everything around him.

"What a lovable fellow you are!" Scacerni remarked with an ironic shrug of his shoulders.

"If people dislike you it's a sign that they know you can't be cheated."

"You talk like a thwarted, wicked old man!" said his father wrathfully. "Look at me. No one has cheated me, as far as I know, and yet I think I may say that I've prospered and won the general affection."

Giuseppe answered with an incredulous look, then his doubtful smile turned into first pity and then derision. Finally he came out with examples: here they were spending too much and there they were saving too little. Hadn't they just paid out so many crowns to the ship-

259

wright from Crespino for caulking the mill when such a one from Francolino or Polesella would have done the job for less?

"How do you know?" his father interrupted.

"Go ask them yourself, and you'll see."

"But the shipwright from Crespino is my friend."

"Ah well, if he's a friend, of course . . ."

"I know he doesn't work as efficiently as he used to, but . . ."

"But he charges as much as he used to and more."

"He's a first-rate craftsman, though."

"No better than the two I just mentioned."

"That may be. But I repeat that he's my friend. In fact he repaired the mill for me after the damage it suffered the day you were born. And that time no one would allow me credit. They all gave me up for lost."

"Then here's hoping it doesn't take him too long to die."

"That's a nice way to reason!"

"I'm just proving to you what it is to enjoy so much affection. And you answer me with nursery tales!"

"At my age, I tell you, a man doesn't like to see new faces."

"Ah, that's a different story. Of course it's up to you."

It was the same thing with the millstones and everything else connected with the mill, especially the price that Scacerni asked for the milling. All the other millers had increased their charges, and he alone was behind the times. Besides, the others all cheated their customers.

"I'm an honest man, in case you want to know it," said Scacerni. "I've always had one price and I'll stick to it."

"Well, if you insist. . . . Of course it's up to you. If you want people to love you still more, you might even bring your price down! You may go bankrupt, but oh, how they'll love you!"

Scacerni lived with one foot out of this world, spending no money on himself and turning all his savings over to Dosolina, who invested them in the land. So when he inquired about he found that prices had indeed increased, on account of both local poverty and the great industrial boom that spread all over Europe between 1830 and 1848. This was something young Giuseppe had not known, for his figures came only from Guarda.

"How can you expect that at my age I should start to increase my prices?" Scacerni said in answer to his son's insistent questions. "All my customers have been with me for years and years and I've always treated them like friends."

"Ah, you have so many friends, have you?"

"Yes," said Scacerni. "So many that since you can't hope for them all to die soon, the best that you can hope for is that I should die soon."

"That's another matter," was all that he got for an answer.

"If I didn't have so much respect for your mother . . ." Scacerni said impatiently.

"Ah well, that's not my concern."

"What do you mean, not your concern?"

"All that concerns me is what happens between the time when I arrived on the scene and the time when I leave it. But nothing that dates from either before or after."

"Either before! . . ." echoed Scacerni with mingled astonishment and disgust.

"Or after! Exactly."

"Then I can only shrug my shoulders."

"It's up to you, as I said before."

At other times Lazzaro lost his patience and accused his son of being a cold-blooded fish.

"Do you know why?" he added. "Because even at your age you're not interested in women! You don't know what it is to fall in love! That's why you spend all your time flirting with pennies. If avarice were a woman you'd marry her and the two of you would breed consumption together!"

Giuseppe did not reply, but swallowed this bitter pill in silence. The scorn in which women held him was undoubtedly the cause of much of his bile. Dosolina tried to persuade herself that this scorn was all due to a feeling of feminine inferiority, since surely there was no woman worthy of her son.

"Go on, now!" she would say. "No woman starts to belittle unless she intends to buy!"

"Don't tell him that, for the love of heaven!" said Scacerni. "He's quite capable of setting a valuation on himself down to the last crown, half-crown and penny!"

Giuseppe gave a wry smile.

Without ever setting foot in the smelly stable or examining an inch of cultivated land he went over his mother's farm accounts as painstakingly as he had analyzed those of the mill, thereby dazzling her completely. Everywhere he found ways of cutting down expenses and building up profits.

In this part of the country there was still some of the imagination that had inspired the sculptor of the figures of strange beings, half animal and half human, on the doors of Ferrara Cathedral. One of the most enduring of these imaginary creatures was that of the werewolf and now, observing Giuseppe's angry rabbitlike face, people called him Were Rabbit. The werewolf was supposedly given to howling at night and jumping at the throat of tardy wayfarers, but Giuseppe, they said, as a Were Rabbit, only squeaked like a bat and preyed upon stray chickens. Giuseppe retaliated for this uncomplimentary legend by telling their children, who were already frightened enough by his bloodshot eyes, that if he found them on the roads after the evening Angelus he would swallow them alive.

Meanwhile Dosolina brooded upon the injustice that was done her boy by not sending him to school. Scacerni had sent him to learn his three R's from Don Bastiano Donzelli, who had a modest pedagogical ability and a way of striking a recalcitrant pupil over the fingers with a ruler which was actually more ticklish than it was painful. Giuseppe had been docile enough as long as he thought these studies had some practical purpose, but as soon as he reached the first stages of the liberal art of grammar he found no point to being rapped over the knuckles any longer and revolted against his teacher with misdirected but extraordinary persistence. Before he prevailed over the priest he had to wage a prolonged battle in the course of which he received in ugly and stubborn silence any number of slaps, tweakings of his ear, canings and raps of the ruler, all culminating in one final kick out the door. Just before the final break he had taken to answering every question with three monotonously repeated syllables:

"I don't know."

"An adjective is a word that cannot stand alone but modifies a noun and agrees with it in gender, case and number."

"I don't know."

"What do you mean, I don't know? Did you understand me or didn't you?"

"I don't know."

"Repeat what you heard me say, then. You're not deaf, are you?"

"I don't know."

"You're the most perverse child I've ever met!"

The obstinately illiterate boy knew that the more he angered his teacher and the longer he stood up against him the shorter time instruction would be forced upon him. He decided to hold out, no matter how painful the punishment, howling under the blows of the cane like a dog at the moon. And in the end he was the stronger.

After this Lazzaro refused to send him to school in Ferrara, saying that he had made quite enough of a donkey of himself at Guarda. Years later Giuseppe had many dealings with lawyers and they said that if the practice of the law consisted only in casuistry and cavilling he had a natural talent for it, especially in view of the fact that he was also a past master of falsehood and perjury.

On Saint Michael's Mill he despised and tormented Malvasone, but reserved his real hate for Schiavetto. He was not jealous of the bond of affection between master and apprentice, which was obviously far stronger than that between father and son, but simply fearful lest Scacerni favor Schiavetto in his will. He affected, as far as lay within his powers, an air of benevolence, trying to inspire Schiavetto with confidence and induce him to take advantage of his master—all this, of course, with the sole aim of catching him red-handed and evicting him from favor. But Schiavetto did not trust Giuseppe's overtures, and even if he had responded to them he would never have stolen a penny because his nature was unequivocally honest. Finding Schiavetto's virtue unassailable, Giuseppe vowed him a cold and enduring hate.

6

During the long period of high water of 1839, then, Saint Michael's Mill was anchored in a sheltered spot behind the Guarda peninsula and the four men took turns watching over the river. For over two months the wind shifted between south and southeast, alternating fierce blasts with a steady pounding, but the air was invariably heavy and oppressive so that three of them lolled about the millstones or in the cabin while the fourth kept watch on the deck, wrapped in a warm cloak with a long-handled harpoon within reach of his hand. He looked out for any cumbersome refuse that might float down the river and at the same time kept an eye on the bar of land, re-enforced by sandbags, on which the mill depended for its protection.

In the shallow lagoon where the mill was anchored the water swirled and gurgled and the wheel had come wearily to a stop. Farther out in the river the main stream rushed furiously by, beating against the point of the sheltering promontory and then, when it was thrown back, veering off toward midstream, leaving a line of eddies behind it as a demarcation between the central current and the relative calm of the backwater.

Strange objects of every kind came floating by, some of them drawn momentarily into the lagoon and tossed about there before they continued downstream. There was always danger that a change in the conformation of the riverbed might alter the course of the current and throw them against the mill. Tree trunks, empty boats, wagons, pieces of furniture carried away from the banks where the frightened peasants had piled them, and the carcasses of domestic animals swept away from low-lying fields all drifted by.

The stubborn fury of the elements stirred something in Lazzaro's memory on which he could not quite put his finger. It came back to him more clearly when the windy, cloud-covered November days became so short that there was only a brief period of light between dawn and dusk. The heavy southeast wind that blew against the current and threw the waters of the Adriatic into the mouth of the Po was an enemy of man comparable to the unforgettable cold of the winter retreat from Moscow. The treacherous Po recalled the murderous Vop and that wild day when he had struggled across it.

All of a sudden an unusually large piece of wreckage came down the river and he saw with astonishment that it was a mill. Fortunately it missed breaking up against the point and paused for a moment before being carried on, with its large hulk pitching and the smaller one rolling, for all the world like a high-spirited horse, reined in tight and pawing the ground impatiently with first one foot and then another. This was how they first saw it, at the very end of the promontory, torn between the main current and the side stream. As it started to be carried on down the river it turned sideways and keeled over so far to one side that it seemed as if it would capsize any moment. Then, staved up by the current, its prow swung around as if it would steer straight for the opposite shore, which it would probably have done had not the impulse given to it from the rush of the water off shore sent it suddenly into the lagoon. Schiavetto jumped onto the skiff with a small anchor by which he arrested its course. Then all four men took oars in the rowboat and towed it to safety. The larger hulk, weighed down by the millstones and half filled with water, was giving way. And yet in spite of its apparent age the mill seemed to be of solid construction. If it was not to sink, it was important to beach it as quickly as possible and this they did without further delay. Then Giuseppe and Schiavetto climbed aboard while Scacerni and Malvasone waited for them in the skiff. With what astonishment did they see Schiavetto reappear with the body of a prostrated young girl in his arms! She was thoroughly soaked, and her bloodless, emaciated face made it seem as if she were exhausted from cold and hunger. The four men were moved to both pity and embarrassment.

"Can she be dead?" asked Schiavetto, lowering her into Scacerni's arms.

"With a woman there's no telling," said Malvasone. "Like cats, they have nine lives."

"We need a woman's help," said Scacerni. "I'll take her to Venusta Chiccoli. Schiavetto, saddle my horse." And a few minutes later, with the still unconscious girl in his arms, he trotted in the direction of the village of Guarda.

Venusta put her to bed with warm blankets and hot-water bottles and brought her around with aromatic spirits of ammonia. The poor girl gave a deep sigh and sank twice back into unconsciousness. Finally, opening her eyes for the second time, she found herself looking into the kindly face of Venusta who was offering her a glass of brandy. She gave a faint smile and said in a weak voice:

"Where am I?"

"Among friends. Have no fear," Venusta answered.

There was such a staring and astonished look in her eyes that Venusta was seriously worried.

"We've brought her back to life, all right, but is she mad? What's she doing now?"

The girl's astonishment had turned into fright and in spite of her weakened condition she tried to get up, calling all the time for her father. Then she opened her eyes wide and fell back as if in another faint. With the return of consciousness had come awareness of an as yet undefined sorrow which reflected itself in her frightened eyes.

"We'll go look for your father," Venusta said reassuringly. "Tell us where you come from and where your mill was anchored. . . . Poor little thing," she added in a whisper to Scacerni, "she's getting a high fever and I shouldn't like to see her mind give way. I don't like those glassy eyes. It would be better if she were to break down and cry. . . . Tell us your father's name."

This time remembrance of her sorrow seemed to restore her reason as well and she started to shed abundant tears.

"That's the way," said Venusta, patting her on the back. "That's the way, my poor girl." And she added after the girl's sobs had subsided: "Tell us what we can do."

The girl shook her head in despair.

264

"You can't do anything. I saw him die before my own eyes."

"Where? When?"

"In the river."

Later on she told the whole story. Her name was Cecilia Rei and she was the daughter of a miller with whom she had lived quite alone ever since her mother had died in giving her birth. The misanthropic old Rei had anchored his mill in a solitary spot and not only did he seldom leave it himself, but because of some incomprehensible jealousy or other extravagance he refused to let his daughter leave it at all. Certainly she had been the apple of his eye, but some people might have said that he carried his love to the point of exaggeration. Cecilia had grown up unacquainted with any human feelings except for her father's possessive passion, for he took umbrage at every greeting she received from his customers or from the rare passers-by on the river, and told her she should make no reply but retire to the cabin where no one would see her. His jealousy took on an even stranger form as she grew up and showed herself aware, in spite of the absence of mirrors, that she was beautiful. What was the use of her beauty, he asked her. He would love her more if she were ugly, and they would lead a much quieter life together. "But why, Father?" she asked him. "Just because," was his only reply.

Had she ever been baptized? There was reason to doubt it, for there was no record of her having been confirmed or admitted to Communion. Indeed her father had never taken her to church for fear that she might exchange a word with a stranger. Such was the odd conduct, unimaginable in any other surroundings, which this savage denizen of the river had chosen to follow. Perhaps the fact that his wife had died in childbirth had affected his brain and his bitterness against the world had turned into this strange form of obsession. The fact is that Cecilia Rei's name was not to be found in any local parish register.

All she knew of the world was confined to the river, and her acquaintance with human kind was limited to the few peasants who had brought their grain to what they called the Madman's Mill, whose owner would not even let them climb aboard. The first time that Cecilia bit into a piece of leavened bread she exclaimed: "How delicious!"

"What? Have you never eaten bread of this kind before?" asked Dosolina in astonishment.

Thus it came out that in order to be completely self-sufficient Rei did not buy bread but simply made a "miller's pie" over the coals or under the ashes of his fire. By dint of hunting and fishing and raising a few vegetables on the nearby shore he had completely emancipated himself from the outside world except for salt and a few raw materials upon which he practiced the arts of a carpenter, a blacksmith, and a tailor all in one.

"A perfect beast!" Giuseppe called him. "An unbeliever, and may God have mercy on him!" said Dosolina. Without making any reply

Lazzaro felt a secret envy for the Mad Miller's way of life. Listening to Cecilia's story he remembered having more than once seen the man as he passed by. At this point the road running along the former riverbank diverged considerably from the shore and unless one caught a glimpse of it from the river the Madman's Mill was hidden by a grove of shady green trees. It stood in shallow, almost stagnant water where the current was barely strong enough to turn the mossy wheel. The old and blackened structure of the mill loomed up with impressive size and something mysterious and forbidding about it, as if it were left over from another age entirely. The steep high roofs of the cabins were made of thatch and often as not grass grew out of them. Scacerni remembered that he had often been curious to know who could live in this apparently deserted and fantastic-looking mill.

And this was what Cecilia told of the events of the last few days. When the water began to rise the old mill floated at first in a sort of pond which formed on the low-lying shore, but finally a new current came along and swept it away. Old Rei had taken no pains to keep his mooring ropes in good condition and when they gave way the mill was carried into the center of the stream before he could make up his mind to jump with his daughter into a skiff and try to reach land.

Was there any truth in Cecilia's heartrending cry just after she had regained consciousness under the roof of Venusta Chiccoli:

"It's my fault that he died!"

As it drifted downstream the mill had come to a curve in the river and was separated only by a narrow, whirling eddy from a portion of the bank that was covered with tall trees. The eddy caused the mill-wheel to start turning and momentarily arrested the mad course of the mill. Rei made a sudden decision to jump overboard with a rope and attempt to attach the mill to one of the nearby trees, but his daughter lost her head, threw her arms around his neck and begged him not to leave her. The old man managed to jump in spite of her, but it was too late. Conscious of her error, the girl saw him clinging to a tree with one hand and trying vainly with the other to put the rope around it. The mill was turning around and the rope became so taut that she thought her father would be torn limb from limb in his effort to hold it. She ran for an axe with which to cut it, signaling to him at the same time to let go. But either Rei could not bear to release it or else he was so overcome by fatigue that he did not know what he was doing and so it was that the rope dragged him into the water and he sank below the surface never to appear again. His daughter started to pull the rope, calling to him now to hold on for dear life, and it was not until she found the end of it slack in her hands that she realized why it had been so easy to haul in.

The mill had resumed its headlong course and Cecilia, weary, desperate, and half starving (since their meager food supplies had for some days been exhausted) had fainted away in the cabin. Thus it was that she arrived, in God's hands, at Guarda. Later on, when she went with Scacerni to examine the exact spot of the riverbank where her father had made his ill-fated attempt to save her, she realized that if he had succeeded the mill would probably have been broken to bits. By virtue of his death the old man had preserved her only inheritance.

Old Rei had called his mill "Bitter Bread," a name with a defiant ring to it, which echoed an old complaint of the common people in the region between the Po and Reno rivers who had so often been forced to do work whose practical or artistic purpose escaped them. They had labored continuously to throw up defenses against the enmity of man and nature, to rebuild and fortify the land as well as to make it more beautiful, in order to please lords and masters who had no conception of what it meant to toil with wheelbarrow and shovel. Whether this name had been handed down to Rei or he had chosen it himself—it had in any case a strange sound, one which reminded Scacerni of the time in his faraway buoyant youth when Subbia had with considerable difficulty dissuaded him from calling his own establishment "Hunger Mill."

From Cecilia's simple and innocent tales of her youth Scacerni came to see that the Mad Miller had had moments of real tenderness toward his daughter. In a storeroom aboard Bitter Bread Mill there were ingenious toys he had fashioned for her when she was a child, and the rustic but tasteful way in which he had decorated her sleeping quarters spoke eloquently of a deep affection.

It took very few words to establish a real bond between Cecilia and Scacerni. She pinned all her faith on this new friend and he in turn said to Dosolina:

"Thanks to Almighty God and the Po, we have a daughter to comfort our old age."

Dosolina turned up her nose, because this was not her idea of a daughter. And the ever amiable Giuseppe set to work calculating the expenses his father had incurred in providing for repairs to Bitter Bread Mill, without even a scrap of paper, not to mention a mortgage, to guarantee any reimbursement.

"'Bitter Bread'! That's a proper name for it," he complained. "This is really the last straw."

"You don't want her," Lazzaro said to Dosolina, "that's clear enough. And as for Were Rabbit, he's the one who gave Our Lord vinegar on the Cross rather than waste a drop of good wine! Very well then, let's say that Almighty God and the Po have given her to me."

Dosolina objected with some reason, in view of the fact that she was his mother, to hearing her son's derogative nickname on her husband's tongue. But there was less justification for her taking offense at the insinuation that he was a miser.

Meanwhile, when the high water had gone down, Bitter Bread Mill was caulked, repainted, and moored alongside the Saint Michael at the latter's old station in front of the dikes.

"Now we've an anchorage to be proud of, Mistress Cecilia!" said Scacerni gaily.

As Cecilia began to recuperate from her shock and grow somewhat

267

more civilized under living conditions of a normal kind such as she had never known before, she acquired the beauty of a delicate wild flower or a proud but shy woodland creature. There was still a certain thorniness to her character, which showed itself particularly toward Giuseppe Scacerni and in some degree toward Dosolina. With everyone else, except for Master Lazzaro, she was exceedingly shy. It was amusing to see the ceremonious relationship, proper to two independent mill owners, that existed between the lame and bearded Lazzaro and this young girl. As soon as Bitter Bread Mill was safely moored in its new anchorage Cecilia declared that she would sleep no longer in the house at Poplar Bridge, because to be on dry land and within four walls gave her a feeling of claustrophobia.

"And where will you sleep then?" asked Dosolina with astonishment.

"Why, on my mill, of course."

"On your mill?" squeaked Giuseppe.

"And whose mill is it then?" Cecilia said resolutely, turning toward Master Lazzaro, who was stroking his beard in tacit approval.

"Yours, my good Mistress, speak up for it loudly," he answered laughing.

"And whose money went to repair it?" asked Dosolina, as if she could read her son's avarice in his eyes.

"What are we to do about that?" Cecilia inquired calmly of Lazzaro. "How are we to settle our accounts?"

"That's easy. Since, thank God, the Saint Michael has more work than it can do, the Bitter Bread will be its apprentice until your debt is paid." And he added, turning to Giuseppe: "We'll keep strict accounts of debit and credit. As you've such a head for figures you can keep the books."

"And who'll set the prices?" asked Giuseppe who, much to his mother's surprise, seemed to approve.

"That we shall agree upon like honest people, without trying to cheat anyone."

"Then Bitter Bread is still mine?" asked Cecilia.

"Of course."

"Good. Otherwise I should feel I must leave here tomorrow."

"Taking your mill along?"

"With the mill or without it."

"Sacramèstul!" Scacerni exclaimed. "That's the kind of talk I like to hear! And do you know the trade?"

"Yes, I know the trade well enough. But not the business end of it, the prices and debits and credits that you were talking about just now."

"But you know how to calculate how many spans of flour will come out of so many spans of grain, don't you?" asked Scacerni, making the gesture of measuring a sack with his extended hand in the conventional manner.

"To within an inch on six three-span bags of grain," Cecilia answered gravely. "My father's span was twice as large as mine," she added, looking sadly at her open hand.

"Capital! You won't be able to get the better of her on that score, Giuseppe, because she knows more than you do. As for the account books, I'll keep an eye on them myself. Have you confidence in me, Mistress?"

"That I have."

"Then let's shake hands on it."

In order to give vent to the indignity she had suffered on behalf of her son Dosolina began to protest against the idea of Cecilia's sleeping on the mill. It was unwise and indecent, she said, and could not fail to be a cause for evil thoughts and scandal.

"What is scandal?" Cecilia asked. "And evil thoughts? What are they?"

"Listen to that, Dosolina!" Scacerni said, with another outburst of laughter. "Evil thoughts are peculiar to old people like ourselves," he added in answer to Cecilia.

"You're only joking because you know your arguments won't stand up against mine," Dosolina grumbled.

Lazzaro was genuinely perplexed, but he said after a moment of reflection:

"Schiavetto and Malvasone are always on the Saint Michael in case of an emergency and they are fellows to count on. As for the rest, I feel sure that if Mother Eurosia were still among us and we were to ask her advice she would say, 'Do no evil and have no fear'."

Any reference to the good nun had a gravity and significance which Lazzaro was chary of invoking except under very unusual circumstances, and then only when the spirit really moved him to do it. Every time he had called upon her name it had inspired Dosolina with reverent awe, reminding her of all the passion and travail of past years, of a long struggle against hate and mortal sin, of dangers and temptations to body and spirit, which had been overcome only by something like a miracle. This holy woman, as she could not forget, had been the emissary of God's grace and pardon, and had also been influential in preserving for her the essential affection and respect of her husband. Summoning up these memories Dosolina rid herself of all the wear and tear of the years and with renewed youthful vigor thanked the Lord for His many favors.

"Do as you like," she said now to Lazzaro, in an access of true humility, which was more effective than any amount of ill humor and never failed to arouse him to grateful response. "You are always the same dear Dosolina," he murmured. "Blessed be the mother that bore you and the day when we plighted our troth!"

A whole world of things hitherto unsuspected rose up before the eyes of the wild and shy Cecilia as she listened to this solemn exchange between husband and wife.

"Master Lazzaro," she exclaimed, "your wife is a good woman and I shall love her."

Among the things she had learned in the days since her rescue, one of those that had most struck her fancy was the custom of the hand-

269

shake, which seemed to lend a sort of virginal freshness to the familiar pledges of gratitude and friendship. She repeated the gesture often and with a warmth that touched Dosolina no less than the others, particularly upon the present occasion when Cecilia said with spontaneous conviction:

"Here's my hand upon it, Mistress Dosolina!"

Dosolina pressed Cecilia's small but powerful hand which was calloused by the rough work of the mill and could not resist giving her a hug and kiss in the bargain. But such effusions were not to Cecilia's taste and she drew back shyly.

Giuseppe was lost in his thoughts. He was wondering, for one thing, whether to consult a lawyer upon the advisability of setting up a guardianship for Cecilia. He knew little of the workings of such an arrangement but he could guess at some of its advantages. Still, weighing these in his mind, he concluded that this was not the ideal solution. His father's idea of allowing her to repay him gradually was not such a bad one. But he didn't fancy his father, much less some perfect stranger, as the girl's guardian. He would have liked to fill this post himself, for he felt a real vocation for looking after the interests of widows and orphans to his own profit. But this was for the moment out of the question. He supposed that such things were regulated by law, although circumstances like the present ones should offer many a loophole. Still it would be all too easy to make a misstep. He leaned instinctively toward extreme prudence where the law was concerned. It was wiser to have recourse to justice only when there was something definite to be gained, and not to quibble just for the sake of quibbling. He decided, therefore, to leave everything up in the air and to insinuate himself little by little into Cecilia's good graces.

Malvasone cherished Cecilia like a faithful dog and Schiavetto gradually came to have a feeling for her of a kind he had never known, a tender, hopeless, mute suffering that he would never have dared call love. The years went by, like the water of the Po, like the spinning of the millwheel on the axle and that of the millstones on their spindles. The flour that was ground by the mill and then made into bread enriched men's blood and roused them to passions which were various and yet ever the same in the passage of time, and indeed time ran on in varied yet equal rhythm from yesterday to tomorrow and from life to death.

Cecilia Rei grew more beautiful every year. She had a robust frame and a somewhat masculine appearance in harmony with her strenuous trade, great agility in her movements, and a bold, proud air. And as she grew more beautiful the adoring Schiavetto fell into greater and greater despair. The very qualities that made him such an excellent and reliable helper fated him to be and aspire to be nothing more. His delicate rustic charm had endeared him to many women without his so much as being aware of the eyes they cast upon him, except in the case of the most enterprising and hence the least worthy among them. And just as his youthful charm faded away and seemed to pass into old age without ever fully coming to flower, so did the only true love of his life, with Cecilia for its object, wither away undeclared. He contented himself with the fervor of his own devotion and the affection with which Cecilia repaid it, for she was unaware that her friendliness had kindled an unrequited passion. She was the only one that failed to guess at his feelings, just as he was the only one to believe them entirely secret. Everyone else could see them quite plainly and said:

"Poor boy! Look what he's got himself in for!"

For although Schiavetto was now a grown man he was of the sort fated to be called "boy" until their manhood is over.

Master Lazzaro was, of course, deeply attached to Schiavetto. Privately he wished he could have had him for a son and in all probability he would remember him in his will. Yet it would never have occurred to him to upset the natural order of things by leaving him the possession of Saint Michael's Mill—("my soul to God and my property to my children" was his motto)—and he could not have imagined Cecilia Rei, a mill owner, marrying a mere hired hand. Schiavetto himself, as we have said before, was the last to contemplate anything so out of the way, and his daydreams served only to paint in brighter colors his picture of a quite impossible happiness. We shall find nothing so strange about his humility if we remember that respect for rank is just as common among the lower classes as among their betters. And this was especially true among the ordinary people of Italy during the last century, coming as they did from an ancient race, still bound by the traditions of Rome.

Dosolina Scacerni and Cecilia learned to respect each other without the least difference arising between them, because they had fundamentally nothing in common and did not pretend otherwise.

As for old Malvasone, one year as the autumn leaves were falling he said: "I'll not live through this winter to see the leaves green again." And he kept his promise, dying just as quietly as he had spoken.

THE FINEST TRADE
IN THE WORLD

1

ABOARD THE two mills and at Poplar Bridge, even after Princivalle Malvegoli had died, they heard more of what was going on in the world because of the news brought home by Giuseppe Scacerni, who went every Monday to market in Ferrara and spent most of the rest of the week going about to local village fairs. He travelled in a broken-down, bumpy cart drawn by a lean, long-haired horse which he had picked up for practically nothing at an auction. As soon as he heard one of the prospective buyers murmur that this equipage was such as to discourage anyone from keeping its driver company he said that in this case it suited him exactly. A typical bit of reasoning on his part, to which there was no ready reply. The horse, whose name was Lightning, was about as quick as the passage of a day of starvation, but this left Giuseppe plenty of time in which to meditate upon his business. He wore long trousers gathered in at the ankles, a short jacket, and a wide-brimmed, upturned hat which formed a sort of pointed visor over his forehead. Cold-blooded and shivery by nature, he swore by the doctrine that it was unhealthy to take off wool clothes too early in the warm weather, with the result that he wore them all summer long, until it was time to pile on still more in the autumn. His body was built along the lines of a barrel, with his short arms growing practically out of his shoulder blades like the wings of a plucked chicken. Sticking out from under his belly were two round, thin legs of equal circumference all the way from the thighs to the ankles. He had light, spread-toed feet, which he threw out to either side when he walked, especially in moments of self-satisfaction, in the fashion of a rooster. As often as not he suffered from boils or pimples on his neck and when this was inflamed by rubbing against his collar he was even more sweet-tempered and amiable than usual.

Giuseppe's business was that of a broker and he dealt for the most part in grain. He had a gift for nosing out the exact moment when a peasant or farmer was obliged by an accumulation of debts or misfortunes or by ill-timed hoarding of his produce to sell it out at a low price. With unerring instinct he knew how to find the sort of unlucky individual who invariably buys inferior merchandise for more than it is worth and sells good things for less than their true value. From Alberone to Lagoscuro lay the territory with which he was best acquainted, but gradually he extended his commerce to the city. His ability secured for him connections with the most important traders in grain and flour on the city markets and he made many business deals on their behalf in the outlying country. His odd appearance and unattractive nickname somehow enhanced his reputation and he was so proud of the latter that when someone asked how to find him he would answer:

"Just inquire for Were Rabbit. Everyone in Ferrara knows that name."

To his father's way of thinking this business stank of usury, gambling, and sheer dishonesty, and Giuseppe, instead of arguing about it, simply threw at him:

"Is it costing you anything? Have I asked you for money?"

"No, you haven't."

"Then what have you to lose?"

"My good name, which happens to be the same as yours. Have you ever thought of that? Shady business like this is bound to lead you to jail."

"I'm sorry, I assure you, but I don't see what I can do about it. If my name's Scacerni, I'm not to blame."

"What's that about blame? Are you implying that I'm to be blamed for the fact that you're not a bastard instead of my legitimate son?"

"As if I cared! You're the one that makes such a fuss about names! Let's put it this way: I'm investing the money and you're lending your name. Your contribution is hardly noticeable, for all the effort it costs you!"

He spoke with such sarcastic scorn of every scruple or obstacle in the way of making money that his father could find nothing to say and hung his head as if he were the one to be ashamed.

"I've known for some time, of course, that you don't like to see me doing business in my own way. While we're on the subject, let's have it out in the open. What can it matter to you? Are you lacking anything because of my gains? I promised to keep the accounts of the mill, and that I've done faithfully. I know what the real trouble is—it's that I don't want to be a miller and to your mind that's the finest trade in the world. How queer people can be! You think it's so very fine and I don't care a rap for it. What more is there to say? Doesn't half the world's charm consist in its variety? Why make such bad blood over a difference of opinion? You'd do better to enjoy yourself, I say."

It was all too true that this was the source of his father's trouble, and when Scacerni heard it thrown at him in this tone of voice he felt ashamed and disgusted with himself because he had not thrashed his son sufficiently when he was a child to cure him of his insolent way of talking.

"A fine trade yours is, you wretched boy!" he grumbled angrily, tugging at his beard.

"Come, come. I don't speak ill of yours, do I? Then you might at least respect mine. Otherwise I'll pull up my stakes and leave home. Thank God, I don't need anyone's help; I'm quite able to make my own living."

This was even more true than anyone could have guessed, for he kept his earnings a dark secret. But the threat he had just made was an idle one, which he had no intention of carrying out. It was meant only to alarm his mother and win her over to his side, which it did most successfully. Dosolina opened her mouth wide with fright, swallowed hard and broke into mute tears, with the result that Lazzaro was sorry he had ever started this useless argument. Let Giuseppe follow his natural bent, whatever it was; however displeasing this might be it was purposeless to upset his mother about it.

"Don't take it so hard, Dosolina," he said embarrassedly. "We were only talking."

"That's right, only talking," echoed Giuseppe, who knew that her tears had bought his immunity. "Don't be so silly as to cry over a few idle words."

"Exactly, don't cry. I still think that the miller's trade is the finest in the world, but that doesn't imply that I think ill of every other. Of course every father likes to think that his son will be his successor. But there's no combatting human nature."

"No more than death and taxes," said Giuseppe with a conciliatory grin, pacing up and down contentedly and scratching a pimple which anxiety had brought to a head.

"It's only that I'd like to see you always in agreement and I can't help being sad when you quarrel," Dosolina said, drying her eyes.

"I didn't know that our boy was so sensitive," said Scacerni laughing.

"Everyone takes pride in his own profession. You as a miller and I as a broker."

Giuseppe's business in the city had given him the idea of looking up his aunt, Argia Malvegoli. He ascertained her whereabouts without making himself known and made discreet inquiries concerning her, which furnished him with the following information.

After Giaour had fled from Ferrara in 1831 Argia had come to enjoy the protection of a man of considerable influence, Cavaliere, or, as he was now titled, Baron Flaminio. Was he genuinely attracted by her or did he take her up for political reasons, with the hope of making her into what he called an informant, or, in plain language, a spy? A close acquaintance with Baron Flaminio would incline us to the opinion that he persisted an even shorter time in the second purpose than in the first. At fifty-five years of age Baron Flaminio may still have had gallant leanings but he could not have persisted long in the illusion that Argia was the sort to be useful to the police.

Now Argia was kept by a certain Freiherr von Bieberfels und Marcktrathau, a lieutenant on duty in the gloomy Fortress. In all likelihood he had been banished there as the result of some youthful indiscretion, for the years went by and he remained in the same post and with the same rank as before, afraid to resign his commission lest his father cut him off from an apparently very handsome allowance. The gayest and wittiest of his companions gathered every evening to drink and make merry in the house rented by Argia Malvegoli in the Strada delle Pettegole, a richly furnished establishment complete with stable and horses. One of the first pleasures which von Bieberfels had shared with Argia was that of riding. She had become a skilled and daring horsewoman and gone on many a racing and hunting expedition, even as far away as the woods of Diamantina, where she probably gallopped any number of times in the vicinity of her day-laborer brothers. But whenever she passed by the old graveyard of the church at Sette Polesini she never failed to visit her mother's humble grave and to leave flowers upon it.

Lieutenant von Bieberfels was unpopular in the city, first because his prolonged stay there had made him conspicuous and second because he had haughty ways and what may have been no more than boredom had all the appearance of disdain. The fact is that his gay riding parties, the horses pawing the paving stones, the conversation in a foreign tongue, and the riders' condescending glances in the direction of the citizenry seemed to aim at creating envy and antagonism. The gilded youth of the city had taken a notion to compete with the Austrians in both fine horse flesh and accomplished riding, with the result that many an arm or shoulder was broken or dislocated in the performance of dare-devil jumps.

Clever rider as she was, Argia could not take place in these frenzied competitions. Nevertheless she had occasion to notice the strong aversion felt for her by the Ferrarese riders, most of them friends of the exiled Giaour. But because she measured everything by one very narrow standard and believed that the one and only cause of dissension among men was that so frankly described by the poet Horace, she attributed their bad feeling to jealousy of the lover of such a beautiful woman as herself. And they, on their part, had no idea that she was not aware of being in their eyes a traitor. Such news would have greatly astonished Argia, but no one passed it on to her, because while she in her vanity fancied herself the disputed lady of a knights' tournament the truth was that everyone shunned her. Bold, shameless, and shocking were some of the milder adjectives which she inspired; she offended the moral code of some people, the patriotism of others, and the decency of all of them together. As she drove out in her carriage she imagined that von Bieberfels was the envy of both men and women and was blissfully unconscious of the fact that the most aristocratic and wealthy families had as little as possible to do with Austrian officers. In some cases they had Liberal sympathies, but even the Papists resented the foreign garrison in the Fortress, especially upon the humiliating occasions when the Austrians stepped in to stave up the faltering power of the Papal government.

Giuseppe Scacerni's sources of information were in the shops and markets of the city, but from these he derived a clear idea of how and in what terms she was judged by the general population. They looked with favor on the risky exploits of the local riding champions, but hated Argia and her luxurious way of living, which offered a flagrant contrast to the widespread poverty of the early years of Pope Gregory XVI's reign and gave ostentatious proof that she was leading an immoral and ungodly life, which was certain to bring down God's wrath upon her.

One of Argia's luxuries, when she was tired of riding, was to drive out in a richly appointed carriage behind a pair of snow-white horses, as stunning as any to be seen in the Vienna Prater, whose favorite gait was an even, high-stepping trot. The fiery, excitable girl who had been Giaour's mistress was now, a few years later, a fully ripened beauty. Her skin was still fresh and clear and although her figure had filled out it was still slender and graceful. She was calmer than before and her eyes, which still had the same lovely coloring, had gained in languor what they had lost in fire. She was very elegantly dressed in the latest Parisian and Viennese fashions and women could not resist turning to look at her as she went by. She had developed respect for social conventions, a correct and reserved manner, and thoroughly bourgeois ideas with a dose of devotion to the Austrian court. This latter came to her not so much from her association with the gallant white-jacketed officers of the garrison as from the precepts of Baron Flaminio, who with advancing years had discreetly taken the post of an elderly beau or fatherly admirer in her house. He too enjoyed the dislike of his fellow citizens, who laughed at the recent vintage of his nobility, hated him for his fanatical persecution of the rebels of 1831 and, even if they were Papists, despised him for his allegiance to the Austrians. Now that Argia's passions were less turbulent than before she had, under the baron's instruction, become devout in her religious practices, to the point of exaggeration.

Now we must say something of the relationship between Baron Flaminio and Virginio Alpi, evil genius of Urbecco and the region between Imola and Faenza, where reactionary "centurions" and "volunteers" matched sticks, knives, and short pistols that they carried under their coats with the "squads" and "maquis" of the Liberals. Virginio was guilty of every sin but hypocrisy. Of Baron Flaminio's political machinations, of his pro-Austrian secret society, the "Ferdinandea," and what he poetically called the new jewel to be added to the crown of Ferdinand, Emperor of Austria and King of Hungary, Bohemia and Lombardy, Virginio had no opinion one way or the other. For the sake of bloodshed and booty he would just as soon have enrolled among the Turks as among the Sanfedisti. And it was for the love of money, which he coveted chiefly in order to spend it, that he thought of putting his devilish talents, which were bound by no ideological fetters, at the service of the wealthy Austrians. He was equally ready to work for Pope or Emperor, and drew the line only where the Liberals, patriots, and Carbonari were concerned. In his enmity to the latter there was a point of honor, of loyalty among thieves, for he had inherited his quality of Sanfedista directly from his father.

His character was printed in large letters on his implacable, muddy, greenish face, where every evil thought and passion seemed to have left a wrinkle or grimace. This face was constantly in convulsive motion, except for the strange, gleaming, malevolent eyes, which stared pitilessly into those of his interlocutor. With them he was able to penetrate all of another man's weaknesses: fear, avarice, lust, and propensities for theft, bloodshed, or tyranny. These low instincts were all he knew of man and all he cared to know, the rest he dismissed as nothing but "words" or "show." He was himself a good talker when occasion demanded, but more often he did not deign to speak. One expletive, "Yellow-belly!" was to him all-inclusive, and for him to apply it to anyone was tantamount to a sentence of death.

It may be that Virginio believed in God; he had never asked himself the question. The religious observances of himself and his fellows, which were only pretexts for bigotry and hatred, added a certain unctuosity to his manner and expression. If he did believe in God, it was after the fashion of a superstitious brigand. His fealty to the Pope, whom he had sworn to defend with his life, turned out to be very hollow indeed when Gregory XVI's successor showed Liberal leanings. In reality the only law he obeyed was an inner compulsion to evil and destruction.

Virginio was of medium height, powerfully built but not heavy. He was adept at the use of all sorts of arms and never went anywhere without carrying a sword cane. When he was alone or among his intimates and there was no necessity of hiding it he enjoyed moving it in and out of its sheath to make sure that he could draw it promptly. This weapon had served him on many an occasion, for in his province of Romagna there were plently of men ready to stand up to him. He had a gift for quick disguises, and most of his skill consisted in dissimulating the snake-like gleam of his eyes, which often he could not resist darting at his enemies, to their discomfiture and his own risk. His strongest single characteristic was a hatred of mankind in general, which came out in his harsh voice and sarcastic language even when he was trying to gloss it over.

For years now, especially after the revolutionary disturbances had died down, he had restlessly travelled about the Romagna region, working for the "good cause" and satisfying his own inclination for troublemaking. Thus it was that he met Baron Flaminio in Ferrara. The baron's ulterior designs and ambitions did not interest him, for he considered all such complexities as mere "show." But he was beginning to suspect that all his disguises and stratagems, all the clubs and scythes of his devoted peasant followers between Forli and Faenza, all the Sanfedisti of Urbecco were not sufficient to save him from the wrath of his victims. Least of all could he trust in the authority of the Papal government which he had scorned and flouted for so long—not without reason, since it had shown itself so lenient toward himself and his accomplices. His jokes at the expense of the government had taken a positively insulting turn when he said defiantly:

"Either the priests must help me exterminate these Liberals, every one, in a second massacre of Saint Bartholomew, or else we're all double-damned . . ."

The choice was unequivocal. As for his language, he chose to make it as scurrilous as possible, especially when he was talking to persons who prided themselves on their formality, like Baron Flaminio, whom he privately called a "stuffed shirt." In Virginio's lingo the highest possible compliment to anyone was to call him a "fast operator," by which he obviously meant a successful bandit.

"His Highness the Duke of Portella has written to me in his own hand . . ." Baron Flaminio would begin in an effort to impress Virginio with one of Metternich's less known titles. . . .

"Ah yes, there's a fast operator for you!" Virginio replied irreverently.

A "fast operator!" The baron choked with indignation.

"Just lately I sent a memorandum to someone in a very high position . . ."

"A scrap of paper, Baron, a scrap of paper!"

"What else am I to write on?"

"Yes, but when you have written, how far does it advance you?"

"Perhaps you can tell me."

And tell him Virginio did, with such pungent words and gestures that never again did Baron Flaminio refer to paper.

The political organization of the "Ferdinandea," in the paper form in which Baron Flaminio showed it to him, seemed to Virginio just good enough to wrap clams in. His chief interests at the moment were money and the possibility of future protection.

"The important thing is to be sure that if we compromise ourselves it is in behalf of a government that will stick by us in time of trouble, that will pull us to safety by our legs if those other wretches throw a noose around our necks," he said excitedly.

The baron shared this preoccupation in the fullest degree, but the language in which the other had phrased it got on his nerves. Alpi had, as usual, measured his man at a single glance and guessed already at his devouring weakness.

"My dear Baron," he asked him, "do you know the whole purpose of politics?"

"I should know, if you will allow me, since my hair's grown grey in political pursuits."

"You've wasted your time."

"How now? What's that? And you say it straight to my face?"

"How else should I say it?"

"I don't think you can prove it so easily," said the baron, with a half disdainful, half offended smile.

"After all you've done, the government is anxious to put you out of Ferrara and the Liberals are anxious to put you out too, in their fashion, with a knife between your ribs."

"Alas!"

"Then wasn't your time wasted?"

"But . . ."

"Don't 'but' me! I understand without any further explanation. Everything that happens to us is our own fault, my dear Baron. With all that you've learned you don't know this, that politics is the art of stirring up muddied waters."

"That's a daring definition!"

"I'm not afraid of men, so why should I be afraid of words?"

And in order to stir up muddied waters, which was the beginning and end of his ambition, Virginio Alpi built up everywhere the fame of the mysterious "Ferdinandea," a secret political society, whose leaders, he said, were high up in the government and controlled the fate of nations. Some of the importance which he attributed to the society was reflected upon himself, and meanwhile he left a train of curiosity and unrest behind him. So it was that just when Baron Flaminio was actually going into a decline and the "Ferdinandea" had no power except in his addled imagination, Virginio's indiscriminate publicity made the baron a target of the ferocious extremists left among the Liberals and Carbonari. They too operated with knives, pistols, and grenades, and the mere mention of an enemy's name was an excuse for them to eliminate him.

Such are the links between cause and effect and this then was the danger overhanging Baron Flaminio at a time when his once dreaded activity was long since over and he was entitled if not to forgiveness at least to oblivion.

2

"Well, Aunt Argia, here I am to pay you a visit. I'll warrant you don't know me."

It was a strange figure of a man, strange in both manner and accoutrement, that Argia Malvegoli saw before her. But his albino eyes and a familiar ring to his voice caused her to recognize her nephew.

"Peppino! You're my sister's son, Peppino!"

"Himself in person!"

"Oh, what a comfort! Who could have imagined it?"

"Turning up like a bad penny, Aunt Argia!"

"Don't say that! I tell you it's a comfort to me! Come along, don't stay in the kitchen; come sit down."

"No, Auntie," said Giuseppe prudently, content with having touched the proper note of family affection. "These hobnailed boots of mine would tear holes in the carpets or make me slide over the varnished floors. Your house is too beautiful. The kitchen is good enough for me. But since I see you've a stable, may I ask for some oats for Lightning, my horse?"

"Of course! All you like, my boy," said Argia, moved and flattered by her nephew's respectful behavior. "What a modest fellow you are. I'll see that your Lightning gets his oats immediately and remember that every time you come by there's always lunch for you in this kitchen. The more often you come the happier you'll make me."

Giuseppe almost forgot to rejoice over the money that his aunt's invitation saved him from spending for his own and his horse's dinner because he was so intent upon regretting the time he had wasted wondering whether to call upon her or no. Convinced by her generosity that she must be very rich, he thought suddenly to himself: "Imagine if in one of these past years she'd been taken ill and died! Of course, she looks strong enough, but there's no telling. And everyone knows how simple it is to have someone draw up a will. To think what we've risked losing, all because of my unworldly parents' absurd scruples. And why should they have felt reticent toward her? It's positively irresponsible of them. What if she had died among strangers, with none of the family around her? They had no right to be so selfish!"

In his case no scruples had held him back, but only calculation and uncertainty as to whether it was worth while to defy the popular animosity of which he knew she was the object. The animosity was universal, but on the sins that were held against her opinions varied. Some people swore that she was wealthy, others that she was in debt up to her ears; some described her as prodigally generous, others as miserably close with her money. All of them exaggerated to the point of discrediting their accusations. An old woman ragpicker who sold her wares near the cathedral porch and was said to be a procuress and moneylender on the side finally helped him to make up his mind:

"My boy, if a woman starts on a career like that and doesn't find someone who's seriously interested in her, then she'll die in the gutter. Do you follow me?"

These words had finally persuaded Giuseppe that he loved his aunt. As a nephew he naturally felt obliged to be extremely discreet and to pay no attention to the sort of people she frequented. And she was grateful to him for being content to stay in the kitchen, in spite of the fact that the stableboy, the coachman, the cook and the chambermaid had plenty to tell him. It didn't take him long to find out that these four servants agreed on only one thing, namely to rob their mistress, and that they were ready to league against him. Without having any notion of Roman history he imitated the policy pursued by Brutus the Elder in order to allay the tyrant's suspicions. The servants took him for a simpleton, played tricks on him at the table, treated him insolently and spoke their minds quite shamelessly in his presence. He drank his wine and nodded tolerantly, and soon he came to know the quantity of oats that was being robbed by the stableboy and the amount of oil spirited away by the cook, all this without their ever suspecting that they were objects of his suspicion.

"Is it true that they call you Were Rabbit?"

"That they do."

"What a funny nickname! But how can they think you're so smart?"

"Smart?" he answered, playing the fool. "Me smart?"

Then they would guffaw until they were near to choking. Baron Flaminio soon came to know Giuseppe and he too held him in low esteem. Whenever he met him on the stairs, Giuseppe bowed with exaggerated obsequiousness, taking off his hat and murmuring: "Your humble servant" in a way that moved the baron to laughter.

"Argia, you have a truly singular relative!"

"Poor boy, he grew up in the country. He doesn't know any better."

Giuseppe took pains that the servants should not overhear when with dissimulated cleverness he insinuated to his aunt that he was a very active broker and one well thought of in the trade.

"What, a simple boy like yourself, so modest and good?"

"Honesty is the best policy, Auntie. That's the only way to win a good reputation."

Then all of a sudden he would throw out tidbits of news and prophecies of what turn business would take next. When these came true his aunt was first incredulous and then astonished.

"Just ask the baron if things didn't go as I said they would. But don't say that I told you."

"Why not?"

"I have my reasons. Watch out, Auntie, and don't forget, unless you want me to be ruined. Secrecy is as important in business as it is in the confessional. Silence is golden. Remember, it's just between ourselves."

This air of mystery never failed to impress her, and the baron was invariably surprised to hear her come out with prognostications about the ups and downs of the grain market.

"That boy has a head on his shoulders," said Argia to her maid one day.

"What boy?" the girl asked, holding back her laughter.

"Mind you speak of him with respect; he's my nephew."

"If he's supposed to get the head on his shoulders from your side of the family, then for your sake I'll respect him."

"You must respect him for himself, my girl!"

"Respect him? Were Rabbit?"

She went into stitches of laughter and Argia put her out the door, where she laughed until later she began to cry over the soft job she had lost because she had let her tongue wag too loosely. In the kitchen the other three servants set upon Giuseppe.

"It's on your account that the mistress sent her away! I'd tie you to the horse's tail, I would!" said the coachman. "And I'd put arsenic in your plate, you double-faced country boy!" said the cook.

"I'm sorry to have made trouble."

"No excuses now! We don't want to see your face around here any longer. Either get the chambermaid back to her job or take your face away from here forever. Why should you batten on your aunt's kindness? A fine nephew you are!"

In the course of this masterfully played scene the three servants discovered Giuseppe's true nature, but too late. They thought when he called his aunt that he meant to capitulate to their demands, but instead he listed the fodder and oil and wine that with the tradesmen's connivance they had stolen from her. In a quarter of an hour it was all over. Argia ran her fingers through her hair and the clumsy thieves stood with downcast faces before her.

"Didn't I tell you I'd put an end to your troubles?" Giuseppe said to them. "Now you've nothing more to say."

"Out with the lot of you!" shouted Argia furiously. "Out of my house, you thieves, this instant, or I'll have you packed off to jail!"

Giuseppe's next step was to have his aunt get rid of her saddle horse, which was eating its head off in the stable without her getting any use out of it. He made himself into her accountant and steward and installed a system of strict economy. The tradesmen had been accustomed to padding their bills and having them paid without a murmur, but now the game was up and they had to answer for every penny of their charges. Argia extolled her nephew to the skies and he found satisfaction in the thought that the money he was saving her would go to increase his eventual inheritance.

"You'll go far," his aunt told him. "I see you one day as a prosperous merchant with offices and warehouses of your own."

"The hard thing is to make a start."

"With talent like yours?"

"I don't know about that. Good luck is better than talent, any day. To tell the truth I need money to set myself up in business. But that's not a woman's concern."

And he studied the effect of these words on her regretful face.

"I'd like to give you the money, you know that, and I'm sure I'd profit handsomely from it. But what am I to do?"

"Don't worry about such things, Auntie. Just enjoy yourself, since you're in a position to do so. I know of a good business deal in the offing; it's a pity to pass it up. But let's not think of it."

"Yes, let's think of it, I say. Perhaps I can help you after all."

Giuseppe was not sure whether to take her seriously or not. Little by little he informed her of the business he had in mind, which was to furnish grain to the Austrian army, known to make prompt and generous payments for all its supplies. But he would have to give guarantees and make deposits, build up funds to pay for his purchases and have a place to store them. Such was the least that could be expected.

"I can think of a very good place for storage," he said, interrupting himself all of a sudden.

"Where's that?" asked his aunt.

"A big loft over your stable."

"I didn't even know it."

"Never mind. I do. One more wasted opportunity. Too bad!"

"Surely it's not for the lack of ready cash that you'll let a fortune escape you?"

"That's just about the size of it. It's happened to others before me."

"Why don't you borrow money in the ghetto?"

"To be ruined by the high rate of interest? No, it wouldn't take so much money, at that."

282

And he looked at her out of the corner of his eye.

"You haven't the money, and I . . ."

"And you? . . ." he interrupted anxiously, holding his breath like a lover awaiting a reply to his declaration.

"I haven't it either."

No, she wasn't teasing; now he knew it. The truth was so simple that he had not even guessed it. Argia had no savings at all; she simply asked her von Bieberfels for money whenever a bill came in. In fact, before her nephew's arrival she had left the payment of bills up to the cook, who had bought a small farm with the profits. Giuseppe looked far more scornful of her careless expenditures than of the source of her income.

"Oh, is that how you conduct your affairs? Congratulations! All you know how to do is throw your money about on food and drink with these friends of yours! Is that it?"

"What else is a woman of my station to do?"

"Are you really asking me? Incredible! Haven't you ever thought, my poor Auntie, of all the things that might happen? Imagine, for instance, if this officer friend of yours tires of the same diet and finds some other woman he likes better than you. You're plump and he dreams of one that's thin; you're blonde and he fancies a brunette! In other words, he walks out on you. Do you think your creditors would come then with hat in hand? I'd like to make you see their hard faces. You'd die of fright!"

And indeed Argia felt faint with fear as, showing the whites of his albino eyes, Were Rabbit brandished his forefinger in her direction.

"How do you know that this paltry beauty in which you take so much pride will always please your lover or that you will find an equally generous successor? Old age is a long way off, you may answer. But what of disease? Smallpox, for instance, that can leave your face as riddled with holes as an old sponge. What good would you be then, except for the rubbish heap?"

"That's true, Peppino! I'd never thought of smallpox!"

"What was I saying? You'd never thought of it, eh? Perhaps you had it as a child."

"No, Peppino, I never had it then."

"Then you're as susceptible to it as the next one. There are cases every day. If you had a good reputation you might have something to fall back on. But here you are surrounded by luxury and grandeur, wallowing like a goose that doesn't know why they're fattening it, going out in your carriage and flaunting yourself like a peacock before the public eye. Do you know what they say about you? 'Shameless' is the mildest word with which I've ever heard you described." Here he spoke in a terrifying whisper: "Don't you know that there are people who simply can't tolerate the sight of these white-jacketed soldiers in our streets? It's no business of mine and I have no part in it, but there are those who are plotting, men who held the reins of government once and may hold them again. Would the Austrians protect you if they came back into power? They'd have other things to worry about, that you can imagine for yourself. I'd like to see what happens to you, come the revolution! And with the popularity you enjoy! You'd count on the baron, would you? But his would be one of the first heads to roll!"

"I understand. Alas, I've heard of these things. The conspirators are everywhere, so the baron says. But the baron is really powerful, you know. He's saved me once already and always remained my friend." Argia clung desperately to this last hope.

"I don't know anything, I repeat. But I've heard them talk of him in the market place. They say that if it weren't for the influence of the Austrians the Papal government would have put him out of the city long ago. He's powerful, you say? I hear that he's lost his prestige and even his credit. His debts are a byword. But that doesn't interest me. All I know is this, that you might be in a position to laugh at them all and instead you're like a goose that can't even call its feathers its own because they'll be plucked for a quilt or pillow before its neck is wrung."

Argia was reduced to tears of despair.

"Are you crying?" asked her nephew. "Why so? Haven't you always laughed? Why not go on laughing? To be quite frank, you make me angry. And all your wealth and luxury and dissipation turn my stomach. Let's look at what you have and get some idea of its value."

So saying he dragged her through the various rooms, planting his hobnailed boots in the carpets, knocking up against the gilded furniture, running his rough, unwashed hands over the silk curtains, pictures, silver and bric-a-brac and estimating the price of everything. In his petulance he scratched savagely at three pimples and caused blood to run over some of his aunt's despised possessions.

"This . . . and this . . . and this. . . . All things that it would cost a fortune to buy but that won't bring in a quarter of their value if you try to sell them. Shame on you! I'm going away!"

And go away he did, so pleased with himself that he flapped his feet sideways as he went out of the door. Later on he had a moment of doubt as to the wisdom of his tirade, but he was quickly reassured.

"Blood's thicker than water," he said to himself as he bumped along in his cart. "A man of feeling can't stand by and let his relatives make one misstep after another."

And he stood on his dignity without trying to see his aunt again until one Monday she sent word to the market place that he should come to hear some good news. She had spoken so highly of his business ability to Baron Flaminio that the baron had arranged for him to lay his grain supply plan before the Austrian Commissary.

"All things considered, for once you've shown yourself less of a goose," was all the thanks he gave her.

But such was Argia's fear of her nephew that she blushed with pleasure.

284

"Without capital I can't start anything," he added crudely, "and that I haven't got."

"Here's some money," said the prodigal sinner, drawing a wad of banknotes out of her bodice and handing them to him. "I hope this is enough to begin with."

"Yes, to begin with that will do," he said after he had counted them. "And what's the rate of interest?"

"There's no interest."

"What do you mean?"

"It's a gift," she said blushing, because in spite of the life she had led her feelings preserved much of their original delicacy.

He made one response more graceless than the next: Who did she think she was? Was her purpose to offend him? Didn't everyone know how she came by her money, with the result that he would be labeled as her fancy man all over the city? Argia broke into disconsolate tears and finally Giuseppe accepted the money simply in order to salve her wounded feelings, on condition however, that it be counted as an advance on the salary due him for handling her affairs. He no longer hung about the kitchen, but took up his post in a small study on the ground floor where every now and then his aunt came to invest more money in his flourishing trade. Soon Giuseppe began to spend more and more time in the city, sleeping in a room next to the study which his aunt saw to it was kept in perfect order. Little by little he began to build her up a fortune, heedless of what anyone, including his own parents, might say.

"I'm not surprised!" was his father's only comment.

Dosolina, however, was deeply shocked and unreservedly proclaimed her woe.

"I've always been a good son to you, haven't I?" was Giuseppe's reply. "Have I ever given you any trouble?"

"You're giving me trouble now!"

"There's no trouble except what you've made up. You are mistress of your house, of course, but when I'm outside I'm my own master. There's no use arguing about it. If you don't want me around any longer I'll go away. But that means for good. I'm a man of my word, you know that."

Dosolina listened with burning shame to this threat, aware that he was quite capable of carrying it out and that she was doomed to give in. And so the subject was closed and Giuseppe returned to making frequent visits to Poplar Bridge, where the proud and beautiful Cecilia was one of the chief attractions. The lust she aroused in him was mingled with avarice, for in all his passions cupidity played a preponderant part. At the moment his prospects were not famous, for she had spoken pungently of his latest activities.

"They say that you're acting as procurer for your aunt. Congratulations!"

"What of it?" he answered sardonically.

"You're right. Perhaps it's the trade that suits you best."

285

"Why so?"

"Because one day or another you'll burst with sheer miserliness."

"What do you care if I burst?"

"Sometimes I'm almost sorry for you."

"You can be sure I'd never think of *you* as a commodity to buy and sell."

"What's that? Me? A commodity?"

"Because if you were for sale I'd want to buy and keep you all for myself."

"Oh, dear me!" she exclaimed laughing.

But there was something in his eyes that cut her laughter short.

"Since we're saying exactly what's on our minds, Cecilia, I'll have you know that I want you to be mine. And by love or by force I'll have you."

"It will take force, I can tell you that. Don't speak to me of love!"

And this, then, was the end of Giuseppe Scacerni's declaration.

Meanwhile the storage of sacks of grain and flour in the loft over Argia's stable had not gone unnoticed. In the section between the Strada delle Pettegole and the Strada San Guglielmo, between Giovecca and the Piazza Nuova gossip had it that, abetted by her nephew, the harlot had turned into an enemy of the people and was trying her best to starve them. This rumor was not only current in the wide, quiet streets of the modern part of the city, but spread in ever amplified form through the ancient, winding, thickly inhabited alleys to Voltapaletto and the market place in the Piazza delle Erbe.

The problem of supplying the Fortress was one of great concern to the Austrian authorities both in Ferrara and beyond the Po, and the revolutionaries, on their side, had always dreamed of starving it out. The theory was widespread among the common people that in case of any disturbance the Austrians would have only to transport all the mills along the Po to the far side of the river in order to throw a ring of hunger around the city, and this long-standing fear was not without foundation. But popular hatred was reserved chiefly for profiteers in grain, who were suspected of eluding the controls and taxes of the Papal government and selling their goods to the occupying forces. There was indeed quite enough smuggling of grain to justify popular suspicion and before the provisory government of 1831 had achieved half its brief span there were rumblings of protest against the issue of permits "to export grain from the country." Now there was a rumor that the supplying of the Fortress covered a large-scale smuggling operation and that Argia Malvegoli and her nephew were shielding the activities of important dealers whose purpose was to enrich themselves and starve their fellow-citizens. Giuseppe Scacerni's reputation had begun to suffer, even more than with all his prudence he ever suspected, and from one night to the next he risked getting a beating.

Argia's Austrian lover had begun to tire of her and kept her on only through force of habit. It was always amusing, of course, to hear her pronounce herself with pursed lips on "ill-advised and seditious political opinions," the "balance of power" and the necessity of defending altar and throne against the "revolutionary dragon." Argia, however, was happy enough to have her nephew to keep her accounts and enrich her. And this he was well on the way to doing, while at the same time he had one eye on the finances of Saint Michael's and Bitter Bread Mills and the yield of his mother's farm lands. In spite of all his faults no one could gainsay Giuseppe's bookkeeping ability. The very sight of him bending over columns of figures gave Lazzaro a headache, but he had to admit that in this respect his son was very helpful.

"Father," Giuseppe said abruptly one day, "are you the Lazzaro Scacerni who on such and such a date (and he named the day, month, and year) received from the hands of a certain Ezekiel Annobon some things deposited with him by a Captain Maurelio Mazzacorati who died in 1812 in Russia?"

"This must be the resurrection of the dead!" Lazzaro exclaimed.

"Ezekiel Annobon died not so many years ago."

"He must have been over a century old!"

"Exactly. So you *are* the man."

"How do you happen to know anything about it?"

"From Ezekiel's sons, with whom I have some business dealings."

"If they're anything like their father then they're honest men. But for all that I'd stay away from them if I were you."

"Why so?"

"Such a memory for names and dates means that they are either very good or very bad."

"Anyhow, it's you they were talking about. They found your signed receipt among their father's papers."

"Very well. I had confidence in the old man and he did not disappoint me. But I could never feel so easy about the sons, after what you've told me. A memory like that is too much of a temptation."

"If I had an evil tongue, I'd say you were afraid."

"Not I. But so much good in the father bodes evil in the sons."

"You have it in for them, haven't you?"

"It's a law of Nature, just the way it is with grapevines, which fall off in quality from one generation to another. And what do these sons of his do?"

"They have an office."

"Are they dentists, or something of the sort?"

"No, they lend money."

"Usurers, is that it?"

"No, bankers. There are things you don't understand."

"I don't even want to understand them."

"And so when you were struggling through the Russian campaign you knew this Maurelio Mazzacorati, did you?"

"What if I did?"

"Oh, it's quite indifferent to me, even if you mulcted him of a fortune."

"A high opinion you have of your father!"

"You're safe, anyhow, on account of what lawyers call prescription."

"What's that?"

Giuseppe explained how the exercise of ownership over a prescribed length of time automatically gives it validity.

"I don't see how an honest man can rejoice over that," said Lazzaro. "Has the law a shorter memory than that of a usurer?"

"Come, come! A banker!"

"Conscience has the longest memory of all, that I can tell you."

"Perhaps so. In any case it's your affair."

"I should hope so."

But this conversation had stirred up too many shadows of the past in Lazzaro's mind for him to let it drop there.

"Some day, perhaps, I may tell you of that poor captain's misadventures in a river far, far away, the Vop . . ."

"It must be quite a story."

Was that all his son had to say, after suspecting him of so serious a crime? There flashed across his mind the suspicion he had seen in the eyes of the dead Annobon, and with it a host of other events that he had not thought of for years. Time could mend and destroy almost anything, even the indignation he had felt when Annobon had implied that he was a murderer, which now rose up in him again for a brief moment, only to subside as quickly as it had risen. He felt replete with years, in spite of the fact that he was not yet really old and no longer suffered as much as before from recurrences of malarial fever.

3

It would be unfair to judge the devout and scholarly but much satirized Gregory XVI only on the basis of his achievements as a temporal ruler during one of the unhappiest periods in the history of the Papal States. In his spiritual and apostolic mission Gregory played an altogether creditable role, which balances the sordid aspects of his political action such as we of necessity see reflected in our story.

The beginning of his reign, as we have already seen, was agitated, and the lull of the years 1835-45 was due rather to general weariness than to his political sagacity. Thereafter confusion and unrest once more prevailed, aggravated by an unusually meager harvest. The lack of bread and ensuing high prices were the direct causes of disorder and uprisings all over the Papal State. Here again the Liberals accused the Gregorians of deliberately fomenting both the scarcity and the rebellion against it, all for the purpose of arousing the people to another Saint Bartholomew's massacre of the kind advocated by Virginio Alpi. The reactionaries, on their side, threw the same bloody accusation at the Liberals and took pains to hammer into the people an old superstition to the effect that Liberal reforms would mean free trade in grain and hence famine. As a matter of fact, the people could see for

288

themselves that wealthy men of both parties, often with the complicity of the customs guards, were going in for smuggling.

The Austrian military command had long made heavy purchases of wheat in Ferrara. When times were good the common people, inspired by ignorance and envy, reproached the dealers with making too much money, and when times were bad they went so far as to charge them with a deliberate attempt to provoke starvation. The impotent Papal government was alternately timid and spiteful; when it did not call upon the Austrians for help it rather enjoyed seeing them discomfited by all these demagogic rumors. In other words, the Papists rejoiced to see the Liberals lose stock and were equally glad to know that the popular mistrust included the little band of pro-Austrian zealots, most of them devoted to the Austrophile Duke of Modena, such as Baron Flaminio. His "Ferdinandea" society, which was little more than a paper organization, under present circumstances struck the general imagination as a band of profiteers and enemies of the people, moved by sheer love of gain and troublemaking.

Meanwhile the baron had taken Giuseppe Scacerni, known as Were Rabbit, under his protection, praising the reliability of his business dealings and recommending him to the Austrian authorities. But the common people called Giuseppe a freak of nature and said that evil thoughts were what caused his splotchy complexion. He was a countryman, they said, who had acquired the vices of the city and now was sucking the blood of the poor. The Austrian Commissary soon had nothing but good words for Giuseppe Scacerni and an unsuccessful rival spread the news of this invidious praise, which rebounded to Giuseppe's discredit. Just as air currents blowing together from different directions make a whirlwind which shoots upward in ever widening circles, so did rumors fly around the head of Were Rabbit.

Baron Flaminio felt the same storm gathering around his head early in 1846, with the death of Francesco IV, Duke of Modena, who had been a scourge of the Liberals and a white hope of the legitimist extremists. Halfway through the same year Gregory XVI also died, and there followed a brief period of uncertainty before the consistory chose his successor.

One day while the baron was mulling over the disappointment visited upon himself and his fellow reactionaries by the election of a Mastai-Ferretti instead of a Lambruschini he was startled by a visit from Virginio Alpi. His visitor was disguised in the habit and wooden sandals of a monk and seeing the perspiration run down his cheeks the baron imagined that the heat of this unaccustomed clothing had put him in a bad humor. Virginio looked grimmer than usual and maintained an uncivil silence while he stripped himself of two pistols and a sword cane which he had hidden under his habit.

"Make yourself at home," said the baron ironically, but the other answered him with no more than a grunt. "What do you think of our new Pope?" the baron added, in order to break the awkward silence.

Virginio Alpi was in so bilious a mood that he still did not reply.

"You must know him well," the baron continued with unshaken composure, "since he was Archbishop of Imola. Apart from this fact, no one seems to have much to say."

"Yes, I know him," said Alpi, with a face that grew greener and more liverish by the moment. "He's a perfect moron."

"What's that?" said the shocked baron, raising his eyebrows. He had never got used to the scurrilous speech affected by the Sanfedisti and applied by them, when they chose, even to the princes of the Church. Such language is common among partisans and fanatics in general, especially when their beliefs compel them to pay respect to rank and form. We may go so far as to say that a history of political insults would undoubtedly show up as the most virulent and charged with hate those proffered by monarchists against the king and by Papists against the Pope. At least this is the only excuse for the excesses of Virginio Alpi, who in any such history would hold an honored place.

"What's that?" the baron repeated, looking askance.

" 'What's that? What's that?' " mimicked Virginio, with an obscene expletive punctuating his words. "I know him well enough to tell you that he's as softhearted as a piece of cheese and that he frowned upon the violence of the Gregorians at Imola. As if it could be called violence, anyhow! No, of this Pius IX we can expect only the worst."

In Virginio's calmer moments he punctuated his discourse with suggestive leers and jokes of every kind and these were transformed into outright obscenities when he was angered.

"For some time now," said the baron, with a superior air, "I've been saying that the Papal government can no longer count on the loyalty or obedience of any of its members, officials, police or militia. Either for cowardice or stupidity or gain, every one of them is ready to betray, and I can prove it a hundred times over."

"You won't tell me all hundred cases, I hope!"

"No, one is quite enough, my esteemed friend. I leave it up to you to judge. You yourself are a case in point, in fact one of the most important."

"I? I am a case in point?"

"Yes, you and your companions, or confederates or conspirators, whatever you choose to call them, *quidquid libet pro licito vindicantes,* you desperadoes of legitimacy. Do you like my Latin?"

"Yes, I do," said Alpi, distracted by his own thoughts.

"Well then," the baron went on, grasping this opportunity to display his powers of argumentation, "I include all you Sanfedisti and Gregorians, centurions and volunteers, all those whose efforts to stave up the Papal State have only precipitated its fall. You prated of order and brought anarchy. As one who has burned the midnight oil over the study of statesmanship and philosophy, I see in you an example of the proverb: 'I can take care of my enemies, but God preserve me from my friends!' "

"I don't know about the enemies, either."

290

"What do you mean by that?" asked the baron, showing surprise.

"I mean that the present government can't seem to take care of either friends or enemies."

"Well spoken!" the baron exclaimed. "You've hit it exactly! You've taken my opinion and improved upon it. If the government had officials worth their salt, the first thing they'd do would be to hang champions of your variety!"

He cut himself short, astonished to see that Alpi, instead of showing any resentment, had burst into loud laughter. After he had regained control of himself he said, putting his forefinger on the baron's chest:

"And what about you?"

"Me?"

"Yes, you! Isn't that secret society of yours, that private police, an affront to the government? And that network of correspondence with Modena and Milan and Vienna? It's true enough that if the government weren't as weak as you say I might be swinging from the gallows. But in that case you'd be wasting away in a dungeon. And here you are, by the grace of God and the Austrians a baron. All because Metternich chose to vent his spite on the clerical government that you have chosen to betray."

The baron bowed his head, while Alpi continued.

"I'm not saying that I blame you. I may even seek the same favor of the Austrians myself. But for the present the best thing is to see what the new Pope has in mind. At the first sign of indulgence toward the Liberals or of severity toward ourselves, then I say the devil take all secret societies, let's offer our services directly to Metternich, or the Duke of Portella, as you choose to call him. There's no other choice, for only Austria can pay us well and guarantee our protection. Are you a good enough friend to recommend me to the Austrian government?"

"What sort of thing are you ready to do?"

"I'm prepared to be an agent, a spy, an assassin, a hangman, or whatever you like! This is no time for delicacy, is it? And then it's one more way of aggravating our cowardly rulers. Have you enough credit with the Austrians to recommend me as a hangman?"

A fine way to spend his credit, Baron Flaminio thought to himself when he heard this sarcastic question, after he had spent thirty years building it up. Still it was only natural that Alpi should think of him as no more than an intermediary.

"I've done in and finished off too many men in my time to expect much better treatment myself in case of trouble," Alpi continued. "But don't go thinking you'll fare much better just because you've always worked with gloves on. Your secret police has done some dirty jobs and they'll handle you just as roughly as they will me. Then the Papal government will sit back and purr over having lost some of its most embarrassing friends. This Ferdinandea of yours is something of no consequence, mind you, but its name alone is quite enough to damn you."

Thus it was that Baron Flaminio recommended Virginio Alpi to the

Austrians. Meanwhile the policy of the new Pope promised to be even more dangerous than the two friends had feared. A few days after the above conversation, on July 16, 1846, when he had been only a month in power, the Pope declared an amnesty of all those who had been warned, exiled or imprisoned, thus raising the curtain on a truly Liberal Papacy, one which was to play a great part in the drama of 1848 and to lay the foundations of a new Italy. Even today, after a hundred years have gone by, the name of Pius IX revives in the memory of every Italian something of the enthusiasm that prevailed during the early years of his reign. But the resentment of the "Gregorians," when they saw themselves and their fanatical cause irrevocably lost, knew no limits, and Virginio Alpi surpassed them all in violence. The story of this feud is buried in documents and pamphlets as dead as the men that wrote them; suffice it to say that the Gregorians' hate was matched only by the charity of the followers of Pius.

The harvest of 1846 was worse than that of the year before and bread was dearer than ever. It looked as if the winter would be severe and the peasants hoarded their wheat while the city population sacked the storehouses and called for confiscatory measures against the hoarders, both procedures as old as the first ancestor of man who hid part of the crop in his cave while his fellows accused him of creating a famine.

In the autumn of 1846 Alpi held forth rabidly in Romagna, the Marches, Umbria, and even in Rome itself, wherever he could exploit remnants of the fanatical Gregorians, popular discontent, or the rebellious spirit nourished among many minor priests and monks against their ecclesiastical superiors. Many country priests were just as unable to accommodate their views to fit in with the policy of the new Pope as their rudest and most rustic parishioners, and their stubborn opposition found expression in such roughly persuasive phrases as:

"Pius IX is giving us reforms. How can we expect him to give us bread as well?"

Things went so far that from many a pulpit there were preached sermons that seemed to incite the congregation against the Pope. Alpi was hard put to it to find enough abusive words in his vocabulary as he argued that a massacre of Liberals, even if not completely successful, would create so much disturbance that the Pope himself would call in the Austrians to restore order. And this time, if the Austrians staged a serious occupation there would be no chance of their withdrawing. That would teach Pope Mastai a lesson! Alpi was abetted by former Sanfedisti as well as smugglers and criminals whom he had protected in the days when he had had a finger in all the administrative and judiciary offices of Romagna. In order either to bolster up his own reputation or to play a sarcastic joke or to win his way into the good graces of the Duke of Portella, he now called himself a knight of the Order of San Sylvester and a count to boot.

In Ferrara and its immediate surroundings a relative quiet prevailed, but the grain question was complicated by the large purchases made by the Austrian garrison. Giuseppe Scacerni heard it said to his face that the new Pope was going to put the "Fritzes" out of the Fortress, which meant an end to the profiteering of those who had sold them all the wheat and thereby caused the price of bread to go so high that no one could afford to buy it. The baron told Giuseppe to pay no attention to these rumors. "A donkey's braying doesn't reach heaven," was the way he dismissed them, reminding Giuseppe also of the fable about the frogs who would not be content with a twig floating on the water for a king and got a two-headed serpent instead. And Alpi, who was present at this conversation, put in a word to the effect that the good people of Ferrara would soon have the two-headed eagle of Austria to cope with.

But the baron took his precautions. He seldom left the house and when he did, it was to slink along close to the walls, wearing a long face that gave Giuseppe Scacerni additional cause for worry.

"I'm an honest man, interested only in my own business," Giuseppe always said, as if to dissociate himself from politics. The crowd in the market place and at the Piazza delle Erbe laughed in his face. And the baron confidentially explained to him his political theory as follows:

"A good government is where one central power keeps order in the streets and everyone's home is his castle. And a bad government is one where in the streets there is anarchy and no man's home is his own, because other people are overrunning it."

"Whose home do you mean?"

"My dear fellow, you heard me!"

"But I didn't understand a thing you said!"

Actually the baron was so afraid of some vaguely impending danger that he buried his head in the sand like an ostrich. From what quarter did he think he was threatened? The mob? Some change in the political picture? An adverse fate? He was afraid of everything and nothing, which meant that he was as afraid as he could possibly be.

"You understood me perfectly!" he insisted to Giuseppe. "Those clumsy shoes of yours don't make me forget that you have a head on your shoulders. What would you say if they came into your storehouse . . ."

"To rob me?"

"That would be the least of your troubles! To ask you exactly how much grain you have, to tell you where to buy and where to sell and at what price. To oblige you to sell your wheat to the people instead of to the Austrians. What would you say to that?"

"The people is a great beast."

"Well spoken. But this is what the people are after, this is what they call liberty and good government, and they'll cheer for whatever party helps them to obtain it."

"I'd sooner set fire to my storehouse."

"That's an heroic remedy. It reminds me of the man, who in order to spite his wife . . ."

"Yes, I know the rest. But can you think of any government that would be better?"

"My idea of a government is one that never slackens the reins on the horse's neck, or jerks the bit in his mouth. I believe in liberty where it's proper to have it. Let one man act for all where the general interest is involved and everyone have a free hand in his own private affairs. That's diametrically opposite to the ways of our present rulers, and to those of the so-called Liberals who still aspire to power. Keep away from one and the other and you'll have no reason to complain; your stores will be safe."

"What government can guarantee the safety of my stores? Only tell me where it is and I'll go to the ends of the earth for it."

"Just have a look on the other side of the bridge at Santa Maria Maddalena!"

This was the bridgehead across from Lagoscuro, in other words the nearest piece of Austria, the beginning and end of all the baron's discourse. There business prospered under an efficient government; the police were severe but not bothersome; the laws were few but respected; in short it was a veritable land of Cockaigne. And as a matter of fact, there was a world of difference between the Austrian administration of the regions of Lombardy and Venice and the unfortunate condition of the Papal State.

Meanwhile Baron Flaminio's fears grew and grew. The reforms instituted by Pius IX gave Italy high hopes in this brief period of 1846-47, which left its mark on history. There were new newspapers and other publications, banquets, fireworks, meetings, new government offices and a housecleaning of the old ones, plans and projects of every kind, a regular Italian revival, so wholeheartedly generous and enthusiastic that it exercised a fascination not only in Italy but in Europe and the rest of the world as well. An ambassador of the Sultan came to Rome, "like the Queen of Sheba coming to pay honor to King Solomon."

It was a time of ardor and inspiration, when the coming Risorgimento seemed to be outlined as a work of art, festive and glorious. In reality its days were counted and other trials and disasters had to be met and overcome before the final achievement. Still a budding like this was necessary. In some such way love is born at first sight and without that one look two human beings might never be bound for life and death together. It was a time when Italy recovered her youth and Italians fell in love with her. Of course discretion is just as essential as passion, but it is acquired inevitably as the years go by, and neither in love or politics or poetry is it of any use unless passion has preceded it.

This happy interval was marked by patriotic celebrations and funds raised for the rehabilitation of the amnestied Liberals. At the end of the year torches were lighted on the crest of the Apennines in honor of the hundredth anniversary of the stone cast at the Austrians by the young Genoese hero, Balilla. Beyond the seas Garibaldi was thinking

294

of setting forth to liberate his country and for a brief moment King Charles Albert and Mazzini were in harmony.

"Watch your step, Italians, I tell you!" muttered the baron to himself. "Sedition is rife all over. Unity and independence, eh? A customs union, an Italian federation! Italians, mind what you write in your papers!"

Thus the baron soliloquized, while every passing day gave him greater cause for concern. He was glad to have the days short because now he only went out at twilight, with the excuse that "in times like these an honest man can't show his face." The goal of his walk was invariably the Fortress. But he did not need now to make a report to the Austrians. The political trend was so obvious that a keen-eyed investigator would have been hard put to it to find anyone who was *not* openly voicing discontent. And so the baron went to the Fortress only to seek release and comfort for himself and to admire the still brightly polished cannons on the ramparts.

"These cannons won't respect the Liberal canons!" he said reviving his own hoary pun, which no longer made anyone laugh. Although he still raised his eyebrows and pursed his lips as if he knew much more than he was authorized to say, he was secretly at a loss as to how to answer Virginio Alpi's outbursts.

"What are the Austrians waiting for?" Virginio asked him. "When are they going to take at least these outlying legations away from the preposterously stupid clerical government?"

"*Loco et tempore,* the proper time and place, my dear friend."

"*Festina lente,* the more haste the less speed, is that it?"

"Exactly."

"I came down in a hurry," said Alpi, who had fallen from his horse. "What's that got to do with anything?"

"It's getting late, and it looks to me as if your Duke of Portella were in his dotage."

The baron did not lower himself to reply to such foolishness. And Virginio Alpi snickeringly told him how here and there in the country around Urbecco and in other villages of Romagna, Umbria, and the Marches he still administered beatings to some Liberal admirers of Pius IX.

"Here's for your Pope!" Virginio's followers cried as they laid about them with whips. "You can thank him for every stroke we're giving you. Here's one for him as he was when he was Mastai! And here's another for His Clemency as Pope Pius!"

Without the satisfaction he got out of these beatings Virginio swore that he would have burst long ago with irritation. His frenzy was such that he could hardly distinguish night from day. He threatened the Austrians with anarchy, his own followers with Austrian intervention, and those "cowardly wretches," the Liberals, with extermination. Virginio was storing up guns and cartridges and at the same time he amused himself with gluing a mustache and goatee onto the pictures of Pius IX in order to tear them off as if they were the badges of a

Liberal. He too wrote to Milan and Vienna, proposing to instigate rural uprisings such as had just been so successfully staged by the "peace-loving" Austrians in the freshly conquered Galicia. *Divide et impera,* as the Latin would have it.

Freiherr von Bieberfels, Argia Malvegoli's lover, had gone away from Ferrara and left her behind him, but she was living comfortably enough because her nephew had deposited a sizeable capital in her name at the bank owned by the sons of Ezekiel Annobon. She was quite happy to be momentarily disengaged and looked ahead with delight to the coming summer holidays. She did not dare speak of such things to Giuseppe, because he was exceedingly strict when it came to spending money on her pleasures, but in her imagination she dreamed of early-morning awakenings in the country after one of the long sleeps which she so cherished, of nightingales singing in the moonlight, of visiting fields and stables and barnyards. The very thought of these rural scenes made her feel young again. If only that nephew of hers were not such a rough lout! Still, now that von Bieberfels had gone, he alone had saved her from the immediate necessity of finding someone else to support her. Whatever he had made her give up, she could now go to sleep early and get up late, curl up cosily in her bed, stretch out her limbs and turn whichever way she would. She was living, in short, like a lady, and in view of the amnesty which Baron Flaminio spent so much of his time deploring, she almost wished that the exiled Giaour might find his way back to Ferrara. Had he not been her first and unforgettable love? One day Giaour did return and someone pointed him out to her on the street. What a disappointment! She had forgotten that so many years had gone by and was shocked to find that the middle-aged man who had gone into banishment was now frankly an old wreck. From a sentimental point of view he could no longer interest her, and so she returned to dreaming about the country.

4

Giuseppe Scacerni always went very early in the morning to the market, and in the section between the Castle, the Volto del Cavallo and Cortevecchia, where he met his fellow merchants and agents and on Mondays the peasants who brought their produce there directly, he was usually the first to appear on the scene. While he waited for business to open he would walk over to the Piazza delle Erbe, where the old woman ragpicker who sold her wares from a hole in the wall near the cathedral porch looked out from behind half-closed shutters with beady, rapacious eyes like a spider weaving a web to catch flies.

Soon the vegetable and fruit sellers came into the square, and their sons and helpers set up the tables and trestles where they displayed their wares. Farmers and peasants arrived with loaded wagons and wheelbarrows, and city boys went around from one to the other, helping them unload, inquiring about the day's prices, repeating bits of gossip, and trying in some way or other to turn a penny. Finally the night watchman, who kept an eye on the sellers' equipment until they arrived to claim it, saw the last-comers straggle in from the direction of the old Contrada San Romano and went off to bed. The relatively prosperous shopkeepers around the square raised their shutters, and among them the old woman, who stood with her back blocking the entrance to her hole in the wall and pulled out of various hiding places the crowns and pennies that she lent for a few days or a week at a rate of interest whose exorbitancy escaped the notice of the borrowers only because most of them had no notions of counting. She hardly knew how to count herself, and only the fact that she kept her capital in one bag and the interest she collected in another gave her an idea of her profit.

People said that once upon a time, in the space alongside the cathedral now occupied by her small shop, repentant courtesans had walled themselves up to pray until they died, subsisting meanwhile on crusts of bread handed to them through a grating by other sinners anxious to benefit from their prayers. Here, then, where these poor creatures had sought to save their souls, this old hag damned the souls of others and her own. When some of her customers teased her on this score she only replied:

"I'm looking after my own business. You look after yours and you'll find that there's place for everybody."

But if they threw it angrily in her face that with her usurious practices she was feeding off the poverty of her neighbors she would retire to the back of her shop so that they could see nothing but her glittering, predatory eyes and shout back at them:

"You care for my soul about as much as I care for yours! There's place for everybody in hell too, if you must know it!"

The wild look in her eyes and the hoarse voice in which she proffered this heresy caused people to accuse her of being a witch, of mixing poisons, casting the spell of the evil eye, and exercising the trade of an abortionist. When her feelings were ruffled no one dared penetrate beyond the threshold, as if she were a cat arching its back and spitting into a corner and might scratch their eyes out. Seldom did the market open without some exchange of harsh words between the old woman and her clients, but soon business began in earnest and her eccentricity was forgotten. When Giuseppe had looked over all the stands and found out the prices of the day he stuck his head into her lair.

"They've provoked you, have they?" he asked her.

"Wretches! May the plague take them all!"

When the Austrians came down from the Fortress with their military vehicles to buy vegetables, lard, bacon and meat they received prompt service and were treated as valuable customers. The little people of the market kept their resentment for the merchants who dealt with the Austrians on a larger scale and particularly those who furnished them with wheat. It wasn't the "Fritzes'" fault if they were born on the other side of the mountains; they had as much right to eat as the next man. But the merchants of Ferrara, who had sent up the price of bread, these were the real enemies. Enemies of their own country, of Italy, people were beginning to call them. Giuseppe Scacerni had a tough hide where such insults were concerned, in fact he had been born impervious to any hard words cast in his direction, but this new phraseology which came into vogue at the beginning of 1848, when the popularity of Pius IX was at its height, did somewhat worry him.

"Love of country, you call it? I say it's just envy!" he retorted, but there were hatchet-faced Liberals in circulation who had the effect of making him swallow his mockery.

The Austrians began to come to the market accompanied by armed guards with turned-up mustaches and fierce expressions, who clicked their heels and the butts of their guns on the paving stones at the loud orders of their sergeants. The more citizens gathered to look on with ironical resentment at this sight, the severer and more forbidding was the soldiers' mien. The garrison had been re-enforced with Croat and Bohemian conscripts, who knew nothing of Italy and were hostile to the Italians.

A provocation, said the patriots who filled the streets, cafés and drawing rooms, an outright defiance of public opinion, a bit of ostentatious insolence that could not be passed over without protest. The politicians held a more prudent language and advised against taking any action that might be considered by the Austrians as a pretext for repressive measures, the proclamation of martial law in the city, and the occupation of all the territory included in the Papal legation.

Those who had or thought they had competence in military matters talked a great deal about the ways and means of capturing the Fortress. They excluded the possibility of taking it by frontal attack for the simple reason that those inside had the cannons at their disposal, and spoke rather of laying siege to it and starving the defenders out. If the Austrians were really to find themselves barricaded inside, deprived of communications with the outer world, hunger might well bring them to their knees. Of this the Austrians themselves were only too well aware.

This was why the question of supplying the Austrians with provisions was such a burning one and had increasingly political implications. The patriots were unanimous in wishing for the formation of a national army and a civic guard which might some day or other lay siege to the beetling Fortress.

One morning Giuseppe Scacerni, with the unconcerned and ignorant expression that he took pains to wear on his face, was watching the clamorous arrival of the Austrian supply vehicles, when an outburst of laughter rang out among the crowd in the Piazza delle Erbe. Mirth ran like wildfire through the square without anyone stopping to ask the reason for it before joining in. Of course it was in itself contagious and besides one look at the astonished and irate demeanor of the

"Fritzes" was enough to start anyone off in gales of laughter. There they stood, trying to hide their discomfiture, with the butts of their rifles resting on the ground and their trousers tucked into their black boots in the style for which they were famous. By chance or mischance turkeys were on sale in the market that morning along with the usual fruit and vegetables, and patriots had gone around telling the vendors to pull out their tail feathers and cause them to emit an angry and painful lament just as the Austrians were clicking their rifles on the paving stones and their porters were opening up the bags in which they carried back their purchases.

"Do you hear what those turkeys are saying?" people asked one another.

"What is it?"

"Pi-us! Pi-us! Pi-us!"

And they all crowded together to listen to this cry and to laugh in the faces of the black-booted soldiers. Soon the laughter spread to the shopkeepers around the square, turned around the cathedral and reached persons who were faring on their own business under the Volto del Cavallo and in front of the Archbishop's Palace. These and many others were impelled to go listen to the seditious turkeys and soon their laughter was added to that of those already in the square, touching off one of the demonstrations in which the people were wont in these days to give vent to their generous but inactive enthusiasm.

"Long live Pius! Pope Pius, hurrah!"

The Austrians did not understand what it was all about, even when an officer arrived from the Fortress and led them away before they had laid in the day's supplies. But later on, at their mess, they became aware that they were on short rations. As they marched clumsily away amid the jeers of the crowd Giuseppe Scacerni followed in their steps somewhat surreptitiously. But near the Archbishop's Palace someone recognized him and shouted, pointing an accusing finger:

"Here's one of those patriotic souls who sell bread to the enemies of Italy!"

"Not I!" Giuseppe answered, genuinely astonished to find himself backed up against the wall with scores of angry faces around him and fists brandished in his direction, among them those of one very powerfully built and notorious public agitator. "I'm no baker!"

"Aren't you Were Rabbit?" asked his accuser, in the tone of Cicero letting out a *quousque tandem* at Catiline. "Don't make any slippery excuses to me! You supply wheat to the enemy, Were Rabbit, and starve the people of your own city!"

"Who is he?" murmured various members of the crowd. "What's happened? Is he a rabbit? A spy? Long live Pope Pius! Did someone say Pius to the gallows? Kill him if he did! Catch him there. Where is he? What's up? Did a turkey get away? No, they've wrung his neck. Whose neck? A rabbit's! The Austrians caught one of our men! No, it's an enemy of the people!"

"Citizens!" thundered the agitator above the general noise and confusion, for he had caught the unfortunate Giuseppe by the collar and was holding him up for all the world like a rabbit for the crowd to see. "Citizens of Ferrara! Fellow Italians!"

"Hurrah for Pope Pius and Italy!" the crowd shouted back in increasing numbers.

"Citizens!" shouted the orator stentoriously. "Today we've seen the minions of tyranny retreat before a flock of turkeys!"

"Hurrah for liberty! Down with the tyrants! Death to Austria!"

"Citizens of Ferrara!"

"Silence! Listen to him! Silence!"

"Citizens of Ferrara, soon the whistles and catcalls with which you accompanied the Austrians' withdrawal will be lead and flame. A word to the wise is sufficient! Away with the barbarians! It is God's will!"

"It is God's will! Long live Pope Pius!"

"Here you have in the pillory," he added, holding the popeyed Giuseppe up to their appraisal, "one of those wretches who shamelessly starve their own people in order to fatten the army of the tyrant. He isn't worth even a turkey!"

"Gobble-gobble-gobble!" chanted some of those who had been present at the beginning of the demonstration. "Even turkeys are more patriotic than that!"

"Good! Well spoken!" said the orator. "He isn't worth even a turkey. And do you know who he is? He isn't a spy, or a traitor or . . ."

"All right! You're stringing it out too long!" shouted someone from the crowd. "We've heard enough. Say who he is and let us go!"

"Were Rabbit, the well-known purveyor of supplies to the Fortress!"

The anticlimax of this long harangue, which had begun so violently, was Giuseppe's salvation. Half suffocated by the prolonged grasp of the agitator's powerful hand, he slipped away among the bored and distracted crowd and arrived, shaking all over, at the house of Argia Malvegoli. As soon as night fell, he told her, he would steal out of Ferrara and make straight for Poplar Bridge. Nothing on earth, he said, could persuade him to wait for dawn of the next day. He vouchsafed no further explanation and when his aunt tried to find out what had happened she had no other recourse than Baron Flaminio. Muttering something about the melancholy times in which they were living, the baron sold out Giuseppe's remaining stock of grain and balanced his accounts, thereby turning over to Argia a considerable sum of money that really belonged to her nephew.

"What shall I do with it?" she asked him.

"Hold it for him until he turns up again."

"And what if he doesn't turn up?"

"He will; never fear. But he showed himself too much of a coward, a true rabbit, as they call him."

"Poor fellow! He grew up in the country, you know, and then quite innocently he found himself among a pack of wolves howling for his head. . . . No one can blame him for losing courage."

"You're not so far from wrong, Argia. That's just what I said to Count von Auersperg, the commander of the Fortress, when he criticized your Giuseppe for his flight. What times, I tell you! What troubles! What universal disorder! Where will it all end, I wonder? A Liberal Pope who decrees an amnesty, it's perfectly absurd. They're asking for a civic guard and probably they'll get it. The government will give them arms which they'll turn against it. Then they'll get their constitution, their parliament, their confederated Italy, and all the rest of it. It's a disaster! It's political suicide!"

The baron did find a ray of hope in Fieldmarshal Radetzki's visit to the Fortress, which took place early in May of the same year. The marshal inspected the garrison, reviewed the troops to the sound of a rousing fanfare, promised that he would increase their number, received the gift of a sword from their officers, and even found time to cheer up Baron Flaminio, assuring him that Austria would never give up her Italian outposts. Austria was Austria, he said to his hesitant questioner, and soon she would prove it. A radical operation, he inferred, was far better than a gradual wasting-away.

The baron took heart, but he did not live to see the fulfillment of these promises. Virginio Alpi had spread rumors of a conspiracy mounted by the Gregorians and Sanfedisti, of a plan to exterminate the Liberal followers of Pope Pius. In Alpi's native Romagna, where partisan passion was always at white heat, there were many who saw in the weary old founder of the "Ferdinandea" the instigator of this black crime. On June 14, at half-past twelve in the night, while the baron was out for a nocturnal stroll in the Strada di San Guglielmo, unknown persons stabbed him in several parts of his body and killed him before he had time even to emit a cry.

<h2 style="text-align:center">5</h2>

Giuseppe Scacerni had always been a man of few words, and now, upon his return to Poplar Bridge, he was as silent as a tomb, in spite of his rage over the money—he knew exactly how much it was—that he had left in the hands of Argia Malvegoli. He carried his assets and liabilities not only in his ledgers but in his head as well, and now he had a dire vision of mismanagement and waste and ruin. Yet he had no mind to set feet in Ferrara and indeed could not bear even the mention of the city's name. The business he had left behind him occupied all his thoughts, and after he had answered with grunts the first questions that had been addressed to him, his family resigned itself to his mutism. When his mother affectionately tried to find out what was his secret sorrow he made rough gestures in her direction without uttering a single word.

Poplar Bridge might have been a hundred miles away from Ferrara and a thousand from the world-shaking events of 1848. Time passed by with the even rhythm of the millstones of St. Michael's and Bitter Bread mills. But toward the end of July an individual appeared on the scene whose face alone was sufficient to disturb the peace. The first person he disturbed was Dosolina, who was lounging about the house in the summer heat, which she held responsible (refusing to hear talk of her age) for a certain lassitude that had lately overcome her. She was alone in the kitchen and through the door came the hum of innumerable chickadees perched on the poplar trees and on the bushes which were dried up by the summer heat. Their hum would have annoyed her if she had paid it any attention, but this is exactly what she did not do.

She had opened the kneading trough to look for something she had misplaced, and now, although she knew that she needed it, she could not even remember what it was. And this too she blamed on the heat. There she stood, holding the cover of the trough in her hand and wondering what she was after.

The man had come in without making a sound. He seemed to be a beggar, dressed in rags. He was trying to hide one snakelike, gleaming eye under the brim of his hat, and the other was covered by a black bandage. There was a rough growth of beard on his face and he gave the impression of being very tired and having sore feet. After gliding noiselessly into the kitchen he stood there, shuffling his feet on the floor until Dosolina started and turned around to look at him, while the cover of the kneading trough escaped from her hand and fell clattering on the floor. The intruder did not move an inch, but a cold mocking light in his eye indicated that he was pleased with the effect he had produced upon her.

"I'm sorry to have frightened you, my good woman," he said.

"What do you want? Are you after charity?" asked Dosolina uncertainly, with visions of thieves and assassins darting across her mind.

"Charity, for the love of God!" he said with an air of false humility that was more offensive than outright profanity. "For the love of God, charity!"

"I can give you a crust of bread."

"God reward you for it, both here and in heaven! Can you tell me where to find a certain Giuseppe Scacerni?"

"Peppino?" Dosolina exclaimed in spite of herself, stopping short when it was already too late.

"Oh, so he lives right here! Come, come, don't be scared. I don't want to eat him! Are you by chance a relative?" He spoke these last words in an increasingly impatient and harsh voice.

"Why have you come? What do you want with Giuseppe Scacerni?"

"A favor that won't cost him anything, and may turn to his advantage. Where is he?"

"Around here, to tell the truth. . . ."

"That's enough, my good woman. I know now that he lives here. Just tell me where he is at the moment. I've no time to waste."

Dosolina nearly took offense, but she was worried about her son and anxious to get rid of this stranger and gain time. When no excuses came into her mind she took a bold resolution and answered:

"And I know that you're not what you're pretending to be. Unless you tell me what you want I shan't help you find him."

"Aha! Then you must be his mother and I understand your solicitude. All I want is to cross the river. A small favor, as you can see. And, as a matter of fact, I'm very much obliged to you already."

"Why so?"

"For having shown me that I've got myself up as too shady a character. Meanwhile, have no fear. Your son knows who I am. Tell him that Baron Flaminio's friend would like a word with him."

Dosolina was racking her brain to see how she could convey a word of warning to Giuseppe, when lo and behold he came through the door in person.

"You see?" the stranger said. "Speak of the devil and he is sure to appear!"

"And what do you mean by that?" asked the surprised Peppino.

"It's too long to explain. You've seen me with your aunt and Baron Flaminio. I was a friend of the poor baron."

"You *were* his friend? Has something happened to him?"

"You don't know? It's just as well."

"I don't know anything."

"There's not much to tell. The poor benighted baron! They knifed him three more times than was strictly necessary, because the first stroke had finished him off. It was all over in less than it's taken me to tell you."

"And Argia Malvegoli?" stuttered Peppino, more concerned than ever for his money. "I can imagine how lost she feels without that good friend to advise her in . . . in various contingencies."

"You almost make me laugh," said the false beggar, while Dosolina frowned at this mention of her sister's name, in spite of her relief over the fact that her son was not in danger. "What do I care for a . . . I mean for your aunt! I'm here to cross the river, and I have my reasons for wanting to stay clear of bridges and ferries. I don't know many people in these parts and so I asked your aunt, who wishes to be remembered to you, where you were to be found. And that's how it is that you see me wearing this false beard. Now I've told you all that's necessary. Can you put me across the river tonight? If you can, so much the better. And if not, it doesn't matter. But in either case mum's the word."

"That goes without saying."

"I wasn't so far off when I took you for a young man of good sense."

"My father will take you across tonight, that is if he consents to do it."

"Do we have to take him into our confidence too?"

"That's something no one has ever had cause to regret. I'm not familiar with the currents and if I took you we'd risk going aground. Besides, it's important to know at what time you're least likely to be seen."

We may note here that Were Rabbit had a long-standing fear of the water.

"Very well, then. Let it be your father. And of course I expect to pay my way."

"If he consents, as I told you."

"Let's go make the arrangements, then."

"If he consents to do it he won't charge you a penny. And if he doesn't no amount of money can persuade him. He has ideas of his own."

"His ideas are agreeable to me, I must say," said Virginio Alpi, whom the reader will already have recognized from his gleaming eye.

"I can't say much for them, myself," sighed Giuseppe.

"Why is that?"

"Because every lost opportunity is lost cash."

"Well, everyone's entitled to his own opinion. But let's go find your father without wasting any more time in discussion. Good day, Mistress."

"Good day, stranger."

When they had come to the mill young Scacerni explained their errand with considerable embarrassment to his father. It was the first time he had asked him for a favor of this kind and he had no idea of Alpi's reasons for escaping. Master Lazzaro stroked his beard, which was a sign of perplexity. He and his son talked in the cabin while Alpi waited on the deck outside.

"Come in here, stranger," called out Master Lazzaro.

"I am Count Virginio Alpi."

"As far as I'm concerned you're only a stranger that wants to cross over to the other side. Here along the river we refuse this service to no one, because we can't afford to make enemies. It's my custom to take anyone across that wants to go, without asking questions or making reservations. For this reason I shall pilot you over tonight."

"You're a man after my own heart, do you know that?" said Alpi with considerable astonishment.

"Don't speak too soon!" said Lazzaro dryly, for he could not in conscience return this expression of liking.

"Upon my word you are! Even if you have a beard that might get you into trouble!"

"What's wrong with my beard?"

"Plenty! If you'd come to Urbecco near Faenza with a beard like that the good people there would have had a carnival! Don't you know that a beard or mustache is the badge of a Liberal? Of course those wretches are at the helm now, with that confounded Pope of theirs. But it wasn't always so and it can't go on much longer. At the time I'm speaking about they'd have torn it off you, whisker by whisker."

"A carnival of that kind would have led them to a hard Lenten penance," Lazzaro observed.

"What? You're not a Liberal, are you?"

"To tell the truth, I don't even know what you mean. But here on the river I've never allowed anyone to lay hands on my beard."

"You've never heard of Urbecco?" said Alpi, who on the eve of indefinite exile had a nostalgic feeling for the only things he was capable of caring about. "You don't know the reputation of the people in those parts?"

"Perhaps it's better all around that I don't."

"Don't say such a thing, unless you want to pass for an admirer of this idiot Pius IX!"

"And you, stranger, learn to curb your tongue. Here aboard this mill you're in my house. And in my house we give honor where honor is due. We bend a knee before the Sacrament and to the Pope we take off our hat. What sort of talk is this, anyhow? And what manner of man are you?"

"Who I am? Ask me rather what manner of man is this Mastai, whom you honor as Pope."

"That's a good one! Isn't he Pope then? To tell the truth I'm beginning to think you must have escaped from the madhouse."

"Your ignorance deserves pity," said Alpi, "and since we have plenty of time before nightfall it may just as well be put to use telling you something about this Pope Mastai."

And Alpi poured out every infamy that he had thought up in recent months with which to besmirch Pius IX, every bit of filth suggested by his violent and sadistic imagination. The epilepsy from which the Pope had suffered in his youth became a sign of imbecility; a love he had cherished before even contemplating the priesthood an example of adulterous or incestuous lust, his piety a sham designed to mask his consuming ambition, and finally the election in which he had been chosen was painted as ruled by evasions, falsifications, and simony.

"Mastai is not a legitimate Pope, I tell you," Alpi concluded. "He pretends to be a Liberal only in order to pull the wool over people's eyes and to build up the number of his supporters in preparation for the day when a council of bishops declares him an anti-Pope, excommunicates him, and sends him to cool his heels in prison. Too bad that he's taken holy orders and hence can't be hanged! But, mark my words, he'll finish *in pace*. Do you know what that means? It's the confinement to which heretics and schismatics are sentenced, men like this excommunicated, free-mason, devil-inspired unbeliever. Is that enough? Or do you need more proof to convince you?"

But the result of his unburdening himself was just the opposite of what he had expected.

"Stranger, I'm convinced that you'll find some other boatman to put you across the Po. For I'll have nothing to do with you or your fellows."

"Oh, that's what you say, is it? Then I'll go my way. But you can take it from me," he added, foaming at the mouth, "that we shall meet again!"

"The later the better. And preferably never."

"For your sake I hope so! Otherwise, goodbye to your beard! You have the word of Virginio Alpi for that. And, unless I've lost all my cunning, you'll go to jail!"

"And you and your false beard to hell! If you don't remove yourself in a hurry I'll have to boot you on your way. *Sacramèstul!*"

Under any other circumstances Alpi would not have taken these words lying down. But he was the guiltiest and most-sought-after figure of the notorious "great conspiracy," which had sought to mark the anniversary of the amnesty decreed by Pius IX with the extermination of the Liberals and the capture and excommunication of the Pope, in other words the *coup d'état* and replica of the massacre of St. Bartholomew plotted by the Sanfedisti. Much of the plot was purely imaginary, but the dangerous ravings of Alpi himself, which he would all too gladly have translated into action, had done much to give the alarm. Now he was fleeing arrest and trial (for his name led the list of enemies posted in Rome and all the other cities of the Papal State), and also the wrath of the people from which he would not easily have escaped unscathed. In short, he was escaping the consequences of his own propaganda, of which he had just given Master Lazzaro such a vivid sample.

Alpi returned to the shore without making any commotion, swallowing his rage in a way to which he had long been accustomed. Were Rabbit slowly came back to himself and not wishing to fall out of Alpi's good graces loaded him on his cart and took him to the border of the Duchy of Modena, whence Alpi soon passed over into Austrian territory and engaged himself in the Imperial service.

"What an odd fish to have come my way!" Master Lazzaro said later, reflectively. "Is this the sort of people you took up with in the city?"

But Were Rabbit only shrugged his shoulders with an evasive smile.

Virginio Alpi was not the last strange acquaintance that Master Lazzaro was to make in that year and the next, which was one of extraordinary happenings. Great events, whose echo reached even Guarda, took place in Ferrara and other towns of the region. The civic guards, who wore a dark-blue uniform with red shoulder tabs and black leather helmets with brass and horsehair decorations, and were called brigands by the Austrians, clashed with the troops in the Fortress. In August the city was occupied by the army and then turned over to the Pope's Swiss Guard. The Pope proclaimed a new constitution, there were rumors of war against Austria, and thousands of turbulent volunteers from all over Italy flocked to Ferrara.

All this news roused astonishment rather than enthusiasm. The women, beginning with Dosolina, deplored the possibility of war, all the more so when the scandalized Don Giuseppe Romagnoli told them that two Barnabite friars, Father Gavazzi and Father Ugo Bassi, self-styled "apostles of freedom," were preaching in the squares to the volunteers, who had sewn crosses on their chests and adopted the title of crusaders. The two friars, then, preached war against Austria, with the slogan "God wills it," and their listeners taunted all slackers by giving them womanly spools of thread and publicly cursed the mothers and wives and daughters who would not let them enroll for the "holy war."

Rumor had it that an army of the King of Naples had come as far as

Ferrara, only to retreat in disorder, that Milan had chased the Austrians away, that Piedmont was at war and that the volunteers of the Free Corps had crossed the Po and King Charles Albert was in victorious pursuit of the foe. All these things seemed far away from peaceful Guarda. But they came nearer in June 1848, when the Free Corps, after suffering defeat at Vicenza, recrossed the Po in panic and crowded into Ferrara. These men were restless and suspicious, as is usually the case with a defeated army. Like all the rest of Italy they were tormented by the conflicting beliefs, hopes and passions that had destroyed the harmony of only a few weeks before. For everything in this fatal year, whether positive or negative, seemed to move with lightning rapidity.

General Durando of the Free Corps tried in vain to impose discipline. But this was achieved only by Garibaldi, the Ligurian sailor, who had just come back from America. Meanwhile Durando was branded a traitor, for, as we have just said, in this year cheers and brickbats followed one another in quick succession. The motley crew of volunteers began to percolate the countryside, many of them, such as the Sicilian followers of La Masa, finding it difficult to make their dialect understood by the citizens of the "continent" or mainland. Scarcity, especially of foodstuffs, prevailed, and rough-and-ready groups of volunteers took to foraging for something to eat. In the course of these expeditions they came to Poplar Bridge and to the two mills on the river.

Before we return to the adventures of the simple people with whom our story is concerned we must note that history is above good and evil and the life and fate of the individual, all of which can be seen in their true perspective only after death has arrested their course. Knowledge of history does not so much incline us to action, which is usually the fruit of passion and necessity, as to moralizing and reflection. It is, then, our historical and poetical duty to say that history brushed these benighted millers at a time when an outsider would necessarily have judged them most unaware of its meaning and most stubbornly ignorant of the ideals for which in this particular year men were fighting and dying.

It was inevitable that Guarda and Poplar Bridge should see not the cream but the scum of the brew in the melting pot, where Italy's future was being decided.

One morning early in July, as Master Lazzaro was riding from his house to the mill, he ran into a group of these disbanded and plundering soldiers. They were standing about, uncertain as to what direction they should take, and it was easy to see from their pale faces, bleary eyes and weary deportment that they had wandered about all night without eating. A good pretext for abusing the peasants and raiding lofts, chicken-coops and cellars was to mount guard over the pontoon bridges at Lagoscuro, Palantone and Francolino, which last was their goal at this moment. Don Giuseppe Romagnoli had been the recipient of their whistles and catcalls, and few of the peasants had escaped their rude visitations.

In the group there were men in the uniforms of the various Free

Corps. Some, who might have been veterans of the Februray uprising in Paris, wore workmen's smocks; others were clad in the new Italian style, with bright-colored scarves around their necks and wide-brimmed hats with plumes stuck in them. They carried guns, knives and sticks, but none of them any longer wore a medal with the picture of Pius IX and they had all ripped off their dusty, tattered shirts and jackets the tricolored crusader's cross, badge of the holy war against Austria. Austria had proved to be quite a mouthful, Scacerni thought to himself as he looked at their ragged condition. Meanwhile they signaled him to stop and started to question him in no gentle terms.

"Listen here, peasant, where do these roads lead to?"

"One way is Guarda and the other is Ro."

"We know that already," said one of them, who was turned out in Italian style, a little more tidily than the rest. "This side road is what we want to know about."

"That goes down to the dikes on the river."

"And where are you going yourself?"

The speaker was a heavy, corpulent man, and his attempts to put on a fierce expression—the thick mustache, beetling brows and tightly drawn lips—only made him slightly ridiculous, like an ineffectual scarecrow, with the black plumes on his hat bedraggled from wind and rain. Moreover the color and spongy texture of the skin of his nose betrayed the fact that he was a tippler.

"I'm going about my own business," said Scacerni calmly. Almost immediately he could feel that the group was not at all displeased to see their overbearing and pretentious leader taken down a peg by a stranger. Meanwhile the leader stuck out his stomach and said sarcastically:

"Oh, you're a lout as well as a peasant, are you? Perhaps you're one of our enemies. And you know how we treat them, don't you?"

"I'm neither enemy nor friend. You asked me where I was going and I told you."

"What is it you said?"

"I said I was going about my business. And what can you say for yourself?"

Some of the men began to laugh behind their hands as their leader retorted:

"I'm fighting for my country, if you must know, and I have every right to ask you what I like."

"And where do you get that right?"

"It's a question of military necessity."

"Pay no attention," said a man sitting on the edge of the ditch, raising his pointed chin to look up at Scacerni, who was on horseback. "His military necessity has a slender neck, a round belly and a cork."

The others laughed, but Scacerni said seriously:

"I'm not a tavern keeper and I have no bottles of wine to sell."

"Oh, Barbastrazzi there would just as soon steal them as find them on sale," said the seated fellow. But Barbastrazzi rejoined truculently:

308

"Go slow there, Vanetta, or we'll not get anywhere at all. Everyone knows quarrelling among ourselves is our worst fault as Italians. If it weren't for that we'd have the world at our mercy."

"At this moment," said Vanetta, "a loaf of bread would suit me better than the world or anything else that's in it."

"You're right there," said a third man, yawning noisily, "judging from the hollow in my stomach."

The yawn was contagious. Barbastrazzi was the only one who, in order to maintain his dignity beneath the cold eye of Vanetta, managed to abstain and keep his mouth shut. He was like a man face to face with the dentist's pincers, trying for vanity's sake to keep up his courage but in reality trembling with fear. It proved impossible for him to outstare his persecutor, who looked at him with sardonic cruelty and a gleam of scornful and malicious laughter in his piercing eyes. The rest of the group, standing or lolling about in knots of two or three, gave signs of fatigue and boredom. Looking down from his horse Scacerni guessed that there was some long-standing grudge between Barbastrazzi and Vanetta which he had not yet fathomed, and out of sheer curiosity he stared at them as if at some cruel but fascinating phenomenon of nature. The scene was like that of a muddy riverbank, foul-smelling under the hot July sun, where a fat toad is surprised by the sudden emergence from the slimy, bubbling water of the darting head, staring eye and writhing neck of a snake, hardly leaving any trace in its wake, so that the spellbound toad knows that it is lost and its faint, disconsolate croak does not cease until the snake has swallowed it alive.

This was the attitude of the swollen and pompous Barbastrazzi before the seated Vanetta, as little by little he grew smaller and smaller under the other's implacable gaze.

"Why have you got it in for me, Vanetta?" he asked mournfully.

The sight was a painful one, but not to Vanetta, who got slowly up, stretched his limbs and patted Barbastrazzi condescendingly on the back.

"You've always been a great clown," he said, "and so far that's been your good fortune. No one thinks you're worth the effort of killing. But mark my words, at Faenza they'll make people like you jump out of their skins. Remember, I'm speaking as a member of the Grand Maquis."

"And what has the Grand Maquis to do with me?" asked Barbastrazzi, while a spasm crossed his face at the name of this dread secret society.

"Aren't you a Saint Hippolyte man yourself?" said Vanetta, referring to the Grand Maquis' milder and more moderate rival.

"The Saint Hippolyte Maquis is second to none when it comes to patriotism, let me tell you that!"

"Do you really dare tell me such a thing?" exclaimed Vanetta, with a lurid gleam in his eyes. "The Pope's lackeys? If you ever set foot in Faenza, you may as well order your coffin in advance."

"What have I done to you?" groaned Barbastrazzi for an answer. "Why, in the name of Heaven? . . ."

"Nothing at all. There's no need for so many whys and wherefores. I'm just warning you, that's all."

"But as your sergeant I've always treated you handsomely. I've thought the world of you . . ."

"Then say it's because you've thought the world of me that I'm out to kill you. How's that?"

"That's no reason," pleaded Barbastrazzi in despair.

"Well, if you haven't caught on yet, let's put it like this: as soon as we get to Faenza we shall see which one of us is first to kill the other. Now, is it clear?"

It was so clear that the unfortunate Barbastrazzi blinked his eyes as if the sun were in them. Then he said in a tearful voice:

"I have a wife and children, dependent on me, Vanetta. That's why I have to get back to my grocery. How else are they to go on? I don't live off an independent income, you know that."

"And I tan skins, don't I?"

"Yes, I know," said Barbastrazzi, in a subdued tone.

"Then perhaps your skin will serve me in my trade. A coward and crybaby like you is a disgrace to our city. If we meet in Faenza I shan't waste so many words upon you. But here we have as much time to spare as that gentleman on his horse there. Don't you know, peasant, that it's rude to listen to other people's conversation?"

"Are you speaking to me?" asked Master Lazzaro, surprised that the attack should be turned on him.

"No, I'm speaking to those swallows."

A whole flight of these light-winged birds darted with gay song across the morning sky, dipping down to brush the swamp grass, from which the heat of the advancing day was already sending up swarms of tiny flies and mosquitoes.

Scacerni counted the men around him, a good three dozen more than the number he might have hoped to handle, standing around with their guns in their hands and their fingers on the triggers. It was a bitter pill to swallow, but he had no choice other than silence. He had no wish to indulge in useless discussion and so he stifled his resentment and kept his peace. He had started to spur his horse and ride away, but Vanetta caught onto the bridle and seven or eight of the others closed in around him.

"What's your hurry?" asked the tanner. "It's time to tell us who you are."

"That's it," chimed in Barbastrazzi. "Who you are, where you're going, and what's your business. For all we know, you may be an Austrian spy. After all, we're at war. And we have to take our precautions. You might be a spy of the priests, for that matter. We've had our experiences."

Scacerni would have been tempted to laugh, had he not been so angry, at the overbearing manner that Barbastrazzi had assumed once

310

more, in the vain hope of reasserting his position in the eyes of Vanetta. He stood there with folded arms as if he were questioning an important prisoner.

"Your name, then?"

"Lazzaro Scacerni," the other was forced to reply.

"And what's your trade."

"I'm a miller."

"And how do you happen to be on horseback?"

"I bought this horse with my own money."

"No one cares about that! Just answer the questions that are asked you! How do you happen to be on this road?"

"I'm on the way to my mill."

"And where is that?"

"On the river. Where else could it be?"

"No comment, please! We're doing no more than our duty, remember that, and now . . ." Barbastrazzi was at a loss what else to ask him. "Why did you stop just here?"

"You stopped me," said Scacerni. "You in person!"

"I did?"

"To the best of my recollection."

"That's right," said Vanetta. "You were the one."

"But I didn't tell you to listen in on our conversation, did I? That's very rude indeed, as my good friend Giovanni Marabini, known as Vanetta, has just told you. He's one of our best soldiers, I'm here to testify to that."

"Did I ask for your testimony?" asked Vanetta, infuriated by this adulation. "Do I need you to speak up for me? I have a notion to kill you off this minute, here on the road. What testimony can you give since every time there was any shooting you took to the bush?"

"The duties of my rank kept me back of the firing line," stammered the sergeant.

"Listen, my good fellow," Vanetta said abruptly to Scacerni, "what's your opinion of this man?"

"He's a fool," said Scacerni with quiet assurance.

"No doubt of it," asserted Vanetta, whose face was remarkable for its inability to show amusement by any other expression than a painful grin. "I just happened to call you 'good fellow,' and I hope you won't disappoint me."

"What is it you want?" asked Scacerni dryly.

"If you're a miller then there must be flour at your mill."

"We might do business on that score."

But the dauntless Barbastrazzi could not resist coming back into the fray.

"Of course! You don't think we're thieves, do you? As soldiers we're entitled to requisition flour."

"Then you no doubt have written orders and can give me a receipt for it," Scacerni answered, and he began to share Vanetta's feelings.

"Can you read?" Barbastrazzi asked with a superior air.

311

"I knew how when I was younger. But, granting you know how to write, I shan't waste time deciphering it. For who's to pay?"

"For whom do you take us?"

"I take it you're down on your luck, the lot of you."

"There you're quite right," said Vanetta, brushing aside the gaping Barbastrazzi's remonstrances. "Show us the way, Miller. Tow sacks are all we need."

They walked along the road, Vanetta and Lazzaro at the head of the line with the "exiles' legion" immediately behind them. Barbastrazzi brought up the rear, limping because of the corns on his feet and muttering that the priests were setting the peasants against the Italian Republic and that such insolence ought to be punished with rope, steel and flame. He talked on uninterruptedly because the rest were too tired to put in a word and some of them, particularly the Sicilian followers of La Masa, did not understand him. If they had understood they would only have felt more bewildered than they did already by the distance they had travelled and the strange circumstances in which they found themselves. The "exiles" talked among themselves of things that made Scacerni shudder. They called themselves "equalitarian communists," spoke of wanting "neither gods nor masters," of dividing all wealth and doing away with "mine and thine" and the "organized theft" that goes under the name of private property. These penniless wretches rambled on in this vein, partly in order to beguile their hunger and partly because it tickled their vanity to play the role of tavern philosophers and shock respectable folks with socialist phrases culled from their party journals. Every now and then they broke into French, recalling to Scacerni that once upon a time he had known a few words of this language himself. But before they could carry their discussion of Proudhon's famous maxim any further they arrived at the mill and Scacerni called out to Schiavetto to bring them two sacks of flour.

He thought that he had got off fairly easy until Dosolina lamented that evening that the same vagabond soldiers had come to Poplar Bridge and with the excuse of baking bread had stolen eggs and some fine capons which she had been fattening up for the family's consumption.

"They insisted on having something to drink, too," she said tearfully. "They broke down the cellar door and opened up the best barrel. Then they made us bake bread and roast the capons and thanked the girls by shouting obscenities at them. That's the way they're behaving all over the country. You'll never catch the Austrians doing such things. I hope they come over to our side of the river soon to stay."

"Cheer up, Dosolina. There are worse things that could happen."

"This was quite bad enough! Didn't you see those heretics?"

"Of course I did. They took the flour at the point of their guns from St. Michael's Mill. I can understand your crying over the capons. But I shouldn't waste any tears over the wine. That vintage of yours. . . ."

312

Well, you know what I think of it. . . . Drinking it will be penance enough for them!"

"There you go again! It may not be a first-rate wine, but it's not so bad as you make it out!"

"Very well, have it your own way! We've argued about it often enough to know that on this point we shall never agree."

"Because you're so hardheaded, Master Lazzaro! But that fat braggart with the plumes in his hat, I wish you could have seen how fast he wrung the necks of my capons! And the language they used! And the filthy things they did! We ought to have the whole house blessed again!"

The open chicken coop, the overturned barrel of wine, half of which had spilled out onto the ground, the musty odor and muddied floor of the cellar and the ugly remains of the orgy scattered over his front yard roused Scacerni to deep resentment of the vagabonds' violence.

Meanwhile the Piedmontese had captured the Fortress of Peschiera and were driving victoriously on, much to Dosolina's consternation. As for Scacerni, he merely said that in time of war there is a shortage of everything but news. And indeed victories alternated with defeats until no one knew what to believe any longer. The more people talked the less they knew, and it was not even clearly established whether or not the Pope was putting his heart into this Austrian war. Toward the end of July the Austrians forced their way across the three bridges and penetrated the Fortress of Ferrara without firing a single shot, since the Free Corps were in no condition to fight and the Pope's soldiers had orders not to resist them. Leaving a small number of troops to garrison the Fortress they marched out of the city again and contented themselves with holding the three fortified bridgeheads at Palantone, Lagoscuro and Francolino. The country people living along the river fell under their control and their patrols went from village to village in battle array, with the oak-leaf badge on their caps, loaded guns, and anger and mistrust written all over their faces. Local gossips with time on their hands to notice every detail of their appearance remarked that it had become stylish since the war for the officers to wear side whiskers and a tuft of beard between the lower lip and the chin. The bridgeheads were guarded by loaded cannons and soldiers constantly on the alert. In short, the Austrians still considered themselves at war with the Pope, in spite of the fact that he had it announced from every pulpit that he was at peace with the whole world. Don Giuseppe Romagnoli, like all his fellows, had orders to preach peace and quiet to the population, while along the Po, from the Bondeno to below Guarda, the Austrians requisitioned boats, which they sent loaded with wheat and flour to the other side, and in some cases transferred the mills along with them. They behaved not as if they were at home, but like conquerors in a foreign land. The rumor spread as far as Rome of a great victory in the field won by King Charles Albert at Sanguinetto, but news came later that he had been defeated at Custozza and was retreating from the

Venetian region. In every village the Austrians looked first for the civic guards, made a hostage of their captain, and threatened that at the first act of hostility they would shoot him. They set up posters on which they proclaimed their intention to maintain law and order and commanded the local population to turn in all their firearms under the one penalty which was recognized by martial law, the penalty of execution. The law was carried out inexorably and when the village of Sermide was nearly razed to the ground it was made abundantly clear what fate awaited those who dared offer any resistance. Late in July a body of militia was sent from Ferrara in the direction of Bologna, for the professed purpose, as usual, of maintaining law and order.

6

It was one of those days early in August when the parched earth seems to communicate to man some of its weariness and both long for the refreshment of a shower. Under two tall elm trees in front of the house at Poplar Bridge there were a rustic table and benches; summoned in haste from the mill Master Lazzaro found them taken over by soldiers with their trousers tucked into their boots who hailed his arrival with a joyful noise. They had laid down their caps, knapsacks, and guns, and appeared to be thoroughly drunk, although they were still drinking copiously. They laughed and shouted words of greeting in their tongue, while those among them, including a corporal, who knew some Italian came forward to meet him. Dosolina stood at the kitchen door with a look of mingled doubt and satisfaction, but it was plain that her anticipation of the Austrians' arrival had given way to anxiety over her cellar and pantry. Now the soldiers suspended their loud joking for a moment while the corporal called gaily out to Dosolina and clapped Scacerni on the shoulder, saying in broken Italian:

"You good Italian! You no swine of civic guard!"

This compliment left Scacerni puzzled, all the more so because one of the soldiers was interpreting the corporal's words to the others and they were repeating them in chorus, punctuated by gales of laughter and hoarse exclamations in their native language. Every time the corporal mentioned the Pope or Italy or Italians, jeers and obscene noises rose from around the table. The hungry and perspiring soldiers guzzled Dosolina's wine out of cups, glasses, pots and recipients of every conceivable kind that they had seized upon in the kitchen. Three soldiers went to and fro between the kitchen and the yard with a huge vat into which the others dipped freely. Down in the cellar Hayseed was having a hard time to keep it filled up.

"See if you can find out what they want," Dosolina murmured to her husband.

"That's plain as the nose on your face. And it doesn't require knowing German to see it. These fellows actually like your wine, Dosolina."

She shrugged her shoulders to conceal her hurt feelings and Scacerni very nearly burst out laughing. Meanwhile the soldiers gave ear-

314

splitting yells because their three cupbearers had lingered too long in the cellar. When he had recaptured their attention the corporal called out:

"We'll to go Rome and liberate the Pope from his enemies. *Pfui!*"

"*Pfui!*" chorused the others. "*Pfui! Dreck!*"

"*Dreck!* We'll take the Pope to Emperor Ferdinand—God save him! —in Vienna! And there the Pope will have to toe the mark."

The soldiers cheered the Emperor's name.

"Then peace will reign and there'll be no more war! No more war, ever! You good Italian! We good Austrians! Everybody good! First hang all bad people! Bad people, *kaput!* Liberals, *kaput!* Civic guards, *kaput!* Heretics, *kaput!* Brigands, *kaput!* Piedmontese, *kaput!* Bad Italians, *kaput!* Good ones like you, *vivat, hoch!*"

His words did not need to be translated in order to be received with wild enthusiasm. Scacerni had to accept an invitation to drink, and then the corporal continued:

"Drink without eating, no good for stomach. Today a great holiday, day for eating. You good people give us good people something to eat. And no more war, ever! You too, *Mutter,* you good old lady! Down with war!"

"Did you understand, Dosolina? They want something to eat!"

"And what shall I give them?"

"Give them some bread and ham. Let's hope that will be enough."

The corporal caught on at once, and shouting: "Good people! Good ham!" he published the news among the rest and started to overpower Lazzaro with drunken embraces, which were applauded by his fellows. Dosolina too reaped her share of applause and the assurance that all of them had old mothers at home who would have no traffic with war. Two hams were not enough, so they were followed by a third, and as for the wine, it seemed to come out of them in perspiration as fast as it went in. Many of them, indeed, regurgitated it in an even more unceremonious fashion on the grass, but their thirst was increased rather than diminished by its loss.

"Don't pull such a long face, Dosolina!" said Scacerni.

"What else do you expect? Am I supposed to laugh?"

"Didn't you hope they'd come back over the Po? Here they are!"

"I'll never forgive those heretics who let them pass!"

"Take it easy, whatever you do; it's no help to be angry."

Under the hot sun a heavy, rank smell hung over the yard, the sweat of the soldiers' bodies mingled with that of the lard they used to polish their leather accoutrements and the tallow with which they waxed their mustaches. These last had a way of dripping into their soup, so that people commonly called them "tallow eaters." Finally they went away, replete with food and drink, insisting loudly that they were the peasants' best friends and singing songs which frequently repeated the names of Italy and Italians and Pope Pius IX in what was doubtless anything but a complimentary fashion.

Similar visits were received by all the country people of the Bondeno, Diamantina, Il Barco, and Polesine di San Giovanni districts, who had to fraternize, willy-nilly, with their conquerors in the same manner. In Ferrara bread was beginning to run short. A few days later, on August 8, when the Austrians were defeated at Montagnola, just short of Bologna, by an improvised citizens' army, their officers ordered them to observe stricter discipline and the men lost much of their good humor.

Master Lazzaro Scacerni went one day on business to Guarda and just before reaching the village he passed near a melon patch lying to one side of the road. The fields all around were bare and shadeless and a dark thatched shed stood out amid the yellow-streaked green leaves of the ripe melons. From inside the shed came the voices of a gay group of peasants singing a licentious song as they downed slices of melon with glasses of wine. Scacerni very nearly laughed at the oddity of their behavior in shutting themselves up to feast and sing in the noontide heat. Around the village square, in the shadow of the church, which lengthened as the sun sank slowly over the parched fields, a large group of hungry and brutish Croat soldiers, who had laid down their knapsacks and stacked their guns, were taking a rest. They had obviously just finished a long, hard march, for they were covered with dust and perspiration and looked dead tired. They were commanded by two sergeants with faces even harder than those of the rest.

"Not one of them knows a word of Italian," said Don Giuseppe, who was at the door of the parish house, to Scacerni. "They say they've lost their way. Here they are, tossed by the fortunes of war into a country they've never seen before. Perhaps they have fought a few days ago near Bologna. It may be that they think our peasants have deliberately misdirected them. The fact is that they are very angry."

"You can see that from their faces," answered Scacerni, looking at them cautiously, since it was evident from their frowning expressions, the words they were muttering between clenched teeth, and the annoyed gestures with which they were shooing away the flies that they were intolerant of the stares of the few passers-by, mostly small boys who gaped at them as if they were so many rare animals.

"I'd like to find someone to guide them to Francolino," the priest added, "but I can't even make them understand what I say. I'd like to see them out of my parish in a hurry."

"Why, Don Giuseppe?"

"They're hardened soldiers, my dear fellow, and full of suspicion. They don't belong to the troops that have been garrisoned here long enough to know us and our ways."

"Not to mention our hams and our wine cellars!" observed Scacerni, remembering the feast in his yard.

"At least that damage can be repaired. But you must know that we priests receive constant hints from the Austrian command to preach peace and quiet to the population. What does that signify?"

316

"That they are ill at ease themselves," answered the lame veteran of Napoleon.

"Exactly. Who knows what these men before us are thinking up this minute. Have you noticed them?"

"I have. And I remember very well what it means for soldiers not to know the language or the roads of the country they are fighting in, to grope their way along with the fear that in every house or behind every tree someone is lying in ambush for them. In Russia we called them partisans."

"And the Austrians call them brigands. That sergeant, now, with the waxed, turned-up mustache, every other word he said to me was 'brigand' or 'pricand' as it sounds with his accent. And their command sends us orders all the time to recommend that people turn in their firearms."

"Very well, and what then, Don Giuseppe?"

"Then . . . well, did you turn in any arms yourself?" the priest asked him.

Scacerni made no more than an evasive gesture in reply.

"In short," Don Giuseppe said, as he walked into the house, "I'd gladly see the last of them."

In the heavy silence that hung over the village square the day was drawing wearily to a close. Even the swallows that had their nests in the church tower seemed too tired to chirp any longer. It was by contrast then that there sounded with a resounding crash a volley of rifle fire from the outskirts of the village. Afraid and angered the soldiers leaped to their feet and snatched up their guns, some of them biting the cartridges before loading and others pulling out their bayonets as they ran in the direction whence the sound had appeared to come. Scacerni and a few others followed them at a discreet distance.

Outside the village the long, straight road and the surrounding fields were deserted. The armed soldiers ran toward the shed in the middle of the melon patch, for the singing voices inside were the only sign of the presence of human beings. Perhaps the soldiers thought that the song was intended to shield the author of the rifle volley; in any case their fear and hate were kindled to a point where there was no stopping them. They stalked through the melon patch trampling down the ripe fruit, moving so silently that they could catch the words of the song from behind the closed door of the shed. Some of them raised their guns, ready to fire or to wield their bayonets at a moment's notice, while their fellows made a circle around it. The sun, which seemed almost too feeble to reach the horizon, lit up the scene with a pale glare. Scacerni called out to an alert boy, one of Chiccoli's sons:

"Go quickly and call Don Giuseppe. But don't let them see you run. If you meet any of them on the way they might shoot you down."

"There are none of them left in the village," the boy answered.

Meanwhile the bloodthirsty soldiers had set fire to the dry reeds of the shed. Four tongues of flame stood out against the pale sunset and four columns of smoke wound up over the edges of the sloping thatch roof and met in the center. The first man out and those that followed (Scacerni counted six of them) found the gun and bayonet points against their chests. Behind them the shed was going up in flames and they still did not know what was happening to them. The fire came out of the door after them and blazed at their backs. Raising their hands imploringly they walked toward the bayonets. They were answered by jeering laughter and the gutturals of a strange language.

The soldiers were disturbed by the heat and glare and moved back, pushing the little group of peasants into the middle of a square formation. Pushing them along with rifle butts at their shoulders and kicks at their legs they forced them to kneel down in a line along the edge of the road. Meanwhile the shed had collapsed and was no more than a mass of burning embers. Three soldiers took up their places in front of every prisoner and with their rifle barrels measured off a distance of four feet from their chests. One of the sergeants pulled out a short sword, stood at the head of the line, and shouted out orders. His gait, voice, and deportment and every motion of the soldiers as they measured out the distance and checked the readiness of their guns were stiff and conventional. In an atmosphere of cold cruelty and horror the approaching misdeed drew nearer and nearer, although the very fulfillment of so many military rites threw an air of improbability around it. The condemned men, if such they could be called, had passed from confusion to stark terror when all of a sudden the resolute young village priest, Don Giuseppe, with his cassock pulled up about his thin legs, came racing down the road.

While the six kneeling peasants were faced each one by three executioners, two aiming at his chest and one, between them, at his temples, the other soldiers lined up at one side ready to present arms when the second sergeant would give the order. Luckily none of the victims had courage or strength to attempt to flee or even to cover his face with his hands, for the slightest move would have precipitated the killing. The first sergeant was about to lower his sword as a command to fire, after which the firing squad was to kneel down and all the soldiers were to bare their heads while one of their number recited a *miserere,* followed by the rolling of drums. This was Austrian military practice.

Now, when he saw the priest running toward him, the sergeant with upraised sword seemed inclined, since all the other elements of justice were lacking, to give him time to grant absolution *in articulo mortis* to those who were about to be shot. Don Giuseppe did not waste a second in words; instead he threw himself on his knees before the first pointed rifles. The sergeant brought his sword slowly down with an air of discontent and embarrassment and the soldiers leaned their guns on the ground as if to indicate not that they had changed their plans but that they had temporarily put off carrying them out. Scacerni and two or three of his companions had drawn cautiously closer and were murmuring the names of the momentarily spared victims, poor ignorant peasants who stood there barely breathing, as limp as half-filled flour sacks. The only one of them to show any sign of life had lowered his face to cry and his shoulders shook with sobbing.

Don Giuseppe stood up and bid the sergeant have pity on his own soul and those of his men by drawing back, before it was too late, from the commission of so excessive a crime. He swore to the innocence of the victims and at the same time said to them between one point and another of his argument in tones of the warmest affection:

"Stay quiet and don't say a word. Don't dream of moving. Most likely they'll shoot me beside you, anyhow."

The sergeant was at a loss. He stood swinging his sword, like a man awakened from a dream who still acts as if he were dreaming. Loutish as he was beneath his tight-fitting uniform and quite unable to understand what the priest was saying, he could not help knowing what was the gist of his words and stopping to think the matter over. The Croats have always been devoutly religious and the priest's garb alone inspired him with a certain respect. Scacerni began to think that Don Giuseppe would have the best of it and with increased confidence he drew nearer. On the soldiers' faces there was written nothing but subordination; they might have been made of painted wood with their long, waxed, upturned mustaches and the perspiration running down their cheeks.

Suddenly the prisoner nearest Don Giuseppe had a mad impulse to leap to his feet and try to get away. All in unison the soldiers once more trained their guns on the chests and temples of the kneeling peasants and at the same time let out a loud grunt expressive of thwarted rage. Master Lazzaro saw their faces transfigured with anger and once more, as amid the orgy in his own front yard, the odor of foreign flesh stank in his nostrils. He was reminded of his painful experiences of hand-to-hand combat and the accompanying stench of blood and sweat and excrement.

With a lightning gesture Don Giuseppe reached out to halt the fugitive, pulled him back down on his knees and caught hold of the three gun barrels pointed against him so that now they were aimed against himself. Thus with action rather than with words he demonstrated readiness to share his fate. An endless minute went by. Then the sergeant barked an order, the soldiers of the firing squad shouldered their rifles and the others returned once more to a position of rest. Don Giuseppe looked into the sergeant's eyes and said "Francolino!" waving his arms to indicate that he offered himself as both a guide and hostage. And so it was that Christian charity won the day.

The soldiers tied the prisoners' hands together; some of their number went to retrieve the knapsacks they had left in the village square and the rest fell into marching formation. Of the shed in the melon patch nothing was left but ashes, and its owner, who was one of the six who had been nearly trapped inside, looked sadly in its direction. Now that he had escaped from the jaws of death his thoughts turned to his material losses. Master Lazzaro limped up to the priest, who was waiting, with a modest and yet radiant look of confidence on his face,

319

for the soldiers to start. Because he could not find words with which to express his thoughts Scacerni took the priest's right hand and kissed it.

"Oh, Master Lazzaro, so you are here too, are you?"

Lazzaro nodded assent with his head several times in succession.

"I sent for you," he finally managed to say, "when I saw that things were taking a bad turn."

"That was an excellent idea. Do you see now that I was right to be worried about the peasants who haven't turned in their arms?"

"Don Giuseppe, you have proved yourself a man! If you hadn't been here . . . All I can say is that you have accomplished a miracle."

"I followed Our Lord's bidding and He came to my help."

"He always helps those who help themselves so courageously," said Lazzaro with a trace of weariness in his voice.

"Then I am doubly obliged to Him, because if I was courageous that also is to His credit. Is there a boy you can send meanwhile to the parish house to get my hat and coat? I must go with these fellows— God forgive them!—to Francolino. Hardheaded, aren't they?"

The Chiccoli boy was standing just behind Scacerni and he darted off to fulfill the priest's request even before it could be repeated to him.

Two days later the prisoners and their savior were freed and it was impressed upon the priest once again that he must tell his parishioners to hand over all arms in their possession, something which they were as reluctant to do as the Austrians were eager to force them. Perhaps Don Giuseppe would have been held as a hostage even longer had not the Cardinal sent a messenger from Ferrara to request his liberation. When he returned to Guarda he told of the precautionary measures and requisitioning and reprisals of the Austrians and quoted the proclamation of their commander-in-chief, Marshal Welden, who had pointed out the ruins of razed Sermide as a warning to the terrified local population and stressed the rigors of martial law and the death penalty.

"They'll never go away," Scacerni thought to himself, without putting it into words, because the very idea caused him an almost bodily discomfort. The foreign odor was still in his nostrils, and in the pit of his stomach there were impotent disgust and resentment not only at the bestial rage with which the soldiers had set fire to the shed but even more at the cold and clock-work precision with which they would have climaxed the atrocity had not the good priest managed to stop them. He objected not so much to their blind anger as to the scorn in which he felt they held the Italian people. This stirred up his blood and moved him to rebellion. To his wife, who still could not see things his way, he said:

"Never mind, you haven't seen and smelled them the way I have. Strange beasts they are, these Croats."

"But who brought it all about? Who asked for trouble and called these strange beasts to avenge it?"

"Not the poor fellows in the melon patch, that's certain."

"Of course not. The innocent had to pay for the guilty, that's the way it always happens. But some people evidently were bored with peace and quiet and shot off their guns. Who were these enemies to God and man?"

"That I don't know. But don't tell me those Croats are God's friends, or man's either!"

The more he thought about it the angrier he grew. Finally it came to him that he had not felt so strongly since he had witnessed from the riverbank at Occhiobello Joachim Murat's attack on the bridgehead of Vallonga. Yes, now as then, he had an itching feeling in his legs and his blood seemed to run faster. When gunfire breaks out on the battle front, echoed by the deep voice of the cannon, an old soldier cannot but be roused to war.

Yes, he had an urge to fight with those Croat mercenaries. He had no political quarrel with Austria or the Austrians; his grudge was only against the particular group of Croats he had seen in the melon patch. He laughed to himself, old and lame as he was, as he remembered the story of the Hungarian horses.

These horses had been sold to some volunteers from Ferrara, at the beginning of the war, by Hungarian deserters from the Imperial Austrian army. But one morning when the volunteers were encamped near Verona the horses heard the bugles of a Hungarian regiment sounding the mess call and so ingrained were their habits that they ran away with their riders and carried them and their leader straight into the Hungarian lines.

"Fine fun that must have been!" he commented to himself, unaware that such stories not only tickled his funnybone, but also made him feel strong and adventurous as he had been in his youth.

Giuseppe Scacerni rarely opened his mouth during these days except to tell some story which threw into a ridiculous light the feelings and deeds of the Liberals in Ferrara, the volunteer crusaders and the Pope's "wooden soldiers," of whom half were neutral and half not.

Giuseppe's political ideas were determined by instinct rather than reason. He lumped together as spoilsports and madmen all those who failed to see that peace was essential to prosperity. It was their fault, he said, that he had been forced to flee from Ferrara, leaving all his worldly goods in his aunt's hands. It was not love for the Austrians that unsealed Giuseppe's mouth. He thought strictly as a merchant, glad to see a good customer's return and perhaps glimpsing in the not-so-distant future the recovery of the money he had given up for lost when he had hastily left it with his aunt in the city. As he wandered about the countryside and visited the local markets, he observed with thwarted greed that prices, especially those of corn and wheat, were steadily rising. His father, who had a particularly keen eye for his faults, could read Giuseppe's mind:

"You're hoping for a poor harvest," he observed.

"I'm hoping for nothing at all. If there is a shortage of grain I'd rather turn a penny myself than see others make a fortune off it."

321

Master Lazzaro unexpectedly remembered the strange words he had overheard on the tongues of the "exiles' legion" and used them to tease his excessively avaricious son. Excessive wealth makes men bad, he said; wealth must be divided among the community; no more of the "organized theft" that goes under the name of private property.

"Who ever put ideas like that into your head?" asked Giuseppe between clenched teeth, while his face grew pale and he raised his hand to scratch his pimples.

"More people hold such ideas than you may think," his father answered, enjoying the situation thoroughly, "and people of good education. They've all been written up in books, too, I believe."

"Then those books should be burned."

"What, the books?"

"Yes, the books and their authors. And those who read them, too. Burned on a slow fire."

"How kind you are! But look here, since you haven't a penny to your name, you should look favorably on a division of wealth."

"That's nothing to go by. I'm not thinking of what I haven't got; I'm thinking of the money I expect to make in the future."

Giuseppe's arguments and the passion he put into them left Master Lazzaro puzzled. All these ideas were actually quite indifferent to him. He looked at the affairs of this world with the eyes of a man who sees more clearly every year, even if he does not say so, that things will always go on the same, old and new, even when he himself is no longer there to witness them.

Autumn was creeping up on the Po Valley and there was serious danger of famine for the winter, especially in the territory of Ferrara. The Austrians, who had set themselves up as protectors of the pathetically feeble Papal government, were raiding and requisitioning at will, strengthening their positions as if they intended to stay and at the same time acting as brutally as if they did not mind leaving famine behind them.

The Austrians' first visit to Poplar Bridge was not their last. First Dosolina had lost her capons to the patriots, then the Austrians came and relieved her of her chickens and setting hens and even the proud rooster. In this case it was clearly theft for theft's sake, for the bird was as old and tough as the cock that crowed at Saint Peter's betrayal. There was no use arguing with the soldiers or begging them to show a little kindness, for they had given up fraternizing and feasting with the peasants and came by now in marching formation with written orders to turn over so much produce as a contribution to the war. As long as there was something for them to carry away they came to get it, always singing songs in which Italy and Pope Pius came in for obscene abuse so blatant that its meaning was conveyed even to those who did not know a word of either Croatian or German. In the cellar, to Dosolina's sorrow, there was left only a little incompletely fermented wine. But Dosolina still stubbornly blamed all the trouble on the patriot unbelievers who had called down the wrath of God on the land south of the Po.

The Austrians paid regular visits to the mill, took definite quantities of corn and wheat and a certain percentage of what already milled flour they could find. Part of this levy was for themselves and part went to the now rationed city of Ferrara. So little was left that Scacerni mumbled about famine.

"Long before you were born, Dosolina," said Scacerni thoughtfully, "we in the country around Ferrara knew that the Austrian eagle has two heads the better to eat with!"

The soldiers left notes promising to pay for what they had plundered, but the peasants began to hoard their grain rather than bring it to the mill. Master Lazzaro should have been prepared for what happened next, for he had heard tell for two months or more what was going on all up and down the river. But when it actually happened to him it was an ugly surprise. Soldiers with their trousers tucked into their boots and papers of authorization in their pockets came to requisition St. Michael's and Bitter Bread Mill.

By the beginning of September the greater part of the Austrians were recrossing the Po, having abandoned the region of Ferrara and the three bridgeheads on the river. Instead of requisitioning mills and boats, they were beginning to give them back to their owners. Just when Scacerni thought that the worst was over, he found the two mills requisitioned under his nose and sent with their workers to the opposite bank of the river to grind grain for the Austrians. And this was no simple matter. How could they hope to find suitable anchorage in so great a hurry? And Subbia had built the mill in such a way as to function most efficiently on the Ferrara side. But even if Scacerni had not remembered from his soldiering days that it was no use arguing against "orders," no matter how unreasonable, the looks on the Austrians' faces were enough to persuade him that his arguments would be thrown away. The best thing was to obey promptly before he was tempted to show the Fritzes the extent of his anger. In order to help him across the river they had sent a small tugboat from Lagoscuro, but he refused to make use of it. He explored the channel in a skiff, then cut the moorings and carried out first one anchor and then another into midstream, pulling the hawsers in around the windlass and kedging his way across, first in the St. Michael and then in the Bitter Bread.

Cecilia Rei, as usual, did a man's work, far more, indeed, than the lazy Giuseppe, who was not at all sorry to cross the Po and take up his station nearer the Austrian Commissary. The prospect so pleased him that he suggested that he be put in charge of St. Michael's Mill until the Austrians chose to return it.

"What if the war starts up again?" asked Dosolina, who was on the verge of tears, so great was her shame. "They might not let you come back."

"It's sure to finish one day."

"But the first thing they'll do will be to commandeer all the boats on the river."

"That's true," said Master Lazzaro, looking out of the corner of his eye at his son. "They'll take what's mine and thine, everything that goes under the name of 'private property' and make it theirs! You see, they're robbers just like the rest! Well, we shall have to wait and see. But tell me, Dosolina, what makes you think the war may start again?"

"I don't know. It's a feeling I have in my bones."

"What a woman you are! The way you used to have a feeling that the gypsies would carry away this boy when he was a baby. It's lucky for the gypsies they didn't take him. By this time he'd have sold the shirts off their backs!"

"Did I ever take anything from you?" Giuseppe asked with his usual wooden expression.

"After all, I'm your own father!"

"Still, if you were in debt to me, I'd feel entitled to collect one way or another."

The two mills, anchored in makeshift fashion on the opposite shore, worked day and night for military consumption. The Austrians would have been good customers if they had not claimed the right to set the price, and because Scacerni was a Papal subject, they set it very low. Scacerni made up for this disadvantage by reinstating the miller's traditional privilege of taking a toll from all the grain that went through his hands. In this way both parties were satisfied. But the more time went by the more he longed for the familiar anchorage on his own side of the river. Cecilia and Schiavetto felt the same way, but Giuseppe became so thoroughly at home with the Austrians that he could even exchange a few words with them in their own tongue.

7

The fatal year of 1848, with its cycle of revolutions and varying fortunes, laden with the passions that had set all Europe topsy-turvy, drew to a close in a deceiving lull, amid a feeling of weariness and oppression on the part of both victors and vanquished. The lull was obviously of the sort that precedes a storm, for there was no real peace in either the military or the political or the social realm. In Vienna Emperor Ferdinand was succeeded by the young Francis Joseph, while in Rome the brutal assassination of Pellegrino Rossi, one of Pius IX's most enlightened ministers, marked the approaching end of the noble but visionary ideal of government by a Liberal and constitutional Pope. It was the end, too, of a whole phase of history, of a day when a variety of small Italian states were bound together by the link of a universal culture, or at least dreamed and schemed of living in such a union.

In Ferrara and its surroundings, where the Austrians ridiculed and violated the nominal Papal authority, and the region suffered all the depredations of war without war being legally declared, confusion reigned.

Disbanded Italian volunteers and Austrian deserters between them made for a large number of crimes all over the countryside. In the city, the discredited local authorities had to put up with disorder in the streets in order not to call for help from the Austrian garrison in the Fortress, whose intention it was to take advantage of the disorder to tighten their hold on the territory which it was their aim to conquer. When Pius IX finally fled to Gaeta, few parts of the Papal State were as battered and weary as Ferrara.

The year was drawing to a close when on the evening of December eighteenth we find our millers, still in exile on the Austrian side of the river, wearily attending to their work of grinding under a clear but darkened winter sky. It was one of the shortest days of the year but the lanterns were lit inside the mill and they did not even notice the fall of darkness. Cecilia was baking corn meal in the oven for them to eat with herring for their supper.

"Mistress Cecilia, it must be time for you to give us something to eat," said Scacerni, opening the cabin door on Bitter Bread Mill. Then he stopped short in amazement. "What is this I see? Is the sun rising in the west? Or has the moon wandered from its orbit?"

In the western sky the clock seemed to have turned back, for there were all the red and gold lights and green glow of a winter sunset. At moments the colors were paler, like those of an unearthly moonrise, and the sky grew white, while the river and its banks were thrown into a cold, dead light, devoid of shadows.

Scacerni called Cecilia and Schiavetto to share his astonishment. Soon the sky to the west and north turned deep violet and burst into flames, as if a crimson cloud were mounting up into the heavens and absorbing the more delicate colors of a few minutes before. But still this outburst cast no shadow and seemed powerless to light up the thin line of the river, which was broken only by cold reflections like shudders running across its surface. Just as during an eclipse of the sun, dogs howled from every farmyard.

Our millers lingered on the deck to observe this phenomenon.

"I seem to remember seeing such a sight before," said Master Lazzaro.

They were attracted not only by the singular splendor of what they saw before them, but also by curiosity as to how it would end and be swallowed up in darkness. So they stood there, torn between hunger and cold on the one hand and curiosity on the other, while the Northern Lights flickered on.

"We saw them more than once in 1831," said Schiavetto with a melancholy smile in Cecilia's direction. "Eighteen years ago, and even then I was no longer a boy. Good Mistress, I've grown old!"

"What's the meaning of it?" Cecilia asked. "In '31 I was a baby and probably I slept through it."

"Ah well," Scacerni answered, "it would take an astrologer to explain it all, or at the very least an almanac. That is, if there's any believing the prophets."

"It must have some meaning," said Schiavetto, "like the comets we see in the sky."

"True, true," Master Lazzaro admitted thoughtfully and with a certain reluctance. "It may mean that the world has gone out of its groove and that it needs even more of a shaking up before it can start running again the way it used to or in some new and better fashion. That's easy enough to say. As we look back on it, the same thing was prophesied in '31 and it certainly came true. Now, here we are again, so plainly things aren't right yet. How is it the litany goes? From pestilence and famine and war, Good Lord, deliver us, eh? That's the best prayer for all of us. We've nothing to gain and everything to lose if disorder persists indefinitely."

But was this really true? He had hardly spoken these words when he half regretted them. Hadn't St. Michael's Mill been built with money that came from a time of unequalled disorder? He thought back to how the Spanish Virgin's treasure had been stolen and how it had come into his hands. This fleeting glimpse at the strange ways of fate caused him more wonder than the spectacle of the Northern Lights. His past life seemed to him like a long dream that had passed by in a flash and the effort to review it left him pensive and disconcerted.

"It would indeed take an astrologer's lore," he said to himself. "And what can that amount to, after all?"

"What about you, Mistress Cecilia?" asked Schiavetto, trying to lighten the tone of their conversation. "Have you no wish to make upon these wild lights?"

"I? What should I wish for?"

"Not even for a scarecrow of a husband?"

"Am I a woman to content herself with a scarecrow?" she tossed back at him jokingly. "Don't I deserve the handsomest young man ever?"

"That you do!" said Schiavetto, who was unable to say more because he was choking with emotion.

"After a man has lived a while in this world and known the good and bad of it," interposed Scacerni, "he sees that life is like a skein of wool. Whether we unravel it or tangle it further is eventually all the same, for only He who made it holds the end in His hands. When we have got this through our heads then we need no longer puzzle over the moon and the stars, over comets and the midnight sun like the one that is shining before us. All we need know is this: In His hands God holds the end of the skein."

So saying he pointed to the Northern Lights, which abruptly went out, leaving him with his forefinger in the air and his companions half afraid in a night of unparalleled darkness.

It is true that the tails of comets and the visitations of the Northern Lights have always given rise to prophecies of great upsets and surprises. And the events of the year following 1848 were such as to

326

justify any forebodings. But since every man feels that the only true version of history is that which he has touched with his own hands, we must say here that never again were the mills on the Po moved from one side of the river to the other. Although at this particular time all hopes of a united Italy were at a low ebb, the day was not far off when both banks of the Po were to be Italian.

Lazzaro Scacerni might have made any number of predictions based upon the appearance of the Northern Lights, but there was one thing that could never have occurred to him, namely that within less than a hundred years there would be no mills at all left on the Po river.

2
Trouble Travels By Water

THE SIEGE OF BOLOGNA

1

A S FAR back as anyone can remember the village of Guarda has had one characteristic, or rather oddity, all its own, namely that the church turns its back to both parish and parishioners. The façade looks toward the river, and between the square in front of the church and the embankment which protects this narrow peninsula there is no room for even the smallest number of human dwellings. The houses are clustered back of the church, and the church seems to protect them from the encroaching river, like a hen covering its chicks. At the time of our story there was a cemetery at the right of the church, but this was neither its first nor its last location. As time went on, it had to be moved farther and farther inland, for the river, not content with harassing the living, seemed intent also on shunting about the dead. To Lazzaro Scacerni this was an unwarranted imposition.

"Let the living struggle for survival, that's what they're here for. But the dead are entitled to sleep in peace."

"A lot of difference it makes for you to say so!" the good people of Guarda replied with a shrug of their shoulders and something between laughter and scorn. "Who do you expect to listen? The Po?"

"All I know is that if the river's going to pursue me even when I'm dead I'd just as soon it carried me away in a flood and buried me in the sand. That way I'd die as I've lived, a miller on the Po."

The landsmen laughed at this dire foreboding.

"We were born here and here we'll be buried," they answered.

"That's all very well for you who claim this for a birthplace. But not for me. There's no place for me in your sunken cemetery."

All Lazzaro's friends in Guarda, especially the Chiccolis, knew of his abhorrence for this cemetery, where one had only to dig down a couple of feet to discover a jet of water. But why did he have to rub it in for the benefit of those who expected to be buried there?

Here in Guarda there was a fateful overtone to any hint that neither for the living nor the dead could peace long endure. After the high water of 1839 the river began to erode this section of the embankment, beginning at Nogarole, where Master Lazzaro had his mills. The dikes of Antonella and San Guglielmo had no more shore to separate them from the river and the waves lapped directly at their base. It was generally agreed that the dikes could offer but little resistance and the authorities were duly informed of this condition. But Lazzaro, whom the villagers knew for both an honest man and an eccentric, only muttered invectives and they contented themselves with shrugging their shoulders.

The older Lazzaro grew the safer he felt aboard his mill. There the sweeping river seemed to him a harsh but honest friend, while ashore he felt that it was plotting evil behind his back. Looking from inland at the eroded dikes he could see the deceivingly quiet aspect that the Po showed to the landsmen. From the mill it appeared more fearsome, but its threat was an open one and did not fill him with the same misgivings. There had been no notable rise in the water since '39 and he wondered how the dikes would stand up against the next flood. He felt a return of the anxiety he had known during his apprenticeship as a miller, when a succession of fat years had given him a premonition that lean ones must follow and bad luck break over his unsuspecting head. Quite unconsciously, now that he was an old hand at his trade, he repeated what the oldsters had so annoyingly predicted to him when he had been a novice: that no one knows the Po who has not seen it raging, that it puts on a mild face only to lull the inexperienced with a false feeling of security, that there are a hundred varieties of flood and a thousand lurking disasters.

"What can any of you know who were mere children in '39?" he said irately.

The young men listened with boredom and impatience, and the old ones, who were practiced in worry, nodded their heads as if they were under a spell. And why did Scacerni insist on boring the ones and worrying the others? Just because in reality he would like to have sold the property at Poplar Bridge, free himself of all servitude to the land, and live with Dosolina and the faithful Schiavetto aboard his own mill, next to that of Cecilia Rei, who was a river dweller like himself. As he grew older his imagination stirred again to the fancies, now impotent, that he had felt in his youth. Once aboard the mill he had only to pull in the anchor and be free! But there was no use mentioning such things, he said, half in jest and half in earnest, to this wife of his, whose heart was set on pigs and chickens and silkworms, not to mention her ever-adored son.

During the months when the mills were under seizure by the Austrians Giuseppe had found business on the opposite shore that reawakened his unquenchable hopes of making money. He began by making up to the simple soldiers who came to have grain ground for military supply, heedless of the fact that the mill owner was a subject of the Pope. Because Master Lazzaro could not brook this imposition he was glad to have his son handle all dealings with these fellows "who wore their trousers tucked into their boots." Were Rabbit learned enough of their language to hold a conversation, and having stabled his cart and his asthmatic and knock-kneed horse, Lightning, in a barn near the village of Guarda on the Venetian side he began to drive to and from Santa Maria Maddalena, at the Venetian end of the bridge of Lagoscuro, where the Austrian Commissary had set up a depot for the collection of supplies intended for the Fortress in Ferrara. He soon renewed his intimacy with their officers, whom he found as preoccupied as they had been when he knew them in the city. Their task was complicated by the fact that during the early months of 1849 Ferrara was part of the Republic and the garrison was to all intents and purposes under siege.

Giuseppe managed to bring in a certain number of bags of flour by dint of the persuasion he exercised upon the peasants. During the disturbances of the preceding year, when the region had been treated to all effects like a conquered territory, the local people had stored away all they could for use in an emergency. It required considerable diplomacy to overcome their mistrust, and the longer they held back the flour the longer Giuseppe held back his crowns and florins. These were coins that dated back to before the time of Pius IX's "constitution," which to the peasants was a piece of trickery and mystification; in other words they were good Imperial money. When the crowns and florins had had their expected effect Giuseppe was able, as we have seen, to send a sizeable amount of grain to General Haynau at Santa Maria Maddalena. Because of the many times he had gone over the pontoon bridge of Lagoscuro and the military one at Francolino he and Lightning were familiar figures all over the region, especially at the port of Polesella, whose opposite number on the Papal side of the river was the main customs station for Guarda.

The crossing of the river at this point was effected by means of a primitive and antiquated system. A barge big enough to carry carts and heavy wagons was tied to the loose end of a rope anchored in midstream. A line of small boats was strung out at regular intervals to hold the rope out of the water and make its use more effective; by moving the oars or rudder in such a way that the current came from the port side, the barge then moved to the starboard and vice versa, the movement being like that of a pendulum, and the principle just the opposite of that which governs navigation by sail. This simple but ingenious system had been adopted in order not to stretch a rope all the way across the river and block the passage of traffic. The crossing was a slow one, but this did not matter to Giuseppe, who was never hurried and liked to meditate on his business affairs along the way.

A quicker way of crossing the river was by rowboat directly to Guarda, but this served only for small groups of people or very light freight. The landing place was known as Guarda Crossing and right on the beach there was a tavern, kept by a certain Orlandini, where two guards and their corporal from the main customs station had their quarters. The tavern keeper was an astute man, nicknamed the Rat, because this rodent is supposed to gnaw at things so quietly that it does not awaken its victim. He was commonly reported to be a hireling of smugglers and their intermediary with the customs guards, and in any case few people ever came to his tavern except those who ordered a glass of poor quality wine while waiting to cross the river. Orlandini was always complaining of his poverty, but the peasants, knowing him to be rich and to practice usury, only laughed at his lamentations. Most of the local people went to the Barchessa tavern in the Piazza Vecchia. A café had sprung up as a competitor just behind the church, but only very young men went there. The older ones, including Scacerni, preferred the Barchessa, which had belonged from time immemorial to the same family. This smoky and fly-ridden room, where good wine was the rule, had been passed down from generation to generation, each one represented by a host who was tidy and round-headed with a tendency to emit bits of homely philosophy, which had won for the entire family the name of Wiseacre. Each host was so like the last that to look at him made a man wonder when he was living.

Orlandini owned and operated the rowboat that crossed the river. He was a taciturn man except when he was bewailing his afflictions and nothing about him betrayed his legendary astuteness except for the fact that he had always something to whine about: that the tavern was empty, the boat did not afford him a living, and so on. And if it was true that he had made as much money from smuggling and usury as people reported he certainly knew how to hide it. Toward Master Lazzaro, Orlandini invariably showed himself unduly obsequious and for this very reason the miller sincerely disliked him and took no pains to conceal it.

Chiccoli, the cobbler, and his wife, Venusta, had aged considerably. He still had an eye for the women, but a teary one, which made his winking a pathetic affair. Venusta had heart murmurs and her legs would no longer carry her on the missions of mercy dictated to her by her homespun but kindly heart. Their numerous children had grown up quite successfully: the oldest boy was wielding an awl in his father's shop and the others had gone to work in the fields or canals. The youngest daughter was of marriageable age and one day Master Lazzaro said to Schiavetto:

"Why don't you step up and take her?"

"I wasn't thinking of getting married for the present," was all that his surprised helper could find to say.

"For the present? If you wait much longer, my boy, you'll be more fit to be a grandfather than a father!"

"I don't want to, that's all."

"But I can't see why. The girl's no beauty, but she's not bad to look at. She has her mother's wit and kindness and some of the ginger of her father. She's been well brought up and is a hard worker. What more can you want? She has no dowry and so besides getting a good wife you'd be doing a good deed that's sure to come back to you some day. Look at me, did I ever have cause to regret that my wife brought me no money? I can promise bread and work for both of you."

If Lazzaro Scacerni had taken to matchmaking it was a sure sign that he was growing old. As for Schiavetto, he was embarrassed and did not know what to do. Cecilia Rei had put in a good word for the marriage too and his heart ached over the fact that she and Master Lazzaro were the only ones who did not know how long he had hopelessly loved her.

334

Master Lazzaro had become impatient with everyone and everything except Cecilia, to whom he was more and more devoted. Now he said angrily to Schiavetto:

"You're missing a golden opportunity if you don't marry her. Don't say I didn't try to push you in the right direction."

"For that I shall always be grateful."

"Such stupidity, and all on account of money! For the sake of a dowry a man goes and marries the wrong kind of woman. You, of all people!"

"I didn't say it was because she hasn't a dowry, did I?"

"What else can it be? Have you any other fault to find with her? Speak up, if you have. If you stand there like a dummy you're positively insulting her!"

"Insulting her? As far as I'm concerned she doesn't even exist!"

"That shows you haven't very good eyes then!"

Schiavetto was so annoyed that for the first time in all these years he came close to ruing the day he had first set foot on St. Michael's Mill. In order to mask his embarrassment he said that there was a squeak in the millstone, and Master Lazzaro, whose hearing up to only a few months ago had been faultless, now felt uncertain and bewildered.

"A squeak, you say? It hasn't seemed to me . . ."

In the same way he had fallen into asking people why they were talking in such a low voice. For all that he had taken an aversion to life on the land and mumbled of retiring to his mill, probably the cold and dampness and discomfort of the winter he had spent aboard had made him hard of hearing besides stiffening his joints in a way which he refused to admit was very painful.

He took out his resentment upon the Northern Lights that had appeared at the end of the last year and swore that they presaged some grave trouble. And when he was finally free to return to his old anchorage and sleep once more in his own bed at Poplar Bridge he complained that the four walls around him were stifling and the barnyard smells unbearable. Everything about the land, including his wife's love for it, rubbed him the wrong way. As soon as the river was the least bit swollen he said that from the land it seemed to him oppressive, as if it were bearing down on his chest and preventing him from breathing. If he had to deal with the river, he said, let it be face to face, on the mill. And those Northern Lights of December 18, 1848, meant that trouble was brewing.

"Haven't we had enough of that already?" asked Dosolina.

"I don't know."

"What you're saying is heretical."

"How so?"

"You should say that it all lies in the hands of Him who is the author of our days, the dispenser of both good and evil."

"That may be . . ."

"What do you mean?"

"I mean that you're quite right, but I've got it into my head that one day or another the Po will break through the dikes!"

"Lord have mercy upon us!"

Dosolina paled, for if the Po were really to break through it would strike first at Poplar Bridge and probably destroy both their lives and the fields she loved so well. This fear Lazzaro did not share, indeed it only annoyed him to hear her enumerate the treasures of the farm for whose safety she was so greatly concerned. Little by little, as she counted them on her fingers, her fear turned into pride in the chickens, pigs, and cows, in the crops of this and other years and the silkworms she had cultivated so carefully. As he smiled disrespectfully into his beard and then relapsed once more into bruiting his notion that the land was no place for him to live and the cemetery unfit even to be dead in, Dosolina thought back to the days of turmoil and the nights of travail and passion they had lived through in the past when they were pitted against Raguseo.

"Lazzaro, I don't think that our saintly Mother Eurosia would approve of your grumbling," she said all of a sudden.

"There's nothing so serious as to warrant disturbing her memory," he answered, shrugging his shoulders in a way that did not conceal how much the mention of this holy name affected him.

Dosolina was worried by his behavior and said as much to Venusta.

"He's not himself any longer," she complained.

"Yes, he has changed, but not altogether."

"Too much for my taste, I tell you. I'm afraid he's ill."

"Well, age is a sort of illness, isn't it? Master Lazzaro and I can both testify to that, since we're considerably older than you are."

Dosolina remained vaguely worried and suspicious, without being able to put her finger on a reason. The long winter she had spent alone while the men were on the other side of the river, not very far away but far enough to disquiet her, had left a painful memory. To be alone after so many years of marriage had affected her and her husband quite differently. Sleeping alone, without her husband, was something to which she was no longer accustomed, it had caused her anxiety and discomfort and chilled her to the marrow. It was not a question of sensuality, for that was a thing of the past, one which had had for a long time now no place in their relationship. Still there was something sensual in their affection, in the habit of sleeping and breathing quietly side by side.

"Sleeping alone makes my blood run cold," she said to herself and longed to repeat to her husband.

Then he came back to her full of queer ideas that caused her still more worry. He took it into his head to sleep aboard the mill and had she not been aware of his queerness she would have imagined that some other woman had revived his youth. She dismissed this unworthy suspicion from her mind, but none the less she was jealous, jealous of the river and the mill and of Cecilia Rei. When Cecilia spoke to Lazzaro of matters concerning the mill he did not make a wry face but listened attentively and answered her with alacrity. Whereas to his wife he lent a distracted ear and wrinkled up his nose. The only good thing he ever had to say to her was:

"Excellent, Dosolina. Whatever you do is well done. You have a head on your shoulders and the farm is strictly your affair."

If the millstone was not grinding properly or a screw was loose anywhere in the mill he was ready enough to discuss what should be done and to get up early in the morning to do it. And all this for a stranger, an intruder. When rust threatened the wheat or anthrax the cattle then he took a hands-off attitude. Such things were strictly the business of his wife and son.

"Let's hope for the best, and prepare ourselves for the worst," he invariably said.

"Is that all you have to say?"

"What else do you expect?"

"Don't you know that anthrax can be fatal? And that it spreads like wildfire? It may mean having to kill off all our stock."

"If something can't be cured there's no use worrying about it."

"Oh, so that's it? I'd like to hear what you'd say if it were a question of the mill! You're not interested in anything but millstones and hoppers. Curses on Saint Michael's and Bitter Bread along with it!"

"Come, come, my good woman," he said laughingly, "by now you must just take me the way I come, like an epidemic among your cows or chickens."

The way he came, indeed! That was an old story! But there was something else that embittered Dosolina and mortified her beyond words, so that she ate her heart out in silence over it, and this was the behavior of her son. He had resumed staying away from home even more than before. Every now and then he came to spend the night or snatch a bite to eat, just as if he were in a hotel except that he had no bill to pay. He arrived late at night and left before dawn and gradually it came out that some market or fair was being held in the neighborhood or there was some piece of business he wanted to settle in connection with his collection of grain. He did not come home for love of his mother, no, never. And during the brief hours he spent there he was careless and distracted, intent only upon the greasy notebook in which he kept his accounts. He was very particular about his food and in spite of the care with which his mother prepared it he termed it "passable peasant fare," and sat at the table disdainfully without saying a word.

"Better so," said his father, "because when he talks he makes me angry."

Dosolina had hoped in silence, without even admitting it to herself, that the troubles her son had gone through when he fled in '48 from Ferrara would cure him of his wanderlust and bring him back to her to stay, for she loved him in the aggressively fatuous fashion of a mother who has spoiled her child. Now she was enduring the fate that is invariably visited upon a mother of this kind, namely ingratitude.

337

Still she considered him a mere boy and suffered because she could not confide her feelings in her husband.

"You brought him up as you saw fit," Lazzaro would say unceremoniously, "and now you have just what you asked for, an egotist."

So Dosolina dared not betray her sorrow. Now she too opposed the "shady business" of "her boy" and finally decided to speak of it to Don Giuseppe Romagnoli, the parish priest of Guarda.

"That boy of mine is going astray, Don Giuseppe. He doesn't even observe the Lord's Day. You must tell him to go to Mass on Sundays and the holy days of obligation."

"I'll tell him, never fear. Just send him to me in the rectory."

"I've no time to go to the rectory," was all the reply that Dosolina had from her son.

Business and money! Didn't he have time to look after his soul? Dosolina arranged for a meeting at Poplar Bridge between the priest and her busy son.

"Fine things I hear about you, Peppino! I'm told you haven't time to listen to your parish priest speak to you of a business more important than any of those here below. Is that true?"

"Is what true?"

"That you haven't time to listen to me? Are you deaf?"

"I haven't time, that's true, and I'm not deaf either."

"Oh, is that the way to answer? Have you fallen so low?"

"I'm only answering the truth."

"Ah? But do you at least remember that there *is* a business more important than any other?"

"Don Giuseppe, I respect you as I should, but let's cut it short. I suppose my mother's been talking to you, poor thing. She must have been blubbering about nothing."

"Blubbering? Let me tell you . . ."

"Let me tell *you*, Don Giuseppe, that I happen to work for the interests of just the business you're speaking of."

The priest was taken aback.

"Are you teaching me something?" he asked. "Are you trying to preach to me?"

"No, I shouldn't presume to do any such thing. I only want to explain and excuse myself, if you still think it's necessary."

"Let's hear your excuse then."

"A few words are enough. And if you weren't a priest I'd not even bother with so many. I never pay any attention to ignoramuses."

Dosolina, who sat in one corner of the kitchen, pretending not to listen, could not contain herself.

"Who's an ignoramus?" she asked.

"The cackling hen," said the insolent Giuseppe, without even bothering to look at her, "is the one that's laid an egg. Let's get down to brass tacks, Don Giuseppe. You know who are enemies to the Pope and to religion, who drove the Holy Father out of Rome, who founded the Republic of Church-haters. The same crew that still occupies Rome,

Bologna, and even Ferrara, although we have the Fortress to hold them at bay and as recently as last February three rounds of cannon fire did the job. Have I said anything amiss?"

"Not yet," admitted the priest, embarrassed by such a display of righteousness.

"I'm glad to hear you say that. Now tell me who are the Church's friends, those who one of these days—and the sooner the better—will cross the Po, not for the first time but for the last, in order to bring law and order, administer justice, and establish who's to command and who's to obey? Who will carry out God's will and bring the Pope back to his throne in St. Peter's? The Austrians! Anything wrong with that?"

"Not so far."

"Well, that's all I have to say. The fact that the 'Fritzes' are coming back over the Po to massacre the Republic is an open secret, but it must stay a secret just the same. It's an open secret too that their army needs wheat and that I am one of those who get it for them. Everyone knows that except my mother. And she doesn't need to know, except inasmuch as she ought to learn to keep her mouth shut and not ask where and when I'm going and what for! Have I made myself clear? But there's one thing I must tell you, Don Giuseppe, just as frankly as if I were in the confessional. This wheat is needed in a hurry and the officers at Santa Maria Maddalena are at my heels for it. Now, when there's a war on, do the soldiers stop fighting on Sundays and holy days of obligation? I observe the Lord's Day by working harder than ever for the good cause. There'll be time enough to rest when we've put the Pope back in Rome! Am I wrong there?"

"No, I can't say you are. Not if things really are the way you describe them."

"Then I'm satisfied. As for you, Mother, I repeat that ignorance is a good enough excuse for one mistake but not for a second. Just put it into your head that these are not things to talk about with anybody. Do we understand one another? Mum's the word."

"Oh, you can count on me!" she said.

"Good. Let's not speak of it again."

But Dosolina was left choked by a host of words she could not say. She was half sorrowful and half afraid, gaping with renewed admiration for this remarkable son of hers, who was to all intents and purposes a soldier.

2

Were Rabbit had not thought up such well-knit doctrinal speeches all by himself. At this very time, when the Austrians were gathering men and supplies at Santa Maria Maddalena in order to march on the former Papal territory and restore its legitimate government, someone had coached him. Just a few days before this conversation with the priest, while he was taking a report to the Commissary's office, he heard someone call him.

"Well, well! Look who's here!"

He opened his eyes with astonishment. The man who had addressed him in these terms was no longer young but under his tight-fitting Austrian uniform it was clear that he had a muscular and agile body. His face was an ugly one, of a yellowish-green bilious hue, covered with a network of grimacing wrinkles, and its salient feature was an angry, piercing, sardonic, snakelike stare. Giuseppe knew that he had seen this most uncomfortable stare before, but the uniform, cap, side whiskers and tuft of beard on the chin, all in the latest Austrian military style, and above all the general noise and confusion threw him off, all the more so because he had no memory for faces. Wondering "where have I seen that mug before," he said, taking off his hat:

"Did you speak to me, sir?"

"Obviously, since we're alone."

"Of course . . ."

"You don't know me, then?"

"I'm not sure . . . No, I haven't the honor . . ."

"That means you haven't a very good memory. A serious fault."

"I'm sorry."

"You don't remember seeing me at the house of your aunt, Argia Malvegoli, along with Baron Flaminio, that is before the baron was dispatched to the next world by a dagger? It's true that I was usually in disguise, in order to keep out of the hands of those wretched Liberals. But I didn't think my face was one so easily forgotten."

"The most honorable Count Virginio Alpi!"

"Himself in person! And the last time you saw me I seemed to have only one eye and a bushy tramp's beard. When you took me to the border of the Duchy of Modena, do you recollect that?"

"I'm embarrassed by my stupidity."

"Well, to show that I have a memory better than yours, let me remind you that on this occasion you did me a real service."

"Just a trifle, that you are very kind, sir, to remember."

"Speaking of beards," Alpi said suddenly, "has your father still got that Liberal, revolutionary monstrosity? You see, my memory is really phenomenal."

"Miraculous, sir."

"Has he still got it?"

"Yes, he has."

"When we've nothing better to do, we'll cut it off."

"Whatever you say, sir."

"Your father rubbed me the wrong way, do you know?"

"I'm truly sorry."

"Never mind, my good fellow. For the time being your father's beard is safe." Alpi leered in a sinister fashion. "We've other scores to settle first. Necks, not beards, are our present concern, necks to fit in the hangman's noose and under the blade of the guillotine. Isn't the guillotine a revolutionary invention? The Liberals and Republicans have no right to complain if we use it on them, have they?"

340

"Allow me, with all due respect, to tell you that my father did not grow his beard as a political emblem."

"I believe you. But still it's unseemly. Political emblems or not, all beards must be done away with. The spirit of '48 is dead and it's time to return to reason. What were you thinking, all of you on the far side of the Po?"

"Personally I didn't think anything at all."

"You thought the Republic was there to stay, did you, you cowards? Those days are gone forever!"

"So I was quite sure."

"Incidentally, what are you doing over here?"

"To the extent of my modest abilities I'm supplying grain to the military."

"Ah? Then I was correct in crediting you with a certain amount of good judgment."

"My trade is that of a go-between and it's to my interest to serve anyone who pays me good money."

"I'm glad to have run into you again and I shall put in a word for you with the Commissary officers."

"The Count is too kind."

Virginio Alpi was no count, but he consented to being called by this title for reasons of utility rather than pride and above all because as one who despised his fellow men he enjoyed seeing them abase themselves in adulation. He was even more pleased when their flattery was a conscious lie, for his overbearing attitude stemmed not only from calculated self-interest but from something like perversion as well. In the history, or rather the police records, of the pontificates of Gregory XVI and Pius IX his career as a Sanfedista, official of the Papal government, and Austrian political agent reads like that of a man given to mere factional violence and vulgar deceit. But within his limited sphere he exercised oppression with a fury almost as intense as that of a large-scale despot. After he had fled to Austria and joined the Imperial army his undeniable energy won him swift promotion until now he was a major attached to the staff of Marshal Franz von Wimpfen, who was preparing to lead an expeditionary force against the Papal territories.

In Ferrara the Republican leaders called for insurrection, the requisition of arms, conscription, and guerrilla warfare in the countryside. They proclaimed that the nation was in peril but confined themselves to inflammatory words rather than action, thereby only creating discontent and discouragement and building up grounds for the Austrians to declare martial law. When people saw the armed might of the Austrian army they shook their heads and said that this was one more proof that northern Europe was the real "reservoir of man power."

As the Austrian preparations for war drew near to completion Giuseppe Scacerni would have liked to consider his supply job done and to retire to private life before the outbreak of hostilities. But Alpi did not let him so much as open his mouth. More energetic and imperious than ever he ordered Scacerni about without giving him any more assurance than an occasional:

"If you serve me well I'll remember you when the war's over and you'll see that your efforts were not wasted."

If there was one trait that Giuseppe had inherited from his father it was a reluctance to serve anyone, and now for the first time he perceived that the independence which he had heretofore taken for granted might be more difficult to retain than he had ever imagined. Having laid up large stocks of wheat and flour Alpi ordered Giuseppe to engage wagoners with their horses and peasant herdsmen, who when they had done the required amount of work for the owners of their property were allowed to hire out the oxen and wagons that went with it.

"There's not too much work on the land at this season," said Alpi. "The women and boys can do the threshing. The peasants on this side of the river have done their share and now it's up to those of the Ferrara district to show some appreciation of the benefits Austria is preparing to bestow on them. When the war is done they'll be nearer the center of things than the others."

"If the peasants suspect that you want to involve them in the fighting they'll not come," Were Rabbit warned him.

"You won't be such a fool as to tell them that, will you? Just hold out the promise of good pay and I'll attend to the rest."

"Forgive me, sir, but what are the benefits you say the Austrians intend to confer upon them?"

"Have you lost your mind? We're going to liberate them from the Republic."

"That holds for the people in the city. But speaking of the Republic, since the peasants live nominally under its laws, how am I to recruit them?"

"Idiot! Or are you afraid? Didn't you just imply that in the country the Republic has no real authority? And are you afraid of the Republic?"

Whether or not it pleased Giuseppe to act as his recruiting agent did not concern Alpi in the least. More often than not he met all objections with a summary "On both sides of the river the Imperial stick and the Imperial gallows are the best medicine!"

Giuseppe went about engaging wagoners and herdsmen, promising them good Austrian pay without specifying what kind of job they were supposed to do.

"The stick to beat up all those who are lazy and the gallows to hang such as display ill will," Alpi echoed when he came back to the subject.

"There'll never be wood enough to make the sticks, or hangmen in sufficient numbers to take care of everyone who needs their attention."

"We'll find enough wood to go around, never fear. And then we can always draw on the firing squads. Two volleys in the chest and one in the temples. Do you know the way it's done?"

Giuseppe had never witnessed an execution, but he had heard his father's vivid description of how some innocent peasants had been very nearly shot for sedition in the melon patch near Guarda by a band of brutal Croats. As for the military punishment of a flogging, which won the Austrians so much hate when they extended it to civilian trials in the occupied countries, Giuseppe had seen it applied often enough in the encampment at Santa Maria Maddalena. At this moment he bitterly repented having got himself into so many complications and wished that, in accordance with his father's wishes, he had been content with the simple life of a miller. Yes, that was the finest trade in the world.

It was May 6, 1849, when Virginio Alpi announced to the group of peasants recruited by Giuseppe Scacerni:

"Tomorrow we cross the Po. The troops are already on the march. You must load the grain tonight and be ready to start. Arrangements have been made to provide you with an armed escort."

"And where are we going, Your Worship?" one of them dared to ask.

"That's no question to ask in time of war. You have only to do what you are told and keep quiet. Do you follow me? Anyone who doesn't know what I mean will have a chance to learn from a dozen strokes across the buttocks. That's all My Worship has to say."

"But we want nothing to do with the war!" another peasant exclaimed. "That's not in our line at all, and if we'd had any idea . . ."

"Perhaps the lesson had better start right now," said Alpi, calling the corporal and four soldiers of the squad that he had brought with him.

The scene was an open space in front of the storehouse. Wagons and carts were lined up on one side, horses and oxen on the other. The sun was sinking slowly on the horizon. In response to a brusque order in German the four soldiers took the muttering peasant by the arm. Strapping fellow as he was he was taken completely by surprise and so were his companions. The soldiers had loaded guns and they did not dare to resist them.

One of the soldiers had already brought a bench and two big sticks. The peasant began to shout and swear and struggle to get free, but to no avail.

"Down with your trousers," said Alpi, "and quickly, unless you want a double dose." And he added, turning to the bystanders, who looked on with bewilderment as their companion was reduced to powerlessness: "Get a rope!"

No one budged. Alpi pointed at Giuseppe Scacerni and said coldly without raising his voice:

"A rope! I'm talking to you."

Scacerni walked slowly over toward the wagons with a straddling step that under other circumstances would have brought laughter upon his head.

"Do you think you're walking on eggs?" Alpi called after him. "Or have you wet your pants in anticipation of a beating that may be in store for you too?"

One of the peasants gave a nervous laugh.

"I see that everyone's in a good humor," said Alpi. "The stick's a sure cure for long faces."

And when Giuseppe came back with the rope he ordered:

"Give it to the corporal, you lout. And let's get on with it. Now you, my fine fellow, do you want twenty-four strokes instead of twelve? You can have enough to kill you if you want them. Down with your trousers and don't make me tell you again!"

He was still speaking in a low voice, and his manner was all the more cold and cutting because of it. The peasant breathed heavily and shook all over, while perspiration broke out on his forehead. Alpi was annoyed by the fact that his head was bowed over and his chin almost touched his chest.

"Look at me!" he said, going nearer. So blinding was his stare that the peasant, as if mesmerized, relaxed from his tense position. "That's more like it," said Alpi, and he motioned to the soldiers to let go his arms.

Listlessly and with uncertain fingers the peasant unbuttoned his trousers. The corporal handed the rope to the soldiers and took one of the two sticks. The bench was so short that when the peasant was laid on it flat on his stomach his head and neck hung over one end. When they had tied his hands and feet together they raised his shirt, exposing an expanse of white skin to the rays of the setting sun. Alpi pretended to have lost interest in the flogging. Beckoning to Giuseppe he proceeded to give him orders as to how he should superintend the loading of the grain. Then he said in an aside to the waiting corporal that he should administer twelve blows of the stick. The first blow fell with a soft thud, that made the bystanders shudder, while the victim writhed in his bonds, raising his head and gasping for breath with a dull cry. After the third and fourth successive blows, which the corporal counted slowly and regularly in German, the prisoner cried out in anticipation of each one to follow, and then his cry passed into an agonized moan. His skin was covered with red welts, which gradually took on a dark purple color.

Giuseppe Scacerni seemed unable to fix his attention upon what his patron was saying, and the latter insisted:

"Mind what I say because I shall hold you responsible for carrying out my orders. This grain is for the troops that are going to occupy Bologna. It must be loaded in such a way that it won't get wet in case of rain and not a single sack of it is lost. I need hardly add that I'm not joking. You've seen what happens to anyone who disobeys me."

These last words were addressed to all those who were standing around him. The punishment was over and the flogged man stood holding up his trousers in a hesitant and comical pose which moved more than one of his fellows to laughter. A flogging of this kind invariably aroused a mixture of mirth and repulsion.

"Do you admit that you had it coming to you?" Alpi asked him.

The man raised his eyes as if he expected some new affliction to descend upon him, nodded assent and broke into shamed tears, which only moved the others to rougher joking. Paying him no further attention Alpi ordered a distribution of cigars and tobacco, thereby light-

344

ening the atmosphere even further. But there was a reason for Alpi's generosity. A movement had sprung up in Milan in 1848 to deprive the Austrian treasury of the money it took in from the government monopoly on tobacco. Patriots who had given up smoking often came to blows with smokers and crossed their knives with the clubs and swords of the police who gave them protection. The Austrian authorities saw fit to combat this seditious boycott by making frequent gifts of cigars to police and people, thus exposing them to opprobrium and revenge and making tobacco into a symbol of all good Italians' suffering and an object of their scorn. Now the oppressors planned to carry this ill-conceived policy into the Papal territory and the clumsiness of it was so obvious that it seemed a harbinger of even more important political missteps.

Of course the wagoners and herdsmen knew nothing of all this; they stuffed their pockets with tobacco and lit up cigars, making mock bows and addressing one another as "Your Lordship" until it was time to start work. Even the man who had been recently flogged lay on his side a little apart from the rest and puffed at a cigar. Giuseppe, who had never smoked in his life, went over to offer him his share of the windfall. The fellow was a herdsman from Guarda and when he came out of his doze he shot his benefactor a look of bitter resentment.

"It's all your fault, you swine and cheat, because you didn't tell me what I was getting into, that I find myself in this condition. But mark my words, as soon as we're out of it I'll pay you back twelve strokes for every one I have received here today."

"That makes a hundred and forty-four!" said a quick-witted fellow standing near by.

The others formed a circle around them and Giuseppe murmured apologetically:

"I didn't know myself what I was engaging you for."

"Oh, you didn't, you swine, is that it? You'd sell Our Lord in person for a few miserable pennies."

"Judas took thirty pieces of silver," put in the wagoner who was arithmetically minded.

"Don't you think I saw you fetching the rope to tie me up with?" said the fellow on the ground. "Here's what I'll do with what you're giving me."

And he threw the tobacco in Giuseppe's face, spitting on the ground to express his contempt. In all the faces before and behind him Giuseppe could read the same hostility.

"No more joking, boys," he said weakly, trying to parry further talk. "You've seen that around here they mean business. Let's get started."

"So this rabbit face wants to give orders, is that it? Do you know that you're pale as a ghost with fright? You'll taste my brand of joke when I give you a beating!"

"Get to work, boys," Giuseppe feebly repeated, looking like a ghost indeed.

"Don't forget," said the flogged man, "that if you spy on me, then instead of giving you . . . how many blows did you say twelve times twelve came to? . . ."

"A hundred and forty-four!" the others chorused.

"Instead of a hundred and forty-four blows a few days from now I'll stick a knife into you tonight and throw your body in the river with a stone around the neck in order to save myself further trouble."

"That's swift and sure," grumbled another one of the company.

The next day the convoy of carts and wagons with its military escort moved slowly over the Lagoscuro bridge behind the troops of Marshal von Wimpfen. Seated on the last vehicle, near to the soldiers who brought up the rear, Giuseppe Scacerni was the most miserable man for miles around. The bells had been taken off the animals' harness or stuffed with straw and the only sounds were those of a few axles creaking for want of oil and a wagon or two groaning under an unaccustomed load. On the still dark and silent road their cadence gave free rein to the imagination.

The unfortunate Giuseppe's imaginings were anything but poetical and there was a bitter taste in his mouth as the convoy stopped to rest below the walls of Ferrara. What had happened to the money he had made as purveyor to the Austrian garrison before the Ferrarese patriots had turned against him and forced him to flee, leaving it with his aunt, Argia Malvegoli? For almost two years mingled scorn and fear had kept him from setting foot in the city and the thought of his money had been one too painful to dwell on. Now he felt a surge of anger with himself for having left his fortune in the hands of a weak and foolish woman. His effort to be an honest go-between, one that didn't poke into other people's affairs, that refused to look for trouble and washed his hands of any which was forced upon his attention had led him into a world of complications. And now when circumstances had led him almost unwittingly to take up the same trade again he found himself in even worse straits than before, with the gallows threatening him on one side and a knife on the other. Yes, his trade had really turned against him, for Alpi would not think twice before hanging him, with or without reason. Now ill luck would have it that he was in charge of this cursed convoy, subject to as much military discipline as if he were a soldier. "Do what you are told and keep quiet." He had seen for himself that these were no idle words.

Was his father right in maintaining that between business and thieving, between so-called fair trade and usury there was little difference? Had he seen clearly when he predicted that trouble and more trouble lay ahead? His father was a man with his head in the clouds. He felt another access of the cold anger with which he had listened to the simple old miller's strictures. Yes, rather than admit himself to be in the wrong he'd take a flogging. And yet the thought of the blows coming down on his back caused him to shiver more than the cool air of the dawn and stayed with him after the convoy had left Ferrara behind and gone on toward the Reno river. At the first village on the other side, which was in Bologna territory, they stopped for rest.

Giuseppe would have liked to run away to Guarda and hide there, but his stomach was queasy and his legs unsteady and he was sure that either Alpi or the peasant with the knife would track him to his lair. There was no escape. After the chilliness and fears of the night he was further indisposed by the heat of the day, for having fallen asleep on his wagon he woke up with a raging headache. As the convoy neared its destination the pace became slower and slower. The road was clogged with men and vehicles and often they had to pull over to one side to let a faster group pass by. The leader of the military escort ordered halts for which they could see no reason and then brusquely ordered them to pursue their weary march. The rumor travelled down the road that the gates of Bologna were closed and the Austrians would have to blast their way in with cannons. It became increasingly clear that the soldiers with their trousers tucked into their boots and the oak leaves on their caps were resentful and splenetic, first because of their strenuous journey and next because of the dangers that awaited them. Their spleen was evident on their faces and in the impatient shouts with which they ordered the convoy to clear the way. The foot soldiers pushed them aside with the butts of their rifles and the cavalrymen with the flat sides of their swords.

Along the side of the road they could see farmhouses in flames and hear cattle lowing from burning stables. Under a clump of trees at a crossroad some rough soldiers had hemmed in a whole group of peasants, pricking the men with their bayonets and leering at the weeping women, whom they then slapped into silence and drew off in twos and threes into the adjacent fields. One of the men who attempted to resist them had his face spattered with shot. While the convoy halted here for a moment before a shrine of the Virgin the wagoners and herdsmen had time to take in this scene with their own eyes. From May 8 to May 16, 1849, or the duration of the siege of Bologna, such episodes were frequent and no one knew whether the Austrian officers were unable to check them or whether they were part of a deliberate policy of striking terror into the population of city and country.

At dawn of May 8 the convoy of grain and flour arrived at the Porta di Galliera. Many of the plainsmen from the lower Po Valley had never seen a mountain, except for the outline of the Apennines in the glow of the setting sun. During all of the previous day they had marvelled at the gradual rise of the foothills around Bologna, covered with green spring vegetation and bathed at dawn in a delicate silvery blue haze and at noon in dazzling light. As they drew nearer they could pick out enticing valleys and at the foot of the hills, between the Savena and Reno rivers, the precise and austere grace of the city of towers, which was then still surrounded by its proud ancient walls. Those of them who had never seen a building higher than the Castle of Ferrara and the leaning belfry of San Benedetto could hardly believe their eyes when they took in the bold thrust of the Asinella tower and the height and bulk of so many other towers and churches in the red and gray, steep, densely constructed city of Bologna. They pointed out to one another the airy villas on the surrounding hills, the extensive structure of San Michele in Bosco and the famous sanctuary of Saint Luke on the highest eminence of all, with the arcade leading up to it like a long enclosed backbone. But great as was their admiration their hunger was even greater, for they had in their stomachs only three slices of bread distributed to them as rations enroute, while the soldiers escorting them had ample reserves to draw on. As they were wondering whether or not anyone would take the trouble to feed them, they heard the bells of the city ring out all together. The sound was intense and agonized, not only because it was calling the alarm of war, fire, and blood, but also because its very urgency seemed to choke and impede it. The bells echoed louder and louder all through the following day and night, until the dawn of May 10, and when they began to slow down they seemed to be sustained by the deep, solemn voice of the bell in the mayor's palace and the other harmonious and no less beautiful voice of San Pietro.

The supply convoy had gone too far ahead and now, on the heels of the soldiers who were massing to attack the city gate, it could move neither one way nor the other. The Austrians had mounted three light artillery pieces in the middle of the road but these were not enough to breach the gate, much less the high, crenellated walls, from which Republican militiamen and armed citizens were maintaining scattered gunfire. And when the cannons from the Montagnola inside the city found the range, the Austrians' light pieces and the soldiers manning them were in serious danger. There was a breaking of ranks among the attackers which led the Bolognese to believe that they were about to withdraw, leaving their artillery pieces behind them. People began to call out that the Austrians were running away and the thing to do was to pursue them.

"Out of the gate and after them! It's time for a sally!" the cry went up from the walls.

Colonel Boldrini, the brave professional soldier in command at the gate, was not of their opinion and did not wish to make a futile sacrifice of his Carabineers, who were the nucleus of the defenders. But when the popular tumult grew louder and branded his men cowards and traitors he had for the sake of military honor to make a sally. Some sixty Carabineers and a group of courageous civilians went after the three Austrian field pieces, but they were attacked from the flank and driven back with heavy losses, including that of Boldrini.

The wagoners and herdsmen had crawled under their vehicles for safety. Similar skirmishes took place at the San Felice and Sargozza gates and as a result the Austrians decided to wait for the arrival of heavier guns from Ferrara and Mantua, while the hotheads among the defenders came to the premature conclusion that the city could never be taken.

At half past twelve Marshal von Wimpfen gave an order to cease fire and sent envoys to establish a two-day truce during which the Bolognese were to make up their minds to surrender. Meanwhile he extended the siege to the remaining gates and to the hills around the city, occupying San Michele in Bosco and the Osservanza and cutting off the acqueduct and the Reno canal which carried the city's water supply and the power to run its flour mills respectively.

The unfortunate wagoners enlisted at Ferrara were dislodged with blows and kicks from their improvised shelters and sent by a roundabout road to a field at Caprara outside the Porta San Felice, which had been turned into an Austrian encampment. There, when they had unloaded their sacks, they received soldiers' rations, fodder for their animals, and space to sleep on the grass.

Fortunately for Giuseppe Scacerni the events of the past two days had distracted his followers from their thoughts of revenge, and the man who had been flogged had made a quick recovery. Giuseppe stuck as close as possible to the Austrians, and in their company he boasted of the authority vested in him by Virginio Alpi. No one, not even the officers, had any idea of how these Ferrarese peasants had come to be among them. They were given nothing but scraps to eat and their miserable animals suffered from the damp night air and the lack of grazing.

After midday of May 10, when the truce was over, there was combat at the Porta delle Lame and Porta San Mamolo. Some small shells and bombs set fire to roof tops in the city, the population refused to discuss surrender, and re-enforcements from the province of Romagna were thrown back by the Austrians outside the Porta Maggiore and the Idice Bridge. All these incidents were reported in a somewhat confused form to the uncomfortable and terrified wagoners.

May 12 was the chief local holiday, when the Bolognese were accustomed to carry the Virgin of Saint Luke's down from its hill and in a procession through the city. Von Wimpfen did not hesitate to remind them, in a tone half fatherly and half threatening, that it was no time for celebration, and dismay grew in all quarters although it was not yet strong enough to prevail against the insistence of the most desperate of the Republican defenders.

On Sunday, May 13, the flogged peasant and a group of his fellows sought out Giuseppe and harangued him as follows:

"Son of Scacerni, why must we stay here? We're wasting our time and the strength of our animals is failing. Why don't they send us home?"

"I know no more than you do, believe me."

"This time we do believe you. And we forgive you for having deceived us as to the terms of our enlistment. As for the threat of giving you a hundred and some blows of the stick, we'd like you to forget about it. We solemnly take back our word." And they added, to the man who had been flogged: "Don't you subscribe to that?"

"I swear it," he answered. "I take back my word, God help me."

"Is this retraction for good, or for just as long as you've the fear of God in you?" Giuseppe asked cautiously.

"It's for a lifetime, but on one condition."

"Let me hear it. I don't want to promise anything I can't fulfill."

"Fair enough! Spoken like the son of an honest man! You must go look for this Count Virginio Alpi with whom you're on such good terms and tell him there's no point to our staying here any longer. We've unloaded our sacks and now it's time to send us back home, where we and our animals have work to do. Isn't that good sense? Tell that fine gentleman to give us our pay and with it leave to go home."

"I'm willing to try if only I can find him. I'll ask him to let you go, for sure, but when it comes to pay I can't bring that up unless he mentions it. And whatever I may say won't carry much weight with him if he's decided not to pay you."

"Just drop him a hint, since with your city manners you know how such things are done."

"Manners are not enough. He's no easy job to handle. What if he loses his temper?"

"The worst thing he can do is to flog you!" observed the one who knew whereof he spoke.

"Listen, Zanocco," Giuseppe said to the herdsman with just the right shade of humility, "if I have to take a beating I'd rather that it should come from one of my own countrymen whom I unwittingly offended."

"You'll have no beating from me, son of Scacerni!" said the simple-hearted herdsman of Guarda. "As far as I'm concerned you need have no fear, here's my word as your countryman upon it."

"Well, I'll do the best I can. Are you satisfied?"

"Yes, we are. We'll close our accounts with you and thank you in the bargain if only you'll get us home. And as for our pay, well, heaven help us!"

Thus was struck up what Giuseppe always said was the most difficult of his bargains. Although he no longer had to fear Zanocco's revenge he still had to cope with that intractable beast of an Alpi, as he secretly called him. He had to satisfy the peasants and at the same time keep the prestige he enjoyed with his patron, to assure his present safety and provide for a future career. The task was so demanding that he tossed sleeplessly on the grass under a wagon all through the night of May 13, trying to think how he should speak to Alpi and discarding every phrase that suggested itself.

It was hard enough to find him, to start with, for all Giuseppe knew was that he was an important adjunct of Marshal von Wimpfen's personal staff, which was quartered at the Villa Spada, not too far away. Once there, Giuseppe said to himself, his real troubles would begin. So anxious was he not to spend his efforts in vain that he started out while it was still dark and arrived at the Villa Spada at an hour when ordinarily he would have found everyone asleep. But the traffic of officers and soldiers was so intense that it was clear that no one had yet gone to bed. Sentries were posted at the gate of the Villa and artillerymen with their gun carriages all along the arcade. Giuseppe had stopped to reflect how he should pass the sentries when someone roughly gripped his shoulder and a voice with a Croat accent asked him in German what he was after. He crumpled up and then timidly stretched out his neck for all the world like a turtle coming out of its shell, and because he had been taken by surprise he said quite bluntly who he was and whom he was seeking. After all the subterfuges he had racked his brains to find, this simple and direct method proved to be the best. After a short time he was informed that Major Virginio Alpi was quartered in a villa called La Cipressina, farther up the hill. Giuseppe proceeded along the arcade to the meadow of San Giuseppe and there he took the narrow road leading to the hilltop. Along the way a civilian gave him precise directions, for the soldiers had told him only the name of the villa. More soldiers and guns lined the arcade, but Giuseppe now realized that the less attention he paid to them the better, and because he looked like a native of the country going about his own business nobody stopped him. The narrow road on which he had swung to the right soon became steep and rocky, climbing up the cultivated side of a small valley whose opposite slope was covered with giant oak trees.

Halfway up the hill a company of artillerymen was struggling to haul a battery of two heavy cannons on heavy low-swung wheels. The horses' hoofs could not get a grip on the steeply rising ground and the men were pulling ropes to help them. Giuseppe was afraid they might enlist him for the job, but either he escaped their notice or they thought him too weak to be of much aid. He called out to some peasants standing in melancholy fashion in front of their farmhouse and they told him that he had nearly reached the place he wanted to find.

The villa was surrounded by a chestnut grove and beyond it were sloping fields and grape arbors looking across at the Colle del Vento, the Church of the Osservanza, and the handsome Villa Aldini. The wide, bare façade, whose simple lines were interrupted only by two large carved stone shells on either side of the pediment, looked over a meadow with a well and a rustic gate at its farther end in the direction of the hill. Two rows of tall cypresses, some ponderous and towering, others slender and pointed like daggers, bordered the meadow, which was equally suited to a tennis game or a summer evening siesta. The tall trees, the grassy sward and the unornamented façade of the house, which was pointed up by green shutters, all combined to create an atmosphere so pleasant that even Giuseppe Scacerni felt its charm, that is, as much as his burden of worry and the sight of some soldiers sitting on the two wide steps in front of the door would allow him.

The soldiers were Lombards and when he asked for Major Virginio Alpi one of them got up and took him inside. A wide hall, characteristic of Bolognese architecture, ran straight through the ground floor, circulating air through the house and providing a cool refuge in summer. Giuseppe was astonished to see that it was filled with broken, half-burned furniture, but he said nothing and pretended not to notice. Alpi was in a smaller meadow, back of the villa, where a semicircular walled terrace afforded a splendid view of the chestnut trees below and the city and the immense plain beyond it in the distance. To the west the blue-green of the countryside under the May sun was broken by a broad curve of the shimmering Reno river and to the east, on the right, Bologna lay nestled among its dark brick walls, with the multitude of its roof tops and dwellings overhung by towers and the naves of churches. Although the sun stood fairly high over the plain and had started to climb the circle of hills, it was still diffusing the warm vermilion and glorious purple lights with which it had illuminated the mist of dawn.

Virginio Alpi stood with a group of Austrian officers on the terrace, speaking to them in Italian and looking mockingly down at the city. Giuseppe and his soldier escort waited for him to finish. He was saying that the best way to induce the Bolognese gentlemen, the constitutionalists of the doctrinaire Liberal party, to surrender was to sack the villas they owned outside the city just as he had sacked La Cipressina. The reason for Alpi's eloquence lay in the fact that he was attached to Austrian headquarters as a political adviser, spy, and informant, in which capacity he drew up lists of suspected persons and displayed an excess of zeal and arrogance in so doing.

There was no doubt about it, he was saying, all the Liberals who infested this center of learning, the second capital of the Papal State, whether of the English parliamentarian or the French Jacobin school, as soon as from the roofs of their city palaces they saw their hillside villas burning would open the gates and surrender. "For the sake of their worldly possessions," he added, leering.

"Of course there are the common people, mere terrorists who waste no time on theory and have neither villas nor anything else to lose. That's where their strength lies, in the fact that they have nothing. The masses are by nature Republican, anarchistic and anxious to see everything topsy-turvy so that they may rob whatever they can lay their hands on. Already once before they've taken the upper hand over the gentlemen theorists; to be exact, it was in September of last year, when the dregs of the Bolognese population went out after Papist spies and betrayers and even after lukewarm Republicans. They operated with knives and pistols and under the noses of their victims' families." (Here Alpi's eyes gleamed, probably because he was reminded of his own deeds of violence when he was a leader of the Sanfedisti in Romagna. But he did not call up his prowess in words.) "They were called *settembrini*, those ruffians, and I take my hat off to them! Of course I'd think still more highly of them if they'd killed off the Liberals entirely. By which I mean that I'd give them a cheer and then stand them up in front of a firing squad! Anyhow, last year those gentlemen constitutionalists and moderates finally put the rebels down. Now the *settembrini* have nothing to lose and they're dead set against surrender. Let the rich Liberals' palaces and villas go to rack and ruin, for all they care. Since they couldn't do the job themselves they're glad to let us do it!"

At this point the faces of his hearers showed clearly that they had little taste for the brutal function which he was assigning to them. But

352

we may note that, aside from his prejudice and bitterness, he had drawn an accurate enough picture of the political scene, which was occupied by passionate supporters of fighting to the death on the one hand and timorous and respectable moderates on the other. Now, seeing that the Austrians were disgusted by the treachery of his speech, Alpi added unctuously:

"Let us thank Divine Providence for the invincible power of our revered Emperor, who will restore law and order and the rightful government of the Holy Father in these fertile provinces where factional strife has too long interfered with the people's happiness."

This was the official apology for the Austrian campaign. But Alpi did not linger long over mouthing such tiresome phrases.

"Hasn't the battery arrived?" he asked impatiently.

"It's on the way," spoke up Giuseppe Scacerni.

"What? Are you here? And what do you know about it?"

"I passed them as I came. They're not far now, but the road is a steep one."

"And what is your business here?" Then he added, without waiting for an answer: "You can tell me that on the way. Gentlemen, for the present there is nothing more we can do. Shall we watch the artillerymen at work?"

Giuseppe tagged along after the officers, although Alpi seemed already to have forgotten his presence. They went through the villa, across the larger meadow and through the gate, where they heard confused murmurs and saw the battery approaching. To the left were some low-lying fields covered with grapevines, fruit trees and rows of tall, green wheat, ripening in the sun. The lower portion of the fields was only a few hundred feet away and one of the cannons was climbing slowly up the grassy opposite slope to a clearing near the oak trees which Giuseppe had noticed on his way. Meanwhile the second cannon was bogged down in a ditch and neither men nor horses could seem to pull it out. Alpi went over to the artillery officers, who at first treated him coldly, as a non-combattant and intruder, but soon saw the wisdom of his advice.

"Go get the peasants down the road," Alpi said to Giuseppe, "and tell them to put the yoke on all the oxen they have in their stable. They've a big farm and must own quite a number of animals. Tell them to bring them here in a hurry. If they raise any objections or it takes you more than a quarter of an hour to go and come back, there'll be trouble. I'll set fire to their hayloft. Double quick, now. I'll count the minutes." And he took a watch out of his pocket.

"Double quick!" muttered Giuseppe, scrambling as best he could in the direction of the peasants' house. "That's all very easy for him to say. What have I got to do with it? The battery's the soldiers' affair, not mine. Is this the sort of luck that's pursuing me?" The time limit impelled him to quicken his pace, but he still mumbled to himself. "Setting fire to the hayloft, that's no joke! And how can I keep track of the minutes if I have no watch? The less taste I have for serving them the

353

more they command me! Must everyone in this world be either a slave or a master?"

Just as anger had driven him to philosophize in this fashion he found himself at his destination. The peasants were still hanging about in front of the house with a melancholy look on their faces.

"Get out your oxen and yoke them in a hurry," shouted Giuseppe breathlessly, scratching the pimples that had broken out on his neck under the stress of his emotion.

"Easy, man, this is my stable," said the head of the family. "What oxen are you talking about?"

"Your stable, is it? *They*'ll soon show you whose stable it is!" And he pointed in the direction from which he had come. "Hitch up the oxen; you've only a quarter of an hour and half of it's gone already."

"You must be mad!" said the peasant, but he looked uneasily about him.

"Mad, am I? I tell you, if you don't go there with your animals this minute they'll set fire to your hayloft."

"Luckily there's very little hay in it at this season," the peasant said slowly.

Then he stopped short, remembering that the loft was, according to Bolognese custom, joined on one side to the house and on the other to the stable.

"Get out the oxen, boys! Yoke them in pairs, and hurry!" he called out.

"Here they are now!" said Giuseppe, as a corporal and four soldiers sent by Alpi to expedite his mission appeared on the scene.

Their arrival, although there was nothing overtly threatening about it, moved the peasants to act quickly. Soon three braces of oxen and four of cows, each led by rings through the animals' noses attached to a rope held by one of the peasant's boys, started along the road. Their owner whipped them so hard that they broke into a clumsy, bovine run and the chains hanging down from their yokes clanged noisily.

Keeping his distance, in the dignified manner to which he now felt entitled, Giuseppe Scacerni, strode along at an almost martial pace, throwing out his feet to either side like a rooster.

"Your orders have been carried out!" he said in soldierly style to Virginio Alpi.

"At a snail's pace, mind you," said Alpi, who could never resist mortifying his underlings. "You've been gone twenty-two minutes, exactly."

The oxen were substituted for the horses, which wandered off to nibble at the grass, and the soldiers stood aside except for a few who held levers under the wheels and axles of the gun carriages. The officers too looked on while the peasants took over. There were four of them in all, two below with the rawhide whip, one looking after the oxen and the other after the cows. Halfway up the line of yoked animals the head of the family gave orders as to how to proceed, while at the head of the line a little boy with a stalk of grass in his mouth led the first brace of them by the nose. The commotion of a few minutes before had given way to the deliberate calm and apparent indifference of the countryman who knows how to handle his job. The scene might have been one of peaceful plowing, with the plowshares ready to cut through the sun-baked earth and turn heavy, shining clods of it over. And the peasant urged the animals on with the slurred syllables he used in plowing, interspersing them with mock reproaches and a trilled *r* sound that seemed to have a particular effect upon them.

"Ho there, Ballarino! Come on, Bigio! Get along, Bianchina! *Rrrrr!* Steady, Solimano, *rrrrr!* Harder now, Ballarino, you son of a cow!"

Ballarino, Solimano, Bianchina and the rest bowed their necks and backs and strained under their yokes to the accompaniment of the voice and whip in alternate doses. When they had all together made their maximum effort the cannon came up out of the ditch and was pulled over the grass to rejoin its fellow, which was already mounted in position. Moving as indifferently as their animals, the peasants prepared to go home. Meanwhile some of the soldiers led the horses to graze in an adjacent field while others cleaned the cannons and prepared the fuses and breechblocks with which to fire them. The officers, in their turn, took out their instruments for finding the range. Through the trees could be glimpsed the tops of the towers in the city as the guns were trained upon their targets and loaded. The whole operation took place in a disciplined silence, which weighed heavily upon the peaceful surroundings and the fresh morning air. It was strange under this overhanging threat to hear the birds singing cheerily away, although in tones that were subdued by the heat of the approaching noon.

Giuseppe had not followed Alpi's previous discussion with the Austrian officers and subsequently he had been forced to concentrate his attention upon the ignominious errand upon which his patron had sent him. Now, all of a sudden, he realized what was the purpose of the maneuver. So horrific did it seem that he could only stare at the set faces and precise gestures of the soldiers and try to persuade himself that it could not be true. Meeting Alpi's eyes he read in them a cold, baleful satisfaction which left him frozen with disgust and indignation to an extent even greater than he was aware.

"Gentlemen," Alpi was saying to the officers, "if by this time tomorrow the Bolognese have rejected our ultimatum we shall open fire upon the city. And you," he added, beckoning to Giuseppe, "what did you come here to tell me?"

"Is it true?" asked the flabbergasted Giuseppe. "Will they shell the city?"

Alpi looked at him with astonishment and gave one of his harsh, cold laughs.

"No, they are here to set off fireworks! Did you come so far just to ask me a stupid question?"

Giuseppe was so terrified by the thought of shells falling on innocent people's houses that his own personal fears took a second place in his mind.

"I came, sir, to tell you that we've unloaded our convoy and would like your permission to return to our homes. The men are needed in the fields and their families will be worried about them. I have ventured to bother you because down in the encampment there's no one in charge of us and we can't find out what to do."

"You did well to come, because I'd completely forgotten about you. You are free to go when you like and I'll see to it that you're given three days' rations. Will that be enough for the trip?"

"More than enough. But we'll need an order with your signature so that the Austrian officers will let us go and give us our rations and . . ."

"You shall have it immediately," Alpi interrupted. "What else can I do for you?"

"There is another matter, yes . . ." Giuseppe, who was feeling encouraged, said cautiously.

"What's that? Out with it."

"It's the matter of pay, since you are so kind . . ."

"You want to be paid, do you?"

"As a matter of fact, we do. Not I, sir, your thanks are enough for me. But the others were promised money, do you remember?"

"You were the one to promise it, then."

"At your orders, sir. I only carried out what you told me. If you remember . . ."

"And what if it pleases me to forget. If . . . if. . . . If and but are fool's excuses."

"I'd just as soon forget about it myself," said Giuseppe, "but those fellows . . ."

"What do those fellows matter to me?"

"Nothing at all. But they'll lay a stick to my shoulders, that's certain."

Virginio Alpi broke out again into disconnected laughter. He stopped short and said solemnly:

"Doesn't it make you laugh, too?"

"If you like I can try, sir."

But the effort was a forced one.

"You're no good at laughing," said Alpi with mock gravity.

"I can do no more than my best. The knowledge that as soon as we start out they'll start beating me up is not exactly conducive to laughter. Forgive me if I've expressed myself crudely."

"Fate has called you to witness an historic event, and you can think only of your shoulders," said Alpi, enjoying the game.

"That's my own history, after all," said Giuseppe, moving him to further laughter.

Alpi ordered a subaltern officer to prepare discharge orders for the wagoners and herdsmen from Ferrara.

"If I put it in writing that you and your men and vehicles were requisitioned for war purposes, that will make your position clear, won't it?"

"I'm afraid none of them knows how to read, sir."

"And what if I'll hear no more of you or them either?"

"Then I'll have to resign myself to a beating."

"That would hardly be fair after you've served me so faithfully and made me laugh in the bargain. How many of you are there?"

"Twenty wagons and fifteen carts."

"I'll give you seventy crowns, two per man, and you can pay them. If you hold back anything for yourself I'll send you straight to jail. Are you satisfied? Is that the way it should be?"

"I beg your pardon, but it should be at least seventy-two."

"Counting yourself, of course. There's no satisfying you. But I'll give you seventy-two. You're lucky to have caught me in a good mood."

Two crowns apiece did not amount to much, but Scacerni thought it best to take what he could and be thankful. The subaltern was ordered to make out a receipt by virtue of which Giuseppe assumed responsibility for paying the men and sending them home. Alpi told him to leave the exact amount a blank, which he would fill in himself, but at that moment a messenger came to call him to the Villa Spada and he went hurriedly away, telling Giuseppe to wait for him.

All afternoon long the Austrians put big guns into position on the slope of the Osservanza, below La Cipressina at the Palazzaccio, and in the meadow of San Giuseppe. The last named was occupied by a large mortar. The afternoon sun warmed the city, suffusing it with blazing light and softening its ancient ruggedness. All its colors were blended together as if in a crucible and the effect was one of torpor, with not a breath of life stirring. For three days the bells had been silent and little gunfire had been exchanged around the walls. Only toward evening did the cannons speak up on either side. Giuseppe slept on a pile of straw with the soldiers, who shared their rations with him, for Alpi did not return until noon the next day.

"What, are you still here?" he asked.

"At your orders, sir."

"At my orders?" He led Scacerni into his office, and the latter, led by the presence of an altar and some holy pictures to think it was a chapel, started to make the sign of the cross.

"Keep your hat on, it's been turned into a library," said Alpi.

Giuseppe could not help baring his head. Taking a pen in hand he looked at the amount Alpi had written on the receipt and read there a hundred crowns.

"Is that what you're giving me, a hundred?" he said with astonishment.

"Seventy-two, I said. Are you trying to cheat me?"

"It's written there . . ."

"Good Lord, I forgot that unfortunately you know how to read."

"Naturally, if I know how to write," said Giuseppe, still holding the pen in his hand.

"These are the drawbacks of education. If you say a word I'll make you sorry. I'll stop at nothing, you know that."

"Yes, I do," said Giuseppe.

"Are you joking, you wretch?" Alpi said, staring at him.

"Not for anything in the world."

"Are you criticizing my arithmetic?"

"Of course not, sir."

"Remember, if you say anything about a hundred crowns, I'll settle with you. And it will be a lesson you'll never forget."

"Why should I say anything about it? By signing this receipt I'm taking a heavy risk and getting nothing out of it."

"What do you mean?"

"Do I need to explain? I'm compromising myself, and to no profit."

"I take off my hat to you. You're cleverer than I thought."

"Not at lining my own pocket, in this case!"

"Don't be impudent! You haven't forgotten that every misplaced word is rewarded with a stroke of the stick, have you?" So saying, he handed over seventy-two crowns and tucked away the receipt for a hundred.

The Austrian officers had gathered on the terrace with field glasses in their hands. Beyond the thick foliage of the oak grove where the two cannons had been located a thick column of smoke and flames was coiling up into the air from a villa behind the grove, which was now on fire. Alpi clapped his hands elatedly.

"Gentlemen, the performance has begun!" he exclaimed, imitating the gestures of the barker at a country fair. "Here we have the Casino Martinelli in flames and if we could see into the Aposa Valley we'd find the Villa Bignami, which belongs to the commander of the Civic Guards of Bologna, in the same condition. I've a list of all the Liberals' names and if they don't surrender we'll turn everything they own into ashes. . . ."

He took his watch out of his pocket.

"It's very nearly noon. In Bologna they boast of their bells and bell ringers. But today they'll listen to a different tune."

His allusion to the pride the Bolognese took in their bells was quite exact, and now it seemed as if, instead of emitting their usual harmony of joyous peals, they were answering his irony with silence. At a moment of suspense like this one such silence spoke eloquently of tragic anxiety and overhanging ruin.

From the Osservanza on top of the Colle del Vento one rustic bell, belonging to a community of poor monks, innocently rang out the Angelus, and its chimes were not yet over before the heavy mortar in the meadow of San Giuseppe came out with its first salvo. It made a dismal sound that climbed up the sun-swept slopes of the hills like a slow rumble of thunder in a clear sky, whose echoes first gather strength and then die away, announcing the advent of a storm.

"There it is!" Alpi shouted. "Well aimed!"

He pointed to a cloud of smoke, dust, and pulverized plaster rising from the center of the city. The first shell had struck the pediment of the Church of San Salvatore, where the damage it did can still be seen today.

The mortar fired five of its destructive shells and with their slow, heavy thuds were mingled the ear-splitting crash of the bronze cannons. From the terrace of La Cipressina the little group that included Virginio Alpi and Giuseppe Scacerni followed the progress of the firing in silence. Most of the projectiles fell on undetermined spots in the most thickly inhabited part of the city and the onlookers' morbid curiosity was heightened by the thought of the men, women, and children who were an integral part of the target. In the case of Alpi this curiosity, rather than his usual hate, was predominant.

The bombardment lasted three quarters of an hour, long enough to demonstrate to the Bolognese not only their enemies' resolution but also their already proved power and the futility of resisting them. On the slender tower that stood above the rest the white flag of surrender was unfurled. Virginio Alpi returned to himself and gave a loud cheer, accompanied by a sample of his insulting laughter, while Giuseppe too pulled himself together and set out as inconspicuously as possible to rejoin and liberate his fellow countrymen. When they had not hoped to receive any money at all they had not grumbled too loudly, but now that they were given two crowns they complained that these were no better than nothing.

"Boys," said Giuseppe, strengthened by his newly won authority and a clear conscience, "I've done the best I could. Why didn't one of you go in my place?"

They had to admit that he had done all he knew how. Of course Giuseppe was the first to confess to himself that Alpi was a profiteer. Two crowns amounted to very little and in his case they were a symbol of complicity with a robber.

"Let's be frank about it," he said. "No pay seems like much when we receive it."

As we have said before, resentment often drove him to philosophize.

Leaving him in this frame of mind for the moment I cannot help recalling that at this time there lived in a house near San Salvatore a respected lawyer to whom on the first day of the siege a son was born. For the sake of safety he had established mother and child in the cellar and she, who up to a late age retained much of her youthful charm, often told of the anxiety she had felt at noon of that day in May 1849 when the first shell fell on the city. My memory is prodded by affection, for the child grew up to be my father. This grandmother of mine was of peasant extraction. Her husband, who was some years her senior, had concluded from the fact that his grandfather's aristocratic and spirited wife had wasted the family fortune that he would do better to marry a humble and modest woman. During those years of childhood when we absorb, all unconsciously, more than we are ever to acquire later by conscious effort, I learned from my grandmother something of the frugal life of an old-fashioned housewife and, in particular, how an apparently humble and remissive character may be enduring and tenacious above all others. Sensible, witty, but unlettered, she lived in the highly cultivated atmosphere of her son's house with just enough knowledge of reading to decipher her prayer book and the daily paper. Her lack of formal education did not mortify her because she never pretended to know more than she did, a talent which books fail to impart and indeed more often destroy. I remember clearly the respect which she enjoyed, without ever asking for it, as a mother and grandmother, and her Christian faith and patience among troubles large and small. Thus it was that I observed and later appreciated a quality of measure and discretion that kept her remote from matters like knowledge, wealth, power, and the clamor of worldly events, which were beyond her understanding, but that never permitted her to fall into embarrassment. Equally removed from ambition and pettiness, she was jealous only of her prerogatives as a housewife.

I venture to hope that my readers will feel as I do the healthy and robust love of life characteristic of the following episode, which she remembered all her days. A few months after the siege of Bologna, when she was out in the fields with her baby in her arms, she met a gypsy, who predicted that she would break a leg, that her child would grow up to be a brilliant public servant, and that she would live to be eighty. After the first two predictions had come true she had such faith in the third that when she fell desperately ill not long before her eightieth birthday she refused to share the doctors' alarm and did indeed confute them with her survival. But after she had entered her eighty-first year, healthy as she was, she would make no plan that extended beyond the next twelve months and she serenely prepared herself for death as a member of an ancient Bolognese lay order known as the Daughters of Saint Catherine. Then, when the last prediction failed to come true, she seemed to forget about death entirely and went back to talking of the future as confidently as a young girl of twenty. All of which was perhaps a trifle superstitious, but, as I was saying, healthy and vigorous, and characteristic of the robust homelife of the day.

How often poetic recreation is a resurrection of the dead and an interpretation of their lives like the one that the gypsy made of my grandmother's, only looking back instead of forward! In this epic of the water mills the writer's endeavor has been to poeticize a century and to celebrate the tenacious humility of the little people of Italy, who have kept faith with themselves and refused to be crushed by the almost overwhelming burden of their history. Here, in this personal connection with the events of almost a hundred years ago, he has found a sure source on which to feed his imagination, a deep human certainty on which he may bank securely, listening to that call of the blood whose nature we cannot fully understand but without which we cannot be men.

THE SMUGGLER OF THE PO

1

WHEN Giuseppe came back to Poplar Bridge he found his mother in the depths of despair, for she had long since given him up for dead.

"How could you imagine anything of the sort?"

"Because you didn't turn up for so long."

"Haven't I often stayed away much longer? You know I'm not one for writing letters. Only great gentlemen have time for that."

"But the other times you stayed away were before the war. If you knew how people have been talking!"

"That's why it's a poor idea to spread gossip or listen to it, either. I believe in few words and less writing."

As he spoke he remembered signing the false receipt and wished he had never learned to write at all.

"Did they make you take part in the war?"

"Oh, the war! Just from the sidelines. And it wasn't so bad as people say."

"What? War isn't so bad?"

Dosolina could not get over her astonishment. Giuseppe told the story of his wanderings from the flogging of the herdsman Zanocco to the bombardment of Bologna with an air of indifference and superiority that made it truly impressive.

His father too listened with interest, stroking his beard and rejoicing that at last Giuseppe had done something a little more manly than his usual trafficking, which he considered a form of polite robbery. Well might he, Lazzaro, the veteran of Napoleon, have bragged of even heavier cannonades, for he had taken part in the firing of Borodino. But Master Lazzaro was not so foolish, just because he had witnessed great deeds, to belittle those witnessed by others. All of us may be tempted to make this mistake, particularly when we are old, but Master Lazzaro was extraordinarily free of envy in any form whatever.

Not only did he rejoice in his son's adventure, but he praised him for virtues that Giuseppe had not even discovered. Giuseppe had omitted the episode of the threats that were tendered to him after Zanocco's flogging, and luckily Zanocco himself who lived only a mile away had not spoken. But Master Lazzaro guessed at something of the sort.

"Your hirelings must have found it hard lines to go off to war for a salary of twelve strokes of the whip," he observed.

"They found it very hard lines indeed."

"I imagine they had it in for you properly!"

"That they did."

"Of course. You were the nearest target. You must have passed some uneasy nights in their company."

"I can't say I always slept very well!"

"It's to your credit that you didn't abandon them. I know what it is to be in fate's hands among enemy soldiers, excited by the smell of gunpowder and by all the ugly and vicious practices of war, among barbarous foreigners who see some intent to cheat them in everything we say, as if every one of us were what was called in Russia a 'partisan.' A soldier can empty his rifle into a civilian's belly whenever he feels like it, knowing there's no penalty to pay. . . ."

"Heaven have mercy upon us!" Dosolina exclaimed trembling. "Holy Mother of God!"

"You haven't said so, but you must have been in a tight spot," said Scacerni.

"It's not up to me to say, Father, but I'm proud to hear it from a man like yourself, who's seen a thing or two and knows what it is to be brave."

"But what if they had really pumped you full of lead?" lamented Dosolina.

"What could I do, Mother?"

"But if they had really killed you?"

"You insist on my being dead, do you, even now that you see me here hale and hearty? You're going to bring me bad luck!"

Giuseppe was half amused and half angry. But in regard to his father this military adventure aroused feelings that neither of them had ever had before or that, much as they would have liked to, neither had ever been able to express. And the intensity of these feelings went beyond the relatively slight importance of the episode from which they had sprung. They were not expressed in words, for neither man knew that there were words to express them, but came out, rather, in small everyday things, or, more properly, in the way of doing them. The father spoke to his son with consideration and the son to his father with affectionate respect, and each one took a new interest in the other's affairs, Lazzaro in the collection and sale of grain and Giuseppe in the mill. Now his son came to help the lame miller when he climbed into the cart to go to work, for he had given up riding and let himself be driven by Hayseed, the peasant, behind a stubborn old donkey that would bite an arm off anyone but its master. And when they all sat around the simple but neatly set dining table Master Lazzaro had a more genial manner of cutting his son's portion of meat and breaking him off a piece of bread after he had served Dosolina. It was with an air of festivity when he was kept late at night on the mill that he welcomed Giuseppe to a dish of unleavened "miller's pie" grilled in oil over a slow fire and to the crude red caviar that had once been a specialty of Malvasone and now was made by Cecilia Rei. Once upon a time Giuseppe had affected scorn for these rustic delicacies, but

362

now he really enjoyed them and praised them to the sky in order to give his father and Cecilia pleasure. Even Cecilia took an interest in the epic of "Giuseppe's war" and listened to Master Lazzaro extoll his son in the presence of Venusta Chiccoli and Dosolina.

"That boy of mine," for thus the miller referred to his thirty-year-old son, "is turning out better than I expected. To tell the truth, I never did him justice. To handle himself so well when dealing with that rough, ugly-mugged gentleman, Virginio Alpi (I've seen him with my own eyes, you know), took not only courage but brains in the bargain. Giuseppe's grown up to be a real man and I think he'll make his way in the world. What does his mother say to that?"

"Haven't I said so from the start?" murmured Dosolina happily.

"Yes, you have. You had keener eyes than I did. But how was I to know? He always seemed to be afraid of the river. There's more than one kind of courage, I reckon, and he just wasn't cut out to be a miller."

"Don't give him a swelled head, now, with this talk of courage, Lazzaro, or else he'll turn into an adventurer and teller of tall tales like you."

"Am I an adventurer and teller of tall tales?"

"We all know what you were as a boy. But Peppino hasn't your good health. He's the sort, as I always told you, that should have studied to become a priest or a lawyer."

"His cleverness has come out even if he hasn't had the benefit of schooling," said Lazzaro, but this veiled reproach left him thoughtful.

"If he'd had more of an education then he wouldn't be in such danger today," Dosolina insisted.

"What danger is he in, my good woman, tell me that?"

"Just danger, that's all I know."

With advancing years Dosolina Scacerni had become slightly addle-pated and what she feared was that Giuseppe might wander about the world, not as a soldier, for even her motherly eye could see that his physique was too miserable for that, but as a purveyor to armies on the march to distant lands. She imagined him called on account of his courage and cleverness to risk his neck in connection with important war business. How many young men, in these calamitous years of 1848 and 1849, had gone away never to come home, dying or disappearing into exile and prison!

Meanwhile, as the months went miserably by, many men, for political reasons or because they had committed some crime, left their homes and regular occupations and went into hiding. A number of them came from the Polesine region north of the Po over to the Ferrara side in order to avoid being drafted into the Austrian army. And as a result of this general upheaval highway robbery was a large-scale menace. The Austrians replied by setting up martial law in Polesine and by instituting the Este Commission which ordered dozens of deserters summarily shot. At Ferrara too an Austrian military court sent many an offender to take a last walk on the terrace of the Fortress, with fettered hands and feet, a kerchief over his eyes, and a priest to exhort him to repentance. After exactly an hour of such walking they sent him up on the ramparts and made him kneel down before the firing squad, for the time had come when, as Alpi had predicted, there were not enough gallows to do the job. The executioners took off their caps and listened on their knees as the priest intoned the *miserere;* then the drums rolled and the dead man was carried away by some lay brothers.

All this severity, however, served only to increase criminal violence, and the countryside was full of bandits and the stories of their misdeeds.

One of the first things the Austrians did upon their arrival in Ferrara was to decree that any hoarder of arms and explosives must be judged by a military court, which might declare him subject to execution. This decree was extended to all the neighboring villages and orders were given to turn in all arms at a central depot in the city.

It was a summer day when this news came to Guarda and the peasants were convinced that it was a serious matter, with the danger of "those fellows with their trousers tucked into their boots" coming to search their houses. They brought out their guns and gaily shot them into the air so as not to have to take time away from their work to carry their gunpowder to Ferrara. Hunters who were usually sparing of their ammunition wasted it that morning on all sorts of birds and prepared to roast even sparrows for their evening meal. A few stubborn disbelievers even took aim at swallows, which commonly enjoyed the Virgin's protection, but found them no easy targets and in any case unfit for eating. As for the guns, almost everyone hid them away. Indeed Master Lazzaro had a special hiding place in his cellar for just such an eventuality.

The seizure of arms was established for military and political reasons but the Papal government had hoped that it would lessen the depredations of bandits and highway robbers. Of course the results were exactly the opposite of what had been intended, and while honest men were disarmed, robbers were bolder than ever. In the body politic as in the physical body it is no use trying to cure symptoms without getting at their cause.

2

On the day, then, when the peasants shot off their guns Master Lazzaro joined them quite happily and then tucked his own arms away in the cellar, joking the while with Giuseppe and Hayseed about the impromptu shooting match. Later he brought home other weapons that he had kept for years on the mill. Only the shotgun he used for duck-shooting would not fit in with the rest and he buried it in the yard.

"A regular arsenal," he said with a laugh.

"What's the use of it?" Giuseppe asked, for he would rather have seen his father comply with the law. But Master Lazzaro misunderstood him.

"Yes," he said, "what use is their edict, anyhow? But military commanders—and I've seen quite a few of them—seem to feel they must issue commands of some sort, for fear of wondering: 'What am I here for, anyhow?'"

"That must be it," said Giuseppe, who made painful efforts to live up to his newly acquired reputation as a brave man.

That very day he had been sorely tried because in the course of a visit to Copparo, the nearest seat of the government, he had heard many stories of the rigors of martial law and seen with his own eyes an impressive example.

When he first entered the town he was glad, after many months of slack trading, to see the market place crowded with people. But he soon found out, to his disappointment, that they were attracted by a towering machine set up on a high platform in the middle of the square. Those who were in the know explained that it was the latest model of guillotine, sent with a special executioner from Bologna to cut off the head of an evildoer of Copparo, who was to serve as an example to all the folk in the surrounding country, much more effectively than if he had been disposed of on the Piazza del Travaglio of Ferrara. The improvement in the guillotine apparently consisted of a moveable plank to which the victim was tied with three straps. When the plank was lowered his neck automatically fitted in the right place and he did not have to be yanked by the hair into position or trussed up like a sausage in case of resistance. The mention of a sausage made the crowd laugh, but the shiny, newly painted, well-oiled machine, fitted out with all the latest wrinkles, sent a cold chill down their spines. One obtrusively knowing individual continued to rave about it, declaring that the plank, now making its first appearance in the Papal States, was copied after an original of the French Revolution.

"You might call it a swing," said one bystander with intent to joke, but his laughter died on his lips.

"Call it a swing then," said the know-it-all. "Here they come out of the jail."

A piercing shriek so uninterrupted that one could not help wondering how it was possible to draw breath between one crescendo and another, emerged from the door of the jail, which was in an old tower next to the governor's palace. As the bestial cry came across the square the crowd stiffened. At the bottom of the stair leading up to the platform it suddenly stopped, or rather turned into mumbled words.

"You promised not to tie me, you murderers!"

"On condition that you behaved yourself," answered a roughly musical loud voice which, amid the breathless silence of the crowd, reached the ears of Giuseppe and all the others on its periphery.

"I have another sin to confess!" shouted the victim.

"Hurry up, then. I've no time to waste and you're in my power. Let this be the last I hear from you. You're in my power, do you understand?"

Giuseppe wondered why the executioner too should raise his voice so high.

"Have you finished?" he asked loudly. "Are you joking?"

"No! You promised me . . ." And the victim's voice died away in a sob.

"I keep my promises, never fear," jeered the other.

And then the condemned man appeared on the stair. The gigantic executioner held the rope around his wrists in the left hand and with the right grasped him by the neck like a rabbit and pushed him forward, half holding him up in the air. Once on the platform he thrust his knees into the victim's back and threw him flat on his stomach on the waiting plank, which was in a vertical position. There two husky assistants strapped him securely while he howled all the while, more like a beast than a man.

The "lord executioner" was dressed, according to the diary of a member of the Brotherhood of Comforters, in all his infernal pomp: a red cap with gold silk ribbons, red trousers, black boots, a short-sleeved red jacket allowing ample play to his muscular arms and a wide black sash from which hung a double-edged sword with a gleaming hilt. He wore a long beard and mustache and had the calm but terrifying aspect of a man who knows his job. Now he drew back to survey the preparations, judged the victim to be too short and ordered the straps loosened so that he could be pushed further up on the plank. This was no easy job, for the fellow resisted and the executioner had to step in and hold him. Finally he was strapped so that his feet did not touch the platform, and so tightly that his cry was strangled in his throat. Perhaps even the know-it-all of a few minutes before was no longer convinced of the perfection of the new instrument of death.

Giuseppe could not endure the sight any longer and closed his eyes until it was over. When he opened them, he saw the plank lying horizontally and blood gushing out of the truncated neck, and felt as if someone had struck him across the face. No one had the heart to transact any business that Friday, although it was the regular market day of Copparo.

With the dead man's blood and the red, black and gold pomp of the executioner fresh in his memory it was natural enough that Giuseppe should be unwilling to flout the authorities. His father had just come out with the argument that the conquerors "must issue commands of some sort" to prove their importance.

"That's no reason for not obeying them!" Giuseppe murmured to himself. "I know perfectly well that they give orders just for the sake of giving orders, but if they have power to cut off my head who's going to stick it back on again? If I had two heads I'd just as soon risk one of them, but as it is, what's the use? Just for a bit of bravado and

366

the pleasure of hiding a few rusty blades and guns in the ground? Of course, I'm supposed to be playing the part of a hero. I was better off as a coward!" And he heaved a cynical sigh.

He told his father of the scene he had just witnessed, with emphasis on the red blood gushing out of the victim's neck, the red, black and gold accoutrement of the executioner and the rough solemnity of his manner.

"Oh, so he's all dressed up nowadays, is he?"

"If you'd seen him you'd know that it's no joking matter."

"I don't mean to joke. I saw another one of his kind once, but he was dressed as simply as you and me and conducted himself like a Christian. He begged the victim's forgiveness and embraced him like a brother. The fellow you're describing sounds like a coward and a sorry clown!"

He spoke from deep in his thoughts. But Giuseppe was still irritable.

"However he's dressed he hacks off heads the same way," he observed, with the voice of the executioner still in his ears.

"You're right," Master Lazzaro said. "It's a terrible sight and one to teach us that our lives hang on a thread and we should look out for our souls."

"And our bodies too, I'd say," muttered Giuseppe, but Master Lazzaro was so absorbed in his memories that he did not even hear him.

"Our souls!" Giuseppe muttered. "Our souls, indeed! We needn't risk our necks just in order to remember them!"

Nevertheless he clung to his newly won reputation, because for the first time Cecilia Rei had departed from the indifference and scorn with which she had always treated him. This fact and his recent change of feelings toward his father, whom he now considered with more affection and less selfishness, combined to rekindle his ardor for Cecilia.

Alas, not even his new and kindly sentiments were altogether divorced from the thought of gain. Now that his father esteemed him he might influence Cecilia in the same direction. So great was the respect in which she held the miller that he could easily win her benevolence toward his son. Giuseppe could not get this idea out of his mind and the uncertainty of his tenuous hopes harassed his acquisitive nature almost more than his former resignation. With inconspicuous skill he maneuvered in such a way that his father should sing his praises to Cecilia, both at home and aboard the mill, and he was so successful that neither one dreamed that he was maneuvering them.

But two people saw through his game and were jealous: Schiavetto on the mill and Dosolina at Poplar Bridge, one who had long ago given up all hope of ever seeing his love requited and the other who thought that the "river gypsy" was no match for her son. Giuseppe's mother gave him little concern, but after spying on Schiavetto and guessing at the state of his feelings, he began to fear that "this cowardly wretch" as he called him, might damage his credit with Cecilia. One day listening shamelessly at the door of the cabin of Bitter Bread Mill he overheard the following conversation.

"This is the last straw, that Were Rabbit should preen himself like a man!" Schiavetto was saying.

"Isn't he a man, Schiavetto?" Cecilia asked mildly, but with what seemed to Giuseppe an overtone of mocking laughter.

"A man with a head on his shoulders and a heart in his breast, is what I mean. But he fancies himself a knight of Charlemagne at the moment!"

"Does he really go so far?"

"Haven't you seen him strutting about? And what are the grounds for it, I ask you? Just because he bamboozled some wagoners and herdsmen, like Zanocco from our own neighborhood, into following him. For a few miserable pennies he exposed them to flogging and all the risks of war. And then of course he prevailed upon the Austrians to release them; that was the least he could do. I happen to know where he got the courage to plead their cause, anyhow."

"You're too hard on him, Schiavetto."

"They threatened him with twelve strokes of the stick for every one given to Zanocco if he didn't get them out of the mess in a hurry. You can figure out for yourself what a beating that would have been!"

"They wanted to kill him, do you mean?"

"I shouldn't be surprised!"

"Schiavetto, now you're being malicious. Under those conditions Were Rabbit could have run away."

"As if they wouldn't have tracked him down! Doesn't Zanocco live near by? I have an idea he was well paid for his pains, even if those fellows got no more than two crowns each. He probably split the difference with that shifty individual who came here with a false beard and quarrelled with Master Lazzaro. Don't you remember that Giuseppe drove him away afterwards?"

"I know nothing about it."

"They've been thick as thieves ever since. Only I've forgotten the individual's name."

"Virginio Alpi, I've heard them call him. They say he's a count."

"A count, my eye! He's a common thief!"

"Have you got it in for him too, Schiavetto?"

"May the devil take him! No, I have it in for Were Rabbit!"

"Why so?"

"Because . . . just because . . . You've never liked him, have you?"

"No, but I think I may have been wrong."

"Wrong? You couldn't have been righter. And if you'll permit me to say so, I'd advise you to steer clear of him in the future."

"I think you're a bit touched in the head, Schiavetto."

"Am I though? Didn't Were Rabbit use to sneak over to the mill and make up to me? He told me that I was the only one he trusted and then he went to see whether I'd stolen any meal or flour. He didn't

368

think I noticed, but I knew perfectly well that if as much as a thimble-ful was missing he'd have denounced me to high heaven. He's been treacherous ever since he was a baby. Thank God, my conscience is clear and I've never taken the slightest advantage of Master Lazzaro."

"I know that, Schiavetto."

"Thank you, Mistress Cecilia. I almost wish Were Rabbit were spy-ing on me this minute. It would do him good to hear the truth about himself."

Giuseppe was there, right enough, and smitten by a paroxysm of rage and hate that was actually more pleasurable than either the spite he felt toward Schiavetto or his stimulated lust for Cecilia. Where another's passion would have been lit up by happy imaginings, his was darkened by bitterly sarcastic scorn. "What do you know about that?" he said to himself. "This good boy and trusted helper is a wolf in sheep's clothing, ready to turn against his masters. And she listens to him! They'll pay me for this!" Suddenly he realized that ever since he had run away from Ferrara he had not indulged in such pleasurable ill feeling. Now the blood coursed through his veins more quickly. "I've been so mild and good of late that they imagined I was a reformed character. I haven't been myself, that's all. They'll see that soon enough. No one can put over anything like that on me." If anyone had asked him as he stood there with his ear to the door what revenge he was planning he would have said with an ugly laugh that he would set a trap to catch a fox in. In the same way, when he was a child, he had delighted in baiting the traps with cornmeal, only to catch not the fox but some sparrow, starving amid the snow. "You have reason to warn her," he thought to himself as Schiavetto went on:

"Don't trust him, Mistress Cecilia, just because he has put on such an air of virtue. That's what he did with me in order to destroy me. He's thinking up some evil trick, you can be sure."

"What harm can he do me? And what motive could he have for doing it?"

"How's that? Haven't you noticed that he's as deeply in love as a red cat in the winter or a donkey in the month of May?"

"What if he is?" said Cecilia, laughing. "That's no reason for doing me harm, is it?"

"You wouldn't say yes to him, would you, Mistress Cecilia?"

Giuseppe listened eagerly in spite of himself to her laughing reply.

"Schiavetto, you're full of strange fancies today, but this is the strangest of them all."

"If you like him, of course, there's nothing I can say. But if not, watch out."

"Like him?" she said, laughing for the third time. "Poor Were Rabbit! He'd be the first one to marvel at what you are saying."

"You'll pay me for this, too," Giuseppe said between clenched teeth. He had heard all that interested him, but out of sheer curiosity he stayed on.

"You know how I love Master Lazzaro, he's for all the world like my father, but I must take him to task when it comes to Giuseppe. Dosolina is a mother, that's some excuse for her blindness, and besides she has about as much sense nowadays as one of her chickens. But I'll take you to task too if you put any trust in Were Rabbit. A wolf, that's what he'd like to be, but he's more like a snake I say. As for Master Lazzaro, I can't help blaming him. . . ."

"And me too," Cecilia answered, screwing up her nose.

"Yes, you too if you think there's any real change in Were Rabbit. Mind what I say, he's just what he used to be."

"You're right there, Schiavetto," Giuseppe said to himself. And just to do something spiteful he removed a large part of the wheat that was just then passing through his father's mill. The millstones whirled idly around and the warning bell began to clang.

"Schiavetto!" called Giuseppe. "Schiavetto, where are you? Where are you hiding?"

Schiavetto came on the run.

"Here I am, Master Peppino, what can I do for you?"

"Do for me? Is this the way you look after the mill? A fine helper you are! My father's away, so I come to take a look at the mill and look what I find? The hopper's empty, the stones are whirring, the bell is ringing, and no one's paying any attention. With all the customers that are waiting, too! Do you want my father to lose all his trade? You eat at our table and that's how you repay us! I'd come straight out and call you a thief, if it weren't that my father still cares for you. But if you go on like this, I'll have to put him wise."

Overcome by surprise and humiliation Schiavetto hung his head and swung his arms in an embarrassed manner.

"Yes, I heard the millstones and the bell," was all he could find to say.

"It's about time! If you're that hard of hearing you'd better find yourself a different job. Or did some other miller bribe you to work against us?"

"I still can't understand how it can have happened. The hopper was full when I went to give a hand to Mistress Cecilia. I don't know why all of a sudden it's empty."

"I think I know. You've been staring at the swallows and disturbing Mistress Cecilia with your chatter. Time always seems to pass quickly for an idler. . . . Excuse me, will you, Cecilia?" he added, seeing her look down with displeasure from the plank that connected the decks of the two mills. Then he went on, angrily: "And what are you doing now? Aren't you going to reload the hopper? Are you slow-witted altogether? You can see for yourself, Mistress Cecilia, that he's guilty of bad faith as well as stupidity. This is the way he rewards the master for treating him like a son!"

From that day on Giuseppe let no occasion go by, whether genuine or brought about by his own guile, of mortifying Schiavetto, particularly when Master Lazzaro or Cecilia Rei was there to see. His zeal impressed itself upon everybody and did not fail to have the desired effect of casting a shadow over the friendship between Schiavetto and Cecilia. Whenever Master Lazzaro came to his helper's defense Giuseppe would say:

"You're the master and of course it's up to you. If it pleases you to have a no-good lazybones in your service, go ahead and keep him. But don't ask me to set foot on Saint Michael's Mill, because I can't bear to see certain things without speaking up about them. And when I speak up, my temper gets the better of me."

Under the torment to which Giuseppe subjected him Schiavetto actually did deteriorate. One look from Were Rabbit was enough to make him forget what he knew perfectly well how to do and throw him into a state of confusion. Giuseppe would fire a succession of orders at him and Schiavetto in his eagerness to carry them out would make every possible mistake. Master Lazzaro did not know what to say. Meanwhile Giuseppe had resumed his trafficking. From dawn to dusk he visited the village markets, driving about under the hot summer sun with a new, fast horse and light cart.

"I'd let Lightning spend the last few months of his life in the stable," Master Lazzaro said when Giuseppe's faithful old nag began to fail him, and Dosolina observed that he could be useful in taking her to Mass in Guarda on Sundays and to do errands in the neighborhood.

But their arguments did not prevail. Giuseppe maintained that he would eat his head off in good hay and they would lose whatever was to be made out of selling his carcass while he was still alive. And so Lightning went off with bowed neck, almost as if he understood what was happening to him, to the slaughterhouse, leaving only his master dry-eyed. Giuseppe worked under the hot summer sun as hard as three men, living as strenuously as if he were intent on wearing himself and everyone he came in contact with to the bone.

"Aren't you afraid of sunstroke?" people asked him. "Only lizards go out at noon."

"There's something of the lizard in me then."

And to this there was no reply.

The summer went by, and it was fall.

"Now I see what's the matter with you," Schiavetto said one day of October, the tenth, to be exact.

For the past forty-eight hours there had been a stifling *scirocco* wind, which exhausted everybody and served to spread the cholera which had been raging in the city, especially among the Austrian troops, ever since early September. Giuseppe laughed at the cholera and the hot wind alike; he swore he had an iron digestion and drank large quantities of water, which was notoriously harmful. The fact is that he was a teetotaller and never touched a drop of anything else.

That afternoon he came home unexpectedly early. Apparently his horse had found the way all alone, for the reins were hanging idle and Giuseppe lay back unconscious and purple-faced on the seat. A recurrent tremor was the only sign that he was alive, and underneath his clothes he was a mass of dysentery. Hayseed's wife, who was the first to catch sight of him, shrieked with fear and could not bear to look at him again. Master Lazzaro and Dosolina came out of the house, but the latter almost fainted away and had to be carried back inside. Summoning up his old strength, Master Lazzaro lifted his son out of the cart and telling the others to stand aside put him down on his bed. There he undressed him and holding up his head put a glass of brandy to his lips.

"Drink all you can hold," he ordered.

At the smell of the alcohol Giuseppe partially came to himself, screwed up his face and turned his head away.

"Drink it down like a man," said his father.

Giuseppe took one swallow and then another and finally the burning liquid seemed to overcome the stony coldness of his body. His eyes lit up and he gulped the brandy down greedily.

"This is a cure I learned about when I was a soldier," said Master Lazzaro. "Taken in time it means salvation."

"I thought I was going to die," stammered Giuseppe. "Ever since morning I've been in pain, but I wouldn't believe it."

"Drink it down to the last drop. When you're really drunk then the danger is over. Can you hold the glass yourself for a moment?"

Dosolina had come back to her senses and was moaning in the kitchen that she must get in to see her dying son. Leaving Giuseppe with another full glass of brandy in his hand, Master Lazzaro came to the bedroom door.

"He's not dying now, good mother, but don't you go near him. If anyone is to catch the disease from him let it be me."

"He's dying, he's dying," shrieked Dosolina.

"He's not, I tell you. In case he has a relapse I'll see to it that you and the priest can bid him goodbye. But don't let the neighbors hear you wailing or we'll have to take him to the quarantine ward in Ferrara and there he'll die for certain."

The mention of this loathsome and terrifying spot was quite enough to silence Dosolina.

"Is he really alive, Lazzaro?" she contented herself with asking.

Lazzaro looked back through the door and saw Giuseppe with an empty glass in his hand, shining eyes and a fatuous smile.

"The alcohol's working on him," he said. "By God's grace the worst of it is over. Send someone to Copparo for a basket of lemons. They'll clean it out of him. And light a candle to Saint Roch, protector of the plague-stricken. Only for heaven's sake don't talk about it, unless you want him put into quarantine."

The calm assurance of Master Lazzaro's words and tone of voice restored confidence to Dosolina and she docilely did what he told her. Kneeling with the other women she prayed before the image of Saint Roch with his dog and pilgrim's staff and plague sore, which she had acquired at the beginning of the epidemic and set up beside the Virgin and Saint Anne in the kitchen.

"Not even cholera can kill him," muttered Schiavetto as he whipped up the horse on his way to get the lemons. "Were Rabbit is tougher than even the plague."

Not that Schiavetto's resentment was carried so far as to make him wish for the death of Giuseppe. This muttering expressed, rather, a perverse satisfaction that Giuseppe was not yet dead and a hope that his cure would be a complete one. In fact, Schiavetto pulled himself up with the suspicion that he was thinking too kindly of his tormentor.

"I don't wish him well on his own account, the wretch," he confided to Hayseed when he came back with the lemons. "But for the sake of his mother and father I pray that Saint Roch will heal him."

"Amen," Hayseed answered.

Drunk as a lord, as the saying goes, Giuseppe muttered and raved, tossing about in a mass of excrement. The heat had come back to his body and he had none of the cramps and vomiting associated with the advanced stages of the dread plague. The violent cure plus the iron constitution that lay beneath his weakling appearance had won the day. When evening came he fell into a deep sleep and snored vigorously.

"Dosolina," said Master Lazzaro, coming into the kitchen with hands outstretched to ward everyone away, "I believe you can thank Saint Roch with complete certainty. He's snoring like a pig. Give me a big piece of bread and some sausage, for I'm extremely hungry. But don't touch me. Better wait until I've washed my hands."

As Dosolina sliced the sausage tears trickled down into the plate. Never had she felt more affection for her husband.

"God bless you, Lazzaro!" she said, handing him his food. "You did what I should have done for him."

"Whichever one of us it was doesn't matter, since we're both his parents. Eat something yourself now, so as not to weaken. And then go have a long sleep."

"And what will you do, Lazzaro?"

"I'll watch over him. And have no fear. A man who's snoring like that has no intention of being taken out of the house feet first, I can tell you!"

Dosolina sent Hayseed and the women to rest and threw herself down with her clothes on. But she could not shut an eye and every now and then she went to listen at Giuseppe's door in order to hear him snoring more distinctly. At one point during the night the snore grew twice as loud and had two distinct notes to it. She smiled in a tender fashion that Lazzaro would have said made her look twenty years younger, half opened the door, propped a chair against it and spent the rest of the night half in prayer, half dozing, with her ear alert for the least sound from her menfolk even when her chin fell sleepily onto her chest. Thunder roared in the distance and lightning played on the dark windows. The distant storm relieved the hot heaviness of the scirocco and left the air refreshed and cool. Toward dawn there was a light rainfall.

The sick man woke up with a raging headache and a feeling of acute nausea.

"Two fingers of brandy right away," said Lazzaro with an authoritative yawn. "That's the only remedy for the after-effects of a bout of drinking."

"Is that something else you learned when you were a soldier?" asked Giuseppe, making faces over the brandy, which however did wonders for his stomach.

"Of course. Second company of pontoneers of the Royal Guard, and I could hold more drink than anyone in the whole company. But the morning after you must always have a hair of the dog that bit you or else you'll never want to touch a drop again. That's the secret of being a successful drinker."

"It did me good, I know that," said Giuseppe, holding out the empty glass. "I'll have to take to drinking myself, out of sheer gratitude."

"Your abstemiousness was the only fault I could find in you," Lazzaro said heartily, "and now I shan't be able to quibble over that any longer. But allow me to tell you that you stink like the devil in person."

Hearing them talk, Dosolina got up and noiselessly took the chair away from the door. Then she signed herself before the holy images and went back into her room. With a motherly feeling toward both men she sought to prevent Lazzaro from finding out that she had substituted him as a watcher.

Lazzaro heaped up a great pile of hemp stalks in the yard. The feast of Our Lady on September 8, which was the date of the harvest, had gone by and the hemp had been soaked and dried. On top of the pile Lazzaro threw a bundle containing the sick man's mattress, sheets, shirt, trousers and filthy underwear. Then he set it afire, while his naked son walked unsteadily across to a tub of water, washed himself thoroughly and thanked God for the clean, invigorating morning air. Flames sprang up from the fire and Dosolina, pretending to have been awakened by their crackling, called cheerfully out of the window:

"Do you want to burn the haystack, you two madmen?"

"Stay inside, Mother," shouted Giuseppe, "I'm stark naked. And throw me something to dry myself with."

"I'm your own mother, after all," Dosolina said laughing, "and after the scare you gave us yesterday I'm entitled to a look at you!"

But she drew in her head and sent out a towel by Lazzaro. When a doctor came from Ro with a government order to take all cholera patients to quarantine, and a sheriff and a couple of Carabinieri to back him up in carrying out the law, he found Giuseppe somewhat thin and pale, but entirely recovered, sitting in the October sun.

"Where's the patient?" the doctor asked.

"It was a bad case of dysentery, that's all," Giuseppe answered.

"Dysentery's a dangerous symptom in days like these," said the doctor. "Where is he? We have orders to put him in quarantine."

"It's not my fault, is it, if I'm already well."

"Oh, you are the man, are you? Congratulations! You've had a narrow escape."

374

Dosolina replaced the two burned-down candles to Saint Roch with new ones in gratitude for the doctor's late arrival.

"Someone must have reported you," Lazzaro said angrily. "If I knew who it was I'd wring his neck."

Who could it have been? Domenico Moia, the sheriff? He was generally disliked, inasmuch as he posted news of levies and taxes and came with customs guards to the mills to set a tax on the grain, which was particularly hateful to both millers and their customers, both of whom felt no scruples about dodging it. Or the tavern keeper at Guarda Crossing, Giulio Orlandini, known as the Rat? We have seen that because of his watered wine, his hypocrisy and his excessive intimacy with both customs guards and smugglers Lazzaro could not abide this man. Still another possibility was Annichini, the owner of the neighboring Antonella farm.

Gaetano Annichini was the head of a hard-working family and were it not for a quarrel he had long ago with Giuseppe over the use of a well, he might have been one of St. Michael's Mill's best customers. As it was, his loss had entailed that of many others. The straightest route to the dikes of Nogarole and the anchorage of the mill branched off from the road between Guarda and Ro and ran through Annichini's farm, from which it derived the name of Strada dell'Antonella. The curve of the other road close to the riverbank made it considerably longer, especially for those coming from Ro, and less convenient for everybody. Annichini might have closed the road completely, but what he did was almost worse. He or one of his family poisoned the ears of everyone that walked through their property with gossip about the wily Giuseppe and his overbearing father. Once upon a time, they said, he might have been an honest miller, but with such a son he must be a thief, and one so skilled as to escape detection. Since for miles around Giuseppe had a reputation for sharp dealing this reasoning carried some weight with it. Master Lazzaro soon became aware that all those who came by the Strada dell'Antonella to the mill were highly suspicious. They measured over and over again the grain they had brought with them and the flour that was milled from it, urged him not to make any mistake and when it was done asked him if he had made any.

When he had put two and two together and noticed that all these suspicious customers came from the same direction he regarded them himself with suspicion.

"Did you come by the Strada dell'Antonella?"

"Yes."

"It's not the best way."

"But for us it happens to be the shortest."

"And it will be the shortest way for you to go back, too, if you've been listening to what Annichini has to say about me."

In any case Annichini indirectly planted suspicion even in people to whom he did not communicate it directly. Many of them decided to travel a longer way to millers in whom they had less trust, just out of resentment for Master Lazzaro's antagonistic manner of speaking. Scacerni did not understand that as the world grew more dishonest it grew more mistrustful as well. The peasants were no longer as ingenuous as they had once been and did not want to be forced to take the word of a miller, even if the miller held that it was a privilege of his trade to be taken at his word. Times, as we say, were changing, as if there were anything else that they could possibly do.

And the man who had reported Giuseppe's cholera was Pietro Vergoli.

3

Why is it that when things are not the way we wish them we put the blame on anyone but ourselves? If between Ro and Guarda times had changed and dishonesty was the order of the day the fault was Pietro Vergoli's. So said Master Lazzaro.

Pietro Vergoli was the grandson of a ditchdigger and the son of a contractor. Starting out with the ownership of a small parcel of land in the vicinity of Ro, he had added to it little by little, with the acumen and industry that accompany a legitimate ambition to attain wealth, reenforced in his case by consciousness of his humble origins and of the difficulties he had overcome in making his first meager profits. He had good business sense and the watchful eye of an administrator who measures every penny but knows when to risk a thousand crowns. He had experience in the care and cultivation of the land and insisted that all such labors be carried out conscientiously, not only for the sake of gain, but also for the cause of general improvement and progress. If we add to this a practical streak, which was very pronounced in spite of his scant schooling, and a natural ability to handle men and command them, we shall see that he was one of those persons who seem to be born into a family in order to raise it to fortune and power. His father had inherited from his original status as the son of a ditchdigger the nickname of "Shovel," and Pietro was originally known as "Shovel's boy." But this sobriquet was used only by those who referred to him disparagingly. By all others, especially his dependents, he was called Vergoli or, more respectfully, Signor Pietro. As his land holdings increased he gradually abandoned his father's contracting business and to everyone's surprise began to buy up land even at exorbitant prices. Most of his purchases encircled some swampy lowlands behind Poplar Bridge and extended as far as the Fossa Lavezzola, a muddy tributary of the Po. At this point of our story he owned a large part of the land between Ro and Guarda, both on the side of the road lying near the river and on the opposite side, stretching toward the Fossa Lavezzola. At Ro itself he had built a country mansion with a fine lawn and shady garden. With an eye to the future of his children, since he had two already and a wife who was quite capable of presenting him with half a dozen more, he had constructed it in such a way as to be able to add on to the wings. In short, with the aid of the local builder he had managed to produce a striking architectural abortion, one which aimed at display rather than decorum.

The ground-floor rooms, including a terrace entrance, had been begun on principles of economy of the kind which usually precede an orgy of extravagance, and were found to be too low-ceilinged. They were therefore turned into offices and pantries and the main house was erected above them, with the ceilings of its first-floor rooms too high by comparison. The stairway between the two floors seemed disproportionately wide when looked at from below, and from above disproportionately narrow. The interior was marred by the decoration painted by an artist from the city, who had covered the walls with landscapes, ruins, and perspectives in a style patterned now after Raphael, now after the Grotesque manner, including cloistered gardens whose fences and trellises were occupied by parrots and monkeys in every conceivable position. The artist boasted descent from the famous School of Bologna and would brook no criticism of his work. But the parrots and monkeys were too much even for Vergoli.

"What are they there for?" he asked, seeing them in ever increasing numbers peering out of the woodwork, climbing everywhere and swinging by their tails from the beams and fixtures of the frescoed interiors as well as from the rocks and trees of the landscapes.

The artist said that this zoo was a symbol of all that was light and fanciful and modern. And when he was asked if no other animal could be equally symbolic he thought for a moment and said:

"How about snakes?"

Snakes are eminently decorative but Signora Vergoli could not bear to see them, even on the walls. And when one of her sons was in bed with typhoid fever the monkeys gave him nightmares and his bedroom had to be whitewashed completely. They said it was a shame, but secretly they envied him the restful absence of color in his room.

At the entrance to his property Vergoli had raised even higher than the main house a bizarre structure supported by two massive wooden columns, which was his own invention. From underneath it seemed like a covered gate and from above a verandah protected by an overhanging, sloping roof like that of a Swiss chalet. But if there was any criticism of Pietro Vergoli's mansion it died down quickly enough when he was appointed mayor of Ro.

The only good feature, and one which might interest a visitor of today, was a wall built around the property with two sentry boxes where armed guards looked out at night for burglars or kidnappers who might be tempted in these troublous times by the mansion's isolated position. Permission to bear arms even after the order to turn them in was accorded to Pietro Vergoli and his hirelings in consideration of his status as mayor, his "known probity" and "blameless political conduct" and the fact that his riches constituted a constant invitation to robbery.

Rome, Ancona, and Venice had fallen, Mazzini had gone back into exile, Garibaldi had escaped, and the new King of Sardinia was not scrapping the Constitution: this, in a nutshell, was the news. When it got around that on August 8, 1849, in Bologna Ugo Bassi had been shot, many persons in and around Ferrara remembered the flaming sermons of this Barnabite priest, the "apostle of freedom," to the Republican "volunteers" of the preceding year, which already seemed like ancient history. On the 10th of the same month Angelo Brunetti, the famous "Ciceruacchio," and his two sons, who had fled from Rome, were caught with arms in their hands at Ca' Tiepolo near the mouth of the Po and summarily shot by the Austrians right on the bank of the river. The execution of Luigi Brunetti was by way of revenge for his assassination of the cabinet minister, Pellegrino Rossi, but that of his thirteen-year-old brother Lorenzo was uncalled for and inexcusably brutal. With their father perished the sincere and generous daring of the revolutionary epoch. The shooting of this family of two men and one child, which took place in the heat of a summer day, far from public knowledge, symbolized the punishment of partisan and sectarian aberrations, the end of many facile enthusiasms, and the martyrdom of Italy. But from this event Pietro Vergoli and the peasant population of Guarda and Ro drew only the conclusion that a wise man sticks to his own business and respects whatever government is in power.

But let us come back to the scene of our story. The property known as La Vallazza, occupying a swamp overgrown with cane and an occasional clump of trees or bushes, which Pietro Vergoli was gradually encircling with his newly bought lands, belonged to Marquis Filippo Macchiavelli, a descendant of the family of Tuscan bankers.

He was a tall, thin man whose agile slenderness bespoke good breeding, and once inspired the flamboyant Sicilian from whom as a youth he took lessons in fencing to say: "Macchiavelli on guard is like the sharp edge of a blade." He had long, lean legs, and small, narrow, high-arched feet, which gave him a light, almost gliding step, like that of a stork or heron. Of these small feet he was a trifle vain, and also of his slender hands. His face was thin but not hollow, in spite of his advanced years, and he wore a silky brown beard that had reddish-gold reflections in it together with a few gray hairs. He had a high, narrow forehead, pale like old ivory but not bloodless, a well-proportioned head, and short, fine hair. He stood very straight when he walked, but did not stick his chest out or hold his head stiffly. His aquiline nose gave him a slightly predatory air, which was mitigated by his warm, brown eyes, which looked penetratingly out of his mobile, finely wrinkled face from under a pair of frequently scowling eyebrows that gave him an expression intended to be gruff but actually acute and bantering. Sparing of gestures, reserved without condescension, smartly turned out in old-fashioned and slightly worn but none the less spotless and faultlessly cut clothes, Filippo Macchiavelli was what is called a gentleman to the manner born. On account of his heritage of wealth, social position, cultivation, fine feelings and respect for both himself and others he had a sure and easy way of doing things, that verged, however, on carelessness and neglect of his own material interests. When a family has been endowed with possessions, for generation after generation, and has had to make no effort to acquire them, its stock is prone to lose its vigor and waste away. The marquis was well aware of this danger. He never worried about it except in moments of laughter and this same laughter served to conceal his worry. The characteristic Macchiavelli voice, which must have been powerful and sonorous in his banker forebears and even louder in their ennobled successors when they commanded a regiment or answered a challenge to their honor, was in the present bearer of the title gentle and veiled. He could not raise it without being overcome by a certain weariness, the same that possessed him when he was irritated, indignant, or angry. His resentment inevitably finished with a shrug of the shoulders, which seemed violent but was in reality resigned and evasive. He would cut short in this way any conversation or discussion that annoyed or saddened him and shut himself up for hours alone in his study. Under these circumstances his wife, children, and friends simply persisted in the opinion which he had failed to contradict, and people with whom he had business dealings proceeded behind his back to turn them to their own advantage. All they had to do was wait for his first ineffectual protest to pass and then, when he was weary, present him with a slightly altered version of the proposition which he had previously rejected.

In this art the managers and stewards of his property were past masters, and his inherited wealth, a tidy sum in spite of various liens and mortgages, had in large part passed into their hands.

"Life is like a stairway," the marquis used to say; "some people are going up and others coming down."

Not very far from Ro, near Cologna, there were some so-called Case della Macchiavella and a tract of land of the same name, which long ago must have belonged to the family. The marquis had got it into his head to trace their history and at the same time to establish once and for all by what ties of blood, if any, he could consider himself a descendant of the great Niccolò Macchiavelli. To this end he went to spend the greater part of several years of his youth studying the archives of Florence, where he indulged himself in thoroughbred horses, gaming, duelling, and affairs of the heart and won the reputation of being a very fine gentleman, a generous lover, and a brilliant hand at cards. Needless to say, the Tuscan origin of his ancestors and their connections with Niccolò remained a secret of the archives he had come to study.

Eventually he married a lady of good birth but moderate means, charming rather than beautiful, and of an eminently kind and patient disposition, whom he held in deep affection and chivalrous respect. They retired to his villa at Ro, Beicamina, a noble pile but fallen into decay, where in the first three years of their marriage she bore him three sons. There they lived comfortably enough, keeping cool in summer and warm in winter, enjoying the great fireplaces and fine old furnishings, the shade trees in the overgrown park, and the orchard and vegetable garden, where the marquis had enthusiastically crossed various strains, only to reduce their fertility to practically nothing. The purpose of his country life was to restore his dilapidated fortune, or such part of it as was left after his years in Florence, and he went about achieving it with enormous but intermittent zeal, spending a great deal of money on agricultural improvements without any rise of income to make up for his expenditures. Then, all of a sudden, he got another historical bee in his bonnet, which led him to study the sojourn of the Macchiavelli family in Modena.

"Everyone knows that when Ferrara fell into the hands of the Pope, its last Duke, Cesare d'Este, carried all his family archives to Modena for safekeeping," Filippo explained.

"And to whom has the gorgeous Giacomina 'fallen'?" asked his friends jokingly.

Giacomina was a notoriously inflammable Venetian beauty, living in Modena, who caused the marquis's good wife to shed many a solitary tear amid the decayed splendor of Beicamina. But eventually this too passed away.

The oldest son left home early. At a time when the Austrians were still intent upon keeping up their Italian connections, Fieldmarshal Nugent, who had many friends in Ferrara, persuaded the marquis to send the boy to the military academy of Vienna. After all, in the armies of the great Eugene of Savoy, a Macchiavelli had been a regimental commander. But Casimiro had been a rachitic child and now he showed a total lack of inclination for a military career and a morbid aversion to horses, which even the famous riding school of the academy could not cure. His mother blamed it all on a fright she had suffered during her pregnancy, but be this as it may, her mild and kindly nature manifested itself in him as an extreme form of caution and inertia. After his brief career as a soldier he was persuaded to marry a highborn and imperious Viennese lady of none too good a moral reputation, who led him by the nose. His wife made one visit to Ferrara, and this was more than enough. The weakly Casimiro had forgotten how to speak Italian and his only occupation was that of an honorary chamberlain at the Imperial court.

The second son, Feliciano, was clever enough, but mean and sceptical. He entered holy orders and went as an abate to the Vatican, where he specialized in intrigue, gallantry and self-aggrandizement. Every now and then he came back to his native parts to settle some question of ecclesiastical properties.

The third, Luigi, was enormously gifted; he had talent, courage, ambition, an agreeable manner and extraordinary good looks. But there was some lack of harmony among all these qualities which prevented his putting them to good use, an excess of initial enthusiasm which soon turned into boredom or disgust. He resembled his father in every way, with so much exaggeration that he was almost a caricature. He was wild for cards, women, and high living, alternately aggressive and indifferent, and Ferrarese society rejected him as being affected, ostentatious, and never pleased with anything. He was pleased least of all with himself, in bad odor with the police because he claimed to be a Liberal, and with the Liberals because without any real faith in their ideals he strove to be the leader of their conspiracies. Having thoroughly misspent his life and spoken ill of all and sundry, Luigi was said to live off gaming and women and to lend himself to the police as an *agent provocateur* in such remote places as Naples, Milan, Paris, and Spain. His family had news of him three times in all. Once, from Vienna, when as a result of having tried to blackmail his sister-in-law he had been told to leave Austrian soil forever. And the next two times from Paris and Madrid, whence he had implored his father to save him from dishonor, for a price that the marquis could not have raised even if he had had twice his actual money.

"There you have a miniature picture of the perversity of the world and its ways," the marquis said after his first bitterness and disillusionment had turned into resigned melancholy. "Right in the bosom of my own family. Casimiro was born for a life of monkish retirement and fate pushed him to try to rival Prince Eugene, with whom he had only a disability in common. Yes, Eugene of Savoy was rachitic too, but that didn't prevent him from becoming *Prinz Eugen, der edle Ritter.* My second son has no religious faith and lo and behold he's an ecclesiastic! As for the third, he has all the qualities that make for success, and instead he has wasted his life and become a thorn in my side. What do you say to that? Good men hang back, and so evil men take over; that's why the world's in such a pickle. At least that's the way to take it philosophically. But ask a father whose sons have turned out badly what consolation there is in philosophy!"

"May it not be a punishment for our sins?" said the marquise timorously, for she could not but see the father's errors reflected in the sons, although of course she inclined to judge the latter more indulgently.

"That's heresy, my good woman! First, because our good and bad deeds are weighed and rewarded not in this world but in the next. Then, because it's uncharitable to damn a son for his father's shortcomings. In your case there'd be no justice at all, since you've never committed a sin in your life."

"No one can say that, Filippo."

"Well, only the most venial variety."

His deeply affectionate relationship with his wife was the only consolation of Filippo Macchiavelli's old age, along with a quiet but strong religious faith, which adversity had never eradicated. He was not unaware of the existence of doubt and the loss of faith, but this only caused him to nurture his own religion the more carefully and to be thankful for the gift of it that God had made him. His devotion was discreet and urbane, as befitted a true Italian nobleman, one of a class which has in its time produced examples of virtue to be set among the very highest.

The marquis was for years mayor of Ro and fulfilled his duties with love and diligence, but his openly demonstrated loyalty to Pope Pius caused the Republicans to remove him from this function. He bore his removal well, and later on the restoration of Papal power gave him less pleasure than he had expected, partly because it did not bring with it recovery of his former office. He was glad to endure this affront to his pride without vanity or affectation, for the sake of convictions to which he had always held so faithfully.

"Better first at Ro than second at Rome," he said. "But even that's gone from me now. I must prove my claim to be an honest man by not allowing disappointed ambition to gnaw at my soul."

And if his interlocutor laughed, as if this were an idle precaution, he added:

"Easy there, my friend, with your scorn! Just turn back the pages of history and look at the ravings that have been inspired by ambition. Read the words of the great tyrants, say Robespierre, for example, who is not too remote from our own day. It's always a case of wounded vanity."

The marquis knew his Latin classics and was even more convinced than Manzoni of the stern wisdom and virile morality of the ancient Romans. A reader of the classics, he maintained, needs no other books, except for one, which is sacred. But the influence of classical imitations, false rhetoric, and debased Roman Republicanism upon the brutal and ridiculous excesses of the French Revolution were such as to show him that even the noblest literature can be dangerous. He did not need to read the confused Taine or the doctrinaire Tocqueville in order to reach this conclusion, for he had personal memories of the Jacobins of Ferrara, "our local Brutuses" as he called them, among whom he remembered most vividly the relentless and unfortunate Maurelio Mazzacorati, "who on account of a tree of liberty shot the priest of San Pietro Bolognese."

What end had Mazzacorati, himself a renegade priest, come to? He found out, quite unexpectedly, from Lazzaro Scacerni, with whom he took pleasure in conversing when business took him to the mill. He had a genuine liking for this old-fashioned miller, who always greeted him with such hearty deference, natural dignity, and true Italian courtesy. As a return for the delicious "miller's pie" that Lazzaro invariably prepared in his honor the marquis gave him permission to hunt in the grounds of La Vallazza, a privilege of which Lazzaro happily availed himself without the least abuse. In spite of the difference in their social positions the two men esteemed one another and had a feeling of friendship deeper than they were aware. For each in his own way had stepped out of another century.

Pietro Vergoli had succeeded Macchiavelli as mayor of Ro and Lazzaro's loyalty to the impoverished nobleman expressed itself in redoubled dislike of the ambitious peasant. The marquis, because he prided himself upon his equanimity, tried to moderate the picturesquely strong language in which Lazzaro spoke his opinion. But he somewhat enjoyed listening to it, even if he judged Vergoli for what he was, a rough but capable fellow who had every reason to make his way in the world.

"He can have every reason you like," Scacerni would say, shrugging his shoulders, "but I can't stand him."

This was not the case with the marquis, who did not particularly object to Vergoli and was unaware of the fact that he was the only person who still called him by his first name instead of "Signor Pietro" and inadvertently treated him without the respect due to his new office. Whenever, as frequently happened, Vergoli felt the need of voicing his pride as a self-made man, he would say:

"Do you remember when I used to be called 'Shovel's boy'?"

"That wasn't so very long ago, was it?" the marquis answered ingenuously, failing to realize that the other did not relish his reply.

Vergoli devoutly hoped that his sons, or at least his grandsons, might acquire this gentlemanly, easygoing, self-assured manner to which he submitted without aspiring to copy it himself. He spent money lavishly on their education and both at school and at home they gave him every satisfaction.

The marquis had an amiable smile whenever Vergoli ingenuously boasted of their scholastic successes or brought them to pay a holiday call.

"I don't envy you your money, Pietro," he said once, and here the thickset, plebeian Vergoli bowed his narrow, stubborn forehead, clenched his massive jaws, and looked sharply up at him, aware that, strangely enough, this was true, "but I do envy you your sons."

And he sighed with such honest pain that Vergoli felt embarrassed, although for reasons of his own.

"Don't let them hear you," he said, "or else their heads will be properly turned."

The boys were enjoying some refreshments given them by the marquise and there was such happiness in Vergoli's expression that Macchiavelli added:

"You're a father, and a good father, too, so you won't take my envy amiss."

At this Vergoli's embarrassment touched upon an apparent sentimentality and he hastened to ask for news of Casimiro, Feliciano and Luigi. The marquis drew himself up and answered with chilly politeness that Marquis Casimiro enjoyed the trust of the Emperor of Austria, Abate Feliciano was equally successful at the Papal court, and Luigi was amusing himself by travelling the world over. Pietro Vergoli did not know what to think.

He wondered at times why, since the marquis visited a miller on his mill and often stopped in to see peasants whose land he, Vergoli, had bought from him, he had never found time to come admire the new mansion at Ro. After it had been decorated for some time in the elaborate fashion which we have described above he said to the marquis one day:

"I should be happy if some time or other you'd stop by to see my house."

"Of course, Pietro, with pleasure."

"Really?" Pietro exclaimed.

"Why not?"

"You've never chosen to . . ."

"But, Pietro, you never asked me . . ."

Oh, that was all, was it? Vergoli sought the advice of the parish priest of Ro and sent him a written invitation, which caused the marquis to smile, as did the profusion of parrots and monkeys on the walls. But he congratulated Vergoli heartily and dropped a few gallantries in the direction of his pretty wife.

"Mind you, though," said the wife, after their caller had gone, "he didn't invite me to Beicamina."

"What ideas can get into a woman's head!"

"How's that? Don't you think I deserve the honor?"

"Come, come! He probably forgot about it."

"We shall see for how long a time he forgets!"

It was true that the marquis had simply not given the matter a thought, but Vergoli's pleasure was spoiled by his concern as to why his wife had not been invited. And this concern rankled the more as he grew in wealth and public consideration.

4

Even Annichini's farm, L'Antonella, had passed into Vergoli's hands.

"Thanks to a succession of poor harvests," observed Scacerni. And when he was told that the Annichinis had declared themselves pleased with this arrangement, happy to have shunted off all responsibility and to live as tenants on the land that had once been their own, he added:

"They're fools to think anyone will believe that. Of course they don't like it. It's as if I had been forced to sell Saint Michael's Mill and hire myself out to the new owner."

He laughed at this supposition, but in somewhat hollow tones, as if his own words had frightened him. They were only words, of course, but the moment of fright had been a real one.

"Better a dry crust of bread of one's own than the crumbs of cake from somebody else's table," he murmured pensively.

And Marquis Macchiavelli chimed in with an echo of the same thought from Ariosto: "Rather a turnip in my own house . . ."

The two men saw eye to eye in preferring poverty to bondage and having no use for wealth without freedom. Without freedom, they agreed, the world is like a piece of rotten fruit, all very fine to look at, but mushy and disgusting within. Pietro Vergoli, on the other hand, had nothing in his head but bonds and bondage. A man who wants to succeed, he repeated to his sons and acquaintances, deals out his favors with an eye to what they will bring him; he must keep the good will of his neighbors and see to it that his name is trumpeted abroad. Let everyone hope to get more out of him than there is any chance of their getting; whenever he meets anyone new he must remember that some day the fellow may be useful. Upon which the marquis and the miller commented between themselves: "Why talk and live like a beggar simply in order to die a rich man?" Vergoli was so fearful of men and gods, so intent upon warding off evil fortune, that he appeared to have no more enjoyment of his riches than a cat that has tangled itself up in the skein it is seeking to unravel.

Neither the marquis nor Lazzaro Scacerni could appreciate the element of strength in Vergoli, the persistence that made him representative of a new class of society. The one who appreciated him most was Giuseppe, whose only regret was that Vergoli did not traffic in grain. There was a reason for this, of which Vergoli made no secret. His father, or Shovel II, as the local wits called him, had solemnly advised him to deal exclusively in land and to sell what was left from his crops without storing it or speculating on an increase of its value. Perhaps the old man shared the peasant superstition that it was dangerous to speculate on the hunger of the poor, to whom bread was the staff of life, or else he had suffered or heard tell of the ill luck that is so often visited upon those who hoard against a time of famine. Be that as it may, among his dying words was a severe warning of the risks of dealing in grain.

Vergoli's present ambitions were, first, to start the cultivation of hemp, which had never been raised in these parts on a large scale, and second, to reclaim the swampy land of La Vallazza. The second was still up his sleeve, but meanwhile the hemp project was particularly irritating to Giuseppe Scacerni. He knew nothing of the gradation of its quality and price, and the very mention of it recalled the misguided business activities of his grandiloquent grandfather, Princivalle Malvegoli. In short, Giuseppe had the same prejudice against hemp that Pietro Vergoli had against grain.

Paradoxically enough, Vergoli had considerable success in raising grain, having introduced new methods of fertilization such as were practiced in Belgium, France, and Lombardy. Giuseppe envied him his handsome granaries, one of which he had built near the boundary line between Poplar Bridge and L'Antonella. There he could have stored all he wanted and have kept it free from worms and mildew for a year or more, on the chance that prices might rise. It made Giuseppe writhe to see him sell his entire crop at the regular price, or even less, thereby winning the blessings of the local population. To Giuseppe this seemed like a waste of God's bounty, and the blessings had an ironical ring to them.

On an early July morning of 1850 the silence of the fields was broken by the shrill, cheerful, imperious sound of a steam whistle and the rhythmical pounding, punctuated by occasional slowdowns, of a threshing machine. Everyone knew at once what it was, for they had been told of Pietro Vergoli's purchase and had seen it arrive at Guarda, still dismantled, on a barge that had brought it from Trieste across the Adriatic and up the Po. After its arrival it had been put together in a large shed beyond La Vallazza, which the local people immediately nicknamed the "Palace of the Machine." On the black belly of the engine was printed in brass letters the name of the English manufacturer, and word soon got around that it would do a hundred times the work of a man. Tons of coal disappeared into its maw, smoke poured out of the smokestack, and it quivered, whistled and pounded away, while the onlookers marvelled at the turning wheel and shiny transmission belt.

"It's come to rob good Christians of their work," said Master Lazzaro. "God help us if ever it explodes; what a slaughter that would be! And it's a dangerous tool to use. If you catch an arm or a leg in it they'll soon enough be reduced to jelly."

"'There's none so blind as he that will not see,'" said Giuseppe, who did not envisage the future of the machine in such a calamitous light. And Lazzaro remembered with dismay how as a young man, when the older millers had predicted disaster on account of the exposed anchorage he had chosen for his mill, he had written this now faded, defiant motto on the bow.

"You don't mean that this method of threshing is as efficient as flails or the hoofs of a good horse, do you?"

"Indeed I do! The machine cuts the ear, separates the wheat from the chaff and pours it into a sack, all in one operation."

"That's the devil's own invention. There must be some catch to it!"

Lazzaro feared, without saying so, that the next thing would be a steam mill, a soulless, greedy machine that would heat and ruin the flour and be the end of millers, himself first of all since he had the bad luck to live near that damned Vergoli. Already there was gossip of such a prospect in the village.

"It won't work," Master Lazzaro insisted. "My father-in-law used to say that in foreign lands, may God damn . . ."

"Damn the foreign lands or damn your father-in-law?"

"God damn the foreign lands and have pity on the soul of my father-in-law. . . . He said they had steam mills in foreign lands, but I say that they must be God-forsaken places, with no water like that of our Po. And the things my father-in-law—God rest his soul!—used to tell were mostly tall tales, anyhow."

But no one remembered Princivalle Malvegoli and the village people continued to gossip about everything new. The next thing was the stink of Pietro Vergoli's hemp, which now that the drying season had come, was poisoning the air of the whole village.

"What a blight!" said Lazzaro. "Here where we've always had such good air from the river. You can't tell me that those fumes aren't bad for the health."

"There are plenty of places around Ferrara where they dry hemp and you don't hear the people complaining."

386

"And the rotten water it's been soaking in, isn't that bound to infect the air?"

Soon after this, rumor had it that Vergoli was setting up a business company with Marquis Macchiavelli for the reclamation of La Vallazza. People asked Lazzaro if he had been told about it, and he shrugged his shoulders incredulously, although he was secretly pleased that they should imagine him to be on such close terms with the marquis. He was so pleased that he risked committing himself to a negative answer, and his shrug of the shoulders turned into an affectedly reticent: "Don't say anything so stupid," which clearly implied that he knew more than he was willing to say.

The time has come to admit that Lazzaro had acquired two definite faults in his old age; one, naturally enough, was the tendency to talk down anything new, the other, more usual in a young man than in an old one, a way of making himself seem important.

These conversations took place at the Barchessa tavern, and when it came out there that the reclamation company was really going ahead, Lazzaro grumbled that it was a mistake to drain the water out of the swamp because it would dry up all the springs. There was some basis for this theory, because it is a known fact that no land needs irrigation as much as that which has been reclaimed, but Lazzaro was of course speaking purely out of his aversion to Pietro Vergoli.

"And you objected to the little bit of stagnant water that the hemp was soaked in!" said his friends teasingly. "Now when it comes to stagnant water, there's enough of that in La Vallazza . . ."

"The water in La Vallazza is natural water!"

"Natural? What does that mean?"

"It means . . . It means natural, of course."

"That's not getting us anywhere."

Scacerni was annoyed.

"I can't talk with people who are so uncouth."

"Master Lazzaro, uncouth we may be, but let's have the truth! You're sorry about La Vallazza because you like wild duck with rice, and coots and woodcocks and the other game birds you go to shoot there!"

The author of this joke was himself known as Woodcock, because he had a small, round, birdlike head with a thin, long nose and eyes set far to each side.

"That's one reason! Of course it is. What are we poor people without some fun after our work?"

"Just beasts of burden," the others agreed.

"And the gentlemen, what sort of gentlemen would they be without their sport? For the most gentlemanly of all sports is hunting."

"Have no fear," said Woodcock, "they'll find another."

"No other so fine. They're likely to fall upon something that's hurtful to themselves and others."

"But are gentlemen really necessary?" Woodcock asked knowingly.

"Would you have everyone poor?"

"I'd like to see the poor less poor and the gentlemen less rich. I'd like to see things fairly divided, Master Lazzaro."

Woodcock was an alert fellow who listened to what was said in the market places of the surrounding villages and Ferrara and this phrase of his left the others at a loss for an answer. But Master Lazzaro accosted him a few days later.

"Woodcock, I've been thinking about your idea of dividing things up," he said.

"It's not my own idea," said Woodcock with false modesty. "I've heard it discussed and it appealed to me."

"I've heard it too, particularly in '48, from some volunteers who came from France. When I was a soldier of Napoleon I learned a bit of their language, you know. One morning on my way to the mill I met these fellows and they were saying in French that private property is theft and that it should be divided equally among all men."

"Then you know more than I do."

"That's not very hard," said Lazzaro. "But do you know what happened that day? Those same fellows came to my house with their guns in their hands to take a sack of flour from me and a dinner of capons and wine from my wife. If they'd had time they'd probably have divided the women and girls among them too, I mean the young and beautiful ones, of course, because no one would be such a fool as to choose the old and ugly. And here, my friends, is where I saw that there was a flaw to their reasoning, because for the flour and capons and wine they gave nothing in return. What sort of division was that, I ask you? It's the same way as it is with the anchorages in the Po. There aren't enough good ones to go around and so it's a question of first come first served. . . ."

"Then give me good luck and let hard work go hang!"

"Hard work has something to do with it too. But I was thinking of luck. The fact is that there is only a small number of anchorages that are no good at all, too. Most of them are a mixture of good and bad together. Isn't that true?"

"Yes, that's true of everything in life."

"That's exactly what I mean. But let's stick to our mills. Let's say a law is passed that they are to be divided. The law is a just enough one, but I know the millers, Woodcock, beginning with myself, because I'm no better than the rest of them. Would I be satisfied with a God-forsaken anchorage, or even a fairly good one? No, I'd want the best of the lot and I'd try by hook or by crook to get it. Out of the idea of justice there would come only injustice, every man would be at war with his neighbor, and I can tell you something about war. There luck is everything, and brute force more than luck. It would be like the Tower of Babel."

He stopped to cool his throat with half a glass of wine, and his opponent, who was wiser than he let it appear, said with a pitying laugh:

"Since you're so domineering by nature, Master Lazzaro, the only thing is to let you have the best anchorage. You deserve it, anyhow, because there's no better miller on the Po."

Lazzaro sat with his glass in his hand, more worried than he was flattered, as the other went on:

"And because a miller of your ability installed in the best anchorage can make enough profit to feed two other families beside his own, then your surplus profit can be given to some of those who are worse off than you are."

"It can, can it? Who's to give it?"

"You yourself."

"I?"

There was such astonishment and incredulity in that "I?" that everyone laughed. This was indeed the most eloquent answer to Woodcock's social system.

"If you won't do it of your own free will, you can be made to, if it's the law."

"Ah, the police, is that it? Is that what you're driving at? To make me work for others and under others' direction, as if I were just a hired man. I'd rather set fire to my mill! Do you think I'm so easy to handle?"

There was resolution in his voice and so much of his old spirit, that no one could make an affirmative answer.

"Then you'd go to jail," said Woodcock coldly.

"Would you put me there?"

There was another outburst of laughter and Scacerni continued triumphantly:

"Can't you see what a Tower of Babel it would be? But don't take me for such a wise man. All that I know about the Tower of Babel I learned from our parish priest, Don Giuseppe Romagnoli. And, Woodcock, you ought to know what sort of a man he was, because you were one of the six fellows whom the Croats very nearly shot at the edge of the melon patch in '48. If Don Giuseppe hadn't faced the guns, what would you have done, you chatterbox?"

"He wet his trousers, didn't you, Woodcock?" the rest of the company sang out in chorus.

"No one can blame him for that," said Lazzaro, with a victor's contemptuous generosity.

This had indeed been the aftermath of the tragedy, but Master Lazzaro and his friends exaggerated their recollections of it on every possible occasion in order to tease Woodcock. His sermonizing was distasteful to them all and so was his lack of religion, which to Scacerni appeared sheer ingratitude toward the good priest who had saved him.

Meanwhile Pietro Vergoli was measuring the area and depth of water in La Vallazza swamp, sticking up poles and pickets and starting to hire diggers and haulers to work on the drainage canals. The miller did not dare speak his opinion to an educated gentleman like the marquis, but the latter must have read it in his face.

"A year from now there'll be no more hunting for either of us in La Vallazza," he said. "Are you sorry, Master Lazzaro?"

"The hunting's the least of it, sir."

"You don't like the idea of reclamation, then?"

"Since you ask me, sir, no, I don't."

"But remember that where two of us had sport before, there'll now be a living for five peasant families."

"There are plenty of peasants in this world," muttered Lazzaro.

"Whereas woodcocks and wild ducks are scarcer every day," said the marquis laughing. "There's a hunter's reasoning for you. I don't say that I fail to understand it."

He stopped laughing abruptly. It was out of necessity that he had made the deal with Vergoli, and since the latter was putting up the capital he had also assured himself a lion's share of the profits. The marquis stood to lose his hunting preserve and to obtain very little money in return. But necessity knows no law.

There came to a head at just this time the consequences of the two poor harvests of 1846 and 1847 and the political upsets of 1848 and 1849. The peasants could not pay their landlords and came to them for financial aid in order to get on with their sowing. Then war had brought requisitioning in its train. On February 18, 1849, the Austrian General Haynau had imposed a levy of 206,000 crowns and on the 25th of the same month the embattled Republicans put through a forced loan on large incomes. Macchiavelli was caught between two fires, mostly on account of a house he owned in Ferrara, whose tenants had long since forgotten to pay their rent. The tax collector never failed to turn up, and he came now on behalf of the restored Papal government, which began with exacting something from all landed estates. Every township had a tax to pay, and salt, always a clue to the cost of living, had gone back to the high price of 1847. The marquis found it hard to sell and harder still to buy. After four years of impairment the affairs of his estate had come to a dead stop and he was faced with the necessity of selling everything in order to meet his obligations.

In return for the right to reclaim La Vallazza Pietro Vergoli offered to take on the administration of all Macchiavelli's properties and to save his financial situation. The marquis hesitated for a long time, for the sake of both form and feeling. He felt that he was abdicating his rights and at the same time betraying the agents, tenants, and peasants who had depended upon him to treat them in easygoing and patriarchal fashion. But one day, under the threat of an imminent seizure of some of his land, he went impulsively to offer Vergoli even more than he had originally asked for, bestowing upon him a general power of attorney and the right to conduct whatever business he saw fit without having to give any accounting. Vergoli was an honest man, he said, and he trusted him completely.

This was true enough, and by means of ruthless tactics such as the marquis would never have employed Vergoli did salvage the situation,

390

at the same time making a handsome profit from the more efficient cultivation of the lands whose management he had taken over. On these the marquis did not set foot again. He was too just a man not to recognize the fact that Vergoli had earned his money, and too generous not to admit his obligation. But he did not realize that his weary way of saying: "You've done a good job; go right ahead," or: "You needn't give me any explanations," or: "Don't bother to show me the receipts, Pietro, I know you're an honest man," gave an effect of disdain. Pietro would have preferred the marquis to take an interest, even a slightly inquisitive one, in his procedures and the results he was obtaining from them. What the marquis meant for a demonstration of confidence and gratitude Pietro mistakenly interpreted as an intended offense, an aristocrat's scorn for the grandson of a ditchdigger.

Meanwhile Master Lazzaro, still affecting to know nothing of what was going on, never lost a chance to slip in a word to the marquis about the sharp business deals that Vergoli was putting across in the surrounding countryside, taking advantage, the miller claimed, of the peasants' poor crops and lack of money. The marquis smiled tolerantly and did not bother to contradict him. But Lazzaro insisted that anyone who had to do with Pietro Vergoli should take warning from the misfortunes of Bastianino Donzelli, nephew of the priest of the same name who had been Don Giuseppe Romagnoli's predecessor.

Bastianino had lived comfortably enough as owner of the piece of land known as The Sisters' Farm, until Vergoli told him that whenever the river was high the drainage from his fields was flooding those next door, belonging to Vergoli, and persuaded him first to deepen his own drainage ditches and next to take part in the construction of a large new canal which would serve both properties. Vergoli lent Bastianino the money for his share of the job and then sued him for its recovery, with the result that Bastianino's farm, with all its ditches, both old and new, passed into his hands and Bastianino was left penniless with five homely daughters on his hands.

The marquis saw plainly enough what Scacerni was driving at with this story.

"I've heard that Bastianino's case was based on false premises and cavilling," he observed.

"So say 'Shovel's Son' and his lawyers."

"But the court decided in his favor."

"Oh well, the court. . . ." said Lazzaro, shrugging his shoulders.

"A court decision, even if it's erroneous, is always better than the conclusion reached by individual outsiders who may, I grant you, know better."

"That's true," admitted Lazzaro, thinking back to the Tower of Babel and to the time when he himself, in his eagerness to see justice done, had narrowly escaped committing a crime.

"They tell me that Bastianino Donzelli is a lazy good-for-nothing, anyhow."

"That's no reason for stripping him of his land. Otherwise . . ."

391

"So lazy, in fact," the marquis continued, "that his uncle, Don Bastiano, failed to bequeath him the field that he himself used to till between one Mass and another. Do you remember?"

"Yes, I do. The priest and Bastianino's father never did get on very well."

"No. Because Bastianino's father was a man of 1796, a Jacobin, and when the revolutionary government expropriated all land belonging to the clergy he bought for a song (speaking of business deals!) the convent site known as The Sisters' Farm."

"That, to tell the truth, I didn't know."

"But you know what they say, that riches acquired by such means do not profit the soul of the buyer, or that of his sons after him."

An uneasy feeling swept over Scacerni, akin to the anxiety of a bad dream, and he said with a forced laugh:

"Then that disbelieving 'son of a Shovel' won't enjoy his new acquisition either!"

"Score a point for you!" said the marquis, amused by the intensity of Lazzaro's feeling and inspired to make a reply in the Voltaire tradition. "Evidently the sins of the fathers are not always visited upon any beyond the second generation. And then Vergoli doesn't belong to the same family."

"I don't follow you, sir."

"So much the better," said Macchiavelli, with such gravity that Lazzaro was embarrassed and fell back into the memories that had troubled him a moment before.

"Do you know my story, too?" he said hazily to the marquis. "I thought I'd never told it outside of confession."

"Come, come, Master Lazzaro, you must be dreaming. What can I know of anything you have told under the seal of the confessional?"

"Because I did accomplish the penance set me by the good Don Bastiano Donzelli, after he had enquired about the danger of excommunication from a theologian at the archbishop's palace."

"Now it's I that can't follow," said the marquis, astonished by this turn in the conversation.

Thus it was that he came to know about the treasure of the Virgin of Spain, the death of Maurelio Mazzacorati, and the beginnings of Saint Michael's Mill. And it would be hard to say which was greater: the lively interest taken by the marquis or Scacerni's relief in unburdening himself all over again.

"Of course I knew nothing of all this," said the marquis when the story was over. "But it's most interesting and instructive. I needn't tell you, especially since you've been absolved of your sin, that I have no intention of putting myself in the place of your confessor. Even if you had not been absolved I should have no right to do that. In short, I don't wish to pass judgment on your affairs or on how you came to build the mill. But it is, I repeat, an interesting and instructive story."

"As long as you weren't bored I'm glad to have told you."

"On the contrary, I enjoyed it immensely."

392

And he equally enjoyed hearing the sequel, the part played by Michele Bergando, known as Raguseo, who had met his end at the hands of Big Brother on the corner of the Strada degli Armari.

"Your life would make a good subject for a book, Master Lazzaro," he observed.

"And what kind of a book would that be?" said Lazzaro, causing his interlocutor to laugh heartily.

But lively as were some of the details of the story, such as Lazzaro's contest of strength with Raguseo, the narrator passed briefly and hurriedly over all matters of feeling, because he had not the vocabulary to express them. He dismissed the emotions he had felt when first Raguseo and then Big Brother were killed before his eyes and his subsequent visit to Mother Eurosia with a few such obscure sentences as: "Of course I went there with a notion to kill him myself. . . . Later I couldn't eat or sleep without a vision of hell yawning before me. . . . Only the saint herself could say what she said to me then. . . ."

His listener did not deeply penetrate Scacerni's innermost soul, an operation which requires a transfer of emotion such as only poetry or divine charity can inspire. Now Lazzaro's story, lively as it was, was anything but poetical and the marquis, in spite of his keen pleasure in it, did not feel called upon to be charitable. So it was in a joking vein that a few days later he informed the miller that Raguseo's empty and supposedly haunted house in the city had been recently bought by a man with a sharp eye for business and no belief in ghosts. Master Lazzaro listened smilingly enough and expressed surprise only at the fact that the Palazzaccio was still standing. If a man wasn't afraid of ghosts, he said, the purchase might well turn out to be a profitable one, as is indicated by the proverb: "A rich man may go to hell, but his heirs are none the less lucky for that."

"But the more I think about it," he concluded, "the surer I am that the buyer is either a saint or a devil."

"He's someone you know," said the marquis.

"Someone I know?"

"Pietro Vergoli!"

The effect of this revelation was not at all what the marquis expected.

"Vergoli, eh?" Lazzaro exclaimed. "Well done! Now I know him for what he is, a second Raguseo. Mind you, though, when his predecessor laid his knife on the table and entered into a discussion, he was honest after a fashion, either an outright friend or an outright enemy. Whereas it's when he comes as friend that this fellow here is particularly dangerous. Before the devil spit him up into the world he cloaked him in hypocrisy. I know what I'm talking about because he wants to buy the little plot of land that belongs to my wife, Dosolina. And since I wouldn't sell it to him for love or money, no doubt he's planning to dig some ditch or canal under the ground and evict me the way he did Bastianino Donzelli. But he'd better watch out. Lazzaro Scacerni wasn't afraid of the first Raguseo, and he was a wolf and a fox, whereas this one is only a weasel and a mole! I know that he's planning to put up a steam mill that will do ten times the work of ours and ruin the flour to boot. Of course the peasants will run to it like flies into a spider's web, but Saint Anthony, the patron saint of millers, won't save his mill when I set it on fire."

"Master Lazzaro! What are you saying?"

Schiavetto and Cecilia Rei, drawn by the loud and angry tone of his voice, had come out of the mill and stood there listening.

"It's enough, I tell you! Enough and too much! And I know what I'm saying."

"You're raving," said the marquis.

"Since it's you that say so, sir, I believe you. But why, at this time of my life, has that damned soul of a Raguseo risen from hell to bring woe to the river and all the land it washes?"

"Come, come now; try to reason."

"I reason according to my own lights, sir."

"Your reasoning's askew, I tell you."

"You are quite right, sir, you and the rest of them. And I alone am in the wrong. Do you know why? Because once upon a time when I was angry I held my tongue, but now I have grown garrulous. Which means that I'm not the man I was. But if the need comes I can turn back the years and once more play the part of a man. I've said for some time that it is not in this earth that my body will rot away."

"What do you mean by that?" asked Macchiavelli severely.

"The potter's field will be my last resting place."

"Come now, Scacerni," said the marquis impatiently. "If you won't listen to reason, let's not talk any further."

The marquis felt embarrassed and ill at ease, as if he shared the blame for these ravings, even only inasmuch as he had not foreseen them. Deep down within perhaps he remembered that in olden days, when local wars and family feuds were the rule in the regions of both Tuscany and Ferrara, a hate like that so inappropriately displayed by the miller would have been considered no more than natural. Perhaps his own ancestors had had devoted partisans of this sort, ready to go to any length in order to achieve revenge.

"Let's speak of it no more, Scacerni," he repeated uneasily. "Because of the esteem in which I hold you I can't bear to see you go in for such loose thinking."

"I'm grateful for your esteem, sir. And I shall say no more. To think that I had to reach this venerable age and have a long white beard hanging down my chest! Schiavetto, ferry the marquis back to the shore."

Macchiavelli had got up from the bench outside the cabin where he was sitting and showed himself ready to go. On all the previous occasions when he had visited the mill Lazzaro had rowed him both ways in person. Now he accompanied him across the deck, doffed his hat and remained stiffly standing, as if pinned there by his lumbago, his face pale and rigid and with a weary expression upon it, as if the vain and tumultuous words with which he had revived his old passion had frozen his veins and drained them of their blood. He was halfway between dreaminess and awakening, in that state when the anxiety we have felt while asleep turns into a fearful waking presentiment.

There is a tragic custom along the Po when a man has drowned in it, which compels the members of his immediate family to keep watch in such places as it seems likely his body will drift ashore. They alone, when he is cast up by the torrent, must receive him in their hands and decently prepare his body. So now, as if the ghost of his past had been cast up by the turbulent water of the years, the weary old Lazzaro stood with his hands outstretched to receive it.

5

Lazzaro was impatient of his old age and these superstitious fears were, as the marquis had claimed, pure ravings. Vergoli had his hands too full with the project of reclaiming La Vallazza to think of acquiring the Poplar Bridge property or of introducing a steam mill to the river. Everyone, including Vergoli himself, when he was told of them, dismissed Lazzaro's complaints as pitiful symptoms of his advancing years, that is, everyone except Bastianino Donzelli, whom Lazzaro despised, and Dosolina, his only remaining confidante.

But Lazzaro was right on one point, of which he spoke out loud where others only whispered, and this was that, like Raguseo, Pietro Vergoli was a smuggler. Of course the two smugglers differed in many ways, but this only made Lazzaro hate the second and subtler of them all the more.

The clever and ambitious Vergoli had embarked on this traffic some time before, when he realized that the fiscal and customs system of the Papal States were such as to choke all his bold enterprises. The government seemed at this time to pursue a policy of deliberate obstruction of commerce and industry, and this for long-standing and singular reasons. Agriculture provided a sufficient living for the frugal peasants and for noble families whose estates were so large as to compensate them for having no liquid money. Manufacturing, if such it could be called, was carried out by artisans in quantities large enough for no more than a local market; while "foreign trade" did not exist and was looked upon as a cause of social disturbance. For the rest, whenever a natural calamity threatened to starve the floating population of the cities religious organizations came to the rescue. With the rents from ecclesiastical holdings and voluntary donations they perpetuated in the name of Christian charity the dole that centuries before the patricians of Rome had handed out to the rabble.

At this time the Church was no longer as wealthy as when a united Christian community had poured gold into its coffers and made it a Renaissance power, but this only shows that economic factors, important as they may be to history, are not everything. At the time of our story, when the defects of the Papal State were greater than its merits and it had entered a process of inevitable decay, the necessity of living on a shoestring made for a temperance of manners which was a kind of virtue and did not stifle either culture or ingenuity.

The governmental tendency to obstruct commercial activity was felt particularly in the northern legations. Here the House of Este had left a tradition of enterprise, the natural wealth of the soil stimulated ambition, and the people had ever before their eyes the example of the more modern and progressive administrations of Lombardy, Venetia, Tuscany, and Modena. In the legations, the system was so at variance with the needs of the population that, in spite of the high taxes raised in them by other means, the revenue from customs duties was even less than that yielded by the infinitely poorer region of Umbria and the province of Rome. This is eloquent proof of the fact that smuggling had become the most common channel of trade.

Pietro Vergoli, as a businessman installed upon the border, which was subject to even more than the usual customs vexations, had soon seen from the records how his business was made to suffer. His income was reduced and his expenses were high; everywhere there were obstacles to his activity, and his sources of gain threatened to wither away. First, the importation of products from abroad was forbidden or else penalized by a heavy tariff; Vergoli would legally have been obliged to buy the wood he used for building at a domestic price considerably higher than that which prevailed on the other side of the Po, and to have had it brought from a longer distance, which meant an additional cost for transportation. It was simpler and less expensive to bribe the customs collectors of Guarda and bring the wood across from Polesella. Altogether a more reasonable procedure, too, or so he argued, but here he was wrong, for no matter how wicked the law may be it is always immoral and hence unreasonable to transgress it. Vergoli was too proud and ambitious to excuse himself with the bad example of others; he chose rather to calculate that with smuggled wood he could build more houses and stables and set up more buildings for the processing of hemp, thus benefiting the peasant population and its livestock and agriculture and developing a new commerce, which should be a source of profit to everyone connected with it. In the long run even the treasury would gain, and in proportions such as to offset the small sums out of which he had cheated the petty and annoying customs. After he had successfully bribed the guards to let pass his wood he applied the same reasoning to the other products he needed for the expansion of his affairs, all of which, both materials and machinery, cost less on the other side of the river.

A second feature of government policy was the attempt to regulate the disposal of local products, which were in this instance hemp and grain. Their exportation, which in the case of grain was blamed by the peasants for the high price of bread, was taxed and when scarcity would have made it most profitable it was actually forbidden. Pietro Vergoli had no sooner decided to go in for the cultivation of hemp on a large scale than he counted up how much it would cost him to defraud the customs and export it rather than contenting himself with the unimportant local market. Hemp spoils after long storage and the Ferrarese variety was greatly in demand, not only in Lombardy and Venetia but also, through merchants in the port of Trieste, as far away as England, France, and the Low Countries. And so it was that he smuggled goods out of the province as well as into it, bribing the customs guards in order to secure the immunity of his traffic in both directions.

The third obstacle to trade was a complicated and often contradictory application of minor taxes, surtaxes, stamps and permits, which varied from one village to another, some new and others of long standing. These were both stupid and annoying, ruinous to a businessman unless he chose to evade them, and in any case of scant utility to the government. When a local industry had been successfully killed off by taxes the government would, paradoxically enough, post a prize for its rehabilitation. In such cases some practical joker as often as not would bring in some item from abroad and win the prize by falsely declaring that it was of local production.

Businessmen of the type of Pietro Vergoli, who were not given to philosophizing, esteemed themselves faithful subjects of the legitimate government because they did not cherish subversive ideas or wish for any change in the governmental structure. But they insisted on evading such of its laws as were damaging to their business. In so doing they did not realize that their loyalty was utterly fictitious and ineffective, and that they were actually guilty of crime.

Conditions were ripe for a revolution, and we can see from the foregoing that this was eventually brought about not only by a group of intellectuals and politicians allied to the nascent House of Savoy but by the necessities of everyday living. The case of Pietro Vergoli (which is largely based on facts) shows how an ambitious man with a newly acquired fortune, one of the rising middle class or *bourgeoisie*, while considering himself a conservative supporter of the Papal government, was in reality a revolutionary.

The basis of his prosperity was the surreptitious introduction of building material and the exportation of hemp down the river and across the Adriatic to Trieste, where one of his correspondents saw to forwarding it overseas. Vergoli did not go in for halfway measures. His illegal traffic was just as carefully organized and accounted for as his more regular activities. For a while he kept all the books himself, but eventually he turned them over to an accountant whom he considered dense enough not to know exactly what was going on. This accountant was a timid weakling who looked as if he had grown up without ever seeing the light of day but had sat from time eternal on a high stool with his head buried in his books. He was for all the world like a grub or ant wrestling with a prey larger than itself and managing by virtue of its pincer-like feelers to tease and tire it out and finally devour it.

Vergoli attended in person to the sale of his hemp and collected the payment for it, and also dealt directly with the customs guards and tax collectors, whose "percentage" he entered in the books as "miscellaneous expenses." He was certain that an accountant such as the one we have described above would never guess at or even wonder about the sources of either his largest assets or his most conspicuous outlays. Long practice of unpunished fraud had given him complete self-confidence and he had no fear at all that the law would ever catch up with him. The local people, with grudging admiration, called him the Smuggler of the Po.

Solimani, the sergeant in charge of the main customs station across from Polesella, and Corporal Barbacinti, who represented him at Guarda Crossing, received regular salaries from Vergoli for closing an eye to all business transacted in his name at either place or in Orlandini's tavern. The tavern building was actually in Vergoli's possession and so was the guards' lodge, formerly a run-down cabin on the sandy shore, which now housed a dozen men. Vergoli had rebuilt this cabin and thrown up a sandbank to protect it from floods, thereby greatly increasing the guards' comfort and security. He also supplied them with food, wine, and wood for their fire, and since they were quiet, good-natured fellows these amply satisfied their needs.

Solimani, known more familiarly as Sergeant Blister, was not to be bought so easily. He was a gross and ignorant but at the same time intrusive man, who hardly knew how to read or write the papers that went through his hands, but had a keen scent for any possible source of money. Greedy, hypocritical, vain, and quick to take offense, he was not content to pocket a bribe and say nothing, but insisted upon enjoying both the public and private intimacy of his master, who would gladly have done without so much embarrassing attention. He had no choice, however, but to receive it and Sergeant Blister was a frequent visitor at the Vergoli mansion, where he walked in without knocking and with his cap on his head, mouthing jokes and friendly greetings in a singularly loud and unpleasant voice. He had followed his occupation on all the boundaries of the Papal States, on mountains and plains, rivers and seas, in the service of the Bourbons, the Estes, the Lorraines and the Hapsburgs, always trampling on the poor and allying himself with the rich and mighty. His subordinate, Corporal Barbacinti, was a prudent man, in constant fear and trembling. They made a curious pair, for the corporal was heavy-set with a ruddy, bearded, leonine face, which concealed a timorous heart, while the bold sergeant was lean and sallow, with a complexion as smooth as a fish's belly and the watchful eyes of a surly cat. Like a fish he was always in motion, turning his eyes this way and that, so that it seemed as if he never closed them even in his sleep. He was from the vicinity of Lagoscuro and knew all the dialects of the border, while Barbacinti came from a region known among its superior neighbors as "the sloppy part of the Marches," whose dialect was broken and singsong, like that of the Abruzzo mountaineers. Speaking, then, with this characteristic accent, he understood little of the talk of the people among whom he was now serving, to which he referred as "damned Ferrarese chatter."

"Corporal Barbacinti," his sergeant invariably told him, "just do as I say, and have no fear. You can leave the worrying to me."

And the corporal, trembling within, let everything go and bothered his head about nothing but Pietro Vergoli's good wine, which enabled him to say to Orlandini, the tavern keeper:

"Keep your poison for your customers, poor devils!"

At certain seasons of the year the riverbank between the main customs station and Guarda Crossing seemed as busy as the port of Lagoscuro, so numerous were the seagoing ships and barges, many of them of Venetian ownership, which were loading and unloading for the benefit of the "smuggler of the Po."

"They're loading things via the customs," the peasants said jokingly, and by now this phrase was synonymous with the absence of custom duties. If any passer-by lingered too long and too curiously Solimani sent one of his men to persuade him to move on.

"What do you want? What are you staring at? Are you looking for trouble?"

And if the passer-by took offense and began to grumble, along came Sergeant Blister in person.

"I'll send you to jail if you don't watch out! Here on the border, remember, we guards come next to God Almighty!"

At Ro and Guarda they only laughed. Call him the smuggler of the Po, if you will, they said, but Pietro Vergoli gives us bread and work; in fact, he's brought us luck and prosperity. If he didn't have his smuggling trade we'd all be the worse off for it. After all, in these circumstances as well as every other, three meals a day were a prime necessity.

And finally it came to the point where Pietro Vergoli threw a bridge over the Antonella canal, widened the road down to the river, and built two ramps solid enough to hold the heaviest wagons over the dikes at Nogarole, right in front of the anchorage of Lazzaro Scacerni's mill. For at this point the river was deep and offered a better landing for the heavy Venetian barges.

During the operation of "loading via the customs" Lazzaro stayed day and night aboard the mill, as he had done as a young man, and carried on an incessant argument with the ship- and barge-masters, telling them to keep a safe distance away because he wanted no disturbance. Otherwise they were quite insolent enough, he thought, to tie up beside the St. Michael and the Bitter Bread and use them as gangplanks to facilitate their loading. Actually all they did was to laugh at his ill humor and say in their drawling Venetian dialect:

"'Bitter Bread!' Who ever heard of such a name?"

"If there were any justice in this world there'd be a worse one than that for you and the man behind you. Keep your distance, I tell you! You're cutting off the flow of water to my mill wheel! Shove off, and let your cable out farther!"

"What are you talking about, Miller?"

"I know what I'm talking about, and that's quite enough. Stay away! I prefer to keep some people at a distance!"

"Are you speaking for our benefit?"

"If the cap fits, put it on. I know for whom I am speaking."

Two men invariably came along at this point to supervise the loading: Sergeant Blister, whom Scacerni remembered for the rigidity with which he was wont to calculate the tax on milled grain, and a certain Olmeda, Pietro's right-hand man and physically so like him that people were reminded of the time when old Shovel had hung about his handsome mother. Olmeda had orders not to aggravate the ageing miller.

"Master Lazzaro," he called out from the beach when he saw the miller's gloomy countenance appear on the deck, "shall we never see a more cheerful look on your face?"

"You yourself? Or are you speaking for someone else?"

"For myself. And for Signor Pietro, who holds you in high esteem."

"I enjoy enough esteem already."

"Proud, aren't you?"

"And as for faces, you have enough of them between you."

"Between whom?"

"You and your master."

"What's that? Aren't you grateful to him for having cleared up the bad air that used to hang over this valley?"

"I liked it better the way it was and breathed it more easily."

"Is that the way to talk? And now he's rebuilt the road so that people can come more easily to your mill."

"He didn't do it for my sake, did he?" Master Lazzaro objected wheezily, and in order not to go too far he let off steam with Cecilia or Schiavetto.

"The cheek of them! They do their loading here because the river laps up against the dikes and gives them more draught for their ships. Now I see why the Po is always threatening to break through at this point. It means there's retribution in store. Raguseo at least tried to hide himself and operated under cover of night. But these shameless fellows carry on in broad daylight and with the customs guards to protect them. Yes, Raguseo had some dignity, by comparison."

Because Scacerni was wont to repeat his lamentations and prophecies at the Barchessa Tavern the revolutionary Woodcock nicknamed him Apocalypse, which of course only caused him to inveigh all the more violently against a generation of sinners. One day when Sergeant Solimani was aboard, walking across a plank from one mill to the other, the plank gave way beneath him and plunged him into the swift and swollen current below. He caught on and was hauled out of the water, dripping, spitting, and swearing in every dialect of the Papal reign.

"You did this to me on purpose, Scacerni," he sputtered.

"I? I've been many a time across that plank and I weigh three times

400

as much as you do, Sergeant. So has Corporal Barbacinti, who's a great ox of a man."

"That's why I say you must have sawed it from underneath."

"There may have been a treacherous knot in the wood, for all I know."

"I say someone cut it, and that not very long ago."

"Then fish up the pieces and prove it," said Lazzaro calmly since he was quite sure that they had by now drifted far down the river.

"I'm positive someone here has hidden arms and I'd like to see him with the Austrian hangman and the lay brothers on either side of him on the terrace of the Fortress."

"Find them if you can," rejoined Master Lazzaro; "at least they'll be useful for something."

The sergeant knew what kind of man he was dealing with and guessed easily enough that the miller would turn his arms on anyone he suspected of having informed upon him. So he kept down his temper along with the river water he had just forcibly swallowed.

Everyone rejoiced over his plunge and he derived from it still another sobriquet, that of Pike, the greediest fish of the river. Even Vergoli agreed that it suited him, but there was nothing he could do to get rid of his accomplice. To get along without paying either the customs or the customs guard would have been too much to expect. It was true that the smugglers of earlier days, such as Raguseo, had bent the guards to their will with knife, stick, and pistol, but this system was no longer in style. It was not adapted to the volume, regularity, and high standing of Vergoli's large-scale business, and moreover it would have been against his conscience. He utterly failed to see any resemblance between his organization and Raguseo's criminal band, whose main activity had not been smuggling so much as kidnapping, rape, extortion, and any kind of violence so long as there was profit in it. Vergoli could not even think of such things without horror and indignation, although he was troubled occasionally by the shadow of an inadmissible doubt. If evil fortune or human perversity were one day to overtake him, if he were faced with the loss of wealth and reputation and a prison sentence on the one hand and a crime on the other, would he not be sorely tempted by the latter?

At such moments he reasoned that his smuggling activities were known to the government and tolerated by it; they were, one might say, a public service. Even if someone were to report and accuse him he would suffer no other punishment but a fine imposed for the sake of stopping gossip. And finally, even if the means were illicit, the end he sought to attain was a good one; indeed his confessor had admitted as much. "I didn't choose to be a smuggler," he said to himself. "The government forced smuggling upon me because of its unreasonable laws. If it would see the light and let up on some of its absurd regulations then I'd be glad enough to call a halt. I don't do it for pleasure." And to add to his justifications the government exaggerated its stupidity. A new tax imposed on goods from overseas made it prohibitive to drink a cup of chocolate or coffee or to buy enough sugar for putting up peach and plum jam. To provide his good wife with sugar for her preserves and to let his friends have chocolate and coffee at a fair price required so little effort that any other course would have shown him lacking in family affection and sociability. With the same means he was able to win the favor of the government officials in Ferrara with whom he had frequent contact now that he had been named prefect of Copparo, a district which included both Ro and Guarda. Was it his fault that such highly placed persons were willing to accept his gifts? He would never have dared offer them had he not been shamelessly solicited. Thus it was that the secretary of the Papal delegate drove down the streets of Ferrara in a stylish tilbury which Pietro Vergoli had passed through the customs, for Milanese carriage work was much in demand but weighed down by excessive duties. The delegate himself, Count Filippo Folicaldi da Bagnacavallo, was a strait-laced individual who frowned on gifts, but he was very much of an exception.

So it came about that along the Po perhaps the only man who was not a professed friend or debtor of Pietro Vergoli was Master Lazzaro Scacerni, the miller, whose dismal prophecies had earned him the nickname of Apocalypse.

And what of Marquis Macchiavelli? The marquis was as well informed as anyone of Vergoli's activities and had the courage to call him Pietro the Smuggler straight to his face. When his interlocutor seemed to be worried or to take umbrage at this appellation he set forth to him a philosophy based on the experience of his own family.

"Don't worry, Pietro. Let me tell you that my ancestors, at the time when they were bankers to the House of Este, enriched themselves with free and easy operations very much like yours and perhaps even less respectable, such as the bribery of magistrates, the lining of their pockets with government contracts and the hoarding of scarce commodities during periods of famine. Their descendants made money in a nobler style, fighting with Montecuccoli and Prince Eugene the world over. I say in a nobler style because they won themselves a fair share of titles and parchments and coats-of-arms, but if the poor folk living in the fields and cities which they laid waste in order to 'make war pay' could have spoken they might tell a different story. Then eventually I came along and undid all my ancestors had achieved. I may be a more delicate spirit than they, but I am assuredly a weaker one. Now you have the will and energy to make your way in the world and most likely your descendants will boast of tracing their origin to the Smuggler of the Po. And then, after a certain number of generations, along will come one of your line who will waste the substance you have with such doubtful means put together. That, my smuggler friend, is the way of the world!"

Vergoli began to avoid meeting the marquis for fear of hearing this or another version of his philosophy, which he mistakenly interpreted as having some recondite malicious meaning.

As for Giuseppe Scacerni, two things conspired to annoy him. First, that Pietro Vergoli did not choose to speculate in grain and in fact had a way of dumping it on the market, and second that Cecilia Rei did not return his love, and indeed despised it. But he did not console himself with saying: "That is the way of the world." He reasoned in the terms of the river country that it takes three fogs to bring a rain and that until it is ripe the fruit cannot fall. On the other hand, even a feather may weigh down a man on a long journey and nothing makes time pass so slowly as an unrequited and hopeless passion.

OF TRICKERY AND GREED,
INTRIGUE AND BLACKMAIL

1

Always turning up, like a bad penny, aren't you? And how is your health, Peppino Scacerni?"

Peppino lifted his head, which hung on his chest as he drove along lost in his thoughts, and his horse spontaneously stopped in front of Pietro Vergoli's mansion in Ro. The voice that had spoken to him was gay in spite of its ironical intonation and the face, ugly as it was, was a smiling one. Peppino took off his hat to Virginio Alpi and to Vergoli, beside whom he was standing.

"What good luck has brought you here, sir?" he asked.

"Exactly what it was on the tip of my tongue to ask you. Get down and come in for a moment, Scacerni, if the master of the house is willing. It will be a pleasure to see you."

Vergoli nodded to indicate his willingness, but showed few signs of pleasure. Alpi's complexion was as green and repellent as ever, but he had shaved off his Austrian-style whiskers and was dressed in a pearl-gray suit of the latest fashion. The English taste in men's clothes had begun to make itself felt, so that collars were lower, ties less voluminous, waistcoats no longer fancy and the lines of jackets and trousers straight instead of pinched in at the waist as they had been before. Beside Alpi's sober elegance, somewhat exaggerated courtly manner, and obvious high spirits Vergoli looked even more awkward, troubled, and ill-humored than usual. He had the expression of a man who has swallowed some bitter medicine and is wondering whether it is more unpleasant to his stomach than it was to his palate a moment before. Giuseppe Scacerni, who had come to know Alpi well, suddenly reflected that the man could never be just himself, for he always seemed to be in disguise. At the moment he was playing the part of a man of the world, but the ugly leer characteristic of his real nature came through like ill-fermented wine seeping out the slats of a barrel, and all his fine dress and elaborate manners were no more than powder intended to camouflage a festering sore. Alpi himself would have subscribed to this description, for often enough, when he had been involved in the conspiracies of the Sanfedisti he had remarked that no make-up could overcome the greenish tint of his skin. Meanwhile the old fox wore a veneer of civility and said politely, although in his usual acute manner:

"Why do you gape at me so, Peppino? Do you remember having

404

seen me in these parts in quite a different guise when the Liberal dogs were hot on my trail?"

And he added, turning to Vergoli, as if he were still acting a part, and pointing at the same time to Giuseppe:

"I acknowledge with rejoicing"—it would have been difficult to find words more hollow and insincere—"that I am indebted to this good man not only for a personal favor he did me in the sad days"—here he drew a deep sigh—"when morality was trampled underfoot and those who kept faith with their legitimate rulers, earthly and divine, were subject to persecution, but also for the invaluable aid he lent to the valiant Austrians to whom we owe . . . What is it, Vergoli, my friend, that we owe them? . . ." and he teasingly interrupted himself like a schoolmaster seeking to trip an unprepared and inattentive pupil.

"We owe them . . . the return of Pope Mastai to power," answered Vergoli guiltily.

But Alpi made a sententious correction:

"We owe them the restoration of His Holiness' legitimate exercise of his sacred and historical rights." (Here Giuseppe could not but remember Alpi's profane railing at this same pontiff in the presence of Baron Flaminio.) "We owe them law and order and salvation from anarchy and revolution. Surely, Vergoli, you have heard of the merits of this fine fellow, whose acquaintance with the grain market and general good will were enormously useful in the difficult task of providing supplies to Marshal von Wimpfen's troops at the siege of Bologna."

"I've heard tell of them, yes," Vergoli muttered.

"Is that all you know? I am really sorry."

"I know that he's an excellent trader in grain."

"No more than that? You really ought to know him better."

"Grain is not Signor Pietro's chief concern," interposed Giuseppe, who was not sure whether he was supposed to take part in the comedy or merely to figure as a spectator.

"You see, Your Excellency," Vergoli said with greater animation, throwing a grateful look in Giuseppe's direction, "what I told you was no more than the truth."

"Who could ever doubt that?" Alpi rejoined, while Giuseppe thought to himself: "He's called 'Excellency' now, is he, the robber? And honesty, they say, is the best policy!"

"I've asked you more than once," Alpi continued, "not to call me by any title. We must talk to one another like good friends. So no more frills, unless you wish to offend me."

Alpi had about as much right to the title of "Excellency" as he did to that of count, both of which were bestowed upon him out of sheer flattery, but had he been to the manner born he could not have shown more gracious and friendly condescension. Vergoli's ill humor only increased and Alpi's way of talking added to it the timidity of a rustic before a gentleman from the city.

405

"I know that it is out of respect for your father's dying wish that you do not concern yourself with grain," Alpi continued, "and I honor you for your scruples. But meanwhile it is just such an honest and experienced man as this one that I need at the moment."

"Were Rabbit?" Vergoli asked with astonishment, adding to himself: "Is this what he's trying to foist upon me? This misshapen, pock-marked creature, the son of my worst enemy?" He had never spoken in such rude terms to Master Lazzaro, and here he was taking out his resentment on Giuseppe, who had never lifted a finger against him. But such is the logic of resentment.

"Yes, Were Rabbit, Peppino Scacerni, of course! It's lucky that I ran into him."

"And may I know the reason why?"

"Of course you may! You have every right to, in fact the most sacred of all rights in view of your conscientious observance of your father's last wishes, God blast it!" This last vulgar exclamation burst from his lips in spite of himself, but he quickly returned to his more unctuous manner: "Of course, no one can trifle with so sacred a matter!"

"That's what I say," said Vergoli between his teeth.

"And yet Fortune, whom men are wont to call blind, has for this once lifted the band from her eyes and sent us this honest fellow."

"We have a saying in these parts," grumbled Vergoli, feeling more at ease after Alpi's outburst of vulgar language, "that if a man's born lucky you can throw him in the Po and he'll come up with a fish in his mouth, but if luck's against him he has only to go into the hat business for babies to be born without heads."

"Very good! First-rate!" Alpi exclaimed, affecting a hearty laugh. "I'm glad to see you once more in good spirits, my friend, because I was just wondering how to tell you" (here he turned dry and dictatorial) "that long faces rub me the wrong way. Take a man with a long face and nine times out of ten he's a malcontent and a conspirator; that's a solid political principle which I have occasion to remember as often as I look at the list of suspect individuals in Ferrara, along with His Excellency Count Folicaldi to whom our venerable and supreme ruler has entrusted the legation. His Excellency doesn't like long faces either, just remember that in your capacity of prefect of Copparo."

From this speech Giuseppe derived a certain amount of reassurance. At least he was not the fish from the river, as he had feared for a moment when Vergoli was telling his story. And he noticed that whenever Alpi touched him Pietro Vergoli cowered like a snail drawing in its horns. What's more he would be obliged from now on to put on a smiling face if he wanted to keep the esteem of those in power.

"Peppino Scacerni, this clever and estimable dealer in grain, is as welcome as butter on a slice of bread, by which I mean that he has come just in time to relieve you of your last conscientious scruple."

"How do you mean?" Vergoli asked, echoing the question that was on the tip of Giuseppe's lips.

"That's easy to explain," Alpi replied. "It would surprise me if you hadn't caught on already, that is, if I didn't know that delicate consciences can never be too fully reassured. Since he is a grain merchant by trade, all he must do is go on with his usual process of buying it up, storing it, and so on. And you can respect your father's last wishes by having nothing to do with it. The rest of the business has no connection with the grain, properly speaking, it's just a little matter of transportation. And you have a political debt to repay. Do you understand me?"

"I'm at Your Excellency's orders . . ."

"No 'Excellency' and no orders to it! I've merely given you a piece of friendly advice. Do we agree? Is your conscience at rest? Answer me frankly, for friendship, honesty, and religious scruples forbid my forcing you to go against it."

"Yes, my conscience is more or less easy . . . more or less . . ." said Vergoli with the strained expression of a man who knows he is being made a fool of but must put a good face upon it.

"Then I too feel easy in my mind."

2

This conversation took place on a fine October day in 1854. Virginio Alpi had been Superintendent of Customs in Ferrara since the beginning of the year, and this was ample time for a man of his kind to make himself known. Among his acquaintances and in his office he alternated his former rude and wild behavior with his newly acquired social graces, developing intimidation into blackmail and extortion into fraud.

"I warn you that I'm a man who stops at nothing," he had a way of saying sententiously.

Upon this point no one contradicted him. As for his superintendency of customs, he exercised it on this principle: that there should be no smuggling at sea, on the Po, or along the border from which he did not derive a rake-off, both from the smugglers and from the guards whom they had corrupted. Whenever, among the latter, he ran into an individual whom avarice or honesty made it hard to deal with, he removed him from his job or made things so unpleasant for him that he either saw reason or else was transferred to another post. His notorious bad temper made everyone tremble, and the threat of: "I'll take it up with Alpi!" was enough to terrify any who attempted to resist his orders or his emissaries. "We'll have to put up with him," said those who resigned themselves unwillingly and "If we have any caution, now is the time to show it," said those who bowed their necks with greater alacrity. Everyone felt powerless to lift a finger against him, knowing that he received a set fee in every department of the vast network of smuggling.

Under the political set-up of the day this fashion of exercising his supervisory functions was not exactly original, but he brought to it a strength and persistence of purpose from which he had profited greatly. In less than a year he had bought a country house on a sizeable tract of land and a string of thoroughbreds. He supported in handsome style his own family, several illegitimate children in Modena and other Austrian possessions, and furnished a luxurious house on the Via Ripagrande in Ferrara.

For some time now Pietro Vergoli had expected the Superintendent of Customs to descend upon him with a regular levy, and Alpi had refrained only because he was hatching another plan in which he needed assistance. On this day then he had put in an appearance at Vergoli's mansion in a smart Milanese gig drawn by a lively and good-natured chestnut mare. Vergoli had ordered the mare unharnessed and taken to feed on oats in the stable, while the superintendent smilingly inspected the garden. When it was time for lunch Alpi had done honor to the groaning board and lingered over his coffee in order to keep the master of the house on tenterhooks a little longer. The coffee, however, provided an occasion for him to let fall an ambiguous phrase:

"Coffee fit for a gourmet, genuine smuggler's coffee! My compliments!" With which he returned to making gallant remarks to Signora Vergoli.

Later, in the ground-floor office, alone with Vergoli, he cut short his compliments and came down to brass tacks. After a brief preamble to the effect that he had come to inform the prefect of the large-scale smuggling that was carried on in his territory he said abruptly:

"Let's examine the situation more closely. Enough of words; now we shall hear the figures speak for themselves. Shall we draw up a balance sheet of the fraud involved?"

In summary fashion, but with exhaustive exactitude and the coldness of a professional accountant, Alpi listed and added up the number of fraudulent imports and exports, the value of the various goods, the amount of money lost to the government and gained by the smuggler, and the size of the fines he should theoretically pay, all of these complete with dates and precise quantities. Only one thing did he omit, at least for the time being, and that was the smuggler's name. Vergoli thought that this torment would never end, until finally Alpi gave a final turn of the screw.

"I know the petty traffic and traffickers, but I don't know the chief one of all, the master mind. That just shows you how clever he is. And I have come to enlist your aid in discovering him."

Did he have to endure such a heavy dose of sarcasm? Vergoli sat with his head hunched between his wide shoulders, like a cow that has received a blow destined to stun it in preparation for his slaughter. Even the sarcasm of this last sentence did not cause him to lift his eyes. Alpi could not have calculated his affairs any more closely if he had read them straight out of the smuggler's books or learned them from Sergeant Blister. The story contained a number of delicate touches, such as the reference to the chocolate supplied to His Excellency the Apostolic Delegate in the Castle of Ferrara, when all the time His Excellency was so severe that he repeatedly asked his Superintendent of Customs to go after smugglers tooth and nail. Or again, the fact that

his own light and elegant gig, mounted on excellent springs high between its two slender wheels, had come in by the same route. For a
moment Vergoli thought that this was a sign that it was time to start
bargaining. He raised his eyes anxiously, quite ready to do away with
himself if only he could put an end to the suspense. But his hopes were
again dashed to the ground.

"I bought it at public auction among a lot of goods seized from the
dealer in carriages who had ordered it smuggled in. But the proceeds
of this forced sale were not sufficient to cover the fine imposed upon
him."

The words "seized," "forced sale," and "fine" struck a chill into Vergoli's heart.

"My friend the Prefect, are you dreaming?" said Alpi rudely.

"I? Ah . . . what's that? Dreaming? Why should I dream?"

Vergoli wondered with terror what Alpi could have come to get out
of him, when all of a sudden the latter changed the subject. Closing the
clasp of the ornate little notebook from which he had read the statistics
on smuggling, he changed the subject completely and began to talk of
the harvests of the years 1853 and 1854, which were so poor as to warrant their being compared not only with the scarcity of 1846 and 1847
but even with the famine of 1815 and 1816, whose terrible memory was
still alive. Wheat and corn were going steadily up in price and it
looked as if during the coming winter they would touch the 1816 price
of forty crowns a bushel. The grapevines too were afflicted. Three years
ago there had descended upon them an epidemic of something called
in local dialect "the white scavenger" and by scientists *oidium*, which
split the grapes open and made them wither on the vine instead of
growing under the August rains, and rot away under the September
sun, just when they should have been ripe. Wine, which a year ago had
cost no more than half a crown per gallon, had gone up to almost ten
times this price.

Pietro Vergoli fell in sincerely enough with this lament. As a man
born in the country he loved it for other things beside money. And so
he nodded his head in a melancholy way and added more pessimistic
figures and prophecies of his own. At a certain point the very desperation of his complaints gave him the courage to say:

"Look, for instance, at my bad luck, Your Excellency. I brought the
first steam threshing machine to these parts, for the general good as
well as my own, and I've committed myself up to my ears in the reclamation of the swamps of La Vallazza, which will also be a public
benefaction. You know that, don't you?"

"I do."

"I introduced the cultivation of hemp and other new crops to the
region, I have always sold grain at a fair price, and here I am threatened by famine. That will be the crowning blow. Must I agree with my
ill-wishers (for because I didn't just twirl my thumbs in other years, I
have put a few crowns aside which they envy me) that my improvements have brought upon us a calamity?"

"Who has said anything so idiotic?"

"Village gossips, poor people who don't know any better," answered Vergoli, thinking with moderate resentment of Master Lazzaro Scacerni.

"Surely you don't pay any attention to what they are saying."

"The way things are turning out forces me to agree with them! And it's the fault of the government . . ."

"Watch your tongue, Vergoli! The government is not to be mentioned, either for good or for ill!"

"It's the taxes, Your Excellency, the taxes! We can't even breathe!"

"They're heavy enough, I'll admit that."

"Positively crushing," and Vergoli sighed as if he were staggering under a heavy load.

"But hasn't hemp gone up to seventy crowns, a price that is absolutely unprecedented?" Alpi asked, giving him a hard stare.

"Yes, but it won't sell. The market is quite dead."

"It's not so hard to sell it, and at a good price, too," said Alpi in an affectedly casual tone, "on the other side of the Po, where the market's very much alive. That is, if it's of really first-rate quality, like yours."

What could Vergoli say? That it was practically forbidden to export hemp, and that what little was allowed had to pay an exit tax that reduced the profit to almost nothing? Alpi would only laugh at that. Or should he proclaim that without the market on the other side of the river to which he smuggled his produce he would long since have been ruined? Either Alpi had come with the express intention of breaking him and it was useless to protest, or else he meant to put him through the wringer, in which case the slightest remark would only add to his perverse amusement. Vergoli hunched farther down in his chair and waited. Alpi returned to philosophical considerations. The famine of 1815-16, he said, was a punishment for the sacrilegious misdeeds of the Revolution, the crimes of the Jacobins, and the tyrannical usurpation of Napoleon. And the scarcity of 1846-47 was to be devoutly considered as a solemn warning and pledge of God's mercy toward a world which was about to plunge once more into revolutionary excesses.

"The warning served no purpose," he said. "And today's shortage is a form of divine retribution."

"Haven't we paid enough for our sins already," Vergoli asked, "with so many disturbances and upheavals? Didn't cholera descend upon us? Now we've all come back to reason, and as for myself, I never took part in any of the excesses you mention. Has God no mercy for me?"

"Come, come! You speak of God's mercy as if it could be calculated along with your accounts or haggled over like a consignment of hemp! Perhaps *expedit ut unus pro populo moriatur*, or, to translate for your benefit, it is necessary that one man be sacrificed for the good of the people."

"And am I to be the scapegoat?" Vergoli interrupted.

"Who am I to know?" asked Alpi rhetorically, and he went on as if he were speaking from the pulpit. "How can any of us be sure? You say that we've come back to reason, but that's not true of all of us, my dear Prefect. Not by a long shot! The impious Liberals are still at work, you know. They work secretly and in the open, now in stubborn silence and now with shameless effrontery, to flout every law of God and man. That's what I often tell His Excellency Count Folicaldi. When I was a young man, you know, in Forlì and Faenza, I fought to the death with the Liberals: I went after them with a knife or a blunderbuss or any other weapon that came to hand. They've never forgiven me, and I owe the fact that I am alive today to the protection of the Austrians. Not to mention the fact that I'd never have the position I have if they hadn't given it to me." Alpi spoke with vehement frankness, adding with a loud laugh: "When I was young I never thought about money, but simply spent everything I had in my pocket. But now I say that before the Austrians go back across the Po—and God grant that may be as late as possible!—I want to put aside enough so that I can send everyone and everything to the devil, particularly the clerical government!" After this outburst he went on in a less violent but still familiar vein: "You too favor the Austrians, I'm sure. You're a man with a head on your shoulders and financial interests to look after. For that reason you know how much we've benefited by the restoration of law and order and a hard currency with which to do business. You can't afford to take Republican money, can you? So you're all for the Austrians, isn't it so? Answer me!"

"I am, Your Excellency, I am. I agree with all that you say."

"Capital! And yet you seemed to have a certain expression on your face . . ."

"I was thinking over what you were saying."

"Good. And is it fair, do you think, that the Austrian Imperial armies, to which you agree we are indebted, should be half starved because of the lack of grain in the crown territories?"

"We're half starving on this side of the Po too," Vergoli objected.

"Not the way they are. And our people here deserve it. What's more, they're ready to pay through the nose."

Alpi's eyes followed those of Vergoli, which, perhaps in an attempt to evade the gaze of his interlocutor, had come to rest on an edict of July 27, 1853, signed by the Papal Secretary of State, Cardinal Antonelli, to the effect that in view of the "not very rich harvest of the year" it was forbidden to export any grain abroad. This text hung on the wall among a number of others, and although it was a year old there were no signs of its having been abrogated.

"I see what you're looking at!" said Alpi, while the other cursed his all-embracing eye. "But I don't see the decree forbidding the exportation of hemp. Still one's the equivalent of the other."

"Curses!" Vergoli thought to himself. "He's always harping on that hemp!"

But Alpi once more, with obvious enjoyment, changed the subject.

411

"Have you read *The Betrothed* by Manzoni, my friend?"

"I've heard tell of it," Vergoli replied modestly, wondering what the devil might be coming next.

"A most precious book and one full of wise maxims and good advice. It's well worth your while to read it. As we grow older we may find time to build up an education to console us for the loss of our youth. In this book, then, there is one truly golden maxim which I recommend to your consideration: 'If a man doesn't tell the truth to his lawyer, he may have to tell it to the judge'."

"That may well be, but I don't understand what connection . . ."

"What connection it has with the matter of which we are speaking? I'll tell you that soon enough. I came here to act as your friend and defender, but you won't give me a chance to do it; you've treated me like a judge and an enemy. Now I said that I am your friend and defender, but I can just as easily be your enemy and, as I needn't remind you, I'm by virtue of office your judge. That, of course, I'd like to forget, but you have forced me to remember."

"*I* have, Your Excellency?"

"Who made me look at that edict on the wall? Who reminded me that I am Superintendent of Customs, charged with imposing respect of the law and punishment of those who break it? You insist, apparently, on talking to the judge for the sake of hiding something from your defender! That's a very poor choice, my friend!"

"Tell me, Your Excellency, what I can do for you, and if it is possible you shall be satisfied."

"Here is a letter from Baron Pasquattini, chief Austrian supply officer in Trieste, asking me as a particular favor for two thousand bushels of grain. If you can fill this order you will be doing a good deed and making a handsome profit, for the baron says that the price is of secondary importance."

"Just tell me one thing to satisfy my curiosity," said Vergoli, letting it be taken for granted that he had accepted Alpi's proposition.

"Anything you want to know."

"Why did Your Excellency's choice happen to fall upon me instead of some other fellow?"

At an earlier time Alpi would have emitted one of his insulting laughs. But now he had learned not only to control his temper, but to put it to good use, either to intimidate or to humiliate those with whom he had dealings. And so he answered his victim's hesitant question sedately.

"I chose you for a reason indicative of my esteem. Because I know you are an honest man and will not take advantage of the situation."

"You do me too great an honor!" exclaimed Vergoli with unconscious irony.

"And you are too modest," Alpi countered quickly. "I need hardly tell you that in my position I have to take special care that the interests of the government I serve shall not be in any way injured."

Vergoli looked up in astonishment. Was this another joke?

412

"How can that be, Your Excellency?"

"Stubborn, aren't you? But I appreciate your scruples. Now tell me, is there any export duty on grain?"

"No."

"Then the treasury is not defrauded."

"But exportation's forbidden."

"Oh, well, the edict's still in force only for the benefit of the masses, for uncouth people who might complain that they are hungry. The government is not abrogating it until the present high price of bread declines. But this year's harvest is better than last's and the shortage promises to end soon. The government is willing to give a great deal more to the Austrians than a mere two thousand bushels of grain, since it owes them its very existence. Only that edict stands in the way and the government can't very well revoke it so brusquely. But, I can reveal a secret: if you satisfy Baron Pasquattini's wishes you will at the same time anticipate those of the government; you will help the government out of an embarrassing situation and serve it better than you would by sticking to the letter of the law. You can't imagine how often a high official thinks to himself: 'Just go ahead and *do* it, but don't say anything.' In short, I'm calling on you for a demonstration of real statesmanship, quite on your own hook."

"But if something were to go wrong, who'd have to take the blame?" asked Vergoli, remaining equally impervious to sarcasm and flattery.

"You would, of course. But if it goes well, yours is the profit."

"It is, is it?" said Vergoli, adding to himself: "And you'll want your cut of it."

"I see that you're a fair and reasonable man," said Alpi, almost as if he were answering Vergoli's unspoken reservation. "And I can tell you something else."

"I'm perfectly content with what I've already heard," Vergoli observed, with an evasive gesture.

"You shouldn't be. I want to treat you for what you are, for a man whose business ability should enable him to deal in much more than a few miserable bales of hemp. Have you often a chance to see Count Folicaldi, the Apostolic Delegate?"

"I'm to see His Excellency in just a few days to give an account of my prefecture. In fact, I've already promised to provide carriages for several of our local priests who wish to report at the archbishop's palace on the spiritual health of their parishes."

This "spiritual health" was measured by "confessional notes," which registered their flocks' observance of the sacraments and served as a measurement not only of their Christian virtues but also of their loyalty to the established government. Archbishop Vannicelli Casoni was a genuinely holy man and would not have dreamed of violating the secrecy of the confessional, but there were ambitious and intriguing persons in the Castle, the Fortress, and even the archbishop's palace who looked for information from this source as to unrest among the population or any evidence of conspiracy. This practice was reminiscent of the days of the ill-famed Cardinal Rivarola, and unfortunately it had now taken on larger proportions and caused the clergy to be accused of profanation. Sincerely devout souls were shaken in their faith, and the enemies of religion and government found an easy target for their abuse, particularly since the government had handed over its function to a foreign power. The priests, whose rule was only nominal, came to be considered not only as impotent administrators but also petty tyrants and spies, who provided fodder for the Austrian guillotine and thus worked against their own people in behalf of the oppressor.

"Well then," Alpi continued, "three days from now, which will be Monday, when you visit His Excellency Count Folicaldi, just come right out and ask him whether you should comply with Baron Pasquattini's request. But, mind what I am saying, you mustn't expect him to answer yes!"

"And if he answers no?"

"In that case, forget all about it. But if he says neither yes nor no, then that's a clear signal for you to go ahead."

"Very well then," said Vergoli. "I promise to do as you say. And shall I ask him nothing more?"

"It would be most indiscreet and in fact stupid for you to do so. And yet I tell you that if our supreme rulers could be bothered over such trifles and you were to ask the Minister of Finance or the Secretary of State, or even, if I may be so bold, His Holiness in person, they would only answer: 'Go ahead, Vergoli, only don't insist that I give you my authorization officially'."

Alpi said these words with a pious air, but his eyes and general expression betrayed the presence of an underlying urge to indulge in mute laughter, of which Vergoli could not but be clearly aware as he sat there, torn between the appeal to his vanity and avarice on the one hand, and a remnant of fear on the other. He knew quite well, however, that by now he had committed himself too far to withdraw his promise.

"There's one more difficulty," he muttered, "but that's a purely personal one."

"Out with it," said Alpi in an impatient tone, as if to signify, "and let it be the last."

It was at this point that Vergoli spoke of the pledge he had given his dying father that he would never traffic in grain.

"That's not my concern," Alpi commented coldly. "You must ask the advice of your spiritual director. If I know my priests, they can smooth over much graver scruples than this one."

He did not betray any loss of patience, but it was clear that he did not wish to be bothered again with such sentimental considerations.

"What did you plan to do today? I've wasted a lot of your time," he said abruptly, as if he meant, "Don't waste any more of mine."

"I meant to attend to a consignment of hemp."

"To Trambusti, eh?" said Alpi, naming the agent who handled Vergoli's illegal cargoes in Trieste.

"Yes, Trambusti," Vergoli admitted with resignation.

"Then let's go attend to it together," said Alpi with a contemptuous smile. "But don't look as if you'd just taken a laxative! Trambusti can serve as your intermediary with Baron Pasquattini."

The two men were on their way to the warehouse where the hemp was stored when Giuseppe Scacerni came by and provided Alpi with a salve to Vergoli's filial conscience. Only one question remained unsettled, and that was what percentage Alpi expected to receive of the profit, and Vergoli did not dare for the moment to raise it. The whole transaction did eventually take place in good order, and as might have been expected, Alpi's share in the loot was no small one.

3

As for Giuseppe Scacerni, when he was asked to get hold of a thousand bushels of grain, he gave a somewhat hesitant answer.

"In a year like this one and in a poor country like ours? I'm nothing but a middleman, you know!" And he ran his hands desperately through his hair.

"You needn't worry about the price," said Alpi.

"Ah?" Giuseppe replied, with a gleam in his eyes.

"You won't complain of your commission, either. Look for the grain here in the neighborhood and as far afield as you like. Only hurry up about it."

"I can find a thousand bushels quickly enough right here, if the price doesn't matter!"

"What? In a poor country like ours, my dear fellow? And in a year like this one? There I have you! But remember, it must be of good quality."

"The very best. In fact, Signor Pietro Vergoli's own!"

"Mine!" Vergoli exclaimed in astonishment. "I sold it all in August. My granaries are empty."

"How did it come into your hands?" asked Alpi, whose curiosity was aroused. "Tell us, will you, unless it's a secret of your trade."

"Well, you see, Signor Pietro; you see, Your Excellency the Count"— he was willing to give Alpi all the titles in the world—"Signor Pietro Vergoli here is a friend to the poor. He sells his grain at a low price, first because he doesn't need the money, and next because he doesn't hesitate to dump it on the market. And what do the poor do? They buy up all they can: one, two, three or four pecks and there they have a bushel. When they can afford to buy it in large quantities, they don't do it in their own names, but hide behind that of a dealer like myself. After which, they store it away and sell it when prices are higher. That's why rich and poor alike bless Signor Pietro!"

"So you're a public benefactor, eh?" said Alpi to Vergoli, bursting into laughter, and he added, turning to Giuseppe: "So a mere middleman like yourself probably has a storehouse full of grain belonging to Signor Pietro."

"I had a storehouse once," Giuseppe answered bitterly, "or rather my aunt had it. You may remember that, sir. But I haven't got it any longer. And the worst of it is that all the money I made was left in the hands of my aunt in Ferrara. God knows where it is now!"

This was the first time in six years that he had mentioned his experiences in the city and he himself was surprised to hear the words come out of his mouth. As he stared dreamily into space Alpi asked with frank curiosity:

"You haven't seen your aunt again, then?"

"Neither her nor the money. I haven't been able to muster up enough courage to face the possibility of disaster."

"She's still plump and prosperous, if you want to know, and her virtue's just as easy as ever," Alpi said without circumlocution. "As for the money, I can help you force it out of her."

"I could kiss the ground Your Excellency walks upon!"

"Then come on Monday to my office in Ferrara."

"If I have to come every inch of the way on my knees!"

"Stupid!" Alpi said with a smile at this exaggeration.

"As you please, sir."

"Wonderful thing, the power of money, Vergoli, isn't it?" Alpi observed to the prefect.

Vergoli nodded with just the right amount of condescending pity, but a wave of disgust came over him as he remembered the blackmail to which he had been submitted and looked at the shabby accomplice who had been forced upon him. Alpi, on the other hand, looked at Giuseppe with a glow of sympathy.

"We haven't met since the siege of Bologna, have we?" he said cordially. "How is your health?"

"I'm just a poor old codger," said Giuseppe in what was a joking local manner, "but that's good enough for me. I had a disease like cholera, but in spite of some unkind souls who wanted to send me to die in the hospital, here I am hale and hearty."

"I don't ask you how well off you are financially, because you'd only tell me a lie."

"I, sir?"

"Would it be the first lie you ever told? Far be it from me to tempt you to that. Have you a wife and family?"

"What girl would want me for a husband? There *is* a girl I care for," he added, feeling embittered as usual and at the same time flattered because Alpi had enquired into his personal affairs, "but she doesn't care for me."

"I can't help you there, but if you get back your money you may find it easier to win her over."

"Money means nothing to her, unfortunately," said Giuseppe.

"And is your father still alive?"

"He's just so much older."

"And has he still that subversive beard?"

"Yes, he still has it."

416

"Remember now, we must cut it off!"

"As you please, sir," said Giuseppe, thinking to himself that this fellow was as stubborn as his father.

And so they left each other that day.

Early the next Monday morning Vergoli, with a goodly number of priests in three carriages, and Giuseppe Scacerni in his cart all set out for Ferrara. The agitated state of mind shared, for different reasons, by Vergoli and Giuseppe, can be easily imagined. As for the priests, a group of rustic and easygoing souls, they looked on the excursion as a great treat and anticipated, after a brief visit to the archbishop's palace, a good dinner in some city tavern. Some of the cruder ones looked perhaps forward to other forms of indulgence. But among the members of this jolly brigade, who pointed out to one another with satisfaction the improved condition of the soil, which promised a good sowing and hopes for the end of the famine, there was one soul in a state of real suffering.

A few months earlier Don Giuseppe Romagnoli, the priest at Guarda, had heard the confession of an unfortunate parishioner who had been hiding in the woods after a quarrel that ended in murder, with a price of twenty crowns (a modest sum, reflecting the misery of the times) on his head. He came to the priest in the dead of night, swearing that he trusted him more than his own brothers. The least of the misdeeds to which he confessed was to have carried messages for certain enemies of the government, whose names he did not know, on the other side of the river.

The "infernal machine" which some ultra-zealous Republicans had exploded in a grocery shop on the Piazza Navona in Rome had put into circulation the idea of other and more dangerous contraptions intended to blow up the College of Cardinals and even the Quirinal Palace with the Pope in it. During this decade wild ideas of the kind filled the heads of would-be tyrannicides and struck unreasoning fear into the hearts of their opponents and the peaceful population. Don Giuseppe Romagnoli's imagination was all the more aroused inasmuch as there were still frequent episodes of throat-cutting inspired by the suppressed revolutionary tradition or simply growing out of the highway robbery that held the countryside in terror along with the punitive measures dealt out by the government in return.

Don Giuseppe did not attach any guilt to the poor fellow's confession of having ignorantly served as a message bearer, but the mere mention of a conspiracy struck him as an obscure public danger, a diabolic and sacrilegious plot, which shattered the tranquillity of his simple conscience. Before such an enormity famine was only a mild example of God's retribution, possibly only a proof that the enormity had been actually contemplated. Some of the things to which the sinner had confessed seemed to him precious weapons against the conspiracy, and as a matter of fact they did not directly enter into the confession. Perhaps, he thought, he could report them without violating the sacrament. In his doubt he decided to consult another priest whom

he admired for his theological learning and also for a better understanding of political affairs. As a matter of fact, this second priest was
an ambitious man, who put his innocent colleague's conscience at rest
and then proceeded to repeat the whole story to the Austrians. They
made an investigation and several arrests, including that of the message bearer. Politically speaking, the whole affair soon fizzled out, but
the guilty fellow already had murder to answer for.

Not long after this, Don Giuseppe Romagnoli, who knew nothing of
the arrests, was called to Ferrara to hear the last confession of a
prisoner condemned to execution. He responded eagerly, touched by
the news that the condemned man would confess to no one else but
himself. And this is what he heard:

"You are the only person in all the world whom I trusted and only to
you did I solemnly confess that I had carried messages. That's not what
they're shooting me for, as it happens, but the reason for their capturing me in the first place was your denunciation."

"Mine?" asked the priest in dismay.

"Yes, yours. You sold me, unimportant as I am, just like Christ, for
thirty pieces of silver. And just because you, in whom I put all my
faith, were the one to betray me, I have no intention of receiving the
sacraments. Christ will have mercy upon me if He sees fit, and if He
sends me to hell I only hope that He'll send you later to join me."

They were in the prison of the Fortress and outside the cell soldiers
were waiting to lead him away. When a prisoner could not walk to his
death unaided they held him up by guns placed under his armpits.
There was no time for Don Giuseppe to reason with the man or appeal
to his feelings.

"May Jesus Christ enlighten you!" he exclaimed. "I swear before
Him that I am innocent."

"I've told my story," said the prisoner. "If anyone knows more let
him add to it."

These words, habitually used by the storytellers at some festive occasion, had an ironical and desperate sound on the prisoner's lips. Don
Giuseppe walked at his side and read the bitterness in his eyes. He
prayed for divine mercy upon this man who imagined that, like Christ,
he had been betrayed, and for a softening of the heart which would
indicate that he was mistaken. For the good priest had begun to doubt
himself and to feel that the prisoner's impenitence was a punishment
for some unconscious misdeed on his part. When the prisoner died
without repenting he felt sure that he had fallen from grace, although
he still did not think he had violated the secrecy of the confessional.

Because such doubts were new to his heretofore simple faith he tormented himself violently about them. When he, in his turn, confessed
the whole story and was told that he had committed no more than an
error of judgment he was assailed by the thought that his trivial error
had resulted in the damnation of a soul, and this led him to doubt
divine justice. Then, hearing from other quarters that over-scrupulous-
ness like this, which led to despair, was his only real sin, he

418

blamed the priestly function that had led him astray and began to deem the Holy Father's edicts unholy. He timorously rebelled against persons and prescriptions that he had hitherto considered infallible, against Pius IX's bull of excommunication and the interference of the clergy in temporal affairs which lay at the root of his trouble. At times he thought that he had lost his faith altogether and at others that he had rediscovered it in some heretical dissent. The solemn words, *Domine non sum dignus,* at the beginning of the Mass seemed to him an accusation and he felt that by his office he profaned the sacrament.

Now this morning, in one of Vergoli's carriages, he heard his brethren commenting indifferently on what they were going to report at the archbishop's palace and making light of what to him was a crucial occasion. For he had decided to ask to be sent to make a retreat in some monastery, and this prospect gave him, if not peace of mind, some slight measure of relief.

At the palace itself, where his heroic defiance of the murderous Croats was not forgotten, he shuddered to hear the praise of himself and his fellows uttered by the abate who read their reports on the spiritual health of their parishioners. And even greater was his disgust when he heard that the government made good use of the information furnished by the local priests in its struggle against anarchy and sedition. The abate in question was none other than Feliciano Macchiavelli, presently on a mission to Ferrara, who was fated to join the reactionary faction of the fanatical Monsignor De Merode, from whom he eventually separated himself in order to embrace a diplomatic career. The abate was the last person in the world to understand the humble Don Giuseppe, who after the audience awkwardly expressed his misgivings and the intention he cherished of making a retreat. The abate displayed first curiosity and then surprise. How could this model priest abandon a flock so needful of his care on account of scruples which he was not even able to express clearly. As he tried to formulate them better Don Giuseppe was terrified by the sound of his own words, which echoed outrageously against the abate's silence. The latter took on a haughtier air, hiding his contempt for such chickenheartedness under an appearance of pity and abounding in good advice with an ironical undertone to it. When Don Giuseppe relapsed into a stubborn silence he lost all patience and labelled him a Jansenist and heretic. The abate threw up his hands in holy horror over such a denial of Papal authority, but his real motive was simply annoyance at having wasted so much time listening to what he took for addlepated ravings. Finally he told Don Giuseppe to go back to his parish until further notice. But it was in vain that his fellow priests, who had arranged to meet at Vergoli's new town house, formerly the Palazzaccio of Raguseo, waited for him to join them.

Standing about in the courtyard they berated the absent member of their company for keeping their distinguished host and themselves waiting. As evening fell they were mindful of the foul play so prevalent on the roads at night. The bandit Sacchetti had been caught and killed but his memory was still green among them, and Passatore, his brutal successor, was still at large. So while they cursed Don Giuseppe for his delay they hesitated to leave him to come home on foot. Because the bandits went about in carts and carriages, the use of all vehicles was prohibited after dusk except by those who could prove a sufficient reason. Like the "safety card" required for going from one town to another and the prohibition of firearms this restriction was more annoying than it was effective. "Honest men travel on foot and unarmed with their safety cards in good order," people said jokingly, "while bandits drive their horses with no identification papers of any kind but with a loaded pistol in their pockets."

The rash or forgetful Don Giuseppe risked having to walk all the way home, that is, unless he hired a public conveyance, and these were known to be too dear for his humble purse. Finally they left without him, thereby arousing the wrath of his devoted parishioners, who accused them of sacrificing the best of their number to an unseemly fear of danger and their haste to eat a good supper.

Don Giuseppe was never seen again, to the consternation of all, particularly of Master Lazzaro Scacerni. Some said that he had abandoned the priesthood, others that he had gone abroad and turned protestant, but the general opinion was that he had been killed by the bandits. At this point the abate, who was the last to have seen him alive, put in a word to the effect that he had seemed somewhat out of his head. Nobody in Guarda would allow such an insult to the good priest's memory, but there were those in the neighborhood who did believe it. He must be shut up in an asylum, some of them said, while others maintained that he had gone to Bologna.

"And why Bologna?"

"Because there are so many madmen there that one more or less makes very little difference."

It never occurred to them that Don Giuseppe might have taken refuge in the penitential life of a monastery, for gossip is not wont to credit anyone with a sense of honor. Even if they had guessed at such a thing, blind common sense would have told them that it was too bold and imaginative a move to have been made by the modest parish priest of Guarda.

As for Pietro Vergoli, following Alpi's instructions he went on that same Monday to ask Count Folicaldi whether he knew anything about a request from the Austrian supply officer at Trieste for a shipment of grain. Before he could even finish his sentence the Apostolic Delegate interrupted him severely:

"I neither know nor wish to know anything about it."

Vergoli was nonplussed, but Alpi, whom he met immediately afterwards in the antechamber, was frankly jubilant.

"Well, how did it go?" he asked.

"He didn't say yes."

"But he didn't say no either, did he? That means full speed ahead."

Alpi knew his superior too well to have any doubts as to the out-

420

come. The Apostolic Delegate was one of those authoritarian persons who make their weight felt by means of impressive phrases. He was often uncertain in his own mind until he had discovered the phrase necessary to cover a given situation, but once he had found it there was no budging him from it. The secret of influencing him, then, was to suggest discreetly such a phrase and then to wait for him to come out with it himself. In short, Count Folicaldi was a so-called "iron man" who could never be taken by storm but who was blissfully unconscious of how little skillfully applied leverage it required to move him from an uncompromising position. Such a character is common among men of great ambition but little real ability to command, for they are wont to make show of the very virtues they do not possess. Folicaldi pretended to be a strong man although he was possessed of only the trappings and illusion of strength. Thus it was that a few days before Alpi had prompted the reply he was to make to Vergoli's question.

After his interview with the count, Vergoli was persuaded that his smuggling enjoyed the blessing of the highest authorities and his heedlessness of danger was greater than ever.

As for Alpi, he proceeded to grant an audience to Giuseppe, who had waited patiently for several hours in the ante-chamber in order to inform his patron that within the last two days, one of which was a Sunday, he had already secured the promise of at least fifty wagonloads of good grain, each one holding an average of four bushels.

Alpi was attracted by any sport of nature and the idea of Giuseppe's being in love intrigued him. The success of the day's business had put him in a good humor and after he had congratulated Giuseppe upon his two hundred and more bushels he advised him to spend the night in Ferrara so that the next day they could, as he put it, devise a trap in which to catch his Aunt Argia Malvegoli. And because he was as curious as a cat he laughingly asked Giuseppe about his unrequited love.

"What do you expect, sir?" said Giuseppe, between annoyance and flattery. "It's been going on for years now with no prospect of success. She floated down the river to us on a mill that was half wrecked by the flood of 1839. Her father had drowned and she was left an orphan. Oh, it's quite a story."

"Very romantic indeed."

"Romantic?" said Giuseppe, raising his eyebrows. He feared that Alpi was teasing him and was overtaken by the angry embarrassment that often accompanies any deep feeling.

"Come now, don't interrupt me at every word you don't understand."

"I apologize, sir, for my ignorance."

"Well then, what next?"

"Well, her father, the Madman of Bitter Bread Mill, had lived for years like a savage alone with his child and she has inherited his wild and shy nature. Now Bitter Bread Mill is anchored alongside my father's and Cecilia has no passion except for the miller's trade."

"That's a curious story. Has this wild woman no human affections?"

421

"None, except for my father."

"What? She's in love with him?"

"No! What are you saying? If I didn't know my place, sir, I'd throw that back in your face. In love with my father? How can you think such a thing?"

"Quite right. I see what you're driving at."

"What's that?"

"That Cecilia loves him like a father."

"And he, good man, loves her like a daughter, too."

"Then there's a chance of your getting a hearing."

"From her, you mean? I've spoken to her enough times already."

"No, I mean from your father. Can't he persuade her? Your intentions are serious, aren't they? I presume you want to marry her."

"And I should speak to my father?"

"Of course! Why are you surprised?"

"It's all very well, sir, for you to say such things, because you don't know the circumstances. My father may care for me after a fashion but he doesn't hold me in very high esteem. He's had it in for me ever since I was a little boy because I was afraid of the water and couldn't learn how to swim. Then he has never thought much of my activities as a middleman . . ."

"You mean as a merchant. . . ."

"If I could get my money back you might call me that. Anyhow my father has about as little use for my trade as I have for his."

Giuseppe spoke without bitterness. The circumstances were of such long standing that he was apparently resigned to them.

"It all goes to show," Alpi commented sententiously, "that things are the same in cities and villages the world over. There's the same conflict between fathers and sons in a royal palace and in a mill on the Po."

"I have no experience of royal palaces," said Giuseppe, who saw no point to talking about Cecilia, "but when I lived in this city of Ferrara I came up against a tough crowd that ran me out of town and forced me to leave all my hard-earned money in the hands of my aunt."

"I told you we'd see to that tomorrow."

"You are too kind, sir."

"Just get it into your head that I've taken a notion to help you."

"Sir, I'm positively embarrassed."

"And I have a notion, too, that I could influence your father."

"That's no easy job," Giuseppe said firmly. "You don't know him."

"Even by giving him the fright of his life?"

"Oh, never! Put that idea out of your head, sir! Lazzaro Scacerni doesn't know what it is to be afraid!" And there was a note of pride in Giuseppe's voice.

"Don't be so sure!" Alpi countered resentfully. "After all, you, his son, are afraid of the water."

"You are free to amuse yourself at my expense, sir," Giuseppe said

422

with quiet insistence, "but you had occasion once to speak to Master Lazzaro, remember that."

"That's just why I'd like to take him down a peg and trim his revolutionary beard! I promised that some time ago and I'm a man of my word."

"I've never got mixed up in politics myself," said Giuseppe stubbornly, "and neither has my father. He wears his beard long because it suits him and anyone who wants to trim it will do so over his dead body."

"Now I have it!" Alpi exclaimed. "Why shouldn't we frighten this Cecilia Rei into marrying you? We can play on her affection for your father and tell her that's the only way to save him from trouble."

As Alpi looked at Giuseppe's ugly face and imagined this forced marriage, another idea, and one worthy of Boccaccio, came into his mind. "Tell me," he said, "is she beautiful?"

"Oh," said Giuseppe, feeling a wave of lust sweep over him, "she may not be beautiful by city standards, but she is to me, that I know."

His dull, albino eyes lit up with a rankling desire to humiliate the proud Cecilia, which was no less violent than his lust.

Alpi contained his amusement, picturing in his imagination the cuckold's horns that would sprout from Giuseppe's ugly head, which was scattered with tufts of straggly hair, as if the moths had been at it.

"But how can we do any such thing," Giuseppe objected with unconscious hypocrisy, "without really harming my father?"

"I suppose he goes in for smuggling," said Alpi meditatively.

"Hardly at all," Giuseppe answered, in a tone that Alpi recognized as sincere. "And then that accusation is not a very damaging one, is it?"

This last remark was obviously true, but it had a daring ring inasmuch as it was addressed to the Superintendent of Customs. But Alpi laughed it off gaily.

"Ah, it isn't damaging? And you say that to me, do you? Very well. Let's admit that it's true. But if this unusual father of yours is neither a Liberal nor a smuggler, he must at least connive with thieves of some sort or other."

He threw this out as an attempt to intimidate his hearer, but Giuseppe answered not without dignity:

"The whole village, beginning with myself, can vouch for the honesty of Lazzaro Scacerni."

Were these barbed words? Alpi suddenly remembered the false receipt he had made Giuseppe sign for the pay of the men who had transported grain to Bologna. Perhaps it was to this flagrant piece of dishonesty that he was now referring. But neither susceptibility nor fear dictated Alpi's reaction; he was moved, rather, by utter scorn for an honest reputation. Other people's virtue did not humiliate him, but provoked him the way a fencer's stroke provokes a return from his opponent. He was a born blackmailer, just as there are born fencers, gamblers, or poets. That Giuseppe should take up the cudgels for vir-

423

tue aroused him to think: "Is this a challenge? Shall I give you a good fright too?" And he promptly answered him aloud:

"Of course, Master Peppino, everyone knows the blameless life and noble feelings of the Scacerni family! I must say, though, that you have inherited some of the boastfulness of your bearded father. And if I thought you could understand me I might quote the Latin proverb: *Excusatio non petita accusatio manifesta*, or, in terms that you can understand, methinks you do protest too much."

This was quite enough to confuse and humble Giuseppe Scacerni and put him with his back against the wall. But Alpi would not let it go at that.

"If when you leave this place you were to be thrown into honorable detention while the alert Austrian military commission carried out an investigation of the house and mill of a certain miller, wouldn't they almost surely find a cache of forbidden arms? You know the penalty for this transgression. Of course, almost everybody has tucked some arms away, and doubtless the Scacerni family among them. Aha! Pale and trembling, are you? Your conscience can't be very easy. If within the twenty-four hours ordained by the law we were to see an honest father and son walking their last mile to execution before the Fortress . . ."

"I know nothing," Giuseppe stuttered, "except that I have no arms, sir, I . . ."

"Tell that to the Austrians, and we shall see whether they believe you. They may be foreigners but they know their Italian and the dialects of Ferrara and Guarda as well."

Giuseppe was utterly lost. He could visualize the discovery of the arms in the cellar and yard at Poplar Bridge and the way he would be marched up to the Fortress. Alpi's piercing gaze, from which he was unable to remove his own, prevented him from thinking of any excuse. He knew something by hearsay of the traffic of information regarding hidden stores of arms and the penalty exacted from those who were found guilty. Gallows and guillotines danced before his eyes. When Alpi saw his victim reduced to such a pitiful condition, huddled up as if he were waiting for another blow to fall, he abruptly changed his tack, laughed, and clapped Giuseppe on the back:

"That was a good scare, wasn't it, my brave fellow? Your face is quite green. I'm sorry I haven't a drink here to revive you. Pull yourself together, now, like a man. Are you sweating? Come, come, what should I care about your hidden arms?"

"You don't care, no, of course . . ." said Giuseppe, wiping the cold sweat from his forehead.

"Then let them lie. You must have more faith in me. I've taken a liking to you, God knows why, and all I ask is that you shouldn't play the braggart." And as Giuseppe looked more confused than ever, he went on in a genial manner: "If you weren't so addled you'd see the point of what I've been saying. After all, you're not a complete fool."

"What point do you mean, sir?"

"With all my joking I've hinted at a way for you to obtain the consent of that wild beauty of yours . . . what's her name?"

"Cecilia Rei."

"Well then, lure Cecilia into some place from which she can't reach your father, and there tell her . . ."

"Where am I to lure her?"

"How should I know, lily-livered fellow? To your aunt's house, for instance."

"She's never been away from the river."

"All the more reason to show her the sights of the city. Then, when the time comes, you can say: 'Either you marry me or else the Austrians will pay a visit to Master Lazzaro and shoot him.' That ought to do the trick if she's so devoted to your father."

"But what if she still says no, sir?"

"Then you may as well give up, because it means she really can't stomach you."

"But they won't really shoot my father, will they?"

"Not if you and I alone are in on the secret!"

Giuseppe was torn between conflicting desires.

"Must I really say that to Cecilia myself, sir?"

"Come, cock of the walk!" said Alpi in superlatively good spirits. "Must I play the pimp for you?"

Torn between lust and fear Giuseppe went out to get some dinner and a room for the night. He was not such a bad son as not to feel some concern for the real danger to his father that was inherent in Alpi's plan. But he was enough of a hypocrite to justify himself by the remembrance that he had advised the old man to turn his arms in rather than hide them. His father had willfully exposed himself to danger and at an age when he should have known better.

"Who led me into this temptation, when you come down to it?" he said to himself. "My father! I didn't tell on him; that devilish Alpi guessed at it. And it's something that everyone knows, he told me. If Alpi really wants to get rid of my father he'll send the Austrians to uncover the arms, anyhow. If I'm too conscientious I risk losing both my father and Cecilia to boot. The only thing is: will she listen to reason?"

But what kept Giuseppe tossing wakefully on his bed was the thought of the proud, disdainful, and ardently desired Cecilia. What kind of a wife would she make him if he were to blackmail her into compliance with his will? Might not she have it in for him forever? He trembled at this thought and at the prospect of informing her of his terms. Trembling with alternate lust and fear he repented his decision and yet at the same time longed to come to the test and get it over with quickly. Finally he fell asleep.

There are times at which to sleep on a difficulty is to solve it, and others when the difficulty seems still more insoluble upon awakening. Giuseppe did not sleep long enough to find any comfort. He woke up with a painful start and jumped out of bed long before his accustomed hour, without getting his money's worth out of what he had paid for the night's lodging.

Memories crowded around him as the convent and monastery bells rang out upon the clear October morning air and the streets (paved with ground pebbles from the river) echoed the creaking wheels of wagons bringing fowl and fruit and vegetables in from the country. Had it really been so long since he had left Ferrara? He knew well enough how long it had been when he remembered the money he had given up and the uncertainty of what his aunt might tell him about it. His steps led him unconsciously to the familiar market place, where his former acquaintances at the stalls were quick to recognize his misshapen body.

"Look who's here! Were Rabbit!" they shouted. "The devil has spit him up out of hell and he's come back along with the famine!"

However their greeting was not without affection and gave him an unexpected feeling of warmth around the heart. He went about shaking hands on every side and saying, not without vanity:

"Now I feel better. I see that in the market place of Ferrara my name is not forgotten."

"Who could ever forget you?" they said, pressing about him.

"I didn't know I had so many good friends. This is a real joy."

They paid him so much attention that it seemed almost as if they were staging a demonstration to make amends for the undignified way in which he had left them, taken by the collar and held up to public derision. Seeing two or three fellow grain merchants he asked them with an air of importance:

"How do today's prices suit you? Those of us who do business in the country wouldn't have anything to complain about if people were a bit richer and less avaricious."

"Didn't we just say that you were a harbinger of famine?" they said laughing.

These words were less pleasing, but he was not taken aback for long.

"Hurrah for Were Rabbit!" someone called out from the crowd and the others took it up in chorus. "Hurrah! Hurrah!"

As they recognized and acclaimed him as one of their own he felt more and more cheerful and when little by little they went back to their stalls and benches he strolled from one to the other, sticking out first his belly and then his buttocks and balancing his barrel-like body on his crooked legs with all the airs and graces of a gentleman of leisure. He seemed for all the world like a general restored to his faithful troops, or rather like a speculator, formerly dismissed as bankrupt, who returns with his credit restored to the arena of his speculations. For it is an obvious truth that the Piazza delle Erbe and the Volto del Cavallo of Ferrara were to Giuseppe Scacerni what the City of London was to Nathan Rothschild or Wall Street to Pierpont Morgan.

In the course of his triumphal walk he arrived at the row of dark little shops near the cathedral porch, in the place known as the Jews' or Junkdealers' Arcade. The door he remembered as belonging to the old ragpicker of whom we have spoken before was walled up and he asked the bystanders what had become of her. They told him that one morning she had been found dead on a filthy old mattress stuffed with bonds of the now defunct Republic, for which she had paid good money in the hope that they might make her rich.

"And then what?" asked Giuseppe, with a sinking feeling in his stomach which he tried to pass off as compassion.

"Don't you know? The bonds were first issued in February of 1849 and by March they were already sold at a twelve per cent discount. That was what tempted the old hag to buy them up. When their value continued to sink she nailed up as a talisman on her door the decree guaranteeing that they would never vary more than three per cent from their original price. People stopped to laugh at these words and, sure enough, by April they were down twenty per cent. And that wasn't the end of it."

"Did they go down still farther?"

"Did they just! No one would have them at any price; they were just like so much waste paper."

"Poor old creature!"

"Why waste your pity on her? You know she made her money by usury. It was only right that she should lose it."

"Still that's always painful."

"She was bound to come to a bad end, wasn't she?"

"Yes, but I can't help feeling for her like a fellow human being."

"After all the ill luck that's come upon honest men, must you waste your sympathy on her? It must have been painful, though, if it killed her! She prospered for years on others' pains."

"Did it actually cause her death?"

"That's right."

"An ugly business. And what about the bonds?"

"The Papal government redeemed them at a loss of thirty-five per cent as an act of charity toward the people who were stuck with them."

Giuseppe stared hard at his informant.

"And what's the value of such bonds today?" he asked.

"What does it matter to you that you should turn so pale? Do you happen to own some?"

"God forbid!" Giuseppe exclaimed, making a sign of the cross.

"It would be too bad if you did. The government has stopped redeeming them altogether and they're good for nothing except to light a pipe with."

Giuseppe grimaced in an attempt to force a smile.

"That's a proper swindle!" he said wryly.

"Worse things than that have happened!"

"I find it hard to believe."

"Some people lost their lives, you know."

"I'd rather lose my life than my money!" said Giuseppe, so fanatically that the bystanders had to laugh.

"Still the same Were Rabbit!" they said.

At this point Giuseppe asked for news of the sons of Ezekiel Annobon and was told that they were still flourishing bankers. The fact that they enjoyed general esteem encouraged him in the idea of resuming relations with them.

"The Republic's over and done with," his informant concluded, "and now we can live in peace. Of course everything, even salt, is dear, and there are many scarcities, including that of bread."

On this point all the bystanders chorused their agreement. Business was languishing; there was a shortage of both cash and commodities.

"And how are your country markets?" they asked Giuseppe.

"Conditions are just the same as here in the city," he answered briefly.

And although they had heard this and repeated it every day for weeks and months in succession, they shook their heads as if they were hearing it for the first time.

It was time to go see his Aunt Argia, but Giuseppe's feet dragged because he had little inclination to do so. Since he was reluctant to pay this call he decided to drop in first at the nearby bank of the sons of Annobon in Via Vignatagliata, behind the same low, nail-studded door at which Lazzaro Scacerni had stooped to knock so many years ago. The sons had opened another and more convenient door in the same house and turned the ground floor into the offices of their bank. These sons were several in number, but Giuseppe had dealt with only one of them, the most insignificant-looking but brainiest of them all.

While Giuseppe goes slowly toward the bank let us look quickly at this Annobon family.

In each successive abundant generation of Annobons there were fated to be examples of every physical and spiritual type of the Jewish race. There was the blond, bloodless type, like the Christ portrayed by painters ever since the sixteenth century, tall and slender, versatile and of refined tastes, but inconclusive. He was often prey to a hypochondriac and suicidal melancholy, which made him the lost hope of his generation. Many of his brothers were equally disappointing. One of them was usually vain and devoured by frustrated but costly ambition; others were hot-blooded, sensual, and quarrelsome, or foolish, or useless, or positively stupid. But there was always one, the most inconspicuous of all, the lean little Jew, dark as a grain of pepper, awkward, flat-footed, stoop-shouldered, with a weary, Oriental quality in his humid, handsome eyes and mild voice and manner. This one did all the work and faced every emergency: gains, losses, good luck and bad, handing out to the rest of them first unheeded advice and then bitter reproaches when trouble had come upon them for having failed to heed him. He alone could relieve their woes after they had run to him with a "You were right, after all," which meant that he had to find the money to pay the creditors or put them off or beg their grudging mercy. He was there for this express purpose, which he knew so well how to fulfill; the whole family recognized his merits and this was supposed to be an ample reward. And indeed it was, for he had no aspiration other than to make himself useful and to win from the old mother whom he venerated in accord with the Mosaic law some such grateful phrase as: "If it weren't for you . . ." which was the equivalent of calling him the Joseph among her sons. And when his difficulties were greatest she could find no other praise than to lament that he should not be gifted with the good looks of one of his brothers, the strength, or ambition, or generous feelings or daring of another, so that the prudence and wisdom which were exclusively his seemed only petty virtues by comparison. To work hard and make money, these were his passions, and the money he had been persuaded since childhood to get along without.

In many cases there grew up beside him his successor in the next generation, whom he trained to take his place in the bank. This was more often a nephew than a son, for his parents had usually married him off to the plainest and most uninteresting of his many cousins, and his own children were apt to be either fools or spendthrifts. The relationship between him and his apprentice, based on their sharing the same experience and the same fate, did not often express itself in words. It came out at crucial moments in an exchange of responsive glances, wherein could be read identical conclusions and premonitions, which were lit up by a ray of irony before both parties half shamefully dropped their eyes.

This had been the part played by Ezekiel Annobon, his son Samuel, and the latter's nephew, David, whose names seemed to sum up, among a race of exiles banished to the ghetto, the dimmed ancient glories of a people of kings and prophets, inspired by divine strength in their exodus from Egypt, in their weeping by the rivers of Babylon, and in the pages of their Holy Book.

4

"Venerable Signor Samuel," said Giuseppe, as he walked into the bank that morning, "here we are, still alive, as your eyes may tell you."

"I am happy, very happy to see you again, Scacerni," said the Jew.

"I am happy to be here," said Giuseppe, but his obsequious manner, which was based not only on self-interest but on a healthy respect for the other's financial position, did not entirely conceal his underlying aversion.

Samuel's nephew, David—young David he was called and would be called until his uncle's death, although he was already in his thirties—was also present, and he now asked:

"Do you wish to return to being our client?"

"Did I ever stop being one?"

"Of course. Your money was withdrawn some time ago. You remember that it was deposited in the name of Argia Malvegoli."

"Some time ago?" asked Giuseppe, with a sinking feeling, as he nodded assent to the depositor's name.

"Do you want to know the exact date of the withdrawal? I can tell you that right away."

"Never mind." He felt positively sick at his stomach. "What do you suppose my aunt did with it?"

"It's no use asking us that. It was deposited in the name of Argia Malvegoli and Argia Malvegoli withdrew it. That's all we need to know."

"Yes, but the money was mine. We were what you might call partners."

"That's not the bank's affair, as you well know."

"Yes, to be sure. I'm just complaining because I have a pain in my stomach. Forgive me if I've said too much."

And he said to himself as he walked away:

"If I hadn't had to leave Ferrara that money would have been as safe there in the bank as eggs under a setting hen. And all this time it would have been increasing day by day; not an hour would have gone by without its earning interest. There my money would be, snug and warm and alive, if I hadn't let it go to ruin just because I was half crazy with fear. Wretched coward that I was!"

His face was a sight to be seen as he let his imagination play around the baby chicks hatched by a setting hen and accused himself of cowardice for having abandoned his money. He quickened his step in the direction of his aunt's house and as he turned the corner into the Strada delle Pettegole he recognized the wall that had formerly enclosed the monks' orchard, the low door and the entrance to the storehouse in which he had once placed such high hopes. His legs threatened to give way beneath him but he pushed desperately forward with the thought: "At least I want to know what kind of a death I must die." The door opened to his knock and he started up the stairs.

"Oh, look who's here! I never expected to see *you*, Peppino!" his aunt exclaimed from above. "I've worried about you, you know, after the shabby way you treated me. Six years without a word of news! But that doesn't matter now that you're here. How long the time has been! Come, let me embrace you. Why are you moving so slowly?"

There were only a few steps from the ground floor to the one above, but with every step Giuseppe's curiosity to hear his fate grew into a mournful presentiment, and he was roused to a passion for revenge. He could hear a tremor in his aunt's voice and a false ring to her affectionate greeting. As he reached the top step he looked up at her from toe to head and found her stout and rosy; perhaps she might no longer inspire a youthful passion, but she still had a large degree of sensual appeal. The florid and well-fed appearance, bright smile, extended arms and the whole attitude of a prostitute with a heart of gold seemed to him a deliberate insult. With one foot still on the next to the top step he raised a threatening forefinger toward his powdered and primped aunt.

"What have you done with it?" he mumbled darkly.

"Done with what, Peppino? What's the matter? Don't you feel well?"

"What have you done with it?" he repeated slowly.

"What are you talking about, my dear? Just when I was so glad to see you!"

"What did you do with the money after you took it out of Ezekiel Annobon's bank?" he thundered.

"Peppino, can't you ever think of anything but money? When I love you, and after all these years . . ."

With a look and a gesture he cut her short. She changed tone abruptly.

"You left me alone and unprotected, Peppino," she said, "with no experience of business. Baron Flaminio told me not to leave the money in the hands of Jews. What was I to do?"

"I asked you what you did with the money. The baron will be rewarded for his good advice in hell."

"What a terrible thought, Peppino! You might at least respect the dead!"

"Neither the dead nor the living!" he shouted, quite beyond himself. "*Where* is the money?"

"Come on up and have a cup of coffee. How can I explain anything to you on the stairs?"

"No!" he shouted hysterically. "I don't want your coffee! Tell me where is the money!"

"I kept it here safely, waiting for the day when you would come back to look after my business and yours. You know what confidence I had in you. Then there was a change of government, you know that. Strange people came to the house, saying strange things. They said there was a Republic and a lot of other things I didn't understand. But I could see that they were quite capable of setting the house afire. And they told me that for the benefit of those who were not good citizens (those were their exact words) they were setting up a guillotine in the square. What was I to do, I ask you? If you'd been here, of course, you could have protected me. But you had run away without even letting me know that you were alive. Tell the truth, now, you were scared. And I was alone and helpless. They made me hand over all the gold and silver and in return they gave me paper, they gave me bonds of the Repub . . . Oh, Peppino! Holy Virgin Mary! What is it?"

Giuseppe's hand fell to his side and he staggered as if he had been hit over the head. Then he raised his arms, waved them convulsively, twisted his lips into a green smile, wheeled halfway about and fell in a dead faint down the steps, one by one. A few hours later he came to himself, lying in bed, with his aching head bound up in wet towels, which his aunt changed at intervals. When she saw him open his eyes and attempted to give him an anxious smile he burst out at her again:

"You won't get me to die so easily."

Argia loved him after a fashion and would have liked to think that he was in a delirium. But there was the intensity of truth in his ravings.

"I'll make it up to you, Peppino," she said. "Whatever's mine's yours. But be quiet, now, and rest."

"Have you someone you can send as a messenger?" said Giuseppe, without paying her any attention. "Yes? Then send him to my father's anchorage in the river. But he mustn't let my father see him. He must go to Cecilia Rei, the mistress of Bitter Bread Mill, and say to her in private that I am badly hurt and need to see her at once. But she must come without letting my father or mother know. Do you understand? Repeat what I have just said."

Argia repeated it after him and added, not without tenderness:

"Don't worry, now. The doctor says there's no danger."

"You needn't have spent money for his visit. I know how to doctor myself. But if Cecilia is reluctant to come to your house . . ."

"Why should she be reluctant, Peppino, if she loves you . . ."

"Pray say no more stupid things. Don't you suppose that even in the country they know your reputation? As I was saying, if she's afraid to come here because she's an honest woman, then the word must be that I have to speak to her of some imminent danger, that there's not a moment to be lost. Do you follow me? Repeat the message again."

After the shock of hearing of the loss of his money and the suffering caused by his fall Giuseppe had awakened with an urge to find some compensation for his pains. He was due not only his aunt's money, or as much as he could get of it, but the possession of Cecilia as well. Everyone has his own way of taking things, and this way was Giuseppe's. All that afternoon and night his conviction grew and at the crack of dawn he awoke to find Cecilia standing anxiously by his bed.

"What has happened? What is the danger of which you sent me word?"

"And what of my accident, Cecilia?" he said mellifluously. "Aren't you even going to notice it?"

"Your aunt tells me you are out of danger."

"I fell head first down the stairs," he said pathetically.

"Is that what you summoned me here for? Is that all?"

"Wouldn't it matter?"

Her annoyance changed to a frank outburst of laughter. Giuseppe took offense and thought to himself: "Is that how you take it? You'll pay me for this."

"Very well, then," he said aloud. "You didn't need to laugh so hard for me to know how little you care for me. But I'm not the only one involved."

"Who else, then?"

"Master Lazzaro. It's a matter of life and death, and his fate is in your hands."

"In my hands?"

"Don't just echo my words. My father has arms hidden in the cellar, you know that very well. And if the Austrians find out he has only twenty-four hours to live. You know that too. Well, a person has found out about them who has the power to tip off the Austrians. If he sends the Austrians they'll discover the arms, and if they discover them . . ."

"You told on him, did you? You spy! Turning in your own father!"

432

"I might remind you that I warned him not to hide them. I am caught between two fires: either he is shot or he and I together. He can't get off in either case. But there's no use wasting precious time in explanations. Mark my words, this is no trifling matter; it's a question of saving my father. The powerful person of whom I've spoken is disposed to forgive him for my sake, that is if you'll give your consent."

"My consent to what?"

"To my proposal of marriage, Cecilia!" And so saying he lifted his bandaged head, batted his eyelids and looked hard at her with such a mixture of lust and supplication, brutality and fear in his albino eyes that Cecilia could not help exclaiming:

"How disgusting! To marry a misshapen creature like you!"

"Words, words," he said icily, stretching himself out again on the bed. "You're wasting time, my proud beauty. If you say any more I'll turn around the other way, and that's all there is to it. I'll have no insolence from you, do you understand? Let justice take its course."

"Would you let your father be killed?"

"You'll be responsible for that, in spite of all your fine talk of how much you love him," said Giuseppe with his eyes turned indifferently toward the ceiling.

"I'll go tell him to throw the arms in the river," she said, starting to leave the room.

"You won't reach him in time," he answered, turning to stare at her.

"Why not?"

"Because the soldiers have set out already on horseback," said Giuseppe, who could lie as coldly as you please when it was to his advantage. "Nothing can stop them now except an order from my friend. You couldn't possibly get there before them."

Poor Cecilia wrung her hands.

"And would you have the courage to look me in the face as your wife?" she asked, unable to escape the fascination of his stare.

"I'm doing just that this minute, am I not?" he asked calmly.

She laughed uneasily and her laugh ended in a sob of repulsion.

"I'm waiting for a reasonable reply," Giuseppe continued dryly.

"Can't you imagine how cordially I'll hate you?" she countered, not so much answering him as making a pledge to herself.

"Don't worry about me. I tell you for the last time that if you choose to spend your time in baby talk and to seal Master Lazzaro's destruction I shall hold my peace. Of course it's hardly a reward for the way he pulled you out of the river and brought you up as his daughter, but that's not my affair. The Austrians must be on their way by now. And if they find the arms not even my protector can stop the law from taking its course. Do you know what that means?"

Cecilia's honest face contracted as she said faintly:

"How am I to know that you haven't made the whole thing up?"

"Just wait and see; then you'll know for sure. But remember it's your responsibility."

"And why does this important person, this protector of yours, take such an interest in a country bumpkin like you and your marriage?"

"You don't want to seal a bargain with your eyes closed, and there you're quite right. I'll get up from my bed and take you to him in the Castle. Then you'll find out whether I've told you the truth. But we must hurry."

He sat on the edge of the bed, darting a cold look from under the bandages around his head at Cecilia. His bow legs and pale, hairy thighs were exposed to her sight as intimately as if he were already her husband. He was making a desperate gamble, for Alpi might well punish him for his bragging by denying the whole story. But the desperate Cecilia lost her head and instead of insisting upon proof of his assertion she broke out indignantly:

"What if I were to strangle you with these two hands?"

"You'd end on the gallows yourself and still not save Master Lazzaro. Instead of a marriage there'd be three funerals. Think it over now, only hurry up, because I don't feel like playing with my father's life because of your whims. If he must die I'd rather know it and get it over with."

His head ached and he threw himself back flat on the bed. At this moment Cecilia seemed to hear in the depths of her conscience the voice of her own father who had drowned in the flood of 1839 trying to save her life. And the voice said that this sacrifice of herself in behalf of Lazzaro Scacerni was the best way to repay him, her real father, for his devotion. The poor, wild girl could not imagine a woman's fate as anything but an attempt to escape a man's violence or unwilling submission to it. She threw open her arms in surrender.

"Do as you think best, Giuseppe Scacerni, and I shall follow."

The fact that she no longer called him by his nickname was in itself a token of her defeat.

But now an unforeseen difficulty arose in Giuseppe's mind. If he were to wait to carry through the procedure of a regular wedding and let Cecilia return in the interim to Guarda she would undoubtedly tell Master Lazzaro the whole story. Yet it would be risky and difficult to keep her in Ferrara and might easily arouse her to suspect something out of the way. He pulled the sheet up under his chin, as if he were suffering from a feverish chill.

"Oh, Cecilia," he said with a weak sigh, "you haven't asked me how I feel or how I got this battered head. You've done nothing but make clear how unwilling you are to marry me. But that won't be a burden to you for long. I have a premonition I shan't linger among the living. One foot is in the next world already."

"I'm sorry for your sake, but for my own it's just as well," said Cecilia with brutal frankness.

"That I know!"

"But now you must send word at once to stop the Austrian soldiers," she said anxiously, with the thought of the old miller's danger once more uppermost in her mind.

434

"That's right," Giuseppe answered; "between my passion for you and the pain in my head I had nearly forgotten. Just go to the door and call Aunt Argia."

Argia came promptly, with an exaggeratedly festive and congratulatory smile on her broad face.

"Send someone immediately to the Castle, Auntie, to take a message to His Excellency Count Virginio Alpi, Superintendent of Customs. If he gives my name as the password they'll let him right in. The message is this: 'Giuseppe Scacerni wants you to know that he has put the deal through.'" And he added, turning to Cecilia: "That will take care of it." And again to his aunt: "If there's time let him add that I can't leave my bed, that I'm at death's door . . ."

"Come, Peppino!" Argia exclaimed. "The doctor said . . ."

"The doctor's a jackass," he interrupted. "I'm at death's door, I tell you, and don't ask me any more questions, because I haven't the strength to answer them."

"If that's so I'll get the doctor to come back at once," said Argia, who had a real affection for her nephew and an almost physical repulsion for even the idea of death.

"Send my message to the Castle if you don't want me to die! That's more important! Have you someone trustworthy?"

"I'll go myself."

"Then go at once, without a second of delay. Never mind about the doctor; I'd like to have a priest. You might tell His Excellency that if he could come to see me here I'd be infinitely obliged to him. I have something important to tell him. If he's not at the Castle, look for him at his house in Via Ripagrande."

Giuseppe's real anxiety gave him a genuinely feverish and commanding air that caused Argia to run to do his bidding and convinced Cecilia that he had told her the truth. She sat down in one corner of the room and closed her eyes in sheer exhaustion. Giuseppe feigned exhaustion too, but watched her on the sly. To him the time seemed long, while she felt sleepy and confused and lost consciousness of where she was.

Alpi's curiosity brought him quickly to Argia's house and the two women retired to another room, both of them anxious for reasons of their own, but without very much to say to one another. Giuseppe had whispered to his aunt to stand guard over Cecilia and threatened her with dire punishment if she let the girl elude her.

"That's what you'd call a real passion for money!" said Alpi when Giuseppe told him how he had fallen down the stairs.

"When I heard about the bonds issued in the name of the Republic I saw stars, I can tell you!"

"What a joke, good Master Peppino! But didn't you expect something of the sort? Didn't you know about them already?"

"Yes and no. I didn't *want* to know. But everything else has gone all right and I've put the money out of my mind. I presumed to ask Your Excellency to come here because my head is really painful and I can't stand up on my legs. I have an idea, if you will be so kind as to listen to it."

"I am so kind. I am all ears."

"To let Cecilia Rei go back to Guarda would be like casting back into the storm a ship that has just reached port."

"Of course."

"Then what am I to do? Keep her here under lock and key?"

"Don't do anything that's contrary to the law, Master Peppino, or I'll let you hang for it! That would amount to kidnapping, don't you realize it?"

"Just what, in my ignorant way, I imagined, sir. That's why I had an idea—tell me frankly if it's all wrong—that my head is battered enough for me to call in a priest . . ."

"Very well, but I don't see . . ."

"I can tell him that I'm afraid I'm going to die, and there's some truth in that . . ."

"And then?"

"In similar cases, if I'm not mistaken, a priest can celebrate a death-bed marriage without the slightest delay. The prospect doesn't altogether please me, because it seems to me a very bad start. But a man can't eat his cake and have it too. I can always tell the priest that I'm under an obligation to marry her, or even that she's no longer a virgin. I'll have plenty of time to repent of any lie."

"I'm only sorry I didn't think this solution up myself," Alpi observed. "I don't know how it squares with canonical law, but I can put my hand on just the priest you need, a fellow without a conscience, who'll do anything I say. And if your marriage gets off to an awkward start you can always patch it up later. Do you know that you're learning the ropes fast?"

"You're too kind," said Giuseppe with mock humility, as if he were practicing the unctuous tone suitable for the profane step he was about to embark upon.

The priest turned up in a very short time, and he was even more contemptible than Alpi had described him. He was a bandit in priest's clothing, given to vices of every kind and to political spying and racketeering. He had been in his time first a Sanfedista and then a Liberal. Now that the wind had changed again he was reduced to selling his services for a few pennies and for his protector, Alpi, there was nothing he would not do. Abate Valmora he was called and he wore trousers instead of a cassock and carried a sword cane. He was dirty and unwashed in a way that blazoned his depravity, and this was the butt of countless jokes on the part of Alpi, who enjoyed seeing other people wrinkle up their noses at his parasitical protégé's smell.

Valmora duly appeared, then, and for a fee of two crowns celebrated a mock marriage between Cecilia Rei and the supposedly dying Giuseppe Scacerni. There were ample grounds for having the marriage annulled and sending the celebrant to prison, but Cecilia never doubted its validity, and besides, her idea of a court was a place where poor and simple folk had nothing to gain and everything to lose. If ever she did have the slightest suspicion of having been tricked it gave her a bitter satisfaction to think that her beloved Master Lazzaro owed her his life. She never said a word to him directly, for she saw no use in stirring up trouble or in worsening the relations between father and son. After all, she was no longer young and her life on the mill had been solitary and hard-working. She had no taste or desire for love-making and could not miss a joy of which she knew so little. In the last resort, so we are told, Giuseppe was no worse than an average husband, indeed better than some, and their marriage was not particularly unhappy. Does this mean that it is better to get off to a poor start than a promising one? Perhaps it was all due to the unfortunate Cecilia's humility and resignation.

Hardly had the unsavory priest left the room than Giuseppe took Cecilia's hand and murmured words that surprised her by their patent sincerity:

"I love you, Cecilia, I've loved you ever since I was a boy. Try to forget the way I persuaded you to marry me, won't you?"

"That's not easy," she said, half dead with fatigue and emotion.

"I know that it's hard and that I'm asking a lot of you. But I knew I was too ugly to please you and yet I couldn't cure myself of my passion."

"Was that my fault?"

"No, but it wasn't mine, either! You are too beautiful, and I couldn't go on suffering. I'll love you so much that you'll forget my ugliness; surely you can see more than skin deep!"

"You're ugly enough," said Cecilia with a faint smile. "But didn't you say you were ready to die?"

"You've enough beauty to do for both of us," said Giuseppe with such ill-concealed longing in his voice that Cecilia had a sudden feeling of shame and fear. "Our children will all look like you. And meanwhile you've brought me back to life."

Argia Malvegoli, who had escorted the abate to the door, came back into the room wreathed in smiles and congratulations.

"My dear nephew, what a joy! How happy I am that you should have chosen my house for your marriage. Let me kiss you again, my dear girl. I shan't let the two of you go so quickly. First Peppino must get well, and then, Cecilia, I wish to make you the gift of a trousseau."

In her big shoes and rough wool dress Cecilia Rei was overcome by the fine words, perfume and other refinements of her newly acquired aunt. Her embarrassment was even greater than the dislike she had originally felt for the simpering Argia, whose profession she knew all too well. As she stood there in a state of confusion Giuseppe said:

"Thank Aunt Argia for her kindness."

Cecilia muttered her thanks and Argia answered:

"Not at all. You needn't thank me; I'm only too happy. Hurry up now and get well, Peppino, because I insist that you spend your honeymoon under my roof."

"What's a honeymoon?" asked Cecilia.

"You'll see, my beauty," said Argia with an oily laugh, her tenderness changing abruptly into lascivious curiosity. "I'll give you some preliminary instructions and Peppino will do the rest."

"An excellent idea, Auntie," said Giuseppe. "She hasn't a relative in the world."

"Poor girl! Then I'll be a mother to her."

"Thank Aunt Argia for her kindness," Giuseppe repeated.

Cecilia thanked her again, feeling more ridiculous and shy than ever. The rich furnishings of the house made her ill at ease now that she looked around at them, and she did not know where to put her clumsy hands and feet. Her discomfort was so great that she edged closer to her husband. Amid these frightening surroundings he at least stood for something familiar. Innocent people have a way of thinking that if vice appears before them it will be in a horrid and immediately recognizable mien, and they are ill prepared to meet it under a bland exterior.

"Ah, love!" Argia sighed. "How lovely! Do you know you've taken years off my shoulders? I have a ticklish sensation all over. Now I want to fix you up an attractive bedroom," she concluded frankly; "that's something I know about. And, Peppino, you must hurry up and get well."

"I feel almost well already," Giuseppe said greedily, touching his bruises and scratching his neck, which had already begun to break out in pimples after all the excitement. And within two days he had recovered, all except for a black bruise on the forehead which did not make him any more good-looking.

Cecilia spent these two days in a sort of stupor, without being clearly aware of what had befallen her or what was about to befall. She no longer had a precise wish to go back to her mill at Guarda, and hung about the house in a state of sheer inertia. Argia was prodigal of caresses and advice regarding the consummation of the marriage, which only threw her into confusion. So it was that on the third evening, after a supper made up of highly seasoned dishes and an unaccustomed abundance of wines, Cecilia found herself before she knew it undressed by her loving aunt and tucked into the bridal bed. A moment later Argia let Giuseppe into the room, having previously counselled him to groom himself carefully and sprayed him with perfume.

"Go to it and good luck to you!" she whispered officiously into his ear, closing the door behind her but putting her ear solicitously to the keyhole.

A fire in the fireplace dispelled the autumnal chill in the bridal chamber and lit up the figure of Giuseppe starting to climb into bed. Cecilia greeted him with an unexpected outburst of laughter.

"I'm glad you're so happy," he said, "but pray tell me why."

"It's the perfume."

"What of that?"

"With your aunt's perfume on you, you too seem like a . . ."

438

Cecilia's vocabulary did not afford her more than one word to describe Argia's profession, and that was a crude one.

Giuseppe gave a wry smile.

"That's something my aunt didn't think of when she sprayed me," he said, crawling in beside her.

"What are you here for?" she asked in alarm.

"I'm here as your husband."

"You can't dream of . . ." said Cecilia, speaking in a disconnected fashion because the wine had gone to her head.

"No, it's not a dream, although so much happiness does make me feel dreamy," he said, stretching out his hands.

But he had more trouble than he had anticipated, for now the wine had begun to exercise a directly opposite effect and Cecilia defended her embattled modesty with a rain of blows from her fists and kicks from a pair of feet hardened by wooden shoes. Rising up on her knees she nailed his shoulders to the bed and said angrily:

"What did you think you were doing? You were mistaken to imagine it would be so easy. It takes a better man than you to bring me to bed!"

Giuseppe submitted quietly to her violence, which indeed aroused in him a certain pleasure. Then he took advantage of a moment when the treacherous softness of the mattress and a sudden dizziness made her hesitate and turned her over. She found herself pinned down by the unexpected strength of her awkward bridegroom's arms. A wave of heat took her by surprise and swept over her before she knew it. The wrench of physical pain and the outrage to her chastity were never erased from her memory and every time her husband approached her she experienced the same submissive resignation. There was an element of disgust in her feelings, but not enough to incite her to revolt against the inevitable or to aspire to a voluptuous pleasure which she was incapable of even imagining.

5

But neither Lazzaro nor Dosolina accepted this marriage in a spirit of resignation. Indeed, for opposite reasons, they greeted it with the same resentment. Lazzaro was prey to a fatherly jealousy which made him feel almost as if Cecilia had betrayed him, and Dosolina, who had never cared for Cecilia, saw her as a daughter-in-law whom she could not possibly bend to her will. While Lazzaro blamed Cecilia for wasting herself on a "paleface" and "half pint," Dosolina taxed Giuseppe with having married a "rum one" and a "gypsy." So it was that both old people, although they could not agree, gave vent to their sorrow. Master Lazzaro deplored the haste with which the ceremony had been performed. No one had been either notified or asked for approval and wagging tongues had it that it had been pushed through so fast because there was urgent need to legalize an improper situation.

"They may be right at that," observed Dosolina, and she might have added that probably Giuseppe was not Cecilia's first lover had not her husband interrupted her.

"I won't let you say that, Dosolina. She's queerer than I thought, the facts prove it. But she was a virtuous girl, I'll stake my head on that; she has a heart as clear as a mirror."

"But Peppino, our own Peppino!" she insisted. "I can still see him as a child! How could he have deceived us?"

"There's no telling about Peppino."

"You have no right to say that, Lazzaro. He wasn't alone in his attempt to deceive, and if a girl can stoop to such evasiveness it doesn't speak well for her ability to make a good wife."

Thus it was that the two of them spoke together when, after a few days' honeymoon in Argia's house, Giuseppe brought his bride back to Poplar Bridge, where Alpi demanded that he turn up some more grain to be sent to the Austrians in Trieste. The two couples, the old and the young, could find little to say to one another, and the chief sufferer was Cecilia, since Lazzaro displayed hurt feelings and Dosolina could not find it in her heart to forgive her. Her father-in-law's unwitting injustice wounded her sensibilities and her mother-in-law's coldness was offensive, and so Cecilia spent as much time as she could aboard her beloved Bitter Bread Mill. The accounts of both mills were still kept by Giuseppe, who was indifferent to the ill humor of both his parents and hence the happiest member of the family. The grain he bought up for Pietro Vergoli yielded him an ample profit and soon he once more had a fat account at the Annobon bank. Wagonloads of wheat and corn crowded the roads leading to Vergoli's granaries. And the connivance of the customs guards was so overt that the loading of the ships anchored near the dikes of Nogarole was carried on at every hour of the day and night.

"There's grain that must be going overseas," the peasants said laughing. They were content because there was well-paid work for all of them to do.

When the export of a certain category of goods was forbidden they could not legally be shipped by either land or water without a "transportation stamp" to be shown to any officers of the law who chose to examine it en route. And there was a "receipt coupon" that had to be signed by the proper official when it reached its destination. Up until the middle of November Vergoli evaded the "transportation stamp" by doing all his shipping undercover and hiding his river cargoes under a layer of bricks. But the easy money they were making induced Vergoli and Alpi to enlarge constantly the scope of their business. The grain they sent to Trieste not only served the Austrian garrison but was forwarded to England and the Netherlands, where there was something near to a famine as well. The profit in pounds sterling and florins was so great that Vergoli hoped within a few months to cover the expenses of reclaiming the swamp of La Vallazza, which was costing him far more than he had calculated and causing him many a sleepless night. He might have parodied Prince Torlonia's words about Lake Fucino

440

and have said: "I'll drain La Vallazza if it doesn't drain me first," but when he struck it rich by smuggling grain he began to think: "I'll stick to it until I've made the twenty-five or thirty thousand crowns that will put through the reclamation project. Then, no matter what Alpi may say, I'll get out. Grain is not my business and it's no use tempting fortune too far."

But every time he incurred some new expense in connection with his various properties it was a temptation to prolong the grain smuggling, with its huge profits. He had greatly extended the radius within which he bought up grain and Giuseppe Scacerni now had another agent to help him cover all the territory between Ferrara and Bologna. Wagons carried the grain over the roads, boats took it down the Volano and Primaro rivers, and strings of barges travelled down the Po to the seaport of Cavanelle. It was no longer a question of a petty evasion of the law; the size of the enterprise called for systematic fraud on a much larger scale and Virginio Alpi was the man to devise it. How often he said to the plaintive Vergoli:

"Nothing venture, nothing have, my friend. Do you remember the day when I first suggested your going into the traffic of grain? You didn't take to the idea at all, and yet it's made your fortune. Let that warn you against hasty judgments."

The new fraud was carried out as follows. Sergeant Solimani of the Guarda customs made out a receipt coupon for the grain that arrived there for embarkation and issued a transportation stamp good for use on the river. Another equally amenable customs guard at a small port a short way down the Po made out another receipt coupon indicating the unloading of the grain, which of course in reality went right on to Trieste. And so to the crime of smuggling was added that of false papers.

"There's grain that must be going overseas," said the peasants between Ro and Guarda.

But Giuseppe Scacerni refused to consider any of this his concern, and indeed he was the only man in the neighborhood who did not joke about it. As long as he was paid for his work he chose to stay in the dark about the purpose it served, whatever evil tongues might say. This was not his father's way.

"I've told you ever since you were a boy that you'd end up in jail some day," he said, still talking like a stern parent to his married son, "and now I see that you've chosen the quickest way to land there."

Giuseppe did not bother so much as to shrug his shoulders. Heaven seemed to have sanctioned Cecilia's humble resignation to her marriage, for she was already pregnant.

6

Month after month the business of Pietro Vergoli, the "smuggler of the Po," continued to prosper. Rumors and accusations of this business and of Alpi's share in it did reach Count Folicaldi's ears, but the

Superintendent of Customs persuaded his chief that they stemmed from the grudge the Liberals held against him because of his devotion to the good cause, or else from a desire for revenge on the part of smugglers whom he had caught red-handed. Folicaldi could not admit that a man whose political leanings coincided with his own could be a liar. After so many years of high office he was convinced that he could infallibly distinguish an honest subordinate from a dishonest one.

Finally, however, an anonymous letter was sent to the Papal Secretary of State and transmitted by him to the Apostolic Delegate. "Virginio Alpi is the biggest smuggler of the region," ran the letter. "Everywhere people know it and within their own four walls they discuss it freely. But it would take a brave man to say the truth aloud and defy the power of a man who has so completely duped Count Folicaldi. Everyone fears the anger and revenge of Virginio Alpi, who says of himself that he stops at nothing. All Ferrara knows what is going on, that is all except the one person who should know it, the honest but foolish and overly credulous Apostolic Delegate."

If the letter had accused him of conniving at Alpi's misdeeds Count Folicaldi would rightly have scorned it. But to be called foolish was the last thing in the world he expected, and his surprise was mingled with curiosity as to how such an unfounded accusation could possibly be brought against him. He was aware that smuggling existed, and on such a large scale that almost everyone had some part in it, but he had not imagined that it had reached the proportions of a public scandal. He was less concerned with putting an end to the illegal traffic than he was with finding out what basis there was to the anonymous letter and demanding that his subordinates maintain at least an appearance of decency and decorum so that their chief's authority should not be undermined. He refused to harbor any suspicion of Alpi, and so it was that he undertook an investigation without even consulting him. And Alpi turned out to be too clever for his own good, since it never occurred to him that Folicaldi's confidence might be excessive.

Alpi had to his credit, besides his vague but none the less important political influence and his reputation of loyalty to the legitimate government, the fact that by bearing down severely upon petty smugglers he had actually brought about an increase in the volume of tax revenue. And this meant that his position as Superintendent of Customs was practically a contract farmed out to him because he was able to make it pay better than any other man in his place. Folicaldi was quite sure that the precarious condition of the Papal State's finances would cause the Secretary of State in Rome to prefer the steady income provided by Alpi's methods to the uncertain yield which would be produced by a more honest or less efficient administrator.

Folicaldi was at rest where his own conscience was concerned. After all, the art of government consists in accomplishing what is possible, and an excess of zeal may be disruptive. But he could not suffer an affront to his prestige, and the accusation of foolishness had cut him to

442

the quick. The more he thought about it the harder it was for him to take.

Besides, he was tired to death of Pietro Vergoli. Because he himself was of a run-down aristocratic family he resented the fact that Vergoli was rolling in wealth and apparently thought that money could buy everything. To call to order and humiliate this upstart seemed to him not only a just retribution but also an indirect way of getting at Alpi, if the substance of the anonymous letter was really true. Indeed, moving from one shaky hypothesis to another he came to the conclusion that perhaps Vergoli had deceived Virginio Alpi. In which case it was up to him to open Alpi's eyes. In order to do everything as discreetly as possible he ordered a humble and inconspicuous employee to gather evidence of the smuggling said to be carried on between Guarda and Ro under Pietro Vergoli's direction. By so doing he hoped to contain the scandal within the limits of prudence and statesmanship.

CECILIA SCACERNI

1

ALTHOUGH THE late autumn sowing went off well and seemed to promise a better harvest for 1855, scarcity continued through the months of December and January, and the hardships suffered by the poor piled up along with their debts to the butcher and baker. Convents and other charitable institutions ministered to an unusual number of beggars. In short, this period went down in history as one of famine.

Naturally enough there was rising resentment against those who hoarded or trafficked in rice, beans, and grain. Of course their exportation was forbidden but everyone knew that the law was flouted, and by those who were supposed to uphold it. Public opinion was mistaken in attributing the entire responsibility for the famine to the practice of smuggling, but the general awareness of an illegal traffic was all too well founded.

Giuseppe Scacerni was clever enough to go about his buying as quietly as he could. As for the peasants of Guarda and Ro, they were glad to find work with Pietro Vergoli during the hard winter months. They affected astonishment when people of the neighboring villages proclaimed the smuggling something shameful and complained of the number of bushels clandestinely exported from the starving country.

"Thieves and leeches!" their neighbors said to them. "You grow fat while we stay hungry, and all on account of Pietro Vergoli, the smuggler of the Po."

"Listen here," the others replied. "If we can draw good pay during the hardest months of the year and in time of famine, why should we look too closely into the business of our employer? We only wish you the good luck of finding a man half as enterprising as he is."

This reasoning did not allay their neighbors' bitterness; in fact it only increased their envy. And so it was that Count Folicaldi's confidential investigator was given all sorts of information in the surroundings, but when he came to the real center of the smuggling activity no one seemed ever to have heard of it. As soon as he broached the subject his interlocutor would say that he attended strictly to his own business and had no intention of calumniating his fellows.

The investigator had almost given up hope of finding out anything when he stumbled upon Vergoli's accountant, a dreamy fellow whose only diversion was to spend his lunch hour in silence in a corner of the gloomy and fly-ridden café in the village of Ro. It had never occurred to the investigator that a man holding this position would be willing to talk. And indeed the accountant would have been the soul of discretion if Vergoli had as much as hinted that such was his duty. But the smuggler had fallen into the habit of considering this man merely an unimportant cog in the machine and did not even think to warn him to hold his tongue. And when the accountant did talk too loosely, one reason was the admiration he felt for his employer and the urge to brag of his wealth.

It happened like this. Just as boredom and discouragement were about to cause the investigator to make a negative report to Ferrara he chanced to exchange a few words with the accountant in the café. For years on end no one in this establishment had paid the accountant any attention; to everybody, as to Pietro Vergoli, his master, he was more of a familiar shadow than a man. The poor fellow unconsciously suffered from this neglect and he overflowed with gratitude toward the stranger for having noticed his existence, and with pride in the prosperity of his master's business. The investigator merely threw out a casual word in his direction:

"They tell me that Signor Vergoli is a rich man."

"Rich, did you say?" threw back the accountant. "*Very* rich, they should have told you. So rich that only he himself and perhaps one other man know the extent of his riches."

"For his sake, I'm glad to hear it," said the investigator, pricking up his ears, "and for the sake of the other man as well. He must have his share of ability too, if what you say is exact."

"If it's exact? What do you mean?"

"I'd like to hear from his lips how rich this Vergoli really is."

"Well, just pretend that I'm the man."

"I know the country around both Ferrara and Bologna pretty thoroughly," said the investigator, who was passing himself off as an itinerant merchant, "and I must say that I've never seen either farms or factories as well kept as this man Vergoli's."

"I'm sure of that!"

"It must cost him a mint of money."

"I'm sure of that too."

"Then in years as lean as these, with business languishing, Signor Vergoli must be running up expenses. I'll wager that he's up to his ears in debt."

"In debt, did you say? Up to his ears?"

"Then let's say up to his chin," and the investigator jokingly touched his lower lip.

"He isn't in debt for as much as a penny. You can ask anywhere either here or in Ferrara how long it takes Signor Vergoli to honor his signature and fulfill his obligations."

"Of course, if you don't want to tell me . . ."

"Go ahead, and ask me anything you like."

"I had an idea you didn't like me to ask you questions."

"On the contrary, I enjoy it."

"Well, I've seen so many men go bankrupt in recent times that I think this Vergoli must have inherited a great pile of money, or else have earned it in better days. He's spending money like water now, for all his brains, I'm sure of that. You know what they say, don't you? He may be draining La Vallazza, but meanwhile La Vallazza's draining his pocket."

"You don't know the size of his brains or the depths of his pocket, or anything about La Vallazza, stranger!"

"Perhaps. But I still have my doubts. Hemp isn't selling well, I know that. Grain would sell, God knows, if anyone had the money to buy it. Am I wrong there?"

"No, you're not wrong. But what makes you think a man like Signor Vergoli could be satisfied with the meager market on this side of the Po?"

"That I can't answer. I've never been on the other side, myself. I didn't know that they sowed beans over there and then reaped crowns."

"Florins, that's what they reap, stranger, gold florins!"

"A land of miracles, eh?"

"For anyone that has Signor Vergoli's brains, it's a land of miracles, if you like."

And in so saying the accountant had not the remotest idea that such miracles were not to be bruited about in public. His interlocutor's pretended ingenuousness so amused him that he could not resist trying to startle him further. So it was that he referred vaguely to the number of bushels of grain sent out in the last cargo and the profit in Austrian florins that had come from it.

"Everyone knows that Signor Vergoli makes good money," he said. "The exact amount is down in his books. Very, very, very rich, that's what they should have told you."

The investigator could not believe in so much good luck after all his days of futile searching.

"I thought that was forbidden," he said half to himself.

"What?"

"The export of grain."

"That may be," said the accountant condescendingly, "but not for Signor Vergoli."

"Aha! And what sort of man is he, then, this Signor Vergoli of yours?"

"He's the greatest power here on the Po. And in the Castle at Ferrara, too, if you really want to know. He's a law unto himself."

"That's a good one! And what about taxes and customs?"

"He runs those from his own house! Some people call him the 'Minister of Finance,' and they aren't so far off, at that."

"I thought the Minister had his offices in Rome."

"In this case Rome's not as powerful as Ro."

"There's but a tiny difference between them," the investigator said, laughing contentedly.

"What did you say?" asked the accountant, slightly taken aback.

"Nothing at all. I was talking to myself—out of astonishment over what you have told me, and what I can now grasp with my hands!"

446

"Are you convinced now of the exactness of my information?"

"Indeed I am. But there's one more thing I'm curious to know—that is, if I'm not boring you."

"No, just ask me quickly, because I must go back to work."

"Exactly what work do you do?" asked the investigator, although he knew the answer already.

"I keep Signor Vergoli's books," said the silly fellow. "But what is it you wanted to know?"

"What do the customs guards say to these goings-on?"

"What do you suppose they say? They dance to Signor Vergoli's tune, as I just told you."

"Oh, of course the local fellows here at Guarda and Ro, I can imagine that. A fistful of money is enough to take care of them. But what about the higher-ups at Ferrara?"

"Pietro Vergoli takes orders from no one; you'd know that if you weren't a stranger. His Excellency Count Virginio Alpi, Superintendent of Customs, is a constant visitor at Signor Vergoli's house. Whatever Signor Vergoli says goes. And I've a notion that's true in Ferrara and Rome as well!"

"Now you're telling me tall tales!"

So it was that Count Folicaldi came to know even more than he wanted to. Attracted by the large reward offered to those who uncovered smuggling and enabled the government to confiscate the smuggled goods, the investigator showered the Apostolic Delegate with precise and circumstantial reports, in which he revealed not only the extent of the illegal traffic, but also the network of complicity that had made it possible and the discredit thrown upon the highest government officials.

We have said that Count Folicaldi was a sober and honest man, one who demanded integrity both of himself and his subordinates. These revelations offended his conscience as well as his vanity and he had no further doubt as to what he should do. Even at the risk of displeasing the Ministry in Rome, which had shown altogether too much tolerance of such shady operations, he resolved to pursue the investigation as far as necessary.

2

Meanwhile, apparently as an effect of the gradual weakening of the population from famine, on February 16, 1855, there came a new wave of cholera, which ever since 1848 had gone from one European country to another. The epidemic started out with heavy enough depredations, grew even more intense during the hot months of the summer, and did not stop until the end of the year. It killed over six thousand persons in all, that is about half of those who caught it. In Ferrara, with its twenty-eight thousand inhabitants, two thousand persons were smitten and half of these, including many entire families, died.

A quarantine ward was opened in the green, airy new part of the city near the Porta San Giovanni, at the Mortara barracks, a former convent whose rustic, austere, and harmoniously proportioned cloister garden had survived years of abandonment.

The cloister and cells of the convent, then, were filled to overflowing with the pitiful horde of desperate and dying cholera victims, to whom the few ministering doctors could bring little comfort. Here the walls echoed the groans and death rattles of the sick and dying and the corridors rang with the footsteps of stretcher bearers bringing in new cases of the dread and disgusting disease and of hooded men who came with hooks to take away the infected bodies of the dead and consign them to an unceremonious and sordid night-time burial.

In the countryside they could at least die in their own beds, that is, if their families did not take fright and put them out of the door, or in the open fields, where as often as not they were struck down with lightning-like rapidity. This was the case with Hayseed, the peasant who worked for Dosolina Scacerni. When he failed to come home from his work his wife went out to look for him and found his body huddled under a hedge, covered with flies. She shouted her grief to high heaven and soon Master Lazzaro and his wife, among others, came to succor her. On the way Dosolina crumpled up and fell to the ground.

"Never mind, friends," said Lazzaro, picking her up in his arms. "Shock has sent the blood to her head. Take poor Hayseed's body home and comfort his wife as best you can. I'll look after the mistress."

The voice in which he spoke these reassuring words trembled and came out of his throat with difficulty, his knees buckled under him and his arms held her up with enormous difficulty. In the effort to carry her home himself and not give her over to others he went through the hardest moments of his hard life; all of a sudden the strength seemed to have gone out of him.

It was a fair March day, when the fruit trees and hawthorns were in blossom. The fields were dotted with daisies, violets peered up from under the grass, and the wheat was putting out its tender shoots. High in the heavens the lark poured out its joy and closer to earth smaller birds chirped an echo. All of nature's beauty seemed to smile and yet at this very moment she turned her face aside, precipitating a night of death and terror.

Master Lazzaro walked at the head of the little line with Dosolina in his arms, her head held up by the young housemaid she had taken to help her. Two men followed, carrying Hayseed by the feet and shoulders, while his hands hung down and brushed the green grass. Then came the silently weeping widow, who burst again into loud sobs when they reached the door of her humble dwelling. From this point Lazzaro, with the housemaid beside him, stumbled on alone.

The dread plague had come again to Poplar Bridge. Lazzaro tried with all his might to banish this thought and imagined that this strain was responsible for his weakness. For a moment it seemed as if he would never reach the door. He was going through a struggle with an invisible adversary, like that which recurs in a dream, when one can see the goal just ahead and yet never reach it. But his anguish was real, not a dream, and all around him were the things he was accustomed to see every day: the rut left by wagon wheels between the two rows of hawthorn, and the flowering plum tree which Dosolina took as a true harbinger of spring. The almond blossoms may be deceived and come out too soon, she always said, but the plum tree never. She had pointed it out to him that very morning, with a reminder that she had planted it during the first year of their marriage.

"Now spring has come for certain," she had said.

Seeing the plum tree now, Lazzaro quickly turned his gaze away. There were the threshing yard, the vegetable garden and the promising orchard on one side and the tool house and the haystack on the other. The hay was half gone, leaving the central pole half bare with its knob sticking out on top. All these things had come to life under her care and now she was about to leave them. The years rolled back as he carried her across the threshold just as he had done on their wedding day, and laid her on the bed where with so much pain and danger she had given birth to their son.

With the housemaid's help he undressed her. Then he went into the dark, smoke-stained kitchen and lit a candle before the image of Our Lady of Sorrows. Again he was reminded of the day when she had suffered in childbirth and he had gone to the rescue of the stormswept mill. On that day of passion and travail he had been reluctant to light a candle because he was in a state of mortal sin, which God's mercy had later forgiven him. Now his hand trembled over the wick and he could hold it steady only through a supreme effort of will. He had only one grace now to implore of God and that was to let him die.

The cattle mooed from the barn and the little maid said with an embarrassment that escaped his notice:

"None of the men is there and the animals are hungry."

"Go to Guarda as fast as you can and tell the priest to come with the last sacrament," he answered.

"Shouldn't I call Mistress Cecilia from the mill?"

"Yes, tell her the mistress is ailing, but don't ask her to come, because it might be"—he did not want to say any more—"because I can take care of her myself." And he added, seeing the terror in her eyes: "No, it isn't what you think. But we must be careful and I can handle it alone. Go first to call the priest."

She was off like the wind, but his attention was taken by a succession of hoarse sobs from the bedroom. He could no longer deceive himself as to the nature of her illness. Holding up her head he could feel a deathly cold steal up his arms to his chest and heart. Suddenly Dosolina had a momentary respite; she recognized him and gave him the same smile she had given him as a timid and loving bride.

"Courage, Dosolina," he said, feeling his soul ebb out in her smile.

"I have plenty of that, Lazzaro," she said in a faint voice that he remembered from the old days. "Have you sent for the priest?"

449

"Yes, just as a precaution. But there's nothing to worry about. He may take some time to come because he's very busy these days. Just keep up your courage."

"That I will, my good man. And I pray that you may have courage too. I have faith that God will have mercy on my soul in purgatory. The time is very near . . . No, don't take on, Lazzaro . . ."

Drawn up to his full height the old man was tearing his hair in utter hopelessness.

"Didn't you tell me to have courage?" she said maternally. "This moment was bound to come. It's hard for me to talk, Lazzaro, and the time is going fast. Just let me say that I've always loved you and if ever I've done anything to displease you I beg your . . . Don't cry now, Lazzaro; at your age it's perfectly shameful!"

With these words she smiled again, and Lazzaro brushed away the tears that had been wrung out of his old eyes.

"You're quite right, Dosolina," he said. "I love you, too, as much as ever. Blessed be the mother that bore you."

"I know how much you love me and I should take comfort from it even if it were less than before. But soon now I shan't be able to say any more. If Cecilia should come, don't let her in. She mustn't expose herself while she is carrying Peppino's child. And you must tell Peppino goodbye for me. Farewell, Lazzaro! You have been my man just as I have been your woman, that much is true. I can't seem to see, Lazzaro, I must be dying. Farewell, Lazzaro, until we meet in the next world."

"Farewell!" stammered Lazzaro. "Farewell!"

Her only response was a last smile that seemed to flicker between her closed eyelids. Perhaps because she did not resist it the cholera took her gently and painlessly away like a fire that goes out for lack of further fuel. Lazzaro, briefly reinvigorated by the very intensity of his suffering, shook like the trunk of an old tree, stripped of the green leaves it had once held out to the sun and with its gnarled branches quivering in the winter wind. He was all alone, for the maid, once she had given the message to the priest, was too scared to return to Poplar Bridge and went off to her own family without taking the news to Cecilia aboard the mill. As for Giuseppe, he had gone to collect grain and had left word that he would not be back for several days.

When the priest knocked at the door the sound echoed as if from an empty house. When he went to open up Lazzaro saw that evening was beginning to fall. He had changed the sheets on the bed and in it Dosolina seemed to be sleeping. Never had she seemed to him so slender and small, not even on their wedding night when her frailty had made him afraid of causing her pain. Feeling as close to her as he did he had not noticed that her barely perceptible breath had ceased altogether. Cholera has a way of cooling and stiffening the body and he hardly realized that out of hers all life was gone.

But the priest, who had other sick calls to answer, did not linger over any unnecessary ceremony and no sooner had he drawn near

450

where Dosolina was lying than he began not to administer the last sacrament but to say the prayers for the dead. Scacerni recognized the penitential psalm, in whose words everything earthly is consumed and enkindled again by an arcane invocation: "*De profundis clamavi ad te, Domine; Domine, exaudi vocem meam. Si iniquitates observaveris, Domine, Domine, quis sustinebit? Speravit anima mea in Domino.*" Without understanding every word, he knew from the *de profundis* what they meant. He admitted that she was dead, without really taking it in, and prayed for mercy on her soul and his, only hoping that he might soon enjoy the same peace. When the priest, after the absolution, turned to say a few words of comfort, he asked firmly:

"Reverend Father, when will you come back for the body?"

"Tomorrow."

"You won't take her alone."

"What are you saying, Master Lazzaro?"

"I shall travel with her."

"Be brave, my friend," said the priest who did not understand the meaning of these words, which Lazzaro had spoken as if in a dream.

"I'd have to be brave indeed if I were to go on living."

"We must resign ourselves to God's will."

"I know that He is too merciful to leave me here alone and I thank Him in advance for His mercy."

"We must always thank Him and place ourselves in His hands."

"That is beyond my powers. Am I sinning?"

"No, you're not sinning, my poor fellow. Forgive me for going so soon. You know what these days are."

"Reverend Father, farewell," said Lazzaro, as if a sort of primitive reserve prevented him from saying more. He did not ask the last sacrament for himself, since his only wish was to be left alone with Dosolina to die.

"Farewell then, Master Lazzaro."

A little later on, after dark, Cecilia and Schiavetto, to whom the priest had sent word, arrived at the house. But Master Lazzaro had locked the door and spoke to them from a dark window.

"You mustn't come in, Cecilia. She said herself before she died that you mustn't expose yourself now that you are carrying a new Lazzaro or a new Dosolina."

"Why do you speak so, Master?"

"You will soon know. Go away, Cecilia; the plague that is in this house knows no mercy."

"But I can't leave you like this."

"We are beyond human help, both of us, dear Cecilia. Go back and take good care of yourself at the mill. For the sake of the love I've had for you ever since I pulled you out of the river."

Cecilia could not open her mouth to speak.

"God bless you, Cecilia, and your child. That is my message to you and that of my dear wife who looks down on us from heaven. Say goodbye for me to my son and take care of your health. I am sure that

451

the Lord will grant my prayer. Don't try to talk, Cecilia, for there's nothing more to say. Yes, one thing . . . Perhaps we did not seem to you to rejoice in your marriage, but now both of us are glad, and it consoles me to know that you, my Cecilia, will be mother of the Scacerni. And now I have done. Goodbye, Schiavetto, we've been through many trials together and you have proved a faithful friend."

Cecilia sobbed under her breath as he closed the window. Schiavetto accompanied her slow, heavy walk back to the mill. Then he returned to Poplar Bridge and sat down on a stone just outside the door.

The March night was cold, reminiscent of winter. Schiavetto looked up at the distant stars and thought back to all the events, both sad and gay, of the years he had spent with Master Lazzaro on the mill. He could not linger long on any one of them, for the silence of the house cried aloud in his heart. But Master Lazzaro insisted upon being obeyed to the very end and upon dying as he had chosen. Already when he was leaning out the window he had felt the pangs of cholera and now, because he did not wish to defile the bed where his beloved was lying, he pulled a mattress over beside it and lay suffering in silence. The very robustness of his frame and his unconscious resistance to the disease seemed to aggravate its spasms. Several times, groping his way along the wall, he went to the backhouse, hoping that he would not die in the usual mass of excrement. His throat ached with thirst, brought on by frequent attacks of vomiting. A chill crept up over him, as if death were invading first one extremity and then another, and he was lying inert on the mattress when the first cramp gripped his leg. Nailed to his bed of pain he felt the succeeding attacks run cruelly through his thighs, arms, shoulders, ribs, and every other part of his body. His sight was blacked out and his eyes rolled wildly in their hollowed sockets. He ground his teeth almost to the point of breaking them rather than cry out, and thus defied his last adversary to the point when he no longer had the breath to utter a sound. When dawn broke he had barely enough strength to make the sign of the cross before he was shaken by a final spasm. Then peace descended upon the house at Poplar Bridge.

As the sun came up in the sky Schiavetto decided to knock at the door. He knocked with both fists and called his master by name, but there was no answer. Finally he took an iron bar and forced his way in.

Dosolina seemed almost incorporeal as she lay on the bed where her husband had closed her eyes. There was something ageless and skeletal about her except for the wax-like pallor of her eyelids, and her gaping mouth was set in a sort of twisted grin. Lazzaro, on the other hand, looked longer than ever lying on the mattress, as if his body had recovered its old strength. His flowing beard hung down over his chest and Schiavetto thought he had never seen it so silvery before. Stepping tremblingly closer he perceived the pointed nose, the clenched jaws, the taut lines of his mouth and the frightening whites of his eyes. His arms were crossed over his chest and his legs stretched out stiff and straight. A heart whose simplicity contained elements of grandeur had ceased to pump the red blood through his veins.

Schiavetto had loved this man as if he were his own father and now, too sad to weep, he bowed his head in remembrance of past years. Then he lifted him up from the mattress, dressed him in fresh clothes and laid him on the bed beside his wife. After this he knew where to find blessed candles and after he had lit two of them at the head of the bed he knelt down to murmur a *requiem* and the Lord's prayer for the souls of Lazzaro and Dosolina, which must now be in purgatory. The candle that Lazzaro had lit before Our Lady of Sorrows in the kitchen had long since burned out. Schiavetto locked the bedroom door so that if Cecilia were to come she would not touch the dead bodies. Such was Master Lazzaro's last wish.

With the oncoming daylight the cows mooed again with hunger from their stalls and Schiavetto went to fill their troughs as the kind mistress whose voice he was never to hear again would have had him do. While he pulled down some fodder with a fork tears at last came into his eyes. He thought of the time when he was a boy and Dosolina had come as a bride to the mill, with her hair as fair as young wheat and her eyes of corn-flower blue. Suddenly he felt old and tired, alone with his memories. Tears veiled his eyes like the dew that during the night had fallen on the yard outside, on the wheat fields, the haystack and the hawthorns. Now the sun had risen over the farm that had belonged to Lazzaro and Dosolina Scacerni and dried the dew from the grass. When everything else we know on the crust of this planet is gone the grass still pushes up, and if ever it ceases to grow there will be an end to all things living.

3

On the night when these events took place at Poplar Bridge a gay party sat up till dawn over a rich supper in Vergoli's mansion at Ro. With the advent of the plague Virginio Alpi (along with all the other city dwellers who could afford it) had sent his family away. Now he spent most of his time gallivanting about the countryside with a former companion in all his excesses, a certain Salvi from Renazzo di Cento, who had been a lieutenant of the "Gregorian volunteers" and was now active in smuggling between Ferrara and the Duchy of Modena. These two went from one country house to another in search of entertainment, and so when Alpi ran into Vergoli one day in the Castle he clapped him on the back and said:

"Come, come, my friend; don't pull that long face! Don't you know that cholera always attacks those who are in low spirits? Good food and drink and pretty girls are the best preventives. Cholera never strikes a man who goes in for high living, and if it does it simply acts as a purge of his system. Three days from now I shall pay you a visit. Gather together our common friends at Ro and tell your cook that we intend to feast until dawn. Cholera descends upon those who are afraid of it, and the sight of a man with a fork and a wine glass in his hand is enough to drive it away."

In his own case, at least, this seemed to be true. Vergoli could only accede ill-humoredly to Alpi's whim, thinking to himself as he gave instructions for preparing the supper that one of these days this uninvited guest would tell him to provide him with pretty girls too.

The company was a select one: Alpi and Salvi, Abate Valmora, Sergeant Solimani, Corporal Barbacinti, Orlandini the tavern keeper, Vergoli's right-hand man, Olmeda, and several other carousing souls of the same low class. Alpi enjoyed associating with such people because of the adulation they heaped upon him, and such occasions were to him like passing all the accomplices of his crimes in review.

Arriving at their host's house around dusk they first drank several glasses of dry white wine for an appetizer. Then they sat down to supper: Vergoli at the head, with Alpi and Salvi on either side of him and the rest around the table. At the far end was Valmora, set apart a little from the others on account of the smell emanating from his unwashed person. Alpi and Salvi poked fun at his filth quite openly, comparing him to everything but a pig, because they said that animal was too clean for comparison. Up to this point the gathering had been a quiet one. Most of the guests stood with their glasses in their hands, while a few of them filled in the pauses with everyday talk, largely about the dread cholera. But when they sat down a complete silence fell upon them, and they leaned with the expressions of pigs or vultures over the steaming soup bowls, into which the boys waiting on the table had carelessly dipped their fingers. The service left much to be desired, but the soup was fragrant and in it floated noodles stuffed with meat and savory herbs. The silence was broken only by the clatter of the guests' spoons in their bowls and the way they licked their chops and mustaches with greedy satisfaction. Even Alpi, who knew better, threw good manners out the window. Four tureens of soup stood on the table for anyone that wanted a second helping and these were soon emptied. Then came a pigeon and liver pie, swimming in butter and flavored with rosemary and sage, into which they dipped pieces of bread and stuffed them with dripping fingers into their mouths. They went at it so hard that Valmora warned them not to spoil their appetites and offend the master of the house by acting as if this was all they were going to have to eat.

"Behave yourselves! Easy there with the bread!" he shouted, but they had fasted for the previous twenty-four hours and many of them had even taken a physic to stimulate their hunger.

They had hardly time to resume conversation before the next course, a choice of roast, fried, or stewed chicken.

"Take all you like," Vergoli exhorted them; "there's plenty for the servants in the kitchen."

The servants loudly echoed this assertion and hastened to bring on a great bowl of vegetable and green salad. It looked for a moment as

454

if the feast were drawing to a premature close, but actually the salad was only meant to revive the guests' hunger for a variety of meat dishes: veal chops and ragout and finally a great roast of beef, which Vergoli proceeded, amid general applause, to carve on the table before them. A few of those present had really had enough, but none of them would admit it.

It was after midnight and they had begun to chew every mouthful slowly, as if to clear the way for the one to follow. Throughout the meal Alpi and Vergoli set the pace. A robust year-old local wine went around the table, poured from earthenware jugs, and made their stomachs tingle. Valmora had pushed aside his glass and appropriated one of the jugs for his own use, thereby arousing general merriment. The jug was so large around that he had to hold it by the handles on either side, and he proclaimed that this was "tweaking the jug's ears," in the manner of a schoolmaster who had submitted him to the same treatment when he was a boy. The mention of schooling made his fellow guests, most of whom were illiterate, stare at him with the mixture of scorn and respect that an impoverished man of letters invariably inspires in those who are wealthy but ignorant. Then they resumed their coarse jokes and loud laughter.

After the roast came some out-of-season and refreshing celery, followed by blood sausage, a specialty of the region. As the first rays of daylight shone through the windows the guests were truly replete, and there was no doubt that the supper had reflected their host's opulence. Custom demanded that he celebrate his ability to give them more than they could possibly hold by one last defiant and gloriously wasteful gesture. And so, in order that they should be not only sated but nauseated as well, Vergoli signalled that platters of roast lamb, pigeon, and guinea hen should be paraded around the table and carried back untouched to the kitchen. His guests feebly shook their heads in refusal, while the servants egged them on to prolong the clash of wills and to prove that their capacity was greater than their host's lavishness. They sipped instead at white wine served in bottles that were packed in bucketfuls of snow, which Vergoli kept all year round in a huge icebox in his cellar. Then they polished off the meal with cake dipped in liqueur and a drink of rum, which reduced them to a stupor and caused several among them to fall asleep with their heads on the table.

"To think that some people still speak ill of smuggling!" exclaimed Salvi, whom drink made loquacious. "With the tariff there is on imported delicacies, how else, I ask you, should anyone in these enlightened Papal States drink such delicious rum? No prince or duke or cardinal could afford it. I doubt if even the Holy Father himself could keep it in stock! Yet without such rum life wouldn't be worth living!"

The irreverence of his words gave them a strange flavor. It was evident that so stalwart a Papist could not open his mouth without making reference to something holy. He might seem guilty of affectation, but such a thing had never entered his mind and the heartiness with which he spoke gave proof of his sincerity. Such mental confusion was typical of Salvi and his fellows, who embraced both smuggling and the cause of the Papacy with equal vigor and were licentious and bigoted together. Both Virginio Alpi and Pietro Vergoli were intelligent enough to see the contradiction between his words and his actions, but the former was amused and the latter ready to close an eye. There was a difference in their points of view, because Vergoli thought to himself: "Here's hoping things go on as they are," while Alpi, more cynically, resolved to go along with them as long as he could. Meanwhile Salvi continued his drunken peroration:

"No one, I may say, is more attached to the person of our Supreme Pontiff and King than I am. I gave ample proof of that as a Gregorian volunteer, when I would sooner have cut a Liberal's head off than miss fasting on Friday! And if this was a sin I don't hesitate to proclaim it! Now they tell me that His Holiness has forbidden smuggling, and in particular the exportation of grain. In that case the undersigned would be a disloyal subject, a traitor. Of course, that's out of the question. And do you know how I square myself with my conscience? If anyone calls me names to my face I beat him up and that settles it, because it's plain that he's a filthy Liberal. And then I tell him: His Holiness is father of all Christians, especially of those who love the Church and its government. Now a father, as we all know, desires the good, not the harm, of his sons. And to whom, I ask you, is smuggling harmful? That I don't know, but I do know, and you do too, to whom it is a benefit. There's no getting away from it: the Holy Father has his reasons, to which we subjects are bound to defer. We must respect his orders, but at the same time we know that he doesn't wish harm upon us. If we were to go looking for harm and trouble we should actually displease him. In so doing, mind you, we should show that we do not believe him to be our king and our father. That would be black heresy! Anyone who talks heresy to me will have to learn his lesson. Of course if there are any Liberal smugglers, they should be punished as enemies to God and man. But, meanwhile, if anyone dares say I shouldn't drink this rum he is a traitor!"

At these words the sun came over the horizon and lit up the drunken weariness of Vergoli's party.

"Well spoken, Salvi, my friend," said Alpi leering. "You are more eloquent than the professors. I never credited you with so much learning. *In vino veritas:* wine has a way of bringing out the truth, or shall we, in this case, give credit to Signor Pietro's excellent rum?"

"Very good! Exactly! Hurrah for the excellent rum of Signor Pietro, the smuggler of the Po!" Salvi tried to rise to his feet as he delivered this toast, but he only staggered and slumped back.

"Better keep your seat," said Vergoli with a forced smile. "You're not quite steady on your pins, and besides you're half seas over."

"Are you insinuating that I am drunk? Who dares say such a thing? Let anyone who does step up and I'll wring his neck like a chicken. Why, I can balance on one foot!"

He got up and stumbled away from the table but soon fell flat, vomited a good part of his supper, and lay prostrate in his vomit. The servants came in with a broom and some sawdust to scatter over the floor and laid him on one of the mattresses which had been providently prepared in the nearby conservatory, where in the winter Vergoli kept young lemon and oleander trees. There several of the guests already lay snoring in every conceivable key from bass to treble.

"Vergoli, you needn't smile so wryly over Salvi's toast," said Alpi, who knew how to hold his wine and had lost none of his pitiless lucidity. "If a friend who has had a drop or two to drink with other friends happens to call you the smuggler of the Po, that's no reason for turning up your nose. What would you do if an officer of the law were accusing you? You must learn to control your feelings better than that. If a man is to rule over others he must learn first to rule over himself. When you have such a hang-dog expression I feel obliged, as Superintendent of Customs, to suspect you of wrongdoing and make an investigation. I don't mind telling you that if you were to pull a face like that in the presence of Count Folicaldi you'd be done for. His Excellency is severe, and justly so, toward those who are suspected of smuggling, and in spite of the friendship I bear you I have to consider the welfare of the government first as soon as I enter his chambers. If you frown and tremble at one heedless word from a man in his cups, I ask you again, how would you face an officer of the law?"

"Alpi! Count Alpi! Sir!" exclaimed Vergoli, sinking lower and lower into adulation to match his rising fear, "I trust you're only joking."

"I'm not a man to joke when I see a chance to give good advice to a friend. You're the one that seems to be joking."

Of course poor Vergoli had no such intentions and he now said in a low voice:

"Have you too heard rumors?"

"Rumors of what?"

"That a stranger has been hanging about here—an itinerant merchant he called himself—and asking all sorts of probing questions about the traffic on the Po. He was particularly curious, they tell me, about the exportation of grain."

"I know nothing about him," Alpi said truthfully, concealing his surprise under a knowing and superior air, which made Vergoli believe that perhaps Alpi himself had sent out a spy in order to lull the Apostolic Delegate's suspicions.

"I tell you this only to prove that where you are concerned I never fail to lay all my cards on the table," said Vergoli, feeling reassured.

"I am sure of that," Alpi rejoined, trying to cover up the uneasiness he felt inside, "but I am glad to hear you say it. And what about the stranger afflicted with so much curiosity?"

"No sooner seen than gone. Whoever sent him on this errand was wasting his time. If the instigator is a friend, he ought to know that here we are all true-blue and have nothing to hide. And if he is an enemy then let him beware, for he risks a thorough beating."

Vergoli spoke in this vein because he was convinced by now that

Alpi had indeed sent the spy, in order to make sure that he was not being cheated of any of the percentage of gain due to him from the illegal operations.

"Well, Vergoli, my friend, if this man or another like him should re-appear I advise beating him for certain, not too roughly of course and with the excuse that he has been mistaken for a chicken thief or a seducer."

"Quite right," murmured Vergoli, thinking to himself: "You'd just as soon throw me overboard as you would let this minion of yours be beaten, that's perfectly clear. In fact you may have chosen this way of warning me, as if I didn't know already that you stop at nothing."

"What are you ruminating about, Vergoli?" asked Alpi, who had been ruminating on his own account.

"I? Am I ruminating?"

"So it seems."

"Well, I've been ruminating that perhaps we should be a little more cautious about this business of ours."

"Business? What business?"

"Is that a question? The common people don't like the looks of it. They say they haven't enough bread to eat, while we . . ."

"Speak for yourself, my friend! And as for the people, don't bother me with their idiotic whims and complaints. If they haven't enough to eat it's a good thing the cholera has come along to lessen the number of mouths to be fed."

"How can you say such a thing?" exclaimed Vergoli with genuine horror.

"I didn't send the cholera, did I? I simply accept it for the good it does, which is considerable. But why don't you raise your sights to the realm of statesmanship? How many times have I told you that the well-being of His Imperial Majesty's troops is at stake? This is no time for quibbling."

"Let's be frank . . ." Vergoli began, intending to state that the smuggling had gone far beyond this purpose and yielded handsome profits to Alpi. But the latter coldly interrupted him:

"I quite agree. There's no need for you to say 'let's be frank' to me. In fact, this is the last time I wish to hear you say it. You are close to giving me offense. I informed you of the Austrian requirements and urged you for various reasons to take them into consideration. But let us indeed be frank. I chose you for your honesty, but if I were ever to find out that you were turning the thing to your own advantage I should not hesitate for a moment to do my duty. If you were to abuse my confidence and that of His Excellency the Apostolic Delegate, I should let you suffer the punishment you deserve and hand you over to the law."

It was quite true, the flabbergasted Vergoli reflected, that Alpi had never said, much less committed to writing, a single word such as to establish his complicity. He had never signed any receipt for his percentage; in fact, he had always pretended that things had gone no

458

farther than the original consignment of grain to the Austrian supply officer. And now, with this indignant protest, he had shown clearly how, in case of trouble, he would deny everything. Vergoli felt a chill run up his spine, which he chose to attribute to the cold morning air blowing in upon the night's dissipation. He would have been even more alarmed if he had known the thoughts that were passing through Virginio Alpi's mind. For Alpi was thoroughly shaken by the news of the mysterious stranger and his uncertainty as to who might have sent him. He felt sure that Folicaldi was still blind to what was going on and feared the interference of a much higher authority, such as the Minister of Finance or the Secretary of State in Rome. After a moment's thought he discarded this supposition in favor of two others. Either Vergoli had been misinformed or else he was trying to put over some form of blackmail. In the one case he was stupid and the best thing was to get rid of him; in the other he was untrustworthy and the only thing to do was to sell him out. It looked bad for Pietro Vergoli, whichever course Alpi chose to follow.

Meanwhile, as day drew on, there was trouble enough of a more immediate kind. Three of the banqueters, Valmora among them, had severe intestinal pains for which either their bout of eating and drinking or the cholera might have been to blame. For safety's sake they were bundled into a cart and sent posthaste to quarantine in Ferrara. Two of them were too far gone to offer any resistance, but Abate Valmora broke in upon the drunken slumber of the remaining guests with cries of terror and profane maundering.

"I refuse to go into quarantine, you wretches! Leave me in a ditch, if you like, but don't take me to that charnel house! I'll never get there alive; I'll die on the road and go straight to hell! Call a priest immediately, or else you, Signor Pietro, you, Alpi and Salvi, will be responsible for my damnation. I'm not afraid to call you by name and I'll call you from hell in the same way. Not even an angel of God, not even Jesus Christ in person will be able to save you. You're damning yourselves to eternity, you can take the word of one who is almost dead and damned already!" And when two husky peasant boys slid poles under the mattress where he was lying in order not to touch him while they loaded him into the cart, he added with fury: "You don't care, eh? Are your hearts as hardened as all that? I shan't confess my sins: I shall die with them all on my conscience, those you know about, which are numerous enough, and others beside them. You, Alpi, made me commit most of them; yes, I mean you. I chose to be damned just so I can drag the rest of you after me to hell. Not a one of you shall be forgiven, you can take a dying man's word for it, wretched cowards that you are!"

"Hurry and load this poor fool in," Alpi ordered the peasants. "And if he keeps on yelling don't hesitate to gag him."

Valmora was choking with rage and vomit and at the gate of Vergoli's mansion they heard him from the retreating cart, through the fresh March air, pouring forth a volley of curses and damning them all to eternity.

"The diet I prescribe as a preventive of cholera is all well and good," observed Alpi impassively, "but there's no use overdoing it like that pig there."

"We all overdid it a bit last night," confessed one of the guests.

"Then let each one of us look to his own belly," Alpi said rudely. "You're a bunch of fools, all of you. And the cholera will most likely be your cathartic."

With such good wishes he gave the signal for the party to break up and they went their ways without so much as thanking their host. Alpi went back to Ferrara to find out what truth there was in the story of the mysterious and curious stranger; Salvi returned, very shakily, to his native village, and Vergoli, having no urge to sleep, decided to get a breath of fresh air by taking a look at the dikes of Nogarole, where an unusually large cargo of grain was scheduled for loading that morning. He started out, with Olmeda and Solimani beside him, and on the way they met Schiavetto who had such a tragic expression on his face that they asked him what was the matter.

"There died an honest man!" Vergoli could not but exclaim with a touch of envy after Schiavetto's broken words had told him the story.

"You're right there, Signor Pietro," said Schiavetto sadly.

"That honest man played me a bad trick, though," said Sergeant Blister.

"Never mind," interposed Olmeda, with a touch of malice, "when it's your turn to die no one will say you were an honest man!"

Vergoli did not speak, but looked volumes. As they all walked together toward the river he said suddenly:

"Keep it in mind, Schiavetto, that I'd like to walk the last mile with the miller and his wife. When are they to be buried?"

"That I don't know. Whenever the priest can find time."

"I understand. But be sure to let me know."

"Of course, Signor Pietro. And, forgive my presumption, but would you do me still another favor?"

"With pleasure."

"Mistress Cecilia is aboard the mill and doesn't yet know that Master Lazzaro is dead. I'm here all alone while her husband is away. Since you know better how to put such things than I do, will you break the news? Master Lazzaro was like a father to her, and he was to me too, so that I can't talk about it."

"I'll do the best I can, Schiavetto. Your sentiments do honor to you and to the memory of your master."

Cecilia was standing anxiously on the Saint Michael's deck.

"Schiavetto!" she called out. "I was afraid you had disappeared."

"I'd like a word with you," Vergoli said, stepping into the skiff.

Cecilia ran back to her own mill and would not hear of any consolation. But Vergoli said what he could, and meant it, for he felt at the moment a genuine envy of the simple life.

Two barges were taking on grain nearby, but he had little wish to watch them and left Olmeda to supervise the job. He himself went, instead, to La Vallazza, in the hope of finding Marquis Macchiavelli. The marquis was there, taking his customary morning walk and looking at the rows of thickly planted green wheat and widely spaced stalks of hemp. Clover and grass had been sown to draw off some of the excessive fertility of the newly reclaimed land and there was still water in the ditches that had been dug to drain it. The impoverished old nobleman hardly knew himself with what feelings the scene inspired him. He was prey to a mixture of affection and resentment, a trace of jealousy without malice, regret for the days when La Vallazza was an overgrown and swampy woodland rich in animal life, and pride in its newly acquired prosperity. His jealousy was like that of an ageing lover toward his last flame; it was mingled with resignation and extended not so much to his lost possessions as to his lost youth. Having no future to which to look forward, he looked back at the past as if it were a mirage and did not even call upon it to return.

"You can say what you like, Pietro," he observed with a gentle smile, "and I know that there is a great deal to be said on your behalf, but I like La Vallazza better the way it used to be."

"Perhaps you are right at that, my dear Marquis," said Vergoli in an unusually melancholy tone.

"Come, come now! Where's your pride? Aren't you going to say that two wild ducks and a woodcock aren't worth a hundred bushels of wheat? But the ducks and the woodcock stand for my youth, you see!"

"We toil away, Marquis, and that's not all, we worry ourselves into sleepless nights and burden our conscience with sins, and all the while life hangs by a single thread."

"What makes you so philosophical this morning?"

"Perhaps because I have just heard that Scacerni and his wife have died of cholera."

The marquis too was deeply affected by this news, and joined the funeral procession. Master Lazzaro was laid to rest in the Guarda cemetery after all, in spite of the many times he had protested against it. Such evil days were not conducive to public gatherings, but all of Guarda was present. As for Giuseppe, when he came back to Poplar Bridge and heard what had happened, he stood stock still and said nothing. Then, under the curious gaze of his neighbors, he unhitched his horse and put it in the stable. The neighbors' curiosity changed to indignation when they heard him whistle, in a way which they mistakenly took for callous insensibility. Actually this was the only time Giuseppe had ever whistled in his life and perhaps he was giving vent in this way to an emotion he knew no other way to express. Anyone who had seen him going about in his cart in the days that followed his father's funeral would have noticed that he let the reins hang idle for long periods of time and slumped down in his seat, absorbed in thoughts that were by no means of money. Meanwhile people judged him to be an unfeeling monster and some went so far as to say that it had been a waste of time to baptize him. This condemnation was repeated to Giuseppe, but he merely shrugged his shoulders.

Cecilia shared the general opinion that he was indifferent to his parents' death, and he did not attempt to persuade her of the contrary. Their marriage was more successful than might have been expected from its inauspicious beginnings, but their tastes grew increasingly apart. The solidity of the house at Poplar Bridge made Cecilia feel shut in, while the motion of the mill on the river caused Giuseppe to be slightly seasick. Cecilia refused to stay in the house even for the birth of her first son, who was born in the cabin of Bitter Bread Mill. No sooner was she delivered than the unspeakable joy of motherhood filled her heart to the exclusion of everything that had gone before.

A midwife from Guarda, who had taken over the function of the now aged Venusta Chiccoli, came to help at the birth.

"It's an odd way of doing things, to give birth to a child aboard a mill when you have a perfectly good house on dry land," she said upon arrival. "You must want him to be a miller."

And holding out the little Lazzaro to Giuseppe:

"He's the image of his grandfather."

"It's customary to say a baby looks like his father," Giuseppe answered with a wry smile, "since the identity of the mother is not a subject of doubt."

"He looks like you too, of course," the midwife added hastily.

Giuseppe handed the baby back to her with a shrug of the shoulders and an unhappy, forced smile.

"Don't be embarrassed," he said. "If he looks like his grandfather he'll be a handsome man. There's no advantage to looking like me, I know that."

Cecilia listened from her bunk in silence. She would have liked to say that she forgave him for everything, that she was grateful to him for having made her a mother and beatifically happy over their new-born son. But words did not come to her easily and the stolid silence in which she had lived with her husband had not made her any more eloquent. The sudden rush of new feelings, along with the milk that flowed into her breasts, left her confused, and there was little encouragement in Giuseppe's stony demeanor. And yet it occurred to her that he might actually suffer from his own coldness, from his inability to mourn his parents' death.

If she could have talked she would have said that now that she was a mother she felt herself to be more truly his wife, that she could not remember a time when she had had no such feeling. In her gratitude she asked for nothing more and did not dream that he could want more of her either. Perhaps this new passionate impulsion toward her suckling babe, the crowning happiness such as she had not felt before, was the expression of a maternal instinct that was deeper than any other and took the place of the sensuality which she was destined never to know. Perhaps her primary function was that of a mother. So it is that spring makes the sap well up in a stem until it bursts into flower and chastely desires that a seed come to fertilize it and crown it with fruit.

462

Did Giuseppe dimly feel that her ardent gratitude defeated his lust and shut him out more than ever from possession of her senses? Unconsciously perhaps he did, and he hopelessly rebelled against his past and future mortification. Her lack of response to his passion transformed it into something weary and deathlike, and all the while his seed in her body grew into paradoxically glorious life.

In his own mute fashion he said within himself at this moment that his marriage gave him the least direct benefit of any of his investments. Let us not condemn him for such meanness of soul, for he was the first to suffer from it. As time went on his neighbors judged him to be just as cold a father as he had been a son. Only Cecilia forgave him, or rather because she had found out now what he could give her, she never pronounced him a poor husband. It was Giuseppe's nature to take a morbid delight in other people's low opinion of him and to disdain their affection.

Giuseppe paid no attention to the cholera, which was spreading with the warm weather. He was convinced that his one attack guaranteed him immunity. More energetic and untiring than ever he went from village to village and from farm to farm to buy up grain from the new harvest. He seemed able to smell it out, the way a hound (or, as some people said, a pig) smells truffles. With quivering nostrils he drove about the plague-stricken countryside and did not even try to conceal his eagerness under the feigned reluctance of a wily and experienced buyer. He attacked the farmers with a sort of fury and frightened them by prophesying a fall in prices and saying that next time he came around he would offer them only half or a quarter of what he was offering now. Because he knew everyone's family circumstances and troubles he used these as a lever of persuasion. He did not hesitate to declare to fathers who had just lost their sons or to weeping widows and orphans that the cholera which had just victimized their families was going to make labor scarce and high-priced and bring them to ruin, that is, of course, unless they sold him their grain.

"Here comes the man whom even the plague does not want," people said when they saw his horse trotting down the dusty roads between the fields of aromatic green hemp or met him walking up to their front door.

The ditchdiggers who were working under the pitiless sun on the reclamation of La Vallazza sang a song which their forefathers had sung before them and which, in spite of the hard labor performed by generation after generation, provided a cheerful accompaniment to the rumbling wheels of their wheelbarrows:

> *Day and night we're digging,*
> *In sunshine and in rain;*
> *Dig in and turn it over,*
> *Over and over again.*
> *We shovel for a living*
> *And whistle for our pain.*

Giuseppe Scacerni looked at them disdainfully, unable to fathom how miserable creatures like these, who had only their strong arms with which to make a living, could manage to sing. Their good cheer seemed to him stupid and insolent. He found it offensive that these humble workers should sing in blissful oblivion of their penniless condition, which it terrified him so much as to see from his cart as he rolled along the road. Because he could not believe that their merriment was sincere he found it positively alarming. Underneath it, he suspected, lay a fierce hatred for anyone who had any money. Sometimes he stopped to talk with them while they rested in the noonday sun, which fermented the muddy bottoms of the freshly dug canals. He felt sorry for them, but they turned the tables on him by saying:

"Haven't you time to take a midday rest, Were Rabbit?" Their sympathy was sincere, but to him it was inconceivable and he interpreted it as an expression of envy.

"You scramble about so hard," they said, "that you forget that some day you too must die. Do you think you can take your money with you to the grave? When you're very rich it will only weigh you down."

There was not only envy, Giuseppe thought, but positive hate in these words. Decidedly they had it in for him. As a matter of fact in these difficult times a certain resentment did smolder among this large and underpaid part of the population, among day laborers and ditchdiggers, harassed by debts and floating about in search of work from place to place with no certainty of finding it on the morrow. They had no share of the benefits provided by Pietro Vergoli, "Shovel's son," whose grandfather had been a ditchdigger like themselves. Their chief complaint was the high price of bread, and measured against their meager wages it was indeed very dear. They laid this fact at the door of those who had made a fortune by shipping grain across the Po. In other words, they looked on bakers, shopkeepers, Pietro Vergoli and Giuseppe Scacerni, his agent, as a band of profiteers. Although they were usually resigned to their miserable lot the present famine had aroused them to irritation and they did not fear to throw Giuseppe's trade in his face.

"Were Rabbit, you and your kind ought to be hanged. And yet they're more likely to hang us if we dare ask for bread and justice. Of course there's a law against selling grain across the river in time of famine, but everyone knows how that law is broken. You know something about it yourself, don't you, Were Rabbit? Look at all the deepsea barges that are loaded every day at Guarda! It's plain enough from the prosperous air of the customs guards what's going on. Meanwhile the price of bread goes up and there's nothing we can do except grin and bear it. John the Baptist found locusts to eat in the desert, but we have absolutely nothing. The government is powerless or shuts an eye, and that's the way it goes! Of course, we can always appeal to the Pope, but how are poor devils like ourselves to reach his ears? Who knows what sort of poppycock his advisers tell him? If the Pope could see what straits we're in he'd make a clean sweep of profiteering. What a happy day that would be! People of your sort are worse than bandits,

464

Were Rabbit! Bandits go after the rich, but you speculate on the hunger of the poor. You're a heretic and a usurer, you're worse than the plague, which puts an end to a man's troubles and that's all there is to it, instead of sucking his blood the way you do."

This was the way Giuseppe heard them talk after they had stood their wheelbarrows in a circle, stuck their shovels in the ground like so many guns, and sat down to eat their meager lunch in the shade of some recently planted tree or under one of the older rows of poplars. Giuseppe was at the same time attracted and repelled by what they were saying; with a crooked smile, half overbearing and half fearful, on his face, he stopped to listen. Finally, when they had finished eating, they would hoist themselves to their feet, pick up the handles of their wheelbarrows and shovels and start again to excavate and carry away the dry, yellowish earth or the black mud that sent up a stench to heaven.

"What's the use of talking?" they invariably concluded. "Such is life. But no wonder the poor are half crazy. Were Rabbit, why didn't you let us take a nap instead of inspiring us to carry on like this?"

Regretting the lost opportunity to sleep, they spit into their hands before they picked up their tools and went back to work. They quickly forgot what they had been saying, but Giuseppe interpreted their attitude as one of scorn and hate, and brooded over it the rest of the day.

4

By the autumn of 1855 the cholera had begun to decline, Pietro Vergoli had forgotten what he had heard about a snooping and mysterious stranger, and Alpi, having been unable to trace the source of the rumor, had decided that it must be the product of a timorous imagination. One fine autumn day when Giuseppe Scacerni arrived at Vergoli's house to report on a consignment of grain which was on its way to embarkation, he ran into something totally unexpected: a magistrate sent at the Apostolic Delegate's orders by the court at Ferrara to examine Vergoli's books and start proceedings against Vergoli, Solimani, Barbacinti, and their minor accomplices.

Astounded and afraid Giuseppe tried in vain to think of a place to hide. He wandered about the garden, asking news of this one and that, like a man who has come late upon the scene of a disaster and finds no answer to his ignorant questions. Soon Domenico Moia, the village sheriff, leaned out of a window, saw Giuseppe and pointed him out to the magistrate's clerk.

"There's the fellow who collected most of the grain," he said.

Giuseppe's knees trembled and he could not move.

"Come up here to the magistrate," said the clerk, and falteringly Giuseppe obeyed him.

The magistrate was sitting in the study, in the chair behind Pietro Vergoli's desk, while Vergoli himself occupied the chair usually reserved for visitors. Vergoli's expression was calm, even calmer than usual, but he sat in a strange position, on the edge of the chair, as if there were pins on it and he only wished he could get up and go away. Another anomaly struck Giuseppe, and this was that in spite of the chilly day and the absence of any fire in the room, Vergoli frequently wiped his forehead. It was obviously bathed in a cold perspiration.

The clerk murmured something to the magistrate and the latter said in reply:

"Very well. Have him wait."

The clerk motioned Giuseppe to a chair in one corner, where without realizing it he sat in the same precarious manner as Vergoli and gave a deep sigh. When Giuseppe had first entered the room, Vergoli shot him a meaningful glance which caused him quickly to lower his eyes. Now he sought to recapture Vergoli's attention and glean some hint as to what to say, but Vergoli was apparently too preoccupied by his own worry to notice. The magistrate was reading aloud from the book listing shipments, mumbling all the small figures concerned with recipients within the boundaries of the legation, but raising his voice and scanning the syllables for emphasis every time there was mention of the customs station of Serravalle or a river crossing. Such notations became more and more frequent and in relation to progressively larger shipments as the book went on. Every time Vergoli held up a piece of paper from a pile in front of him and said:

"Here's the regular receipt coupon released by the Serravalle customs."

Whereupon the magistrate took the coupon and laid it down with those that had gone before. Every now and then there was mention of a shipment to Trieste or to the steam mill at Duino and then Vergoli took a paper from another file.

"Here's the export permit," he said.

Many of these shipments did appear to have been effected with regular permits made out in Vergoli's name or passed on to him by dealers in grain, but they could not compare in numbers to the coupons from Serravalle.

"It's very odd," the magistrate said finally, "that a settlement of no more than a dozen families, lost in the swamps, should devour enough grain to feed a whole city."

"If some of the grain went from Serravalle to other localities, or even abroad," Vergoli said with an air of contemptuous assurance, "that was not my affair. If I have coupons testifying that the grain was unloaded at Serravalle then there is no load on my conscience either."

"You have a free and easy way of speaking of your conscience," the magistrate observed.

"My conscience is clear. I shall demand an explanation from higher up of this insulting manner of coming to poke about in my books."

"You may do whatever you see fit to safeguard your reputation. I'm only obeying orders."

"It's the orders that I resent," Vergoli said. "I have nothing against you personally."

466

Giuseppe took courage and began to believe that the magistrate was conducting his search halfheartedly and was anything but pleased with his findings. But now the magistrate showed genuine annoyance.

"The coupons are in order, to be sure, but at Serravalle they all disclaim having seen any grain unloaded at the customs. Can shipments of such a size have been handled secretly? What does Signor Vergoli say to that?"

But Vergoli had a ready answer, which revived Giuseppe's spirits.

"When has 'Signor Vergoli' claimed or been burdened with any responsibility for the conduct of the customs guards at Serravalle? Once I had the coupon I was not concerned with the actual unloading of the grain. The burden of proof that the coupons are false is incumbent upon the law, not upon me. If you mean to bring suit against the customs, then 'Signor Vergoli' is not involved."

These last words were sarcastic and defiant. And the expression on the magistrate's face showed clearly that he was vastly annoyed to find himself entangled in a piece of business that would almost surely win him the enmity of a man like Virginio Alpi. Alpi's name was in the minds of both men, and Vergoli continued unctuously:

"In my humble opinion, the whole thing is up to the Superintendent of Customs. That is, unless he is the one on trial."

The magistrate betrayed a momentary perplexity. This thought was obviously a strange one.

"Who can dream of such a thing?" he said abruptly.

"Not I!" exclaimed Vergoli, in a tone which seemed to imply: "Why are we wasting our time over this comedy?"

But the magistrate pulled himself together and said sententiously:

"For your information, let me tell you that when the law moves against government employees such as the customs guards it is through the Criminal Division of the Apostolic Chamber of Rome. Do you understand?"

"Thank you for vouchsafing me this information."

"For what?"

"For taking such pains to instruct me," said Vergoli with patent irony.

"Meanwhile," the magistrate continued, "let Signor Vergoli explain why all the shipments to either Serravalle or Trieste were addressed to a certain Trambusti."

"That's simple enough. Trambusti was the man through whom I had the honor of making authorized consignments of grain to the Austrian supply officer in Trieste."

"Yes, Trieste is his residence, but not Serravalle."

"What of that? The consignments that passed through Serravalle were ordered by the same Trambusti."

"Didn't you see there an unusual and suspicious coincidence?"

"How do you mean, suspicious?"

"Didn't this seem to indicate that the grain nominally delivered to

Serravalle went on to Trieste?" The judge was annoyed at having to answer his own questions.

"The coupons were my only concern," Vergoli protested. "Tell me, what would you think of me if I were so presumptuous as to raise doubts about trusted government servants? As far as I knew the grain was unloaded at Serravalle. I neither know nor wish to know anything more about it."

Did not these last words exactly echo those of Count Folicaldi? Vergoli could not but smile to himself at the memory. Meanwhile the examination of the books went forward and it became more and more clear that the customs officials and hence their chief, Virginio Alpi, were mixed up in the affair. The magistrate did not wish to go further into anything so compromising without precise instructions from the Apostolic Delegate in person.

For this reason he did not question Giuseppe Scacerni, much less Sergeant Solimani and Corporal Barbacinti, who arrived upon the scene a few minutes after the magistrate's departure. These two caught sight of Moia, the sheriff, coming out of the garden with his tail between his legs on the way back to Guarda. They hailed him loudly and made fun of his hangdog air, branding him a contented cuckold and laughing uproariously over the foolhardiness he had shown in setting himself up against Pietro Vergoli and locking horns (here they made the appropriate gesture under his nose) with so powerful a man as Virginio Alpi.

"You'll see how he breaks you," shouted the irate Solimani. "You'll find out the price of betrayal. I wouldn't give a penny for your hide, even if they do say donkey skins made good drums."

Moia was no saint, but they stood around him like the Jews in the High Priest's house around Jesus and very nearly struck him in the face in order to make up for their recent anxiety. He was a minor cause of their woe but they had a mind to take it out on him because he had exceeded the role of a mere officer of the law and tried to win promotion by passing on information about things that were, after all, common knowledge, and by presuming to sit in judgment upon them.

"Here you are left empty-handed because the chickens have flown the coop," jeered the sergeant. "And when they come home to roost you'll be worse off than before."

Pietro Vergoli looked on at the scene with the offended expression of a man who has been unjustly put upon and does not deign to revile his lying accuser. And Moia too was painfully silent, as if he were just awakening to the enormity of his miscalculation.

"Let him go," Vergoli said contemptuously. "I don't want to see him around here any longer."

Giuseppe told at this point what malicious joy Moia always displayed when he came to the mill to announce a new tax. One might have thought it was going into his own pockets.

"Some of it does stick there, you can be sure," said Sergeant Solimani. "Never you mind, we'll catch him red-handed some day."

468

"I feel quite certain," Giuseppe added, "that during the previous cholera epidemic he was the one who spied on me and tried to send me to my death in quarantine."

"Naturally, of course, who else could it be?" Corporal Barbacinti said gravely. Usually he had only to open his mouth to arouse general laughter. But this time everyone nodded assent and he was encouraged to say something more.

"If I didn't know that we have Virginio Alpi to protect us I'd be scared stiff. I might even make my way to safety across the river."

The way his listeners jumped on him in reply only betrayed their own nervousness.

"What sort of stupid talk is that? Why should anyone cross the river? There's nothing to be scared of. It's all fixed up now. You must be joking, Corporal Barbacinti."

And Sergeant Blister said in an oily voice:

"Corporal, we're all honest men."

"Not quite *all*, Sergeant," the corporal answered

"Ask Signor Pietro," said Solimani, pointing to him. "If he's honest, then it's safe to say all the rest of us are."

As Vergoli went over the questioning in his mind he felt sure that he had said just the right thing, not a word too much or too little. He was as pleased with himself as he had been worried a few minutes before. For no sooner had he taken cover behind the name of Virginio Alpi than the magistrate seemed to have lost all enthusiasm for his task and it looked as if his inquiry would go no further. But his satisfaction on this score was marred by the thought that Alpi would undoubtedly ask for a larger cut of his profits. And he was annoyed by the impudent familiarity of Solimani, Alpi's awkward and servile subordinate.

"Sergeant," he said abruptly, "for some time now I've meant to tell you to talk less freely and to behave in a more dignified manner. I have nothing to discuss with you."

"What's the matter?" asked the sergeant insolently. "Do you mind hearing it said that Virginio Alpi is our protector and that we are honest men?"

"You talk too much, that's all, and if you must know, I'm tired of seeing you hang about the house. Your place is down at the customs."

"As you please," said Solimani, shifting to a servile tone. "I didn't think I had said anything amiss . . ."

"You talk too much, that's all I was saying, but there are times when it amounts to the same thing. These are days that call for the exercise of discretion. There's bound to be a lot of gossip about the magistrate's visit," he added, speaking to all those who stood around him, "and the thing for all of you to do if you are asked any questions is to answer that you weren't present and know nothing about it. Is that clear?"

"Perfectly," they said with conviction, each one going about his own business.

But Pietro Vergoli's worries were not over, for at this point the Apostolic Delegate was powerless to prevent the investigation from running its course, in spite of the fact that it had taken a turn quite different from anything he had expected.

At the first inkling he had of the reality of the situation he merely reiterated to himself his conviction that Alpi had nothing to do with it and was on no account to be suspected. The reader has become acquainted with Folicaldi's character well enough to know that having once made up his mind on a subject it was almost impossible to budge him. After all, what were the sources of the accusations? Rumor and anonymous letters.

"There is no surer proof that an official is performing his duty than the fact that the public maligns him," he concluded.

Relying on this maxim, whose only defect was its erroneous application, he considered every new piece of evidence against his subordinate as a further proof of innocence. But his stubborn guilelessness struck the public as an indication that he was conniving with Alpi or that the latter enjoyed protection in even higher places.

"The whole thing will be stifled in the usual way," people said at the end of every one of the numerous discussions of the case which were taking place in Ferrara and along the banks of the Po.

Toward Vergoli, Folicaldi had with unconscious perversity adopted just the contrary attitude. Instead of saying that a rich man's honesty is proved by the extent of the envy he arouses, he observed sententiously:

"*De nihilo nihil.* There's no smoke without fire, and general indignation can't be entirely without a basis. Public opinion, *consensus gentium* or *vox populi*, whichever you choose to call it, is not a mere *flatus vocis* or waste of breath. When people begin to wonder about the origins of a suddenly acquired fortune, experience teaches us that their suspicions are usually well founded."

If anyone had called to Folicaldi's attention that Virginio Alpi was living in a luxury far beyond what his salary as Superintendent of Customs would have permitted, it might have made him stop to consider. But nobody wanted to risk getting in Alpi's disfavor, his shameless self-assurance having strengthened the impression that he was all-powerful. Alpi's own confidence was so sincere that he cheered up the fearful Vergoli by telling him that if any further inquiry were to be made into smuggling at Guarda he himself would be called upon to make it.

"What about the magistrate's visit?" Vergoli asked wryly. "Did you send him?"

"That was a mere formality, a gesture to satisfy the idle gossip of the region. As for the magistrate, he took it all too seriously. You can lay your head on your pillow without fear."

470

"There are nettles in my pillow, unfortunately," groaned Vergoli, "if you know what I mean."

Alpi answered with a boisterous laugh that was not, however, without a false note. For he knew that the police and the judiciary not only operated outside his sphere of influence, but that they were actually jealous of his boastful and interfering management of his own office. Alpi had friends in Milan as well as in Rome, and he made frequent trips to one or the other, returning with all sorts of confidential messages and missions, which raised his credit with the Apostolic Delegate but made him very unpopular with the regular police. They strongly desired, even if they did not say so, to unseat him and get him out of Ferrara altogether.

"Vergoli, my fine friend, my nettled friend," he threw out contemptuously. "Folicaldi doesn't do anything without consulting me. And you can leave it to me to put everything straight with him if need be."

Not even the cleverest man can think of everything, and so it came as a complete surprise to Vergoli when Count Folicaldi, his faith in Alpi still intact, abruptly detained him one morning after a routine report on the affairs of his prefecture.

"Vergoli, your misdeeds are known to the law. You can hope for no mercy unless you make a complete confession."

"What misdeeds, Your Excellency?"

"Don't quibble. I am waiting for you to confess. Either you'll do so of your own free will, or else you'll not leave the building."

"Your Excellency, what is it?" stammered Vergoli, overcome by emotion.

"Let your conscience tell you," Folicaldi said coldly, "that is, if it isn't so hardened that you don't know what happens to those who violate and make mockery of the law."

"I violate the law?" Vergoli exclaimed, and then with real sincerity, "I make mockery of it?"

"Yes, you," said Folicaldi in a manner that showed he would neither brook further delay nor show the least indulgence.

"Since I'm completely in the dark," said Vergoli with the courage of despair, "I can only tell you that I've done nothing more than Signor Alpi, the Superintendent of Customs, advised, or rather commanded me to do."

"What?" exclaimed Folicaldi, passing from severity to indignation. "Do you dare accuse an innocent man, one whose only fault is to have trusted you too blindly?"

"I can go farther than that, Your Excellency, if the truth is going to be held against me, whatever I say."

"Farther than that? What could go farther, I ask you?"

"I've done nothing that Your Excellency hasn't known about and conveyed to me that I should do."

"Who conveyed it to you?"

"Your Excellency in person." And because Folicaldi was speechless with anger, he added, "Hear me out, Your Excellency, before you make any pronouncement. The day I told Your Excellency that Baron Pasquattini had requested grain for the Imperial Austrian troops, you gave the answer: 'I neither know nor wish to know anything about it'."

"Exactly! Of course that was my answer," Folicaldi said, unaware of what was coming next.

"Well, I thought that you meant I was to accede to Pasquattini's request without forcing Your Excellency to say either yes or . . ."

"What can you be saying?"

". . . either yes or no. In short, I believed you were telling me to exercise my own discretion without bothering you further. What else could I believe, Your Excellency, when the request came to me straight from . . ."

"From whom?" asked Folicaldi, as if he felt himself to be on the edge of a precipice.

"From the Superintendent of Customs. What was I to think?"

"Are you asking me that?"

The question was charged with astonishment and scorn, and yet even while he was voicing it Folicaldi realized that Vergoli had spoken with a certain amount of logic.

"Whom else *could* I ask, Your Excellency? After I had received what I thought was your authorization, I didn't presume to ask anyone."

If my writer's intuition has not led me astray I may at this point hazard a guess that nothing is harder for a politician or statesman to bear than a misinterpretation of his orders. Hearing his own words thrown back at him, Folicaldi was placed in this unbearable position, and the more he thought about them the angrier he grew. Vergoli was virtually accusing him of stupidity, and if Vergoli was in earnest then his stupidity was all the greater.

"Who authorized you to interpret my words in this outrageous fashion?"

"Only the words themselves, Your Excellency. And let me add this. Even if Your Excellency sends me to prison I shall never believe that anything he says or does is wrong."

"Granting then—although I don't agree—that you mistakenly took my words for an authorization, you must admit that you abused it and carried the thing to a length that is positively disgraceful."

"That's what the magistrate claimed."

"And what did you answer?"

"That my shipments to Trieste were made by virtue of a regular permit, a statement which is perfectly true."

"And what about the thousands of bushels sent through the customs station of Guarda to Serravalle?"

"I showed him the receipt coupons from the Serravalle customs."

"All that grain for Serravalle? Do you expect me to believe that?"

"I can tell Your Excellency something which I thought best not to mention to the magistrate."

"Best for whom?"

"For the reputation of Your Excellency. This system of false 'receipt

472

coupons' was thought up to meet the request of Baron Pasquattini, which was for a quantity of grain much larger than that allowed by any export permit. In fact, the quantity was so large that I had to buy it up from other merchants, at considerable loss to myself, just so as not to fail the baron and his brave Austrian troops. Until now I thought Your Excellency would prefer me to keep silent about these things, but now that Your Excellency has chosen to heed idle gossip about me, treat me like a criminal and threaten me with ruin, I shall ask permission to tell the magistrate the whole story. Your Excellency is too kind to deny me the right to defend myself. Incidentally, the Superintendent knows all about the receipt coupons too."

Folicaldi had more than one reason for feeling acute embarrassment. His own words had come back to haunt him and the consequences of the whole affair promised to be exceedingly unpleasant. Without any official phraseology to fall back on he relapsed into his characteristic indecision. In this state of mind he was even ready to admit that Vergoli might have been tempted to evildoing by a misinterpretation— malicious or not—of the words he had just quoted. And injustice was alien to his highly religious conscience. Without realizing it he demeaned himself by saying disgustedly:

"I must allow you to furnish excuses—even if they are not valid— for your outrageous mistake."

"My mistake or yours?" Vergoli thought ironically to himself, but the irony was out of place because there was no doubt of the enormity of his crime.

"I don't want to hark back to the past or to know how much money you made from the export of this grain. In consideration of your services as a prefect and the good faith you have just affirmed, I am willing to suspend all proceedings against you. That is, if you admit your error and prove that you are sorry by coming to terms and paying the proper fine to the treasury."

It shot through Vergoli's mind that the "terms" would be arranged by Virginio Alpi and he would get out of the whole thing at the cost of a few crowns. With renewed assurance he plaintively protested that any mistake he had made was in perfect good faith, that it was hard lines for him to have to bear the consequences all alone, and that he preferred a ruinous court trial to a humiliating settlement, and poverty to any spot on the reputation of his father's name and that of his sons. He carried on so tearfully that he made the Apostolic Delegate feel ill at ease and indeed conscience-stricken at having been unwittingly responsible for a simple-minded man's error. The more he thought of the obligations imposed upon him by his own superior intelligence the more disposed he was to indulgence and pity. To admit his own role, even if it was not a guilty one, in Vergoli's mistake salved both his conscience and his vanity.

"Alas, it is the fate of those in high places," he said gravely, "to suffer misunderstanding and unintentionally to allow evil to come out of good." And he sighed before adding: "I said that there were attenuating circumstances, among them the fact that I spoke to you in words too hard for you to understand, in phrases too abstract, epigrammatic and statesmanlike for the capacities of a rural prefect."

Vergoli was quick to assume the look and gestures of one deferring to statesmanship and wisdom.

"I place myself in Your Excellency's paternal hands. I shall not move a finger unless Your Excellency so orders."

Folicaldi sighed again, and now his embarrassment was increased by the suspicion that the Minister of Finance, the Cardinal Secretary of State, and His Holiness himself would not hold him in very high esteem. Pius IX was known among his intimates for his biting wit, which had taken on an even bitterer note after the disappointments of 1848, and for his sudden and stubborn fits of anger. Folicaldi had enough experience of government to realize that the long-standing humiliation to which the Pope and his reign had been submitted by the Austrians would throw the present affair into a more serious light than it deserved. After all the Papal government had had to put up with, an untimely display of servility toward the Austrians (and such, he now perceived, was the supply of grain to General Pasquattini) might be the straw that broke the camel's back. And a superintendent who superintended infractions of the law might be said to carry things a good bit too far.

While Vergoli complained the Apostolic Delegate mulled these things over and became so anxious to hush the whole thing up that he was unaware of the fact that he was begging rather than ordering Vergoli to come to terms.

The affair came to a perfect, if grotesque, conclusion when Folicaldi summoned Virginio Alpi, informed him of what he already knew, and instructed him to see that Vergoli came to financial terms such as to make amends for his misdeeds and cover the payment of his derelict taxes. He had been led to believe that this was the proper thing to do by political considerations and by the sincere repentance of the guilty man. Now he awaited only a word of advice from the Superintendent of Customs.

Alpi listened to him with an expression whose severity was tempered by respect for the infinite wisdom of his superior.

"It is meet and right, I say, since I am called upon for an opinion, that as appointed governor of the legation of Ferrara Your Excellency should have a heart open to mercy. But mercy is the prerogative of rulers; I who am a mere official can take into account nothing but the proper functioning of my office. Since Your Excellency has ordered me to speak and it is my duty promptly to obey, I feel obliged to state that in the face of such large-scale smuggling and the falsification of legal papers, wrapped up, of course, with truly fearful dishonesty and profiteering, my duty is all too clear. I must find out exactly what private and public damage has been done, punish all the guilty, and see that the treasury is reimbursed as it should be. *Debellare superbos*, or in other words, strike down the proud!"

Vergoli shot a keen look at the speaker of these words. Could he possibly mean them or was he merely joking? Folicaldi, on his part, covered his uncertainty behind a solemn and frowning expression. He leaned his chin on his left hand, which was propped up on the table, and with his right gripped the arm of his heavy gilded chair, on whose back were embroidered the crown and keys of the Papal emblem.

"Quite right, and beautifully expressed in the bargain," he said, swallowing hard, "but still I incline toward mercy."

"Then your inclination is my command," Alpi said smugly. "And my motto *parcere subiectis,* to spare those who have been laid low."

Vergoli's sigh of relief was so deep that it rustled some of the papers on Folicaldi's table. The Apostolic Delegate had a sudden stabbing memory that Alpi himself was at the bottom of the fraud. He blushed with shame, aware that he did not have the courage to put the discussion on the proper plane.

"What terms does the defendant offer by way of reparation?" Alpi continued.

"Twelve hundred crowns," breathed Vergoli.

"From Your Excellency's brief account of his crime, I should call that a ridiculous sum," Alpi said, adding before his superior could make any comment, "but ridiculous as it may be, it is up to Your Excellency's mercy. If Your Excellency commands me to transmit it to the Ministry of Finance in Rome I shall do so without delay. But I should like to make a humble suggestion."

"You may."

"If this offer were accompanied by the full story, such as Your Excellency tells me the magistrate uncovered, then it would seem quite out of proportion to the extent of his dishonesty. In fact, our whole conduct of the affair would be discredited."

Vergoli was again thrown into consternation while Folicaldi approved what Alpi was saying. And Alpi went on to suggest further that the Apostolic Delegate order the magistrate to desist from his inquiry and give him time to forward Vergoli's terms after phrasing them in an appropriate manner. This proposal was accepted, and as soon as Vergoli and Alpi had joined forces outside the delegate's office Alpi exclaimed, rubbing his hands:

"Now we have him just where we want him."

"How do you mean?" asked Vergoli without enthusiasm.

"Don't you see? If the inquiry is stifled and he consents to sending an inexact report to Rome, then we can hold it over him for the rest of his days."

"I'm not so demanding. All I ask is to get out of it by the skin of my teeth. Good Lord, the fright I've been through!"

"What a chickenhearted fellow you are!" And he added, laughing: "Yes, yes, just think, twelve hundred crowns . . ."

"Twelve hundred crowns . . . Exactly."

"A mess of pottage!" Alpi exclaimed. "A mess of pottage in return for Esau's rights as the first-born! Why, my dear fellow, you're positively a miser! Think that over, after all the political wisdom you've heard from the lips of our exalted Apostolic Delegate! Remember that you ought to go to jail for your corruption!"

"*My* corruption?"

"If you had any accomplices, pray name them!" said Alpi boldly. "But let's stick to the point. For the crime of smuggling alone you are subject to the following penalties: first, repayment of everything of which you have defrauded the customs; second, confiscation of all your smuggled goods; third, since the goods are out of reach, *in partibus infidelium,* a reimbursement of their full value; fourth, a fine amounting to three times this value; fifth . . . But you can see without adding it all up that it comes to many tens of thousands of crowns!"

Vergoli shuddered.

"And you, Alpi," he asked so solemnly that his interlocutor could not help laughing, "aren't you bothered by the mention of such astronomical sums?"

"My friend, I've stood up for you right along and shall continue to do so. But I don't intend to be taken for your accomplice."

"But aren't you just that?"

"I advise you to rid yourself of such illusions at once unless you wish to lose them later in a far more painful fashion. And in case you contemplate blackmailing me, remember that such things nauseate as well as amuse me, and I don't usually leave them unpunished. If, on the contrary, you behave decently, I'll go to Rome myself to plead your cause and persuade them to close the case upon your miserly payment of twelve hundred crowns. Otherwise . . . well, do you remember that I said to you the first time we met: *Expedit ut unus pro populo morietur,* it is necessary that one man be sacrificed for the good of the people? Now I add that it may suit *my* convenience to let both you and the people be scapegoats."

And to Rome Alpi went, in the winter of 1856, to traffic in every conceivable fashion. He handed out bribes where they were acceptable, held himself out to the Minister of Finance as a faithful public servant and to the Secretary of State as a judicious politician, softened any blame that he could not escape, falsified accusations that he could not deny and enlarged everything that spoke in his favor. As an explanation of the whole affair he broached the suspicion that revolutionary and Liberal intriguers were trying to cast out of Ferrara the long-standing enemy who had broken so many of their ribs when he was a Gregorian volunteer and Sanfedista.

Alpi had friends of old vintage and new in all the government offices, and these he rallied to his support. He flaunted himself as a scourge of the Liberals and a trusted adviser of the Austrian staff. So it was that eventually he was able to write to Vergoli and Salvi that the little matter of smuggling had been buried under a stone so heavy that it would not be lifted before Judgment Day. The boastful and talkative Salvi proceeded to extoll the power and prestige of Virginio Alpi,

476

threatening and making fun of all those who had ever doubted them. Soon this was common gossip in the cafés of Ferrara.

The magistrate's inquiry was quite obviously leading into the ground. Times were better and Vergoli smuggled no more than was necessary for his ordinary business, having given up all dealing in grain. Giuseppe Scacerni mourned the loss of his profitable trade.

"Those were the days!" he sighed whenever he met Pietro Vergoli.

But Vergoli answered:

"To tell the truth, Scacerni, I'm glad to have put aside something that I never liked doing."

Giuseppe shrugged his shoulders. Now that Vergoli's barges no longer loaded their cargoes there, the dikes of Nogarole had returned to being the quiet anchorage of the old Saint Michael's and the still older Bitter Bread Mill. How many millstones had been flattened and worn down, how many joints and nails and screws replaced since their mill wheels had been turning. Over the oak door of the cabin on the larger of St. Michael's hulks Master Lazzaro had printed with a red-hot nail the date of the mill's launching, that of his son's birth, and the major floods of his time. Cecilia, who had never learned to read and write, although she carried in her head all the mill's accounts, begged her husband to continue this tradition. But when he asked her the date of Bitter Bread's construction she was at a loss to answer him.

"That's like asking about the age of the moon," observed Schiavetto.

Schiavetto had long since resigned himself to Cecilia's marriage, to the point, indeed, where he no longer remembered having loved her. His natural respect forbade anything else, and besides he had begun to age and was shot through with rheumatic pains. Giuseppe would have liked to discharge him, but Cecilia would hear no word of it.

"You'd treat a human being the way you treated your poor old horse, Lightning."

"That's what it would really be practical to do when a man's no more use."

"Don't think of it again. I'll engage a boy to help Schiavetto with his work. If for no other reason, I'd do it out of respect for the memory of your father, a man who made only one mistake all his life long."

"The mistake of having a son like me, I suppose you mean. Speak freely; I shan't take offense."

The fact is that Cecilia ruled over the mills. She slept aboard them most of the time, spending only an occasional night in the house at Poplar Bridge, as a concession to her husband's special request and to her own longing for more children. As for Giuseppe, he claimed that he could not properly play the part of a husband on the water. Another one of his peculiarities, and a truly ludicrous one!

Meanwhile, as we have said, the judicial inquiry proceeded at a snail's pace, with the hearing of any number of witnesses from Guarda and Ro, most of whom swore they knew nothing, although a few admitted to having heard rumors about the smuggling of grain and some people took advantage of the occasion to give vent to their ire over the bullying attitude of Solimani, or Sergeant Blister. Giuseppe Scacerni was one of those questioned and his statement was among the shortest.

"If they loaded grain down at the Nogarole dikes I should have been the first to know about it, because that's the anchorage of my wife's mill and mine. Occasionally, when the water was too shallow at the regular customs landing, a barge did come to load in the vicinity and grapple onto the mills. So that if smuggling on a large scale had been going on I could hardly have failed to see it. But I should never have countenanced such a thing. Do you think I'd risk going to jail for someone else's sake? No, sir, not I."

Vergoli's right-hand man, Olmeda, testified that nothing out of the way could have happened at Nogarole, because the dikes were plainly visible from the customs station. And when finally a surveyor came to measure this distance and others connected with the scene of the crime, everyone caught on to the fact that the inquiry was being dragged out only in order to throw dust in the public's eyes.

Meanwhile, however, the tombstone that Alpi had promised would seal the affair forever failed to arrive from Rome. Alpi himself did come back and swaggered about in such an ostentatious manner that wise men began to say that he must be less sure than he seemed.

6

If anyone has the curiosity to look through files of crumbling documents he will find written in faded ink on the back of one of them that in an audience of May 14, 1856, His Holiness the Pope turned down an offer of twelve hundred crowns in amends for smuggling in the region of Ferrara, which smuggling was concerned with 12,000 bushels of wheat, 2000 bushels of beans, and 40,000 pounds of rice. We read that His Holiness was "deeply interested in the prosecution of the case" and wished it to be carried through regardless of fear or favor. This meant that it would eventually pass into the hands of the Criminal Division of the Apostolic Chamber of Rome.

The Pope's decision meant the ruin of Vergoli, who, considering the prevalence of this particular kind of corruption, did not deserve so hard a fate, and the punishment of Alpi, who merited no indulgence whatsoever.

The Peace of Paris was signed in the same month of March, thereby putting an end to the Crimean War, and the year that followed was among the most important of this eventful decade when Italian national unity was in the making. After the conclusion of the peace treaty Cavour gave the signatories a demonstration of statesmanship so subtle that not all of them knew what he was driving at. For political genius lies in taking advantage of existing situations and turning them to profit in such a way that the will of a single man appears to be that of history. Heedless of superficialities and armed with the

478

fateful assurance of a prophet Cavour laid Italy's case on the table. And the immediate result of this bold action was to discredit the Papal government, whose inability to rule and unsteady dependence on French and Austrian garrisons was a positive menace to the peace of Europe. The Vienna treaties of 1815 had tried to impose the idea that the neutrality of the Papacy and the restoration of the various parts of Italy to legitimate kings were conducive to law and order and to the balance of European power. Now a newly awakened national feeling throughout the peninsula threatened to upset everything.

So it was that the Piedmontese Cavour used his diplomatic genius to persuade Austria that by striving to maintain its position of influence in Italy it was sacrificing the principle of balance of power in Europe. And at the same time he worked upon the cabinets in London and Paris to urge the Papal government to follow a stronger and yet more Liberal policy, knowing perfectly well that it would never accede to their solicitations. Indeed, the Holy See's refusal, as voiced by Pius IX himself and Cardinal Antonelli, was even angrier than Cavour could have hoped for, which indicated how completely the Papal government was under Austrian domination and how powerless it was to take any independent action.

The Pope and his Secretary of State could not help obscurely realizing that their policy, together with that of the various Italian princelings, was losing prestige every day and degenerating into a negative and jealous fear of the growing power of Piedmont. They took refuge in the true but overly sentimental assertion that they enjoyed "the affection of the people," a phrase unhappily reminiscent of Metternich and the period of "enlightened despotism." Pius IX failed to realize even during his trip through the provinces in the spring of 1857 that this affection was of a religious character, unconnected with his political conduct, to which the masses were indifferent and persons of intelligence actively opposed. As for the princelings, they were neither enlightened nor despotic, but simply a group of weak men huddled under Austrian protection.

All this was in the air in the spring of 1856 when the Pope received a report of the guilt of Virginio Alpi, whom he already knew as an enraged Sanfedista and profane critic, a troublemaker during the Liberal reforms and a pillar of the ensuing reaction. Now the Pope might be grateful for the support of Austria, but not to one of his own subjects who had turned into an Austrian agent and used Austrian influence to secure an official position, which he was now accused of brazenly abusing.

Just because a man—either a sovereign or a private individual—has put up with a great deal from someone stronger than himself, it does not follow that he will submit to every attempt to get the better of him. And we may presume that the excuse of supplying grain to the Austrian supply officer, which had so effectively quieted Folicaldi, struck Pius IX as a bit of provocative insolence. It was symptomatic of the disorganization and weakness of the government that a public official should have violated its tariff policy to his own profit with such shameless impunity.

It is deeply satisfying to dig out of dusty files this evidence of a case where the Pope took decisive action and ordered justice to be done, for his government had too often let itself be hoodwinked on the pretext of *quieta non movere*, or let sleeping dogs lie. It would have been even better, in this case, to act with speed instead of letting the case drag on while Alpi, who was sure that the Austrians would protect him, maintained his cocky demeanor until he heard that a mandate for his arrest had been issued. Up to the very last minute he hung on to his office and tried to bluff and bribe his way to safety.

There is satisfaction in this example of justice because we have for too long witnessed a tendency to belittle the governments of the last century, those that preceded the nation's final unification. To some extent they deserve to be judged harshly, but the habit of underestimating them has been carried too far and led to an unconscious abasement of the Italian character. A time comes when discussion colored by party strife must give way to history and when to drag it out further is a proof of ungenerous and ridiculous prejudice, a revenge taken upon those who are not only defeated but dead. God is pure love and justice and His kingdom is not of this world, but an earthly government, if it is to be strong and successful, must proceed on just the opposite principles. So let us not charge the Papal government with iniquity simply because it was weak. For my own part I must admit that I should have been distressed to hear such a charge even in the mouth of Cavour. And yet Cavour was right. Which is one of the reasons why I have chosen to be the historian of the plain people of Italy, who knew little of political conflicts and cared less. These, through trials and tribulations, have kept their own morality, religion and civilization, and above all a language with which to defend and glorify them. For the glory of the Italian language is due no less to the plain people than to the illustrious writers. And considering the adverse circumstances under which the people preserved and handed down this inheritance their achievement partakes of the miraculous.

7

Virginio Alpi, with his guilt fastened upon him, chose to run away rather than face arrest, thus stripping "the Ferrarese smuggling case," as it was called in the court records in Rome, of its political interest and leaving Vergoli to bear the brunt of the penalty. Vergoli too, for a time, contemplated fleeing, but finally he was granted a safe-conduct with which to appear before the court of his own free will and defend himself without being previously thrown into jail. Apparently the court was inclined to treat him leniently. Meanwhile Alpi crossed the border, never to return, and ended his days living in obscurity at Graz and drawing an Austrian pension. This was the final proof, if any was needed, of his betrayal. And we shall see him no more.

Up to the time of Alpi's escape (which took place in September of 1856) Giuseppe Scacerni lay low. He had profited handsomely from the affair, having deposited a certain amount of money in the Annobon bank and bought a piece of land adjacent to his own which brought the boundaries of Poplar Bridge Farm right up to the road.

This piece of land, whose actual value was very small, had for many years attracted first Dosolina then her son. But the owners, a family from Ro, had caught on to the fact that their neighbors valued it for more than its intrinsic worth and resolved not to give it up so easily. Every time that Dosolina and Giuseppe had to take the path through this property in order to reach the road they cast cautious but acquisitive eyes at the few square rods of earth on either side that excited their envy. Many a time they would have put out feelers for its purchase had they not feared putting "those people"—who were constantly on their minds and rarely on their tongues—even more on the defensive. For "those people" were already vigilant and when third parties approached them with an offer for the land they said they were far too attached to it to contemplate selling. So year after year went by and Dosolina never attained her desire. Indeed the matter had occasioned something very like a quarrel between Dosolina and Giuseppe on one side and Lazzaro on the other. One day when Lazzaro, who had little interest in questions of money and gain, was walking along the path with Giuseppe he called out to his neighbor:

"Hello there, Dal Pero" (for such was the neighbor's name), "hello!"

"At your service, Master Lazzaro. What is it?"

And Giuseppe shuddered to hear his father laugh into his beard and answer:

"At yours, Dal Pero, whenever you need me. Meanwhile just sell me this bit of land, because my wife and son are dying to have it. Their tongues hang out as if they were a pair of dogs every time they go by. Help me to escape from their nagging, there's a good fellow."

Dal Pero and his sons joined in Master Lazzaro's laughter and so did Giuseppe, who was green with rage within. He and his mother were convinced that the miller had thus ruined their chances once and for all. But Master Lazzaro said:

"Come, come, don't you suppose Dal Pero already knew? If he were really so stupid, one glance at your faces would tell him. You look as if you had a bellyache!" And he laughed again, irritating them all the more.

Later on came the famine and Dal Pero was reduced to misery. He offered his land to Pietro Vergoli, who had no use for it and advised him to sell it to Giuseppe Scacerni. To Giuseppe this was an opportunity for revenge.

"My mother suffered too much from your obstinacy," he said. "You knew how much she wanted your land and took delight in thwarting her. And all the time it mattered to you very little."

"I was just looking after my own interest, God help me."

"And I am looking after mine, God help me, too!"

"But we've no bread, we're starving, Scacerni. It's a question of Christian charity. Think of my little grandchildren who are crying for something to eat. God grant that in your house you may never hear such a cry."

"I'm disposed to show you Christian charity," Giuseppe said hypocritically, "but I've something on my conscience."

"What's that? To let your neighbor die when you have the power to save him so easily?"

"My mother died with this unfulfilled longing. You don't know how she ate her heart out over it for forty long years. That's what brought about her early death."

"Come now, Scacerni. The good woman died of cholera, didn't she, God rest her soul!"

Giuseppe realized that he had gone too far and took another tack, equally hypocritical.

"I say it was your fault if she died unhappy. And she left instructions to me in her will that I should not compromise on the price of your land. So that no matter how charitably I may be inclined I can't trespass against her memory. If I were to offer you a single crown more I'd feel that I was adding to her pains in purgatory."

With this sanctimonious reasoning he offered a shameful price, which Dal Pero had to accept, murmuring the while that Giuseppe was the sort to give away the bone of the corn meal, that just as the miller had once said, he was like the soldier who gave Our Lord vinegar rather than waste a drop of good wine.

Giuseppe Scacerni had a good head for business, and the next to discover it was Pietro Vergoli. When Vergoli found himself in trouble he took Giuseppe aside one day and spoke to him about a farm known as the Ca' Morgosa, between the Strada dell'Antonella and the road between the river and Ro.

"Look here, Scacerni," he said, "the Ca' Morgosa is coming up for sale, and you can see that it's to my advantage to buy it to add to the adjoining Antonella."

"Yes, Signor Pietro, I see."

"Then you can see something else, besides, without my stopping to explain it to you."

But it was Giuseppe's principle never to appear to understand anything.

"I am an ignorant man, Signor Pietro. Your explanation won't offend me." And he twisted his fingers with a stupid air.

Vergoli had his back to the wall. The police were examining his affairs and the magistrate was drawing up a case against him, based on the testimony of his neighbors. In fact, it was just at this time that Vergoli was thinking of fleeing abroad. He was in no mood to argue over trifles and Giuseppe's attitude struck him as being sincerely humble rather than malicious. And so he said patiently:

"With this devilish case against me, it's no time for me to spend

482

money on land. What would people say? Besides, since the court is accusing me . . ."

"What?" said Giuseppe. "Are you in trouble before the court, Signor Pietro?"

"No," Vergoli answered nervously. "It's my enemies. My enemies are conspiring against me, but they'll never dare come out with it. Everything will be all right in the end . . ."

Here a sly look from Giuseppe caused him to repeat in a louder voice:

"It will be all right in the end, but meanwhile I must be prudent."

"Yes, prudence is always advisable. And even if your friends don't dare come out against you, supposing the magistrate suspects you of having hidden assets and for safety's sake puts a lien on your visible holdings . . ."

"What? How do you know about such things?"

"Oh, I'm a poor country bumpkin," said Giuseppe, but there was a touch of self-esteem beneath his affected humility. "Although my good mother used to say I was cut out to be a lawyer."

"Surely they'll not have the cheek to put a lien on my properties!" Vergoli shouted in alarm.

"Nobody says that," said Giuseppe evasively.

"I say it myself!"

"Who could have the preposterous notion of putting a lien on the properties of Signor Pietro Vergoli?"

"Unfortunately there *are* people who air this preposterous notion," said Vergoli sadly, "and that's just why it would be imprudent for me to . . ." and he fumbled for the word to express what he meant.

"To make yourself conspicuous by adding to your holdings, is that it?" supplied Giuseppe.

"Exactly. Of course I'm sure everything will turn out all right eventually, because I have Count Alpi and the Minister of Finance and the Secretary of State in Rome all on my side. That's something, isn't it?"

"I don't know the last two gentlemen you mention," said Giuseppe with a sleepy expression on his face because the lids were half lowered over his colorless eyes, "but I've seen more than enough of the first, I can tell you."

"So have I!" Vergoli exclaimed without thinking, then he recovered himself and added without conviction: "You must be joking. I hold him in esteem."

Several days before, on July 8, 1856, Folicaldi had been relieved of the post of Apostolic Delegate and transferred as a state councillor to Rome. And his hasty, almost surreptitious departure had given rise to considerable gossip, some people maintaining that Alpi's head would be the next to fall and others pointing out Folicaldi's departure as the latest of Alpi's successful machinations and a punishment for the delegate's failure to stifle the investigation. Vergoli's position was insecure and he muttered more for his own benefit than for that of Giuseppe:

"Meanwhile Folicaldi's paid a stiff price."

"I don't know any gentleman of that name, either."

Pietro Vergoli lost patience completely.

"Nobody asked whether you know him or not. What should it matter to me?"

"I simply mean that you're wasting your breath when you try to impress me with so many great names." Giuseppe's words were almost insolent, but he preserved a downcast look and a humble tone. "I came to hear how I can best serve you, Signor Pietro," he added.

"Good. That's the right idea. I have chosen you because I know you for an honest man and the son of an honest man."

"You are too kind."

"The point is this: I'll give you the money and you must buy Ca' Morgosa. Later on, when all the fuss has died down, we'll make out a bill of sale from you to me. Of course, you'll be rewarded for your pains."

"That's the least of my worries. But what will people say to my being able to spend so much in the first place?"

"Everyone says you're a prosperous man."

"That's just the chatter of idle tongues, the product of unbridled imagination."

"Then you won't do me this favor?"

"I don't say no. But I too must move with circumspection."

"Has the magistrate questioned you lately?"

"Not since that first time at your house, when I said no smuggling could have gone on near the mill without my seeing it."

"An excellent answer. I shan't forget that, either. As a matter of fact, all the witnesses, even if they aren't as quick-witted as you, have testified in my favor."

"Then how is it that so many of them have gone to jail?" Giuseppe asked maliciously.

"Because they're stupid louts who don't know how to express themselves the way you do, and get all mixed up when they're called into court, or else they try to be clever and end up in even greater confusion. Some have gone to jail, it's true, but they'll not stay there long, and meanwhile I send them extra food through the prison warden."

"Very generous of you. But if I were in their shoes I'd cause you no such expense."

"You have nothing to fear, I assure you."

"Of course, if I have the assurance of a man as educated as you are . . ."

"You can trust me absolutely."

"I trust you well enough, but you must give me some cash to cover current expenses, to pay the peasants and make a few necessary improvements. When a piece of property changes hands, there's always work to be done. And I know the Ca' Morgosa. It's been badly neglected, the farm buildings are in disrepair, the drainage ditches are choked up, the fields are fallow, and there aren't enough hands to take

484

care of it. It's the kind of place where the owner settles his accounts on New Year's Eve instead of Saint Michael's Day."

In the Ferrara region it was customary to date the year's financial transactions from the feast of Saint Michael; hence the saying: "If Saint Michael's Day is of good cheer, it means a full belly all the year." But certain avaricious and dishonest landowners, who found it advantageous that the peasants should be perpetually in debt and have to borrow money at interest instead of receiving their just due, refused to settle accounts with them before the New Year. In this way they could charge them for their purchase of daily necessities at the highest possible price, whether it was the one prevailing at the time of the harvest or at the end of the year. And Giuseppe knew that Pietro Vergoli did not condone this ungenerous practice.

"Do you know so much about farming?" Vergoli asked him with a mixture of satisfaction and uneasiness.

"Just what I picked up when I kept accounts for my mother."

"I'm not asking you to go to any trouble," said Vergoli. "You needn't as much as set foot on the Ca' Morgosa farm. My man Olmeda will take care of all that."

"What sort of figure shall I cut under such circumstances?"

"You'll be paid for that too," said Vergoli impatiently.

"A pretty poor figure, I say. But never mind about that, as long as it's to please you. Only what will people say?"

"What does that matter?"

"They'll say that you're the real owner."

"I don't give a hang what they say. What matters is that for the time being my name should not appear on the bill of sale."

"Yes, of course. As long as the wind is blowing from the wrong direction," said Giuseppe pensively.

For Pietro Vergoli's sake, Giuseppe did what was asked of him. But a little more than a week later Olmeda crossed the river in order to avoid going to jail. Soon after, before it was time for sowing, fate overtook Virginio Alpi and he too disappeared, followed, although not permanently, by Vergoli. So it was that Giuseppe took charge of the Ca' Morgosa farm after all. He saw to it that the clods of earth upturned by the August plowing should be broken by the hoe and the harrow, properly fertilized, and then laid out in rows such as to facilitate drainage, which was always a problem to achieve so near to the banks of the river. It was a race with time to accomplish the sowing before a change in the weather.

The finishing touches to the preparation of the soil reflected the experience of centuries and were given by the oldest of the peasants, who went over the furrows with the point of the shovel. The furrows spread in a network over the fields in the wake of numberless tiny veins of water. These they now followed, now turned away from, while piled up on either side of them was the fertile gray earth of the Po Valley, broken now into clods of the proper size that emanated a delicate but rich smell. The peasant possessed the inherited art of knowing the

485

land inch by inch and of being able to tell from the color of the soil or the sprouting of an unsuspected blade of grass that in such and such a spot the moisture seeped through from the river or stood in a stagnant pool after rain, where it might stunt the growth of hemp or wheat or whatever the crop might be. Following these signs he used the point of the shovel to trace minute canals to draw off the water of the autumn rains, the winter snows and the spring showers and lead it into progressively larger drainage ditches. Instinctively and without the aid of any instrument he knew how to make an incline of a few inches along a hundred-yard furrow. This was the peasant's final working-over of the earth before he opened his bag of seed and scattered it in handfuls with the practiced gesture of the sower, at the head of a line of men, women and children, who covered it lightly over with rakes and hoes until the day when it should push up out of the earth, bearing the hope of the next year's harvest. And at the end of every row they planted a cross made of wood or hemp stalks that had been blessed by the priest.

Giuseppe Scacerni followed the peasant's work on a fine October day, which boded well for the sowing, and the two of them exchanged a few words of observation and advice, and cautious good-luck wishes. Strangely enough Giuseppe felt a sudden and violent affection for Ca' Morgosa such as his own Poplar Bridge property had never inspired. Leaning over every now and then to pick up a clod of earth, crumble it between his fingers and smell it, he had for the first time an urge to be a farmer. When Pietro Vergoli came back, he reflected, he would receive a cash reward for his work, and yet he began to wish, half unconsciously, that Vergoli would never come.

While he indulged in this half-formulated reflection he saw a man start along the path winding among the furrows and soon recognized him as Moia, the hated sheriff, who signalled that he wanted a word with him. Giuseppe did not respond, but waited for him to come closer.

"You might have saved me this bit of walking," Moia said angrily as he came upon the scene.

"When I come to see you then you may set the rules for my behavior, but when you're a visitor on my property . . ."

"So this property is yours, is it?"

"As far as you're concerned it is."

"Go on with you! As if everybody didn't know that it belongs to someone who's moved away for the sake of his health."

"Everybody may know it, Moia, but that's no reason why you should know."

"Why not?"

"Because in your business there's something I can tell you to your advantage. In this field you'll see wheat sprouting, but not sneaks and spies. When one of them is laid away in the ground he'll not sprout again, you can take my word for it."

Giuseppe's voice must have echoed some of the resolution of his father's, for Moia did not pursue the argument further, but contented himself with announcing:

"Giuseppe Scacerni, otherwise known as Were Rabbit, the honorable magistrate of the court is at Guarda today, together with his clerk, and he requests your presence there immediately."

"What does he want with me?"

"He'll tell you that himself."

"Very well. I'll come along."

Giuseppe presented himself before the magistrate with no misgivings. He was sure that the questions would be the same as before and he had only to give the same answers. Instead, after a few vague preliminaries, the magistrate said to him harshly:

"Giuseppe Scacerni, you've made a lot of money."

"Yes, by working hard at my trade," Giuseppe answered promptly.

"Is that all?"

"What do you mean, sir? I was a middleman and buyer, and I had no business asking questions."

"In fact your curiosity was so slight that you didn't even notice the loading of grain at the Nogarole dikes or at Guarda Crossing."

"I had no occasion to hang about either of those places," said Giuseppe. "My business required me to travel around the country. I was a commission agent and as such . . ."

"You must have made some very handsome commissions," the magistrate interrupted.

Giuseppe goggled. Did the magistrate know or suspect under what circumstances he had bought the Ca' Morgosa farm? Was he speaking ironically? As a matter of fact, the magistrate was simply trying another approach to the question of how much merchandise had actually been smuggled out of the country.

"I had no reason to know anything . . ." Giuseppe added weakly, but the magistrate interrupted.

"Listen carefully," he said. "I'm indicting you for complicity in the proven crime of smuggling and illegal exportation of large quantities of grain through both the Polesella customs station and Guarda Crossing, in violation of the decree of His Eminence the Cardinal Secretary of State dated the 27th of July, *anno millesimo octingentesimo et quinquagesimo tertio recuperatae salutis.*"

These Latin words achieved Giuseppe's confusion and he blinked his eyes as if he were listening to a sentence of execution.

"A poor buyer like myself . . ." he stammered.

"An honest buyer, working for an honest commission, doesn't suddenly make enough money to purchase large pieces of land."

Through his confusion Giuseppe obscurely realized the necessity of justifying the transaction of the Ca' Morgosa farm.

"Don't forget that I have just come into the money left me by my father," he offered.

"Don't bring your father into it; he was an honest man!" the judge said severely, more persuaded than ever that Giuseppe was directly involved in the smuggling.

But Giuseppe persisted in putting his foot in it.

"You see, sir, it was just as you said . . ."

487

"What did I say?"

"I earned large commissions because I bought up commodities on a large scale: hundreds of wagonloads and thousands of bushels of wheat and rice and beans . . ."

"And you said before that you didn't know they were being shipped down the river or what was their destination? That was so patently false a statement as to count against you from the start."

"Perhaps when you questioned me before, my memory failed me or I was too anxious to save others from being hurt . . ."

"It didn't require much memory when the loading was still going on, and just at the site of your mills."

"Well, when the water level was low at the Crossing, perhaps they made some use of our anchorage. . . . I was afraid when you called me in last time and couldn't think clearly."

"Very well," said the magistrate, cutting short Giuseppe's floundering attempts to justify his gains. "Meanwhile I place you under arrest as a reluctant and false witness, such as you have just confessed yourself to be."

"I can't believe . . ."

"You'll be locked up this very day in the San Paolo prison in Ferrara. Clerk, let me have the verbatim record you have been keeping."

When he had signed the record and made Scacerni sign it, the magistrate ordered the horses to be hitched to his carriage and turned Giuseppe over to the gendarmes. From the front of the house came a clamor of peasant voices.

"They're taking Were Rabbit to jail!"

At first the clamor was a festive one, as if to greet some pleasant surprise like the arrival of an itinerant sword swallower or a miraculous medicine man. But the magistrate's carriage was old and rusty and it took some time to put the horses in harness. Gradually the clamor lost its simple and joyful sound and took on the malicious tone of delight in another's misfortune. This delight was all the keener because several men from Guarda had been arrested for false testimony or failure to testify and it had seemed as if Giuseppe alone enjoyed some sort of impunity. Not that anyone took the jail sentences very seriously, for they were all convinced that the investigation would peter out and that all those who had suffered for Pietro Vergoli's sake would receive abundant compensation. Indeed the news of the good food he had sent to the prisoners, which rumor had magnified beyond its modest proportions, had consolidated his reputation for generosity and made many of the peasants say they only wished they could have some of the same treatment. As for Giuseppe, no one in the village saw much of him, for he never set foot in the tavern and did not linger after early Mass on Sunday morning. Now, all of a sudden, seeing him in trouble they shouted:

"They're taking Were Rabbit to jail!"

Giuseppe's arrest first aroused their curiosity and then reawakened their long-standing dislike for his ugly face and strange ways. They

488

interpreted the isolation in which he lived as a pretense of smug superiority and credited him not with mere loyalty to Pietro Vergoli but with some ignoble crime of his own. Smuggler or no smuggler, Vergoli had given them bread and work, while Were Rabbit had put his illicit profits in the bank and continued to buy up grain and take the food out of their hungry mouths. They felt a sudden passion for justice and applauded its unexpected visitation upon their unpopular neighbor.

"They're taking Were Rabbit to jail!" they cried again.

We have said that it was a slow process to attach the horses with their stiff harness to the heavy shafts of the carriage. But there was more than time enough for the little crowd that had gathered in front of the local gendarmes' post to crystallize the accumulated resentment of the years into a collective expression of indignation. And fuel was added to the flames by the appearance, between two gendarmes, of Giuseppe in person. Hearing the crowd shouting against him Giuseppe had regained control of himself, and putting off his meek and guilty air he looked at them with some of the contempt he felt for all human kind. They stood tiptoe in order to scrutinize him more carefully and passed quickly from surprise to increased anger. For a mob is more likely to show indulgence to a discomfited guilty man than to one who is oversure of his innocence. Now they had a good look at his face because the carriage had two open seats behind the coachman's box, and in one of these sat the magistrate and his clerk while the other was reserved for the prisoner and his two guards.

"See that ugly mug on him!" a boy called out and the crowd took up his cry. "Ugly mug! Sourface! Bloodsucker!" they cried. "You've fattened on our misery long enough! Now you'll have to spit it all up; the good times are over. Go put your neck in the hangman's noose!"

And they crowded threateningly around him with clenched fists, ribald gestures and laughter.

"You'd think they expected my misfortune to line their pockets, the silly fools," Giuseppe said to his guards.

"Don't let them hear you," answered one of the gendarmes. "They might tear you limb from limb. What have you done to make them dislike you so heartily?"

"It's sheer envy," said Giuseppe.

"Well, you're welcome to think what you like, but we'd best be getting away. Is the coachman drunk again?"

Scarafuna, the coachman attached to the court of Ferrara, had lost his hat and whip and was, as usual, under the influence of liquor. The magistrate showed signs of impatience and only Giuseppe kept calm, almost as if he were enjoying the taunts from the crowd.

"If they knew how little I cared about their mockery," he said, shrugging his shoulders.

Meanwhile boys shouted in chorus:

"Were Rabbit is going away in a horse and carriage, like a great gentleman! Oh, Were Rabbit!"

Even the white-haired and decrepit Venusta Chiccoli came out into the square and shouted:

"Your father would die of shame to see you! I can tell you that because I was there when you were born!"

Surprised by the source of this attack Giuseppe put his forefinger to his forehead to signify that she had lost her mind. This was true enough as everyone knew, but they preferred to ignore it for the moment. One fellow, who was either naturally excitable or else had caught the hysteria of Venusta, cried out:

"He's insulting the woman who helped bring him into the world and held him up for baptism. Antichrist, I call him!"

The crowd was in a mood to be intoxicated with words, the bigger the better.

"Antichrist! Antichrist!" they echoed.

The magistrate was annoyed and said to his clerk:

"Antichrist, that's laying it on too thick! Thank God, here's that wretch Scarafuna, and we needn't listen to any more such nonsense."

In the last years of his life Lazzaro Scacerni had been called "Apocalypse," and now his son was branded with the epithet of "Antichrist." The coincidence is worthy of note in passing. Meanwhile Scarafuna had struggled up onto his box, cracked his whip, and shouted:

"Make way for the majesty of the law!"

The carriage started slowly to move over the rough road, but finally the horses broke into a trot and the wheels creaked so loudly that they covered up the clamor made by the good people of Guarda.

Eventually they reached the Ferrara prison, which was housed in a dispossessed Carmelite convent, and Giuseppe was turned over to the warden. He could not yet fully take in what had befallen him and the interrogation to which he had been subjected became hazy in his mind and finally faded away into a disappearing point in the distance. Probably he had made too unpremeditated and honest answers to the questions they had asked him, and these had been his undoing. In his imagination he interrogated himself all over again, answering everything in a brilliant and plausible manner. But unfortunately the questions were of his own rather than of the magistrate's devising! Meanwhile the warden entered Giuseppe's name in large and slowly-formed letters in the prison register.

"Come with me," he said, picking up a bunch of keys and leading Giuseppe through the courtyard of the former convent.

Giuseppe followed him docilely, with a guard at his side. At the end of the courtyard they went up a flight of worn stairs and stopped in front of what had once been a nun's cell.

"You're lucky to find this cell free," said the warden, "because it gets a lot of sun and air."

The narrow funnel-shaped window seemed to Giuseppe a mere mockery, through which he could see only a tiny square of twilight sky.

"Here's a mattress and you'll find a pot in the corner. You can have bed linen sent to you from home if you like. And you'll be taken down to the courtyard to wash. By the way, will you take the prison fare or do you want food brought in from a restaurant outside?"

"From a restaurant."

"A wise choice. Our fare is not bad: soup, beans, bread and water, with meat and wine on Sundays and holidays. But it's monotonous."

"You don't think I intend to stay here very long, do you?" Scacerni asked angrily.

"Is this your first time?"

"I should say it is!"

"Then take my advice and act as if you were here to stay. Otherwise the time will go by even more slowly. Meanwhile I'll pass on your order to the restaurant."

No doubt this slow-moving and hypocritical fellow took a fat fee for exploiting the prisoners' hunger, Giuseppe thought to himself, but he said nothing.

"Does your family know where you are?" asked the warden.

"No, but probably the village people have told them."

"If not, we can have them informed, that is for a small consideration."

"There's no need of that."

"So much the better. Now empty your pockets."

Giuseppe pulled out his famous notebook, a penknife, and some small change. He was sure that he would never see his money again and glad that he had so little of it on his person. The warden also took away Giuseppe's peasant hat, with the old-fashioned wide, upturned brim that was a distinctive mark of his appearance. Running his hands over Giuseppe's person to make sure he was not holding anything back, the warden was surprised to find how many layers of wool he was wearing.

"Are you so cold-blooded?" he asked him.

"Have you finished your search?" said Giuseppe without making an answer, for he was irritated by this physical contact and the questioning.

"See here, my man," said the warden, "the restaurant keeper will want a deposit and what you've given me will do for no more than a couple of days."

"That's enough, I hope! Do you want me to grow old and gray here?"

"I'm warning you, that's all. Don't be surprised if you are served beans and bread and water."

"My wife will come to see me soon and I can tell her what I need."

The idea of Cecilia's paying him a visit filled him with an unexpected tenderness and made him wish to be alone so as to think of her the better.

"I am allowed to see her, am I not?" he asked anxiously.

"We'll arrange it. Don't go thinking there's no Christian charity among us. And I'll have your supper sent in soon."

Followed by the guard, the warden left the cell, turning the key three times in the lock behind him. The lock was old and rusty and the harsh sound of the key turning in it rang cruelly in the new prisoner's ears. His eyes travelled from the heavy bars of the window to the securely locked door and he had an impulse to tug at the bars with his bare hands and break the door down by throwing his shoulder against it. Yet an instant later he was aware that no amount of brute strength would serve and that, like a caged animal, he could do no more than gnaw at the walls of his prison. He threw himself down on the mattress, wringing his hands in a gesture of obscure terror, with just enough reason left to warn him that he had lost his head.

From the window's narrow opening, along with the rapidly darkening autumnal sky, he was conscious of the buzz of the city, so near and yet so inaccessible, which intensified by contrast the gloomy silence of his cell. Before barriers of iron and stone had cut him off from them he had not appreciated the beauties of nature and freedom. He tried to think coolly, but he could not get away from the idea that he was done for, that once more it was his fate to lose everything just as he was on the point of obtaining it. And what of Cecilia? She was about to give birth to their third child and he wondered if she would be able to come see him. He put his doubt in these terms in order not to wonder whether she would *want* to come. Well might he despair of her too, since he had tricked and trapped her into marriage. He was not so much penitent as he was afraid. If she did not love him there was no way he could force her to do so. She had resigned herself to the married state and taken advantage of it to satisfy her deep maternal instinct, but now that she had children what need had she of a hated and derided husband, one who had fallen afoul of the law and now risked years of prison and the loss of all his worldly goods? All the things of which it was possible to accuse him surged up in his bewildered imagination, twice as large as they were in reality, and pointed a frightening finger. He was convinced that Vergoli, Alpi, and all the other powerful persons involved would get off scot free and that, as the proverb has it, the poorest must pay. Yes, they would make him the scapegoat. And what of justice? To Giuseppe this was just a word worthy of disillusioned scorn, like honesty, kindness, and the rest of the so-called human virtues, not to mention the love of women, including Cecilia. Here was a chance for her to find revenge and freedom and she would be silly if she did not take advantage of it.

Giuseppe judged Cecilia, as he did everyone and everything else, by himself and his own dark nature, which fed on greed and suspicion. This is the dire punishment that is visited upon souls like his, which are easily thrown into despair and insensible to any motives save those of avarice. He fell so rapidly into this abyss that before the last rays of the sun had sunk below the horizon he was a broken man, and when his supper arrived his throat was too choked with emotion for him to swallow it.

"Don't take it so hard," the guard said to him, "or you'll make your imprisonment unbearable. You must learn to be patient."

"I can't," Giuseppe moaned. "Take this food away; I can't get it down."

"The restaurant won't take it back and it's already been paid for."

"Yes, I paid for it and you'll be the one to eat it!"

The fact that in the midst of such a predicament he could bewail the waste of his money may invite laughter, but it was indicative of his shaken and tormented state of mind.

"That's always the way," he muttered as the guard removed his supper. "It's my fate to buy all my troubles and pay for them."

And this reflection, instead of admitting a ray of light to his closed spirit, only made the cell seem to shut in around him more hermetically. He would have liked to bash his head against the wall but did not have the courage to do it.

Now night had come. He lay down without undressing on the mattress, hoping to snatch a little sleep. But at that moment, from every crack in the masonry and woodwork, a bloodthirsty army of bedbugs descended upon him. He scratched himself and tossed from side to side until dawn put them to flight and allowed him to doze off. He had time to realize that worry would have caused him still greater torment, and came to the typical conclusion that he was indebted to the bedbugs. And when he woke up, as if from a forgotten bad dream, he had regained his courage and had a healthy appetite. As for Cecilia, he began to think it might be better if she were not to come. There are times when a woman is in the way.

8

As soon as Cecilia heard what had happened she sent Schiavetto to hitch up the horse at Poplar Bridge and had him drive her to Guarda to ask the advice of the priest. She found the village still excited over the happenings of the day and indignant over the haughty attitude struck up by Were Rabbit.

"Your husband can thank his lucky stars that he had the gendarmes to protect him and that the carriage finally went a little faster," the sharp-tongued Woodcock told her, "or else even the gendarmes couldn't have saved him from getting the lesson he deserved."

"And who'd have given it to him? You, by chance, Woodcock?"

She did not need to say any more, for Woodcock was not known for his bravery. And Cecilia's voice, somewhat husky and masculine from her long habit of living on the river, expressed such succinct scorn that the bystanders could not help laughing.

"If you want my opinion," Cecilia added, "I wouldn't puff myself up so much for jumping on someone who has had a piece of bad luck and is being taken away to prison."

Many of them agreed with her on that and either said so openly or showed it in their faces.

"Oh well, you're his wife," said Woodcock. "You can't fail to take up for him."

"That's quite aside from the point," she answered dryly. "But I didn't come here to waste time chattering."

Another person whom Cecilia handled with dispatch was Venusta Chiccoli, who railed from her doorway against Giuseppe Scacerni and his most unfortunate wife. The cheerfully grumbling and helpful Venusta of years gone by, slightly bizarre in her ways, but fundamentally sound, showed no bodily effects of old age but a startling reduction in her former heavy weight. As for her mind, it was not actually weakened, but rather exhausted by the accumulation of misfortunes visited upon her numerous children and grandchildren and the extreme poverty in which she had been left after her husband's death. She was dominated by one deluded notion, and that was that her fellow villagers, when they gave her an occasional crust of bread, were guilty of black ingratitude. During the years of famine no one had bread to spare, but ungrateful as people generally are for past favors she had no real reason to complain. White-haired, wrinkled, and careless of her appearance to the point of being actually dirty, she carried on a constant flow of curses, threats and accusations against her own family and her neighbors. The peasants, with childish cruelty, nicknamed her "Drunken Death's-head" and tossed her a crust of bread not so much out of pity but because they feared she might visit ill luck upon them as she went from kitchen to kitchen, from the church in the Piazza Vecchia to the hovels of the so-called village ghetto, where she had her own miserable dwelling. Now she called out to Cecilia:

"What's this, Cecilia, before my eyes? How miserable it is to grow old, only to witness such infamy! His father, who was a man cut from a pattern that's long since lost, would have died of shame to see him in the hands of the police. I shouted it to his face, the Antichrist! And he, whom I held in my hands when he came into the world, turned on me and said I was in my dotage! Would he had never come into the world at all, I say! If I hadn't known his sainted mother I'd wonder whose son he was, for it's hard to believe such a coward could descend from such a brave father. He never gave his father anything but trouble, and when the old man died he didn't shed as much as a tear for him. I say he'd better never have been born, and I say it for your sake too, my poor Cecilia. You were forced into marrying him (I know you've never said so but such things always leak out) and now you must swallow the bitter pill of being a common thief's wife!"

She raved on at such a rate that it was several minutes before Cecilia could stop her.

"Even if all you say were true, it's not up to you to say it or to me to listen."

"And what might you mean by that?"

"I mean that you, my good woman, have lived too long."

"I? How can you speak like that to me when I brought you back to life after you were dragged out of the river? Is this your gratitude, Mistress Cecilia?"

494

"This harping on gratitude has turned you into a public nuisance, Venusta. If you insist upon gratitude I'd almost rather I had nothing to be grateful for."

"You mean I have no right to speak as I do?"

"Surely I'm not the only one to tell you that."

"The only one, that's what you are, except for bad people."

"Then you have no other friends sincere enough to tell you the truth. And now that I've told it to you I must be on my way."

And she left Venusta half aware that she had indeed no right to speak as she had and to hurt the feelings of a tried friend. For in all these years during which Venusta had been transformed by old age into "Drunken Death's-head" Cecilia alone had shown her compassion and understanding. Why did Venusta hold such a grudge against Giuseppe Scacerni, some reader may ask if he is dissatisfied with the explanation that she had it in for everyone and was in fact half crazy. Reason must always look for reasonable meanings, even at the cost of being unreasonable. Perhaps Venusta had no motive at all. And again it may be that a well told story does not necessarily answer all the reader's questions. The truth is that the parents' best friends are often not those of the children, and that they may be more critical of them than the parents themselves. Such is the inevitable clash between the generations.

The priest of course told Cecilia to look for a lawyer, that is if her husband did not have one already, and early the next morning she had Schiavetto drive her to the city, with clean linen and money for the prisoner and several baskets of fruit, one of which she took at once to Argia Malvegoli in the Strada delle Pettegole.

The ageing sinner, who had not set eyes on Cecilia since the strange marriage consummated under her roof, pretended to take the news with indifference, but the idea that her half beloved and half feared Peppino was in prison disturbed her.

"What's that?" she stammered. "You shouldn't have bothered to bring me the fruit. All I ask from you and Peppino is your affection. . . . You're at your third child, are you?" she added, pointing to Cecilia's obviously pregnant condition. "A shame that this one should be born with the father in prison. Heaven help us poor women in our sorrow! Where shall I turn for aid?"

Argia stood twisting and turning, with the basket of fruit in her hands, as if her only trouble were that she did not know where to set it down.

"Have no fear, Aunt Argia."

"That's all very well for you to say, but I have more sensitive feelings."

"Of course. You've been brought up among the refinements of the city."

"But do you know what they accuse him of?" Argia asked, finally putting down the basket and then, as if the worst were over, sinking with a deep sigh into an armchair.

"I know very little," admitted Cecilia.

"Yes, Peppino always was very close-mouthed. He never opens up to anyone."

"I'm quite sure he's committed no crime for which he should be hanged."

"Heaven forbid!"

"And I believe it has to do with smuggling."

"That's the peccadillo of all of you there on the river!"

"And I know some influential persons are connected with it."

"That's hopeful. Who are they?"

"Signor Pietro Vergoli."

"Never heard of him."

"And Count Alpi."

"Oh, he's a friend of mine. I have only to send him word . . ."

"You don't know, then, that he's run away?"

"Run away?" And here Argia's embarrassment changed to speechless dismay. "Alpi has run away?"

For some time now the fast fading Argia had had no occasion to see persons in high places. She was overcome by receiving such a piece of news from a simple countrywoman and painfully aware that her failure to have heard it was a mark of her social decline.

"I came only to ask you if you know a good lawyer," said Cecilia.

"Yes, dozens of them," said Argia, seizing this chance to regain importance, at least in her own eyes. And she mentioned various names which she evaluated simply on the basis of gossip. Neither woman could write, and so Argia called in a manservant who printed a list, complete with addresses. Bearing this in her hands Cecilia went to the prison and obtained permission to see her husband.

"Out of consideration for your condition," the warden said. "Because ordinarily it's strictly forbidden."

Husband and wife did not go in for any effusions.

"So you're here, are you, Peppino?" she said when he appeared pale and puffy before her.

"One of life's little tricks. And what brings you to see me, Cecilia?"

"I've brought you some linen, a basket of fruit and twenty crowns."

"Quietly! Lower your voice!"

"Have I done wrong?"

"No, and I thank you. The linen is very useful and you can give the fruit to the warden. But as for the twenty crowns, let me whisper in your ear: take them home and forget about them. In fact, you can tell the warden that you brought him the fruit because you had no money, and that you just managed to put three crowns together for the restaurant keeper, whom you had best pay in person. Here we're like so many geese, and this is the plucking season. Do you see what I mean?"

"I see. Shall I give the restaurant keeper a basket of fruit too?"

"He's a thief. Give him nothing."

"Your aunt sends you her love and a list of the best lawyers of Ferrara."

"Lawyers? What good to me are they?"

"To defend you in court. The priest at Guarda gave me the same advice."

"Tell the priest to keep his mind on his Masses and my aunt to reflect upon her sins. I can defend myself without any lawyer."

"Whatever you say. Be brave and patient, for I must go back to the mill, and I shan't be able to come to see you again before the birth of our child."

"May Saint Anne be with you in your travail, Cecilia. Thank you for your visit. I know your merits and how well you deserve of me. There's no need for me to tell you to look after the mills, because you do that better than I do. But don't neglect the farm at Poplar Bridge and the land at Ca' Morgosa that's ready for sowing. Of course I hope I'm not going to stay here very long."

"God grant you a quick release. Don't lose heart, and I shall take care of everything as well as I can."

"I know you will, Cecilia. And when you give the basket of fruit to the warden, ask him to send me some breakfast. I'm hungry as a bear this morning."

"Is that all?"

"Remind them of my breakfast at the restaurant, too. Thank you for your trouble."

The night had refreshed Giuseppe's memory and after a copious breakfast his mind was completely clear. The magistrate had not found any guilt in his transactions with Vergoli; he had suspected him of taking part in the operation of smuggling, with which he had no connection. All he had needed to do was to deny everything. And instead, losing his head over the mention of smuggling, he had contradicted himself in the attempt to be clever. "The only real cleverness is to pretend I remember nothing," he said to himself. And from then on this was what he did. When the magistrate questioned him about his money he replied that it represented years of honest transactions in grain, and to the accusation of complicity in the smuggling he would not budge an inch from what he had said before.

"Has the law any proof that my father's son had anything to do with boats and barges and loading grain at the customs? I know no more about that than anyone else. When my father's son sent a consignment of wheat to Signor Vergoli all the necessary papers were in order. What happened at Guarda Crossing was not his affair."

"His father's son" was so tedious with his repeated denials that finally the magistrate was happy to release him and send him away. But this was not until spring, when Cecilia's third child, her first daughter, was already born.

If anyone had asked Giuseppe how he had managed to avoid all intimacy with the "smuggler of the Po," the Superintendent of Customs and their friends, he would have answered: "They and their company were given to too much feasting and dissipation. And I prefer to keep to myself." This was the strict truth and lucky for him that it was. Vergoli himself could have borne witness to the sad results of keeping bad company.

Giuseppe's denial that he had ever seen grain loaded at Nogarole, within sight of the mill, was too much for anyone to swallow, and he had contradicted himself on this score upon his second questioning. On this point he corrected himself in the forced tranquillity of the prison. In the course of his meditations, without any lawyer to help him, he came to the conclusion that he could not deny having lied the first time and contradicted himself the second. And when the magistrate asked him why he had originally passed the matter over in silence he said:

"The customs guards saw with their own eyes what was going on at the Nogarole dikes just as well as I did. So why should I have worried?"

"That's no reason for your original denial."

"There I admit I was mistaken. I was too clever for my own good."

"Explain yourself further."

"That I can do in a very few words. When I was first called up I had heard people talk of smuggling and illegal exportation. I reasoned that if the customs guards, the sergeant, and the Superintendent of Customs had winked at the whole thing, they must have good motives to do so. Perhaps they were carrying out orders, and in that case I should do well to pretend I had seen nothing. Your Honor knows very well that where politics and government are concerned I prefer not to hold any opinion."

"The first time you were questioned you were told that it was your duty to tell the truth, the whole truth, and nothing but the truth. How, then, do you account for your untruthful answer?"

"That's something I've only just now discovered," said Giuseppe in what might have seemed a somewhat brazen manner. "The lesson has cost me dear," he added more humbly, "and now I have really told you all that I know."

Eventually, because so many minor witnesses had been thrown into jail and political considerations made it seem wise to release them, Giuseppe, along with the rest, got off scot free. The investigation dragged on at Rome for another year and Vergoli stayed so long in hiding that Giuseppe had time to become more and more interested in farming and to feel that he was the legitimate owner of the land he had put under cultivation at Ca' Morgosa.

9

Twice Giuseppe Scacerni had reaped the harvest and plowed the land, and now, in the autumn of 1858, he was preparing for another sowing. Now the land is in this way, as in many others, like a woman, for if it inspires real passion in a man it becomes with habit more and more dear. Like a passionate adulterer Giuseppe was by now so accustomed to ruling over the Ca' Morgosa farm that he hardly remembered that it belonged to somebody else. The preceding summer, when at last Pietro Vergoli was sentenced to three years of prison and the payment of large damages and a heavy fine, Giuseppe could not help rejoicing.

"That means he'll stay in hiding indefinitely. Or if he does give himself up I can count on the next three years. Besides, the shock of going to jail may very well be fatal. In three years—although far be it from me to wish him ill!—almost anything can happen."

It is a common superstition that to wish another man to die only has the result of prolonging his life, and for this reason Giuseppe did not go quite so far. He was sure of having three years of grace, and one day just three months after the announcement of Vergoli's sentence, when he was roaming about the farm, feasting his eyes upon some tender shoots of green brought up by a timely fall of rain, the arrival of a visitor took him entirely by surprise. He was so absorbed in pleasantly possessive thoughts that he did not hear the footsteps behind him until a voice said from close by:

"Hello there, Scacerni!"

Giuseppe knew the voice but he was unwilling to admit it and refused to turn around.

"Hello," he threw back over his shoulder; "who's there?"

"Look and see!" said the voice of Pietro Vergoli.

Vergoli was a changed man. It was plain that if his troubles had not weakened his energy and fighting spirit they had nevertheless put him to a severe test. He smiled, something in itself very unusual, and in a melancholy fashion.

"Did you expect never to see me alive again?" he asked.

"A pleasant surprise, Signor Pietro, but I thought you were sentenced to three years in jail."

"His Holiness suspended the sentence upon my payment of a larger fine."

"I congratulate you on having obtained such a pardon," said Giuseppe with a funereal expression.

"Thanks. The fact is, my dear Scacerni, that I am very nearly ruined, and if it weren't for my children I'd almost rather be in prison. I've had to pay lawyers' fees for several years and this last fine, which is only a drop in the bucket, comes to thirty thousand crowns, in itself a small fortune."

Giuseppe was thoughtful as Vergoli went on:

"That would be the least of my worries, if I hadn't lost my credit as well. I'll have to sell my mortgaged land, and before I finish paying off my fine and what I owe to various creditors I shan't have much left."

"I understand," said Giuseppe, adding to himself, "Why does he come with all this to me? Hasn't he relatives?"

"I'm glad of that," said Vergoli, breaking in on his thoughts.

"Glad of what?"

"That you understand. Let me tell you that one of my few consolations is to see how well you've handled the land here at Ca' Morgosa. If I hadn't had the sense to put it in your name, the treasury or my creditors would long since have laid hands on it."

"There you are!" Giuseppe said once more to himself. "That's friendship for you! There's always money at the bottom of it; don't forget that, Peppino!" But he answered out loud:

"Don't be discouraged, Signor Pietro. A man like you! You can take it from an ignorant peasant like myself, that you're sure to recoup your losses."

"I'd like to think so, and perhaps your confidence will bring me good luck. Meanwhile I'm glad to know that you're a decent fellow. If you knew how many people there are who owe me gratitude and pretend not to recognize me!"

"Those are fair-weather friends."

"But you're not of their number."

"Let us be just, Signor Pietro."

"What do you mean?"

"Let us be just to your creditors. You know, of course, what people are saying all over Ro and Guarda and Ferrara."

"No, please tell me."

"A poor ignorant peasant like myself? Now you're joking. They say that you have many more mortgages than those that appear. They have evil tongues, perhaps, but you can't get it out of their heads that Pietro Vergoli has money tucked away somewhere, so securely that neither rain nor sun nor the law can fall upon it."

"That's slander."

"Oh, I'm ready to take your word for it. But they say you own land, good land, that is registered under another name. I don't know much about the law, but I suppose that if this turned out to be true your creditors would send you to jail for it, along with the wretch who had lent you his name and thus helped you cheat them of their rights."

"All slander, I tell you. And anyhow . . ."

"Your word is quite enough for me. I wish no further proof . . ."

"Anyhow you needn't worry on your own account. No one suspects you . . ."

"I'm not worried in the least, Signor Pietro. My conscience is clean as a whistle, although for your sake I had to spend some time in prison."

"I shall not forget that, nor the danger to which you exposed yourself by doing me a favor. Not to mention the good care you've taken of this place; I'd hardly know it. You shall be recompensed for everything."

"I want no recompense and ask for none. As I said to the magistrate, whatever I did, I did out of the kindness of my heart. I have nothing to fear."

"I felt from what you said a few minutes ago that you were worried about our agreement . . ."

"There's no question of any agreement between us."

"What? There's no question . . ."

"That's mere slander! You said so yourself, Signor Pietro, and I believe you. If this land weren't really mine, there would be cause for worry, for *you* to worry, that is. I've heard that in a case like this the man who lends his name to the transaction gets off with a few months, but the principal is sure to go to jail for at least three years. And this time His Holiness is not so apt to give you a pardon."

"Excuse me, Scacerni . . ." said Vergoli, trying to interrupt the other's flow of words.

"A gentleman of your stamp mustn't stoop to excuse himself to a peasant like me."

"For the love of heaven!" Vergoli exclaimed, "whose is this land, anyhow?"

"Oh, it belongs to my father's son. Shall I show you the bill of sale?"

"Is this the kind of an honest man you are?"

"With all your education surely you'll not lower yourself by losing your temper in the presence of an inferior."

"And the money? You wretch, who gave you the money?"

"I'll stand by the legal papers. All I know is that I signed them."

"You cheat!"

"You can't mean what you say, Signor Pietro. Unless, as rumor has it, you're a bad man, one capable of any evil action. But that I refuse to believe; it's nothing but slander. Not even you yourself can persuade me to insult you, no, not even at the point of a knife. Even when I was in prison I stood up for you, if you must know. That's the sort of fellow I am."

"You ought to be hanged."

"When a man is in trouble he often loses control of his tongue. Anyhow, we should be hanged together. But that's not really necessary and I shan't let it happen to you. At this minute I care more for you than you do yourself. You must be patient, that's all, Signor Vergoli."

Looking into Giuseppe's eyes Vergoli saw that he must be very patient indeed; he had no other choice, for Were Rabbit had made an ironbound decision and with an apparently clear conscience intended to stick by it.

"For your sake I bore false witness . . ." Giuseppe continued implacably.

"I'll pay you for that," shouted Vergoli; "I'll pay you for bearing false witness!"

"I went to prison . . ."

"I'll pay you for that too!"

"I didn't go to prison just for the love of you. It was because you played an ugly trick on me, leaving me holding the bag and ignorant of the detours of the law."

"What do you mean, you ugly bloodsucker?"

"Come, come; you'll have to pay me for your bad language, besides the rest. I shan't be satisfied with the Ca' Morgosa farm alone. Don't you know why I was arrested? Because they were suspicious of my having a valuable piece of land. Justice isn't always blind, you know. They suspected me of being a smuggler! Can you imagine that? My father's son!"

501

"What are you raving about now?"

"I'm not raving. You are. But, to be brief, you can add the item of kindheartedness to my bill."

"Many thanks!"

"I still have kindly feelings toward you, in spite of the fact that you deceived me. Just remember the money I've had to spend putting the farm in order, just as if it were mine, and the difference . . ."

"What difference?"

"The difference of price. You know, land has gone up lately and if I am to resell Ca' Morgosa I can expect to make a profit."

"Well, I'm ready to give you credit for that, and for the improvements you've made," said Vergoli, with a ray of hope that perhaps the blackmail would go no farther.

"And the shock I suffered when I was arrested, the money I lost when I was in jail, not to mention the damage to my reputation. It's never quite the same when one has such a stain on one's record, and my father's son is extremely sensitive. Let's make it what's called a lump price, like the good friends we are, Signor Pietro. You must admit that I've fully earned my right to Ca' Morgosa farm."

"And do you really believe it?" asked Vergoli, almost admiringly, raising his arms to the sky.

"Do I believe it?"

"Do you now, honestly?"

"Why not?"

"What a shameless monkey you are. And do you think that's all there is to it?"

"Yes, as far as I'm concerned. You'll never hear me speak of it again."

Vergoli went away too angry to say another word, but there was nothing he could do. And Giuseppe made a round seven thousand crowns. Later on, Vergoli, who had done so much to modernize the agriculture of the Ferrara region, turned with characteristic vigor to building up industry in another part of the country, although he never regained all the wealth he had lost. He wrote off the loss of Ca' Morgosa along with many others and never set foot again at Guarda or Ro. Looking back on his misfortunes Vergoli used to say that if a man pulls too hard on a rope he does not make allowance for the impact of his fall to the ground when the rope is broken.

Marquis Filippo Macchiavelli too felt the effects of Vergoli's disaster, for La Vallazza was drained without being reclaimed, and indeed left at a point where considerable money would have been needed in order to complete the operation. Since the marquis did not have sufficient funds to carry on, the land fell into ugliness and neglect. The ditches filled up with mud and stagnant water, vegetation decayed, sunshine and rain were equally powerless to make anything grow but a tangled mass of weeds, and the peasants were discouraged and easily prey to fever. La Vallazza was a heavy liability to the marquis and he ended his days in poverty. But never did he take it out on Pietro Vergoli.

"Vergoli paid a heavy price for his excessively enterprising spirit and

502

the real passion he had for this land," the marquis used to say. "He wasn't after money alone, and the proof is that he did a great deal of good, some of which still remains. Let us leave it to the law to pass a final judgment upon him. In the course of my genealogical studies I've seen many similar cases. I shan't waste the few years that remain to me in condemning this man. If he hadn't been so ambitious our part of the country would not enjoy many of the benefits it has today."

Considering that Vergoli was indirectly the cause of the marquis's final ruin, we can only admire such equity. For the old man never departed from his reserve until the day when he went to join his good wife in the local cemetery, under a magnificent but broken-down stone, covered all the year around with wild grass and in spring with an abundance of buttercups.

And the marquis's opinion was shared by most of the simpler people of the countryside. Whenever they referred to Vergoli, and I can personally remember one of the old men who conserved his memory, it was to say: "Signor Pietro was a man who gave work and bread to a great many of us in these parts!"

There is humanity to this judgment, if we contrast it with the rigid conclusions of law and economics; but of course science cannot take human values into account and justice must often condemn them in order to safeguard the welfare of the population.

Naturally the peasants soon figured out how Giuseppe Scacerni had come into possession of the Ca' Morgosa farm, and they mumbled again that he was the Antichrist in person. But we do not wish to let envy dictate the final terms of our moral appraisal.

10

During the last two years of the Papal government the legations enjoyed relative peace and quiet. History treated them with the regard that nature often displays for the old and afflicted, affording them a moment of respite before their passage into oblivion. Such figures of speech are beset with obvious inconsistencies, but in this instance we may go a step further and recall Plato's famous comparison between the social organism of the Republic and the physical body of man. We may speak in these terms of what went on in Rome, the most ancient fief of St. Peter, during the last decade before the eclipse of the Pope's temporal power. For the feverish activity of the ultra-montane party, the crusade waged by De Merode and his fanatical adherents against the "Moslem" supporters of Liberalism and national unity, and their ill-advised complicity with the brigands of the defunct Bourbon regime were all symptoms of fever in an organism that was condemned to perish. But to pursue the simile any further would distract us from our story.

It was inevitable that in 1859 the legations should quietly detach themselves from the Papal State. For some time they had carried on a political, economic and intellectual life of their own almost in defiance

503

of an increasingly weaker central government, which was based solely on external trappings rather than real substance. When their gradual detachment became a concrete reality they were bound to gravitate toward the rising force of a united Italian nation. We have already seen how the Papal government in Ferrara, in an attempt to correct abuse of its power, revealed its own weakness and dependence on the Austrians, and how private initiative could only flourish by circumventing unnecessarily restrictive laws.

Meanwhile, before the precipitation of events in 1859, there were several good harvests, and in 1857 the annual Fair at Ferrara took on a luster which it had not had for some years. Political affairs were quiescent when on May 4, 1857, the Pope started out by carriage to make his quarterly tour of the provinces, and was greeted by devoted and at times wildly enthusiastic crowds. It would be unfair to accuse Pius IX of mistaking their veneration of his holy office for support of his temporal power. Actually the crowds themselves had no such distinction in mind, but two years later they made no effort to defend him as a ruler, in large part because the Austrian occupation had discredited his authority even among his most faithful supporters. If it is true, as Pius IX said after the Breach of Porta Pia in 1870 had forced the reality of the new situation upon him, that the Church cannot exist without liberty, then we may ask what liberty the Church actually did enjoy under an impotent Papal government. The hollow character of nineteenth-century Papal power, which had fallen so far from the theological pre-eminence of the Middle Ages and the bold leadership of the Renaissance, was actually a threat to the spiritual influence of the Church, and the acclaim which Pius IX received in the provinces clearly reflected religious and not political feeling.

The Pope came to Ferrara on the tenth of July and was received at the Porta San Giorgio by the flower of the local nobility, who turned out in their most elaborate coaches and carriages to greet him. He proceeded hence to a *Te Deum* at the Cathedral and in the evening was honored by fireworks and band music in the public squares, and feasting, half solemn, half gay, in private houses. On the next day, which was Saturday, people from all over the region crowded the roads to Ferrara, long lines of them as far as the eye could see from the four towers of the Castle and the crooked belfry of San Benedetto. Most of them brought enough food for two days with them and planned to sleep under the cloudless summer sky. As they drew nearer and nearer their goal it seemed as if the whole population were on the march. Ever since the day before, Austrian guns had shot salvos from the Fortress, echoed by the Papal cannons on the walls, and the church bells of the city accompanied those of the outlying villages in a salutation to the throng. The peasants wore Sunday dress and moved along in dignified yet festive fashion, their pace somewhat slowing down as under the hot sun their numbers swelled beyond what anyone could have expected, and sporadic bursts of gunfire greeted their passage from the surrounding fields and hedges.

504

On the evening of July 11 the Holy Father was to impart his blessing from the balcony of the archbishop's palace, which overlooked both the Piazza del Duomo and the Piazza del Commercio, and among the crowd of those seeking to win a special indulgence were Giuseppe and Cecilia Scacerni. The two squares were illuminated for the first time by electric arc lights, and the absence of flaming wicks impressed the crowd as something like a miracle. The lighting effect was stronger than any to which the people were accustomed, as it fell upon the majestic white robe and serene, noble face of Pius IX. The immense silence was broken only by a faint buzz caused by the new light bulbs, as the musical voice for which the Pope was famous uttered the words of benediction.

The kneeling crowd had just stood up, clapping and acclaiming the Pope as he started to go inside, when there was a distinct earthquake tremor. The moment of silence which followed was quite different from the one that had gone before; it was pregnant with icy fear. There were at first only occasional and barely visible ripples among the closely-packed crowd, like those produced by the subaqueous motion of a vast body of water. Some people standing on the fringes ran away under the low arches of the Camerini, but they were soon ashamed of their fear and came back to join the crowd, which with recovered aplomb was applauding the Pope even more loudly than before.

This untimely visitation of a familiar danger, instead of throwing the people into panic, only added a purposeful note to their rejoicings. The carefree threw their hats higher up into the air than before and the religiously inclined gave thanks for their deliverance and prayed that the earthquake might not be repeated. When it became clear that no damage whatsoever had been done, there was talk of a miracle.

The Pope had hardly withdrawn from sight when Giuseppe Scacerni elbowed his way out of the crowd, which murmured against his haste, dragging Cecilia behind him.

"Let's go away from here," he said roughly.

"Go where?" Cecilia asked with a touch of irony that only added to his ill humor.

"Somewhere in the open, outside the walls. It stifles me to be closed in like this during an earthquake, especially in the darkness."

Cecilia was a kind wife if ever there was one, but when there was any question of courage her bright black eyes shone with a light that was more eloquent than words.

"We might just as well go home," said Giuseppe with annoyance, whereas Cecilia had just acceded to the idea of waiting in the fields until the earthquake made its intentions more plain.

"You can go home by yourself if you like," she said calmly, adding the acute observation, "Giovecca is such a broad street and the houses on either side are so low that if we walk in the middle the earthquake is powerless to hurt us, even if the whole of Ferrara is levelled to the ground."

"What a thing to say! What an outrageous thought! Ferrara levelled to the ground!" Giuseppe puffed angrily, but her words had so struck his imagination that he could not help measuring the width of Giovecca with his eye. "Can you see me walking down the middle of the street with a crowd of urchins laughing behind me? Of course, I know you're quite capable of going back among the crowd around the Cathedral. The Cathedral's so old that, earthquake or no earthquake, I don't know how it remains standing."

"If it's stood all these centuries it certainly won't crumble on a day of indulgence and blessing like this one. And I must say I'd like another taste of the festivities."

"Just a bit of cornice or a loose stone would do enough harm when there's a crowd too thick to get out of it quickly."

"You're afraid to go back to the square, that's all; you're the only coward among so vast a multitude. Yes, I remember your father telling me how you used to shrink back from the water."

"Please don't take the name of the dead in vain."

"Very well, then. But didn't you see how calm the Pope was?"

"The Pope? If he could hear what I'm saying he'd tell me I was quite right."

"That's a fine one!"

"Of course he would. You don't think the Pope wants his people to be exposed to danger, do you? But he didn't want the crowd to disperse and suffer disappointment so he concealed his own fear. Otherwise he'd have sent them home in a hurry; after all, he's supposed to have better judgment than the rest of us and he must know that to run an unnecessary risk is contrary to good judgment."

"Well, it was a very small earthquake! And I'd like to see the fireworks," said Cecilia, tugging at her husband's sleeve.

"A small earthquake! Isn't that enough for you? But I'm less worried about the tremor that has already gone by than I am about the one that may follow."

"Do you know what it means?" Cecilia said with sudden gravity. "The devil was giving vent to his spite at the vision of so many souls wrapped up in devotion to God and to the Holy Father. He hoped some of these souls would be so cowardly as to run away from the earthquake and give him an occasion for laughter. But if anyone were to die today he'd be very close to heaven."

Giuseppe fell into an awkward silence. Cecilia rarely expressed her religious feelings but when she did so it was with startling directness, with a clean-cut distinction between good and evil, between the things of God and the things of Mammon, with genuine fear of the devil and all his works and awareness of the necessity of saving her soul before Christ came to sit in judgment upon it. These sentiments were in tune with her wild and shy nature.

Already on the way to the city husband and wife had fallen out over Giuseppe's wish to dine and sleep at the house of Argia Malvegoli.

506

"She'll be glad to see us after we've neglected her for so long," Giuseppe insisted.

"I say let's go to see her another day."

"And who knows when that will be?"

"Why is it that you feel this sudden tenderness for your aunt?"

"We should save the price of our dinner, as well. Who knows how much the restaurants are charging on a day like this?"

"I see. There's a string to your benevolence. But I've taken a vow to fast today in order to atone for my sins and make myself worthy of the Papal benediction. I don't wish to be so presumptuous as to pass judgment upon your aunt, but on this holy occasion her house is the last place in the world I want to go."

"You sound for all the world like a missionary."

"Peppino, don't make me angry or I may say something you'll be sorry to hear. If you don't mend your ways your avarice may be your undoing. Enough now, I don't want to fall from grace by losing my temper."

But after they had come to the end of the broad Giovecca Giuseppe regained his courage and, influenced perhaps by curiosity about the fireworks, which were now being set off near the Castle, and a desire to take a second look at the arc lights, he gave in to his wife's wishes. They strolled up and down among the gay crowd until, shortly after eleven o'clock, the earthquake shook the city a second time. This was too much for Giuseppe to bear, and he put the sleepy Cecilia into his cart and whipped the tired horse into a slow trot until they reached home. When he had no money in his pockets he was not afraid of highway robbers, and at this date their depredations were definitely on the decline. His prudence was so to speak rewarded when around midnight there was a third tremor. There were antipapists in the city who acclaimed with joy this disturbance of the pious celebrations, but Giuseppe was wise enough not to show any pleasure over the fulfillment of his prophecy for fear of arousing the ire of the devout country people.

After the birth of her third child Cecilia found life aboard the mill too uncomfortable and regretfully moved to the house at Poplar Bridge. Living in closer contact with her husband she had come to know his niggardly character better, and this explains why she upbraided him with it that evening in Ferrara. But Giuseppe valued her opinion on any subject and did not take offense. Just because he was close-mouthed with strangers he found satisfaction in opening his heart to Cecilia and he told her, among other things, the terms of the agreement he had made with Vergoli for the pretended purchase of the Ca' Morgosa farm. Ignorant as she was of the law she thought that Giuseppe was doing a good deed in coming to Pietro Vergoli's assistance. It never occurred to her to criticize Vergoli's smuggling, for to the river dwellers this was an accepted practice and the government and all its laws were enemies by definition. She herself, in her management of the two mills, put all her feminine wile into paying as little taxes as possible. And so she never gave a second thought to the Ca' Morgosa transaction, imagining that both parties had agreed to keep it secret.

In this year of 1857, when things in the legations were as peaceful as we have described them above and the courts were shifted from Austrian to Papal jurisdiction, Ferrara was ruled by Monsignor Gramiccia and in Milan old Radetzki was tranquilly nearing the end of his days and contributing to the general somnolence. The weather too was propitious and one good season followed another. In October, when Giuseppe had finished the sowing, the river was so low that Cecilia ordered Schiavetto and his two helpers, Coxcomb and Lazybones, to install in front of the mills the long, heavy sluice gate which by stemming the current diverted it to the mill wheel with a stronger impact. This clumsy apparatus was lowered into the water by means of a windlass.

On the twenty-first of October it was as warm as a summer day. There was a dust cloud on the horizon, but this seemed to presage continued dryness, and indeed, in spite of all efforts to accelerate the mill wheels, they were barely able to function.

"At this rate the river will soon be dry," said Cecilia to her helpers, looking out over the sandbanks plainly visible under the water even in midstream.

The two new boys were very young and their first thought was that they could lie abed late in the morning with no work to do. Besides, they did not have their mistress' instinctive and unerring eye and ear for the least motion of the river.

"There's something in the air that I don't like," Cecilia continued.

"It makes me feel heavy and drowsy, that's all," said Lazybones with a yawn.

"That name of yours suits you down to the ground," Cecilia answered. "Sh!" And from the narrow foredeck she peered with taut nerves up the river.

"Something in the air. . . . Don't you feel it too, Schiavetto?"

"Yes, a vague something. . . ."

The air was motionless, but it underwent an intangible change of consistency and hung less heavily over the dry banks of the river. A new smell was exhaled by the mud flats, and there was a glow in the gray western sky. The leaves of the poplar trees began to quiver.

"The water is changing color!" Cecilia and Schiavetto exclaimed simultaneously.

Indeed, the water had lost its previous calm transparency, which had left the green weeds on the bottom plainly visible, and was filled with a multitude of tiny rivulets of mud, emitting the odor characteristic of a flood.

"It can't be a flood in this dry weather!" exclaimed Cecilia, taking the words out of Schiavetto's mouth.

"The river has its source so very far away," said Schiavetto, sniffing the air. "They say it comes from those mountains." He pointed westward with a gesture that seemed to illustrate its mighty flow. "We don't know what the weather may be there in the distance and yet we are bound to feel its effects."

"Do you think we should pull up the sluice gate?" Cecilia interrupted.

"It might be safer. I've already experienced one totally unexpected flood, of the kind the old millers have made famous in story."

"Let's haul both sluice gates in at once," Cecilia said brusquely as the current started to swish about them and gain volume with unforeseen speed. "Watch how it's rising, Schiavetto!"

Schiavetto had already begun to turn the windlass, but the heavy sluice gate had apparently sunk deep into the mud, because it would not be budged from the river bed. Meanwhile the gathering current swept over the mud flats, leaving a pattern behind it like that traced by the wind on the desert sands and then, surging up again, broke into thousands of tiny streams which soon all ran together, so that the separate pools of water, which had first multiplied their numbers, now diminished them and formed one solid sheet all the way across the river. From the shore, which was usually so quiet as to appear uninhabited, arose a confused murmur of voices and finally one clear watchword like that of a group of boys at play:

"The flood! The flood!"

A man who had been digging sand from the bars in mid-stream was suddenly marooned, and as he whipped up his horse to seek safety on the Venetian shore the water rose to the axles of his wagon wheels and then almost to the horse's withers. Another stray laborer, no longer able to touch bottom, came swimming downstream and Cecilia threw him a rope by which he pulled himself aboard the mill. Still the unfortunate sluice gate stuck fast and the action of the ropes pulled the bow of the mill down into the water. The current rose up between the two hulks and threatened to top the mill wheel and flood the holds. Boards quivered and creaked under the strain, while Cecilia and the new arrival, still in his soaking clothes, applied their strength to turning the windlass, but all in vain.

The river was high now, and flowed majestically between its accustomed banks. Whirling eddies of cold air, brought by the onrush of water, made the reeds and woodland growths back of the shore rustle, although all around the horizon they were ringed by the same heavy heat as before. The bow of Saint Michael's Mill bobbed up and down in the water until the ropes of the windlass were broken and the mill floated on the surface of the water, in danger, however, of being staved in if its keel struck some protuberance of the half-sunken sluice gate. The jerk of the breaking rope made the gangplank between the two mills fall into the river, and although they were not so far apart as to make it impossible to jump from one to the other the forward list of the Bitter Bread and the mobility of the Saint Michael presented a considerable hazard.

"Let go!" Cecilia shouted.

The Bitter Bread's windlass let the rope roll out until it was slack and the bow came up, leaving the mill to float as freely as its companion but with a less violent up and down motion because it was in deeper water and was not so much affected by the surge of the current against the obstacle below. St. Michael's was obviously in greater danger.

"Who'll jump?" Cecilia called out resolutely.

Cecilia's old admirer, Schiavetto, had never seen her more beautiful than she was now with her flushed cheeks, keen eyes, quivering body, and her long black hair released from a loosened kerchief and flying in the wind. With an instinctive gesture like that of a woman who has just left her lover's arms she searched her hair for a hairpin, then rapidly coiled it around her head.

"Who'll jump over and shorten the hawser of the Saint Michael's anchor?" she asked again.

Coxcomb did not have long enough legs and Lazybones showed no eagerness to put his to the test. As for the rescued man, he was willing enough to help but he had little inclination for risking another plunge into the water. Schiavetto stepped forward but Cecilia held up her hand.

"No, you mustn't go. You must stay with these two boys."

She spoke in an affectionate, almost filial tone but with a certain authority. Then, without a moment's hesitation, she kicked off her wooden shoes and raised her skirt above a pair of round knees and strong, agile, slightly curved legs, worthy of being celebrated in the amorous verse of some classical and pastoral poet. In these days it was most unusual to see a woman's bare limbs, and Schiavetto felt a pang of jealousy which made him say to the staring boys:

"To work, young pups!"

Cecilia took a few steps backward and then nimbly jumped across to Saint Michael's Mill. Beside the long chain of wooden blocks at the stern each mill was held by an anchor off the bow and when Cecilia and Schiavetto had pulled in their respective hawsers on the windlass and loosened the lateral mooring ropes, the Saint Michael and the Bitter Bread were both out of the channel in which they had risked colliding with the half-sunken sluice gates. Another gangplank was secured between them, and after this everything appeared in a more cheerful light, although there was still danger that some unusually large drifting object might be thrown by the sudden flood against the hulks or wheels of the mills.

The flood was rising now just as rapidly and angrily as it had started, with the subdued roar that expresses the released might of a great lowland river. Pushing against the embankments on either side and prevented by them from breaking over the plains it seemed to roar with thwarted fury. This was the familiar noise of a major flood, which filled the air to the exclusion of every other sound. The little group aboard the mills could feel it swelling under the keels and they stood ready with poles and harpoons to shove away any piece of dangerous drifting

510

wreckage. Cecilia and Lazybones watched from the Saint Michael and the others from the Bitter Bread, under the command of Schiavetto.

"God have mercy upon us!" Schiavetto cried. "I've never before seen it rise so fast. Holy souls in purgatory, come to our aid!"

This prayer illustrates one of the deep meanings of the Christian religion, which gives man faith in God's mercy at a critical juncture like this, where a pagan would be overcome by the blind violence of nature and call it fate or else a piece of treachery on the part of his capricious deities. For no one could see this condition of the Po without feeling that it was the expression of some immense and evil will.

"Courage, Schiavetto!" answered Cecilia. "Our patron, Saint Anthony, has not forgotten us. He is pleading now that we be spared."

"May God listen to his prayers and yours," said Schiavetto, crossing himself, "now and at the hour of our death!"

Within an incredibly short time the river had risen halfway up the banks, from which the mills were quite far away. Suddenly Giuseppe Scacerni appeared on the scene and called out to Cecilia:

"Is there anything I can do?"

"Yes, find a pair of stout fellows to relieve us tonight."

"Have no fear; I shall find them."

They were badly needed indeed, for it was a strain to watch over the mills, and the flood was too high to dream of taking them to shelter on the other side of the Guarda peninsula, where the waves were breaking hard on the shore. As evening came the two men sent by Giuseppe were brought over in the skiff and mounted guard with lanterns. But had it not been for faith in Saint Anthony the prospects seemed gloomy.

The water continued to rise, and before it grew dark Schiavetto noted the markers set up to commemorate the heights reached by previous floods and began to think that this would go higher than the famous one of 1839 when the drifting Bitter Bread Mill had brought the orphaned Cecilia to Master Lazzaro's protection. All night long there was going to and fro on the dikes, and the sound of horns and voices. The Waterway Commission had been taken by surprise and was now tardily dispatching sentinels and squads of workers ready to carry out any necessary repairs to the dikes in case of a break-through.

The October night was a long one and by dawn the level of the flood had risen to the eighty-eight inches of 1839. Fortunately no east wind blew the river water back from the sea, for in this case it would surely have overflowed, and there were none of the squalls that often came from the south. The autumnal sun rose out of a golden haze and shone over the parched fields and the tawny surface of the river. There was a weary beauty in its light and something like a malicious smile. It was ironical that after a long dry spell, which had left the earth greedily thirsty, this mass of water should course between the riverbanks only to lose itself in the sterile salt sea.

The Po stayed high for two days, but by the evening of the third it began to go down as rapidly as it had risen. Cecilia decided to wait until later to recuperate the sunken sluice gates and, having sent the extra workers home and the boys to sleep in their cabins, she went herself in the cart in which her husband came to fetch her to sleep at Poplar Bridge. Giuseppe had been for some time on the dikes and from the mills they had seen him go down to the shore after the water level had begun to subside and start poking about with a cane at some fragments of an old wall that had been turned up by the flood. He went up on the dikes again to talk gesticulatingly to the representatives of the Waterway Commission and then brought one of them down with him to the river, where he continued to busy himself, for all the world like a big crab, crawling first one way and then the other, on the narrow strip of sand just left dry by the receding water. Cecilia was too busy aboard the mill to wonder what he was doing and when she finally came ashore she was too tired to ask him. She hardly had time to swallow her dinner when her head began to nod and the servant girl had to put her to bed as if she were a baby.

She fell happily enough into a deep sleep, but the next morning in spite of being thoroughly rested she had a vague feeling of worry, which she at first attributed to some forgotten bad dream and thought she would shake off as soon as she plunged her face into a basin of cold water. But it continued to haunt her, and although she had won her three-day struggle, now in retrospect she saw dangers to which she had given no thought when they were actually overhanging and succumbed to them in her imagination. The unaccustomed fear in the voice of the faithful Schiavetto echoed clearly in her ears and seemed to enfold her, like that fear of fear which so often leads a man, for want of a more reasonable kind of courage, to commit suicide. In earthquake countries there are people who are said to suffer from "earthquake shock," a mistrust of the stability of the earth beneath their feet that lasts long after the quake itself is over. A similar feeling toward the river on whose banks she had always lived now came over Cecilia as she seemed to hear again Schiavetto's desperate cry: "Holy souls in purgatory, come to our aid!"

She tried to laugh and to persuade herself that the danger was gone, but to no avail. Instead, she saw before her all the more vividly, like an ocean voyager dizzy from taking his first few steps on land, the relentless wrath of the mighty Po, which could only have been instigated by the author of all evil, to whom, as litanies and rogations tell us, has been given power to provoke the great catastrophes of nature.

We must note here that Cecilia, whose drowned father had brought her up in almost savage solitude, had acquired her religious imagery not only from her ingenuous imagination, but from the comparatively late age, the age of reason, when she had first received any doctrinal instruction. She had been impressed by the descriptions of the end of the world such as are to be found in the Apocalypse and the *Dies irae*, and particularly, of course, by the picture of fearful angels in the waters. These religious conceptions are commonly associated with the Middle Ages, which immortalized them in paint and stone, but they also entered into the faith of Cecilia's day and had been handed down to her by Lazzaro Scacerni, her foster father. To while away the long days on the mill and teach her something of the rude life of the millers of days gone by Master Lazzaro had told this serious child many tales of his own adventures. But when it came to the most perilous of them all he did not know how to explain the murderous passion that had for a time enslaved him, and he glossed it over by saying that he had been tempted by the devil. The very reticence of this sentence inspired her imagination, and all the more so when, after a brief pause, he added that only the grace of God had saved him. He found it irreverent to add any details to this simple statement, and its very succinctness impressed it clearly upon her.

And now that she had suddenly lost faith in her beloved Po her simple soul reflected the tragic old pagan superstition, which caused a mortal staggering under a succession of troubles to accredit them to the perfidy of the gods. That her own river should have visited destruction and fear upon her seemed something like a divine betrayal and she might have harbored doubts of God's mercy had not her husband come along and interrupted this tortuous train of thought.

"Do you remember, Cecilia, how my father used to say that ever since the flood of '39 the river had been sapping the dikes' foundations?"

"I remember very well indeed."

"Some day or other, he said, it was sure to break through. He said many other things that are better forgotten, but it made a particular impression on me to hear him say he didn't want to be buried in land that one day would be under water. Of course, people had some reason for calling him 'Apocalypse' after such dire prophecies, and with all due respect for the dead he did have some odd quirks to his character. But for understanding the river there was never a man like him."

"That's true."

"I paid more attention than he realized to what he was saying. Of course, I know he was often vexed with me for what he thought was indifference on my part. Was it his fault or mine? We weren't cut out to get along together, that's all, and may God rest his soul."

"Amen!"

"One of the things he taught me was that the banks of the river are in an especially perilous condition when the flood comes after a long period of drought."

"Yes, I remember that too."

"He blamed in part the holes burrowed by moles and rats and the cracks opened by the dry weather. But above all he said that if the embankment isn't built out of tightly packed, homogeneous earth but has veins of sand and peat in it, or, worse yet, if it rests upon a clay foundation, then after a drought has dried up the moisture that held it together a sudden flood will easily penetrate it and before you know it there will be a break."

"Yes, he used to say that the embankment is like a pistol, and that if you don't change the cartridges every so often you'll find they don't go off when you need them."

"Exactly. And that these dikes are the most loosely packed portion of the banks, made out of mixed varieties of dirt and built over the rubble of some earlier construction whose stones are bared every time the water rises and presses against them. That's why you may have seen me yesterday pointing out the condition of the base of the dikes to the representatives of the Commission."

"Yes, I saw you," said Cecilia, with a presentiment of disaster to come.

"Those people on the Commission aren't good for anything except spending the taxpayers' money," Giuseppe went on. "But it was my duty to tell them about the condition of the dikes. And you can imagine how concerned I was when I saw the flood rising after such a long drought as we had last summer."

"That concerned you more than the fact that I was all alone there on the mill, did it?" asked Cecilia, half laughing.

"You're a woman able to deal with anything that comes along," he said hastily. "And besides, if the dikes are broken through it's not the mills that are in danger. I'm thinking about my land!"

"Even Schiavetto said he'd never seen an uglier flood in all his years on the river. Were you worried about our children here at Poplar Bridge?" she asked, not without emotion.

"Well, it's all over now," Giuseppe grumbled. "But the condition of the dikes is just as bad as it was before and what worries me is the thought of my land that lies just behind them. One fine day a sudden squall may wash it all away."

"But your father used to say that Poplar Bridge was well protected by the road, which is built over an older dike with a solid foundation."

"Who said anything about Poplar Bridge?"

"You referred to your land, didn't you?" said Cecilia, somewhat surprised.

"I said . . . that is, I meant to say . . ." Giuseppe stammered, realizing that he had revealed more than he intended.

"What *did* you mean then?"

"I meant the Ca' Morgosa farm."

"But that belongs to Pietro Vergoli, doesn't it? Didn't you tell me? . . ."

"Yes, I told you it was Pietro Vergoli's. But I sowed it at my own expense, and this year's crop is mine."

Cecilia felt uneasy without knowing why.

"You told me you'd bought Ca' Morgosa for him and with his money."

"Yes, I did!" exclaimed Giuseppe, who was somewhat put out. Then, regaining his self-control he added unctuously: "Wasn't it right for me to help him out of his trouble?"

"That doesn't sound like you, Peppino. What you said before rings more true."

"What's that?"

"When you referred to Ca' Morgosa as your land."

"That's what it is to talk to a woman. She can't help sticking her nose into everything and if you give her an inch she'll take an ell. I'm always in the wrong, am I? What's all this about what rings true and what doesn't?"

"You know very well what I mean."

"What if I didn't know at all?"

"When money's at stake you're not likely to be moved by pity. And from what you let slip I suspect something even worse."

"What's that?"

"If the land is yours then I don't know where you found the money to pay for it, and if you didn't find the money I don't see how you can call it yours."

"I feel as if I were up before the magistrate again for cross-examination!"

"I hope you won't actually come up before him again!"

"So you incline to think that I'm a thief and a cheat, do you?"

Cecilia started to say that one must speak no ill, even of the devil, but checked herself and remarked mildly:

"It must be a very sore point for you to be so angry about it!"

"Haven't I reason to be offended?"

"Not if you can tell me that you have done no wrong and have no intention of doing any."

"Imagine having my own wife suspect me, and just on the basis of a careless word!"

"You're not careless by nature. I only say that if the cap fits put it on."

"Never mind so many proverbs. It's positively evilminded of you to be so suspicious. And it's not at all in keeping with your religion."

"You taught me to mistrust you, if memory serves me right, by the way you tricked me into marriage."

"That was a scurvy trick, I admit. But if I were to play one on a stranger, what would it matter to you?"

"You see! Wasn't I right to suspect you?"

"But if the risk—granting there is any—and all the bother and inconvenience are mine, while you and the children stand to profit, surely you've no objection. There's a proverb to cover that too: 'A rich man may go to hell, but his heirs are none the less lucky for that.'"

"But what about honesty and conscience?"

"Have I asked you to do anything dishonest?"

"After all, I'm your wife."

"Say you're sorry for that, if you like."

"I say I'm your wife, that's all, and I know my obligations. But do you know the difference between right and wrong, that's what I wonder."

Giuseppe's only answer was to shrug his shoulders.

When Cecilia heard it confirmed by Venusta Chiccoli and others that Giuseppe had to all intents and purposes stolen another man's property she fell prey again to her half-repressed fear of the river, which was increased by pangs of conscience over her husband's misdeed and the certainty that ill-gotten gains would bring some terrible retribution. Such retribution would come from the river, this she knew, because she had been born in a land where everything, including the land itself, came from the river and by the river was taken away, so that the river was synonymous with fate. The honest Cecilia's convictions on this score were far more substantial than the doubtful tribute which worldly folk pay to fortune, holding it responsible for more of both good and evil than it can possibly give.

That the devil's flour is quick to rot is a saying known in every part of the globe where men mill wheat and eat bread, and this is exactly what Cecilia thought of Giuseppe's newly acquired riches. But now that she had faced the situation squarely and realized that it called for atonement she was delivered from her oppressive fear. For a passion for justice is so deeply rooted in the human breast that it strengthens us and inspires us to exact a penalty from our own selves, even when, as in this case, we are only partially guilty of a crime.

What share, we may ask, did Cecilia have in her husband's guilt, that she should feel the necessity of making expiation? This question was one of a kind that might have led to other doubts and fears, that might even have disturbed her Christian humility and turned it into that all too human pride which thinks to defy the justice of the Almighty, although it actually does no more than try His endless patience.

But if Cecilia did not ask herself any such question the reason was a very simple one: it would never have occurred to her. Since marriage had caused her to share her husband's life and luck, to let him down in time of need would have struck her as being equivalent to a soldier's desertion of his comrades, even if they had got him into trouble. Her naturally good character plus a thorough schooling in virtue had made her just the opposite of the stupid Pharisee, who comparing himself to the publican thanked God that he was not like other men. For her scorn of Giuseppe's evil actions did not make her feel superior to him; on the contrary, she resigned herself to sharing whatever punishment it might please God to send his way.

Strange as it may seem to moderns, law, custom and religion all conspired to imbue a woman of her race and time with unalterable conviction of the sacred indissolubility of the marriage bond. Passion might strain but never break it, and no amount of specious reasoning could furnish an excuse for its circumvention. If the reader protests that I am foisting excessively deep feelings upon my rustic heroine, this only goes to show that moral principles and sentiments are more often to be found in a simple soul than in a complex one. There is an heroic cast to the Italian's temperament which inclines him when in love to say: "Forever!" rather than: "Let's try it and see!" Of course this does not apply to Cecilia's case because she was not in love with her husband, but for

516

this reason her loyalty was all the nobler; it was a tribute to the sacrament of matrimony and the responsibilities of motherhood.

Meanwhile, day by day and month by month, time went by. The winter of '58 went down in history for its fierce cold. The Po froze over and people walked and rode over it, which was all very amusing except to the millers, who had to battle the ice day and night to keep their wheels in motion. This job was made inhumanly difficult by the record cold, and when finally the mill wheels stopped there was a shortage of flour in the region. Pietro Vergoli had set up, near Ferrara, the steam mill whose advent had aroused such scorn in Master Lazzaro, and this turned out to be a precious aid in the emergency. The old miller, had he been alive, would have said that the freeze was a work of the devil and that Vergoli was still capitalizing on the misfortunes of his fellows. But he would have been mistaken. For in spite of his errors, this stubborn and energetic man still provided bread and work for all who sought them.

The freeze completely ruined the crop which Giuseppe had sown on the Ca' Morgosa farm. But instead of losing courage he planted it all over again with different varieties of seeds and said to the peasant:

"It was time for a change, and had it not been for this incentive we might never have made it. God never slams a door without opening a window."

As for Master Lazzaro, he would have had no time for mere words under circumstances such as those faced that winter by his beloved Cecilia. Looking out over the glaring white expanse of water she and her helpers worked with iron-tipped wooden poles to break the encroaching ice before it could get a grip on the wheels of the mills. And when at last the spring thaw came, bringing with it a rush of high water, they still had to fend off any drifting blocks and splinters of ice that might have pierced holes in the hulks.

By God's grace this trial, too, passed away. Yet it was worthy of being immortalized in a song like the one which celebrates the labor the humble Italian immigrant has put into the building of cities all over the globe, where his contribution has for the most part gone unrecorded. For the miller, like the immigrant, is "unknown to fame."

LAZZARINO

1

"BEANS! A thousand bags of beans! Gentlemen, your offers!"
The auctioneer was haranguing a small crowd in a courtyard
inside the Ferrara Fortress. He stood behind a table and back
of him were piled up bales, barrels, and pieces of furniture, the kitchen-
wares and supplies of the Austrian garrison, which had just left the
city. The day, June 29, was a hot one.

"I'm waiting for your bids, gentlemen. First quality dried beans.
Come see them for yourselves," and he ordered one of his assistants to
open up a bag.

Foodstuffs along with furniture, doors, windows, and all removable
trimmings of the Fortress were on the auction block, for the Austrian
and Papal troops had been gone a week, and the provisional government
of the province of Emilia, heartily backed up by public opinion, had
decreed that the Fortress should be razed to the ground. People were
streaming over the walls, barracks, batteries, shooting ranges, and
storerooms for arms and ammunition within its vast five-pointed star.
Only a few of them stopped to watch the gesticulations of the auctioneer.

"Let me have an opening bid!"

If there had been a larger crowd looking on the first bidder would
not have had the courage to name so low a price, but finding himself
among friends he came out with:

"Three crowns!"

"Ridiculous!" said the auctioneer with the scornful look that was part
of his stock in trade. "If someone doesn't offer me more than that I'll
take the beans off sale. Three crowns! You must be joking."

"Three crowns and two coppers!" said another. And a thousand bags
came to well over a ton.

"Gentlemen, we're not here just for the fun of it."

He saw before him twenty or thirty cautious faces with an expression of indifference and absent-mindedness that was meant to mask
their eagerness to buy, but only made it stand out the more clearly.
The owners were like so many schoolboys who have not done their
lesson and therefore put on studiedly obtuse expressions which fail to
conceal their fear that the teacher will ask them a question. It was hot,
as we have said above, and they were all perspiring.

The prospective buyers were recruited from the moneylenders, speculators, and junk dealers of the city, who invariably turned up at any
sale of this kind in order to divide the pickings of a bankruptcy or

518

disaster. In spite of their rivalry there was a tacit understanding among them with a view to keeping prices down, a sort of professional alliance directed against any outsider who might offer a fair amount and thereby, in their estimation, ruin the business.

"Three crowns and a half," said a third bidder, condescendingly.

"Four," said another, as if he were waking up from a dream.

The auctioneer was looking the other way, as if he had lost all interest in the proceedings.

"Four crowns and six coppers."

"Gentlemen, I'll give orders to sound the trumpet."

This instrument stood alongside the auctioneer's hammer, ready to "trumpet" the sale and invite the general public to compete in the bidding.

"You gentlemen know how loudly my trumpeter blows."

An alarmed silence fell over the little group. The presence of the public might be a threat to low prices and to their reputation and safety as well.

For people were vastly excited over recent events: the victorious war, the Austrian defeat, the end of the Papal rule, the ingress of a provisory government, and the prospect of becoming part of the new Italian nation. In this mood they might well turn against anyone who was trying to buy up the goods left behind by the oppressors in order to make money on them in the market. The crowd had penetrated the cellars and every other musty, abandoned corner of the Fortress, as if they could not get enough of their new liberty to curse, deride, defile, and generally trespass upon this pile which had so long been a symbol of tyranny. They exchanged apocryphal tales of the most lurid variety and began to search for dungeons, torture chambers, trap doors and other horrors which they attributed not only to the lately departed Austrians but to the Papal garrison of older days as well, although history tells us that the latter was a very tame affair, so tame that Bonaparte found it commanded by a monk who cared less for guns and gunpowder than for the sacred functions he performed in the little Chapel of the Annunciation within the walls. But popular opinion now insisted that in the shadow of the beetling Fortress no one could breathe freely, even those who had apparently been breathing all their life long. In short, the crowd's anger could not be assuaged except by the destruction of the Fortress.

Let us, however, return to the auction. If a single voice were to proclaim that the usual profiteers and money-lenders were turning it to their own ends and sucking the blood of the people there was serious danger that it would end in a free-for-all fight. And so, in order to prevent the trumpet from making a public announcement, one of the little group of buyers raised seven fingers, indicating a bid of seven crowns. The others sighed, torn between avarice and greed, sorry that they had come, and yet unable to tear themselves away. The bidding went very slowly up and finally the customary three strokes of the hammer dis-

519

posed of the beans at a low price. And there followed in the same way cheeses, sugar, coffee, oil, vinegar, soap, coal, wood, dried and preserved fish, rice, oats, corn meal, flour, furnishings and fixtures of every kind, including chairs, beds, tables, and prison benches.

Indignation reigned during the following days in the city, when it came out at what low prices all these things had been sold. And since there is always someone who is wise after the event, people who had not bothered to notice the sale when it was underneath their eyes now rose up to say that it should be annulled, that everything sold should be recuperated and put up at auction again. But of course by now most of it had already been resold, and Giuseppe Scacerni, for one, had put away a number of sacks of flour in a storeroom on the Ca' Morgosa farm. Luckily the people's attention was soon distracted by the joyful task of tearing down the Fortress.

2

There were several of Giuseppe's market-place acquaintances at the auction and he had been unable to resist the temptation of attending it himself. He was attracted half by curiosity and half by the memory of the time when he had sold grain to the garrison. But once he was there neither his own memories nor the joyous tumult of the crowd could distract him. He was all eyes and ears for the auction, as if he were determined to do one last piece of good business with the Austrians. And when flour and cereals came up on the block there was no more cautious bidder. Naming a separate price for every bag and every bushel he succeeded in irritating all those present and especially the auctioneer, who once more threatened to sound the trumpet.

"Nobody knows what I've suffered on account of the Austrians!" Giuseppe explained with an air of wounded dignity. "It's only fair that now the shoe should be on the other foot. The profit I may make in pennies won't make up for the crowns they've cost me. Not to mention the trouble I've seen; for that no money can repay."

In these days everyone had taken to vociferating about the wrongs they had suffered at the Austrians' hands. And now one of the bidders asked ironically:

"What troubles may those be, my good man?"

"I'm not given to bragging," Giuseppe answered promptly. "But I came very near to a flogging. Have you any idea what it is to get twenty-four strokes of the stick from those krauts?"

"Not I."

"Well, I have, and it's a miracle that I escaped them."

None of the other speculators could boast any such distinction, and they looked on Giuseppe with increased respect, including the auctioneer, who once more gave up the idea of sounding the trumpet. Giuseppe had a remarkable gift for what we have learned to call wishful thinking, and in this instance, by passing himself off as a patriot, he succeeded in obtaining the auctioned flour at a rock-bottom price. Some of those present might have remembered the turkey episode of 1848, when Giuseppe had been laughed out of the market place, but about this there was a conspiracy of silence. Without going so far as to hold himself up as a last-minute hero Giuseppe actually persuaded himself and hence others that he deserved some compensation for the flogging he had escaped so narrowly and the miscellaneous difficulties of the last ten years. Just as a moralistic millionaire is sure that his moneybags will win him a place in heaven, so was Giuseppe convinced that what he wanted was no more than his just due, although in his case the conviction arose out of his personal temperament rather than any theological principle. Now, having established a patriotic reputation, he proceeded to go into business again in the market place of Ferrara, where he soon made so much money that when Vergoli put the Antonella farm up for sale he was able to add it to the adjacent Ca' Morgosa and become a landowner on a large scale.

The first years of the Kingdom of Italy, and indeed many of those to follow, were weighed down by the financial burdens of a war and something like a social revolution. Only a small minority of the people were prepared for unity, independence, and political freedom, and it was not long before the majority were grumbling: "Things were not so bad the way they used to be."

Little people, in particular, felt oppressed by the civil and military obligations incumbent upon a modern nation, which fell upon their shoulders before they received any advantage from their new condition, or were even aware of its meaning. They were subject to high taxes, a rise in the cost of living, and military conscription, and as a result they began to belittle their right to vote and all the rest of their constitutional liberties. There was some spite in this attitude, but also a degree of justification, since most of the new privileges were enjoyed by the wealthy and aristocratic few, while the drawbacks were felt by everybody, especially the poor. They could not help mourning the evasive clauses of the old constitution while the virtues of the new one were still so theoretical that the promise of them only aroused discontent, as if they were being told to look at a reflection of the moon in the water, when there was a rising tide of petty annoyances about them.

These were the humble beginnings of the Kingdom of Italy, which command our respect because they were built upon everyday small sacrifices, not always the easiest to make and yet providing a solid base for the growth of a national character. The common people, it is true, played no large part in the events of the Risorgimento,* but they were called upon to pay its debts and did so courageously.

Just as they became acquainted with the faults and abuses of the parliamentary system before its merits tardily dawned upon them, so did they suffer the economic crises inherent to capitalism before experiencing, at least by hearsay, the benefits that attach to it. This was par-

* The movement for political unity in Italy; literally, the Revival.

ticularly true in the former Papal States, whose economic structure was particularly backward because it had been designed to preserve social stability in an environment of scarce capital, low prices, and a total lack of business enterprise or initiative.

In the Ferrara region, after 1860, land reclamation was resumed on a large scale, with capital from other parts of Italy and even from abroad. The speculative purpose of such investment was the division of large estates and their subsequent purchase in small lots by the peasants. But the process was a long one and much more expensive than had been anticipated. Some of the land previously reclaimed was in good, dry condition, but it was still unready for agricultural use for it needed trees, roads, farm buildings, drainage ditches, and fresh water to run through the irrigation canals and clean out the stagnant pools with which they were filled. These canals, locally known as "straight-line swamps," had come to breed just as much malaria as the vast bogs which they had replaced. And drinking water was another urgent need, for this still had to be hauled for both men and beasts all the long way from the Po. This was the heritage of the first reclamation efforts of some thirty or forty years before the time at which we have now arrived in our story. Now that the work was taken up again on a vaster scale, labor was hard to come by and expensive, and landowners, both large and small, had a difficult time of it. Meanwhile the rapidly mounting cost of living prevented even the laborers from enjoying their high salaries. This is an inevitable result when a pioneering enterprise is undertaken in a region where there is, as yet, no industry. An old balance is broken and there is as yet no new one to take its place, so that needs and wants are stimulated without there being any possibility of their finding satisfaction.

Richer parts of the country profited by the economic revival and the people of poorer sections embraced the heroic solution of emigration. But the province of Emilia and the country around Ferrara were neither sufficiently rich to start with nor (if it were human to say so) sufficiently poor. So it was that they remained in a state of uneasiness and turmoil. Their disorders were never aggravated by rebellious poverty on the one hand, or channelled into peaceful progress on the other, and the people, while more hot-blooded than their prosperous neighbors to the north, were at the same time more rational than the struggling masses to the south.

It is the human side of this economic picture that leads me, perhaps to the reader's surprise, to depart from the well-trodden ways of the novel and embark upon a background panorama. But what is a novel's style, or any style at all that is worth having, except the intonation of a man who is seeking to surmount the difficulties of conveying the truth and whose only pride lies in his awareness of how unequal he is to this glorious task?

Giuseppe Scacerni (God forgive him, as his wife would have said!) had become the owner of several pieces of land with a long history behind them. Although as a merchant he was quick to profit by higher prices and free trade, as a landowner and miller, with heavy taxes to pay, he took advantage of the new liberties, which he had never dreamed of possessing during the Pope's reign, to belittle the new government that was their author. Of course, when he heard his own accusations echoed by the poor, he not only failed to recognize them but actually called upon the government to act more severely against those who complained about it.

Giuseppe paid no attention to politics except when he heard criticism of the new government, and of this, both public and private, there was plenty. The common people, particularly in the country, were faithful to the priests, and these, with a bitterness unworthy of their sacred calling, cursed and fought the king and the government for the sacrilege of having confiscated ecclesiastical wealth. They struck fear into the hearts of the timorous and aroused the women to anger, seeking to enlarge every gesture of discontent and even advising ways of evading military service and taxes. In retaliation, the Liberal monarchists and moderates of the government party harked back to the attitude of Voltaire, which stemmed from the Jacobin and libertine philosophy of the eighteenth century.

For reasons which we have more than once touched upon before—the lack of sound philosophical doctrine even among persons of learning and taste, and the spiritual damage done by the Church's temporal power—it was inevitable that the former Papal States should be the scene of the bitterest fight between clericals and anti-clericals, neither of which factions showed very much use of reason. Religious fanatics often offended the spirit of religion, while the supposed Liberals were simply people without faith and reverence. There was something cowardly about their affectation of sceptical indifference, something that made them less worthy of respect than the free-masons and militant anti-Catholics scattered throughout their ranks who, however rudely, did face the problem instead of debasing their characters by evading it.

The government was handicapped by its inexperience and by the dead weight of inherited financial and moral problems, by a series of wars and revolutions and a rustiness of the governmental machinery, which gave rise to much abuse, scandal, and suspicion. Great moral damage was done by the conspicuous success of recent converts to the new government, while the veterans of the Risorgimento were pushed aside and often persecuted. The latter did require some control, for they had a tendency to continue acting like conspirators outside the law. But they were treated in such varying and unpredictable ways, first with excessive tolerance and then with sudden severity that, inevitable as the mistake may have been, people could not help thinking that the whole thing was a game and a pretense, that the government did not expect its orders to be taken seriously, and that public life was ruled by the principle of concealing one's thoughts and dissembling one's intentions. The widespread belief in this inferior form of Machiavellian strategy wrought great moral damage, as did an excess of favoritism, in which even King Victor Emmanuel indulged.

The nation was prey to sloth and malice. After centuries of forced prudence and dissimulation there was an orgy of abuse of free speech. Instead of the healthy practice of liberty, this was a superficial ebullience with all the hectic and deceiving excitement of a fever. It was a period of jokes and cartoons, of mudslinging and defamation carried to such a sickly extreme that they weakened by excessive stimulation the moral and intellectual fiber of the Italian people.

3

One of the questions that created most bitterness between Garibaldi and Cavour was that of the irregular Garibaldi volunteers, or *Garibaldini*, who could no longer be tolerated by the government and therefore considered themselves victims of neglect and injustice. There was one of these at Guarda, a good fellow called Stump because he had lost his forearm in the battle of the Volturno River. Even after 1866, when the Austrians ceded his native province of Venetia to Italy, he did not return there but stayed on at Guarda as a river watcher. He was a great talker and never ceased praising General Garibaldi and lamenting the fact that his mutilated arm brought him such an insignificant pension. He found another good case against the pettiness of the government in the fact that the military medal struck off in 1865 in commemoration of the wars for the liberation and unification of Italy was given only to those who had served with a regular army formation and (to the contemporary cartoonists' delight) cost all others the round sum of six liras. He maintained that if Garibaldi had been in command of the army then the battles of Custozza and Lissa would have had a very different outcome, and since it is very easy to be wise after the event, especially when it has turned out badly, he had no trouble in finding an audience for his strictures.

"If Garibaldi wants a Republic, what's the matter with that?" he concluded. "Let him be king, pope, emperor or whatever he chooses!"

"We poor shall always be in trouble, anyhow," chimed in Woodcock, who was among those who, disappointed in their revolutionary hopes, had taken refuge in bitterness and sarcasm.

This state of mind had already shown itself in outbreaks of mob violence in Sicily after Garibaldi's passage there on his way to Rome and also in Milan, at the opposite end of the peninsula, where there was still an enthusiastic reaction to the cry of "Death to the rich!" And there was a new element in the political picture in Bologna and vicinity, where this period witnessed the stirrings of the First International, known under an equalitarian, anarchical, communistic label or under the name of its originator, Bakunin, the Russian idealist and agitator. Here the theory of unlimited progress so dear to the nineteenth century found a ready response among Italian peasants who hoped to see the revolution in their country carried further. Their justified discontent easily fitted into this theory and its far-fetched elucubrations, which brought together radical intellectuals and simple souls completely ignorant of politics. These had in common a bent for excessive and illogical simplification such as is often found among the very poor and the very fanatical, the ignorant and those who go in for abstract learning.

An unemployed and conceited comic actor recruited for the new movement in Bologna, and as it became known throughout the provinces of Emilia and Romagna Woodcock naturally became one of its adherents. He shocked his neighbors with the profane slogan "No more gods either on earth or in heaven!" and even told poor Stump, the river watcher, that Garibaldi and his ideas were outdated.

"What?" said Stump, almost mute with astonishment. "Garibaldi outdated?"

"Yes, and Mazzini too."

"Garibaldi, let me tell you, is like good bread. When every other kind of food ruins the stomach a loaf of bread will always stay with you."

"If you talk that way it's a sign that you too are superannuated."

"Who's superannuated?"

"You and all the rest of the devotees of Garibaldi and Mazzini."

"And just what do you mean by that?"

"You overthrew one tyrant only to acquire another."

"Garibaldi's not a tyrant, he's a god."

"That's it, exactly! A god and a tyrant are the same thing."

His audience was stunned by this dialectic.

"It's no use Mazzini's being against the Pope if he only wants to take his place or be president of a bourgeois Republic, which amounts to the same thing."

"I can't follow your argument, but I ask you, hasn't Garibaldi always fought for freedom?"

"Yes, he has, but if you say that he's infallible and honor him like a king, then your freedom's gone out the window."

"A man must pin his faith on someone," said Stump with embarrassment.

"I have faith in no man."

"What's that?"

"My only faith is in the idea of a free human race."

"Explain that idea to me better."

"No gods either on earth or in heaven, all men brothers, with no one to command or obey; the earth and all its wealth divided in equal shares; no money or kow-towing to authority, that's what I'm talking about. God is an invention of the priests to enable them to divide the world between themselves and the kings or the bourgeois government that has taken their place."

At this point even those who had listened to him most sympathetically were taken aback by the violence of his atheism.

"Even if Garibaldi were king, he'd be a kind master, I can swear to that."

"That's the worst thing of all."

"That's a fine one! What in heaven's name do you mean?"

"Because a wicked tyrant bends the people to his will with brute force, but a kind one throws the spell of his love over them, and that's far stronger. There's never been a kinder man than Jesus Christ, has there? And for eighteen centuries the world has been under His yoke."

"That's because He's been taken over by the priests," said Stump, who had heard some of Garibaldi's speeches and pronouncements against the Church.

"Any man who serves another has himself to blame for it. And, I repeat, a good master is worse than a bad one, because he lulls people into contentment. If you want to have a genuine, worldwide social revolution (don't report me to the carabineers!) . . ." and he lowered his voice as if he were speaking of a powerful secret army, ". . . then you must have a band of men driven to desperation."

"Dogs without a master, that's all," interrupted Sapienza, the proprietor of the Barchessa tavern, adding crudely: "Just put a juicy bone or a bitch that's in heat among them and you'll see what their brotherhood amounts to."

"That's slaves' talk," said Woodcock disgustedly.

"Then go ahead and talk like a madman if you will. But I want to keep out of trouble with the carabineers, so I'll thank you to do your talking outside my tavern."

The new café at Guarda proved to be equally inhospitable, and besides the carabineers had their post next door, just behind the church. This was the good fortune of Orlandini, known as the Rat, the tavern keeper at Guarda Crossing, whose business had gone to pieces because with the new government there was no more smuggling across the Po and also because he stubbornly refused to better the quality of his wine. The malcontents, what few of them were not scared away by fear of the law or the wine's effect on their stomachs, chose this for their hangout, and the younger men were particularly attracted by its isolated and almost conspiratorial position down on the shore, between the riverbank and the water. As for the Rat, he was not in the least worried about the carabineers, for the simple reason that he made regular reports to them on who came to his tavern and what was the subject of their conversation. Of course he took pains to be discreet about it for fear that his customers might beat him up or duck his head in the river.

So it was that a band of would-be anarchist desperadoes took shape at Guarda. They were conspicuously absent from the church and at the hour of Sunday Mass they gathered defiantly on the green and mocked the devout, older peasants who wore up-turned caps like Giuseppe Scacerni's and gold earrings. But the latter did not choose to pay any attention.

526

Giuseppe, as it happened, was a frequent visitor at the Rat's tavern, not for the sake of the drink or the conversation but in order to find Stump, the river watcher, who still held forth against Woodcock in defense of Garibaldi, and to take him to look at the rapid crumbling and disintegration of the dikes.

"I see perfectly. You're quite right," Stump invariably assented.

"Very well! You don't need to say that to me; I know it already!"

"Then why do you call me to look?" Stump asked.

"So that you'll inform your superiors."

"Come, come, my dear man! They only see what they want to see; otherwise they wouldn't be where they are."

"But have you told them that one fine day there'll be a break?"

"Haven't you told them yourself?"

"At least a dozen times!"

"And did they pay any attention?"

"But now I'm telling *you*, and I shall hold you responsible. The safety of the whole village is at stake."

"If your land weren't in such an exposed condition I doubt if you'd worry very much about the safety of the village!"

"You ought to be hauled into court for saying that!" Giuseppe shouted. "Let the river break through, then, and submerge the countryside, if you people want to spite me!"

Giuseppe added on this score to his notoriety, and even those who shared his fears did not say so but amused themselves by goading him to anger.

"Once upon a time there were gallows set up every ten miles along the river to teach a lesson to those who neglected the care of the banks!" Giuseppe shouted.

"When was that, 'once upon a time'?" they asked, leading him on.

"Under the rule of the Pope. And may God punish those who've robbed him of his due!"

"You forget that I'm one of them," Stump answered proudly, "and that I lost half an arm for the sake of putting Italy together!"

"I'd give a whole arm and half a leg besides to take it apart again!" Giuseppe foamed. "The gallows, you swine! You belong on the gallows!"

"You're a little daft, and I'm sorry for you," said the *Garibaldino*. "Who's ever heard of these gallows along the river?"

"My father saw them with his own eyes and counted them all the way from here to Lagoscuro. There was one every ten miles, I tell you."

Of course there had never been any such thing, but in his rage Giuseppe believed what he was saying and so did poor Stump, who shook his head gravely and said to the bystanders:

"There's the Pope's tyranny for you! Imagine so many gallows! Well, we've all heard tell of the Inquisition, haven't we? Did you know that they tortured people by making them swallow melted lead?"

"That's good brandy compared to what I'd like to force down the

527

throats of certain people of this neighborhood. Lucky for you that the gallows have gone!"

So Giuseppe added a reputation for being a reactionary to the bad name he already enjoyed as a profiteer. But he was among the most prosperous men of the neighborhood and because people had to come to him for a loan or an advance of money they kept their dislike of him to themselves and were content to look on with amusement at his frequent attacks of bad temper. The chief sufferer from his father's unpopularity was Lazzarino, his oldest son, who everyone agreed was a very fine boy.

In the early summer of 1866 Lazzarino was just eleven years old, a quick and precociously intelligent little fellow. His father had taught him to read and write; Schiavetto swore that he was already adept at the miller's trade, and Cecilia was proud to have him for a helper. From early childhood he had been unusually strong and brave and between his eleventh and his twelfth years he shot up in a way that caused all those who had known his grandfather to say that one day he would surpass him in stature as well as in heart and brains. Some wooden shoes stored aboard Saint Michael's Mill, which had been too large for anyone to wear since Master Lazzaro's death, fitted Lazzarino to perfection and, to the general astonishment, some of his grandfather's old clothes, although too big around the waist, were almost right for his long legs and broad shoulders.

On the day he tried these things on the boy was a trifle embarrassed over the sudden increase in his size. He was simple, frank, and shy, with a sensitive openheartedness which together with his mature judgment and the high spirits natural to his age made him a favorite with everyone. His playmates idolized him because he was at the same time muscular and good, and the villagers were happy to see him whenever he accompanied his father on his rounds. Lazzarino liked to drive or ride his father's horse, to row a boat, to swim across the river, even when the waves were high, and to talk to the peasants about their work on the Ca' Morgosa and Antonella farms. It would be quite superfluous to say how much his mother adored him, but what was more remarkable was the exaggerated and almost savage love which he inspired in his father. This was all the deeper because Giuseppe could not express it and because it contained an element of repentance for his own shortcomings together with the hope that he might atone for them through the merits of his son. Thanks to Lazzarino, Giuseppe was able to pray, and the one grace he asked of God was the assurance of his beloved boy's prosperity and preservation.

Even in this unselfishness there was something sinful, for of all the seven children whom Cecilia bore him, Lazzarino was the only one he cared for, and the rest of them he shamelessly neglected. Cecilia was perfectly aware of this, but since she could hardly reproach him for loving Lazzarino, she simply did the best she could to make up for his indifference toward the others. If ever she showed any severity toward her first-born and indulgence toward the rest Giuseppe was almost sure to make a scene. Lazzarino suffered from this state of affairs and with instinctive tact and delicacy sought to calm his father and to console his brothers and sisters with proofs of his affection. He and his mother understood one another at a glance, which of course made Giuseppe very jealous.

"His father is positively mad about the boy," Cecilia often said, "but he's not to be blamed for that."

And the local people had a way of saying to Lazzarino's face:

"The only worthwhile thing Were Rabbit ever did was to have a son like you."

Lazzarino was offended by the nickname bestowed upon his father and threatened to wring the neck of the next person who used it in his presence. Because it was clear that very soon he would be quite strong enough to carry this out there were some people malicious enough, in the short respite that was left them, to try to hurt Giuseppe on the only score where he was the least bit sensitive, namely his son. For Giuseppe had made himself more hated than ever for the last couple of years, ever since the government engineers had finally decided to strengthen the dikes at Nogarole.

They chose to build what they called a crown, that is a secondary bank back of the old one, a large part of which was to be on Giuseppe's land. At the prospect of having hundreds of laborers digging up his good earth for months on end Giuseppe complained that they wanted to ruin him and insisted, besides, that it would cost them less money to stave up the actual dikes directly on the water. The land was not suitable, he said, for supporting a second bank, and also this would create an unnatural curve in the river. He collected signatures for a petition in which he set forth these arguments, some of which were true, but since he himself was the only injured party he had a hard time to find anyone that would sign it. By the time he had it ready the legal period before the beginning of the actual work was over, and he had wasted his time and effort, not to mention the expense of the notary's seal, to which the other signatories had not wished to contribute.

He found another cause for annoyance in the question of the indemnity he was supposed to receive for his expropriated land. On this score he made such a fuss that finally, on the basis of a public utility law of 1865, he was sentenced to have his land taken from him and to accept whatever indemnity the government chose to offer. The only alternative was a costly lawsuit, with the chances against his winning. Even his lawyer, who was expert at cavilling and had a passion for lost causes, told him as much. But Giuseppe was unconquerably stubborn. He wanted to bring suit against the government.

"I'd rather endure a flood than the government's intrusion," he said to all and sundry.

"Speak for yourself," they answered him at Guarda. "Did you know that a break in the dikes might put half the province under water?"

529

"Devil take the province, I say!"

"Is that the way to talk?" said one, and, "He speaks like a jackass," said another.

"You can die every last one of you, for all I care," said Giuseppe. "I'm willing to die myself."

"Like Samson with the Philistines, is that it? Meanwhile you're making us die of laughter."

The work had already begun, with almost a thousand laborers overrunning Giuseppe's property. They stole chickens, pigs, fruit and grain and turned the place into something like a community forest, where everyone can cut down to his heart's content. Every clod they turned up tore at Giuseppe's heartstrings and he was so thwarted by his inability to defend himself and so exasperated by his neighbors' laughter that he forbid anyone to glean the remains of the harvests of wheat and flax that year. The poor were authorized by an ancient custom to gather up what they could after the season was over and no one could believe until he saw it with his own eyes that Giuseppe had actually imposed such a prohibition and stood by with a club to enforce it because none of his peasants would take part in such a profanation. Two widows came hopefully along, and he shouted:

"Away with you, women! I didn't kill your husbands, did I? Why should I be responsible for your feeding?"

And to the orphans:

"Get away, ragamuffins! With the excuse of gleaning the wheat you steal my cherries, and in the flax season you take my grapes. And I didn't bring you into the world, did I, you bastards?"

Some old beggars, men and women, could not take in the fact that he actually meant it.

"We've always been allowed to come here. You yourself . . ."

"I've changed my mind."

"But it's our right!" they exclaimed.

"Examine the law and you'll find no such thing. It's my right to call the police if you insist on gleaning off my land without permission."

"What can you do with a few ears of wheat left on the ground? Surely you're too God-fearing to have them gathered up just to spite us." (For they knew that his peasants had refused to do so.)

"Leave that worry to me!"

And they saw him lean over and shake the dry stalks to get what he could from them. Surely it was worse than usury or theft to rob the hunger of the poor. Antichrist, that's what he was!

Even Cecilia came to beg him to desist, but to no avail.

"Your father has the ugliest mug we've ever seen," the villagers said openly to Lazzarino.

"He should have let you glean, I know, but it's your own fault for mocking him," Lazzarino replied with sorrow.

"He doesn't need the money. He's just a mad dog."

"Don't call him names, I beg of you." And the boy was close to tears.

"We shouldn't speak so of him to you, but this has been too much for us to bear. After all, we're men, not mice."

As the work went on, iron accumulated in Giuseppe's soul and bad blood between him and the peasants. He was obsessed like a damned soul and could not take either his eyes or his thoughts away from the damage that was being done to his land. First of all the contractor to whom the government had given the job had had the necessary part of Giuseppe's land knocked down to him on the auction block and chopped off over 100,000 liras from the 350,000 estimate of expenses made by the government engineers.

"And you can be sure they kept their figures low enough," Giuseppe grumbled. "It would take 400,000 liras to do the job properly; I've calculated it for myself. So what is this contractor doing? Where's he getting the 150,000 liras difference?"

"That's easy; he's stealing them."

"And from whom?"

"From the government, of course. He wouldn't be the first, would he?"

"I don't mind if he steals from the government. In fact, I'm glad of it."

"Well then, what's wrong? He's making a profit and you're glad, so everyone should be satisfied."

"What do you mean, satisfied? I'm eating my heart out over it, that's all."

"You don't have to, do you? Why don't you stick to your own affairs?"

"I do; that's just the point. After all, it's on my land. But I'll not be the only one to suffer, and you know it. Only sheer spite keeps you from being on my side. You'll see, when it's too late. In order to put 100,000 liras in his pocket the contractor is doing a sloppy job and his crown won't stand up, I promise you!"

And he flitted like a bat from one to the other, clutching at their coats and jackets and imploring them to listen. Constant agitation had ringed his neck with boils and pimples, and these were so irritated from scratching that blood streamed down from them over his collar. The fear that the contractor might sue him for libel or take some even more direct form of retaliation caused him to lower his voice, which came out hoarse and squeaking.

"Just take a look at the kind of construction they're doing on the crown, and you'll be even more afraid than I am. When this man has finished the job he'll go away and we'll never see him again. But we'll be stuck with his handiwork and some day it may cost us our lives."

Everyone could verify the accuracy of what he was saying. They knew that, from the start, the engineers had done no more than test the earth by boring a few shallow holes with a worn auger. Because this earth had formerly been part of the river bed it was by definition untrustworthy. And afterwards it had been the bottom of a swamp, thereby adding to an insecure sand and clay foundation the accumulated rot of decayed plants and grasses. These generate what is known as marsh gas, and when water opens up a vein of it there occurs something like an explosion, after which the foundation is completely undermined and the river is certain to crack it and sweep right through. Giuseppe added to this description lurid details which rang true to anyone who had lived near the river.

"All of us know what kind of earth that is," he said. "It was the river bed when the river ran along the old bank on which is now built the road from Guarda to Ro. That's one point to take into consideration!" And he waggled the thumb of his left hand threateningly to emphasize what he was saying. "And when my father anchored at the Nogarole dikes he said that Ca' Morgosa was an island in a swamp and that the foundation of the Antonella farm was definitely marshy. Point two! A river bed and swamp, there you have it."

"Too bad Pietro Vergoli isn't here to drain it," the villagers said, looking at Giuseppe out of the corners of their eyes. "Too bad that after he built his nest another bird should have laid eggs in it."

Giuseppe only shrugged his shoulders and waggled his thumb and forefinger.

"This is no time for idle chatter. Since the land has been mine I've raised hemp on it, and you can count on its being chock-full of decayed roots from that. Point three!"

And he held up his middle finger, which like the rest had short, thick joints and a long hooked nail. The three fingers waggling in the air were reminiscent of the three fateful words that appeared on the wall to mar Belshazzar's feasting.

"And it's on this triply treacherous terrain that they've chosen to build their crown, using the earth that's nearest at hand, made of clay, sand, frozen clods, mud, rot and so on, just so they won't have to fetch something more solid from farther away. When there's a ditch to be filled, instead of cleaning it out they just stuff it with grass and reeds and cover it up without any more trouble. And they're not packing the earth tight either; they simply dump it out of their wheelbarrows and level it off with the backs of their shovels. A gust of wind is enough to destroy a bank of this kind, I tell you."

His hearers blanched. Of course they knew that almost every construction job has some portent of bad luck like this harangue of Were Rabbit. But the crown did seem ill-fated from the start; even the laborers spoke of it disparagingly, and so did the contractor's assistants, who continually accused one another of laxity and then made their complaints a matter of public knowledge. There were even some laborers who swore that they had sacks of good earth in reserve, so that when the government engineer was scheduled to make an inspection they would be ready to throw this over the bad and cover up its deficiencies. In fact this engineer, Manghetti, was openly called a gullible jackass.

"We're working just the way you'd expect from the pay we're getting. It's dog's pay and dog's work, and there you have it."

At a certain point a night shift was set up in order to hasten the job's completion and with this the boldest of the laborers declared:

"The only witnesses to our night work are the stars. And if you don't like the quality of our work that's your lookout, not ours. When we've done we'll shoulder our shovels and say goodbye. We're recruited to work all over the country, like soldiers. And why should poor day laborers like ourselves worry about you peasants who live on the fat of the land?" And they mockingly sang the old song:

> Day and night we're digging,
> In sunshine and in rain;
> Dig in and turn it over,
> Over and over again.
> We shovel for a living
> And whistle for our pain.

"Where is the police? Call the carabineers!" Giuseppe shouted when he saw the seditious look on their faces. And he added: "They say that Schiappazza was the last of the highwaymen. Nowadays robbers work on the embankment of the river, and the worst among them are full-fledged contractors."

This Schiappazza was the last man to be guillotined in the Piazza del Travaglio in Ferrara and the memory of his depredations was still green in the river country.

"Come, come, Were Rabbit!" the villagers said mockingly. "There's a man we all know who's raising a tremendous racket over the safety of some land he owns just behind the dikes. But if anyone asks him where he got that land he doesn't seem to have any answer."

"Of whom are you speaking?"

"You mean to say you don't know?"

"And I don't care either. I don't believe in speaking ill of my neighbors."

Giuseppe's failure to answer them annoyed the villagers even more than the faulty construction of the crown. And they could not forgive him for haranguing them about things they knew very well already. What could be his purpose? They knew, yes, but since there was nothing they could do they preferred to forget the matter entirely. Hadn't the embankments along the Po always been built of whatever material was closest to hand and then gradually solidified with the passage of time? If every bit of badly constructed embankment had been fated to give way, then Ferrara would not still be standing. And why didn't he take his troubles straight to the government instead of trying to intimidate the countryside? If he was so sure of himself he had only to speak to the proper authorities.

"Very well, I will," said Giuseppe. "I'll be the first to petition for an investigation, but you must sign the petition after me."

At this point they backed down, because they did not wish to be bothered.

"Petitions never accomplish anything," they murmured.

"Then you're putting the whole thing on me, are you, you cowards?"

They were irritated, and besides they knew that the grounds of the petition were true, and had a bad conscience over their failure to sign it. So they answered all the more sharply that he should hold his tongue. The only reason they tolerated him at all, they said, was because they knew he was half mad and not responsible for what he was saying. To which Giuseppe only made obscene gestures and did not attempt to reply.

It was plain by now that (to draw an illustrious parallel) his neighbors hated Giuseppe for the same reason that the Trojans hated Cassandra, to whom Apollo gave the divine but ungrateful gift of prophecy.

Because Giuseppe's feelings were encased in such a hard shell that they found it impossible to wound him, they took it out on his son. And this with the cowardly anonymity of the group, all of them taking part, but none of them taking responsibility. They made continual, vague, derogatory insinuations, which they interrupted with a wink or a nudge or a smile as if out of respect for Lazzarino's presence, to a miserly usurer and profiteer who had stolen land from Signor Pietro Vergoli. No one, they said, had anything against Signor Pietro; he was a benefactor of the village and his entanglement with the law, if any blame attached to it, was under the now superseded Papal government, whereas the malefactor of whom they were speaking still walked among them in insolent immunity. They talked in this vein on the public square and the church green and in the tavern, and although Lazzarino swore more than once that he would stay away and pay them no attention his humiliation brought him back over and over again.

"That man should be put out of the way like a mad dog," he heard them say, "if it weren't that no one can help being sorry for his children."

Lazzarino felt, even when his back was turned, the contemptuous looks that Giuseppe did not deign to notice. And his suffering increased as he gradually abandoned his original intention of taking revenge and teaching a thorough lesson to his father's detractors. His sudden growth actually seemed to weaken rather than to strengthen him. Limbs and muscles were soft; brain and spirit torpid. The least effort tired him and although his anger was quickly aroused it collapsed just as quickly in an emergency. He wanted experience with women, but was not brave enough to stand up under the eyes of those who had begun to look at him with a certain curiosity. In the same way he swore angrily to himself that he would pick up a stick and lay about him in defense of his father's good name and then the next time he heard it insulted he stood there like a bump on a log, without raising his hand, or saying a word, or even wondering what to do. Naturally, in retrospect he had a deathly fear of having acted like a coward.

Woodcock was one of the slanderers, insisting that Giuseppe was a Papist reactionary, a fossil, and a profiteer who had sucked the blood of the people. To which Stump, the river watcher, replied by singing the praises of Garibaldi, whose name was very prominent during the spring and summer of 1867 because great events were in the making: the gathering of volunteers in the Sabine country, the invasion of the Papal States, and the liberation of Rome.

"Once Garibaldi starts moving," Stump said, "the victory is as good as won."

"If the regular army is sent against him there'll be a revolution," said Woodcock, with greater subtlety. "And this time it won't stop where the wealthy want it to."

Giuseppe shrugged his shoulders.

"Of course we all know what you think," Stump remarked.

"I think only of my own business."

"And your own stomach! There's patriotism for you! If everyone were the way you are . . ."

"The world would be better off, and there would be less senseless chatter."

Then they all joined forces against Giuseppe and taxed him with cowardice. Young Lazzarino listened eagerly to Stump's stories, in which above the bloody and confused tumult of battle there emerged the shining red, blue, and blond figure of Garibaldi.

"That voice and smile sent you into the cannon's mouth as if into a woman's arms," Stump asserted.

As a matter of fact he was quite sincere, just as he was when he declared that he did not miss his forearm.

"I gave it for Garibaldi, and I'm not sorry."

Lazzarino was enflamed by these words and began to think that he could rescue his father from the neighbors' malice and himself from shame if only he could join Garibaldi.

"What age must one be to volunteer?" he asked Stump.

"In my day it didn't matter. I've seen boys that weren't nearly as tall as their guns. I ran away from home myself to join up when I was no more than your age. But nowadays boys aren't the same."

He did not know Lazzarino's exact age and the boy's height made him overestimate it just as he underestimated, out of vanity, the age of his own enlistment.

"How does one go about joining?"

"Why? Do you want to do it?"

At this question the seven or eight men present burst into laughter. The boy paled, with wounded pride stabbing at his chest. So they could read on his face that he was a coward. He turned redder than if someone had struck him. Just at that moment his father came back into the tavern and asked what they were laughing at.

"Your son wants to enlist with Garibaldi! Who would have ever thought it?"

"If anyone's putting him up to that he'll have to settle accounts with me!"

"That's just what we meant. You're like a goose that sees a handsome little black swan among its goslings."

"He'll have to settle accounts with me, I say."

"And what will you do to him?"

"What will I do? I'll . . . I'll report him to the carabineers."

They laughed even louder.

"You are frightening us out of our wits! Let's all run for safety! Heaven help us!"

"As for the carabineers," added the knowing Woodcock, when he could make himself heard above the clamor, "I can inform you that they close an eye to what's going on and that there's a recruiting committee right in Ferrara. When you have a paper from the committee you have only to show it to the train conductor in order to ride free. You travel to a place called Terni, or another one near by, Narni I think is the name, and there Garibaldi's officers admit you to the mess, give you a national guardsman's gun and train you until you're ready to march on Rome. There Garibaldi will set up a republic, and if the government tries to stop him there'll be a lot of trouble. And trouble will serve the purposes of certain people who have deeper aims than even Garibaldi can imagine. For if there's enough trouble the republic will take a socialist turn."

It was a matter of common knowledge that volunteers were being recruited by Garibaldi in something like this way. But Giuseppe felt a sudden vague terror.

"May God strike you dumb, you loud-mouthed fools!" he exclaimed. "Which one of *you* is enlisting?" And seeing that they were taken aback, he added: "Not a single one! Your flag-waving is confined strictly to chatter. A bunch of cowards, that's what you are!"

"Take that back!" they shouted all together.

"I'm not taking back anything."

"Look out! You'll eat those words!"

"Eat your own . . . !"

Decency forbids printing what he invited them to eat. They kicked him out of the tavern and he stumbled over his spindly legs and rolled over on the ground. Lazzarino, who attempted to stand up for his father, was evicted with not much more ceremony. He ran to pick up Giuseppe and then started to go back inside to avenge the insult. But his father held him by the arm.

"Let them go to the devil!" he said. "What do they matter to you?"

"But they threw you out!"

"Never mind. I had my say. The main thing is that you shouldn't see them again."

The boy's heart bled and he had a desperate desire to cry, in which all his anger was swept away.

"They'll be calling *us* cowards now," he said.

"Let them call us what they choose. You stay here with me."

So saying he held his son with one hand, while with the other he brushed the dry September dust off his clothes. And he added passionately, as if he were afraid to see Lazzarino get away from him:

"You won't go off to die for Garibaldi, promise me that!"

"I hadn't dreamed of it," said the boy, drying his tears. "But I can't bear to be called a coward."

"It's better to live like a coward than to be brave and die," said Giuseppe with an uncommonly insistent manner. "Swear that you won't leave me!"

"There's no need to swear, Father."

Giuseppe decided that it would be unwise to insist and he let it go at that, with the intention of watching the boy closely. But that same night Lazzarino ran away to Ferrara, where he had no trouble finding the recruiting committee, and enlisted as a Garibaldi volunteer.

4

Soon afterwards, when Garibaldi began to penetrate the territory around Rome, Lazzarino had acquired some notion of how to load the broken gun they had given him at Narni. He had cheerfully slept outdoors and tightened his belt when he was hungry; in fact he was in better mental and physical health than before, not so much on account of the open-air life, which was not new to him, as on account of his pride in wearing a red shirt and the stimulation he received from taking part in an enterprise of daring. Fortunately he had profited by a remark of Stump's and brought with him two pairs of stout shoes from home. A good *Garibaldino*, the old veteran used to say, had best provide himself with shoes, as everything else he will find on the way. With good shoes on their feet Garibaldi's men would go to the ends of the earth without anyone's stopping them.

This advice was probably the offshoot of some painful marching experience, and allowing for some exaggeration, it did in humble fashion illustrate the weakness of the supply system of the Garibaldi forces. Indeed, one of the defeats impending at this time hinged in part upon a delay in the advance from Monterotondo caused by the necessity of distributing shoes to Menotti Garibaldi's barefoot volunteers.

Lazzarino thought of Guarda only in connection with the worry he knew he must be causing his parents and this did not weigh upon him very heavily in comparison with his impatience for the moment when Garibaldi would arrive from Caprera and lead the march on Rome. That neither this period of waiting nor the campaign itself would be a long one was the general opinion of the volunteers encamped around Terni and Narni in so miserable a fashion. There were some veterans of better days and some genuinely enthusiastic new recruits among them, but the majority were not of very good quality because they had not been as carefully chosen as the famous "Thousand" who, as the noble-hearted Ippolito Nievo tells us, were pledged to a "desperate battle" with no other hope than that of laying down their lives for the cause.

The present assembly included a large number of foolish and ignorant souls, beside various ambitious intriguers and charlatans, whom there had been no time to sort out, much less to discipline. There were even some almost criminal types with no real political ideals, gathered up from the sidewalks of the big cities, around whom the foolish and ignorant clustered. Many of these were to be found in the band led by a certain "Colonel Callimaco," who had taken this name from an older *Garibaldino*, Callimaco Zambianchi, notorious for his bloody violence, who in 1860 had led an incursion into Papal territory from Talamone. The end of this obscure episode had given rise to much speculation. In the course of the next year Cavour had shipped Zambianchi off to America and he had died on the way, by poison his namesake declared, poison ordered for him by Cavour in the form of so-called "Scotti pills," which had the property of quieting those who were inclined to do too much talking. This suspicion was typical of the mania of persecution growing out of partisan passion, which saw in the period of Italian history from 1848 on nothing but an "infernal plot" woven by the Piedmontese in order to avert a more profound revolution. This "Colonel Callimaco" claimed the purpose of avenging his predecessor's death and also of emulating the reputation for violence which he had won by the number of monks and priests he had murdered in Rome in 1849.

This will serve to show exactly what expectations "Colonel Callimaco" and his ferocious followers cherished in connection with the fall of Rome. Their band had been swollen in numbers not only by its attraction for kindred evil spirits, but also by virtue of the fact that other leaders recommended it to the most unruly of their own men. They behaved like so many brigands, stealing food where they could find it, and insulting and maltreating the local peasants and priests, especially after the first days of October, when they passed over into Papal territory. "Colonel Callimaco" struck up the attitude of a Marat and promised his followers an orgy of violence in Rome, and they were stirred by his inflammatory talk to indulge ahead of time in rape and assassination. It was only because they were on the march and never stopped anywhere for more than three days that they managed to escape bloody retaliation.

Chance and confusion brought Lazzarino Scacerni into the strange company of these men, and their ugly, vicious expressions relaxed into benevolent smiles at the sight of his tanned, healthy face and the good, honest soul that shone through it.

Lazzarino was unaware of his companions' crimes, not only because he was so innocent but also because they respected his innocence and hid the worst from his knowledge. Indeed there was something deeply touching in the contrast between his great simplicity and the ferment of evil passions about him. Perhaps it was his naturally friendly disposition and his prompt compliance with such military discipline as existed among "Colonel Callimaco's" band; and even more than his blithe ignorance of evil it was his modest refusal to set himself up as better than anyone else.

Several of the roughest fellows of the lot, among them the very worst of all, nicknamed Barabbas, were attracted to Lazzarino as bad natures often are to good, that is when they are not utterly repelled by them. There is something desperate about such attractions, perhaps because

538

they arise from an inability to hate in normal fashion. So it was that Lazzarino was the especial favorite of the ugly Barabbas and the mascot of "Colonel Callimaco's" company.

Meanwhile Garibaldi eluded the vigilance of the ships of the royal navy deployed around Caprera and came to take command of this ill-trained army. Lazzarino had undergone his baptism of fire at Monterotondo and felt a sort of joyful intoxication over his victorious emergence from the trial. Like a young man after his first experience of love he was eager for a second taste of the same medicine and chaste as he was he remembered in this connection Stump's comparison between the cannon's mouth and a woman's arms.

After Garibaldi's arrival came the march on Rome and the forced retreat after an insurrection had failed to materialize in the city. The sacrifice of Villa Glori, the French support of the Pope, an abundance of uncertain and contradictory news and an appalling lack of discipline conspired to dishearten the volunteers and progressively thin their ranks until the day when Garibaldi set out again on the Via Nomentana.

"Colonel Callimaco's" band was marching near the head of the column. The ancient road ran gently up and down along the wooded slopes of the Cornicolani Mountains and afforded no clear view of what was ahead. The cool air made it agreeable to walk and Lazzarino, with Barabbas at his side, was in a mood of childlike gaiety and laughter.

Rumors were circulating to the effect that they were going not to Rome, but to Tivoli in order to stir up a nationwide revolution and thus punish the king for having betrayed Garibaldi by failing to declare war on the French Emperor. And in this case the French and Papal troops would not oppose them. "Colonel Callimaco" rejoiced loudly over the prospect of a civil war, because in this case, he said, the regular army would desert rather than fire upon fellow countrymen.

At this point they saw on top of a low hill the round towers of Mentana and the upward curve of the road leading to it.

"Where are you going, Lazzarino?" asked Barabbas.

"To shoot off my gun!" Lazzarino answered, brandishing his unserviceable musket.

From the town itself and from golden haystacks that stood out against gray-green olive groves and brown autumnal fields rifle fire was hailing down on Garibaldi's men. Along with the sound of this fire an angry and confused sound of volunteers' voices travelled down the column. They were all doing the same thing as Lazzarino, stepping out of line in the disorderly way that inevitably leads to military disaster, running, bumping into one another and shouting incomprehensible words that they were not even aware of shouting. This was the beginning of a battle in which, as eyewitnesses tell us, every man was a law unto himself, thus making defeat not only inevitable but also catastrophic.

Lazzarino Scacerni ran briskly ahead of the rest, with his curly black hair ruffled by the breeze, unaware of the steepness of the road and of the fact that he was ahead of his few scattered companions. The impudent whistle of bullets in the air made his blood run more quickly, and Barabbas and the others had difficulty in keeping up with him.

Wounded and dead bodies lay in the road and the fields on either side, but Lazzarino seemed not to see them, nor did he notice the fighting among the haystacks. All he saw was the empty road ahead and the short distance that separated him from the first house of Mentana. He gave a sharp cry like that of an angry eagle and started to run forward. At this moment the Papal troops withdrew from the fields and fell back on the Villa Santucci at the edge of the village. Seeing them on the road before him he stopped to check if his rifle was working and was overtaken by the massed volunteers moving on to attack the Villa. He was piqued, like a boy who loses a race just as he thinks he has won it, and as if he had been pushed from behind, he jumped over a crumbled wall. From behind a gnarled tree, only a few yards away, he felt some cause of physical uneasiness; it was an eye at the sight of a gun that was pointed straight at him, a glittering and ironical eye.

Suddenly he was deafened by a volley of gunfire which left him amazed to find himself still standing. He thought the soldier behind the tree must have fired at him and did not connect the volley with the unexpected sight of this heretofore unseen body lying prostrate on the ground and kicking convulsively. Finding himself left behind he started to run again, with Barabbas at his heels. Perhaps Barabbas was his savior. But he could not put his mind on any of these things; he felt as if he did not know where he was going but was in a tremendous hurry to get there. Coming out of one field into another he joined a line of his fellows who were firing at the enemy clustered at the entrance to the village. The air filled with smoke, and he had a sudden impulse to throw away his useless gun and get away from all the noise and smell. Barabbas was still beside him, with a gravely eloquent look on his face, as if he had many things to say. Lazzarino wildly imagined that he had fallen into enemy hands, that the cluster of soldiers across the way had ceased firing and started to bear down on him. It shot through his mind that if he were to fall they would step on his body. Just then Barabbas caught hold of his resisting arm and almost jerked him off his feet.

"The Zouaves!" he shouted, and all the others echoed the cry.

Squeezed by their companions on either side Lazzarino and Barabbas were pushed backwards. Lazzarino did not fully come to himself until the first moment of panic was over and he found himself finally released from the pressure of other bodies, standing breathlessly near the haystacks.

"Halt there, boys!" he heard shouted desperately by a white-bearded old man with sword in hand, taller than the group in which he was standing. "Halt there, and charge them!"

He pointed with his sword in the direction of the enemy, but no one moved to obey. The gunfire was tremendous, seeming to crackle from every direction. While the old man, General Fabrizi, continued to shout, Barabbas grabbed Lazzarino's arm again and practically threw him over a low wall into an olive grove.

"If we stayed there we were done for," he muttered.

But the olive grove was not much safer, with bullets rustling through the trees. A little group of men were pulling a rope and pushing the wheel of a cannon that was stuck in the ground, one of two artillery pieces captured at Monterotondo, which were all that Garibaldi's expedition possessed.

"Give us a hand, you two!" an officer called out. His voice and manner were reassuringly serene.

"Now, pull all together," he ordered, when they had joined the group.

It seemed from his confident tone that nothing had any importance except the immediate job of moving the cannon. And yet this was the moment when the French Zouaves were encircling the volunteers with their deathly *chassepots* or breech-loading guns. The raging battle, from which stray missiles struck the upper branches of the olive trees, seemed by reason of the interposed wall to be far in the distance. They tugged hard at the rope, but the wheel was buried to the axle and would not move.

"Try pulling in jerks," the officer suggested. "Are you ready? Now go to it!"

But it was no use.

"We need some more help," said the officer as if to himself, walking toward the wall to call across it. His pace was as casual as if he had all the time in the world, but as soon as he turned his back the men he left behind him lost heart. One dropped the rope, two fell wounded to the ground and one was struck dead on the spot, leaving only Barabbas and Lazzarino. The officer came back toward the cannon with a dazed air, as if he could not believe his own eyes.

"It's all over," he said. "Our men are on the run."

A fading sound of voices and shots came from the road they had marched up that morning. The officer leaned wearily against the cannon.

"What next?" Barabbas said to Lazzarino.

"What do you say?" asked the boy, looking as if he were about to burst into tears, in a way that usually causes adults to smile.

"Wherever you go, I'll go too," said Barabbas.

Lazzarino frowned.

"I'm obeying the officer," he said stiffly.

The officer looked dreamily around and, as if he were seeing him for the first time, asked:

"How old are you, anyhow?"

The gunfire slowed down and died away among the houses of the village. A chill breeze made the leaves of the trees quiver, bringing out the melancholy of the November afternoon and restoring peace to the grove. But fate always has a parting shot in reserve, a bullet that has gone astray. With a tiny red hole in his forehead, Lazzarino Scacerni fell noiselessly, his arms outstretched, to the ground, answering the officer's friendly question with the most radiant and youthful of his smiles.

His mother had never lost faith in his return. She suffered as only a mother can, but she was sure that she would see him again in heaven. But Giuseppe spent the two months that went by without news in implacable silence, remembering his own brief experience of the horrors of war and refusing to see any hope of Lazzarino's salvation. He shrugged his shoulders furiously and only opened his mouth to say:

"He'll never come back alive! That would be too good to be true."

As a matter of fact, not even Lazzarino's dead body came back. He carried no identification papers, and Barabbas and the rest of his companions had quickly dispersed. So he was buried in a ditch near where he had fallen.

"You'll see him in heaven," said the parish priest.

"I want to see him here," Giuseppe answered.

"Just what do you mean?"

"That other place you speak of, Father, means very little to me."

"Come, now. I have pity on your affliction, but what you've said there is blasphemy. You should offer your grief to the Lord."

"He's taken enough from me already," muttered Giuseppe half insanely, passing from raging sorrow to dull pain.

Woodcock and Stump had a warning of the disorder that was brewing in Giuseppe's mind when he appeared one day at Orlandini's tavern with a shotgun in his hand. They were singing a drinking song inside, but they stopped short when he opened the ill-repaired door.

"Make way," he said, with his gun in hand. "I came to get Woodcock and Stump. Keep out of my path if you want to steer clear of trouble. As for you two," he added, pointing the gun at them, "start saying your prayers. I don't give a rap for your souls or mine, but that will make your agony last a little longer. Make way, the rest of you, this gun is loaded with buckshot, and it isn't exactly healthy."

The drinkers shrank back against the wall. Woodcock's teeth chattered noisily and Stump grew pale, although he controlled himself somewhat better.

"Very well," said Giuseppe. "I'm satisfied to see that you're a bunch of cowards. The first one of you that moves will be shot down. But you two, who send boys to their death, must die. Still there!"

No one stirred. Giuseppe aimed his gun first at Stump and then at Woodcock, from forehead to chest and back to forehead.

"It's on your account that Lazzarino was killed," he said with a ghastly grin. "He heard you insult me and was ashamed to be my son. If I'd shot you down the day you threw me out of the tavern he would never have gone away. Better late than never. You two must pay. But I'd like to hear first what you have to say. Woodcock, you've always been a great talker."

"For the love of your dear departed . . ." said Woodcock feebly, causing Giuseppe to laugh.

"And you, Stump, what's on your mind? Something equally silly?"

"I have nothing to say," said Stump with a certain fortitude.

"What do you mean, nothing? That's no answer."

The fact was that he had talked too much himself already and he did not really have the heart to carry out his cruel jest. The gun trembled in his hands, and the most courageous of the bystanders finally spoke up.

"Scacerni, none of us sent your Lazzarino to his death. We loved him and are among the first to regret it. If he went off with Garibaldi it just shows that he was a brave boy. Don't give us credit for his courage. He was quite capable of making his own decisions."

"And I haven't the courage to shoot you," said Giuseppe childishly. "Go on and report me to the police."

And he went out the way he had come, foolishly shaking his head. They did not dream of reporting him, but came to the conclusion that it was either a bad joke or a sign that he was demented and were torn between resentment and compassion. Giuseppe himself seemed to forget the whole thing, except when occasionally he muttered for no particular reason:

"Wolves must howl and rabbits tremble."

People said that he had lost his mind, although as far as business was concerned he was more acute than ever, and certainly far more cruel, without an ounce of Christian charity left in him. When he could take advantage of a poor man's need to lend him money and then brusquely demand repayment, bombarding the fellow with legal papers, injunctions, seizures, and threats of bankruptcy proceedings, he seemed to be motivated less by a love of gain than by an irresistible urge to express his deep hate for the human race. There was talk at this time of doing away with the penalty of imprisonment for debt (which was actually abolished ten years later), and when Giuseppe was discussing with his lawyers in Ferrara some new and infernal method of torturing his debtors he seethed with indignation.

"That would be worse than showing mercy to thieves," he protested. "At least thieves don't pretend to be honest men. But when a man borrows money with no intention of returning it . . ."

"All borrowers don't have that intention," the lawyers argued.

"If they don't have it to start with they usually acquire it along the way."

"Some people have plain bad luck."

"And am I supposed to suffer the penalty?"

"But if your debtors have no money what use is it to throw them into jail?"

"To teach them a good lesson."

"What lesson is that?"

"To keep their bad luck to themselves. Otherwise they're tempted to unload it on somebody else."

"Pray God, Were Rabbit, that you'll never be in need!"

"I'll do the best I can. But if ever a defaulting debtor gets me into a tight hole I'll be the first one to call for the gallows. I'll even knot the rope around my own neck."

And indeed many people who saw Giuseppe's peculiar ways began to think that one day he would commit suicide. Among his family he lived quite apart, making strange sounds and signs, like a deaf-mute, that is except when he broke out into cursing and swearing and beat his children unmercifully without any reason. For a long time his wife fulfilled her duty of respecting him. She was herself a strict disciplinarian, but his behavior made her blood boil over. Gradually, when his unfairness was too great to bear, she began to upbraid him tactfully, but it was clear that he took delight in injustice and deliberately tried to terrify his children by turning his albino eyes upon them and keeping them in perpetual uncertainty as to whether or not they had fallen under his displeasure. Still Cecilia tried to inspire her three sons and three daughters with the proper consideration.

"After all, he's your father," she said, and when he was at his worst she added, "Sorrow has made him a bit queer."

Since Giuseppe had a way of coming home unexpectedly and in a bad mood to the house at Poplar Bridge Cecilia did not leave her children there any more than necessary, but took them with her to the mill. The miller's trade was the one for them, in her estimation, this was the real source of the Scacerni family's good luck and prosperity, not the obscure and mad business dealings of Were Rabbit. Like a mother hen she gathered her chicks around her and saved them from their father's cruelty. At such times it was plain that he wanted to strike her, but once when he threateningly raised his hand she took hold of his wrist and made him feel the strength of her muscles.

"There's a limit even to madness, Were Rabbit," she said. "If you do that again I'll straighten out the hump in your back and put some reason into your head."

One day when she had left her children at home because he was supposed to be away in Ferrara she came back from the mill to find the house door locked and a child crying inside to the accompaniment of a rain of mad blows.

"If you open the door I'll kill you," called out Giuseppe.

"Have pity, Father, or I shall die!" she heard one of her little girls shouting.

Cecilia raised a ladder to a window of the barn, which was connected with the house inside, and in a moment she was upon the scene. Giuseppe, covered with blood from the little girl's nose, was still beating her half-naked body. Around the dark kitchen walls the wide-open terrified eyes of her brothers and sisters seemed like those of a family of owls. Cecilia leaped at her husband, caught hold of his rough woolen jacket and lifted him up by it as if he were a puppy. Turning him around she knocked his body against the door without saying a word. Giuseppe might have come to a bad end, had not she been interrupted by her children calling:

"Mother! Mother!"

When she ran to succor the injured girl Giuseppe fell on his hands and knees to the floor and howled into the night like a mad wolf. And darkness reigned indeed in his diseased mind.

From this time on Giuseppe no longer lived at Poplar Bridge but lodged himself and his horse in the stable at the Ca' Morgosa farm. When Cecilia and he met they barely spoke to one another. She supported her children with the profits of the mill, while Giuseppe went his own way, with a wild and unkempt look about him that boded complete collapse.

<h2 style="text-align:center">6</h2>

"Pray God, Were Rabbit . . ."

But did he still believe in God? This was a question he did not even ask himself. And as his mind continued to deteriorate most people simply blamed his well-known bad character.

Toward the end of 1871 the new crown embankment was finally completed and the next operation was to make openings in the old dikes and gradually let the river into the intervening basin. One cold and foggy winter night Giuseppe Scacerni went to seek out an old woman known as Dame Blackface and commonly considered to be a witch. The peasants looked on her with a mixture of hate, fear, and superstitious belief, telling of miraculous cures she had made of persons given up for dead, of winning lottery numbers which she had predicted, of rats and other foul beasts of which she had rid their farms and even of ghosts banished by her incantations where even the priest's exorcism and blessing had failed to dispel them. She was said to attend the witches' sabbath and to worship Satan; a feeble-minded woman of the village swore to having seen her rise stark naked out of a chimney and fly away on a broomstick to some unholy meeting. Some people said that as a girl Dame Blackface had cast her spell over a young man and made him die of love, then in order to get him back she had made herself into a witch and sold her soul to the devil in return for his teaching her the black arts. In all these tales there was a combination of lust and unbridled imagination, and on long winter evenings in the stables they took on a macabre character that made the peasants tremble and draw closer to their smoky lanterns, which threw pale rays on the wide backs and sides of the cows placidly chewing their cuds in the semidarkness. At night everyone gave her miserable hut a wide berth, but most of the time the peasants bothered very little about her except when they sought some household or barnyard remedy. And the faith they had in her on such occasions they deemed no more than a venial sin. They paid her with gifts of their produce or, if she was recalcitrant, with the threat of a beating. More than once the threat had been translated into reality, when they suspected her of being responsible for the decline of a dear one's mental or physical health or for having cast the evil eye upon their crops and livestock. Hence there were hate and fear on both sides, which might have added up to a sort of rough justice, were it not that evil matching evil and ignorance matching ignorance make a picture too ugly to deserve this name.

The old Nogarole and Antonella dikes had been cut in two places and Cecilia, after so many years in one anchorage, had been forced to move temporarily her mills farther down the river. Only a small rise in the water level was sufficient to fill the wide space between the dikes and the crown embankment with stagnant water. The dikes were fated to be gradually washed away, but meanwhile hardly had the crown been touched by the water than parts of its surface visibly slipped. This time Giuseppe's petition asking for the rehabilitation of the dike until the crown was strengthened did not want for signatures. But the engineers' answer was that such a difficult and expensive job would be quite useless. Such slipping was the rule with any newly constructed embankment, and alarm and complaints were only to be expected. And in this there was some truth. When the slips had been repaired the priests of Guarda and Ro, followed by the population of their respective villages, came to bless the crown. And it was this ceremony that inspired Giuseppe Scacerni to knock one winter night at the door of the witch's hut.

The old woman asked his name and let him in. She was a horrible sight, tall and skinny like the trunk of a stripped, dead tree, with a long, wrinkled neck, toothless mouth, bald head, and a concave, leathery, bloodless face lit up only by two hollow, colorless eyes, out of which shone a sort of obscene madness.

"And what can a fine gentleman like yourself seek in my palace?" she asked him, in the sarcastically pompous and mysterious tone that he already knew.

But he had never set foot in her "palace," and he gazed curiously about him, without seeing in the dim light anything but evidence of poverty and decay. The word reminded him of the story of how someone entering her accursed door had once seen the smoky kitchen change before his eyes into a sumptuous basilica with marble instead of dirt paving, gold and marble walls illuminated by glittering candelabra, and in place of the stove where she brewed her philters the throne of Satan himself, surrounded by cloven-footed witches and devils bringing an obscene tribute to their master. The bearer of this tale was never anyone alive or within reach, for if any of those who told it secondhand had claimed to be an eyewitness to such a scene he would have been dismissed as a trickster. However the legend had gained credence with age, and indeed from time immemorial Dame Blackface had been described as one hundred and seventeen years old.

"Then next year she'll be a hundred and eighteen," some wit was tempted to say.

"No, she stays at a hundred and seventeen," the villagers replied with an evasive smile.

"How do you account for that?"

"She derives her age from her master" (meaning the devil), was the reply.

"And what of that?"

"You don't think that he calculates his dates from the birth of Our Lord, do you?"

And thus the would-be wit was silenced. At any rate, the hut was not transformed into a palace for Were Rabbit's benefit, although looking at the old hag he was ready to credit her with a hundred years and some left over.

"I came to ask you a favor, one for which I am prepared to pay," he said in answer to her question.

"I can read your mind," said Dame Blackface, either because she really had some necromantic power or else had made a good guess at Giuseppe's preoccupation. "What you are going to ask is anything but easy."

"Why?" he asked, half curious, half incredulous, but he blanched to hear her reply:

"Because the priests have already blessed it with holy water. My incantations are worthless unless . . . Don't bother to cross yourself; you will only upset my lord and master! . . ."

"Unless what, then?" stammered Were Rabbit.

"Unless you go up on the embankment with me at midnight and say amen to my ejaculations, making the sign of the cross backwards and with your left hand."

"Do I have to go there in person?"

"Of course. You must first wipe out the blessing if you seek a grace from my lord and master."

"Can't you do that alone?"

"Yes and no. It would be very insolent to ask my lord and master a favor if you grudge him an act of adoration. As for me, I'm not afraid even if the Po breaks through. I've no lands to lose."

"Yes, to be sure. And is it true that you know how to fly through the air?"

"Let's stick to the business at hand."

"I understand," he said, strengthened in his conviction that she had power to help him. "The person to whom you refer . . ."

"Call him my lord and master, or he'll not listen."

"Your lord and master, then. I understand that he can do great things, but can he do this one?"

"Don't you know that he commands winds and rain, earthquake and flood?"

"But will he keep his word? If he is so powerful he can afford to break it."

"Just have faith. Didn't I give you a proof of his power when I read your mind? No one else could have revealed to me what you would ask."

"No one must know."

"Have no fear on that score. My lord and master doesn't make his mysteries known in the market place."

Bitterness, superstition, insanity, and a persistent wild desire to triumph over the new embankment swept the last of Giuseppe's doubts away.

"I'll do what you say. This very night."

"It's too late. It's almost midnight already and we shouldn't get there in time."

"Tomorrow night, then."

"If it is written in the stars. And if the night is dark and cloudy."

The stars were propitious by their absence, and the old hag came wrapped in a cloak to keep the appointment. She made signs in the air, flayed the water, traced symbols on the ground and made Were Rabbit stand in them while she chanted the praises of Astaroth and Beelzebub. At the end of every period, Were Rabbit made the response she had taught him.

"Here he is!" she exclaimed after a long interval, gripping Giuseppe's right arm. "I see the great prince, my lord and master. Cross yourself with your left hand!"

Tremblingly Giuseppe obeyed. The witch went through other rites and incantations, pocketed the two gold pieces Giuseppe had promised her, and disappeared into the fog, leaving him alone. Fearful as he had been when in a moment of transfiguration the witch had announced the "great prince," Giuseppe had felt the pride in her words, the obstinate and glorious pride of a visionary and a soul possessed. Curiosity overcame his fear, while a teasing light wind blew through the frosty air and drove the fog away from the river and over the land. Looking inland from the top of the crown he could see only trees and chimney tops, while the stars came out in the cleared sky above. He could guess at the river, swollen halfway to the flood mark, by the sound of its rapid flow through the two cuts in the old dikes, whose summits stood out as black masses on the other side of the newly-formed lagoon. Here there were still a few wisps of fog, and air currents gently rippled the surface.

Suddenly the diabolic pride of the old woman began to stir echoes in Giuseppe's turbid soul and his curiosity gave way to a sinful desire to share her occult power and join the worshippers of Satan. He walked away from the embankment, turning his toes out and puffing up his chest like a rooster. With the passage of the years he had acquired a fat belly and protruding buttocks and these, contrasting with his scrawny legs, gave him the air of a double hunchback, sticking out both before and behind. Too bad that no one was there to see him strutting along, boasting to himself:

"They built that crown to spite me, but now I've put it in good hands and there's no danger that it will crumble. Presumptuous fools!"

And in this appellation he included the whole world, above and below, the village gossips, the government engineers, the contractor, the machinations of fate against him, the ministers of God, the saints and God Himself, whom he had now so rashly denied. So they thought they had put something over on him, did they? In his demented state he was unaware of the fact that he was laughing and the harsh cackle that rang in his ears seemed to him to come from somewhere else, perhaps from Satan himself just over his shoulder. He was bathed in cold sweat and closed his eyes in terror. A desperate sigh—his own—blew across his face and he broke into a run, with the echo of his own footsteps pursuing him. When he reached the Ca' Morgosa stable he fell prostrate on his bed with his head between his arms and all night long he heard the devil prowl outside and sniff at the door. But Dame Blackface had warned him not to breathe a single prayer for three consecutive days, unless he wished his compact with the prince of darkness to be broken. Greed was stronger than fear, and with his face buried in the pillow he shouted to the intruder:

"Mind you abide by your word! Make all the racket you like, but you have given your promise. And curses upon whichever one of us breaks faith!"

When the cock crew Giuseppe went out into the fields and rejoiced to see them look so fair. The preceding winter of 1870-71 had been unusually cold, but this one gave indications of being temperate. He had sown his wheat in good dry weather and it had received the benefit of the autumn rains, so that now it was growing just the way it should.

> *Dry cold in January*
> *Build an oaken granary.*

The land set aside for hemp, which was due to come up by the feast of the Annunciation in late March, had received all the necessary preparation, including a large amount of manure. Giuseppe knew that a successful farmer must give every detail his personal attention, and now he rubbed his hands happily together in the crisp morning air.

"Land as good as this is worth a bit of heresy. And what's so bad about what I did last night? I've put the land under powerful protection and bound the devil to my service, and that can't be displeasing to God Almighty."

This theology was of his own invention, and he voiced it with so much assurance as to arouse compassion. But there was some basis for it in the local legend of Blow-hard and the sorcerer Chiozzini, who renewed a pact with the devil in order to stave off a flood. The figure of speech in which Giuseppe spoke of having bound the devil to his service recalls the stories sculptured on many an historical monument of the region of the Po and its tributaries, between the Apennines and the sea. Here along the Via Emilia, one of the Roman roads, there was a great flowering in the Middle Ages, when abbots, bishops, feudal lords and common men of tenacious ingenuity rescued the country from the destruction in which the barbarian invaders had left it, with the unchecked river flooding the land and turning it into swampy wastes. Amid the struggle between Pope and Emperor great universities and religious orders came into being, but the age was so doctrinal that it found artistic expression in stone rather than in poetry, and hence we have the sculptured marvels of the cathedrals and churches of Piacenza, San Gimignano, San Donnino, Parma, and Ferrara, which was Saint George's city.

To the passionate spectator these sculptures reveal not only a biblical and theological epic, but a vigorous and earthy style, rich in rustic invention. Here we have Adam, with Eve at his side, shedding the first sweat of his brow as he breaks clods of earth; the work and games appropriate to the various seasons; the pleasures of the flesh and their degeneration into sin; domestic animals; everyday customs and costumes; fables from Aesop and legends of the Carolingian and Arthurian cycles; and sometimes a whole novel, such as the sculpture at Modena of the knight who sold his soul to the devil and then finally found repentance and exorcism.

In the handing down of tradition, language, dress, and taste we see a constant and enriching exchange between art and life. This rustic fancy, this robustly earthy and carnal touch smiling out of the sculptured figures, were looked at by generation after generation and passed down from one to the other along with the proverbs and fables that are told over and over again to children. Thus they were stamped indelibly on the popular imagination.

Were Rabbit had a direct physical resemblance to the greedy misers, to the sinners half crazed with lust whom we see sculptured on cathedral doors, before we enter the abode of holiness and prayer inside. His very nickname, with its mocking implication of bad luck, arose from a superstitious belief widespread in the Middle Ages. His contemporaries had imposed it upon him just as monks who got their learning from the medieval bestiaries had suggested the figures from which it stemmed to the stonecutters of their day. And because a man often conforms to the name that has been given him, who knows what an influence this one played upon Were Rabbit's embittered and sorrowful life? His former restlessness and anxiety were now more tortured and crazed than ever, and yet he seemed very well pleased as he preened himself over his infernal bargain, laughing and muttering incomprehensible exclamations.

The pale winter sun did not melt the frost covering the hard ground, which crackled under his heavy boots. Along the ditches it was as thick and white as snow and there was a paper-thin coat of ice over the pools of water left in them from the last rain. He sniffed the subtle odor of the frozen earth and delighted in the pale sprouts of sturdy wheat, the thick dark-green clover and herb known sometimes as "monk's rhubarb" and sometimes as "devil's flax." He pouted and puffed and laughed as if he were teased by a wild physical pleasure, and yet all the time he was broken and decayed within. If anyone could have penetrated his benighted inner solitude, by virtue of which his suffering was far greater than his sin, he would surely have been reminded of the agony of the human spirit sculptured by the great Wiligelmus upon one of the churches we have mentioned above and the compassionate Latin words that go with it: *"Hic gemit, hic plorat, nimis iste laborat,* here he groans and cries and labors."

But who was there to care for Were Rabbit, or to discern under his avarice and madness the sorrow of a father mourning for his dead son?

THE BREAK-THROUGH

1

Like swallows that come in May
And go in September . . .

THE SWALLOWS had come, and throughout the region of Ferrara there were still prospects of a good harvest. High winds are to be expected in March, and this year they blew themselves out without doing any harm; April showers speeded the growth of the wheat and it stood tall and pale green by May, so that the farmers' hope was transformed into confidence.

There is a local proverb, particularly pleasing to girls with good complexions, which says: "The March sun lightens; the April sun brightens." And this was what happened to the wheat that May, when the smiling weather tinged the green with gold. The hemp, too, grew thick and tall; and the fruit trees flowered abundantly. It seemed, indeed, as if the circling swallows were inviting men to be of good cheer. Even the new embankment, settled by the spring rains, seemed so solid that no one was surprised when Giuseppe Scacerni gave up his prophecies of doom. He was no longer seen in the church or square or tavern and apparently talked to no one except on business.

As the old dikes of Nogarole and Antonella started to disappear the river seemed to have settled into its new bed and after a minor rise of water in May failed to weaken the crown. Cecilia began to hope that she could soon bring the mills back to their original anchorage. It is important to say at this point that the high water of May and those that had immediately preceded it had worried Cecilia and all those who knew the river well by their suddenness, increased frequency, impetus, and the fact that they brought with them great quantities of mud and driftwood. This was proof of the rumor that was circulating all along the valley about the large-scale destruction of forests up in the Apennines, a fatal and shortsighted error, and one which was to be paid dear in spite of the immediate gains it afforded a few speculators.

The old governments had pursued a sterner and wiser course, setting guards to enforce strict laws against deforestation in both the Alps and the Apennines. And the forests were further protected by the lack of roads, trade, and transportation, as well as the general ignorance that prevailed in the mountainous regions. The advent of progress and the stimulation of business in the new Kingdom of Italy, the need for wood and the afflux of speculators' money to buy it soon brought on private abuse to the detriment of the public good. The lawmakers themselves made the situation worse by their misplaced Liberal faith and ex-

551

aggerated respect for the doctrine of unbridled free enterprise; they wiped out the previous restrictive legislation and failed to provide or to enforce any to take its place. Within a few years a vast patrimony, which it would take decades to recreate, was lost, and the woodlands of the Apennines were transformed into sliding and sterile wastes of clay.

Some people even said that the climate of the region was affected, that it was more changeable than before, and the country exposed to the violence of the *scirocco* wind. Certainly the aridity of the mountains, caused by the removal of such a reservoir of vegetation, did dry up the underground springs of the plains below. The chief effect was the abrupt discharge of the melted winter snow and spring rain into the river, but fishermen also complained that the mud in the water was killing off one of their chief sources of wealth, the sturgeon. What was clearly visible to all, and further confirmed by measurement made by the engineers, was the widening of the river bed, the piling up of mud in the delta, and the periodical rise of the water to flood level.

The clogging of the delta, especially when south and east winds blew the tide back from the sea, as they did at the time of the spring floods, was conspicuous even at Guarda. The fact that the river was now wider in front of the new crown embankment meant that a larger surface was exposed to the south wind so dreaded by the millers. Instinct and prudence combined to make Cecilia decide to wait and see how things were going before she moved back, in spite of the fact that her temporary anchorage was shallow and difficult to reach.

A week had elapsed since the mid-May high water when the phenomenon was repeated and the level rose to seventy-six inches. But this was not a frightening height, and besides the water showed signs of subsiding. This was the opinion of the two river watchers, appointed to keep an eye on the two cuts in the old dikes, through the lower of which the high water was now flowing. They were talking to Were Rabbit, who had gone to stretch his legs after lunch, at about two o'clock in the afternoon.

"These two rises had to come," said one of them. "For your sake too, Scacerni."

"For my sake?"

"Aren't you the one that made the most trouble?"

"Yes," echoed his companion. "You said that the crown was badly built and wouldn't stand."

"I did say so, that's true."

"Well, now the water has risen twice and the crown has held fast."

"They do say some water filtered through the first time," objected Giuseppe.

"But it isn't filtering now, is it?"

"No. Apparently it's tight enough."

"Well, what did I tell you?"

"There's a ditch that overflowed not far from here, at the boundary between the Ca' Morgosa and Antonella farms . . ."

552

"On your good land, eh?" the other watcher interrupted laughing.

"I'm not speaking in my own interest alone. Have you any idea what a break-through would mean?"

"Heaven help us!" both men exclaimed together, looking down at the powerful rushing river muddily swirling just below. "Don't mention it even in joking!"

"A good joke, that's what it would be if all that water spilled out into the fields. The Po might even make itself another permanent channel, the way it did with the historical Siccardi break, a thousand years ago. Then it's goodbye to the farms and villages we have known!"

"And goodbye to the three of us, to start with!" exclaimed the first watcher, while the mere prospect made his head reel, his stomach turn over, and the ground seem to slip away under his feet.

"What I say is that if you, Scacerni, of all people, can stand here and joke about it, then you must really feel secure."

"Wasn't there a stagnant ditch down by The Sisters' Farm in which the water suddenly churned up and began flowing?" Giuseppe insisted.

"But a few cartloads of dirt were enough to stop it and now it's no longer leaking."

"True."

"Every time the water rises something of the sort happens."

"That's true, too."

"Then how can you wear so indifferent a face while you make such dire prophecies?"

"Ever since the second rise I've felt as secure as a babe at its mother's breast," said Giuseppe, causing his interlocutors to laugh at the image of him in any such position. Then they separated to walk their beats, one of them going downstream where the old dikes were joined onto the new embankment, and his fellow upstream to examine the other cut. Giuseppe joined the second watcher, but they had not taken more than a hundred steps before they were startled by a sudden cry.

"What's that?" asked the watcher, gripping Giuseppe's arm.

"The devil! . . ."

"Go along with you! This is no time for more joking."

"Has the devil broken his word?" Giuseppe stammered to himself.

From the lower cut which they had just left behind rose a tremendous soot-black column of water, and they could hear the other watcher shouting:

"The river! The river!"

"It's all my fault!" Giuseppe raved. "I never told him to protect the dikes."

His companion did not heed him but spoke later of Giuseppe's having seemed to go quite mad at that moment. Meanwhile they both stared incredulously at what was going on before their eyes, as in the vicinity of the jet of water the dike gave way and seemed to sink into the waves.

"Let's get away!" the watcher shouted. "The dike is being swallowed up by the river!"

But Giuseppe, with a sudden access of strength, held him back. Together they saw the water pour through the widened opening into the inner basin, beat against the new embankment and surge over it. It was worse than they could have imagined, for the crown was broken and the river started to overrun the green countryside, along a row of fruit trees which bent over and disappeared one by one from view as if they had been swallowed.

Giuseppe stood rooted to the spot as if by enchantment. He saw the water swirl around a house and the peasants scramble up on the roof like ants coming out of an ant-hill. There was a rumbling noise like that of distant thunder—but alas it was near and did not end—which seemed to come from the bowels of the earth and make its surface tremble. The aspect of the countryside was one of stunned surprise rather than panic, like the lull that precedes a storm. Finally men's voices rose from the fields and rang through the still innocent May afternoon.

"The river! The river! Here it comes!"

They seemed to call not out of fear but simply in order to give a warning, the way a miner proclaims that he has lit a powder train and bids his fellows stand away from the explosion. It was the time of day when the peasants go home for a siesta, and now other roof tops could be seen crowded with men and women holding children in their arms, while along hedged paths and ditches men and animals fled before the flood. The vegetation of the fields gradually sank out of view and some peasants who were caught at their work struggled to extricate themselves from the mud. A few groups and lone figures took refuge on mounds or banks or in the branches of trees, whence they made desperate gestures as they saw the river rising inexorably around them. The spectator's eye, dazzled by the water, sought with almost cruel curiosity to distinguish them.

The river poured through the break in the embankment with a swift, even flow, or at least so it appeared to those looking down at it from a roof top. The first house to be struck was still standing, for the initial jet had thrown a large amount of earth around it and this now served to cushion the assault. The current was deflected down the valley in the direction of Guarda, and the Antonella and Ca' Morgosa farms, which lay farther upstream, escaped it entirely. Giuseppe let go the watcher's arm, which the horror of the sight had made him grasp so tightly.

"My land is dry!" he said triumphantly.

"What do I care?" said the other. "What does it matter to me?" Then waking up to the unholy joy of Giuseppe's words and gestures, he added: "Were Rabbit, you're a damned soul if ever there was one! If you should die today I warrant you'd go straight to hell."

"All I have is safe!" Giuseppe repeated beating his breast as if he had not heard him.

"Nothing is safe today!" replied the watcher, running desperately away.

Over Giuseppe's wrinkled face, which had come to look more like a weasel's than a rabbit's, there hovered a fatuous smile. From the Anto-

554

nella farm and its dependencies peasant families with livestock and wagons on which were loaded all their household goods streamed in the direction of the embankment. In the distance the road from Ro to Guarda was black with refugees.

"The river! The river's coming!" echoed their cry.

Hoarse sounds of distress came from the stables where some of the animals were left imprisoned and from the fields where others wandered about with the water rising to their knees and chest and shoulders. And tolling church bells voiced the general complaint, with Guarda, which had never rung so loud and despairingly, giving the answer to Ro. Giuseppe was heedless of everything except the fact that the water had passed by his land and swept on toward the village. Standing where the Strada dell'Antonella met the embankment he watched his own peasants hurrying toward him, still too astonished to demonstrate any sorrow. Giuseppe praised the foresightedness of one old herdsman, who was leading the best brace of cattle from one of the Ca' Morgosa stables.

"Foresightedness do you call it, Master?" said the white-haired old man. "The water was coming, that's all!"

"Well, it won't come here, that I can tell you."

"Are you joking, Master?"

"Joking? It's going down the valley, isn't it?"

"Half the countryside around Ferrara will be submerged at this rate. My father's father knew what he was saying."

"And what was that, if you'll pardon my ignorance?"

"Trouble travels by water," the peasant said hurriedly, running after a cow that had strayed from the herd.

Giuseppe listened to the proverb with a scornful shrug of the shoulders and an annoyed smile. He stood aside to let the peasants pass by as they stumbled over one another to climb up the embankment. The road was steep and narrow; it was a tight squeeze for the wagons, and the hurry they were in did not help them to go any faster. They struggled for precedence, but if one wagon proved to be heavier or less manageable than the rest they all put a shoulder to the wheel. Fear united them where Christian charity failed.

"Stupid fools!" muttered Giuseppe to himself, standing with his chest thrown out and his hands on his hips as if he were the only one not to have lost his head in the emergency. He would have been laughable had the situation not been so acute and left so little time for anyone to notice him. "Stupid fools! What a mess they're in!"

There was a little space on top of the embankment in which the wagons could turn, and because it had not been strewn with gravel or planted with grass their wheels made deep furrows in the earth and many of them stuck fast. Those behind them thought that now that their fellows had reached safety they were taking it easy and began to shout all the louder, thereby adding to Giuseppe's scorn.

"The idiots haven't even seen that the water is pouring down in the opposite direction and that they are perfectly safe. In fact, they could just as well have stayed at home."

As they reached the top of the embankment the peasants glanced with timid resignation at the rushing river as if it were the embodiment of their fate. But as their fear momentarily abated and they looked back at the houses and fields they had left behind them their eyes lingered longer, reflecting anxiety as to when they would see them again and in what condition.

The group was not so large as it had at first seemed, for many people had chosen to take refuge on the raised road between Guarda and Ro, a place of proved safety and one farther from the river. Giuseppe found himself almost alone at one end of the embankment and decided to retrace his steps and see what the break-through looked like.

It was a sunny day and one of the longest of the year.

Puffed up with his insane self-assurance, forgetful of wife and children and even of self, and rejoicing in the fulfillment of his prophecy and the good piece of business he had done with the devil, he walked along the upper part of the dike, which was still standing. Perhaps, in the state he was in, he thought that this had always been the lay of the land, or at least that it didn't matter, as long as his own property was safe, if the Po went in a new channel to the sea. Finally he came upon the break in the dike, opposite which was a corresponding break in the new crown embankment. Not far away he could see the mills, riding at their temporary anchorage farther down the river, but not even this sight could disturb or distract him.

By now the triangle of land between the old Guarda road and the river was filled with water. Most of the drainage ditches through which the river had poured into the Lavezzola canal had been broken down by its impact, and now the Po was beating upon the road itself. Just as he arrived at the break, the water pouring through it struck the stagnant mass and then ran up against the peasant's house which had first blocked its way. There was a furious shock as the force of the river crumbled the earthen rampart that had risen around it and started off in another direction along the outer circumference of the crown until it poured into the fields of Giuseppe Scacerni.

All in all no more than an hour had gone by, but there are occasions when the clock can provide no exact measurement of time. Now, under Giuseppe's eyes, a few minutes were enough to spread the two torrents through the valley. The nearer one, ever widening, threatened to crumble the walls on either side of the break, just below his feet, and he was very nearly swallowed up alive. Meanwhile the water overran the fields higher and higher. Two new foaming muddy rivulets grew and grew, narrowing the space between them until they were one, which boiled up angrily for the last time and then settled into an even more menacing solid flow.

Giuseppe's thoughts, if any, were feverish to the point of delirium. Later on witnesses said that they had seen him from afar dancing like a soul possessed. He stared incredulously at the running water and the still, as if he could not believe his eyes, until evening fell and hid him from the view of anyone who might have been looking.

The slope of the land toward the sea is so slight in this region that the overflowed water soon began to wander off to various parts of the map. One current, running along the outer edge of the crown, went in the opposite direction to that of the Po, toward the depressed localities of Fossa d'Albero and Ruina, and would have gone all the way to the Francolino road and the Porta San Giovanni of Ferrara had not the road between Ro and Guarda been broken just near Poplar Bridge by a current that crossed the reclaimed land of La Vallazza and jumped the Lavezzola canal. This was the third new stream created by the overflowing river.

Surrounded and eaten away on both sides the crown embankment collapsed again farther upstream. The new break reversed the previous succession of events and in its turn enlarged the second cut in the dike. During the following night the great basin between the dikes and the crown was filled with seething masses and currents of water. By the light of the next day there appeared, then, two pairs of outlets. From the upper pair the water flowed directly out over the land; from the lower one, instead, since the break in the crown was not wide enough to let it all through, the water flowed partly back into the basin and then ricocheted with a tremendous gurgle through the upper.

The dawn was somber and sad, promising rain and bad weather, and revealing the fact that over half the Po was now flowing calmly in a new bed through the lowlands of La Vallazza. It was then that someone saw a man's figure clinging to a remaining dry summit of the dikes and called out to Cecilia, who was aboard one of the mills:

"Mistress Cecilia, unless my eyes deceive me, there's your husband!"

2

During the last months before the break-through Cecilia had not wasted her time in fear and cursing, although she too heard the rumors about the faulty construction of the crown. (Here let us note, for the record, that the break-through came not in the crown but in the dike, perhaps because of an eruption of marsh gas.) Mindful of this rumor she had waited no longer than the first high water of the year to transfer her children to the mills where she was sure of their safety, for she had heard also that if the crown gave way the river would be thrown into La Vallazza, and in this case the farm at Poplar Bridge would be in its path. Of course not even the mills would have been safe if they had been near the actual break, and for this reason she thanked Saint Anthony Abbot for having caused her to shift her anchorage while the crown was under construction. Like old Master Lazzaro she felt more secure on the water than on land. Aboard the mills she was light-footed, alert, and ready to fight against danger, while in the farmhouse she had a trapped feeling. There were rats that had nested for years in the old Bitter Bread Mill and Cecilia likened herself to them.

"I'm of river rat stock," she said. "I could never be happy with the moles that burrow under the land."

The death of Lazzarino and Giuseppe's madness, which inspired her with disgust as well as pity, made Cecilia feel easy in her mind only when all her brood was gathered about her. There was no telling how wildly their father might behave and she dreaded a visit from him as much as that of a werewolf. The sight of him torturing his little daughter had left an ineradicable impression on her memory, rousing all her maternal instincts to the defense of her young. This horrible creature (to give him his right name) had to all intents and purposes deserted the family anyhow, since he no longer contributed anything to their support.

"It's just as well," thought Cecilia. "If he does turn up it can only bode harm."

But in order to bring up her six children she had to increase the earnings she made from the mills. And the laborers who had come to work on the new embankment, instead of bringing her more work actually brought her less. The mills operated slowly and according to the force of the current, and as a result the bakers of Ro and Guarda took their trade to Vergoli's steam mill, near Ferrara, where they could get as much flour from his storehouse as they wanted in a hurry. Frascari, the baker of Guarda, told her quite frankly how things were with him.

"What can you expect, Mistress Cecilia? We had only a few customers and then all of a sudden there were the mouths of two hundred laborers to feed. We took all our reserves of flour to make dough and hurry it into the oven, and then what were we to do? We couldn't count on your slow-moving mill wheel to stock us up again in twenty-four hours, could we?"

"Slow but steady, that's it."

"You can't say that to a hungry man, you know!"

Frascari had a somewhat fawning and evasive manner and he did not say that the number of laborers might drop sharply from one day to the next, leaving him with a surplus of flour that was almost sure to rot. Someone might have suggested that he had better provide himself with better storage facilities, and actually he found it more convenient to patronize Pietro Vergoli. There were even advantages to compensate for the expense of transportation all the way from Ferrara.

"I'm not saying that the flour milled on the Po isn't by far the best. That's what's given the bread baked in the Ferrara region the reputation of being the tastiest in the whole wide world. But there's no use speaking ill of everything new. I'll warrant that many of those who belittle the steam mill wouldn't know how to tell the flour of one mill from another!"

Here was a customer lost to Cecilia, and not the only one. The new anchorage was harder to reach and the road leading to it was thrown into disrepair during the construction of the crown. The peasants did not want to push their way through the laborers, and once they had gone to another mill they were apt to go back there again, often for no more substantial a reason than because there was a tavern along the

558

way that was to their liking. So it is that some of man's vastest enterprises are no more lasting than an intricately woven spider web. Cecilia's mills had built up their clientèle over a period of half a century and yet at the first breath of an adverse wind everything threatened to blow away.

Another reason for Cecilia's living on the river lay in the fact that the peasants liked to see the miller's face before they came to terms over something so precious as their wheat. The reader will remember that Bitter Bread Mill was a vast structure whose steep roof was covered with a sort of thatch made of marsh reeds, with moss and grass growing on top of it. Under the roof there was space for an attic room, and there Cecilia lodged her three boys: Giovanni, named after her father; Princivalle, named after the grandfather of Giuseppe, and Antonio, named for the patron saint of the river mills. This attic was reached by a ladder from the deck leading to a sort of dormer window, which provided endless amusement for the three boys. The first night that they all spent aboard Cecilia could not help thinking of the absent one, poor dead Lazzarino, but in order not to mar the others' innocent pleasure she held back her tears until she could shed them into her own pillow.

She concentrated on the smaller hulk of Saint Michael's Mill the forge, the carpenter's bench, and all the tools of the miller's trade, besides the equipment left by Master Lazzaro for fishing and hunting, and kept the Bitter Bread for the kitchen and sleeping quarters. Her two older daughters, Dosolina and Maria, named for their grandmothers, were lodged in bunks one above the other, like those aboard ship. Cecilia did not know her own mother's name, since she had died in childbirth, but Maria is the heritage of every Christian woman. Her third daughter she called Berta, because when she was a little girl her father had told her stories from the Carolingian cycle and she particularly liked the one about Milon d'Anglante and Berta, the sister of Charlemagne, whose son, Roland, was born in a grotto at Sutri. Indeed she often compared in her mind the prowess of Roland with that of her lost Lazzarino. Berta slept in the small bed which Cecilia's father had made for her when she was herself a baby and carved with rustic designs and ornaments which were a perpetual reminder of the great affection bestowed upon her by the half-savage Madman of Bitter Bread Mill.

So it was then that Cecilia had moved her whole family to the shore.

Often a passer-by on the banks paused to look with agreeable surprise at the happy play of so many children aboard these blackened and frowning constructions, one of which was positively ancient. The two pairs of hulks dipping deep into the water were like four ploughshares in an endless furrow, one that never grew longer but closed in again as soon as it was opened. The prows bobbing rhythmically in the river seemed to be living things, rocking back and forth with impatience, mildly discontented with their state of perpetual motion because it did not enable them to move an inch from where they had started. And is this fate so very different from that of man, as he imagines himself making a furrow in time, and looking over his shoulder see it unroll behind him just as it unrolls before? But a mother who has six children to feed has scant occasion to examine the past or speculate about the future; it is more than enough for her to cope with the problems of the day. A customer bringing his sacks of wheat to the mill had put it to her this way:

"Mistress Cecilia, you've a cargo of holy innocents!"

"May their innocence be their fortune!"

"Have no fear! Your merits are so great that God is sure to protect you."

"My trust is in the innocence of my children."

There were some who went so far as to hope that she might be left a widow, for there was something very vital and attractive about her. Such an idea would have made Cecilia laugh with astonishment. Her deep-seated desire for children was now satisfied, and just as the original spring of water in a well disappears from view under the quiet un-rippled flow that surges up with the years, so now her urge for mother-hood found another outlet in devotion to the creatures she had borne. At this point a husband would have seemed intrusive and incongruous, and as sexual pleasure had always been a closed book to her she almost forgot the existence of man altogether.

In the evening, after a hard day's work, when she had put the three girls to bed and the boys had repaired to the attic, often so sleepy that Schiavetto had to hoist them up the ladder, Cecilia's head would nod and rest on the table. Then hers was a cargo of innocents indeed, with Schiavetto, now a white-haired old man, smoking his clay pipe and keeping watch over it until he too went to sleep near the mill stones, with the cord within reach of his hand so that he could regulate the flow of grain through the hopper. On Saint Michael's Mill Coxcomb and Lazybones took turns keeping vigil. They were now full-grown apprentices, not expert at the trade, but useful enough in their way.

God's protection of the innocents was plain for all to see at the time of the break-through, for had they been in the house at Poplar Bridge the river would have swept them away as it poured through La Vallazza. Of the house built by Lazzaro and Dosolina nothing remained. The walls and even the foundation were gone, and when the flood subsided all that could be seen in the place of the fields and garden was a barren space littered with sand and stones, like the dried-up bed of a river. Cecilia thanked Saint Anthony for having delivered her and her children from this fate, fully aware as she looked upon this scene of desolation, that had they been on land even their bones would have perished forever.

With the gloomy dawn that followed the disaster Cecilia breathed again after a night of sleepless listening to the roar of the river. And then it was that someone called out to her that the man marooned on the dike was her husband.

"The river may swallow him up from one moment to the next," called out her informant.

560

"Why doesn't he come away?" Cecilia asked.

"There are two more breaks higher up the river, didn't you know? Now he's cut off entirely."

"How was I to know that?"

"Well, now you've been told. His only hope is for someone to take him off in a boat. And it will have to be someone who cares a great deal for him!"

These last words were hardly necessary. It was obvious that to venture near the break was extremely dangerous, and the very fact that the main body of the river was flowing more slowly and at a lower level than usual proved that most of its force was now pouring through the new outlet. The ironical meaning of the man's words was clear. He implied that no one on the mainland cared enough for Giuseppe to go to his rescue, and that perhaps not even his wife cared enough either. Cecilia was offended.

Accompanied by Schiavetto she went hurriedly ashore, where she found her interlocutor talking to an engineer and the first of the watchers in whose company Giuseppe had been the day before. Across the two or three hundred foot width of the break, on an isolated piece of the dike, they could see Giuseppe, sitting with his head in his hands and his elbows on his knees, surrounded by the rushing water and looking as if he had sat there all his life long. The despairing pose of his dark form seemed as permanent as that of a dead man in the grave. His desperate immobility spoke more loudly of the disaster than even the ravaged landscape about him; he was the personification of human woe against a background of unfeeling and pitiless nature. The watcher spoke of him as if he were a dead man as he pointed him out to the engineer:

"That man was here when the column of water first shot up in the air." And he added, to Cecilia: "He must be your husband."

"How did he happen to stay on that spur?"

"I can't tell you. I ran off to give warning. Perhaps he was rooted to the ground by sheer despair. The land just back of the crown was his, you know."

And he pointed to the lake of water behind them with the roofs of a few houses and scattered tree trunks still standing out above it. Two muddy streams were clearly to be seen running together, plowing up Giuseppe's fields. In the distance the road was still black with refugees, and from a nearby roof top a peasant family called out for someone to come to their assistance.

"We can go for them in a boat easily enough," said the watcher, "because around their house the water is still. But that fellow there between the two breaks . . ." And he shot a questioning look at Cecilia.

"We must go for him too," she declared firmly.

"Quite so, we must," he answered. "But the water's pouring out very swiftly, as you can see. If the boat is caught in the entanglement of rocks and tree trunks underneath there, which cause the presence of so many swirls and eddies, and the oars can't free it, then it will soon have a hole in the bottom and sink like a stone with whoever's in it."

"The thing to do is to approach him from the river," said Cecilia, adding as if to herself, "to make a wide circle and get between the two breaks without coming to grief."

"Of course," said the watcher. "But who can tell anything about the currents in the river after this upheaval? Just look at the pressure of the water coming through the breaks!"

Between the internal lake and the river, cross currents swirled and clashed together, first attracted by the breaks, then thrown angrily back before they were finally sucked in by a vast whirlpool consisting of myriad small eddies gathered into one.

"To be pulled into something like that . . ." the watcher continued. "If only those people on the roof would leave off their shouting . . ." he interrupted himself impatiently. "They can wait. While that fellow there's sure to be swallowed up soon by the river. Why is he so quiet? But he can't be dead if he's sitting in that position. What I want to know is who'll dare to go out to him?"

Looking dreamily around and speaking in a subdued voice Schiavetto said with a touch of malice:

"If he were here and his wife were out there he wouldn't go for her, I can tell you."

Cecilia was startled to have an outsider say something that struck home to her conscience.

"I could never give that excuse to his children," she said, and as Schiavetto bowed his head she went on, "If one day they were to ask me why I abandoned their father to his fate, what could I say then, Schiavetto? There's no time to be lost!" And there was cheerfulness in her decisive tone of voice.

"I'm ready," said Schiavetto.

"I knew I could count on you," she said.

"But there's no need for you to come, Mistress Cecilia."

"Do you want me to show fear? Where's your head this morning, Schiavetto?"

"I'm thinking of your six innocent children, if you must know."

"If I were to die here in the river I could recommend them with a clear conscience to Our Lord and His Mother," Cecilia said stoically. "There are men of good will who I am sure would take care of them. And since we're old hands with the river we shall know how to handle it and make the trip out and back safely." Then, as she went back to the small boat she had left anchored on the shore she added, "There's another point to consider. If I go, then the two helpers will feel they too must lend a hand. We need them at the oars, because you're no longer twenty, you know, Schiavetto!"

"Or thirty, either!" said the old man, echoing her good cheer. "I should have known that you're sure to get your way."

"Because I'm so stubborn, is that it?"

"Because you are both wise and kind."

The boat was readied, and almost immediately after, as if to prove the truth of what Cecilia had said, Lazybones appeared on the scene and asked who was going. When they told him it was Coxcomb, he could not bear to be outdone and said that two were better than one. Meanwhile Cecilia slipped on some old trousers she wore about the house and came to join them. She jumped into the boat and each of the two apprentices took an oar. At the last minute Cecilia thought she heard Berta crying on the mill and sent Schiavetto to see what was wrong. When he came back to report that all was well the boat had already drawn away from the shore. Cecilia was sitting at one of the oars near the bow with Lazybones at the other. Coxcomb was the more experienced rower and she directed him to take command, standing up to steer with the pair of oars at the stern.

"Pull away, boys!" she shouted, dipping her own oar into the water.

The boat was long and slender, a little dangerous because it was so light, but for this very reason easy to maneuver and suited to the delicate task that lay before them. With four powerful strokes of the left oar Coxcomb aimed it at the opposite shore and now it glided diagonally over the water.

"Ho there, Mistress Cecilia!" called out Schiavetto from the deck of Bitter Bread Mill.

"The children!" Cecilia shouted back between one oar stroke and another. "If anything happens I leave them in your charge!"

"That's the way to talk," said Coxcomb approvingly. "We've no time to waste in words."

Coxcomb was short-bodied, long-armed, and awkward in the manner of a bear, but with a bear's strength and agility. His number had been drawn for conscription and in a few months he was to leave for service in the navy. In his strong hands the heavy oars in their high oarlocks literally flew. Meanwhile Schiavetto stood with his hands in his pockets, leaning against the cabin of Bitter Bread Mill. It was impossible to tell at this distance whether the expression on his face was one of resentment or humiliation, and they had not a minute to throw away in guessing at his state of mind.

The upper break was now attracting the greater volume of water, and before veering through it the river made a wide semicircle rimmed by swirling eddies. Their plan was to row up the river along the opposite shore and then come back downstream along the edge of the semicircle without being sucked into it. At the same time, as they made for the remaining segment of the dike, where Giuseppe was sitting, they had to take care not to be pulled into the current of the lower break, which churned up dangerously in the newly formed lake between the dikes and the crown and promised certain disaster. The problem, then, was to steer a straight course between these two perils. Returning diagonally again across the river, this time headed downstream, Coxcomb showed himself to be an excellent pilot. Now the boat balanced for a moment on the dividing line between the two currents while Coxcomb pointed it straight across the semicircle and the forward rowers sent it with clean strokes through to safety, just as neatly as if it were the ferry barge that crossed the river on a rope. They landed on the segment of the dike at a point of comparative calm.

"Good work, Coxcomb!" said Cecilia, jumping ashore.

Giuseppe sat there motionless and did not respond to her call. She ran anxiously toward him and a moment later the two apprentices heard her shout for help. Tying the boat to an oar stuck vertically into the sand they ran to join her. Cecilia pointed to her crouching husband who looked into the water and laughed, unconscious of anyone's presence. There was a vacant look in his eyes, as if they had been washed by the flood. Perhaps he had lost his mind as well as his possessions in the water.

"The devil broke his word to me . . . My land . . . My money . . ." he muttered, staring vacantly ahead of him.

"Never mind about your money, Master Peppino," said the two apprentices. "Come, we must get away."

"My money . . ." he repeated. "A bag of silver crowns and thousands of liras in paper, all buried."

"Buried where?" asked Cecilia.

"You'd like to know in order to steal them, would you? But the river got there before you!" And this was the only time that he paid attention to what they were saying or made any answer.

Had he really buried some money or was he merely raving? At this point it was of little matter. He stood up on his feet and appeared comparatively calm. Then he stuck his hands into his pockets, pulled them out full of coins, and threw them into the river.

"Take these too!" he shouted. "And I hope you choke on them."

"What rotten luck!" exclaimed the apprentices, who at any other time might have laughed, as they saw the gold ducats flying through the air.

When they started to restrain him and lead him away he struggled so violently that it was all both of them could do to hold him. Cecilia ran to get the rope, shoving the boat up on the sand until they could get back to it. Then they tied his legs together and his arms to his sides, winding the rope around and around him in order that there should be no danger of his overturning the boat.

"He bites worse than a pike," Lazybones muttered.

Because his head was the only part of him free, Giuseppe was actually trying to bite them.

"He's madder than a mad dog," observed Coxcomb.

Reduced to this humiliating position, Giuseppe began to howl like a wolf, as Cecilia had heard him do before.

"He's mad beyond any cure," Coxcomb added. "Was it really worth risking our lives on the river to bring back such a human wreck, especially now that he's thrown away his ducats?"

"He's a werewolf, for certain," said Lazybones fearfully.

"The devil is in him," answered Coxcomb. "What are we to do, Mistress Cecilia?"

"How can you ask?" said Cecilia, shaking herself out of a daze. "We must put him on the boat."

564

"He may well bring us bad luck," objected the superstitious Coxcomb, "or make us capsize. Look at the way he's struggling."

"The rope's long enough to tie him to the bottom."

And this was what they did, raising their voices above his loud howl to consult one another.

"Look at the people that have come to see what kind of an animal we're bringing back with us," Coxcomb said with annoyance.

"They've come to admire your bravery," said Cecilia severely. "Stop all this foolish talk."

Now Coxcomb had other things on his mind, for it was up to him to pilot them back. This time there was less danger from the undertow of the upper break than from that of the lower. He ordered them to row with quick, short strokes and so doing they reached the middle of the river. Then all of a sudden Cecilia's oar broke.

"Don't be afraid!" Coxcomb said, adding to Lazybones, who was idling as he waited for an order: "Don't stroke too hard and I'll manage to balance you."

Now Coxcomb had most of the work to do and he was quite a sight to see, with his face as red as his name implied and the veins standing out on his neck and temples. His powerful stocky body seemed to be one with the boat as he engaged in a life-and-death struggle with the river.

"Backstroke, Lazybones!" he shouted at just the right moment, turning the boat right around and aiming for the nearby Bitter Bread Mill.

As he at last relaxed he turned pale and perspiration streamed down his cheeks. Now he felt entitled to give vent to his feelings, for Giuseppe had made more noise on the boat than he had on the dike.

"If that madman would only keep his trap shut!" he exclaimed, and as they drew close to the mill he took advantage of his last moment of authority to call out: "Schiavetto, see what a fine sausage we've brought you!"

"That's enough, Coxcomb!" said Cecilia, half in anger and half in sorrow. "Show some respect for a man who's suffering such a calamity."

"I'm sorry if I've spoken too rudely. But I know a medicine that's sure to cure him."

No one enquired what the cure might be while they toiled over disembarking the trussed and howling Giuseppe, taking care lest he fasten his foaming mouth upon them and sink his teeth into their flesh. So Coxcomb raised his voice again:

"Something's gone to his head, that's all, but nothing serious. I say to dip him half a dozen times in the river and all his mad ideas will be swept away."

"Come, come, you brute!" said Schiavetto, leaning over to haul up the writhing body.

"Schiavetto!" Cecilia called. "Put the children inside!"

The hapless children followed Schiavetto into the cabin in order that they might be spared the sad sight of their father's return. Then the old helper went back on deck, where the two apprentices were having a hard time holding Giuseppe down.

"He'd better be tied with rags," he advised them. "The rope may cut and wound him."

They untied and tied him up again, then lowered him into the hold of Saint Michael's Mill and laid him on a mattress. The darkness seemed to have a calming effect, for his howling tapered off into an intermittent moan.

3

Their relief, if such it could be called, did not last long, for they had to take counsel immediately as to where they should transport him to be cared for ashore. If they were to leave him in his present condition there was danger of his either strangling himself or dying of starvation. Unfortunately Schiavetto had heard news of how difficult it was to travel by land after the ravage of the flood.

All the way to the flooded village of Guarda the riverbank was practically deserted. Most people had chosen to take refuge on the old raised road that had saved Guarda before. With the instinct of homing birds they had gone up the river rather than down. But a terrified rumor came up from the section devastated by the new river as it swelled ditches and canals to the breaking point and plowed its way through fields and villages in a headlong rush to the sea. This rumor had it that the flood, having gone through La Vallazza, jumped the Lavezzola canal and spread out in the direction of Francolino, was now breaking down the walls of the Canal Bianco and forcing its way through to the Volano river and the Ambrogio valley. Ditches were clogged up, bridges swept away, and, worst of all, the roads, which many had considered places of safety, were repeatedly broken. As boats went about rescuing people who had climbed onto roofs and trees the roads were more and more crowded with peasants and their animals and household goods. It was easy to imagine that this crush, similar to that of a defeated army, would by now prevent the passage of a single cart or even an individual on foot. Even where the roads were not broken people clung to them and were reluctant to move for fear of finding themselves in a place less secure. This cowardliness, half stubborn and half weary, this refusal to move on or even to make room for another, were well known from the stories of previous disasters of the same kind, they were as traditional as the instinct to seek out a high place on the banks or along the roads, preferably farther up the river than the break-through. When Cecilia went ashore to find out how they could transport the madman to more suitable quarters, she was told everywhere about this congestion. One man whom she questioned pointed to the dark clouds to the east and south.

"Pretty soon it will be raining," he said. "Over there it's pouring already in a way that gets into your bones. That's the last straw! And to think of those people on the roads, crowded together as if they were stuck with glue!"

The day of the break-through had been sunny, but the gloomy dawn that followed led on to one of those complete changes of weather in which the month of June does not live up to its character and dampness rusts the wheat just when it is in the greatest need of sun. This was the prospect at that very moment, with gusts of alternate north and south wind displacing huge masses of rain-laden clouds. The air became heavy and cold, and before there was time to say that a storm was gathering it was actually upon them, a mixture of rain and hail. One downpour followed another, without any hope of clearing or of respite for the population of the countryside, who had already been the victims of one visitation of divine anger. The rain and wind put out their meager improvised fires and all they could do was to crawl under a canvas or a cart or some dripping tree.

"Even if you could get through," they said to Cecilia, "who would be able to lend you a cart or in fact any vehicle at all? The only thing is for you to take the poor fellow across the Po and then come back by the bridge at Lagoscuro, if it's still standing. We know nothing of conditions there, and God seems to remember us only for the purpose of subjecting us to punishment."

Such pessimism was, however, exaggerated, since even if the pontoon bridge at Lagoscuro had been broken there was a new iron bridge carrying the railway line between Bologna and Venice.

"And what's happened to the people who were on that roof?" asked Cecilia, trying to consider other people's troubles even if she could not really take her mind off her own.

"The doctor came and took them off in his boat . . ."

"Dr. Lupacchioli," interposed Schiavetto, who seemed equally relieved to change the subject. "And there's a really fine man. Just imagine, Mistress Cecilia, last night he lost his only daughter, his pride and joy, and no sooner had he closed her eyes than he went out in his boat over the flooded countryside, to bandage wounds, save lives, and distribute food and medicine. What's more, his wife is doing the same thing. Their good work is needed, for fear and cold have laid many people low with fever. Yes, Signora Lupacchioli's a fine woman, too, even if she has a way of saying exactly what she thinks and of smoking a cigar for all the world like a man."

"Yes, the doctor . . ." said Cecilia. "We must get the doctor to come see him."

"What good would that do? He's no case for a doctor. It's a visitation of God that's upon him."

"Schiavetto," Cecilia ordered him dryly as if she had not heard what he was saying, "go look for Dr. Lupacchioli and tell him to come as soon as he can to my husband." And she added as an apology for her brusqueness, "I'm sorry to send you in this weather."

"This is no time to worry about the rain. I'll go at once, Mistress Cecilia," Schiavetto said obediently.

It was coming down in sheets as the old man, wrapped in his cloak, went off along the bank toward Guarda. Aboard the mill Giuseppe continued to moan to the accompaniment of the thunder. But what tugged most at Cecilia's heartstrings was to hear the children softly singing a little rainy day invocation to the sun:

> God's little swallow, take the rain away;
> God's little swallow, bring the sun to stay!

Their plaintive song was like whistling in the dark to keep up their courage, and Cecilia did not go in lest they should see her tears and take fright. She cried alone on the deck of the mill in anticipation of what the doctor was sure to say.

"There's nothing to do but put him away as quickly as possible. Otherwise . . . And yet that might be the best thing of all."

"What do you mean?"

"For him to die, my good woman. Why should a madman go on living? When you think how young people die in their prime and here this man may live to the turn of the century when he'd be better off dead! When we think of the young ones . . ."

"Yes, Doctor, we know of your misfortune, and we're all heartily sorry for you. And even today you have not failed to show your kindness."

"Thank you, my good woman. That is the only way to keep me from despairing. Now let's come back to you and your own troubles. I'll write a letter to the head of the asylum at Ferrara and tell him to admit your husband immediately."

"I have neither pen nor ink here on the mill."

"I'll use a pencil; don't worry about that. But how are you going to take him there?"

"I'll take him across the river and then back over the bridge at Lagoscuro. Surely I'll find some vehicle from there to Ferrara."

"Yes, probably that's the best you can do. Goodbye, Mistress Cecilia."

"Goodbye, Doctor."

The doctor was a small, slender man, with a straggly beard and a colorless face which bore the marks of his recent fatigue upon it. There was a lost expression in his tired, pale eyes, which like those of a suffering animal reflected a grief of which he was powerless to speak. But while his eyes seemed to ask mutely what was the reason for so much human woe, his voice and gestures were both energetic and kindly, and by sheer fortitude of spirit he was able to overcome his physical frailty and the affliction which had just overtaken him.

"The doctor doesn't go to Mass," said Schiavetto, after he had ferried him ashore, "but all the same he's a saint."

His wife was a strange woman, of masculine build and manners, with a quarrelsome disposition, given to hunting and smoking. When a sick man came to see her husband she often took affairs into her own hands and as soon as she had heard the diagnosis she prescribed a cure and followed up its execution. No one called her a saint, but she did a great deal of good in her own way even if her brusqueness often aroused antagonism. She had a habit of throwing the premise and unfavorable conclusion of an argument at the person to whom she was talking before he could catch his breath:

"You're bound to disregard what I'm telling you," she would say, "because you're such a jackass."

She too did not go to Mass and was a freethinker, a most astonishing thing in those days for a woman living in the country. But if a hothead like Woodcock claimed that she shared his political opinions she pulled him up very short indeed.

"Don't try to pass yourself off as a philosopher," she said. "If anyone were to squeeze your brain, all that would come out of it would be a little watery pumpkin juice."

In Signora Lupacchioli's opinion the world was made up of pumpkin heads and rascals in equal number. She was the epitome of willfullness and self-assurance, quite unaware that her theories were far removed from reality and verged on the chimerical and the inane. Sometimes she confined herself to reproaching some poor peasant for having more faith in the magical draughts and incantations of Dame Blackface, the witch, than in a good dose of quinine, but such a case did not give full play to her convictions, which she often felt compelled to express in vehement and theatrical language. Malicious neighbors had it that with a wife of this sort Dr. Lupacchioli could not help being either a saint or an assassin. And yet she did do good in her own fashion, especially on the day of the flood. Having said a last farewell to her daughter, whom she had always tyrannized, and given the body over to two pious women, she set out in a boat among the half-submerged houses and flooded fields to rescue as many of the peasants as she could, berating them thoroughly if she found them downhearted.

She taxed Stump with inattention to his duty of inspection, threatened to shoot the sheriff for his cowardice, and then went on to discover that the oven of Frascari, the baker, which stood on a raised platform, had not been flooded. His wood supply was drenched but she secured wood from a neighbor and lit his fire with her own hands until soon its lone column of smoke could be seen from far away. Frascari himself had climbed up in the eaves of his barn but she made him come down and start baking bread.

Not long after this, Signora Lupacchioli made a frontal attack on the parish priest, a humble and not very highly educated man, who had ordered the church bells rung in order that the faithful should come implore God's mercy. She accused him so violently of contributing to the general demoralization that finally he lashed back at her:

"Don't forget that the bell will toll for your daughter's funeral soon!"

"There's work to be done, and this is no time for whining litanies!" she answered. "And there's no use tolling the bell if she can't even be buried. You pious pumpkin heads didn't have the sense to build your cemetery on a hillside, and now it's under water."

"We pray for souls, not bodies, if you must know, and your words smack of idolatry!" the priest exclaimed.

"As soon as the water subsides we'll turn the church into a refuge. That way it will be useful for something beside selling indulgences!"

"This is blasphemy! How do you dare say such a thing? I'd like to see you touch it!"

"I'll have it requisitioned by due process of law!"

The priest was leaning out of the rectory window, while Signora Lupacchioli stood in her boat on the flooded square. The water level was beginning to fall, for the main impetus of the flood had spent itself in another direction. Many of the refugees had come back to their houses, and while bewailing the damage done they had already started to repair it and in parts of the village they had restored communications by means of planks from one emergent area to another. Around noon the boats of the doctor and his wife crossed and under a heavy downpour of rain he told her the sad story of Cecilia and her mad husband.

"Mad, is he?" she said scornfully. "I'd like to see that for myself."

"He's completely out of his head, I tell you."

"He may find it convenient to pretend just in order not to pay taxes."

The doctor shrugged his shoulders and she steered her fishing boat toward the river. Gathering her cape about her and pulling her mannish hat down over her forehead to protect her against the wind she walked along the shore in the direction of the mills. She had real respect for Cecilia, but finding her in an uncomfortable situation she could not resist acting in her usual high-handed manner.

"Come, let me see if he's as mad as he makes out," she said brusquely.

She had Giuseppe brought up from the hold to the cabin of the still creaking Saint Michael's Mill. He had fallen into a sort of torpor and moaned with his eyes tight shut.

"Open your eyes and look me in the face, Were Rabbit!" commanded Signora Lupacchioli, laying aside her wet cape and baring her ruffled gray head.

The madman obeyed her, with sheer terror veiling his glassy eyes and his face turning an ashen color.

"Remember that even madmen have to watch their step with me and answer when I speak to them," she said sternly.

"This must be the devil with skirts on!" Giuseppe exclaimed wildly, causing Coxcomb, who was standing by, to burst into laughter.

"You mannerless bumpkin!" thundered the would-be healer, feeling her therapeutic authority undermined. "Traitor and gallows bird! How do you dare to laugh?"

"I laugh when I please," he said rudely, between one fit of choking and another, "and if I ever go mad I'll surely come to you to be cured."

"Out of my sight, you rascal!"

Coxcomb went over to the other mill, whence from time to time there echoed a gale of laughter, and Signora Lupacchioli, affecting not to hear, applied herself once more to the task of dealing with Giuseppe. Now the scene took on a mock-heroic character, with the opponents shouting and trying to stare one another down. Giuseppe emitted bestial howls and obscene noises and in order to shout him down Signora Lupacchioli scolded and insulted him in a shriller and shriller tone of voice. The madman struggled with his bonds and bit at the air, simply because he could not sink his teeth into his enemy, while she stood with her hands on her hips, shouting at the top of her iron lungs as if she were commanding an army on the field of battle. The one who was confessedly crazy was the first to tire of the struggle, close his eyes and resume moaning, but his surrender seemed to be eminently sensible.

"Now we must take him to the asylum," said Signora Lupacchioli undauntedly.

There was no use telling her she could have saved time by admitting this in the first place, without provoking such unreasonable fury.

"I know that for myself," said Cecilia. "I'd be on the way already, if . . ." "If you hadn't come upon the scene," was what she started to say, but she restrained herself.

"If there weren't such suspicious characters out on the river," said Schiavetto lamely.

"And who might they be?" said the doctor's wife, angrily wheeling upon him, as if she feared he might be alluding to her own person.

Schiavetto explained that several boatloads of ugly-looking individuals had gone by, the sort that always turn up after a disaster for the purpose of robbing abandoned houses and holding up any stray and helpless persons they may meet on their way.

"There's flour and grain here on the mills and they may believe there's money too, which it would be an easy job for them to take away from a woman with six children. It's safe enough during the day, but what about nightfall?"

"Do you expect the police to pay special attention to you on such an eventful day?" Signora Lupacchioli asked angrily.

"I expect nothing of the sort. But I say it's impossible to go to Ferrara and back before night and the mills can't be left unprotected."

"It looks to me as if you were afraid, my man," she insisted, "but at least you talk sense. If you can get the patient across the river I'll do the rest."

"If you think I'm afraid . . ." said Schiavetto heatedly, but then he cut himself short. "I've had a long experience of the river, that's all," he said. "Meanwhile your offer is indeed a kind one."

"That it is," said Cecilia.

"I know a fellow on the Venetian side," said Signora Lupacchioli, "who will surely lend me a horse. You're right to say that you had best stay here. In fact, I advise you to keep your guns loaded, because I've heard it from other sources too that there are ugly faces roaming about the neighborhood. Cecilia, will you be good enough to send word to the doctor that I'll not be home until late? And give the same message to the women who are watching over my poor daughter's body. Do you know of my misfortune?"

The intense and dry-eyed sorrow portrayed on her rough, bronzed face was sudden and striking. But before Cecilia could utter a word of compassion she added:

"Don't speak of it. If I let myself go I'll be as mad as Were Rabbit and madder."

"May God recompense you in His good time."

"Never mind about that."

The scene of violence threatened to start again, but everyone was by now too tired to suffer. Schiavetto and Coxcomb ferried Signora Lupacchioli and Giuseppe across the river in a burst of rain from the darkening clouds. On the way back to the mills Coxcomb had the last word as he spit the rain water out of his mouth:

"They're equally mad," he said, "only one of them isn't tied up, that's all."

"Keep your trap shut, you fool," said Schiavetto.

And as for Were Rabbit, he was not to come back to Guarda alive.

4

It took a far-reaching acquaintance with the history of the Po to recall a disaster of the magnitude of this one. The closest parallel was one a thousand years old, still kept alive in legend, the Siccardi breakthrough, which had caused the river to change its path just at the bend of Ficarolo. The lesson of the former flood was clear. Unless an attempt was made to repair the breaks right away it would be impossible to deflect the river from its new course, or at least too late to preserve the land from excessive damage. The nature of the terrain led to this conclusion, because it was so flat that there was nothing to prevent the river from spreading indefinitely, especially in this late spring season when melted snow was pouring down from the mountains. The Po continued to be swollen, and about half its volume poured through the breaks, overran the Canal Bianco and caused the Volano in its turn to overflow. The district of San Giovanni and the land between the Volano and the Po all the way to the Ambrogio Valley was flooded, 175,000 acres of land, with a population of some 40,000 souls, now homeless under the protracted rain.

Aboard Cecilia's two mills there was just enough work to keep things going, and she was lucky, at that. She had brought with her from the house at Poplar Bridge a few pieces of simple gold jewelry, some everyday furniture and clothing for herself and her children, but no money. What grief she felt for the loss of the farm was far less than her sense of liberation in the knowledge that Ca' Morgosa and Antonella had been swept away, for these two pieces of land had always seemed to her to lie under a curse because of the way Giuseppe had acquired them. Were it not for his madness she would have allowed herself the satisfaction of the "I told you so" which to most of us is so gratifying that we do not care at what cost to ourselves we have won the right to say it.

As it was, she saw Giuseppe's madness as a sort of divine retribution and could not think of it without trembling. About Poplar Bridge she did have some sentiment, because it was connected with her memories of Lazzaro and Dosolina, even if the former had affected to despise it.

Yes, it was from his mother that Giuseppe had inherited the lust for land which had brought upon him such exemplary punishment. In her mixed feelings about both her husband and mother-in-law Cecilia displayed a bit of human weakness. In any case she was moved to mingled horror and pity by the memory of Master Lazzaro's reluctance to be buried in the Guarda cemetery and the doleful prophecies which in his old age had won him the name of Apocalypse. After all, they had in large measure come true. And this only made her fonder of the mills and her life on the river, including all the dangers that went with it. In the same way the sailor loves the sea and the mountaineer the mountains, not only in fair weather but in foul. And Cecilia certainly cared more for her dead father-in-law than for her wreck of a husband.

She felt a certain unconscious pride during these days, when the general population was so sorely afflicted, in the fact that she and her family could rely on the mills instead of on a dole from the government. Such peasants as had saved some of their cattle had to go in boats to clip sprigs of wheat and leaves off the trees with which to feed them. Those who had no resources at all drifted toward the city, where shelters had been opened and help was pouring in from all over Italy and from other countries as well. According to the fashion of the times, artistic and musical galas were held for the benefit of the refugees and there was even talk of drawing up an "international list of lovers of music and drama contributing to the relief fund." Such is the role of the ridiculous in human affairs.

In their weakened condition the refugees were an easy prey to a recrudescent epidemic of smallpox, as well as to waves of typhoid fever and malaria. By some irony of fate the flood brought with it an abundance of fish, but cooking facilities were poor and much of it spoiled and was a source of infection. Diarrhea and dysentery on a large scale started up the rumor that cholera was once more on the march. And another adverse factor was the lack of unpolluted drinking water.

Signora Lupacchioli was charged with the distribution of food, clothing, and medicine at Guarda. She arranged for the transportation of the sick and needy to the hospital and shelters in Ferrara and this was often a cause of bad feeling, for prejudice was still strong among the country people against everything that smacked of an institution. Signora Lupacchioli was quite right in combatting their ignorance, but she did not always do so in the most tactful manner.

"You know nothing of hygiene!" she told them.

It was true that they neither knew nor cared, but was this the right moment to tell them so?

"Priests and tyrants have kept you in a state of ignorance and superstition. You live and die in filth and mud, like your pigs!"

"My pigs have all drowned," said one peasant bitterly. "And they were a fine lot, the dozen of them, especially the male, who had proved his worth with the sows."

"Are you joking?" Signora Lupacchioli asked angrily.

"Joking, at a time like this?" And he shrugged his shoulders. "What I want to know is whether you can raise them up again?"

The bystanders could not help smiling.

"You pumpkin heads seem to believe that the hospital's the gateway to hell, and the doctor an assassin!"

"Not quite, but he does the best he can!"

"You don't deserve to have anyone look after you."

"There you may be right," admitted the peasant more humbly, but Signora Lupacchioli could not let it go at that.

"You show neither conscience nor gratitude! And yet an international relief fund has been collected for you."

"Is that where our miserable ration of bread comes from? It might be kinder to let us starve than to keep us barely alive. And meanwhile nothing's being done about mending the breaks in the embankment."

"Ignorance and presumptuousness always go together! Do you claim to know more than the engineers?"

Here she had hit the wrong note, for on other occasions she herself had blamed the engineers for the recent disaster. And they were bold enough to answer her all together:

"That would be easy! The break-through proved what the engineers amount to, with that wonderful crown of theirs! They were the only ones too blind to see how it would turn out, and all because they were splitting fees with a thieving contractor. Are you telling us to respect that jackass Manghetti?"

Their anger tapered off into a bitter laugh, for this title had by general consent been fastened upon the engineer responsible for inspecting the finished job and also for giving the order to cut the dikes and fill the basin in between with water.

"You called him a jackass yourself," said another one of the group to Signora Lupacchioli. "And it was even published in the most advanced papers."

"Just because one was a fool doesn't mean that all the rest were too," she shot back at them.

"Yes, but he alone did quite enough damage. One swallow doesn't make a summer, but in this case one jackass was sufficient to bring on our ruin."

"That's no way to reason."

"Then they're all thieves: government, engineers, and contractors, since usually they divide the job among them. And when it's time to pay they clap another on the taxpayer. Poor Pantaloon must always foot the bill!"

The peasants had cleverly enough turned Signora Lupacchioli's radical political beliefs against her. In spite of all her good intentions she aggravated them by failing to understand how loth they were to let their dear ones go to the hospital, no matter how sick they might be.

"Society has to protect itself against contagion," she insisted. "Good health is not a right but a duty and disease is a form of crime. Can't you do anything but pray to Saint Roch about it? Instead of worshipping false relics you should look up to the new martyrs of science."

Weeping women and men silent with grief stared at her in astonishment.

"What's all this got to do with smallpox?" they asked her.

"Smallpox can have its use as a scientific experiment if you take it to the doctor. Hygiene should be the order of the day."

"We'll settle for our good health!" they retorted.

"You're egotists, all of you!"

"What's that?"

"Pumpkin heads! Ignoramuses! Science is the new religion!"

But they simply stood with their mouths hanging open.

In these days politics entered into everything. First the long period of comparative peace under paternalistic governments after the peace treaty of Aix-la-Chapelle had been interrupted by the meteoric intervention of Napoleon in Italian affairs; then the unwelcome Austrian rule had brought tyranny and the answering revolutionary disorders of 1848. Now Italians found themselves in possession of political liberty and a constitutional form of government for which they were totally unprepared. They threw themselves intoxicatedly into party strife, with the old revolutionary groups that had no reason to out-live the Risorgimento lined up against the equally anachronistic reactionaries. In this atmosphere of intemperate controversy they forgot that true freedom has its roots in civic discipline and respect for tradition. I refer to the members of the new upper class, who vaingloriously spoke of themselves as called upon for leadership and as a result of limited suffrage actually did use or rather misuse governmental powers. Because they were new to its exercise they could not be expected to have any tradition behind them, and they proceeded to act in a way that hardly favored its establishment. By constantly bringing doctrinaire political considerations to bear on every problem, they ensured the survival of factional party spirit, which was damaging enough even though expressed in wordy arguments rather than deeds of violence.

The simple and unlettered poor had a bulwark of tradition in the Catholic Church, from which they had derived their moral code and general outlook upon the world. Shaped by the daily life of centuries, this tradition had been rounded and polished by an inherited civilization just the way the Italian language is rounded and polished by its derivation from Latin. Now, all of a sudden, the covert hostility between Church and State threatened to give their religious beliefs the character of sedition. And because their Christian views traditionally kept them remote from politics the people looked with mistrust and annoyance at the current political strife, and made an effort only to understand and join in it for reasons of economic necessity. The government was quite organized enough to impose the taxes necessary to its existence, and the humble heroes of this period were those who had to shoulder the burden of paying off the public debt and balancing the budget. In this connection the government bore down upon the poor with an authority more legal than moral, more rigorous than persuasive, and yet the people came through this trial as they had come through so many others before.

Meanwhile, by the end of June, the village of Guarda, which had suffered comparatively little damage from the flood, was completely dry. Against its return every householder had raised an individual wall in front of his own dwelling, and under this halfway protection begun to put things in order. The villagers were fairly lucky, although their poverty was great and the rations of food allotted to them did not satisfy their hunger any more than did the meager salaries given to the laborers on the embankment, whom the contractor had hired for ridiculously little because there was widespread unemployment. Some peasants preferred to apply for a dole to Signora Lupacchioli than to work hard and be unable to eat as much as they needed. Once the general dismay over the tragedy had subsided and each one could better measure his personal damage, a spirit of mistrust and resentment began to prevail. Signora Lupacchioli was suspected of partiality and Woodcock was one of the most active in spreading rumors against her. He had plenty of time to do so since he refused to work, not because he was lazy but simply on general principles.

"Let the rich look after us," he said. "They'll only be giving back a little of what they've taken away from the poor. Now is the time to square accounts with them."

Woodcock did not stand in line like a beggar asking for charity but posed as an avenger of social injustice and a militant in the class struggle. Unlike Signora Lupacchioli he even approved the laborers when they streamed away from their ill-paid work on the repair of the embankment in order to attend a Mass on the midsummer feast of Saint John the Baptist.

"The worse things get the better they will eventually be," he insisted. "When poverty becomes really unbearable then we shall have a social revolution. Either we go the whole hog, or there's no use lifting a finger."

He was active in spreading discontent with the contractor's miserable pay, and when several hundred laborers went so far as to go on strike he organized them and encouraged their belief that this was the only way for them to achieve concrete gains. To this end he set up a sort of flying squad which went about the village enlightening the people as to the aims of the strike and asking them not to let themselves be hired as substitutes for the strikers.

"That would amount to betraying your comrades and stabbing them in the back. If you can't understand the point for yourselves we'll make you understand it!"

The arguments of the notoriously poor pay and the betrayal of their comrades were persuasively backed up by the stout sticks with which Woodcock armed his propagandists. The contractor was unable to find any strikebreakers and had to increase the laborers' pay. The success of

576

the strike made many converts to Woodcock's methods, although some people looked askance at the members of the flying squad because they did not break up, and instead of going back to work demanded extra rations from those distributed to the laborers' families.

"What's left for you to do now?" the laborers said to Woodcock and his men.

"To protect you from the rear."

"But the strike's over."

"It wouldn't be over if it weren't for us, would it?"

"That's all very well, but now . . ."

"If we don't keep watch the contractor will find a hundred beggars to put in your place. He'll kick you out, take them on at a lower pay, and get great satisfaction out of having evened the score. Is that what you want? If it is, just say so."

"No, of course not. We just want you to come back to work with us, because we can't have you fed at our expense for days and weeks and months, in fact indefinitely!"

Woodcock soon found a reply to the protest of these unregenerate souls. When the laborers engaged by the day came to work in the morning or started in again after lunch, their shovels and wheelbarrows were in a different place from the one where they had left them, and the piece-workers found their sandbags empty or their fencing cut, or a pile they were hammering mysteriously split down the middle. Under these circumstances the foreman very often accused them of negligence and fired them on the spot, much to Woodcock's amusement. When some such victims of his displeasure hinted that they might report him for sabotaging their work he saw that they were dealt with outside working hours.

"If you don't stop spreading gossip, you'll be sorry."

"And what will you do about it?"

The answer was a sound beating and the threat:

"Next time the dose will be stiffer!"

So it was that, before the Irish Land League gave the ugly practice its name, the "boycott" came into use at Guarda on the Po. The dole was given to those who were unable to work but not to those who were discharged from their jobs for incompetence, and hence the "boycotted" men went hungry.

Signora Lupacchioli could not bear either Woodcock or his followers and they could never get their rations from her without a quarrel. So instead of standing in line with the others they went from house to house and demanded their share.

"While we were engaged in protecting you from the rear we got ourselves into trouble and Signora Lupacchioli won't give us our due."

She was relieved by their absence and mistakenly rejoiced in it:

"I've weeded out a lot of good-for-nothings who claimed bread like the rest without being willing to work for it. What I call a good riddance!"

She would not have been so pleased with herself had she known what was really going on. But what could she have done about it? When a man starts asking himself a question of the kind he loses all desire to try to govern his fellows. This is clear enough in the last words—"The comedy is over!"—of a ruler who set up the most enlightened political, juridical and social system of all time. Signora Lupacchioli had not the wisdom of a Caesar Augustus, and she was far more of a despot, and an unreasonable one at that. She insisted that the enjoyment of the most elementary human rights be accorded by her benevolence and she had no respect for any human institution except a Utopian republic. Her only principle was that next to God she should reign supreme over Guarda. And in God she had no belief whatsoever.

5

Cecilia was faced with the necessity of finding a new anchorage for the mills. The place where she had taken refuge was no more than a temporary expedient, and the work being done to restore the embankment farther up the river made the flow of water uneven and clogged the roads with too much traffic to permit her customers to circulate freely. She went out in a skiff to explore the possibilities of the region, with Schiavetto to advise her. He was strong enough to navigate the skiff downstream, but when it was time to buck the current Cecilia had to take an oar. At first he would not admit the disabilities of his age, but a shooting pain in the ribs that almost took his breath away finally got the better of him.

"It's nothing," he protested. "The wet weather of this unlucky month of June has got into my bones."

"It's nothing at all," echoed Cecilia. "You'll get over it."

But his wasted gray face, the sudden pain that seemed to stab him from within, and his shrinking appetite were anything but encouraging. Of course Schiavetto never complained.

"If only I could get a good night's sleep," he said, "I'd be well in a trice. This pain is like an owl that comes out at night." But he would not see a doctor. "It's only a touch of rheumatism and good Master Lazzaro taught me how to cure that. A thorough sweat would take it all away."

Master Lazzaro's prescription was a plaster on the chest and back and a draught of medicated hot wine before going to bed. But Schiavetto could not seem to raise a sweat and the pain did not go away.

After a minute study of the current and the conformation of the banks of the river Cecilia and Schiavetto agreed on a site two miles below the village of Guarda. There was a steady flow of water, a safe landing-place in case of danger, sheltered by the Guarda peninsula, and a network of good roads, which would serve her old customers as well as the new. Three other mills were anchored not far away, but they had more business than they could handle and the millers welcomed her arrival. She did not threaten to take away their established clientele and they might even hope gradually to attract hers, although they would have cherished no such hope had they known her better. All in all, the site seemed to be a good one and Cecilia finally persuaded Schiavetto, who had pointed out the disadvantages of every place they had visited, to make a definite choice. They could not stay much longer where they were and the old anchorage at Nogarole was wiped away. It was a mid-August day when they came to a decision and on their way home they hugged the shore. In the purple and gold light of the sunset they saw hundreds of peasants filling barrels with river water, for the flood had played havoc with their wells.

"Do you see how many people there are in this vicinity, Mistress Cecilia?" said Schiavetto, more cheerfully than he had spoken in a long time. "Communications must be good, because I can tell that some of them have come from far away. There are two tests of an anchorage, you know: a steady flow of the river and plenty of roads converging upon it." And he went on to sing the praises of the new anchorage with unexpected enthusiasm. "The land down here was hardly touched by the flood and yet it's not so far away that our faithful customers will desert you. As for the Nogarole dikes, there must have been a curse hanging over them all along. Just look what happened to poor Master Giuseppe! Better for him if the river had carried him away!"

Cecilia shuddered. She had gone to visit her husband at the insane asylum of Ferrara, but they would not let her see him. From the heavy ironbound doors she had heard the inmates shouting and now memory made this sad noise echo in her ears. She said nothing and Schiavetto was encouraged to go on.

"This new anchorage is better than the old," he said emphatically.

"Do you really think so?" asked Cecilia quietly.

The weariness returned to Schiavetto's voice.

"What else can I say?" he muttered, pulling feebly at his oar. "I was thinking of you, who have years of activity ahead of you and your children to look after. With you it's a case of necessity and the sooner you become attached to the new place the better. With me it's a different story. The loss of the Nogarole dikes is something I simply can't get over; with every passing day I grow too old to try. You know how an old cat will cling to a house even after it's torn down and die rather than move away." He tried to speak lightly and across his gaunt, wrinkled face flickered the smile he had had as a boy. But there was no one to recognize it, for all the friends of his youth were dead and when he had first come to Master Lazzaro Cecilia was not yet born. "Yes," he added, "if I had my way I'd die there where I've lived for so long."

But something in his smile did draw Cecilia's attention and she looked at him half uncomprehendingly as if at an object that has fallen into the water and shimmers uncertainly before we can determine whether it will rise or fall. Schiavetto was overcome now by a host of memories.

"Like a cat, that's it exactly," he said, leaping from one subject to another, as if the flow of his words rather than the pain in his side and the weariness of his arms were causing him to breathe so hard. "I can remember the cats on the roof of Saint Michael's Mill. What a story! You've heard most of it yourself. It was the morning after the night when the soles of Big Brother's feet were toasted. What men there were in those days! And what about the cats? O yes, they were up on the roof. That morning Master Lazzaro made me go back with him to the mill and look Beffa in the eye. He knew what he was doing and understood that this was the only way for me to get over my fear. Yes, now that I remember, I felt sick at my stomach, but I tried not to show it. We were engaged in a struggle to the death with Raguseo, you know. The mere mention of his name made everyone tremble, and they were giants of courage in those days, both good men and bad. They took their courage jokingly, but underneath the joking you could hear the sound of steel striking steel. Well, I couldn't make it out that morning, when no sooner had that accursed Beffa stuck his ugly head out the window than Master Lazzaro capriciously called for a thorough cleaning of the mill. It was more than a cleaning, it was a tempest! He turned everything upside down and told us to sweep and wash and polish (don't forget it was a cold winter day, too!) and then to grease all the machinery. All the while he stood in the middle of the turmoil, shouting and making a fuss. Now I can see what he was driving at: he wanted to purge the mill of the sinister goings-on of the night before and to make me more afraid of him than of that hellbound Beffa. His strategy worked out perfectly, too, because I was hustling about so fast that I entirely forgot my original fear."

"And what about the cats on the roof?"

"The cats? Oh yes, of course, those splendid creatures that long ago mated with the ones you brought with you on the Bitter Bread Mill. Well, the dust was flying so fast that they took refuge on the roof and gazed at us with astonishment. A little later, when one of them started playing with a mouse, Master Lazzaro looked hard at Beffa and in fact stared him down, saying that we should name that cat Raguseo. And not so long after the good master himself played the part of the cat, while Beffa and Raguseo and Big Brother were the mice in the picture. Although they do say that God forgave Big Brother for his sins because he repented just before his execution."

With this Schiavetto turned back into an old, old man, and the pains in his sides and back were so acute that he let fall his oar and said with calm resignation:

"I have a feeling this ailment of mine will save me from grieving over the move to a new anchorage." And to forestall Cecilia's protest he added, "You don't really need me any more. I should only be a burden and eat bread I couldn't earn any longer. Of course I know you'd never send me away, any more than Master Lazzaro, whom I always looked on as a father. But you've hard years ahead after the losses you've suffered from the break-through and what with the job of bringing up so many children. It would be too much if you had an extra mouth to feed. The last thing I can do is to assure you that the new anchorage is a good one. But I shan't be down there for long." (By "down there" he meant below the Guarda peninsula.) "With the autumn rains I'll be going to a land where there's no need of eating bread, and a good thing it is, too."

Schiavetto had a touch of fever, and this was what led him to say something that Cecilia might otherwise never have known. He was further encouraged by the darkness of the night that had fallen around them and Cecilia's affectionate words:

"I've always looked on you as a brother, you know that, Schiavetto."

"Yes, I do. And haven't you wondered why I never took a wife?"

"No, to tell the truth, I haven't."

"Because the only woman I ever cared for was the owner of a mill and I was not worthy of her hand. Don't scold me, Mistress Cecilia, for having loved her so deeply."

"And you tell me that at my age?" Cecilia exclaimed. She was both touched and amused, but most of all she wanted to cheer him up by turning the whole thing into a joke.

"It's *my* age that gives me an excuse to tell you," said Schiavetto, tactfully restoring their relationship to normal.

6

The writer, with pen in hand, admits that he is loth to take leave of Schiavetto, and hopes that the reader who has followed the story so far will share his regret. The autumn rains came and Schiavetto did not see the end of them.

For two months now the mills had been tied up at the new anchorage. The millstones were in good order, neither bearing down too heavily at the edges nor too lightly at the center. Their balance was perfect and they were not so worn as to require the process called "dressing the furrows."

But 1872 was set upon being an unlucky year. Rain continued to pour down every day, mingled with violent wind and spells of thunder and lightning. There was even a most unseasonal hailstorm, which seemed like a curse hurled from on high upon a portion of the earth that had no more to lose. For weeks on end the sun did not shine, and one gloomy day followed another, shedding only a feeble light over the washed-out fields, the staved-up houses and muddy roads. Hadn't the flood done enough damage, without this further visitation? The few peasants who had any grain to bring to the mills were unable to travel on account of the bad weather, and Cecilia had barely enough corn-meal mush and bread to feed her children. The baker was in no position to extend her credit and she had more fear of indebtedness than of hunger. Unemployment was on the increase and the peasants soon used up their reserves of grain which were already low when the flood swept away the crops they were so close to harvesting. Many of them became dependent upon public charity.

The new anchorage, known as Dwarf's Landing, a name which it shared with a bridge over the road near by, had most inauspicious beginnings. On a rainy day, when there was no bread to eat, Schiavetto was carried ashore, after a mercifully brief illness, from Saint Michael's Mill. Cecilia and the oldest of her sons, Giovanni, went with the body. The river was running high, the sky was heavy with clouds, and the fields were half under water, almost as if the *dies irae* or day of judgment were at hand. The pallbearers walked as fast as they could, shaking the mud from their shoes at every step, while the priest found it wise to wait for them in the church. Torrents of rain poured down on the crude coffin and soaked Cecilia and her boy, while the wind threatened to turn their oilcloth umbrellas inside out and blow them away. A heavy fog hung over the river and the day was so dark that they could not see the church even when they heard the dull tolling of the bell. The priest stood all alone at the church door, for Schiavetto had concentrated his life so completely on the mills that he had not had time to make friends in the village. Yet now was the time when a friend would have stood him in good stead. A grave had been dug beside that of Master Lazzaro, but it was filled with mud and water and the sexton said to the priest:

"We'd better wait a few hours, at least until it stops raining."

"That may not be for some time."

It was hardly necessary to look out at the weather in order to grasp his meaning. Even the sorely tried earth seemed to refuse the old man's body. They had to bail out the grave with a bucket as if it were a sinking ship—another agony—and then to dig deeper. The earth clung to the shovel. And if it had first been recalcitrant in leaving the ditch, now it seemed to refuse to return to it. It stuck, and each shovelful had to be shaken off with effort, so that the entombment led to degrading and offensive scenes. Cecilia could almost hear Master Lazzaro saying as he had done when they called him Apocalypse, that he did not want to be buried there below the water level. And then she had the humiliating experience of asking the priest and the sexton to let her off temporarily from the payment of their modest fees.

"Today I've no bread to give my children, but tomorrow or the next day a peasant is bringing grain to the mill and I shall be able to fulfill my obligations."

"Don't worry about that," said the priest, whose share was a small one.

"It's an unlucky year," said the sexton, shaking his head. "Of course I'll wait, but you know how badly off I am."

"I'll not forget, I promise you."

"And I know your word is good, Mistress Cecilia."

The title of mistress rang ironically in her ear. Mistress of what? Of hunger? Her few simple jewels had gone to guarantee the money she owed the shopkeepers, for although Coxcomb had been conscripted to serve in the navy she still had Lazybones to feed, and he was indispensable now that Schiavetto was no longer there. In fact she prayed God that there might be no further disaster, that the river might not continue to rise as it had begun to do since early in October. But God seemed to be in a wrathful mood and the *dies irae* was still hanging over them. This was the first day that Cecilia had found herself with the larder bare and she shuddered at the prospect of going back empty-handed to face her hungry children. They hadn't yet complained but at noon the day before the littlest girl had said:

"Mother, aren't we going to eat today?"

And while the others silently echoed this innocent question, Maria, who was unusually mature for her years, had coaxed them into a game of blindman's buff. While she dressed Schiavetto for his funeral she could hear them singing in the cabin of Bitter Bread Mill:

Catch me, catch me!
You can't watch me!

But later little Berta slipped the scarf off her eyes to ask her:

"Mother, is it true that Schiavetto's dead?"

"Yes, poor dear fellow, he is."

"And what's it mean that he's dead?"

"That he's gone to a better world than ours."

"Then why do you call him 'poor fellow'?" asked the precocious Maria.

Aboard the Saint Michael they were nailing down the lid of the coffin.

Now that the burial was over Cecilia did not have the heart to face their questioning again. She did not know where to turn for help until she suddenly thought of the doctor's wife. Signora Lupacchioli was in charge of distributing relief to all those who had suffered from the flood and so it was a question not of charity but of justice. This was what lent Cecilia assurance when she knocked at the doctor's door. Indeed she taxed herself with her failure to have taken advantage of this resource long ago.

"There's no reason why I should feel ashamed," she murmured deep down in her heart. "My children are hungry and I'm only claiming my just due."

Cold, hunger, and fatigue lent a sort of aggressive petulance to her train of thought and gave her an almost cocky air.

"She can't say no. Of course she'll give me bread. It would be an outrage if she didn't."

Signora Lupacchioli came to open the door, and having a certain esteem for Cecilia she took her to warm herself up by the fire, where a pot was boiling. Cecilia told her story in plain words, interrupted only by Signora Lupacchioli's exclamations of dismay:

"Just think of that! Poor dear, to have sunk so low!"

"So low, exactly. I'm not ashamed to say so, because the fault's not mine."

"Of course not, dear Cecilia. There's no question of fault. Think how many thousands of people are worse off than yourself."

"Ah no," Cecilia said peremptorily. "No one's worse off than I am."

"Oh yes. What about those who haven't even a roof over their head? Those who have been stricken with smallpox and typhoid and dysentery?"

"There's no end to human misery. But a mother who has no bread to give her children . . ."

583

"I'm sorry for you, really sorry, and besides you know how high you stand in my esteem."

Cecilia did not wish to waste any more time in talk and so she came out brusquely with her request.

"I'm sorry, really very, very sorry, but the bread I get from the central committee in Ferrara is measured out to me loaf by loaf. You're intelligent enough to know what I mean. During the first days after the flood everyone was in the same position, rich and poor alike, and we handed out what bread we had to all of them. But to continue on such a basis would have meant putting a premium on laziness, encouraging abuse, and taking food out of the mouth of the really needy."

"And am I not one of these?" said Cecilia, who vaguely understood the other's point, but still could not admit it. "But I'm not speaking for myself; I'd never have come to you on my own account. It's my children that are in need."

"Yes, yours is a case worth looking into."

"What's that you say?"

"I say it's worth investigating and thinking over."

Cecilia was not so much indignant as she was astounded, but Signora Lupacchioli took her expression for one of devout attention.

"The central committee wants to be sure that not a single kilogram of bread is wasted," she continued didactically.

"What's a kilogram?" Cecilia asked absently.

"How slow you country people are to appreciate the beauties of the metric system. But I can't go into that just now."

This was true enough, and Cecilia was left gaping, as if at the skill of a magician or juggler.

"To put it in the old-fashioned way," said Signora Lupacchioli, "not a single *pound* of the committee's bread must go astray. Do you follow me?"

"Yes, I follow you."

"I was sure you would. We don't distribute our charity in a haphazard fashion, like those religious souls who say that God is mindful of the giver's intention rather than of the concrete results of his giving. No, we don't claim to be God, and so we can't be as wasteful as He or some of His long-robed administrators. We don't go in for so-called charity at all; we distribute donations on a businesslike basis. Do you understand?"

"No," said poor Cecilia, "but I grasp your point just the same."

"It isn't the same at all!" Signora Lupacchioli protested. "But this is no time for argument. To put it in simple terms, let me tell you that in some localities, such as Guarda, bread is lacking, while in others, like Mesola, where the priest is in charge of the distribution, there's too much bread and it's actually rotting away. That's the point I made just recently at the meeting of all the branch organizations with the central committee."

Now it must be admitted that Signora Lupacchioli had prepared a large part of the preceding speech for the meeting in question and that limitations of time had prevented her from the presentation of anything more than a few statistics and left her with a feeling of frustration. "All well and good," she declared to her comrades of the Workers' Improvement Association, "but statistics cannot satisfy the spirit. In my view it was the presence of a priest that caused the chairman of the meeting to castrate and cut short my peroration. There's no excuse for it that I can see, except the ever present sinister influence of the Jesuits!"

Sitting under the hood of the fireplace, where the embers no longer gave out any heat, although they did make her wet skirt steam, Cecilia took in very little of what she had heard. Her ears were tuned to the fateful sound of the wind and rain outside, to which she attributed her overwhelming weariness and her reluctance to set forth in the early autumnal darkness and return empty-handed to her miserable brood. Every now and then lightning flashed across the window, and she was obsessed by one desperate and mortifying reflection: "I came here just to be made a fool of."

"We have had to list the persons damaged by the flood according to various categories," Signora Lupacchioli blithely concluded. "Old people, men incapacitated for work, women and children with no visible means of support, etc. We had to draw a distinction between people of substance and those totally indigent, etc., etc." (She threw out *etceteras* like sneezes.)

"What does 'totally indigent' mean?" asked Cecilia.

"Someone that has nothing at all."

"And haven't I nothing?"

"My good woman, to be quite truthful, you have two mills!"

"Be as truthful as you like!" exclaimed Cecilia indignantly. "But what are they worth to me if no one brings me grain?"

"That's not the committee's affair."

"Oh, it's not the committee's affair! But it's my affair if my family and I must starve! Who would lend me a penny in times like these on the strength of the mills, even if I offered them for kindling wood? And if I did sell them what would I have to live on? I'd better die and have done with it. I should never have come here, that's plain, and now even if you were to offer me what I asked for I wouldn't take it, except that . . ."

Cecilia wept with rage and mortification; she was angry at herself for affording Signora Lupacchioli the sight of her emotion and resentful of the hostile attitude which the outside world had apparently struck up against her. Her own son stared at her in silence, his eyes wide open with astonishment.

"That's all then," she said, rising to her feet and choking back her tears. "I gather from what you've said that for me there is neither bread nor compassion. Forgive me for having disturbed you."

Beneath her crusty and literal-minded way of speaking Signora Lupacchioli was not really unkind, and Cecilia's plight did touch her.

"I too am a mother, or was before my poor girl died," she said, "and if I had any bread in the house I'd take it upon myself to give it to you. But the fact is that the distribution has taken place already and there's not a single loaf left."

This was clear speaking at last and Cecilia, instead of saying: "Why didn't you tell me so in the first place?" only voiced her gratitude for the privilege of warming herself at the fire.

"God's will be done!" she said with resignation.

"I'd give you bread of my own," Signora Lupacchioli continued, "but I'm actually short of that, too."

"I'm not asking for anything of the sort," said Cecilia in a humble fashion that took the edge of pride out of her words.

"You probably know that my husband makes very little money in this village, but you can't imagine *how* little. And there's so much poverty around us that I've had to make it a rule not to give any away. Besides, in your case it would be only a drop in the bucket. My heart grieves for you, Cecilia, but let me confess that we too are in debt to the butcher and baker. When my husband comes back wet and hungry from work I can't very well let him go without a bowl of hot soup. Just look for yourself at what's boiling in my pot."

So saying she abruptly took off the cover. Inside were a few bare bones and the feet of a chicken. The two women looked each other in the eyes, for the pot was more eloquent than anything they might say. Cecilia, the more miserable of the two, felt sorry for her more prosperous sister and Signora Lupacchioli was ashamed of having hurt the other's feelings. Even so, the odor coming out of the pot had a strong attraction for the pale and hungry Giovanni.

"Give us something to eat, for the love of God Almighty!" he said, holding out his hand like a beggar.

Signora Lupacchioli got up from her bench beside the fire as if her bony body were creaking. She went over to the bread box, filled a cloth with pieces of bread and gave it to Giovanni.

"Bring me back the cloth at your convenience, when the weather is better," she said gruffly. "And now be on your way home. Goodbye."

What could they say? Mother and son raised their voices together:

"God bless you for your kindness!"

7

We shall not tell at length how the good doctor's soup tasted better to him than ever after his wife had told him of the gift she had made to Cecilia. Even someone who has never done a good deed in his life—if there be such an unlikely character—can imagine the satisfaction that comes in its wake. Signora Lupacchioli was almost apologetic for having emptied her larder and left the supper table bare, but he cut her short with a "well done" and began to discuss the terrible days through which they were living and the damage done by floods all over the country.

In the region of Ferrara alone, the Po, the Reno, and the Panaro had overrun their banks and swept up toward the Bondeno. The city itself was in a state of terror, with barricades thrown up at the gates most exposed to the rivers. Day and night crowds gathered in the streets, cafés, squares, and around the Castle, anxious to hear the latest news. The railway had returned all the freight at its depot to the senders, and stripped its offices of all their furniture. At a meeting of the provincial council the engineering corps was blamed for the break-through of the Po near Guarda, but other imminent and perhaps greater disasters turned recriminations into complaints, which served to spread mistrust and fear even farther. And yet everyone knew that the much maligned engineers were working twenty-four hours a day to combat the danger. That evening, October 22, 1872, not even Signora Lupacchioli could speak against them.

At Lagoscuro the Po had risen ninety-nine inches above the normal level, that is nine inches above its former record. To describe it in terms of inches is a matter-of-fact affair, which gives no idea of the state of mind of people huddled in the shadow of peril, weighing in the light of experience the threat of every successive inch and the implications of an overflow, or a leak, or a break-through. The names of the weakest spots and of those that had given away on previous occasions were on everyone's lips and the banks of the river seemed a feeble defense against the mighty sweep of its waters, which threatened men and lands both near and far. Very few people found anything but sporadic sleep that night. Through the fields and from village to village ran terror left by the disaster of a few months before and all those preceding it, together with anxiety about the possibilities of what was to come.

On her way back to the mill Cecilia had either the east wind in her face or the south wind against her side, both of them gusty and laden with hail and rain. The river came all the way up to the edge of the shore, quiet at times as if it were lying mysteriously in ambush, but more often swelling up under the impact of the wind and splashing against the bank with alternately short, pounding waves and longer ones that rolled back all the way across the river. This was a sign that down at the delta the sea was beating in and further increasing the volume of water. Every miller knew that this meant a storm on the Po. More than once Cecilia and her boy felt spray in their faces or found themselves walking in water that had come over the top. Behind them, in the direction of Ferrara, there were continuous thunder and lightning, but although the latter lit up the sky, earth and water remained dark and terrifying.

"You shall not perish!" said a voice deep down in Cecilia's heart. "You shall not be abandoned."

If she had thought that these words came from her own heart alone they would have yielded her scanty encouragement, but accrediting them to a higher source she accepted them with a gentle submissiveness that was actually stronger than any amount of courage. Hadn't she been given bread just when all hope seemed lost? This gift was a token of the reassuring promise which she had just received, and she was pervaded by a sense of sweetness that easily overcame her previous horror. Now the memory of her short-lived despair only made her smile secretly to herself over her own childish presumption. If she had known how to put her thoughts into words she would have said that the fate of herself and her children and the mills and indeed the whole village was in the hands of the Almighty, in whom she for one put all her trust.

"Thou art our help when other helpers fail," she would have said to Him. "And now things have come to such a pass that Thou must assume our burden."

There was something defiant in her unvoiced prayer, like the wager a daughter makes with her father. She was powerless now to lose her newly found faith or the joy of distributing the bread of charity and good cheer among the brood that waited for her around the table aboard the Bitter Bread Mill. As she watched them bite happily into it she quite forgot her own hunger. How far gone one must be to appreciate the true worth of bread! Now the flickering lamp warned her that she had no more kerosene to put in it and soon they would be left in darkness. As for drinking, there was nothing but foul and muddy river water, for in the confusion of Schiavetto's funeral she had forgotten to put any aside to filter in a porous earthenware jar and it was unlikely that the slipshod Lazybones should have repaired her omission. Suddenly it occurred to her that fortune might deal her one final blow if this evening or the next day Lazybones were to decide to go away, leaving her alone with both mills. But when she spoke to him it was not to betray this fear, but rather to apologize for the meager supper and to make amends for having unjustly doubted his good will and intelligence since he had filtered the water after all and it was ready for them to drink at the table. Only a trifle, to be sure, but the difficult circumstances lent it meaning.

"Bread and water, eh, Lazybones?" she said. "I'm sorry we've neither meat nor wine. But we shouldn't have even the bread if it hadn't been given to Giovanni for charity."

She was sorry but unashamed, and even her humility bore the stamp of pride. She was anxious but unafraid; her newly tapped source of courage inspired her with the certainty that even without the help of Lazybones or that of any other human hand the help on high in which she trusted so implicitly would not fail. Indeed she almost wished to hasten the moment when she would stand alone, for already she could feel her anxiety passing over into a good cheer far stronger than all the elements arrayed against her. She was about to tell Lazybones that he must go seek work at a mill in less desperate straits than this one when for the second time he seemed to read her thoughts and answered her before she had spoken.

"This bread and water are quite good enough for me, and appetite is the best sauce to give them flavor. And there's something else I'd like to say."

"Speak up, Lazybones," she said with resignation.

"I want to tell you that better times must surely be coming. We've fallen so low that we've hit rock bottom and there's nothing left for us to do but to rise again." And he added, chewing vigorously on a mouthful of bread, "Even if times stay bad for a long time or for some unknown reason worsen, you can be sure that I shan't give out on you, bread or no bread with which to fill my belly. I may be a bloody idiot from a practical point of view, but my father never taught me to be yellow."

"Then I say God bless your father," said Cecilia with contained emotion.

"Amen. Now I've said what I had to say. As for my wages, you can pay me those later."

"You've a good and generous heart, Lazybones, and I'm glad to have had this chance to know you better. Thank you most warmly."

"There's no reason for you to thank me."

"Yes, there is too! And no one could blame you if you chose to go away."

"I'd blame myself, that's all."

Cecilia was shaken to realize that after she had twice misjudged him this boy had been chosen as the channel of God's mercy. And she reproached herself for having called upon this mercy in an aggressive fashion instead of with due humility and submission. There was something like retribution in the fact that Lazybones, whom she had heretofore looked upon as an ignorant dolt, should now have been chosen to save her and her children. Meanwhile the latter were almost overcome by sleep.

"It's time to say your prayers," she told them. "You had better keep your clothes on and sleep here in the cabin, so that if anything happens we shall all be together."

"Well spoken," said Lazybones.

"And don't forget in your prayers to thank God for His mercy," Cecilia added.

"To thank God for what?" asked little Berta.

"For the bread we had to eat and for the fact that Lazybones has proved himself a true friend."

The little girl had a sort of adoration for Lazybones already and now she opened wide her sleepy eyes:

"Are you a true friend, Lazybones?" she asked ingenuously.

Quite unexpectedly they all burst into healthy laughter, Lazybones, Cecilia, and every one of the children, down to Berta herself. Then by the dying rays of the kerosene lamp the children lay down to sleep.

Hail and rain beat noisily against the roof. The river threw itself headlong at the bows of the mills, churning under them and pushing them up into the air or wedging its way turbulently between them as if to tear them apart so that the connecting beams creaked alarmingly. The turning mill wheels made the millstones whirl idly. Whistling gusts of south wind raised choppy waves against the sides, while the still more powerful blasts from the east, coming up the river from the sea, made the bows bob furiously up and down in the water. This jerking motion endangered the wheels and caused Cecilia to wonder what damage would have been done to them by dawn. Just now there were no lanterns to see by, and if some floating piece of wreckage were to drift into either mill and tear a hole in the hulk there were not enough strong arms to push it away and no lights by which to make their way to safety. The threat of such a disaster was a very real one.

"Lazybones, you must snatch a few hours sleep while I keep watch. Then it will be your turn. If anything happens we'll simply jump into the boat and trust in God's good grace."

"The boat is ready, Mistress Cecilia; it's tied to a stanchion on the deck. But I'm not sleepy; why don't you let me take the first watch?"

"I'd be glad to sleep, I admit, but how can I close an eye when I know these poor creatures are at the mercy of the river?" And by the light of the flickering lantern, which was shaken by the pitching and rolling of the mill, she pointed to the sleeping heads on the floor.

"Try to rest, anyhow," said Lazybones, going to stand guard up on deck.

Cecilia knew that she was weary, but she had no idea of how fast she would fall into a dead sleep, with on her lips the stifled words: "Give us this day our daily bread!"

And she slept long after the lantern had gone out, until the first fitful light of dawn.

"Lazybones!" she called out of the cabin. "Why didn't you wake me when it was my turn?"

"Don't think of that again, Mistress Cecilia, as long as you had some good of it. This night has gone well and so will those to come, although no man, dead or alive, has ever seen the Po swollen like this, not even Schiavetto, God rest his soul, who knew all there was to know of the river. Look out over it now, and see what it is that's our salvation!"

The sight that met Cecilia's eyes was indeed a strange one. With the dying down of the wind the current had been carried by its own impetus and the configuration of the river bed to concentrate its turbulent flow in midstream. And the early morning light revealed that it was carrying with it at a safe distance from the shore enough wreckage to have rammed a dozen mills. Close to the banks the water was now calm, and Lazybones said between a yawn and a laugh:

"For once the Po is not as cruel as it makes itself out to be. I'd say it had a soft spot in its heart for us. Do you see?"

"I see. You're quite right."

Then Cecilia turned to look at the muddy shore. The water was so high that they seemed to be looking down at the land from an observation tower, and she felt almost dizzy. There was a group of watchers on the bank and some laborers piling up sandbags for future protection.

"Ahoy there, aboard the mills!" called a voice which she took to belong to one of the laborers.

"Ahoy, ahoy!" Lazybones replied.

"Step lively!"

"Here we are! What can we do for you?" shouted Lazybones half ironically, holding his hands to his mouth like a horn.

"You can grind our wheat, idiot!" came the reply.

Little did the stranger know that he was saving their lives, and after

Lazybones had rowed him across to the mill with his sacks he observed casually:

"In wild weather like this I'd have preferred to wait a little longer. But the days are quick to go by and I might have been left without any flour. It's better to get wet in the rain than to have to cook up raw wheat, after all. And the weather shows no signs of clearing. I only hope I'm causing you no inconvenience."

"Not the least in the world! Everyone's afraid to venture out and so all my hoppers are empty. I'll send you home in no time with flour and corn meal better than any your wife has ever had for her baking."

"Good! My only worry is for those two oxen I've left standing with their feet in the water."

"Lazybones, take some flour bags and throw them over the animals' backs. That will be better than nothing. Then go get some sleep, for I'm perfectly able to load the hoppers myself."

Never in all her life had Cecilia felt so strong and hopeful, and no sooner had the millstones started to grind the grain than the river seemed to harness itself to the good work and to answer her prayer of the night before: "Give us this day our daily bread!" *Hac voce tollitur*, as the commentator of the Vulgate tells us; with these words we are relieved of all anxiety for the morrow.

The heart of the humble Cecilia Scacerni beat steadily and her courage was high as she stood pouring the grain into the hoppers. Her happiness was deep and pure, for without knowing it she had been called upon to fight a difficult battle and in no uncertain terms she had borne away the victory.